P9-DYA-833

LEGACY

Also by Shannon Messenger

The KEEPER OF THE LOST CITIES Series
Keeper of the Lost Cities
Exile
Everblaze
Neverseen
Lodestar
Nightfall
Flashback

The SKY FALL Series
Let the Sky Fall
Let the Storm Break
Let the Wind Rise

KEEPER
OF THE LOST CITIES
LEGACY

SHANNON MESSENGER

Aladdin
New York London Toronto Sydney New Delhi

This book is a work of fiction. Any references to historical events, real people, or real places are used fictitiously. Other names, characters, places, and events are products of the author's imagination, and any resemblance to actual events or places or persons, living or dead, is entirely coincidental.

ALADDIN

An imprint of Simon & Schuster Children's Publishing Division
1230 Avenue of the Americas, New York, NY 10020
First Aladdin hardcover edition November 2019
Text copyright © 2019 by Shannon Messenger
Jacket illustration copyright © 2019 by Jason Chan
All rights reserved, including the right of reproduction in whole or in part in any form.
ALADDIN and related logo are registered trademarks of Simon & Schuster, Inc.
For information about special discounts for bulk purchases, please contact
Simon & Schuster Special Sales at 1-866-506-1949 or business@simonandschuster.com.
The Simon & Schuster Speakers Bureau can bring authors to your live event.
For more information or to book an event contact the Simon & Schuster Speakers Bureau
at 1-866-248-3049 or visit our website at www.simonspeakers.com.
Jacket designed by Karin Paprocki
Interior designed by Mike Rosamilia
The text of this book was set in Scala.
Manufactured in the United States of America 0919 FFG
2 4 6 8 10 9 7 5 3 1
Full CIP data for this book is available from the Library of Congress.
ISBN 978-1-5344-2733-4 (hc)
ISBN 978-1-5344-2735-8 (eBook)

For Debra Driza
Because I *never* would've finished this book
without your steady support, brilliant brainstorming
sessions, and tiny chocolate chip cookies
(And FYI, readers: The cliff-hanger was Deb's idea!)
☺

PREFACE

WE CAN'T KEEP DOING THIS.

The words pulsed through Sophie's mind. Gaining volume—gaining momentum— as the arguments raged around her.

All the strategizing and analyzing and agonizing.

It never worked.

No matter how clever or careful their plans were.

Their enemies were always smarter.

Stronger.

Ready with some brutal, unexpected twist.

Leaving them stumbling and scrambling.

"We can't keep doing this."

This time the words had a voice, and it took Sophie a second to realize they'd come from her.

And she didn't regret them.

It was time to try something new.

Time to take a stand.

Even if it risked everything.

And maybe if they worked together—and were really, *really* lucky . . .

This would be their new legacy.

Saving Keefe from his.

ONE

Y OU LOOK CONFUSED," MR. FORKLE said, and the lilt of his tone made Sophie wonder if his lips were twitching with a smile—but she couldn't pull her eyes away from the round, gilded door he'd brought her to, tucked into the side of a rolling, grassy hill.

The place reminded her of a hobbit hole. But Sophie had been living in the Lost Cities long enough to know better than to voice that observation. All it would earn her was laughter. Or perhaps some impossible-to-believe story about how Mr. Forkle had once brought J. R. R. Tolkien there and provided him with the inspiration.

"I thought you were taking me to your office," she told him, shifting her gaze toward the windblown meadow and searching the swaying wildflowers for clues as to where they were.

"I did."

Sophie opened her mouth to argue—then realized what he meant.

He'd brought her to *his* office. Not Magnate Leto's office at Foxfire, like she'd been expecting. Which was an easy mistake to make, considering the fact that Mr. Forkle and Magnate Leto were actually the same person—and "Mr. Forkle" was his much more enigmatic side.

"So, this is your *secret* office," she clarified, feeling goose bumps prickle her skin at the thought.

"One of them," Mr. Forkle confirmed, winking as he shuffled his ruckleberry-bloated body closer to the door. He leaned in and licked a spot on the left side of the door, which must've been a camouflaged DNA sensor because a rectangular panel slid open in the center, revealing five spinning, fist-size cogs lined up in a neat row: one silver, one copper, one iron, one bronze, and one steel.

"Did Tinker design this place?" Sophie asked, remembering the abundance of gleaming gears she'd seen decorating the walls of Widgetmoor, as well as the Technopath's clear fondness for the number five. But that wasn't the question she should've been focusing on, so she quickly added, "And why are we here?"

Mr. Forkle twisted the cogs one by one, entering some sort of complicated combination. "You said we needed to talk. Isn't that why you requested this meeting?"

"It is, but . . ." Sophie's words trailed off as the last cog clicked into place, making the ground rumble and the golden door sink into a slit that appeared in the damp earth. Cold air blasted her face from the dark room beyond, blowing strands of her blond hair into her eyes as she took an eager step forward and—

"Stop!" a familiar squeaky voice shouted behind her.

Sophie froze.

She'd learned that it was much easier to let the seven-foot-tall, heavily armed gray goblin lead the way—along with a hulking ogre warrior and a tiny green-toothed gnome. Sandor, Bo, and Flori were three of her five multispeciesial bodyguards, and they took their jobs *very* seriously.

So did her other bodyguards, of course. But Nubiti kept watch from a position deep underground, since dwarves' eyes were highly sensitive to light. And Tarina still hadn't been allowed to return to duty after what everyone was calling the "Scandal at Everglen"—though "scandal" really wasn't a strong enough word. It didn't capture the shock that came with discovering an illegal troll hive hidden at the estate of one of their world's most prominent families. And it *definitely* didn't evoke the horror of the genetically altered, bloodthirsty trolls who went on a murderous rampage once the door to the hive was opened.

Both the elvin and trollish worlds were still reeling from the disaster, since the Neverseen had managed to broadcast the nightmarish battle to everyone gathered for the Celestial Festival. And no one could agree on how to punish those who'd been involved. A Tribunal had already been held for Luzia Vacker, but her sentence had yet to be finalized. And numerous additional investigations seemed to be endlessly "ongoing." Foxfire, the elves' most prestigious academy, had even been put on an extended hiatus because parents were worried the school might be targeted. Plus, treaty renegotiations still needed to be arranged between the elvin Council and the trolls' supreme leader, but everyone was wary of another Peace Summit after what happened at the last one.

"This office is perfectly safe," Mr. Forkle assured Sophie's bodyguards. "Watchward Heath is protected by five different kinds of security. And only six people in the world know how to find it. Well, *seven* now, given Miss Foster's knack for teleporting."

"Then the office should have no problem passing my inspection," Sandor called over his shoulder as he drew his massive curved sword and marched through the doorway, followed by Bo and Flori. He'd always been overprotective, but his paranoia had reached new levels of exhausting after the Neverseen's recent brutal attack—and Sophie couldn't blame him, since she and Fitz had ended up bedridden in the Healing Center for weeks. Her right hand still ached whenever she pushed herself too hard, and Fitz occasionally walked with a slight limp. But Elwin kept assuring them that they'd make a full recovery. Certain wounds were just trickier than others—and theirs had been some of the worst, thanks to the creepy echoes caused by their exposure to shadowflux.

The rare sixth element was darkness in its purest form. Only the strongest Shades could control it. And shadowflux changed everything it touched.

Shadowflux was also somehow so vital to whatever the Neverseen were planning that when their Shade was killed at Everglen, Lady Gisela threatened Tam until he agreed to serve as Umber's replacement. Sophie and Keefe had begged Tam not to go, but he swore he could handle himself. And Lady Gisela had warned them that any attempt at rescue would only put Tam and his twin sister, Linh, in greater danger. So Tam was on his own with the Neverseen—and it killed Sophie every time she thought about it.

Each passing week made her heart heavier. Her nightmares more vivid. Her brain more convinced that she'd never see her friend again.

Or worse: that Tam would join the enemy for real.

If you hear us out, I guarantee you'll realize that we are the only ones with an actual solution to the problems in this world, and that you've been wasting your talent serving the wrong side, Lady Gisela had told him. And she'd proven time and again that she was a master of mind games and manipulation.

"All clear!" Sandor called, and Sophie squared her shoulders and took a long, steadying breath.

She could go back to worrying about Tam later. Right now, she needed to focus on the conversation ahead—a conversation she'd been rehearsing for the last nine days. Ever since she'd gone to Atlantis and . . .

Well.

Things had *not* gone according to plan.

She could still see the pitying looks on the matchmakers' faces as they'd shown her the ugly red words on the screen.

Words that would define her—*destroy* her—if people found out about them.

That was why she'd begged for this meeting. If she could convince Mr. Forkle to give her one tiny piece of information—something she *deserved* to know anyway—everything would get back on track.

She'd been gearing up for a fight, since getting information from the Black Swan was a lot like prying open the jaws of a thrashing verminion. But if he trusted her enough to bring her to his secret office . . .

"Shall we?" Mr. Forkle asked, gesturing to the entrance.

Sophie nodded and crossed the threshold, shivering as a blast of cold, metallic-tinged air seeped through the thin fabric of her lavender tunic. The room was too dark to see, but it felt like stepping into a refrigerator, and she pulled her dove gray cape tighter around her shoulders, wishing she'd worn thicker gloves, instead of the silk ones she'd chosen.

The light flared to life when Mr. Forkle followed, as if the sensor only responded to him. "You don't look impressed," he noted as Sophie blinked in the sudden brightness.

"It's just . . . not what I was expecting."

She'd been imagining his secret office for years—and she'd always pictured a cross between a spaceship and Hogwarts, with fancy architecture and all kinds of high-tech gadgets and mysterious contraptions. Plus clues to who Mr. Forkle truly was, and plenty of hints about Project Moonlark. Instead, she'd found herself in a curved white room that made her feel like she was standing inside a giant underground egg. Soft light poured from a single bulb, which dangled off the end of a thin chain above a round, silver table. The walls were smooth and bare—as was the floor—and several small grates in the ceiling flooded the room with icy drafts.

That was it.

No windows. No doors—except the one they'd come through, which had sealed silently behind them. Nowhere to sit. No decor of any kind. Not even any books or scrolls, despite Mr. Forkle's love of research.

"And here I thought you'd learned that things in the Lost Cities are rarely what they seem," Mr. Forkle said, pressing his palm against the wall. The light bulb flickered twice before it flared much brighter and projected a grid of images across every surface of the room, as if the office was tapping into thousands of camera feeds displaying elves, goblins, ogres, trolls, dwarves, gnomes, and humans going about their daily lives. Every few seconds the images shifted, making Sophie wonder whether she'd catch a glimpse of the entire planet if she stood there long enough.

"Still nothing?" Mr. Forkle asked.

She shrugged. "It's not *that* different from Quinlin's office in Atlantis. And I'm pretty sure a lot of human leaders have rooms like this too—not showing all the other species, but . . . you know what I mean."

"Do I?" Mr. Forkle tapped the wall to make the images disappear before he placed his palm flat against the silver table. "What about this, then?"

The metal surface rippled at his touch, stretching and splitting into a million thin wires that made it look like a giant version of one of those pin art toys Sophie used to play with as a kid. He tapped his fingers in a quick rhythm, and the pins shifted and sank, forming highs and lows and smooth, flat stretches. Sophie couldn't figure out what she was seeing until he tapped a few additional beats and tiny pricks of light flared at the ends of each wire, bathing the scene in vibrant colors and marking everything with glowing labels.

"It's a map," she murmured, making a slow circle around the table.

And not just any map.

A 3-D map of the Lost Cities.

She'd never seen her world like that before, with everything spread out across the planet in relation to everything else. Eternalia, the elvin capital that had likely inspired the human myths of Shangri-la, was much closer to the Sanctuary than she'd realized, nestled into one of the valleys of the Himalayas—while the special animal preserve was hidden inside the hollowed-out mountains. Atlantis was deep under the Mediterranean Sea, just like the human legends described, and it looked like Mysterium was somewhere in the Bermuda Triangle. The Gateway to Exile was in the middle of the Sahara desert—though the prison itself was buried in the center of the earth. And Lumenaria . . .

"Wait. Is Lumenaria one of the Channel Islands?" she asked, trying to compare what she was seeing against the maps she'd memorized in her human geography classes.

"Yes and no. It's technically part of the same archipelago. But we've kept that particular island hidden, so humans have no idea it exists—well, beyond the convoluted stories we've occasionally leaked to cause confusion."

"Huh." Lumenaria *had* reminded her of Camelot when she'd been there, so that must be where some of those legends came from. The elves liked to play with the lore of their world, weaving in conflicting fantastical details, to make it that much harder for humans to believe in it.

She leaned closer, wondering how accurate the map's details were. She hadn't been to Lumenaria since the collapse, and it looked like the glowing castle was now fully rebuilt—with much higher walls. A new tree also stood next to the Four Seasons Tree, perhaps as a memorial for those who'd died in the attack. "And humans really haven't found the island? It's *right* by France and the United Kingdom—and boats go through the channel all the time."

"You've seen how powerful our illusions are," Mr. Forkle reminded her.

Sophie's stomach soured.

Vespera had designed most of the optical illusions that shielded the Lost Cities from detection. And out of all the Neverseen's leaders, she was the most ruthless. She saw violence as a *solution*—and was always claiming that Sophie and Keefe would never be "ready."

For what, they didn't know. But it seemed safe to assume it had something to do with Keefe's "legacy."

"It helps to see our world this way, doesn't it?" Mr. Forkle asked, moving to Sophie's side. "I've been coming here a lot lately to strategize."

"Does that mean you have a plan?" she asked, even though she was pretty sure she already knew the answer.

"It's a work in progress." He sighed when her hands curled into fists. "I understand your impatience, Miss Foster. But some things cannot be rushed."

Her laugh sounded as bitter as she felt.

They'd been trying to take down the Neverseen the entire time she'd been living in the Lost Cities. And here they were, *years* later, still with no clue what the Neverseen were up to or where they were hiding.

She and her friends had been trying to figure out how to make their next move ever since Tam was taken, but all they had to go on were the same worthless leads they'd wasted too much time on already.

Fake caches.

A missing starstone.

Way too many confusing symbols.

The key to Lady Gisela's Archetype, but not the book that the key opened.

Tiny fragments of shattered memories that didn't make any sense.

And no matter what truths they pieced together or what risks they took, the Neverseen were always five million steps ahead of them.

Put simply: They were losing.

And Sophie was sick of it.

"The Neverseen have proven to be more formidable than we expected," Mr. Forkle admitted. "And their changes in leadership have made anticipating their tactics particularly complicated."

"We have too many enemies," Sophie muttered.

"We do indeed. And their individual visions do not always perfectly align, which has caused additional confusion. But we still know far more than you're letting yourself admit."

"Like what?" She turned to face him, crossing her arms. "I'm serious. Tell me *one* useful thing we've learned."

"I can name many, Miss Foster. And so can you. You're simply overlooking them because you're upset that you haven't gotten the answers you *want*—and I understand that inclination. But you're far too smart for such ill-reasoned logic. Which is why I brought you here, to make sure you're seeing the bigger picture."

He tapped another rhythm against the table, and the pins shifted, making new landmarks emerge among all the others: Gildingham, the goblins' golden capital, which seemed to be tucked among the Andes Mountains—and probably inspired the human myths of El Dorado. Ravagog, the ogre stronghold on the Eventide River, which was apparently hidden in the lushest part of central Asia. Loamnore, a city Sophie assumed was the dwarven capital, since the enormous metropolis was *under* the Gobi desert rather than above it. And Marintrylla, an island near New Zealand that was probably the trollish capital and seemed to be an intricate network of caves and bridges.

"What do you see?" Mr. Forkle asked.

Sophie's eyes narrowed. "I'm assuming you're looking for a better answer than 'a bunch of cities.'"

Flori giggled.

Sandor and Bo snorted.

Mr. Forkle grumbled something under his breath that started with "You kids."

"Why don't you just tell me what you want me to say?" Sophie suggested.

"Because I'm trying to teach you, Miss Foster. Your friends look to you for guidance, and lately all I've seen you display is despair and frustration. If you're going to lead them, you need to do better."

"Lead them." The phrase felt heavy on Sophie's tongue. "Is *that* your big plan, then? Dump all the responsibility on me, because I'm the moonlark?"

"Need I remind you that you're the one who chose to involve your friends? I'm not criticizing you for that—your friends have proven invaluable to our efforts. But you can't ignore the responsibility that you took on when you recruited them."

Sophie's insides twisted.

She'd never intended to "recruit" her friends. They just kept asking questions about what she was doing and offering to help. And eventually, she'd realized she needed them.

But now everything that happened wasn't just her responsibility—it was her *fault*. Like when Lady Gisela knocked Tam out cold and dragged him away, even though he'd already agreed to cooperate.

"I know what you're thinking," Mr. Forkle said gently. "And not because I'm violating the rules of telepathy, in case you're worried. The burden you're carrying is written in every shadow on your face—and you must *not* blame yourself."

Sophie forced herself to nod.

Guilt was dangerous for elves—almost as sanity-shattering as violence.

But it sure wasn't easy to let go of.

"I want Mr. Tam home safely every bit as much as you do," Mr. Forkle assured her. "As does the rest of the Black Swan. But that cannot be our only goal. So I need you to step back and remember what we're fighting for."

"What *are* we fighting for?" Sophie countered. "It feels like all we ever do is . . . try not to die—and sometimes we're not even very good at that."

Mr. Forkle looked away, blinking hard, and Sophie was sorry she'd brought up what had happened to his twin brother. But . . . if they didn't change something, it was only a matter of time before they lost someone else.

"We've been playing defense for far too long," he said, clearing the thickness from his throat. "And that is never a good way to win. That's why I need you to look at the map again—*truly* look—and tell me what you see."

Sophie dragged out her sigh and tilted her head, trying to guess what he expected her to say. "I see . . . a divided world."

"An *unevenly* divided world," Bo added.

He had a point. The elves had a bunch of huge cities—and that wasn't counting their individual estates scattered all over the planet. Meanwhile, the other species seemed to be much more confined to their capitals—except the gnomes, who lived with the elves.

"The ancient Council felt it would be easier to ensure that each leader upheld the tenets of their treaties if the various species were separated from each other," Mr. Forkle explained. "So they did their best to keep everyone confined to their respective homelands." A quick series of taps made glowing lines appear across the map, outlining the invisible boundaries around each species' territory—and their lands were much vaster than Sophie had realized, with borders extending well beyond their capitals. "And the arrangement has had its share of success. We scattered our cities to better keep an eye on everything. And no *major* wars have erupted among the intelligent species—though what happened with Serenvale was a close call."

Bo shifted his weight, not looking happy to hear a reminder of how the ancient ogres stole the gnomes' homeland and forced them to flee to the Lost Cities.

Flori looked even less thrilled.

Mr. Forkle kept his focus on the map. "Time, however, has complicated things. Populations have grown. Resources have been depleted. And many are beginning to feel *restricted* by their boundaries. Particularly when you consider this."

He tapped a rapid rhythm against the metal, and thousands more cities appeared across the parts of the map that had previously been empty, most scrunched so closely together that their labels overlapped in a tangle of letters. But Sophie could still tell she was looking at the Forbidden Cities.

Human cities.

"The Council let each intelligent species choose their homeland— and kept land for ourselves and the Neutral Territories," Mr. Forkle continued quietly. "But they left the rest of the planet to humans, because they're so much more prolific. And many now feel that decision was a mistake. Some have even begun calling for drastic changes. I believe you've heard about the proposal for building a Human Sanctuary that circulated a few decades back, haven't you, Miss Foster?"

"Alden mentioned it a while ago," Sophie agreed. And the thought of moving all the humans to what would basically be an enormous prison still made her queasy. "Was that the Neverseen's idea?"

"It's hard to say where the murmurings originated. But the idea gained some powerful supporters, even among those considered to be respectable and influential. And though the Council shut it down, they failed to address the larger conundrum that's been festering beneath the surface of all of our worlds for centuries now." He turned to meet her gaze. "We're spiraling toward war. And not an isolated battle. A global conflict involving every living being." He let that sink in before he added, "*That's* why the Black Swan was formed—and why Alden and Quinlin have carried out so many of their own secret investigations throughout the last few decades. But it's *also* why the Neverseen exist. And why King Dimitar forged an alliance with them and unleashed the plague upon the gnomes. I suspect it's even why the trolls enlisted Luzia Vacker to help them experiment on their newborns. We're all reacting to the same problem. Only our solutions separate us."

"But . . . why?" Sophie had to ask, pointing to the map. "I thought we could make anywhere inhabitable. So if this is all just about space, couldn't we hollow out more mountains or sink more cities under the ocean or—"

"We could," Mr. Forkle interrupted. "But who would live there? Not every territory is ideally situated for that kind of expansion—and people generally don't like leaving the place they've come to think of as *home*. There's also no telling what complications might arise from scattering the species. But even if we resolved all of that, it wouldn't address the fact that humans are polluting our planet and stripping it of its natural resources while simultaneously building weapons that could destroy everyone."

"My queen has expressed *many* concerns about that," Sandor noted.

"As has my king," Bo agreed.

"And rightfully so," Mr. Forkle told them. "It's an incredibly disturbing situation. And I assure you, the Black Swan has been hard at work on a solution."

His gaze drifted toward Sophie again, and she took a step away.

"*That's* what Project Moonlark's about? I'm supposed to . . ." She wasn't sure how to finish that sentence, but she had a horrible feeling it ended with something like "save the human race."

"Project Moonlark was about gaining a valuable new perspective," Mr. Forkle corrected, "in the hope that fresh eyes might help us spot something we've been missing—both for this issue and for some of the internal injustices in our own society. Any action beyond that was never meant to rest solely on your shoulders. You're a part of our *order*. We face these challenges together."

Somehow that was both a relief *and* a disappointment.

Sophie didn't want to be the answer to *everything*. But she wouldn't mind being the answer to *something*, after all the sacrifices she'd had to make.

Mr. Forkle rested a hand on her shoulder. "You're incredibly special, Miss Foster. And there are other roles you'll be asked to play someday—but for now, I need you to concentrate on this." He pointed to the map. "Given everything I've just told you, and everything you see here, what do *you* think the Neverseen's next move will be?"

She stared at the map so long, the colors blurred.

"Okay, let's try it this way," he said. "What do you think the Neverseen truly want? I'm talking about the order as a whole, not the personal agendas of their individual leaders."

The only answer Sophie could come up with was: "Power?"

"Exactly. *They* want to be in control—that's one of the primary ways our orders differ from one another. The Black Swan resorted to rebellion because we had no other means of pursuing necessary solutions. And our ultimate hope has been—and always will be—to work hand in hand with the Council as we address these complicated challenges. But the Neverseen have always desired to take over."

"So . . . you're saying their next move is to overthrow the Council?" Sophie asked, really hoping she was wrong.

"I believe that's their endgame—but I also believe they're wise enough to know they're not ready for that step. Think about what would happen if they took out the Council now. Would they prove themselves mighty? Or simply show the leaders of the other species that the Lost Cities are ripe for a takeover?" He tapped another rhythm against the table and made every landmark on the map disappear except Gildingham, Ravagog, Loamnore, and Marintrylla. "That's the piece I fear you've been ignoring. Ruling our planet involves so much more than leading the elves. And the Neverseen cannot afford to weaken the Lost Cities until they've first weakened all of the other worlds."

"They'll never weaken us," Bo huffed, his knuckles cracking as he squeezed the hilt of his sword.

Mr. Forkle shook his head. "They already have. What happened when they tricked your king into unleashing the plague upon the gnomes?"

Sophie wasn't sure if it was a good idea to remind Bo that she and her friends had been forced to flood half of Ravagog in order to escape the ogre city after they snuck in to steal the cure from King Dimitar. But Bo's grip loosened on his weapon, and his mottled skin paled as he said, "We lost many great warriors."

"You did indeed. And others defected to the Neverseen afterward. You've also had half of a city to rebuild—which is still a work in progress, as I understand it." Mr. Forkle tapped Ravagog on the map, and the lights dimmed around the ogre capital.

"We can still protect ourselves," Bo argued.

"I never said you couldn't. But we all know that your king changed strategies after the flood, shifting his focus away from the larger world and centering his attention on his people—which is what the Neverseen require. They need the other leaders to be distracted and disorganized, so they won't notice the turmoil in the Lost Cities— or have the means to take advantage—until things stabilize. And that's exactly what they've now made happen for Empress Pernille. By exposing Luzia Vacker's involvement with the experimental hive, the Neverseen cost the empress her secret ally, as well as the lives of those newborn soldiers, and the facility where they were created. *And* they've forced the empress to face numerous treaty violations, which will keep her far too busy to concern herself with whatever's happening in our world for a good long while."

Another tap darkened Marintrylla on the map.

"That leaves the goblins and the dwarves," Sophie murmured, feeling her stomach churn with a thick, sloshy dread. "Though . . . I guess they already took out a bunch of goblins in Lumenaria."

"That was hardly a dent in our forces," Sandor argued. "Our army is immense."

"It is," Mr. Forkle agreed.

But he still darkened Gildingham on the map with an ominous tap.

"My gut tells me," he explained, "that the Neverseen will save any targeted move against Queen Hylda until they're ready to take down the Council, since the goblins serve as the Councillors' bodyguards. And before they can take down the Council, they must *also* win over the majority of our people—otherwise their rule will be rejected, and our world will dissolve into rebellion. That's why each of the Neverseen's moves has also been designed to make them appear mighty while making our current Councillors look weak and foolish, and caused many in our world to question the Council's power and authority."

"But everyone saw Vespera, Ruy, and Gethen cowering under their little force field during the Celestial Festival," Sophie reminded him. "And abandoning Umber without even bothering to see if she was still alive."

"Yes, they made a grave mistake there—which is a credit to you and your friends." He moved closer, placing both hands on her shoulders and bending to her eye level. "I realize how easy it is to see our defeats. But don't overlook what we've achieved. We've dulled the effectiveness of each and every one of the Neverseen's schemes.

And this time? We're going to thwart them much more completely."

All eyes focused on Loamnore, glowing like a beacon on the otherwise dark map.

Glowing like a *target*.

And yet, Sophie still had to ask, "How can you be so certain?"

They'd been wrong about the Neverseen's plans so many times before. In fact, she was pretty sure they'd never actually been *right*.

"I can be certain, Miss Foster, because this time the Neverseen tipped their hand. Taking Mr. Tam was devastating—but not just for us. In fact, it dealt a far larger blow to them. Now we know that shadows will play a role in the next stage of their plan."

"Shadow*flux*," Sophie corrected.

"I'm sure that will be crucial, yes. But I doubt they would limit themselves to one aspect of Mr. Tam's ability when they can utilize the full scope, particularly since Shades are so powerful. So I think it's best if we keep our focus wider and assume that the key will be darkness, in all of its varied forms. And where would darkness be more valuable than an underground city inhabited by creatures who rarely step into the light?"

A tingly sort of energy hummed under Sophie's skin as he moved back to the map and tapped the table with a new rhythm. The pins zoomed in on the dwarven capital, which reminded Sophie of an ant farm—a maze of carefully arranged tunnels snaking deep into the earth and leading to underground plazas and marketplaces, or to the scattered bubble-shaped living quarters. It was somehow both bigger and smaller than she'd been expecting. Grady had told her once that the most recent census showed only three hundred and twenty-nine dwarves on the entire planet—and that was before thirty went missing, and others were lost in the battle on Mount Everest. But it was strange to see so few homes in Loamnore—especially since their tunnels stretched for miles and miles and miles.

"Okay," she said, almost afraid to admit that he'd made a decent point. She was getting a floaty feeling in her heart that felt a lot like *hope*—and hope was an emotion that had led them astray far too many times. "Assuming you're right, how are we supposed to know what the Neverseen are planning to do to the dwarves? Like . . . *specifically*? Because I'm seeing thousands of underground paths, and any of them could be used in an attack."

"*That* is what I want you and your friends to figure out. You all have extra time while Foxfire remains on hiatus."

"Uh . . . how are we supposed to do that?"

"By determining how the Neverseen can use shadowflux—and shadows or darkness in general—to weaken the dwarves while bringing further scandal to the Council."

"Oh, is that all?" she asked, her heart crashing back to reality. "And here I thought you were going to be vague."

"I think you'll find that those guidelines narrow the options far more significantly than you're expecting. Particularly when you also consider the fact that this attack will likely be targeted at you and your friends."

Sophie's mouth turned dry, giving her voice a hint of rasp as she asked, "Aren't we always one of the targets?"

"In a way. But up until this point, they've mostly tried to test you or control you. This time, I believe they'll be aiming to . . . well, I suppose the best way to put it is to 'crush your spirit'—because their broadcast at the Celestial Festival backfired. Not only did everyone see members of the Neverseen cower and flee, but they also saw you and your friends stand strong and keep fighting. And that made many in our world begin to see what the Black Swan and I have seen all along: the true future we should be focusing on."

A fresh set of goose bumps prickled Sophie's arms. But these ones felt itchier. Almost demanding.

"Yes," Mr. Forkle told her. "It's a tremendous responsibility. One that every young generation must learn to carry. Adults may have wisdom and experience. But our youth are bold and brave and willing to fight for what they believe in with a formidable kind of energy. And you and your friends showed everyone precisely how to be a true force for change. So I suspect the Neverseen will try to counter that by putting you in a situation where you will be forced to surrender in a very public way. And I realize that's not easy to hear—"

"No, it's fine," Sophie interrupted, hugging herself to squeeze back some of the queasiness. "Who doesn't love being told they have an evil band of villains trying to crush their spirit?"

"But they never will," Flori said, placing her hand over Sophie's. Her green thumb traced circles across the back of Sophie's gloved palm as she hummed a soft melody that whispered through the air like warm spring rain.

Sophie closed her eyes, letting the song sink into her mind, washing away some of the panic.

"It's okay to be afraid, Miss Foster," Mr. Forkle told her. "I am."

That didn't make her feel any better. In fact, it made her wish she could go back to being a little kid, believing the grown-ups in her life would take care of everything.

Flori hummed another verse of the soft melody, letting the

whispery sounds flutter around them before she said, "The trick is to acknowledge your fear and let it fuel you to fight harder."

"I'm already fighting as hard as I can!" Sophie argued.

"So it's time to fight *smarter*," Mr. Forkle told her. "The Neverseen took your friend, and now they're going to use him to strike at you where you're most vulnerable. Their plan will center on something that affects you, the Council, *and* the dwarves. If you consider all three goals, I've no doubt that you and your friends can determine the shape and direction of the threat we're facing."

"Shouldn't someone also warn King Enki?" Sandor asked, leaning closer to squint at the map.

"I have," Mr. Forkle assured him. "He's already taking precautions. But several of the dwarves who defected to the Neverseen were key strategists behind the city's security. So we'll definitely have our work cut out for us. But we must rise to the challenge. We cannot let the Neverseen weaken the dwarves. It would bring our world far too close to their ultimate endgame. Plus, the dwarves are a vital resource. Without them, we never would've been able to rebuild so quickly after the Neverseen's attacks."

"You've had a lot of help from my people as well," Flori reminded him. "Don't count us out."

"I haven't. And I'm sure the Neverseen haven't either. In fact, I'm certain they'll strike against the gnomes again when the time is right. That's why I've allowed you—and Miss Foster's other guards—to be present for this meeting."

Sandor and Bo both snorted "allowed" under their breath.

Mr. Forkle smiled. "Oh, I assure you—if I didn't want you in my office, I could cast you out before you could even draw your weapons. It's my favorite security feature that Tinker designed. But I haven't used it, because I'm counting on you three to make sure your people are ready, in case the Neverseen attempt to weaken your worlds further while they're targeting the dwarves. I'll update the Council as well, and convince them to take their own precautions. And while we're doing all of that"—he shifted back toward Sophie—"I need you and your friends to focus on what we've discussed. I'd recommend starting with Mr. Tam. Think about *his* strengths and *your* weaknesses, since where they overlap likely lies the Neverseen's plan."

Sophie swallowed hard, but it couldn't dislodge the lump in her throat as she forced herself to ask the question she'd been dreading. "So . . . you think Tam's going to do what they want him to? You don't think he'll find a way to resist?"

Mr. Forkle looked away. "I think, if it comes down to it, there are very few things Mr. Tam wouldn't do to protect his sister. And Lady Gisela knows that all too well."

Sophie wished she could argue. But she'd been worrying about the same thing.

Tam had already left the Lost Cities so that Linh wouldn't have to be alone after the Council banished her. And the two of them spent years living in shoddy tents and nearly starving in the Neutral Territories. He even joined the Black Swan mostly for her.

It made him incredibly brave and sweet and noble and . . .

A *little* scary—at least in his present situation.

"He needs your help," Mr. Forkle told her. "*You* can save Mr. Tam from facing an impossible decision. So I suggest you get to work. Compare what you and your friends each know about him. Then talk to Lady Zillah and find out everything she's taught Mr. Tam—and everything she knows about shadowflux. I'd also recommend familiarizing yourself with Loamnore. Miss Linh lived there for a brief time, so she might have some ideas about the city's vulnerabilities. And you should ask Nubiti as well. Feel free to share my theories with her—if she hasn't been listening to us already—and see if she can provide any insights. I'll of course arrange a visit between you and King Enki, along with a tour of Loamnore as soon as I can."

Sophie nodded, telling herself to feel relieved as he pounded his fist against the table, making the metal flatten back into a smooth, empty surface. This was the earliest they'd ever had a concrete strategy for stopping the Neverseen—and she hadn't even had to pry it out of him, or follow a bunch of mysterious clues and notes before he trusted her.

This was progress!

But . . . was it *enough*?

And how would her friends feel about focusing on Tam?

She suspected that would *not* go over well, but . . . at least it would give her a perfect excuse not to talk about—

"Wait," she said as the door slid open and Mr. Forkle pulled his pathfinder from his cape pocket. She'd gotten so distracted by the map and his theories about the dwarves and Tam that she'd forgotten the reason she'd asked for the meeting in the first place. "None of this is why I said we needed to talk."

He spun the crystal at the end of the silver wand. "Well, surely you can agree that this is far more important."

It was and it wasn't.

Compared to everything going on, her personal life did rank pretty low.

But . . . she'd waited nine days for this opportunity. She wasn't about to waste it.

"This will only take a minute," she promised, squaring her shoulders and trying to project confidence as she switched to the speech she'd prepared. "I know you haven't wanted to tell me certain things about who I am, and what your plans for me are, and where I come from, and what's happened in my past. And I know you think you're protecting me—but I can handle that stuff now. And I'm worried that the reason we keep failing is because of all of the secrets between us. It makes trusting you really hard sometimes—and it leaves me without some pretty important information. So I think it's time for us to agree that we need to solve all of those mysteries."

She let out a breath.

There.

She'd said it.

Now she needed him to argue that he couldn't possibly tell her *everything*—because this was Mr. Forkle, after all—and then she'd offer a compromise and make him agree to answer at least one question.

They'd made a similar deal before—and she knew exactly what question she'd ask.

But Mr. Forkle didn't follow the script.

"I'm sorry, Miss Foster." His eyes stayed focused on his pathfinder as he locked the crystal into place. "I can't tell you what you want to know."

"You don't even *know* what I want to know," she pointed out.

"Actually, I do. You . . . want to know who your biological parents are."

Sophie blinked. "How did you—"

"I know you far better than you realize. Which is why I *also* know that you won't be happy with me when I tell you that, unfortunately, the answer to your question is 'no.'"

"*Why?*"

He sighed. "I can't tell you that, either."

She gritted her teeth. "I deserve to know."

"You do. But that doesn't change the fact that I can't tell you— because it doesn't *only* affect you. The ramifications are too huge. I'm sorry, I realize that's not what you want to hear. But it's the best I can do."

His tone made it clear that they'd reached the end of the conversation.

But Sophie couldn't let it go. She had to make him understand that there were huge ramifications for her, too—even if it meant saying the words she'd been bottling up since that horrible day in Atlantis, when she'd stumbled out of the matchmakers' office with a fake smile plastered across her face, pretending everything was okay.

"I'm unmatchable."

It came out as a whisper, but she knew everyone heard her. They all sucked in breaths. Even Bo, who probably didn't understand the full enormity of that statement.

The elves didn't discriminate because of skin color or money, like so many humans did. But anyone who was part of a bad match faced scorn for the rest of their lives—and so would their kids. It mostly happened to the Talentless, since the matchmakers focused on pairing up those with the strongest abilities in the hope that their children would be equally powerful. But the foundation of the matchmaking system was genetics, to ensure that no distant relatives were intermarrying, which could happen all too easily in a world where everyone stayed beautiful and healthy for thousands of years.

So if Sophie couldn't provide the names of the male and female whose DNA she carried, the matchmakers could do nothing except give her a sympathetic pat on the head and send her away in shame.

She honestly wasn't sure how she'd made it out of that room without bursting into tears—and couldn't remember what she'd told her parents to explain why she wasn't carrying a match packet as she rejoined them in the main lobby and headed home.

It was all a horrible, sickening blur—and the nine days that followed had been even more unbearable. She'd had to avoid her friends, afraid they might be able to tell that something had happened, all while her brain kept imagining the many ways her life was about to implode. The only thing that had gotten her through was waiting for this moment—this chance to avert the disaster.

"Please," she said, ready to drop to her knees and beg. "I won't tell anyone and—"

"You'd *have* to," Mr. Forkle interrupted. "The information would only be useful if it were part of your official records. And that cannot happen."

"*But I'm unmatchable!*" she repeated, much louder this time. And she couldn't help noticing that he didn't flinch.

That's when she realized . . .

"You knew."

She should've figured that out before.

He was the one who filled out her Inception Certificate and left off that crucial information.

Of *course* he knew what that would mean for her someday.

"What is this?" she demanded. "Another way that Project Moonlark is manipulating my *perspective* so I'll see the follies of our world? Am I supposed to be the poster girl for the dark side of matchmaking?"

"Of course not! Though, as I recall, you have had quite a few issues with the system. You even considered not participating."

She had.

Matchmaking was disappointingly unromantic, and inherently problematic—but that was before . . .

She couldn't think about it without wanting to throw up. And yet her mind still flashed to a pair of beautiful teal eyes.

Fitz had looked so adorably earnest—so honest—when he'd said the six words that changed everything.

I want it to be you.

The boy she'd liked from the moment he'd found her on her class field trip and showed her where she truly belonged—the boy who was so impossibly out of her league that it was almost laughable— told her he wanted to see her name on his match lists. And whether she agreed with matchmaking or not, she needed her name to be there so they could be together.

But she was unmatchable.

"Please," she said again. "There has to be a way to fix this."

"I wish there were."

The sorrow in his voice sounded genuine.

But that didn't help.

"I realize at your age," he said carefully, "dating and relationships can feel like *everything*. But it's truly only one small fraction of your life—and something you definitely don't need to be rushing into. Perhaps in a few hundred years—"

"A few *hundred* years," Sophie repeated, suddenly despising the elves' indefinite life span with the passion of a thousand fiery suns.

It didn't matter how he was planning to finish that sentence. In a few hundred years, everyone she knew would already be matched up.

Actually, they'd probably all be matched in the next decade. Fitz definitely would be. Even with all the drama surrounding his family, he was still basically elvin royalty. And he was handsome, and charming, and talented, and sweet, and thoughtful, and powerful, and—

"Time is relative," Mr. Forkle said, interrupting her mental swooning. "Things can feel so urgent, and yet be so small in the grand scheme. I realize that's a difficult concept to grasp at such a young age—and I'm sure it's even harder for you, given your upbringing."

"The upbringing you forced on me," she spat back at him.

"Yes, that *is* one of the few things we didn't give you a choice in. And yet, I suspect you wouldn't trade the time you spent with your human parents and sister."

"I wouldn't," she conceded. "But that doesn't mean I don't deserve to know who my biological family is—especially since not knowing them ruins everything."

"Not everything," he corrected. "And not *ruins*. It simply *complicates* certain things."

Sophie shook her head.

It would ruin what she had with Fitz. That was more than enough.

"Please don't do this to me," she whispered to him as Flori started humming again, trying to keep her calm.

Mr. Forkle dragged a palm down his face. "I'm not *doing* anything. We're just . . . at an impasse. And I wish I could change that. But right now, this is where we must stand—and given everything going on, I'm begging you to put this out of your mind. You cannot let it distract you from everything we've been discussing. Focus on the dwarves. There's too much at stake. Too many people we care about who could get hurt. I know you're smart enough to see that, so I won't say any more."

Sophie turned away, counting her breaths and willing herself not to cry. But she could still feel the tears burning behind her eyes as Mr. Forkle tilted her chin back toward him.

"You're the strongest, most resourceful person I've ever known, Miss Foster. And after everything you've survived, I know you can survive this."

He was wrong.

This was officially too much.

But . . .

Maybe he was also right.

She *was* strong and resourceful.

And she wasn't backing down.

She'd spent the last few years learning how to focus on multiple challenges at the same time. She had multitasking down to an art.

So she let him lead her and her bodyguards into the sunlit meadow and pulled her home crystal out from under her tunic. She had to light leap out of there fast, before he caught a glimpse of the new plan forming in her mind.

If he wouldn't tell her who her genetic parents were, she'd find the answer herself.

TWO

SO HOW'D IT GO?" GRADY CALLED AS Sophie and her bodyguards glittered onto the flower-lined path at Havenfield—and it took Sophie a second to spot her adoptive father standing near the triceratops pen, along with her adoptive mother, Edaline.

Havenfield was one of the rehabilitation centers for the Sanctuary, so there was always an abundance of bizarre animals milling about the lush pastures that stretched all the way to the steep ocean cliffs bordering the property. And one of Sophie's favorite creatures was bounding around Grady and Edaline on wobbly legs, flapping his blue-tipped wings and shaking his gleaming mane.

Wynn wasn't just adorable. He was a true miracle baby, since he and his twin sister, Luna, were the first alicorns to ever be born in the Lost Cities. And with their birth nearly two weeks earlier, they'd doubled the population of their severely endangered species and reset the Timeline to Extinction. Both the babies and their mama had only survived the incredibly high-risk delivery thanks to the help of the trolls and Luzia Vacker—which was one of the reasons the Council kept struggling to find the right punishment for what happened with the illegal hive at Everglen.

The line between hero and criminal was sometimes very gray.

"What's all that for?" Sophie asked, pointing to the large spool of glowing wire that Grady was holding, and the bulging sack Edaline had slung over one of her shoulders.

Grady tipped his chin toward Wynn. "The gnomes are helping us baby-alicorn-proof the gorgodon enclosure, since this guy seems to think the gorgodon is his new best friend—and it turns out he's scrawny enough to wriggle through the bars."

"I nearly had a heart attack when I found him trotting around in there this morning," Edaline added as Wynn reared back with a whinny.

"Is he okay?" Sophie asked, sprinting over and searching Wynn's silvery body for signs of injury.

"He's fine," Edaline assured her, stroking Wynn's forehead right where his nubby horn jutted out of his wild mane. "Don't ask me *how*, but he didn't get a scratch on him."

Sophie couldn't understand it either. The gorgodon was the last of the mutant hybrid beasts that Lady Gisela had created as creepy guard dogs for her version of the Nightfall facility. Part flareadon, part gorgonops, part eurypterid, and part argentavis—it was huge, ugly, and as deadly as possible. It could fly, could breathe underwater, *and* had enormous claws, fangs, and a stinging scorpion tail. The gnomes were always fixing giant gouges in the bars from the beast thrashing against its cage—and feeding time was super challenging.

"Will that really be strong enough?" Sophie asked, frowning at the glowing wire. It looked so thin, she had a feeling even her weak right hand could bend it.

"Oh yeah." Grady shook the spool, filling the air with a clinking noise that reminded Sophie of ringing bells. "This is iron tempered with lumenite. Even an angry T. rex couldn't break it."

"But you might also want to let Silveny know what her son's been up to," Edaline suggested. "Wynn's already tried to sneak back to the gorgodon three times since I lured him out of there, and I think a nice long mama lecture will put some proper fear into him."

Sophie nodded.

One of the many unique aspects of her enhanced telepathy was her ability to communicate with animals—and Silveny was particularly easy to understand, because the Black Swan loosely modeled Sophie's genetic enhancements on alicorn DNA. She almost wished she could tell that to the matchmakers and see if it made them decide that her biological parents didn't matter, since her genes had been so drastically manipulated. Which showed how desperate she was, if becoming "the horse girl"—on *official record*—suddenly sounded appealing.

"Everything okay?" Edaline asked, her turquoise eyes narrowing and her delicate eyebrows pressing together. It was a look she'd been giving Sophie a lot lately. Ever since Sophie had stepped out of the matchmakers' office empty-handed. And Sophie had a feeling it meant her parents had guessed that *something* had happened in Atlantis—but she was hoping their theory had to do with her changing her mind about registering and being too embarrassed to admit it.

She was determined to avoid clarifying the situation for as long as she possibly could.

"You didn't answer Grady's question about how it went with Mr. Forkle," Edaline reminded her.

Sophie shrugged. "It was Mr. Forkle. How do you think it went?"

Grady grinned. "That bad, huh?"

"Pretty much." She told them about the weird egg-shaped office, the 3-D map of the Lost Cities, and Mr. Forkle's theory about the dwarves being the Neverseen's next target—but couldn't bring herself to repeat his fears about Tam. She also decided not to mention the fact that she and her friends might be attacked much more personally.

"That's more information than he usually gives you," Edaline noted when Sophie had finished.

"I know. But . . . it still feels like we've narrowed it down from a million possibilities to a thousand—and that's assuming Mr. Forkle's even right."

"I think he is," Grady said, his gaze focusing on some invisible point in the distance. "It would explain some of the things I've been looking into with the dwarves."

"What things?" Sophie asked, glancing at Edaline, who looked equally curious.

Grady blew out a breath, knocking a few strands of his blond hair off of his forehead. "I'm not sure how much I'm allowed to share. My assignments were classified—and I'm not saying I won't tell you, so no need to give me that look, kiddo. I just think I should speak with the Council first, to save us a whole lot of drama. I'll head to Eternalia as soon as I make sure Wynn can't become a gorgodon snack."

Wynn nickered in protest.

"The gnomes and I can finish up without you," Edaline offered, reaching for his bundle of glowing wire.

Grady pivoted away. "This is much heavier than it looks."

"So?"

When he still wouldn't hand it to her, Edaline snapped her fingers, making the spool disappear. Edaline was a Conjurer, so she could pull things back and forth through the void—or hide something in the nothingness and drag it back when she needed it.

A second snap did the same to the sack she'd had over her shoulder.

"Should've thought of that earlier," Edaline said, smoothing her amber-colored hair. "Sometimes I forget that I don't have to do things the way you do."

Sophie occasionally had the same problem. It didn't always feel natural to rely on her abilities—and she was even worse at remembering to use any of her elvin skills. Things like telekinesis, levitating, channeling, darkness vision, breath control, and body temperature regulation were all feats that every single elf was capable of achieving. But their world put so much emphasis on special abilities that people rarely used their skills—or even thought about them—and that was turning out to be a dangerous mistake. Particularly since the Neverseen made their members train in their skills every day.

Fitz and Biana's traitorous older brother, Alvar, had even used breath control and body temperature regulation to cheat death in the troll hive at Everglen. And Sophie was dreading the day she'd have to face him again. She hadn't *trusted* Alvar, but . . . she hadn't been as suspicious of him as she should've been either. So she'd stopped Fitz from knocking Alvar unconscious when Alvar started acting strange on the night of the Celestial Festival.

A tiny part of her wasn't sure if Fitz had truly forgiven her for that mistake—and she wouldn't blame him if he hadn't. Alvar had been the one to let the Neverseen in through Everglen's gates and brought them to the illegal troll hive. He'd claimed he was trying to expose the "Vacker legacy," but Sophie still didn't understand exactly what that meant. It felt like there was still some larger revelation coming—and knowing Alvar, it wasn't going to be good news.

"Go shower and change," Edaline told Grady, brushing green Verdi feathers off of his black tunic. "You can't meet with the Council smelling like a wet dinosaur."

"See, and I think that'll make it more fun," Grady countered. But he headed toward their shimmering glass-and-gold manor without further protest.

"And you should tell your friends to come over," Edaline said to Sophie. "That way they're here when Grady gets home and fills you in on what he's been working on."

"Yeah, that'd probably save some time," Sophie agreed.

Her voice was a touch too high-pitched, though, and Edaline's eyes narrowed again. "You haven't had anyone over in more than a week . . . ," she said slowly.

"I haven't?" Sophie asked, trying Keefe's trick of answering questions with questions.

It didn't work.

"Nope. Not since we came home from Atlantis." Edaline added an eyebrow raise to hint at the part she wasn't saying.

Sophie focused on stroking Wynn's velvet-soft nose.

"I thought you would've at least wanted to spend a little time with Fitz," Edaline pressed. "The last time he was here—"

"I know," Sophie interrupted, trying not to think about how tightly Fitz had held her as he'd spun her around to celebrate the safe arrival of Wynn and Luna.

She knew she couldn't hide her "unmatchable" status forever—especially since she and Fitz were Cognates, and the rare telepathic connection required absolute honesty in order to work most effectively. But . . . she'd been trying to hold off on telling him until she had an actual solution to share. And she'd wasted too much time counting on Mr. Forkle, so now she needed to come up with a plan for finding out who her genetic parents were—fast.

And sadly, she didn't have much to go on. The only clues Mr. Forkle had given her over the years were that her genetic parents had no connection to each other, and hadn't been told who the other was—which meant she'd have to look for them individually, instead of searching for a couple. He'd also sworn that *he* wasn't her genetic father, since there'd been a time when she'd wondered. And he'd ruled out the two other theories she'd come up with: Grady and Edaline's daughter, Jolie, and Councillor Kenric.

Of course, that was assuming he'd actually told her the truth about any of that, which was a fifty-fifty bet.

And even without all the matchmaking misery, she honestly wasn't sure how to act around Fitz. They weren't *dating*—but they weren't *not* dating either. Some of their friends knew. Some *suspected*. And at least one might not be very excited when he found out for sure.

Basically, everything was a mess, and the whole "romance" thing was turning out to be *way* less awesome than it had looked in human TV shows and movies.

Edaline sighed. "I wish you'd tell me what's going on. I know there's something."

"I can tell you," Bo offered, reminding Sophie why he was her least favorite bodyguard.

"No, you can't," Sandor snapped. "Our ability to protect Miss Foster would be severely hindered if she felt she couldn't speak freely around us."

"Does that mean all three of you know what she's not saying?" Edaline asked Sandor, Bo, and Flori.

"I'm just worried about Tam," Sophie jumped in, trying to distract with a different confession. "Mr. Forkle thinks the Neverseen are going to force Tam to do something really bad, so he wants us to focus on Tam's strengths when we're trying to figure out their plan. And I'm not sure how everyone's going to feel about that."

Edaline wrapped her arm around Sophie's shoulders. "I'm sure they'll feel the same way you do: anxious for their friend—but also eager to do whatever it takes to get Tam out of there safely. Just like you guys did when Keefe was in the same position."

"Yeah, but Keefe was different. He *chose* to run off and join the Neverseen without anyone threatening him." He'd foolishly thought he could take them down by pretending to be on their side. "*And* he had nothing to lose. Tam has Linh."

"I think Keefe had more to lose than you realize," Edaline said, her lips curling into one of those annoying parent smiles that always seemed to say, *You'll understand when you're older.* "He still does. But my point was, he got out of there before it was too late."

"Barely," Sophie mumbled.

And Lady Gisela had claimed that the real reason Keefe remained alive was because he was her son and benefited from her protection.

Tam didn't have that advantage.

"It's a tricky situation," Edaline admitted. "But the good news is, Tam has a group of smart, dedicated friends to help him through this—and I'm sure they're just as eager to get to work as you are. So don't be afraid to lean on them."

Sophie nodded, watching Wynn chase his tail in stumbling circles. "I guess I should hail them and explain what's going on."

She could hear the dread in her voice and was certain Edaline had picked up on it. But Edaline didn't bring it up as she kissed Sophie's cheek and lowered her arm.

"I should get over to the gorgodon enclosure and see how the gnomes are doing," Edaline said, taking a couple of steps down the path before she turned back to Sophie. "Oh, but in case you were wondering, I know there's still something you're not telling me. And if you don't want to talk about it, that's fine. I'm not going to pressure you. But I figured I should at least tell you that I'm onto you."

She said it with a smile, but Sophie still had to fight the urge to tug out an itchy eyelash—her much-too-noticeable nervous habit. Discussing boy troubles with her mom was about as fun as being dropped into a pile of sparkly alicorn poop.

Plus . . .

Grady and Edaline had already lived through all kinds of bad match drama with Brant and Jolie—and it had *not* ended well. She didn't want her situation to send them back to the miserable place they'd been in when she first met them.

"You can tell me *anything*," Edaline assured her, as if she'd guessed part of Sophie's worries. "I realize I haven't always been as strong as you needed me to be—"

"You're *very* strong," Sophie interrupted, scrambling for an explanation that wouldn't hurt Edaline's feelings. "I just . . . want to be strong too."

Edaline stepped closer, taking Sophie's gloved hands. "You're the strongest person I've ever met. I *know* you can handle anything. But you're carrying such heavy burdens for someone so young. I wish you'd unload some of them on me. I understand if you'd rather face it alone. I guess I just want you to know that you don't *have* to."

Sophie's heart felt like it was pressing against her throat, and for a second, she was tempted to blurt out everything. But . . . she was *also* worried about how Grady and Edaline would react to her plan to fix her matchmaking situation.

They'd never been bothered by her connection to her human parents, but her biological parents might be a different story. They were elves, living somewhere in the Lost Cities. And once Sophie knew who they were, it would probably change things. Not that she'd want to live with either of them—or even want to talk to them, honestly.

These were people who'd been okay with letting their child be part of an *experiment*, knowing it would likely put her in constant danger. People who'd let her grow up in a forbidden world without them. People who hadn't made any attempt at contacting her now that she was back in the Lost Cities. In fact, for all she knew, she saw them all the time and they never gave her the slightest clue that she meant anything to them.

Probably because she *didn't*.

She wasn't their daughter.

She was the Black Swan's *creation.*

And as far as Sophie was concerned, they were nothing more than DNA donors.

That was why she didn't care about Mr. Forkle's reasons for keeping their identities secret. Her genetic parents *chose* to be a part of Project Moonlark. Nobody forced them to do it. So if having people know about their involvement caused problems for them, that was their own fault.

She shouldn't have to deal with a lifetime of scorn just to protect them from facing the consequences of their decision.

"Well," Edaline said, straightening up, "you know where to find me if you need me."

"Same," Sophie told her, turning to Wynn and transmitting an order to stay far, far away from the gorgodon.

The tiny alicorn responded with a bouncy nicker that wasn't very reassuring.

Sophie was definitely going to need to have a chat with Silveny about her son's poor survival instincts. But she had bigger things to focus on as she headed inside. Havenfield's elegant mansion overlooked the ocean, and Sophie spent the climb up to her third-floor bedroom watching the waves through the etched glass walls and trying to figure out how she was going to tell her friends about Tam.

But even after Sandor, Bo, and Flori had finished their endless security sweep—inspecting every closet, shadow, and petal in her flowered carpet—she still hadn't found the right words. In fact, the more she'd repeated Mr. Forkle's plan in her head, the more pointless it had started to sound.

Why would she sit around brainstorming ways that Tam's power could be used against her and her friends, when she could reach out to him the same way she used to reach out to Keefe when he was with the Neverseen and see if Tam could tell her anything that might help?

She hadn't tried to contact him before, because she hadn't wanted to put Tam in a difficult situation. But if Mr. Forkle was right, then Tam was already in so far over his head that it'd be worth the risk.

And it was certainly a lot smarter than wasting weeks or months on theories that might not even be on the right track.

Before she could change her mind, she plopped down on her enormous canopied bed and stared at the crystal stars dangling from her ceiling, watching them sparkle in the bright afternoon sunlight as she gathered her mental strength. The warm energy churned inside her head, humming as it grew stronger and stronger and stronger. And when she could feel it buzzing against the backs of her eyes, she shoved it out of her head, along with the loudest call she could muster.

TAM—CAN YOU HEAR ME? IT'S SOPHIE!

She repeated the words over and over, imagining the force like thick syrup pouring across the sky in every direction—covering the world. And as her consciousness spread, she closed her eyes and tried to feel for . . .

Actually, she wasn't sure.

She hadn't communicated telepathically with Tam very often, so she didn't know how to recognize his thoughts the way she could with Fitz and Keefe.

TAM! PLEASE, I NEED TO TALK TO YOU!

A headache prickled the edge of her consciousness, but she gave herself several long, slow breaths and timed her next transmissions with each exhale, keeping the message shorter to save her energy.

Tam.

Tam!

TAM!

Still nothing—and she could feel her concentration draining to the dregs.

If Fitz were there, he could've given her a mental boost, the way he always did when they worked together. But she'd let her silly matchmaking worries keep him away. She had to stop that—had to figure out how to keep things balanced and—

Sophie?

The voice was a ghost in the shadows—cold and whispery.

TAM!

Yeah. But I shouldn't be talking to you like this. It's way too dangerous.

I know, but—

There's no "but," Tam interrupted, and the feel of his thoughts shifted with the words, like the darkness was crystalizing into ice. *Gethen checks my memories constantly.*

Sophie's heart screeched to a stop.

She'd forgotten that the Neverseen's only Telepath had been in the Black Swan's custody when Keefe had been living with the enemy. So they hadn't had to worry about anyone discovering their conversations unless someone caught them in the act and somehow figured out what was happening.

They also hadn't had to worry about Keefe unwittingly revealing anything he wasn't supposed to.

Has Gethen probed your mind? she asked, trying to keep the transmission as quiet as possible.

Of course. That was the first thing he did.

Bile burned Sophie's throat.

Probing was a type of deep mental search that could uncover pretty much anything when performed by a skilled Telepath.

And Tam knew all of their secrets.

All.

Of.

Them.

So if Gethen had probed his mind . . .

Then the Neverseen now knew that Sophie was an Enhancer. And that Mr. Forkle was still technically alive—and that Magnate Leto and Sir Astin were two of his alter egos. And that Granite and Squall—two other members of the Black Swan's Collective— were Sir Tiergan and Juline Dizznee. And they knew every single lead that Sophie and her friends had uncovered—and everything they *didn't* know as well, like how to open Councillor Kenric's cache if they ever got their hands on the real one again. And how little Sophie had learned, from healing Prentice's mind and from searching Wylie's memories, about what had happened the day Wylie's mom died.

This is so bad, she thought, reaching up to rub her temples.

Did Tam know where they'd hidden her human family after they'd rescued them from Nightfall?

And how much did he know about the security at Havenfield?

Were Silveny, Greyfell, and the babies still safe there?

I'm sorry, Tam's mind murmured, and the frigidness of his voice thawed a little. *I tried to block him, but . . . Gethen's too powerful.*

He was.

Sophie had faced off against him several times, and it had never gone well—and she was a Telepath with an impenetrable mind.

It's not your fault, she promised, wanting to punch herself for not figuring this out earlier. If she had, they could've started taking precautions from the moment Tam had left.

Actually, she should've thought of it before he turned himself over. Maybe he wouldn't have gone if he'd known how much he was going to compromise the Black Swan in the process. After all, Tam had been to some of the Black Swan's hideouts. He knew the oath they made when they swore fealty, and what weapons and fighting techniques Sophie and her friends had been practicing during their battle training, and—

Yeah, Tam thought, interrupting her ever-spiraling panic. *Now you get why I can't talk. He's going to know everything you tell me, and he's already learned enough.*

Okay. She took a deep breath, reminding herself that she couldn't change what had already happened.

Time to focus on damage control.

You can still tell ME something, she reminded him. *Even if they know you told me, they'll have to change their plans—and that'll buy us some time.*

His thoughts froze again. *Uh, you think they tell me anything important?*

There must be something. Maybe some clue to where you are, like a landmark you recognize?

Nope. I'm in a cave. All I've seen are rocks.

What color are they?

They're rocks, Sophie. There's nothing special about them.

Are you sure it's a cave and not somewhere underground?

Underground might mean he was close to Loamnore.

I don't know. All I can tell is that it's dark and stuffy.

So it's hot? Like . . . maybe you're in a desert?

I seriously have no idea. The Neverseen are smart. They're not going to let me learn anything that would give their hideout away. His mental voice stayed soft and whispery, but there was a sharpness to his thoughts that Sophie had never experienced. It felt like each word was a shard of darkness, slicing into her head.

But she wasn't going to let him scare her away. *Have you met any other members of the order?*

A couple—but they wear cloaks and use code names, and barely say two words to me when we train, so I can't tell you anything about them.

Wait—you're training with them? Does that mean there's another Shade?

No. I don't know what these guys can do. Or maybe they're female. I can't tell. Lady Gisela keeps me alone in a corner, practicing from Umber's journals.

A shiver rippled down Sophie's spine. *Umber had journals?*

Lots of them. And I have to work through all of her exercises.

Well . . . *that* was terrifying.

What kind of exercises? Sophie asked—and when he hesitated, she added, *Shadowflux training, right?*

Obviously.

The response bothered her more than a single word should—but it was the icy confidence behind it.

The Tam she knew had been reluctant to train in the dark element. Almost afraid of its strange power. And now he sounded . . . proud.

You need to be careful, she warned him. *You don't know how Umber's training will affect you. She was one of the creepiest people I've ever met.*

The bones in her hand throbbed, remembering the way Umber had shattered them one by one.

I AM being careful, Tam assured her. *But the training is unavoidable.*

Then tell me what they're having you do so I can figure out what they're planning and get you out of there. You're already going to be in trouble for talking to me, right? Why not make it worth it?

Uh, because they can make their punishments WAY worse.

Don't worry—Linh's safe. Tiergan's added a ton of security to his house to make sure of it.

You and I both know that doesn't mean anything. And even if she IS okay right now, they have plenty of ways they can punish ME.

Sophie was certain they did. And she hated putting him in that position. But leaving him with the Neverseen was feeling beyond scary. She had to find a way to get him out of there, before they made him do something terrifying.

Please, she begged. *You know what's at stake—especially if you're studying Umber's journals.*

I DO know what's at stake. My sister's LIFE.

The coldness wrapping each thought sank all the way to her bones. *We'll protect her.*

Yeah. I've seen how well that protection works. I can't take that risk.

So . . . what? You'll just do whatever creepy things the Neverseen tell you to do and hang the consequences?

I don't know.

That's not good enough!

Well, it's going to have to be!

Sophie locked her jaw to stop her teeth from chattering. *I can already feel a change in you, Tam. Just from your mind. I think Umber's training is affecting you.*

I can handle it.

You know Keefe said the same thing, right? Sophie asked.

She'd hoped that would knock some sense into him, given the strange animosity between the two boys. But Tam's thoughts were frozen claws as he said, *I guess I get where he was coming from now.*

Tam—

No—just stop! You're making everything worse. Leave me alone. His thoughts stirred like an arctic flurry.

I can't do that.

Well, you're going to have to. If you try reaching out to me again, I'll run straight to Gethen so he can hear everything you say. I can't put Linh at risk.

Meanwhile, you're putting Linh's safety ahead of everyone else's—do you really think she wants you to do that?

I don't care. I'm her twin. Protecting her is my job. And I think you're forgetting that I also saved Silveny and Greyfell—and their babies—by agreeing to cooperate.

I could've saved them another way.

How? I'm sure you've spent the last couple of weeks replaying what happened over and over—can you honestly tell me you've thought of anything else that would've cured them in time?

She hadn't.

But she couldn't admit that.

You've seen the kind of cruelty the Neverseen are capable of, Tam. You really want to be a part of that?

The mental flurry picked up speed, hurling each word at her. *I don't have a choice!*

There's always a choice!

Well, right now, I'm choosing to be done with this conversation.

Tam—

No, it's time for you to leave me alone, Sophie. Get out of my head— or I'll make you go away.

Tam, please—

The flurry spun into a hurricane—a black storm crashing into her brain. And Tam's booming voice was thunder amid the tempest.

I'M SORRY—I DIDN'T MEAN ANY OF THAT. I HAD TO PUT ON A GOOD SHOW SO GETHEN WON'T GET SUSPICIOUS WHEN HE CHECKS MY MEMORIES LATER. AND I NEEDED TIME TO GATHER THE SHADOWFLUX I'M USING TO SHROUD THIS THOUGHT, SO HE CAN'T HEAR ANYTHING I'M SAYING. HE'LL PROBABLY STILL BE ABLE TO SEE THAT I SENT SOMETHING, SO I CAN'T TELL YOU MUCH— AND YOU CAN'T REACH OUT TO ME LIKE THIS AGAIN. IT'S WAY TOO DANGEROUS FOR EVERYONE. JUST . . . TRUST ME TO HANDLE THIS. I HAVE THINGS UNDER CONTROL— OR I WILL, IF YOU DO ONE FAVOR FOR ME. I NEED YOU TO KEEP KEEFE AWAY UNTIL THIS IS OVER. IF YOU CAN'T CONVINCE HIM TO COOPERATE, MAKE UP A FAKE PROJECT TO DISTRACT HIM. OR LOCK HIM UP SOMEWHERE IF YOU HAVE TO. I DON'T CARE. JUST DON'T LET HIM GET

NEAR THE NEVERSEEN—AND DEFINITELY DON'T LET HIM GET NEAR ME.

Why not? Sophie asked, struggling to pick his words out of the frozen chaos. Her heart was pounding as hard as her head, drowning out everything with the *thump! thump! thump!*

But she still managed to catch when Tam said, *BECAUSE HIS MOM ORDERED ME TO KILL HIM.*

THREE

HAT? SOPHIE TRANSMITTED—though she should've asked, *WHEN?*

Or, *HOW?*

Actually, the best question would've been, *WHY?* But it didn't matter.

The storm faded from her mind, and her connection to Tam vanished with it. Only a few wisps of shadow remained, swirling around her brain like icy smoke. But instead of dissipating, the inky threads coiled together, twisting and tangling with glimmers of darkness she'd thought were long since buried and gone. Morphing into something black and shivery and *much* too familiar.

Sophie shook her head—hard—and ripped her eyes open, hoping the burning light could sear away the darkness before it took over. She'd spent months haunted by an eerie shadow beast—her mind's way of processing the lingering echoes from the shadowflux she'd been exposed to during Umber's attack. And there was no way she was letting that terrifying monster come back to life.

But the shadows sharpened and stretched. Growing claws and fangs.

"Flori!" she shouted, never so grateful to have the loyal gnome stationed outside of her doorway.

"What's wrong?" Flori asked as she rushed to Sophie's side.

Sophie curled into a ball, hugging Ella—the bright blue Hawaiian-shirt-wearing stuffed elephant she'd brought with her from her human life. "I need you to sing that song you wrote to quiet the echoes."

Flori clearly had *lots* of questions, but said nothing as she reached for Sophie's face, brushing her fingers softly down Sophie's cheeks and humming the first notes of the melody. She sang the lyrics in an ancient, earthy language that slipped under Sophie's skin, turning warm and wonderful as each verse sank into her mind and heart. And as the air thickened with a sweet floral perfume, it felt like the sun rose inside her, melting the cold darkness and flooding her with tingly light.

"Did that help?" Flori whispered, studying Sophie with worried gray eyes.

"I . . . think so." Sophie flexed the fingers on her right hand to test for pain, breathing a sigh of relief when there wasn't any—and the weakness didn't feel like it had worsened. But as the last of the song's warmth faded, a bone-deep weariness nestled in, making her wish she could burrow under her blankets and soak up the sweet, heady scent from the flowers growing across her canopy for the rest of the day. Each of the four types of blossoms had inspired part of the lyrics for the healing verses, and the vines had grown much more fragrant with Flori's singing.

But Tam's message had left a different type of echo—the kind where the words kept crashing around in her head, knocking loose stabbing slivers of worry. And while her brain wanted to rebel—wanted to scream that there had to be some horrible misunderstanding—it also kept repeating what Mr. Forkle had said about Tam earlier.

They're going to use him to strike at you where you're most vulnerable.

"Easy," Flori warned as Sophie stumbled to her feet.

"What's going on?" Sandor demanded, catching Sophie by her shoulders to hold her steady.

"Nothing," she assured him.

"That wasn't *nothing,*" Flori said gently. "Something stirred your echoes."

"Yeah, but you fixed me." She flashed a grateful smile, and Flori gave her a green-toothed grin in return.

But Sandor stopped her from pulling away. "Where do you think you're going?"

"I need to talk to Keefe."

His jaw locked with a furious *click.* "What has that boy done now?"

"Nothing." All of her bodyguards looked dubious—which was fair, considering the amount of chaos that Keefe had caused over the years. "I'm serious."

"You were perfectly fine—and then you started doing your Telepath tricks, and suddenly you were begging for Flori's help," Sandor argued. "Don't expect me to believe the two have no connection."

"They *are* connected," Sophie admitted. "But I wasn't talking to Keefe."

"Then who were you talking to?" Bo called from the doorway.

Sophie sighed, knowing the truth would cost her precious time. But when she tried to pull free again, Sandor was much too strong. "I . . . reached out to Tam."

Sandor's grip tightened and he leaned back, studying her from head to toe like he was searching for injuries. "What did that traitor do to you?"

"Nothing!"

"Stop using that word as your answer for everything!" he snapped.

"But it's true! And he's not a traitor!" She twisted free of his grasp—anger bringing back her strength. "You *know* Tam. How can you call him that?"

And yet, even as she asked the question, she could hear Mr. Forkle telling her, *There are very few things Mr. Tam wouldn't do to protect his sister.*

And *that* didn't even take into consideration how the shadowflux might influence him.

She wasn't going to forget the sharpness of his thoughts—or the chill—for a very long time.

"As your bodyguard, I must view anyone choosing to live with the enemy as a traitor," Sandor insisted. "And what he did to you today proves why that distinction is necessary."

"He didn't *do* anything," she argued, clinging to the reminder with an iron grasp. "He used shadowflux to pass along an important warning—at huge risk to himself. And I guess whatever's left of my echoes reacted to it. It's not a big deal."

"It's a *very* big deal," Sandor argued. "He should've known that would happen and—"

"Well, he didn't," she interrupted. "Or . . . maybe he did and figured it was worth the risk—which is the same thing *I* did when I reached out to him telepathically."

She was trying very hard not to think about what the Neverseen might do to punish Tam for their conversation. Hopefully the show Tam put on would convince Gethen that he'd remained loyal.

"And it's a good thing we talked," she added, "because Mr. Forkle was right. The Neverseen *are* planning to use Tam for something. That's why I have to talk to Keefe."

Sandor blocked her as she headed for the door. "You can hail Mr. Sencen on your Imparter if you'd like. But you're staying here. And you're getting back into bed."

Sophie shook her head.

This wasn't the kind of conversation she could have through a tiny handheld screen. She needed to be there in person, to make sure that Keefe was *really* listening—and so he couldn't turn off his Imparter if they ended up arguing.

And to give him a good long hug if he needed it too.

"I'll rest when I get back," she promised.

"Perhaps we should see how your mother feels about that plan," Sandor countered, blocking her again. "Do you really think she'd want you leaving this room after how close you came to a major setback to your recovery?"

He had a point.

But Sophie couldn't afford to be babied right now. "I know my limits. I wouldn't go if I couldn't handle it."

Sandor snorted. "Right, because you never push yourself too hard."

"Maybe it would help if you explained what's so urgent," Flori suggested when Sandor blocked Sophie yet *again*—and she seriously considered kicking him in the shin. "What do you need to tell Mr. Sencen that can't wait until morning?"

Tam's horrible warning lodged in Sophie's throat, and she knew she wouldn't have the energy to repeat the words more than once. So she reached for her temples, pretending to feel faint, and waited until Sandor moved to steady her—then launched past him with a spin move that was shockingly graceful, given her general clumsiness.

"See?" she called over her shoulder. "I'm fine!"

Bo raised his arms to barricade the door, but Sophie ducked underneath, earning herself lots of growls as she raced up the stairs to Havenfield's gleaming fourth-floor cupola, which existed mostly to house the large sparkling orb hanging from the ceiling, made up of hundreds of small round crystals dangling off nearly invisible cords.

The Leapmaster 500.

None of the crystals would take Sophie where she needed to go, but they weren't the reason she'd headed there.

"Absolutely not!" Sandor bellowed as she made her way to the largest window and flipped the latch to open the glass. "You're not jumping off of any towers today."

"I wasn't planning on jumping."

The fourth floor probably wasn't tall enough to give her the momentum she'd need to teleport, so she was going to have to levitate higher first. Usually she leaped off of one of the cliffs at the edge of the property, but this was closer and faster—or it would've been, if she didn't have two gorilla-size bodyguards shoving their way in front of her and forming a wall of impenetrable muscle.

"Tell. Me. What's. Going. On!" Sandor demanded.

"You'll find out when we get there." A hint of a smirk curled her lips when his scowl softened. "What? You thought I wasn't going to take you with me?"

"Past experience has shown that to be your preference," he noted.

"Yeah, well, I've learned to pick my battles. So can we go now? Or do you want to keep wasting time and being super annoying?" She offered him her left hand.

Bo grabbed it first.

"We're just going to Keefe's house," Sophie reminded him, trying to wriggle free without losing her glove. "I don't need to bring the whole cavalry."

"Nowhere is safe," Bo argued.

She couldn't necessarily disagree, considering all the "safe" places where she'd ended up getting attacked over the last few years. But that didn't change the basic physics of their situation. "My levitating's only strong enough to carry one of you."

"Then you should bring *me*," Bo insisted. "My senses are far superior. As are my fighting techniques."

Sandor snorted a squeaky laugh.

"If you go," Sophie jumped in before she had to suffer through another round of the ogres-versus-goblins debate, "I'm sure Keefe will make you listen to more of *The Ballad of Bo and Ro*."

Bo's lips curled back, revealing his pointed teeth.

His relationship with Keefe's ogre-princess bodyguard was equal parts tumultuous and complicated, a fact that Keefe never missed an opportunity to torment the two of them about—generally in the form of an epic poem that kept getting mushier with each new stanza. And Sophie couldn't blame Keefe for the teasing. Not only did Bo's and Ro's names rhyme, but it turned out that they were also secretly married, thanks to a betrothal arranged by Ro's father— King Dimitar—in an attempt to protect them when his time as king was over. The ogre seat of power was *earned* instead of *inherited*, and Dimitar didn't want either of his top warriors fighting against each other in the battles-to-the-death that would follow his surrender or demise—not when they would be so much more powerful ruling together. So he made them marry, hoping the alliance would spur one of them to back down whenever the time came.

Instead, they seemed even more intent on killing each other.

"The last verse I heard Keefe working on had a *lot* of Bo-Ro snug- gling," Sophie added when Bo didn't let go. "Pretty sure there was some kissing, too."

Bo muttered an impressive string of ogre curses as he released her arm. "Fine. I'll remain behind—but tell Romhilda she needs to get better control of her charge!"

"Oh sure, I'll get right on that." She said it with enough sarcasm to make it clear that he didn't exactly have a lot of control over *his* charge either. "Ready?" she asked Sandor.

He reluctantly took her hand. "I can't decide how I feel about the strong-willed teenager you're becoming."

"Neither can I," Sophie admitted. Sometimes she felt so much braver than the wide-eyed girl she'd been when Fitz first brought her to the Lost Cities. But deep down, she was just as terrified. Maybe more so, now that she understood what she was up against.

"I trust you'll begin the evening patrols while we're gone?" Sandor asked Bo—though it was more of an order than a request.

Bo nodded. "I expect a full report when you return."

"Of course." Sandor turned to Flori. "And will you let Lady Ruewen know where we've gone, so she doesn't worry?"

Flori dipped into a quick bow and turned to head down the stairs.

"Wait!" Sophie called after her as the much more pressing worry hit her, and she wanted to smack herself for letting the echoes and Tam's warning distract her. "I need you to give her an urgent message. Tell her that Gethen probed Tam's memories the first day they took him."

Sandor flinched. "Does that mean what I think it means?"

"Unfortunately, yeah. The Neverseen know everything Tam knows."

More muttered curses filled the air—a mix of ogre, goblin, and gnomish words this time. And Sophie definitely shared their sentiments.

"Would you like me to notify the Black Swan?" Flori offered.

"Probably smart." Sophie shouldn't have been surprised that Flori knew how to contact the Collective—Flori's great-great-grandaunt Calla had been part of the order, *and* part of Project Moonlark, before she sacrificed herself to become the cure for her species in the form of a Panakes tree.

Calla had even been the one to choose Project Moonlark's name.

"I'm assuming the news we're bringing Mr. Sencen is equally dire?" Sandor asked quietly.

Sophie nodded.

She was still trying to wrap her head around it—trying to understand what Lady Gisela could possibly be thinking with such a cruel, unexpected order. But Tam had seemed pretty desperate, so there was no way she was letting Keefe ignore the warning, no matter how much he whined or resisted.

"Count on being there for a while," she told Sandor.

He heaved a squeaky sigh. "And you're sure you're up for teleporting?"

"Teleporting will be the easy part." She glanced at the ground far below, then closed her eyes, searching for the slight tug of gravity coursing through her cells. If she concentrated hard enough on the sensation, she could push against it with her mind and take control. "Okay. Here we go. One . . . two . . . *three!*"

Their feet floated off the ground—slowly at first. Then much, much faster. So fast, they would've crashed into the Leapmaster if Sophie hadn't done a whole lot of awkward flailing. That was the problem with levitating. There was no traction in the air, so she was stuck flapping her arms and kicking her legs like a fledgling flare-adon until the momentum dragged them out of the window. And once they were clear of the cupola, the strong ocean winds took over, launching them up so fast, Sandor made several squealy sounds that Sophie couldn't wait to tease him about later.

"Please tell me we're high enough now," he begged over the roar of rushing air.

Sophie peered down, trying to decide if it was the height or the conversation ahead that was making her dizzy.

SOPHIE! FRIEND! FLY! Silveny transmitted, nearly breaking Sophie's concentration.

Not today! Sophie told her, wishing she had more time. Flying with Silveny was the best way to clear her head and let her biggest worries go. *Right now, I have to talk to Keefe!*

Even that high up, she could hear Silveny's giddy whinny. And as her mind filled with a whole lot of *KEEFE! KEEFE! KEEFE!*

Sophie tried to share some of the mama alicorn's enthusiasm.

But all she felt was dread as she let gravity take back over, dropping them faster faster faster, until her concentration tore open the sky and they crashed into the black nothingness of the void.

"Miss Foster," Lord Cassius said, offering one of his unsettling, oily smiles as he stepped aside to let Sophie and Sandor into his home.

The Shores of Solace would've lived up to its name if Keefe's dad weren't such miserable company. The single sprawling level had glistening mother-of-pearl walls and vine-draped arches that formed a series of brightly lit rooms and sunbaked patios, all decorated in soothing tones of blue and gray to match the panoramic ocean views from every window. It truly was one of the most breathtaking estates that Sophie had visited in the Lost Cities. But she always wished she could leave the second she got there.

"I'm assuming you're here to visit my son?" Lord Cassius asked, smoothing his blond hair—which was already immaculate. As were his cream-colored jerkin and ruby-encrusted cape. "He's in his room, where he's *supposed* to be working through the empathy exercises I created for him this morning. But I think we can safely assume he'll be doing anything but what I've asked."

That sounded like Keefe—not that Lord Cassius deserved Keefe's cooperation.

Father of the Year he most definitely was *not*.

In fact, Sophie could barely look at him without wanting to fling something at his head for every hurtful word he'd ever said to his son. Much like how she despised every gorgeous room in that house, since Lord Cassius had hidden it for most of Keefe's life in order to use it as an "escape" from his family. Keefe was only living there now because Lord Cassius had refused to provide crucial intel to find Sophie's missing human parents unless Keefe agreed to move in—and not because he missed Keefe or was worried about Keefe living on his own. He'd simply wanted to put an end to the gossip about his runaway son after Keefe fled the Neverseen.

"That way," Lord Cassius told her, pointing to a polished driftwood door at the end of a long, shimmering hallway.

It took Sophie a second to realize the words were an invitation.

The few other times she'd visited Keefe, they'd sat outside on the cushioned swings dangling from the cover over the back patio. She'd never been in his room. And for some reason the idea of going there made her cheeks warm.

But she could feel Lord Cassius watching her, so she tilted her chin up and motioned for Sandor to follow her down the hall, which was dotted with shards of green, blue, and clear sea glass arranged in swirling patterns.

Her knock was wimpier than she meant it to be—so wimpy that there was a second where she wasn't sure if Keefe had actually heard her. But then he called out, "Back to nag me already? You seriously need to get yourself a hobby. I hear spelunking's fun. Oooh, or you could try swimming with the krakens! I *doubt* they'd eat you—but maybe we'll get lucky!"

Which wasn't exactly a "come in." But Sophie still grabbed the silver handle and turned it—realizing only as she was yanking the door open that she should've made sure Keefe was dressed before she barged in.

Thankfully, he was.

Mostly . . .

He lay sprawled across a huge bed that rested on a pedestal made of lacy bleached coral, wearing fuzzy blue pajama bottoms covered in tiny black gremlins, with his head propped against a familiar green gulon stuffed animal.

"Foster?" he asked, jolting upright—which only drew more attention to the fact that he was currently shirtless. He crossed his arms, his cheeks flushing with a hint of pink when his ice blue eyes focused on her. "I . . . um . . . what are you doing here?"

Ro snickered from the corner, where she lounged on a cushioned chaise, painting her claws the same purple she must have recently dyed the ends of her choppy pink pigtails. "Smooth, Lord Hunky-hair. Smoooooooooooooooooooth."

The nickname was a remnant from one of Keefe and Ro's many bets—though it seemed especially fitting at the moment. Keefe's hair was always artfully mussed, but there was something wilder about it than usual, as if he'd spent the morning swimming in the salty waves and let it dry in the sun—and the beachy look *really* worked for him.

Not that Keefe needed improvement.

All elves were jaw-droppingly gorgeous, but there was something particularly handsome about Keefe Sencen—and the boy was *well* aware of it. Though he seemed a little off his game at the moment. His smug smirk was noticeably absent as he scrounged around his blankets, searching for something.

"Here," Ro said, tossing Keefe a wrinkled black tunic from the floor. "Bet you're wishing it didn't smell so much like sweaty boy in here, huh?"

"It's fine," Sophie promised, even if the room could definitely use some airing out.

A good cleaning would work wonders too. Everywhere she looked were piles of crumpled clothes and scattered shoes and stacks of papers and plates of half-eaten food. And all the thick curtains were drawn tight, leaving the space dim and stuffy. The room was clearly designed to be beautiful, with marble floors broken up by rugs woven to look like pristine sand, and seafoam walls inlaid with starfish and anemone shells. But under Keefe's care, it was a disaster zone. Even the furniture had a strange randomness to the arrangement that made Sophie wonder if he'd moved it all just to bug his dad.

"Let this be a lesson to you," Lord Cassius said as Keefe wrestled with the tunic, which was refusing to turn right side out. "You should always keep your room—and yourself—at your best, since you never know when you'll need to make an impression."

Keefe rolled his eyes. "Whatever. Foster's used to me."

Sophie was.

But she was also wishing he'd get that tunic on. Her gaze kept straying to the long thin scar just below his rib cage—a gift from King Dimitar after Keefe challenged the ogre king to a brutal sparring match. Even though Keefe had pulled off a desperate victory, Sophie had still been ready to strangle him for risking his life so recklessly. They'd had one of their worst fights afterward—which did *not* bode well for the conversation ahead.

Lord Cassius cleared his throat. "Well. My son may like to pretend he's above everything. But I hope you won't hold his laziness against him, Miss Foster. Or his sloppiness. I know how much he values your friendship."

"Keep it up, Dad, and Foster's going to get jealous of all the sweet things you say about me. Not everyone gets to be so lucky, after all!"

"You *are* lucky," Lord Cassius informed him. "Far more than you know."

"Yep, everyone wishes they had my family." Keefe yanked his tunic over his head a little harder than necessary. "And, uh, you can go now."

"Oh, I can, can I?" Lord Cassius's mouth twitched in a way that *almost* looked like he might be teasing—and it made the resemblance between father and son much stronger. "Perhaps I should stay. We all know the princess rarely serves as a proper chaperone."

"I don't need to," Ro said, adjusting her metal breastplate as she sat up straighter. "Gigantor does enough fun-killing for everybody. Plus, our girl's still rocking the 'adorably oblivious' thing—which, I gotta say, gets less adorable by the day." Her eyes narrowed at Sophie. "I'd be happy to spell it all out for you if you want. We could make a pros and cons list together!"

"Pros and cons of what?" Sophie asked.

Ro sighed dramatically, glancing at Keefe as she said, "See what I mean?"

Keefe threw Mrs. Stinkbottom at her head, but Ro swatted the stuffed green gulon right back at him—and when he ducked, it knocked into one of the lanterns lining Keefe's bedside table, sending it crashing to the floor.

Sandor rubbed the center of his forehead. "It's going to be a long afternoon."

"It is," Lord Cassius agreed, "and I think I've endured all I can manage. But I expect to be kept informed—assuming Miss Foster is here to discuss something of importance. If this visit is *personal*"—he raised his eyebrows in a way that had Sophie fidgeting and Keefe glowering—"then I suppose the less I know, the better. But if it pertains to the Black Swan, don't forget that I, too, am a member."

He was.

And Sophie hated it.

Joining the order had been another one of his conditions before he'd shared the information Sophie needed to rescue her human parents. Leave it to Lord Cassius to barter with innocent lives in order to further his own agenda.

"Then you can ask the *Black Swan* for an update," Ro told him, plucking one of the daggers from the holsters strapped to her thighs and aiming it at Lord Cassius's head. "Right now, it's time to go, Daddio."

Lord Cassius narrowed his eyes. But he left without another word, closing the door behind him.

"Sooo . . . ," Sophie said, dragging out the word as she stared at the way her boots sank into the rug, which looked uncannily like stepping on real sand. "Sorry to drop by unannounced, but I—"

"Hang on," Keefe interrupted, sliding off his bed and tiptoeing across his room. He paused near the door, pressing his finger to his lips in the universal *shhhhh* sign before he grabbed the handle and shoved his shoulder against the wood as hard as he could.

A startled yelp echoed from the hallway, followed by a thud that could only be the sound of a body hitting the floor.

"You have ten seconds before I let Ro unleash some of her new little bacteria buddies on you," Keefe warned as he slammed the door hard enough to rattle the wall. "I hear they leave a gnarly rash!"

He waited until the sound of footsteps had retreated down the hall before he turned back to Sophie and lowered his voice. "That won't keep him away for long, so better spill it quick, Foster. Tell me why you have that cute little crease between your eyebrows. And why I'm feeling"—he waved his hands through the air—"hmm. Feels like the usual mix of worry, anger, and panic—though there's something underneath that's a little . . . I can't figure out how to describe it. Fluttery?"

"Oooh, let's focus on that one!" Ro jumped in. "It'll be *much* more interesting than all the blah-blah-blah-the-Neverseen-are-trying-to-kill-everybody-blah-blah."

"It's not *everybody* this time," Sophie corrected, trying to keep the conversation on track. "I mean . . . I'm sure that's still their plan for the long run. But at the moment . . ."

Her voice trailed off as she locked eyes with Keefe.

How in the world was she supposed to tell him this?

She couldn't just blurt out, *Your mom ordered Tam to murder you*—could she?

But . . . was there a delicate way of putting that?

"Aaaaaaaaaand the worry reaches the so-queasy-I-might-vomit level," Keefe said, clutching his stomach and dropping back onto his bed. "Gotta say, it's not my favorite emotion to share with you, Foster. Seriously—how do you ever eat?"

"Sometimes it's not easy," she admitted, swallowing the sour taste in her mouth. "And sorry."

She took a step back, trying to put some distance between them. Most Empaths had to make physical contact in order to pick up what someone was feeling. But Keefe was different—with her, at least. At first she'd thought it meant something about the strength of her emotions, but Keefe's father was able to do the same thing—and other Empaths couldn't. So the Sencens also seemed to have extra-powerful empathy.

Keefe patted the empty side of the bed. "I'm fine, Foster. And clearly you're going to need to sit down for this." When she didn't move toward him, he raised one eyebrow. "Uh, it's not like we've never done the News of Doom thing before."

They had.

Way too many times.

But one of these days, they were going to hit his breaking point—and this could easily be the moment.

"Need me to calm you down?" he offered, holding out his hand.

They'd discovered that if she enhanced him, he could use his ability to fill her mind with softly colored breezes and soothe her emotions. But the last thing he should be doing right then was comforting *her*. So she kept her gloves on as she made her way closer and sank onto the edge of the bed, keeping as much space between them as possible.

"Okay," she said, fussing with the frilly sleeves on her tunic. "I . . . talked to Tam today."

"Ugh, I should've known Bangs Boy was going to be a part of this," Keefe grumbled. "And I'm assuming by 'talked,' you mean one of your Look-at-my-fancy-Telepath-tricks! kind of chats, right? Mommy Dearest didn't send him to deliver a special message, did she?" He sat up straighter. "Wait. He didn't blow up anything, did he?"

"No, so far only *you've* destroyed anything for the Neverseen," Sandor growled.

He was, of course, referring to the time that Keefe exploded the glass pyramid at Foxfire—while Sophie was in it—in order to prove his loyalty to the Neverseen's cause. It . . . hadn't been one of his better life choices, even if he *had* given Sophie his cloak to make sure she'd be safe.

Keefe bent down and snatched Mrs. Stinkbottom off the floor, tossing the stuffed gulon from hand to hand like a furry basketball. "So what did good old Tammy have to say? Let me guess—he has no idea where they're keeping him, and everyone's wearing cloaks and using code names and ignoring his questions, so he's pretty much useless to us."

"Sorta," Sophie admitted. "He managed to learn one thing."

"And I'm assuming it has to do with me—and it's the reason for all the vomit vibes floating around in here?" Keefe guessed.

She nodded.

He set Mrs. Stinkbottom on the bed between them. "Then let's get this over with, shall we? I'm not sure my stomach can hold on much longer. Just blurt it all out when I count to three—it'll be fun!"

It wouldn't. But he was trying so hard to make this easier for her that she made herself agree. And when Keefe got to her cue, she held his stare and told him *everything*, starting with the map in Mr. Forkle's office and his theories about the dwarves, straight on to Tam's horrible warning.

Her throat felt raw by the time she'd finished. And Keefe . . .

Keefe was *silent*.

So was Sandor—though he was scanning the room like he expected Tam to jump out of the shadows any second.

Ro was doing the same, but she was muttering a whole lot of creative words under her breath.

And Keefe just kept sitting there.

Not talking.

Or moving.

Or blinking.

Sophie grabbed Mrs. Stinkbottom and scooted closer, placing the gulon in Keefe's lap in a pose where the shiny eyes seemed to look right at him. She'd had Elwin buy Keefe the so-ugly-it's-cute stuffed animal back when he was struggling with the possibility that his mom might've been killed in an ogre prison, hoping it would help Keefe feel a little less alone. And at the time, she'd thought there couldn't be anything harder than having to figure out how to mourn a mother who'd proven to be so terrible.

But *this* was awful on a whole other level.

"I'm sorry," she murmured, reaching for his hand.

Keefe watched her gloved fingers cover his palm, and for a second, he turned his hand and held on as tight as he could. Then he sighed and let go, scooting away from her. "I'm fine, Foster. We all knew this was coming."

"We did?" Ro asked, beating Sophie to the question.

"Uh, yeah." Keefe stood so fast that Mrs. Stinkbottom made a nosedive to the floor. "I keep failing my mom's creepy tests, so it was only a matter of time before she realized I was never going to 'fulfill my legacy' or whatever. And once she figured that out, she'd have to get rid of me."

"Why?" Sophie wondered.

That was the part that kept tripping her up.

Why was Keefe's mom being so extreme—and why now, all of a sudden?

It wasn't like Lady Gisela hadn't had chances to take Keefe out during their last few confrontations. She'd had weapons aimed right at his head and never came close to pulling the trigger.

So what changed?

And why make Tam do it when she could give the job to someone reliably evil, like Vespera or Gethen?

Keefe tapped one of his temples. "Because if I'm not on her side—and never will be—then I'm a liability. I could piece together the memories she took from me, find what she's hiding, and use that to beat her."

"I guess," Sophie mumbled, trying to figure out how to word the next part gently, since it had proven to be a sensitive subject. "But . . . she had those memories *shattered* instead of *washed*, so nothing can trigger them."

And no matter what telepathy tricks Sophie and Fitz had tried, they hadn't been able to recover enough shards to learn anything useful—and neither had Tiergan.

"That just proves the memories are important," Keefe insisted, turning to pace and sending clothes and papers flying as he kicked them out of the way. "I think something happened in London— something *big*, otherwise she wouldn't have gone to so much trouble to erase it. And I bet she told Bangs Boy to off me because I'm finally getting close to figuring out what it was."

"You are?" Sophie asked, frowning when Keefe nodded. "Since when?"

He chewed his lip for a second, then stalked over to a dresser that was shoved haphazardly into a corner and yanked the bottom drawer open, pulling out wrinkled tunics and tossing them onto the floor.

"You already know my mom gave me a letter to deliver to a house in London with a green door," he reminded Sophie as she made her way over. "And you said Fintan told you she sent me there to recruit somebody."

"He did," she agreed, peering over his shoulder as he removed the last of the shirts. "He also said that it was one of her side projects, so she didn't tell him much about it. And that the recruiting didn't work out—and you were never supposed to recover that memory."

"Guess it's a good thing I found another piece, then," he said, pushing on one of the corners of the drawer and making what must've been a false bottom lift ever so slightly on the opposite side—enough for him to get a grip on the edge. Slowly he raised the thin wooden panel, stopping after a few inches to slide a finger underneath and feel around for . . .

"Is that a trip wire?" Sophie asked as he unhooked a thin strand of silver from the underside of the panel.

"Can't be too careful with Lord Nosypants around," he confirmed, pulling the panel free and revealing four notebooks—one brown, one gold, one silver, and one green—with a cloudy vial sitting on top of them, attached to the other end of the wire.

"That tube is filled with one of my favorite airborne microbes," Ro explained, flashing all of her pointed teeth when Sophie backed up a step. "Those little guys know how to have a *party* in your sinuses."

Sophie's nose burned just imagining it, and she held her breath as Keefe finished unhooking the vial and set it aside—not *nearly* as carefully as she would've liked—before carrying the journals over to the bed. He left the brown, green, and gold notebooks resting on the quilt and flipped open the silver one, turning the pages so fast that Sophie couldn't recognize anything. But she could tell the book was filled with Keefe's amazing sketches.

"I've switched from making lists of memories to drawing them, since it helps me see it all a lot better, and I can't do the fancy projecting thing like *some* people," he explained, his cheeks flushing the way they often did when he talked about his art. "And it's a lot to keep track of, so I started sorting it into different categories."

"Does that mean *all* of these are filled with memories?" Sophie asked, wondering when he'd found the time to do so many drawings—and why he hadn't told her what he was up to or asked her to help.

"Yeah, but they're not full or anything—at least not yet. And it's not all stuff I've recovered. I've been logging *everything*, trying to arrange it in order, hoping it'll help me find the gaps, so I can see where to focus. But it's a lot to work through. You know how it is with a photographic memory. . . ."

She did.

She also knew how it felt to have someone mess with her head. In fact, she still hadn't found all the snippets of information that the Black Swan had hidden in her brain to prepare her to be the moonlark—nor had she filled in one of the blank spots that Mr. Forkle created when he erased the memory of her first allergy attack.

"Do the colors of the journals mean something?" she asked.

His cheeks flushed even brighter. "Kinda. I use the silver one for anything that feels important, since that's the same color as the last elite level. Green is hard stuff, since we wear it at plantings. Brown is happy stuff, since . . . I don't know. It was the one I had left."

He noticeably didn't explain the gold. And Sophie was pretty sure she could guess the reason.

Before she and Fitz had tried to help Keefe recover more shattered memories, Tiergan had taught Keefe a trick to mark the things he didn't want them to look at while they were inside his mind. And Keefe had gilded all of his secret memories—which made Sophie very tempted to grab the gold journal and teleport away before he could catch her.

Somehow she found the willpower to resist.

Keefe glanced at the gold notebook, like he suspected what she'd been thinking. But he said nothing, instead going back to flipping through the silver one. And after a few more pages, he paused, pressing the book against his chest to hide what he was looking at. "Okay. Before I show you this, I swear I was *going* to tell you about it. I just . . . wanted to make a little more progress on my own first— which you do all the time, so please don't go all Foster Rage on me."

Sophie crossed her arms, not feeling ready to make any promises.

"You've also been super busy lately," he reminded her. "And . . ."

"And what?" she asked when he didn't finish.

"Never mind. All that matters is: I haven't done anything dangerous. I've just been doing the mental exercises Tiergan taught me."

"So you haven't been taking fathomlethes?" she pressed, sighing when Keefe looked away guiltily. "Ugh. You *know* those things are super unreliable."

They'd also made him cover the walls of his room at one of the Black Swan's hideouts in tiny scribbled-on scraps of paper like a serial killer's lair—which explained the abundance of drawings he'd managed to get done so quickly.

The rare river pearls were known for causing frenzied dreams and flashbacks.

"I was careful," he promised.

"And it was *hilarious*," Ro added. "One night he got out of bed and started doing a wiggle dance in his sleep and singing about Prattles pins. And another time he decided he was a baby alicorn and dropped to his hands and knees and galloped all over the house, whinnying. Greatest thing I've ever seen."

Sandor choked back a laugh—but Sophie only felt more worried.

"It was worth it," Keefe assured her, his face now brighter than Ro's hair. "It helped me remember this."

He flipped the silver notebook over and held out a photo-realistic drawing of . . .

A really nerdy-looking guy.

Between the tweed blazer and the bow tie and the ruddy cheeks and the wild hair, he looked like some sort of professor stereotype. All he was missing was a pair of thick spectacles and . . .

"He's human," Sophie realized, focusing on the man's deep brown eyes.

She'd gotten so used to being surrounded by blue-eyed elves that it was almost jarring to see someone with the same eye color as her—and someone with deep smile lines and strands of gray peppered through his messy red hair.

The elves remained ageless after they became adults. Only their ears changed with time, growing points along the tops after a few thousand years.

"Look at what he's holding," Keefe told her, pointing to the man's left hand, which held an envelope sealed with a symbol they'd only seen one other time: two crescents forming a loose circle around a glowing star.

"That's the letter your mom gave you," Sophie murmured.

"Yep. Looks like I didn't follow Mommy's delivery instructions as strictly as she wanted me to."

"Which surprises *no one*," Ro jumped in.

"Of course not," Keefe agreed, a hint of his smirk returning. "But now we know for sure that I *did* deliver the letter. And I saw the guy she was contacting. And now that I know what he looks like? I can track him down again and find out what Mommy Dearest wanted from him."

FOUR

BUT . . . YOU KNOW HOW MANY HUMANS there are in London, right?" Sophie had to ask, even though she hated being the hope crusher. "It's a *huge* city. Like, millions and millions of people."

And the man that Keefe had drawn was a pretty generic-looking British guy—from his bright ginger hair down to the elbow patches on his blazer. There were probably ten men on every block who looked similar to him—not that wandering the zillions of London streets trying to find someone more unique would honestly be much easier.

"That's where Dex comes in," Keefe said, snapping the silver notebook shut with a smug grin. "I did some research—which, uh, *don't* tell the Forklenator about, by the way. I'll never hear the end of it if he finds out—and it turns out, London has *lots* of surveillance cameras. So Dex is going to hack into their system and set it up to search for anyone who looks like my drawing. He says the art is detailed enough that he should be able to find an exact match—*and* it'll tell him which camera caught the image, so we'll know right where the guy is. All Dex needs is a few minutes with one of their computers so he can do his thing, and then we just sit back and wait for the alerts to go off."

Sophie wanted to point out that they were assuming the guy was still living in London, and he could've easily moved away in the years that had passed. But her brain was too busy getting stuck on something that was probably way less important.

"You've been working on this with Dex?"

She managed to leave off the "without me." But the unspoken words still felt like they were staring them down, demanding to be acknowledged.

Keefe tapped his fingers against the spine of the silver notebook. "Well . . . I needed a Technopath. And Dex is the best."

"He is," Sophie agreed.

He was also her best friend.

And she knew it wasn't fair to feel left out after all the times she'd chosen to hide what she was working on from everybody. But that didn't stop a piece of her heart from turning very prickly.

"I was *going* to tell you," Keefe assured her.

"When?"

"Soon."

That didn't feel like a good enough answer—and Keefe must've known it, because he reminded her again, "You've been super busy. I haven't seen you in over a week."

"Well, I would've been here if you'd told me what you were doing! And if Dex has to go to London, you're going to need me to teleport him there."

Sandor cleared his throat.

"We'll figure out how to bring you along if we have to," she promised.

"You *will*," Sandor agreed. "There is no 'if.'"

"And that's what we were already planning on," Keefe told her, which didn't make Sophie feel any better. If anything, it kinda proved that they'd been waiting until they *had* to clue her in.

"It also would've been way faster if you'd let me project your memories for you," she pointed out, feeling more tempted than ever to grab the gold notebook and steal a good long look at everything he was hiding.

She snatched the brown one instead.

Keefe cringed as she flipped to the first carefully sketched memory—but didn't try to stop her.

He also didn't offer to let her start helping him now that she knew what he was working on, she noticed—but then she didn't care anymore, because his art was even more amazing than she'd expected. He'd used a medium she didn't recognize—not paint, but the colors were too vibrant for pencil, and the details seemed to shift with the way the light hit the paper. It felt like she was actually watching Keefe sneak through the grounds of Foxfire at night, carrying a wiggling green creature, and playing tackle bramble with Fitz while Biana cheered them on, and sitting with all of the Vackers, gazing at the colorful flames of an aurenflare. The drawing after that showed Lord Cassius covered in some sort of thick, sticky slime. And the rest of the pages seemed to be blank, save for a barely started pencil sketch toward the middle of the notebook, where the bodies had only been vaguely blocked out. It was impossible to tell who the figures were, but the memory looked like it might have taken place in Keefe's favorite ditching spot at Foxfire.

"I haven't spent as much time on my happy memories," Keefe explained quietly, "since they never have my mom in them, so they're not as important, you know?"

The raw truth in those words softened some of the prickles in Sophie's chest. And she was about to hand back the notebook when a sketch hidden near the end caught her attention—a drawing she was surprised to recognize herself in.

She sat with Keefe on the staircase at Havenfield, the light from the chandelier forming a soft halo around her as she leaned toward him, clinging to his hand while he turned away, his eyes slightly watery. It didn't look like a happy scene, and it took her a second to realize she was seeing the moment she'd told him what little she'd learned from Fintan about Keefe's shattered London memory. But underneath the sketch, in neat, bold letters, he'd written the words she remembered telling him that day:

Lots of people care about you, Keefe.

"We do," she said quietly. "And we can help if you let us. *I* can help.

Keefe cleared his throat. "I know."

"Then why are you keeping me away?"

He took the brown notebook from her and added it back to the pile with the green and gold. "I'm not. It's just . . ."

"That's not an answer," she pointed out when he didn't continue. "And that's the second time you've stopped yourself from telling me something."

"Is it?"

"Yep—and don't even try the whole answering-questions-with-questions thing on me."

He tore a hand through his hair. "It's not a big deal."

"Seems like it *is*, if it's making you not trust me."

"I never said I don't trust you."

"You didn't have to. It's pretty obvious."

Ro clicked her tongue. "Hmm. This sounds a *lot* like something I warned you would happen, doesn't it, Hunkyhair?"

Keefe shot her a withering glare before turning back to Sophie. "I *do* trust you. I'm just . . ."

His voice trailed off, and the prickliness in Sophie's heart came back with a vengeance. "Please tell me what's wrong. Did I do something, or say something, or . . . ?"

Keefe dragged a hand down his face, making a sound that would probably be best described as "frustrated ferret." "It's not you. I'm just . . . trying to do the right thing."

"What does that mean?" She glanced at Ro for translation when Keefe stayed silent.

"Don't look at me," Ro told her. "I've never understood it."

Keefe sank onto the bed, making more ferret noises. "It means . . . it's different now, you know?"

"Not really," Sophie admitted.

Unless he meant . . . Fitz.

Or *her and Fitz.*

That was the only thing that was different.

But it also *wasn't.*

He sighed. "You're going to make me say it, aren't you?"

"I think you have to," she admitted. "Because I don't really get what would be *wrong.*"

Ro giggled. "The adorable obliviousness strikes again!"

Keefe rolled his eyes and tugged on the hem of his tunic—which was still inside out, Sophie realized. "Fine. Now that you and Fitz are dating—"

"We're not," she interrupted.

"I know, I know—not *officially*. But come on, Foster. You guys are totally a 'thing.' Fitz told me the whole sappy story about his big confession. And *yours*." He kicked one of his shoes across the room.

"That's ten minutes of my life I'll never get back," Ro added as Sophie's cheeks reached nuclear levels of heat. "Though I *did* enjoy the part where you bailed on Pretty Boy right before all the smooching."

"I didn't *bail* on him," Sophie mumbled, refusing to look at anybody. "Silveny went into labor, and we had to go save her and the babies."

"Don't you just hate when that happens?" Ro teased. "And that doesn't explain why you and Swoony Boy *still* haven't . . ." She puckered her lips and made horrifyingly loud kissy sounds. "Or *have* you?"

They . . . hadn't—but no *way* was Sophie answering that question. "I still don't get why any of this means I can't help with your memories."

A rhythmic thumping sound followed.

Maybe Keefe kicking the bed?

Or banging his head against the wall?

Sophie was far too busy studying the grains of sand in the rug to check.

"It's just . . . now that you guys are *together*," he eventually said, making her jump a little, "I figured it might be a bad idea for you and me to work on such a time-consuming project—especially since Fitz is obsessed with finding Alvar right now, so he won't want to help."

It took a beat for Sophie to piece together what he meant. "Fitz won't care if we work on this without him."

"You sure about that? 'Cause he *also* told me he hasn't seen you since Wynn and Luna were born—and that you haven't been hailing him or doing any of your little secret Telepath convos. He sounded kinda bummed about it. And he got a little less pouty after I told him I hadn't heard from you either, so . . ."

"Why is that, by the way?" Ro jumped in as a whole other kind of nausea flooded Sophie's system. "Shouldn't you guys be, like, all Fitzphie all the time?"

The urge to tug on her eyelashes was *strong*. But somehow Sophie resisted. "I have a lot going on."

"Like what? Something *you* haven't included *us* in?" Ro pressed.

"No! It's . . ."

"It's what?" Ro asked, refusing to let it go.

Sophie sighed. "It's . . . personal."

"Is it, now?" Ro patted the chaise next to her. "Well then, why don't you sit right here and tell Auntie Ro all about it?"

"Auntie Ro?" Sophie, Sandor, and Keefe all asked in unison.

Ro shrugged. "What? I can be nurturing when I want to be."

That would've been a lot easier to believe if she weren't using a dagger to clean beneath her claws.

"Don't look so afraid," she told Sophie. "Personal stuff is my specialty! Need some smooching advice? Because you're probably over-thinking it. You just—"

"NO!" Sophie interrupted, definitely not wanting to hear the end of that sentence.

"See why I didn't want to bring this up?" Keefe asked. "It's like, just when you think it can't possibly get any worse—it does!"

Yes, *yes*, it did.

But . . . now that they were *there*, Sophie had to know. "You really think Fitz would be *bothered* by us working together?"

Keefe shrugged. "Seems like he might be."

Ro snorted. "Of *course* he would! He'd be super, super jealous!"

"Don't," Keefe told her.

"No—I can't take it anymore!" Ro stalked toward Sophie and tapped her on the nose with a calloused fingertip. "I repeat: Yes, your Captain Perfectpants would be jealous! He scraped together the courage to get all share-y about his feelings, and now you're ignoring him, and being all mysterious about why, and telling everyone who asks that you're not dating him. And I'm not saying that's a bad call. Trust your instincts! Hopefully they'll lead you out of the oblivion. But in the meantime, count on your teal-eyed Wonderboy feeling a little insecure, particularly if he finds out you're spending lots of quality time with other dudes. And you know what? That's good for him. We all know that boy could use a little help in the humility department. So make him sweat a little. And *you*"—she spun back toward Keefe—"need to stop being so afraid."

"Afraid of what?" Sophie asked.

"I'm *not* afraid," Keefe argued. "I'm being a good friend."

"And how's that working out?" Ro countered.

"Awesome!" Keefe spat back.

"Yeah, it looks super awesome watching you draw until your fingers cramp every night because you're giving up without even trying."

"Giving up?" Sophie asked.

Keefe flopped back on the bed and covered his face with his hands. "Ugh, I'm so over this conversation!"

"So am I," Sandor agreed. "Aren't we supposed to be discussing the fact that your mother has given an order to have you killed by one of your friends?"

Suffocating silence followed.

"I wouldn't say Bangs Boy and I are *friends*," Keefe eventually muttered as he slowly sat back up. "More like *frenemies*. So I guess Mom kinda got that part right."

"No, she didn't," Sophie said, trying to decide if she should go sit beside him. They were back to the brutal topic, but . . . it felt *so* awkward. "I'll never understand why you and Tam have your ridiculous feud going on, but he took a huge risk to warn you to stay away."

"Yeah, I'm all warm and fuzzy about it. What was it he said again? Lock me up if you have to? What a good buddy!"

"Keefe—"

"Uh-uh, Foster. I know what you're thinking—and I don't care what Bangs Boy said. I'm *not* sitting any of this out! And if you try to lock me up, it's *on*."

"Anyone else kinda want to see that?" Ro asked, raising her hand. "Come on—you know you're curious, Gigantor. Our girl's got a feisty side to her that's gonna be *epic* when she fully unleashes it."

Keefe rolled his eyes but kept his focus on Sophie. "Do you really believe my mom would let something crucial like this leak? She's totally playing us! If she actually planned on killing me, she wouldn't breathe a word about it until it was time to give the death order—and there's no way she'd leave it up to Mr. Happy Shadow

Thoughts. He's a sulky know-it-all with ridiculous hair, but . . . he's not a murderer."

Sophie truly wanted to believe that.

But her brain kept picturing the same horrifying scenario: *Linh and Keefe both prisoners—strapped to some sort of brutal countdown contraption—and the only way for Tam to save one is to kill the other.*

Sure, it sounded like the final showdown in a cheesy human spy movie, but . . . they were living in a reality with cloaked villains setting unstoppable fires and unleashing genetically engineered beasts and flooding cities.

And even if it wasn't something quite so dramatic, if Tam had to choose between Keefe and his sister . . .

"Huh," Keefe said, fanning the air. "So . . . you think Tammy Boy would—dare I say it—do the 'dark deed'?"

"I think I don't want to find out what happens if he's faced with an impossible decision," Sophie corrected, scratching at her arms to rub away the chills. "And I'm sure Tam doesn't either. That's why he gave me that warning."

"But it's not a real warning! I bet you anything my mom *ordered* him to tell you that, so you'd get all protective and distracted."

"Then why was your first reaction to say you knew this would happen?" Sophie wondered aloud. "You said you're a *liability*."

"I *am* a liability. But *this* isn't how she's going to get rid of me. This is just her trying to keep me out of her way or scare me into cooperating, because some tiny part of her is still hoping I'll change my mind and be who she wants me to be. Once that hope's gone, or once she realizes how much progress I'm making on my memories, she *will* try to off me. And I guarantee *that* plan won't come with a warning. She'll just make her move and . . . I guess we'll see if I survive it."

He said the last part with a shrug, but his voice cracked ever so slightly. And it helped Sophie scrape together the courage to sit down beside him.

"I will *never* let her hurt you," she promised.

"Neither will I!" Ro flung her dagger, nailing the center of one of the starfish set into the wall. "And FYI—the next time I see Mommy Dearest, I'm aiming for her head."

"Perfect! Problem solved!" Keefe told her. And his expression was probably supposed to be a smirk—but Sophie could see the wince underneath.

No matter how much he hated or feared his mom, some tiny, reluctant part of him was always going to care about her a little.

"Anyway," he added, clearing his throat, "I guess that means we agree. I have all the protection I need."

"Um, that's not what we said," Sophie argued. "I—"

"I appreciate the crinkly forehead concern," Keefe interrupted. "More than you know."

"*Way* more than you know," Ro emphasized.

Keefe's jaw tightened. "But you're not going to change my mind on this, Foster. If something goes down in Loamnore like Forkle's predicting, I *will* be there with you guys. Just like I'll be there for anything else that happens—so let's not make this into a fight, okay?"

"Kee—"

"Nope! No more 'Keefe-ing' me. I get that you're worried, but . . . think about what you're asking. You want me to hide like some frightened sasquatch while everyone I care about keeps right on risking their lives. How am I supposed to live with myself if something bad goes down and I wasn't there to help?"

"And how are any of us supposed to live with ourselves if something happens to you?" Sophie countered.

"Easy. You'll say, 'Wow, that's the hottest Wanderling I've ever seen! Who knew a tree could have awesome hair?' And then you'll all sit under my stunning leaves and write poems about my general amazingness."

Sophie shook her head. "I can't believe you're trying to joke about this."

"Well, believe it, Miss F. I can joke about *anything*!" He nudged her with his elbow, but she refused to smile. And she hated her brain for suddenly picturing his Wanderling. But she could see it so clearly now. The tree would have yellow spiky leaves and ice blue flowers and pale bark—and it would be lopsided somehow, mirroring his crooked smirk.

"The thought of you dying will *never* be funny," she whispered, wishing her eyes weren't burning.

Keefe sighed and scooted closer, keeping only a sliver of space separating them. "If it makes you feel any better, I'd really prefer to keep living."

"Then stay away from the Neverseen!"

"See, I *knew* you were going to say that. And I *swear* I'll be *careful*, but—"

"No! There's no 'but,' Keefe! You can't ignore vital intel just because you don't like what it means."

"Is that so? Then tell me this: If Bangs Boy's warning had been about *you*, would you be like, 'Cool, guys, I'll be over here chilling at home while you go take on the Neverseen without me'?"

"Yes," Sandor told him.

"No," Sophie corrected. "But that's different."

"Why?" Keefe pressed. "And don't say because you're the moonlark—"

"But I *am* the moonlark! I was literally *designed* to be a part of everything that's happening."

"Yeah, well, so was I. I mean, no one gave *me* a cool code name, or a million fancy abilities—which is a serious bummer, by the way—but we both know my mom's been preparing me for my *legacy* my entire life."

"All that means is she's been preparing you to be on *her* side—not ours."

As soon as the words left her mouth, Sophie wished she could suck them back in. "Sorry."

Keefe picked up his silver notebook, slapping the side against his palm with a steady *thwap! thwap! thwap!* "No need to apologize. You're right. I *am* supposed to be part of the bad guys."

"That doesn't mean—"

"Relax, Foster. I'm not going to freak out on you. I'm aware of my situation—the question is, are you?" He thwapped the notebook harder. "I can swear fealty to anyone I want. Be friends with anyone I want. Fight on any side I want. That's *my* choice, no matter what my mom wants—and I say, 'Go, Team Good-Guys!' *But.* I don't get to stop being the dude who was raised by one of the leaders of the Neverseen. And it doesn't make whatever plans my mom has for me go away. Just like it doesn't erase the things she's already had me do—like delivering that letter. Who knows what other stuff I've done and don't remember?" *Thwap! Thwap! Thwap!* "*That's* why I can't let Mommy Dearest scare me away. We're always complaining that we don't have any good leads. But *I'm* the lead. And I can't help you guys if I'm hiding."

"Nobody said anything about hiding," Sophie argued.

"No, you just talked about locking me up."

"That was Tam," Sophie corrected. "And I'm pretty sure he was joking. Or using hyperbole."

"But I wouldn't be opposed to the idea," Sandor noted.

"Neither would I," Ro agreed.

"All I'm saying," Sophie said, snatching the silver notebook from Keefe's hands, "is that you don't have to be *with* us to *help* us. You've done a huge thing already. You remembered the guy's face! Now Dex and I can work on hacking the security feed in London, and—"

"Oh, so I'm not invited to London now?" Keefe asked, lunging to steal back his notebook—but Sophie was faster.

She tucked the silver book into the inner pocket of her cape. "No, you'll be staying here doing something way more important."

"If you say research—"

"Nope. You'll be adding to these." She put the brown, gold, and green notebooks into his lap. "This was a good plan, Keefe. I mean . . . I wish you'd lay off the fathomlethes. But cataloging your memories already worked, so keep at it! Plus, you're making some seriously gorgeous art."

"Oh sure, *now* you want me drawing until my hands cramp! What happened to the whole 'I could've helped you project your memories' thing, with the sad eyes and the 'Why don't you trust me?' I guess you're fine with me working alone now that you found a reason to ditch me?"

"The boy does make a valid point," Ro noted.

"I'm not *ditching* you."

"Good! Because, to quote Gigantor"—Keefe shifted his voice into an uncanny impersonation of Sandor's squeaky tone—"I go where you go."

"I don't sound like that," Sandor huffed.

Ro snickered. "You totally do."

Sophie sighed. "I'm *not* trying to ditch you, Keefe."

"Awesome, because there's no way you're investigating *my* past without *me*."

"It won't be *without* you. You'll be working harder than any of us. Kinda like how Dex works on his own when he's doing his Technopath thing—"

"Yeah, because Dex *never* feels left out."

"Okay, but Dex is . . . sensitive."

"You were going to say 'pouty,' weren't you?" Ro asked.

"Hey, don't dis the Dexinator!" Keefe told her. "He's my hero. Master elixir maker, ultimate gadget manipulator, *and* he scored a Foster kiss before Fitzy."

Ro's eyes widened. "He *did*?"

"It's not what it sounds like," Sophie mumbled. "It was . . . never mind—stop trying to distract me, Keefe! Working alone doesn't make what you're doing any less important. And I'll keep you updated on *everything*. I'll check in as many times as you want me to, answer all your questions—I'll even project everything I learn into a memory log so you can see it all for yourself. It'll be exactly like you were there, only better because you'll be safe."

Keefe whistled. "Wow, you say that like you honestly expect me to go along with this plan. It's like you don't even *know* me."

"Oh, I know you," Sophie said through a sigh. "I'll just never stop hoping you'll decide to play things smart for once."

"See, but 'smart' really isn't my brand. I'm more 'reckless dream guy without a care'! It's part of my whole 'bad boy' image." He tossed his hair. "And don't think I won't tackle you to get my silver notebook back—I will."

"Okay," Ro jumped in, before Sophie could respond. "Fun as it is to watch you two try to make each other's heads explode, I had big plans for napping before some serious pranking this evening. So how about I settle this for you guys and you let me get my beauty rest?"

"If you're still on the 'lock me up' plan, that's never gonna happen," Keefe warned.

Ro sauntered closer and pinched both of his cheeks. "You're so cute when you think you're being all tough and rebellious. But let's get real for a second, shall we? You get away with the things I *let* you get away with, because I don't care enough to fight you on them. And ignoring solid intel that someone's threatened to murder my charge? That's a big bodyguarding no-no. I may not care *that* much about what happens to you, but if you get yourself killed on my watch, it makes *me* look bad—especially if I had advance notice. So, I can't have that. Plus, I can also demand something fun from your little girlie while I'm at it!"

"Wait—what?" Sophie asked.

"Uh, yeah, my help doesn't come for free. I can take care of your Hunkyhair problem. But it'll cost you."

"If you're about to propose one of your ridiculous bets—" Sandor cut in.

"Not a bet," Ro assured him. "I'm talking about a straight bargain. Miss F gives me something, and I give her an obedient Keefster."

Keefe snort-laughed. "Good luck with that."

"See, but I don't need luck. Because *you* still owe me a dare."

The color drained from Keefe's face.

"Thaaaaaaaaaaaaat's right, Hunkyhair! You lost our last bet—and what were the terms again? Oh, that's right! If I won, I get to dare you to do anything I want, and you *have* to agree. So if I dare you to stay away from the Neverseen, guess who's not allowed to go near the creepy cloaked dudes? And yes, that *does* include places they *might* be."

"You realize, by that logic, I can't go *anywhere*," Keefe pointed out.

"Hmm, I guess you're right. Maybe I should drag you off to a cave, then. Oh! Or to my dad's palace! No one's breached the security there in centuries."

"Sounds fun," Keefe retorted. "I can teach King Daddy *The Ballad of Bo and Ro!*"

"Not if I lock you in the dungeon. The palace has a *really* awesome one. And given your delicate elvin senses, I'm betting the smell would break you in less than a day. Face it, Funkyhair—you have two choices: You can cooperate, and still get to leave the house to see your friends occasionally. *Or* I can finally get out of sparkle town and take you back to Ravagog with me—and before you go getting too smiley, Miss F, don't forget that you haven't heard your side of this bargain. You don't think I'd trade in my prizewinning dare for something easy, do you?"

"What do you want?" Sophie asked, and her mind made a quick list of possible demands.

But she definitely wasn't expecting the ogre princess to plop back onto the chaise, pat the cushion next to her, and say, "I want you to tell Auntie Ro why you looked ready to spew all over the floor when I asked what's been keeping you so busy lately."

"Seriously?" Sophie and Keefe both asked.

"Why?" Sandor added.

Ro shrugged. "Because I'm curious. And I enjoy meddling. It's the only fun I get to have here in elf land, and I have a hunch that this is the kind of secret that could be a game changer."

"It's not," Sophie assured her.

"Well then, I guess you're getting the deal of the century, aren't you? Oh, but if you lie, I'm sure Hunkyhair will call you out on it."

"I will," Keefe agreed.

"You realize she's bargaining for your freedom, right?" Sophie reminded him.

"Yup! But I can't stop her, so I might as well let her take you down with me."

Sandor leaned closer, whispering in Sophie's ear. "Admit it. You're tempted to let the Neverseen have him now, aren't you?"

A tiny, tiny part of her was.

But the larger part—the part that always had to be annoyingly practical—knew this was a way better solution than any promise she might force Keefe into making after who knew how many more hours of arguing.

And . . . it wasn't like her secret would stay hidden forever.

"Do we have a deal?" Ro asked.

"You *swear* you'll keep him away from the Neverseen?" Sophie clarified. "Like, you realize how impossible that's going to be?"

"Yes, I'm familiar with your boy's stubbornness—and his tendency to think he's outsmarting everybody. But he'll behave. Because he knows the consequences for breaking a bet—and I can always put him on a leash if I have to. I have the perfect harness. It chafes in some particularly unpleasant places. So what do you say?" She patted the chaise again.

Sophie closed her eyes, needing a few more seconds to remind herself that this was the best way to keep Keefe safe. Then slowly, painfully, she made her way over and sank onto the cushion. "I don't know why you care so much about this."

"I'm not totally sure either," Ro admitted. "But a deal's a deal, so spill it, girlie, and let's hope it's something juicy."

"Hang on," Keefe said, grabbing the chair from his desk and dragging it over. He plopped down right in front of Sophie, resting his elbows on his knees and propping his chin on his palms in the ultimate *I'm listening* pose. "Okay, let's solve one of the Foster Mysteries."

Sophie shot him a look that hopefully said *I hate you so much right now*. And she really hoped he was picking up on all of her vomit-churning as she closed her eyes and took a long breath.

"Anytime now," Ro prompted.

Sophie's hands balled into fists. "Fine. A little more than a week ago, I . . . went to see the matchmakers. And I tried to pick up my match packet. But . . . they wouldn't let me. Apparently, I'm"—she needed another breath—"I'm . . . unmatchable."

She squeezed her eyes tighter to make sure she wouldn't have to see the looks on their faces.

"Hmm," Ro said after several agonizing seconds. "That's not what I was expecting. But it should still do the trick."

"What trick?" Sophie asked, wishing Keefe would say something. His silence was seriously killing her.

"Don't worry your pretty little head about it," Ro told her. "And you're being awfully quiet over there, Hunkyhair. Nothing you want to say?"

Breathing became impossible.

It felt like three entire lifetimes passed before Keefe cleared his throat and asked, "So . . . you decided to register?"

"Really?" Ro demanded. "*That's* what you're going with? Of all the wasted opportunities!"

"What?" Keefe snapped back. "I just thought she still had mixed feelings about it!"

"I did," Sophie agreed. "But . . ."

"Yeah . . . ," Keefe mumbled.

Neither of them bothered to say that she'd done it for Fitz.

Because it didn't matter anymore.

"Whoa." The strain in Keefe's voice made Sophie finally open her eyes—and she found him clutching his chest, face twisted with pain. "Um, what's with all the heartache, Foster?"

Sophie crossed her arms, wishing she could physically hold back her stupid, too-strong emotions. "What do you mean?"

"I mean, it feels like you think . . ." His eyebrows crushed together as he tilted his head to study her. "You think Fitz is going to care about this?"

"Of course he's going to care! I'm unmatchable!" Saying it again definitely did not make it easier.

"Yeah, but . . . only for right now," Keefe told her. "Once you know who your biological parents are, you'll be fine."

The sentence had to tumble around her brain a few times before she could figure out why it felt weird.

She hadn't told him *why* she was unmatchable. Just that she was.

"You knew?" she whispered.

He stared at his foot as he kicked at the floor. "Well . . . I saw your Inception Certificate. And matchmaking's all about genetics, so . . . I sorta assumed. And I'm sure Fitz did too."

Sophie blew out a breath.

Was she seriously the only one who'd been too clueless to realize what that had meant?

No.

She couldn't be.

Because Fitz had said . . .

"He doesn't know," she assured Keefe, crossing her arms tighter. "Fitz gave me this big speech about how there's no way he and I wouldn't be on each other's lists."

Ro snorted. "Wow. Is *that* what you elves call romance? 'Don't worry, my love, a bunch of snooty intellectuals are totally going to put your name on a piece of paper and give us permission to date each other'? Ugh, no wonder you haven't felt ready for any smooching."

Sophie's cheeks went nuclear again. But when Ro put it that way, it did sound pretty awful—though that was also a strange observation coming from someone stuck in an arranged marriage.

And she really didn't know what to do with the whole "my love" thing.

Keefe, meanwhile, was kicking the floor with enough gusto that Sophie wondered if he was trying to tunnel his way out of there.

"I'm sure Fitz was just assuming you'd wait to register until after the Black Swan gave you that information," he mumbled. "I mean, it's not like they're never going to tell you who your biological parents are."

Sophie barked a laugh. "Wanna bet? That's why I met with Forkle today—I was trying to get him to tell me. And do you know what he said? *'Perhaps in a few hundred years.'*"

Ro whistled. "Harsh."

Sophie nodded. "I even told him what happened at the matchmakers', to make sure he knew the stakes—but of course he did. And then he launched into a speech about how I should be focusing on protecting the dwarves and saving Tam instead of dating. He didn't care that . . ."

Nope.

She was *not* going to cry in front of Keefe.

Especially not about Fitz.

Keefe let out a sigh that sounded like a balloon deflating and leaned closer. "This isn't going to change anything."

She looked away, blinking hard and choking down the giant knot of nerves trying to close off her throat. "Right. Because being a bad match is no big deal around here—and I'm not even that. I'm *unmatchable*! How much you wanna bet I'm the first person that's ever happened to?"

"You *do* seem to be a trendsetter," he admitted. "But, um . . . you realize there are more ways to find out who your biological parents are than just asking Forkle, right? I mean, you're Sophie Freaking

Foster. Where's that stubborn streak we all know and fear a little? You've told the Councillors where they could shove their rules how many times? And don't even get me started on all the almost dying. Are you seriously telling me it hasn't occurred to you that you can solve this on your own?"

"It has," Sophie admitted. "I just . . . don't know where to start. Mr. Forkle hasn't exactly given me much to go on."

"Well then, I guess it's a good thing you're friends with someone who's mastered the art of breaking rules to get what they want," Ro told her. "I'm sure Hunkyhair can help you come up with a plan."

Sandor cleared his throat.

"Oh, relax, Gigantor, she already said she was going to be working on this anyway," Ro reminded him. "Isn't it better if she has some help?"

Help.

The word felt like a spark—but it snuffed out just as fast when she realized Keefe wasn't exactly volunteering.

"It's okay," she told him after a beat of awkward silence. "You should be focusing on your memories."

"I should," he agreed, and her heart felt like it sank into her sloshy stomach. "But . . . thanks to my lovely bodyguard here, it looks like I'll be sitting out on all the scheming you'll be doing about the dwarves and Tammy Boy. So I'll have some extra time to kill—and you know I'd never pass up a chance to get one up on the Forklenator."

"You don't have to," she told him when his smirk looked a tiny bit forced.

"I want to. Seriously."

She met his eyes, and there was an intensity in his stare that made her heart change rhythm.

"I'm *always* here for whatever you need, Sophie," he said quietly. "And I gotta say, Team Foster-Keefe is going to *crush this*. But . . . I need you to promise me one thing, okay?"

She nodded.

He looked away, kicking the ground again. "You have to tell Fitz what we're doing—and *why*. Just to make sure there're no misunderstandings, you know?"

"I know," she mumbled. "I've been planning to tell him anyway. I was only waiting until I had an actual plan, so he wouldn't freak out as badly."

"He won't freak out," Keefe assured her.

"Uh, this is Fitz," Sophie reminded him. "Reacting to bad news isn't exactly his strong suit."

"Yeah, I guess that's true." He stood and strode over to his desk, grabbing another notebook—a pale blue one this time—and a pen before plopping down on his bed. "Okay then, Miss F. Let's figure out how to solve the ultimate Foster Mystery!"

FIVE

WOW. YOU WEREN'T KIDDING about not having much to go on," Keefe said, squinting at the notes he'd scribbled down while Sophie had paced his room and told him everything she knew about her biological parents.

He hadn't even filled half of a page.

And everything had question marks by it, in case Mr. Forkle had been lying.

So *technically*, they might have nothing.

Keefe scooted farther back on his bed and propped Mrs. Stinkbottom behind his head, looking *way* more relaxed than Sophie was feeling at the moment. "Okay, I *have* to ask . . . how do you feel about bending the rules of telepathy a little?"

"You mean *breaking* the rules of telepathy," Sophie corrected, number one of which was *No reading someone's mind without their permission.*

He shrugged. "I'm just saying, I'm pretty positive that you and Fitzy could solve this thing in five minutes if you went all *Cognate—RAWR* on Forkle's memories. You've broken through his blocking before."

"Yeah, but I'm sure he has other defenses he'd start using once he figured out what we were trying to do."

"And *that's* why you do it when he's asleep."

Sophie frowned. "We don't know where he lives—and even if we did, I'm sure he has all kinds of security and . . ."

Her voice trailed off as Keefe exchanged a look with Ro that seemed to say, *Isn't our moonlark the cutest?*

"You don't have to go to his house. You already know where he works," Ro reminded her.

"But Foxfire's on hiatus—and he doesn't sleep there anyway," Sophie argued.

Keefe laughed. "I kinda love that I have to explain this to you. It's like proof that no matter how feisty you get, you'll still always be our sweet little Foster."

Sophie's cheeks burned, but whether she was embarrassed or touched, she couldn't tell. Either way, she hoped he didn't notice.

"You know those sedative things you hate so much?" he asked. "We'd slip one into the Forklenator's lunch when school's back in session and he's in Magnate Leto mode. Then you and Fitz would ditch your afternoon sessions, let me work my mad skills on the lock to his office, and ta-da! One conked-out Forkle drooling on his giant desk, just waiting to have his memories explored. You guys would have plenty of time to do your Telepath thing and slip back to study hall before he wakes up. I doubt he'd even know anything happened."

"Absolutely not!" Sandor snapped. "No one will be ditching sessions or drugging anybody!"

Sophie had to agree, even if the less-than-noble part of herself couldn't deny that the plan was solid.

"I'm not saying it wouldn't work," she told Keefe. "But . . . it'd be icky."

"Icky?" Ro repeated.

Sophie nodded. "Keefe and I both know how it feels to have someone invade our minds and mess with our memories. I'm not doing that to anyone else."

"Even if you wouldn't be 'messing' with anything?" Keefe countered. "You'd just be learning information you should've been given anyway because it's about *your* life. And let's not forget that you'd be learning it from the person who stole some of your memories and planted all kinds of other stuff without telling you. I mean, if anyone deserves to have their privacy violated . . ."

Sophie sighed.

He wasn't wrong.

But that didn't make it *right*.

The fact that he'd used the word "violated" said more than enough.

"How about we call that plan Z?" she suggested. "And I'll *consider* it once Foxfire is back in session, if literally every other idea has failed and we have no other options."

Ro muttered something about "no fun." But Keefe grinned. "Fair enough. And . . . never change, Foster. You keep us honest."

Sophie's face burned even hotter as he flipped to the last page of the blue notebook and wrote, "PLAN Z: UNLEASH THE FITZPHIE!!!" Then he turned back to the half-full first page and labeled it "PLAN A."

"Okay . . . since right now the only information we have is about who it's *not*," he said, scanning his notes again, "the first thing we need to do is make a list of people it actually could be. Then we'll decide how to rule them out."

Sophie sighed. "Technically it could be anybody."

"Nah, we can rule out a bunch of people. Like Grady and Edaline, since there'd be no reason to keep that hidden. And my dad, since he'd never give up control of his kid like that—or be able to go this long without bragging about you. And everyone in the Neverseen, since they'd never help the Black Swan—and hey, good news! That means you're not my sister."

Sophie stopped pacing. "Did you actually think I was?"

"Nope." He smirked. "But admit it. You're worrying about Fitzy now, huh?"

She hadn't been.

But now that he mentioned it . . .

Keefe cracked up. "I'm kidding! Alden wouldn't have been involved with Prentice's memory break if he was your dad—and Della would've stopped him from searching for you if she was your mom."

"I guess," Sophie mumbled, leaning against the nearest wall, her brain spinning spinning spinning.

What if a different Vacker was her biological parent?

She could be Fitz's cousin.

Or his aunt, thanks to the weirdness of the elvin life span.

In fact, for all she knew, her biological father could be Fallon Vacker and she'd be Fitz's great-grandmother. Sort of, at least.

"Whoa, deep breaths!" Keefe said, rushing over to her side. "It was just a joke."

"Not your smoothest moment," Ro told him. "Come on, Hunky-hair, don't blow this!"

Keefe ignored her, squatting a little to meet Sophie's eyes. "You're *not* a Vacker, Foster."

"You don't know that," she argued. "It could be the reason Forkle won't tell me, because it'd bring too much scandal to the family. Or because Fallon used to be with the Council or—"

"Fallon?" Keefe interrupted. "Wow, you've gone deep, deep conspiracy on me."

"You have to admit it's possible, right?"

She held her breath as Keefe considered, her mouth turning sourer and sourer with each passing second.

Eventually Keefe shook his head. "Nah, I don't buy it. Forkle would've snuffed out your Fitz feelings a loooooooooong time ago if you had any Vacker-family connection—and yes, I'm sure he knew about your crush. You *really* weren't that great at hiding it."

Sophie tried to glare, but she was pretty sure it mostly looked sulky.

"Seriously," he told her. "I'm one-hundred-percent positive about this. See? No Vackers on the list."

He held up the blue notebook, showing her the still mostly blank pages.

There were no names on the list at all—but Keefe had put "Foster Mommy" on one side and "Foster Daddy" on the other.

"Gah, what's wrong now?" he asked, wrapping an arm around her shoulders to steady her as her knees wobbled.

"She needs to rest!" Sandor snapped. "I told her she wasn't up for this. Her conversation with Tam nearly brought back her echoes."

"It did?" Keefe asked.

"I'm fine," Sophie insisted, but the words were too breathless to be convincing, and she didn't have the energy to fight Keefe as he guided her over to the bed. She even bent at the waist once she was sitting, trying to keep blood flowing to her darkening brain.

"You need water," Keefe told her, grabbing a bottle of Youth off the floor and handing it to her. "I've had a few sips from this, but if I head to the kitchen for a fresh one, Lord Annoyingpants will be waiting there with *questions*."

Sophie nodded, taking the bottle with shaky hands and downing the whole thing in one long swig. And the cool sweetness did clear most of the fog from her head. "Sorry," she mumbled. "I don't know what happened."

"Preeeeeeeetty sure it's called freaking out," Keefe said, sinking onto the bed beside her. "The question is, *why?*"

Sophie sighed, leaning back to stare at the ceiling. She hadn't noticed the skylights scattered around the room, or how their thick blue glass made it feel like she was peering up at the sky from somewhere deep underwater—which wasn't a helpful observation. It made the tightness in her chest feel even more like she was drowning. "I guess . . . it's just hitting me that we're really doing this. We're *really* trying to find my biological parents."

"That's what you want, isn't it?" Keefe asked.

She nodded.

Then shook her head.

"No. I *need* to know who they are. But . . . if I didn't . . . I'd be good with just pretending they don't exist. And the thought of maybe having to face them someday makes me sick."

"Yeah, I got that when you almost blacked out on me. And I think my stomach's going to need a week to recover from all of this.

But don't apologize," he added when she was about to do just that. "You're allowed to freak out—this is a *huge* thing."

"It is," Sophie mumbled, relieved he understood. "We're trying to find the people who volunteered to give up their DNA so their child could be turned into some freak—"

"You're not a freak," Keefe interrupted. "You're *special*. There's a huge difference."

She shrugged, not sure if she should agree to that.

But she really wished she could.

"Either way, they didn't know how I'd turn out when they signed me up for this," she argued. "For all they knew, I could've ended up with two heads or three arms or something."

"Ohhhhhh, that would've been amazing!" Ro jumped in. "The Black Swan should totally make that happen someday!"

"I'm pretty sure everyone involved with Project Moonlark trusted that Forkle knew what he was doing," Keefe said, ignoring his bodyguard. "He's supersmart when he's not being all curmudgeon-y."

"Maybe. But it still seems like my parents can't be very awesome people if they were willing to gamble like that with their kid. Especially since they also knew how dangerous this would be."

Keefe hesitated a second before he reached for her gloved hand. "I definitely know how it feels to have a not-so-awesome family. But like you're always telling me, that doesn't change anything about *you*. And . . . I have a feeling your biological parents signed up for this because they knew Project Moonlark was going to create something amazing, and they wanted to be a part of it, even if they had to do it secretly and trust the Black Swan to keep their daughter safe."

"I hope you're right," she whispered, and silence settled between them—until Keefe started to pull his hand away. She tightened her hold, needing that extra bit of support to ask, "Do you think I already know them?"

Keefe chewed his lip. "I kinda feel like Forkle might've tried to avoid that. Most people can't pull off hiding something so huge."

"I guess that's true." She sucked in a steadying breath before she could admit, "I think . . . I'm going to hate them. Especially if I *have* met them and they've pretended like I'm nobody. *That's* the part I'm dreading. If it's someone I thought I liked . . ."

"I get that," Keefe told her. "But . . . you found a way to make it work with Forkle, right? After you found out he wasn't just the nosy old human guy who lived next door like you thought, you figured out how to deal with him as your 'creator.' And Calla was part of Project Moonlark, and you two were super close. So . . . I'm not saying it won't be weird at first, but with a little time it might get easier."

"Maybe. But this feels bigger than all of that, you know? I mean, they're my *biological parents*. They were supposed to *love* me. And I know how awful I sound right now, since I've gotten to live with *two* super-awesome families and you've been stuck with your mom and dad. I realize how lucky I am. And I shouldn't need anything else. I just . . . it's hard to explain."

"I get what you mean, though," Keefe told her, twining their fingers together. "And I wish I was better at the whole 'saying smart stuff' thing. But . . . whether you know your biological parents, or don't know them, like them, hate them—whatever—I *know* you'll find a way to get through this. It's one of the things I'm always jealous of about you. You just . . . *handle* stuff. No running away or making a bunch of huge mistakes. Somehow you keep your head clear and just dig in and deal. It's pretty amazing."

A smile peeked out of the corners of Sophie's lips. "Thanks."

He nodded. "And if you need any help, I'm here."

"I may take you up on that," she told him, clinging to him a little tighter before she forced herself to let go of his hand. She sat up straighter. "I guess we should get back to plan A, huh?"

Keefe grabbed the blue notebook and pen, tapping his fingers against the blank lists he'd created.

Tap tap tap tap.

"You know, Foster," he said quietly, "you don't have to do this if you don't want to."

"What do you mean?"

"I mean . . . I can feel how much you're dreading it—and I don't blame you for that. So . . . if you want to keep one unsolved mystery about your past, I just want to make sure you know that no one will judge you."

She frowned. "Pretty sure they will."

Keefe sighed. "If you're worrying about all the matchmaking crud—don't. No one's going to care that you're unmatchable. At least not anyone who matters."

"Yes, they will," she argued. "You *know* they will. Especially . . ."

She couldn't bring herself to use the name.

Keefe looked away, tapping the notebook harder—*tap tap tap tap tap*—before he blurted out, "Fitz'll get over it."

Ro sighed *super* loudly, but Keefe shook his head and turned back to Sophie. "I'm his best friend. I know these things. I mean, he's Fitz, so yeah, odds are he'll need a *little* time to get used to everything—and I'll be right there to make sure he doesn't say something he regrets while he's adjusting. But he's liked you for a really long time—longer than he even realizes. So trust the Empath—a piece of paper with or without your name on it isn't going to change that. Fitz has also had to deal with being related to *Alvar*, so he'll understand why you might not feel ready to go exploring the sketchier parts of your biological family tree."

Sophie wanted to scoop up the words and hug each and every one of them—and then hug Keefe for being sweet enough to say them.

But that didn't mean she believed him.

"Come on, Keefe. We both know I'm already the weird human girl with the wrong color eyes who keeps getting caught up in a ton of drama. The whole time I've lived here, people have blamed me for the bad stuff that's been happening and threatened to banish or exile me. So if I'm *also* unmatchable—and someone dates me anyway? It'll be like . . . the scandal of the century."

"Maybe," he agreed. "But that won't matter to anyone who cares about you. It *won't*," he insisted, before she could argue. "And honestly . . . don't you think that's how it should be?"

Yes.

She really did.

But she'd also been through enough to know that life didn't always work out the way it *should.*

"The thing is," she said quietly, scraping together a truth she rarely even admitted to herself, "I'm not sure if I can handle the drama of being unmatchable either. I know you think I'm a pro at dealing with stuff, but . . . I'm tired of always being the exception to everything. All I've ever wanted to do is *belong.* And having my name on match lists feels like the best proof I'll ever have that I really am supposed to be here, you know? It's not *just* about crushes and dating."

Keefe studied her for a long second, like he was testing her resolve. Then he held up the blue journal. "Okay. On with plan A, then! But I agree with Gigantor. You need to rest. No offense, but . . . you look super wiped—and by the way, I'm going to need more info on the whole Bangs-Boy-stirring-up-your-echoes thing so I know how hard I need to smack Tammy the next time I see him. But we'll get to that later. Right now, you're going home, and I'll stop by tomorrow with the lists so we can start working on a strategy."

Sophie shook her head. "Uh, to quote you, 'There's no way you're investigating *my* past without *me*.'"

He smirked. "Yeah, that argument's going to work about as well for you as it did for me. And come on, Foster, do you really think you're up for spending hours brainstorming bio-mommy-and-daddy names? You almost passed out after two minutes—and I'd probably do the same thing. This is rough stuff. And you're already beat. So let me help. All I'm doing is making lists."

Her stubborn side wanted to keep arguing, but *annoyingly* he was right. "Fine. But you better not show those lists to *anybody*, or talk to *anyone* on them without me."

"Don't worry, Blondie. I won't let him screw this up," Ro promised.

"Does that mean we're leaving?" Sandor asked, holding out his hand.

Sophie stood and fished out her home crystal. "Yeah, I guess it does."

But when she looked over at Keefe and thought about the roller coaster of complicated conversations they'd just been through, she couldn't leave quite yet. Not without doing one more thing.

And she didn't care if it was awkward. Or what anyone might think.

She leaned over, pulling Keefe into the tightest hug possible, and whispered, "Thank you."

It took him a second to hug her back, and his arms felt a little stiff. But his breath was warm in her ear as he told her, "Anytime, Foster. I'm *always* here."

"Everything okay?" Edaline asked, running over to where Sophie and Sandor had arrived in the Havenfield pastures, and Sophie briefly wondered why her mom was covered in verminion fur—but forgot about it when Edaline added, "Flori told me what's going on—or everything she knew, anyway."

"*I'll* tell you the rest," Sandor said, steering Sophie toward the front door.

Sophie locked her knees. "No, you won't!"

"You and I both know you don't have the energy to go through the whole conversation again," Sandor argued. And when Sophie still didn't relent, he leaned down and whispered, "Don't fight me on this, and I'll keep your matchmaking secrets—though you're going to need to fill her in soon, now that you've involved Keefe and the princess."

"I know," she whispered back, needing a quick eyelash tug to settle her nerves. "And fine. But I have one question first—*then* I'll go to bed."

Sandor's sigh-growl made her ears ring.

But he let her turn back to Edaline and ask, "Is Grady still with the Council?"

Edaline nodded. "But only because he went back to warn them after I shared what Flori told me about Gethen probing Tam's memories. And she was able to get ahold of the Black Swan as well, in case you're wondering. Mr. Forkle said he'll let you know how they're going to manage the situation once he's gotten a few things in motion. I'm sure the Council will have lots of questions about what Tam knows when you meet with them tomorrow too."

Sophie's eyebrows shot up. "I'm meeting with the Council tomorrow?"

"You are. They've asked you to come to Eternalia at midday."

Sophie waited for her to add more, but Edaline had busied herself with brushing the shaggy purple fur off the front of her tunic in slow, methodical strokes. "Is everything okay?"

"Of course! I just feel like I should wait for Grady to be home before I say anything else." She stole a quick glance at Sophie. "But you're not going to let it go now that I've said something, are you?"

"You know me well," Sophie agreed.

"Fine," Edaline decided. "But I'll only tell you *after* you've showered, gotten into bed, and let me bring you something to eat—and I've had a chance to get some updates from Sandor. That's the deal. Take it or leave it."

It was Sophie's turn to sigh-growl.

But she knew a losing battle when she saw one. So she hurried inside and took what might've been the fastest shower she'd ever taken in her entire life. Her pajamas were bunched all weird as she stumbled into bed, because she'd tugged them on over her still-damp skin, and her hair was probably sticking out in a hundred directions. But she didn't care, because meeting with the Council was rarely a good thing.

And meeting with them in Eternalia had her brain screaming, *DANGER! DANGER! DANGER!*

"So what does the Council want?" she asked as Edaline snapped her fingers, making a tray appear in her lap filled with colorful, mushy foods that would taste way better than they looked.

"Take a few bites first," Edaline told her, which wasn't technically part of their deal. But it was easier to snarf down a few spoonfuls of pinkish-greenish goo than to argue—and bonus, it tasted like the most amazing macaroni and cheese.

Edaline sighed and sat beside her, tucking a soggy strand of Sophie's hair behind her ear.

"The Council has agreed to share the classified details of Grady's dwarven assignments with you. But only if you agree to work with them in a more official capacity, so that they can demand you take proper responsibility."

Sophie paused with the spoon halfway to her mouth. "Do I want to know what a 'more official capacity' means?"

"You do. It's good news—though it's definitely also a little strange and might take some adjusting." Edaline's smile was somehow equal parts proud and wary as she added, "It means they want to appoint you as a Regent in the nobility."

SIX

REGENT," SOPHIE REPEATED.

"You have no idea what that means, do you?" Edaline guessed, smoothing another strand of Sophie's wild post-shower hair.

"Not really," Sophie admitted.

She knew Vika Heks was a Regent, and that Regents were technically less "important" than Emissaries. But she honestly didn't know what being an Emissary meant either—despite Grady having the title.

All nobility-related stuff fell into the category of Weird Elf-y Things She Didn't Understand. She'd been forced to accept the fact that she was probably always going to be playing catch-up when it came to knowledge about the Lost Cities.

But she did remember one important detail. "I thought someone had to complete the elite levels at Foxfire before they could be part of the nobility."

"Normally that's true," Edaline agreed. "To be offered the title at your age is unprecedented."

"Oh good." So she'd get to have everyone grumbling about how she wasn't qualified for that kind of fancy status—and she couldn't even blame them for being upset.

The Talentless weren't allowed to join the nobility, in part because they couldn't take part in the elite levels without manifesting a special ability. So why should the weird girl raised by humans get to skip ahead?

Yes, she *did* have a special ability—five of them, actually. But once people found out that she was unmatchable . . .

"I promise, this is good news," Edaline said as Sophie scooted her tray to the foot of the bed so she could curl her knees into her chest and become a Sophie-ball. "I know it sounds intimidating. But it really might be the best way to protect the dwarves—and Tam—from whatever the Neverseen are planning."

Maybe it was.

But Sophie doubted that would matter once she was caught up in some huge gossipy scandal.

"Will you *please* tell me what's wrong?" Edaline asked, leaning down to make Sophie look at her. "I know this isn't just about becoming a Regent."

Lying was tempting.

As was ignoring.

But Sandor was right. Now that Keefe and Ro knew her secret, it was only a matter of time before the truth was "out there"—and her parents needed to know, in case she was right about all the ways being unmatchable would ruin her life.

So she reached for Ella, needing something to hide her face behind as she forced herself to explain what had *really* happened in Atlantis.

"Oh, sweetheart," Edaline whispered, pulling Sophie into her lap and hugging her as tight as she could. "Please don't cry—it's going to be okay."

"Sorry," Sophie mumbled, hating herself for getting all sniffly. She'd held it together pretty well with Keefe and Mr. Forkle. But for some reason, saying it to her mom made her a puddle of snot and tears.

"Don't be sorry," Edaline told her, wiping Sophie's cheeks. "*I'm* sorry that life always has to be so complicated for you. I was really hoping it wouldn't come to this."

Sophie pulled back to study her. "Wait. *You* knew I'd be unmatchable too?"

She was officially starting to hate everybody. And herself. And the world. And—

"I didn't," Edaline assured her, reaching out to brush away more of Sophie's tears. "But . . . I guess Grady's been worried for a while. He never mentioned it to me until you started avoiding your friends after we got back from Atlantis."

"I'd been holding out hope that the Black Swan had provided your genetic information to the matchmakers," Grady said from the doorway, making both Sophie and Edaline jump, "since their records are far more secure than the registry."

"They are?" Sophie asked, swiping at her runny nose and wishing she had a tissue.

Edaline snapped her fingers, conjuring up a silky handkerchief for her. "Controlling who people marry is fraught with challenges—as you well know. And the Council needs people to trust the system without question. So only the matchmakers themselves are allowed to know anything about their process, or the reasons behind their specific decisions. No one can access their own file, or the file of anyone else."

"That's why I kept hoping their record for you might be complete," Grady added as he made his way over to the bed, "but I should've known the Black Swan wouldn't take any risks. I don't understand why they're keeping your genetic parents secret, but I'm sure they have their reasons. Hopefully someday they'll share them. In the meantime"—he pulled Sophie and Edaline into a family group hug—"I need you to know that as far as your mom and I are concerned, this changes *nothing*. You're amazing. We love you. And we will support whatever decisions you make. Okay?"

Sophie hugged them tighter, barely managing to choke out, "Okay."

"And hey," Grady added, "if this makes you decide to put the whole dating thing on hold for a while, I can definitely get behind that—OW!"

He pulled back from the hug, rubbing the tender part of his arm where Edaline must have pinched him.

"What your overprotective father—who, unfortunately, will always struggle with the idea of you growing up—is *trying* to say, is that we're here for anything you need," Edaline clarified. "And that includes whatever investigating you might be planning to do into your biological family. I'm assuming that's why you went to talk to Mr. Forkle today? And I'm guessing he was less than cooperative, and now you're determined to find out what you can on your own while you also look into all the other important things going on?"

"Something like that," Sophie admitted, picking at the tiny silver gadgets covering her index fingernails and her thumbnails. Tinker had designed them to control her enhancing, so she wouldn't always have to wear gloves—though she still wore gloves most of the time as an extra precaution. "That . . . doesn't bother you guys?"

"It does if the search is going to cause more Elwin visits or Tribunals," Grady told her.

"Avoiding anything dangerous or illegal would be best," Edaline agreed. "But again—translating for your overprotective father—of course it doesn't bother us. We know your past is complicated. And we *never* want you to feel like you have to deny or hide any part of it. So if there's some way we can help, just say the word—and *please* never worry that it's going to upset us."

"Thanks," Sophie mumbled, blinking hard to fight off the fresh burn of tears. "Right now, I don't have much of a plan. Keefe's making some lists, but—"

"You told That Boy about this?" Grady interrupted. "He didn't make you feel embarrassed, did he? Or pressure you to—"

"Actually, he told me no one would care about the unmatchable thing," Sophie corrected. "Well, not anyone who mattered, at least."

Edaline's smile practically glowed. "That was very sweet of him—not that I'm surprised."

Grady snorted.

"And he's absolutely right," Edaline added, elbowing Grady in the ribs.

Sophie shrugged, still not convinced. She stared at her lap and folded and unfolded the handkerchief. "He actually tried to talk me out of finding my biological parents when he realized how weird it was going to be for me. But . . . I have to."

"No, you don't." Edaline tilted Sophie's chin up. "Seriously, Sophie—and I'm not saying that because I don't want you finding them. I just want to make sure you know that if your current match-making status is a deal-breaker for someone, they don't deserve you. Yes, being unmatchable will bring its share of challenges. But those challenges will mean *nothing* if someone truly loves you."

"How can you say that after what happened with . . ." Sophie stopped herself from blurting out the name, worried she was about to cross a line.

"What happened with Jolie was a tragedy," Edaline finished quietly. "And there's no excuse for what Brant did—even if it was a horrible accident. But . . . part of me will always wonder what would've happened if I hadn't put so much emphasis on matchmaking. I'll never know if things would be different if I'd truly supported their relationship—one hundred percent—from the moment Jolie picked up her final list and found that Brant's name still wasn't on it. That's why I'm not making that mistake again. I understand why the matchmaking system exists. And I'm grateful every day that it steered me toward Grady." She reached for her husband's hand, clinging tight. "But . . . the system definitely has its flaws. And if it's going to exclude you for something you can't control—especially since I *know* Mr. Forkle would never let you form an attachment to someone you're related to—I hope you'll trust yourself enough to know what you truly want and ignore the rest. And Grady and I will support you every single step of the way."

"We will," Grady agreed. "Though I gotta say, I hear staying single can be *amazing.*" He yanked his hand free before Edaline could pinch him again.

Sophie rolled her eyes. "You know this isn't *just* about dating, right? Everyone's going to freak when they find out. And I'm sure the Council will take back their fancy appointment faster than you can say 'Regent.'"

Maybe they'd even kick her out of Foxfire. . . .

"Why?" Grady asked. "Marriage has nothing to do with the nobility. In fact, some Regents and Emissaries are even advised to stay single—that way they'll have the option of becoming a Councillor someday, should an opening arise."

The Councillors weren't allowed to have any immediate family ties because it could hinder their ability to make objective decisions.

"Okay," Sophie said, wishing it could be that simple, "but . . . how many bad matches have been appointed to the nobility?"

Grady and Edaline shared a look.

"I . . . can't think of anyone," Edaline admitted. "But it's hard to keep up with all the Regents, Mentors, and Emissaries."

"I'm sure it is," Sophie conceded. "But, given the way people treat bad matches, I'm betting there haven't been any. And even if there have been . . . I'm *unmatchable*. I'll be stuck with that label whether I date or not—*and* I'm sure it's never happened to anyone before, so that's going to make it an even bigger deal. Which means, once the news gets out—and you know it will, given how many people have already figured it out without me telling them—it's going to turn into this huge drama. And if I'm a Regent, I'm sure they'll demand the title be taken away, and then I'll be the Girl Who Got Kicked Out of the Nobility and—"

"Whoa, easy there," Grady interrupted, wrapping an arm around her shoulders. "I think you're forgetting that power and talent will always reign supreme around here. How else would someone as grumpy as Bronte end up on the Council? And no one—*no one*—can deny the value of your abilities. Or how much we need your help with the huge problems we're up against."

Edaline reached for Sophie's hand. "I know people haven't always been as welcoming, or as accepting of you as they should've been. Our world wasn't prepared for the challenges we're now facing. And many unfairly blamed you, because you were new and different and completely unexpected. But they're beginning to see how very much we *need* you."

"That's actually another reason the Council is offering you this appointment," Grady added as Sophie's skin turned prickly with responsibility. "They want to send a message—loud and clear—that you're officially on their side."

Sophie chewed her lip. *"Am* I on their side, though?"

"I think it's time for you to be," Grady admitted. "If the Neverseen are working to sway the public to *their* side, then the best thing you can do—for yourself, the Black Swan, *and* the Council—is prove that you're not some rogue rebel circumventing our weak leaders. Show everyone that you're a valuable ally working in unison with the Councillors because you respect and trust their authority. Make the Council look *good*, if you can. And take advantage of the resources that only a Regent is entitled to have."

"Like what?" she asked. "I still don't even know what a Regent is."

"Their specific duties and privileges vary," Edaline told her. "So try to think of it more as 'redefining your relationship with the Council.' You'd be one step closer to being their equal, and as such, they'd grant you the power to make certain decisions that an ordinary citizen wouldn't be authorized to make. Like . . . choosing moments to bend the rules of telepathy—or break them. Or when to teleport to important places, even if they're technically forbidden."

"So . . . things you already do—but now you wouldn't get in trouble for them," Grady teased, jostling her gently. "And there's a *lot* more to it than that. But, like Edaline said, it's hard to know the specifics until you have your first assignment."

"They're going to give me an *assignment?*"

"They're going to give you *lots* of assignments," Grady corrected. "That's why the nobility exists—to provide the Councillors with reliable people who can assist them with the projects they either don't have time for, or that require special skills. The title just provides you the clearance to access classified secrets and the authority to act on the Council's behalf."

"Lady Sophie," Edaline said, her voice all singsongy.

Sophie winced.

Keefe would have *way* too much fun with that.

"Please tell me people won't have to curtsy to me," she mumbled.

Grady laughed. "They won't *have* to unless you demand it. But they'll probably do it on their own. Or bow."

She groaned.

It was bad enough walking through the halls of Foxfire surrounded by all of her bodyguards. If people were dipping curtsies or bowing, she might as well ask Magnate Leto to set up a permanent spotlight to follow her around.

"What happens if I don't want to be a Regent?" she whispered.

"Then you won't be a Regent," Grady said simply. "No one's going to force you to accept the appointment. But at least hear the Council out before you make up your mind, okay? I know they've made some *huge* mistakes, so I don't blame you for having reservations. I'm sure you remember how hard I resisted becoming an Emissary again after what happened with Jolie. But . . . I think the problems we're facing with the Neverseen are reaching a point where having the Council on your side is going to be essential. For example, the title will be a huge help when you're dealing with King Enki. He responds better to those with obvious authority."

"Will the Council tell me what my first assignment will be before I have to decide?"

She'd have to make sure it wouldn't interfere with everything Mr. Forkle needed her to work on—and the search for her genetic parents—and Keefe's missing memories—and Tam—and . . .

"I know you have a lot going on," Grady promised. "And so does the Council. I got the impression that their assignment will be right in line with everything you're already tackling. But we'll find out more tomorrow. They wanted to explain everything to you personally."

She blew out a breath, wishing she didn't have to ask her next question. "Will I have to tell them I'm unmatchable?"

"That's up to you," Edaline jumped in. "If you're worried that there will be problems once they find out, then it might set your mind at ease to clue them in and see what they say. But it's also private information—*and* it's a status that may very easily change if you track down your biological parents. So, you're definitely not required to share."

"Take the night and sleep on it," Grady recommended, leaning in and kissing her on the forehead. "You've had a long day. I'm sure everything will feel clearer in the morning."

Sophie grabbed his wrist to stop him from leaving. "Wait. You didn't tell me what the Councillors said about the Neverseen probing Tam's memories."

She was really getting tired of all the matchmaking drama sidetracking her from the bigger problems they were facing.

But Grady shrugged. "They actually weren't worried—but that might be because Tam doesn't know anything that specifically compromises the Council."

"I take it that means you didn't tell them I lost Kenric's cache?" Sophie asked, even if "lost" wasn't technically the right word to describe what happened.

"I didn't," Grady agreed, "because if the Neverseen had a way to open the cache, they would've used it already. And that's actually what the Council said about *all* the secrets that were stolen from Tam. The Neverseen have had that knowledge for long enough to do something with it, and yet nothing's changed. So the Councillors feel that the more important lesson is for the Black Swan to be much more open with them in the future, to ensure that our enemies never have more knowledge than our leaders."

"But shouldn't we—"

"I'll update Grady on all the things Sandor told me about Tam and Keefe while you get some sleep," Edaline interrupted, snapping her fingers to make Sophie's dinner tray disappear. "Try not to stress. You've done all you can for today."

"But—"

"You need to rest," Edaline insisted, pulling the covers back so Sophie could crawl underneath. "Sandor told me what happened with your echoes—and thank goodness Flori's song was able to calm them again. But that was still an incredibly close call, and you need to let your body recover."

Sophie wanted to argue, but . . . she *was* pretty wiped.

The exhaustion hit even harder when Edaline turned off the lights.

"Sleep," Edaline told her. "That way you can get back to work tomorrow feeling as strong as possible."

"Sweet dreams," Grady added, which should've been impossible, given her current list of worries. But Silveny reached out telepathically after Grady and Edaline left, filling Sophie's head with soothing scenes of Wynn and Luna snuggling.

The nuzzle-filled memories left Sophie just enough concentration to warn Silveny to keep Wynn away from the gorgodon. Then she drifted off into dreams filled with cuddly alicorn babies.

Somewhere in the night, though, the scenes shifted to glittering castles and cheering faces. And among them were two blurry figures—one male, one female—standing apart but somehow also together.

"We're so proud of you!" they shouted in unison, stretching out their arms like they wanted to hug her.

By the time she'd fought her way through the crowd, they were gone.

"If this is how I'm going to have to dress all the time, I'm definitely passing on the Regent appointment," Sophie grumbled, trying to lift her dark blue gown as she walked—but there were so many tiers of tulle, she couldn't find the right layer of fabric to grab. It would only be a matter of time before her much-too-narrow heels caught on the hem and she ended up sprawled across the shimmering sidewalk.

Sure, the gown was also gorgeous. The skirt had an ombré effect that made it look like wisps of twilight were floating around her, and the waist was dotted with dozens of tiny diamond stars—the same stars that decorated the halter neckline and sparkled along the edges of her gloves. More diamonds formed a glittering galaxy across the velvet cape covering her shoulders. And Vertina—the tiny talking face programmed into her spectral mirror—had even managed to convince Sophie to brush a little smoky powder across her eyelids and tie back the front part of her hair with strands of silver tinsel.

But Sophie would never *not* be annoyed that she'd had to play Pretty Princess Dress-Up when she could've used the time to update her friends about Tam, or to check in with Keefe about his memories.

Plus, leggings, boots, and tunics were *so* much more comfortable.

"How much farther do we have to walk?" she asked, wishing Sandor would move a little slower so she could hide behind his massive muscles. Eternalia wasn't as bustling of a city as Atlantis, but there were still plenty of people staring as she followed Grady down a street lined with enormous jeweled buildings.

Bo, Flori, and Edaline hadn't been invited to join them.

"Just a few more blocks," Grady promised, looking particularly regal in his burgundy jerkin with silver leaf embroidery, starched gray trousers, and smoky gray cape.

Their leap had brought them to the glassy river that divided the main city from the twelve identical crystal castles that served as the Councillors' offices, and they'd spent the majority of their walk on a meandering path along the shore, bathed in the shade of the towering palmlike trees called "the Pures." But now they'd headed into a section that was more like the capital's "downtown"—nothing but wall-to-wall sparkly buildings for block after block. And each street was a mix of *before* and *after*. The solid-colored buildings built from bricks of a single gemstone were the "originals" that had survived Fintan's Everblaze attack. The newer replacement buildings were elaborate, multicolored jeweled mosaics.

Either way, the wealth on display was staggering.

Sophie had only been to Eternalia a few times, and most of those visits had involved dramatic, life-changing rulings from the Council, so she found herself huffing out a sigh of relief once they'd passed the emerald walls of Tribunal Hall—one of the few buildings that had been rebuilt to look exactly the way it had looked before: huge and green and intimidating. But her chest tightened back up when she realized their path was heading toward one of the largest structures in the city: a sprawling diamond palace framed by four domed towers.

The building glittered so brightly in the midday sunlight that Sophie had to shield her eyes as they drew closer. If Ro had been there, she would've called it "sparkle overload." And honestly? She would've been right.

"This is the Seat of Eminence," Grady explained as they made their way up the palace's wide diamond steps. "Think of it as the hub of the nobility." He pressed his palm against the rectangular door, which looked like it had been made from threads of gold and silver woven together. "Only Regents, Emissaries, and Mentors may enter. But the Council has granted you early access today since they're offering you an appointment."

He leaned in to lick the DNA sensor that appeared next to his thumb, and Sophie's insides squirmed as the doors swung inward to reveal . . .

. . . a whole lot of darkness.

She might've been staring into an unlit foyer. Or a corridor. Or a dungeon. There was no way to tell.

"Where does all of the light go?" she asked, trailing her hand over the outer wall, which was sparkly and clear and should've been flooding the interior with sunshine.

"The diamonds are cut with a specific pattern of facets that reflects all of the light away. It's one of the ways the Seat of Eminence remains untouched by any outside force or influence. The palace is also a place of peace, where even the Councillors' own bodyguards aren't meant to follow—but they've made an exception for Sandor because they want you to feel safe. Their only requirement is that your weapons must remain stowed," he warned as Sandor pushed past them to take the lead.

"Places of peace are generally the most vulnerable," Sandor countered, gripping the hilt of his sword. But he kept the blade sheathed when he strode through the doorway.

Sophie expected his body to be swallowed by the shadows, but as soon as Sandor crossed the threshold, a thread of fuzzy grayish light flared around him, forming a spotlight that looked like he was standing in the center of a glowing lasso.

A similar light coiled around Grady when he followed—except his glow was orange.

Sophie's was vivid red.

"Do the colors mean something?" she asked when she noticed the way Grady was studying her.

He nodded. "Different talents flare in different shades. And given your multiple abilities, I'd assumed your light would be nearly white, from the spectrum blending together. Or if one ability was going to dominate, I'd figured you'd glow blue, like the other Telepaths."

"Which ability is red?" she asked, even though she was pretty sure she could guess.

"I think it's inflicting—but the Councillors always glow silver when they're here, to ensure they present as equals, so I've never seen what shade Bronte would flare on his own."

Sophie sighed.

She wasn't a huge fan of her inflicting ability, given how intense the power was—and how impossible it was to control. And it definitely didn't help that now it made her look like some sort of possessed girl from a human horror movie.

"Come on, kiddo," Grady said, hooking an arm around her shoulders. "The Council's waiting."

Sandor kept his place in the lead, and Sophie had no idea how he knew which way to go. Even with their strange spotlights, the darkness remained so thick that she couldn't see more than a few feet in front of her in any direction.

"Not saying I don't appreciate the ominous aesthetic they have going on here," she said after several minutes of walking. "But isn't this kind of a waste of space?"

Also a waste of time—but she stopped herself from saying that in case the Council was somehow listening. This process was already taking much longer than she'd wanted, and it technically hadn't even started yet.

"The design is meant to ensure that by the time we reach the main chambers, we've cleared our minds of everything except the reason we're here," Grady explained—which she was absolutely failing at. "Serving in the nobility means disconnecting from your daily life and fully immersing yourself in your duties to the Council. I realize that may be extra challenging for you," he added, obviously knowing her way too well. "You're carrying a ton of truly daunting responsibilities—more than I probably know about. But try to remember that what we're here to discuss could help with some of those problems—if you decide you feel comfortable accepting the appointment, that is."

"I know. It's just . . ." Sophie's voice trailed off as the fuzzy glow of another spotlight became visible up ahead.

The light looked white from a distance, but as they drew closer, it took on a greenish tint. And when the figure in the center finally came into focus . . .

"Dex?" Sophie whispered, blinking to make sure the strawberry-blond boy with periwinkle eyes wasn't some sort of mirage. "What are you doing here?"

"No idea," he admitted with a smile that was a tad too nervous to reach his dimples. "I was just about to ask you the same thing."

"Are you here alone?" Grady asked.

The answer seemed pretty obvious, given that there were no other spotlights—until a familiar female voice declared, "Nope!" and Biana appeared next to Dex in a halo of flickering violet light.

Her magenta gown was much simpler than the styles Biana usually favored. The only adornment was an embroidered teal sash that matched her stunning eyes—not that it stopped Biana from looking more glamorous and gorgeous than anyone else ever could. The gown was also sleeveless, with a V-shaped neckline that left the scars on Biana's arms, shoulders, and back prominently displayed. She'd hidden the marks for a while, but now she didn't look the least bit bothered by the way the thin, jagged lines almost glowed in the strange lighting. And it made Sophie want to hug her really, really hard.

"How did you guys get into this building?" Grady asked them.

"And where are your bodyguards?" Sandor demanded. Biana was notorious for ditching poor Woltzer, but Dex and Lovise usually stuck together.

"They weren't invited," a third voice said as another violet spotlight flickered to life and Della appeared next to her daughter wearing a peacock blue gown with shimmering gold beading that was almost as stunningly beautiful as she was.

Sandor muttered something about Vanishers as Sophie clutched her chest. But her racing pulse had more to do with the possibility of a blue spotlight appearing in the darkness.

"Fitz wasn't invited either," Biana told her, guessing why Sophie was scanning the shadows. "And boy, was he pouty about it. He's going to flip when he finds out you were here."

Dex's grin shifted to full dimple mode. "Can I be the one to tell him?"

Sophie shot him a glare that hopefully said *Don't start* before she turned to Grady. "Why didn't you tell me they'd be here?"

"I didn't know," Grady promised.

"Neither did we, until about an hour ago," Della said, adjusting one of the jeweled combs she'd set into her dark, wavy hair. "A messenger showed up at Everglen with a scroll telling me to pick up Dex from Rimeshire and bring him and Biana here by midday."

"We received a similar summons," an equally familiar—but much less friendly—voice huffed behind them.

Sophie's jaw locked as she spun around to find two tall figures striding toward them, lit by baby pink spotlights: Vika Heks, in a fitted yellow gown that matched her sour expression. And her daughter, Stina, whose gown was covered in so many jewels, it probably weighed more than she did.

"What's the matter, Foster?" Stina asked, tossing her curly hair and crossing her bony arms. "You didn't think you're the only one who gets special messages from the Council, did you? Or are you just mad that neither of your boyfriends seem to have made the guest list?"

"That's true," Dex murmured. "Keefe's not here. If he was, I'm sure he'd have a *lot* to say about his pretty pink spotlight."

Biana giggled. "Maybe he's on his way."

"Ro won't let him come, even if he *is* invited," Sophie realized, then transmitted to Dex and Biana, *It's a long story. I saw Mr. Forkle yesterday and . . . there's a lot going on—I promise I'll catch you up on everything as soon as we're done here,* before she turned back to Stina and added, "and I don't have a boyfriend."

"You don't?" Della asked, then flushed and shook her head. "Never mind. Forget I said anything."

Sophie wished she could.

She also wished she hadn't noticed the way Biana was frowning at her.

Or how relieved Grady looked.

Or the way Stina was smirking like a cat that had just trapped a tiny, helpless bird.

"Did your invitations explain why the Council was calling you here?" Grady asked Della and Vika, mercifully changing the subject.

"Ours didn't," yet another voice announced behind them.

Everyone turned to find Sir Tiergan illuminated by a spotlight that glowed in the same deep blue as his eyes. The bold color somehow made the contrast between his olive complexion and pale blond hair look even more severe than usual, but the effect softened when he offered Sophie a kind smile.

"It wasn't an *invitation*," his adopted son, Wylie, corrected, tugging on the front of his sunset-toned cape. "It was an *order*." Wylie's spotlight shifted colors with the words: peach one second, yellow the next, then purple—each halo so bright that it tinted his dark skin the same shade—and Sophie couldn't tell if that was happening naturally, or if Wylie was using his ability as a Flasher to control it. "And some of us had things we needed to do today."

He turned to pace, and Sophie understood his impatience. But now he had her worried that something was going on that she didn't know about—maybe with his father—or Linh.

"What did you need to do?" she asked.

Wylie glanced at the others before he shook his head. "I'll tell you later."

Stina snorted. "It's cute how you think we care about your boring secrets. We *don't*."

"Let's hope that will not always be the case," a rich, velvety voice boomed from somewhere in the shadows, making everyone suck in a breath.

The words reverberated through the room as twelve spotlights flared in a wide circle around their group, illuminating each of the Councillors with a nearly blinding halo of silver. Sophie was usually able to tell the Councillors apart, since they comprised a wide mix of skin colors and hairstyles and facial features. But between the strange lighting and their matching outfits, they looked eerily alike. Their tailored silver suits and pulled-back hair even made it hard to distinguish between the different genders. And they were wearing identical diamond crowns instead of their individual gemstone circlets.

Their long silver cloaks were all pinned with clasps shaped like glowing golden keys—a style Sophie had only seen the Councillors wear one other time. The day she moved to the Lost Cities and found herself facing a test that decided her future with the elves.

Her stomach turned very flippy at the reminder, and she scanned each of the Councillors' faces, searching for Oralie—one of her strongest allies on the Council—finally picking her out on the right side of the circle thanks to a soft blond ringlet that had broken free from her tight bun.

But Oralie didn't look her way.

And there was something off about her expression—a strange tension in her pretty features. As if she were as anxious to be done with this process as Sophie was.

"Welcome to the Seat of Eminence," Councillor Emery said as the spotlights dimmed enough to make the Councillors more recognizable. All heads turned toward the dark-skinned elf who served as spokesperson for the Council, and his sapphire eyes flicked from face to face as he stepped forward and folded his hands. "We apologize for the somewhat last-minute nature of this meeting, and realize that you all likely have many questions about why we've brought you here—particularly since this place is accessible only to those who bear titles for the oaths they've sworn to our service. And *that* is not changing, in case you were wondering. Those of you who required an escort to gain access today will not be permitted to visit again, unless you have a title of your own."

Vika gasped. "Does that mean . . . ?"

Her voice choked off when Emery cleared his throat.

"I'll explain what it means in a moment," he told her. "But first, we must verify something." His gaze turned to Sophie. "Is it safe to assume, Miss Foster, that your father has explained his reason for bringing you here?"

Sophie nodded, fighting the urge to duck behind Grady.

"And will you be accepting our offer?" Emery asked.

Every single bit of moisture in Sophie's mouth evaporated. "I . . . thought you guys were going to give me more information about what you need me to do before I had to decide."

"We will be happy to answer your questions. But certain things have changed, and we need to know if you're interested before we continue."

Sophie glanced at Grady for help.

"No one has ever had to make an oath with so little information," he reminded the Councillors.

"We're not asking for her *oath*. We're asking if she's *willing*," Emery clarified, which . . . didn't actually sound all that different to Sophie. "And we're asking now, because if she isn't, there's no point in continuing with any of this."

"Any of what?" Tiergan demanded.

Emery reached up to rub his temples, moderating the other Councillors telepathically.

"Very well," he said after a painful beat of silence. "I'd hoped to avoid an interruption-filled discussion. But it seems we must do this out of order." He cleared his throat. "Yesterday, in light of several serious developments that Lord Grady brought to our attention, we decided to redefine the qualifications for the nobility in order to extend an invitation to Miss Foster. Our plan was to appoint her as a Regent today, so that she can pair her unique talents with the resources available to our nobles, and assist us with these pressing challenges more fully." He paused to let that sink in before he added, "But upon further discussion, we discovered that we'd made one crucial miscalculation. Miss Foster's greatest successes are rarely hers alone. She's most valuable when working in tandem with others—which is not an insult to you, Miss Foster. As Councillors, we are far better as a united group of twelve than we could ever be as individuals. But because of that, we realized the best way to utilize you would be to place you with a team—one carefully selected, arranged, and monitored by us, to ensure maximum efficiency."

Dex, Biana, Wylie, and Sophie all looked at each other.

Then they looked at Stina Heks.

And Stina summed it up for them. "You have to be kidding me."

"We're not," Councillor Emery assured her. "We've invited the five of you here today because you've each been chosen for this revolutionary new approach to the Regency—but the arrangement hinges on Miss Foster's willingness to accept the position of leader."

"Leader," Sophie repeated, liking that term even less when the Council was the one assigning it to her.

"Yes," Councillor Emery said, pausing to glance at each of the other Councillors before he added. "The leader of Team Prodigious."

SEVEN

S O, QUESTION," DEX SAID, BREAKING THE uncomfortable silence. "Can we get a cooler name? Because 'Team Prodigious' is an epic fail."

"I'm not even a prodigy anymore," Wylie added.

Sophie knew she should probably worry that Wylie would be annoyed that *he* wasn't being put in charge, given that he was the eldest of their group, and the only one of them who'd actually taken the elite levels—and was therefore the only one legitimately qualified to be a Regent. But her brain was too stuck on the fact that *she* was expected to officially be the leader.

Of Team Prodigious.

Her nose crinkled.

Dex was right. That name had to go.

"It's not a reference to prodigies," Councillor Emery tried to explain. "'Prodigious' means 'extraordinary.'"

"It also means 'abnormal,'" Councillor Bronte informed them, with the closest thing to a smile that his sharp-featured face was capable of making.

"Yeah, well, whatever your boring reasons are," Dex said through a feigned yawn, "the name's still a deal-breaker for me."

"Me too," Biana agreed. "I think we should be Team Sparkles, because we'll make everything better!"

Dex snort-laughed—then frowned. "Wait, was that a serious suggestion?"

Biana's eyes narrowed. "I don't hear you coming up with any better ideas."

"I was getting to that!" Dex scratched his chin and tapped his foot for several beats. "Okay. What if we went with something cool and space-y, like . . . Team Nebula?"

"You realize that would technically make us Team Swirling-Cloud-of-Gas, right?" Biana asked, earning a choked laugh from Grady.

Even with his green spotlight, Sophie could see Dex's blush spread all the way to the tips of his ears. "Is that what 'nebula' means?" he mumbled. "I always get it confused with 'galaxy.' But hey . . . nothing wrong with a little gas, am I right?"

"Everyone has it," Wylie agreed.

Stina groaned. "Are you hearing this?" she asked the Councillors. "Why would you pick these losers for something so important?"

"Uh, because these *losers* have taken on the Neverseen how many times now?" Dex snapped back.

"And *lost* how many times?" Stina countered. "Oh, that's right—all of them."

"We haven't *lost*," Biana argued.

"Well, you certainly haven't won." She pointed to Biana's scars, and Biana—to her credit—didn't flinch.

Della, on the other hand, looked like she'd gone into full mama-bear mode and was imagining the many ways she could use her fancy defense training to drop-kick Stina across the room and then step on her with the spikes of her heels.

"Yeah, well, what have *you* done?" Dex asked, stepping into Stina's personal space. He was still shorter than her. But almost everyone was.

Stina got even taller when she straightened to her full height and said, "Uh, how about I saved the alicorn babies and reset the Timeline to Extinction?"

"Um, the people who saved those babies were Sophie, my brother, and the trolls," Biana corrected.

"Do not underestimate the role my daughter and I played that day!" Vika snapped.

"Maybe *you* did important stuff," Dex told her. "But I heard Stina put out some blankets or something? Good job! No one else could've done *that*."

"There was a lot more to it," Stina argued. "And what was the last gadget you made that actually worked right? Because *I* heard a bunch of things failed at the Celestial Festival."

"That wasn't Dex's fault," Sophie mumbled. "The null that Tinker designed for me interfered."

"And a *Technopath* couldn't tell that was going to happen?" Stina asked, clicking her tongue. "If Dex was any good, he would've been prepared."

Dex snorted. "Yeah, well, at least I actually fought back that night. What were you doing? Hiding behind Mommy and Daddy?"

One of the Councillors sighed—Sophie was pretty sure it was Councillor Zarina because she looked like she wanted to zap all of them with lightning. "I'm starting to remember why we don't work with teenagers."

"It's going to be an exercise in patience," Councillor Darek agreed, tearing a hand through his dark, curly hair.

"Hey, we'd be fine without Stina," Biana pointed out. "She's the one causing all the drama."

"And Keefe's a way more powerful Empath than she is," Dex added. "So it's a super-easy fix."

"I can't believe I'm saying this," Grady said, "but . . . Keefe *would* be a better fit for this."

Councillor Emery shook his head. "Mr. Sencen's ties to the Neverseen pose too great of a risk."

"Keefe's on our side," Sophie argued—even though this was exactly the kind of assignment she had to keep Keefe far away from. But that didn't mean they needed to be stuck with Stina Heks in Team Whatever-They-Were-Going-to-Call-It—assuming she was willing to go along with this. "Shouldn't we get to pick who we work with?"

"Absolutely not!" Councillor Bronte said, shaking his head so hard, the points of his Ancient ears flapped against his crown. "You chose your group for the Black Swan—and we've all seen how far from ideal things have gone for you. A change in strategy is essential for you to become truly successful."

"And *Stina Heks* is your big solution?" Dex asked. "Like . . . for real?"

"I don't appreciate the way you all keep singling out my daughter!" Vika snapped.

"Um, your daughter was the first to complain," Biana reminded her. "She also called us losers, so . . ."

"Right, and you guys weren't already looking at me like you'd rather work with a muskog," Stina countered.

Dex flashed his most wicked grin. "A muskog *would* smell better."

Grady coughed through another laugh—and Sandor's shoulders shook like he was holding in a fit of goblin giggles.

"Enough!" Councillor Emery cut in, before Stina could respond, and Sophie was grateful for the outburst.

They couldn't afford to waste the rest of the day cracking jokes and bickering—even if it *was* mildly entertaining.

"Miss Heks is a talented Empath who's proven to be clearheaded under pressure," Emery continued. "And since her father is already affiliated with the Black Swan—"

Vika sucked in a breath. "That information isn't meant to be public knowledge."

"Yes, well, *we* are not the public." The diamonds in Emery's crown seemed to shine brighter with the words. "And we're working hard to remove the veils of secrecy separating ourselves from that order. Which is why we felt it would be best to draw from a family with an existing connection to the Black Swan, since that would make for a smoother process when we need to rely on the Collective for these projects. And we have no doubt that once the five of you learn to work together"—he turned back to Sophie, Biana, Dex, Wylie, and Stina, eyeing them each in turn—"Miss Heks will prove to be a valuable teammate."

"She will," Vika agreed. "But I don't understand how this is such a big 'change in strategy.' You're pulling almost everyone from the same failing group that Sophie already works with."

"They haven't *failed*," Councillor Terik corrected, taking a slow step forward. His prosthetic leg still wobbled—and he still leaned heavily on his cane—but the movement did seem smoother than it did the last time Sophie had seen him. "And Miss Foster needs to trust her teammates—and trust takes time to build. Time we cannot afford to lose, given the severity of the challenges we're facing. So yes, we did pull primarily from the core group of friends that we knew Miss Foster would be most comfortable with—but we specifically selected those whom she doesn't rely on as closely. Those whom we believe have far more to give than what they've currently been allowed to offer."

"Uh, I rely on Dex and Biana all the time," Sophie argued, holding up her hand—and then realizing the panic-switch ring that Dex had designed for her was hidden under her glove. "The only reason I haven't relied on Wylie as much is because he's newer to working with the Black Swan."

She glanced at her friends, expecting to find them nodding along. But they were all staring at their feet. "What?"

"Well . . . I mean . . . you do leave us out sometimes," Biana mumbled. "Or you only include us if we *force* you to."

"And it's never like that for Keefe and Fitz," Dex added.

"It totally is for Keefe," Sophie argued. "He just doesn't take no for an answer—you know how Keefe is. Plus, we're fighting his *mom*. And Fitz and I are Cognates—"

"Yes, we're all *very* aware of that connection," Councillor Alina jumped in, tilting her head just so, to make the highlights in her dark hair gleam under the spotlight. "And sometimes it can be quite useful. So if it turns out that we need Mr. Vacker, we'll add a sixth member to your team. But we also fear that you've come to rely on your telepathy as a crutch—and no one is saying the ability isn't valuable," she added, before anyone could protest, "or that we don't want you using it. All we're saying is that if it was the only ability that mattered, your order wouldn't have gone to such great lengths to give you *four* others. Isn't that right, Tiergan?" She flashed a gleaming smile when she noticed the frowns on Vika's and Stina's faces. "I'm guessing your husband never told you that Tiergan is a member of the Black Swan's Collective?"

"Timkin doesn't know," Tiergan corrected. "And since you seem bent on outing those of us in the order today, I feel the need to add that just because the Neverseen have some extra knowledge about our members, that doesn't mean we want you to share that information whenever and wherever you please."

"Why do the Neverseen know . . . ?" Biana started to ask—but then her eyes widened. "Did Tam tell them?"

"It wasn't his fault," Sophie assured her. "Gethen probed his memories."

She didn't have to use her telepathy to see the news snowballing inside her friends' minds.

"Does that mean you've talked to him?" Biana asked.

"And didn't tell us?" Dex added.

"See?" Councillor Terik said when Sophie nodded. "This proves my point."

"No it doesn't," Sophie argued. "I talked to Tam *yesterday*—and I would've told them about it by now if you guys hadn't made me come here today."

"And you haven't told Fitz?" Biana clarified. "Or Keefe?"

There was something pointed about the way she said the second name—something that made Sophie a little nervous to admit, "I . . . actually talked to Keefe last night—but you'll understand why once I explain what's going on. As soon as we're done here, I'll—"

"Why wait?" Stina interrupted. "Sounds like pretty crucial information. And I'm part of the team now, so . . ."

"Technically not yet," Sophie reminded her. "I haven't agreed to be the leader."

Stina rolled her eyes. "But we all know you're going to. That's what you do. You pout and stall for a while—but eventually you give in because you can't help being the good little moonlark! So I should be there for the big explanation."

"We *all* should," Councillor Emery added. "Team Prodigious is meant to be a collaboration between the five of you *and* the twelve of us."

"Dude, you *have* to stop calling it that," Dex told him. "How about Team T. Rex?"

"Or Team Alicorn?" Biana added.

"If we go that route, why don't we just call ourselves the Order of the Phoenix?" Sophie couldn't resist suggesting—but of course no one appreciated her reference. "Never mind."

"Human thing?" Dex guessed.

"A super-famous one," she agreed, kinda wishing she had a few more shared life experiences with her friends.

At least Stina wasn't still pushing for information.

They'd managed to sidestep that for the moment.

"What about Linh?" Wylie asked, and it took Sophie a second to realize he wasn't suggesting that as a team name. "She should be a part of this. She's way more powerful than I am. Probably more powerful than all of us—except Sophie."

"She is," Emery agreed. "But the Neverseen have control of her brother, which makes her vulnerable at best and completely unreliable at worst. Not to mention the fact that we *also* selected each of you for your unique abilities, and hydrokinesis will serve us little use in the desert."

"Desert?" Dex, Biana, and Wylie repeated.

Councillor Emery glanced at Sophie. "I assume you *also* have yet to tell them about Mr. Forkle's suspicions regarding Loamnore?"

Sophie sighed when she saw the scowls on her friends' faces. "I was going to cover everything at once."

"Well then," Emery said, "no time like the present."

All eyes focused on Sophie, and she could tell that no one was going to let her drop this. So she gave them the bullet points of Mr. Forkle's theory, even though it felt wrong discussing Black Swan stuff with so many extra people. And when Biana started to argue that Tam would never play a role in something like what Sophie was fearing, she went ahead and told them about the warning Tam had given her and the basic details of the deal she'd made with Ro to keep Keefe safe. The only stuff she left out was the matchmaking nightmare, because there was no way she was admitting *that* to Stina Heks—or letting Della and Biana hear it before Fitz.

Wylie turned away when she'd finished, his spotlight fading to a dull gray. "I should be the one to explain this to Linh."

Sophie wasn't about to argue. She didn't know how to define Linh and Wylie's friendship, but the two of them were very close. And since Linh lived with Wylie's adoptive father, they spent a lot of time together.

"Do you want us to be there when you talk to her?" Biana offered.

Wylie shook his head. "It might be better one-on-one, so she won't feel like she has to be brave. But I'll let you know if I change my mind."

"Thank you," Sophie told him.

His smile looked grim.

"Well," Councillor Emery said, clapping his hands to call everyone's attention back to him. "This is all the more reason for you five to get to work. The first assignment we'd planned to give you was to meet with King Enki in Loamnore, so he can show you his security concerns and catch you up on the projects we've already been assisting him with in recent months—a meeting the Black Swan would never be able to properly arrange, regardless of what they might claim. In case you still need proof that it's both necessary and beneficial for you to begin your own investigation into the threat on the dwarves through our more official channel. And yes, Grady, you would be there for that meeting. But before we can move forward with scheduling that, we need Miss Foster to accept her role as leader. And if she does, we need all five of you to swear your oath as Regents."

"And if I don't accept?" Sophie had to know.

Emery rubbed his temples. "We would ask you to reconsider."

"We realize you struggle with authority," Councillor Terik added, before Sophie could push the issue. "Particularly *our* authority. And I, at least, won't deny that you're justified to feel that way. But . . . the dwarves need to be handled with care in order to avoid any interspeciesial incidents—ask your father to share his stories about some of his more interesting encounters with King Enki if you don't believe me."

"Okay, but . . . you guys remember this is *Sophie*, right?" Stina jumped in. "The girl who almost started a war with the ogres—twice. Or was it three times? And she formed an alliance with the trolls without getting anyone's permission. I also doubt the goblins are thrilled that one of their best soldiers keeps almost dying while trying to protect her—especially since she's supposed to be this all-powerful *thing* who can protect herself."

"Protecting Miss Foster is my *honor*," Sandor assured her.

"If you say so," Stina told him. "All I'm saying is, if you want her on the team because she's the moonlark—fine. I sorta get that. I still think she's overrated, but . . . whatever. But what I *don't* understand is why you'd make her our leader—especially since it sounds like King Enki's going to be tough to deal with. Shouldn't you go with someone who isn't a walking interspeciesial disaster?"

"Sophie is *far* from a disaster," Grady argued, placing a reassuring hand on Sophie's shoulder.

"Yeah, the only disaster I see here is *you*," Dex told Stina. "And let me guess. You think *you'd* be a better leader?"

Stina laughed. "You think I want that kind of responsibility? Uh, yeah, *hard* pass. Wylie's the obvious choice. He's older, with more training and experience, and—"

"Not necessarily," Wylie interrupted. "Sophie may be younger, but she's lived through more than all of us combined."

"Since when is 'not dying' a qualification for leadership?" Stina countered.

"That's not what I meant," Wylie argued. "Though you should try braving a few attempts on *your* life before you discount the wisdom and strength gained from that kind of experience—"

"Ugh, if you're going to be all grumpy, never mind," Stina interrupted. "Forget I suggested it."

"We *will*," Councillor Emery told her. "And let me make this clear: Sophie *must* be the leader of Team Prodigious in order for it to exist. That is nonnegotiable—and why we tried to gauge her commitment before we started this conversation. The public will likely consider the formation of this team to be a rather odd decision on our part, given your ages and levels of experience. And Sophie is the key to winning them over. She's gained a level of notoriety in our world—and lately, a bit of respect. It's time we send the message that the Council sees her value and is utilizing her to the fullest extent possible."

The words didn't want to fit in Sophie's brain—even though they matched things that Grady and Mr. Forkle had already told her.

After years of threats and Tribunals, did the Council actually . . . like her?

Or believe in her, at least?

And why did that feel like both a good thing *and* a bad thing?

"Okay, but what about the team name?" Dex asked. "You *have* to let us change it. Trust me, if you announce that you formed *Team Prodigious*, people are going to laugh."

"They really will," Biana agreed.

Councillor Emery's sigh sounded like a muffled scream as it bounced around the room. "Fine. You may call yourselves whatever you'd like, on two conditions," he told them, holding up a hand and counting off his fingers. "One: You must choose something *respectable*—something befitting the noble status the team will bear. And two: We must approve your selection."

Dex's dimples returned. "I can live with that."

"Good. Does that mean we have a deal?" Emery's gaze homed in on Sophie.

"Your choice, kiddo," Grady whispered as he leaned in. "I'll back you up, whatever you choose."

She nodded, fighting the urge to tug on her eyelashes as she turned toward Dex, Biana, Wylie, and Stina. "If I'm the leader of this . . . group thing . . . I'm going to have to give you guys orders. Won't that be weird?"

"Uh, I don't know if you realize this," Dex told her, "but . . . you already boss us around all the time."

Biana grinned. "Exactly. Nothing new there!"

"As long as you let us have some input, we should be good," Wylie added.

Stina bit her lip.

"You'd have to listen to me," Sophie pressed, not letting her off the hook. "Even if you don't like it."

"Not if you're wrong," Stina countered.

"Actually, working as a team sometimes means going against your own judgment," Councillor Emery told her. "You can voice your dissent—*respectfully*—but if you disagree with Sophie's ultimate decision, you will still be expected to complete whatever orders she gives you."

"Fine," Stina said, tilting up her chin. "But if I turn out to be right, expect a *lot* of 'I told you so's.'"

Sophie had *zero* doubt of that.

"We're also going to have to spend a lot more time together," Biana reminded Stina. "So . . . you'll have to be nice to us."

"And *you'll* have to be nice to *me*," Stina reminded her.

No one looked particularly happy about these revelations.

"We don't expect you to become best friends," Emery assured them. "But we do expect you to be respectful."

Stina shrugged. "I guess I can live with that."

"But . . . why?" Sophie had to ask. "You've never wanted to be involved with this kind of stuff before."

"Isn't it obvious?" Dex cut in. "She wants the title."

"Like you don't!" Stina snapped back.

Dex didn't deny it. And the intensity in his eyes made Sophie realize how much this opportunity had to mean to him.

He'd spent his whole life being bullied because his parents were a bad match and his siblings were triplets. In fact, that was probably why Della had to be the one to bring him to Eternalia with Biana, since neither of his parents had access to the Seat of Eminence.

So to go from *that* to being one of the youngest Regents ever?

Appointed to the nobility before even completing the elite levels?

To be *Lord* Dex.

Even Biana looked pretty dazzled by the title, and she'd grown up with the elitest of the elite.

"There's nothing wrong with wanting recognition for your talents," Della told all of them. "But make sure you aren't forgetting the serious responsibilities you'll be taking on if you agree to this—and I don't mean the danger. Most of you are getting frighteningly used to that. But for this, you'll not only be swearing an oath to put the needs of our world, and its people, ahead of your own lives, but you'll also be vowing to give complete allegiance to the Council. That's not something to take lightly."

"It isn't," Councillor Emery agreed. "But it's also nothing to fear. We're on the same side."

"Are we?" Tiergan asked, beating Sophie to the question. "Truly?"

"Yes," all twelve Councillors said in unison.

"Unity is our best chance for survival," Councillor Emery added. "Our foes are divided. Always changing out leaders and sniping at each other over the differences in their visions. So this"—he gestured between the twelve of them and the five soon-to-be teammates—"is how we stand strong against them. And to prove our commitment to that statement, we're willing to make a new oath as well—an oath that will only be made to the five of you."

Lots of eyebrows rose at that.

"What will the oath say?" Vika asked.

"That's between us and Team Prodigious," Councillor Emery said, glancing at Dex and reluctantly adding, "or Team Whatever-They-Decide-to-Call-Themselves. But it's an oath to assure them that trust will not simply be demanded from them—it will be given. And we're ready to make the vow now, if they're ready to commit as well."

Sophie, Dex, Biana, Wylie, and Stina shared another long look, and Sophie could see the resolve in their eyes.

But before she agreed, she had to address one final concern.

"It sounds like this is going to involve a lot of classified information," she told the Council. "And I don't see how that's not going to damage my Cognate connection with Fitz."

"As Councillor Alina already said," Emery told her, "if excluding Fitz from the team becomes a problem, we're willing to add another member. But we'd like to try it without him first."

"And keep in mind," Oralie added, finally turning her azure eyes toward Sophie, "*true* trust does not require absolute transparency. There is incredible power in accepting that there are some things you cannot know—and being willing to maintain your commitment to that person despite the secrets."

"She has a point," Tiergan agreed. "I've always considered that to be the ultimate level of Cognatedom."

Sophie frowned. "But you said—"

"I know what I've said in our lessons," Tiergan interrupted. "And uninhibited sharing is still the most vital way to build and maintain the connection between Cognates. But once the connection exists— and once you reach a level of maturity with your partner—you can work your way to a new sort of relationship. One that acknowledges that there are pieces of yourself that you may occasionally have to hold back, and that doing so changes absolutely nothing between the two of you. In fact, accepting the other person's limitations actually enhances your bond. Put simply, it's reaching a point where you both know beyond any shadow of doubt that you trust each other *no matter what*. I doubt you and Fitz have achieved that level of commitment yet, given how young you both are. But working toward it can be the new focus for our training."

"Does that satisfy your concern?" Emery asked as Sophie struggled to process what Tiergan was saying—and wondered why it made her palms feel so very sweaty.

One quick glance at each of her friends told her what she needed to say. "Okay. Count me in for Team Whatever-Our-Name-Is."

EIGHT

YOU REALIZE I'M NEVER GOING TO remember to call you guys lords and ladies, right?" Sophie whispered, trying to keep herself distracted as she, Dex, Biana, Stina, and Wylie followed a single-file line of all twelve Councillors down a very dark, very quiet hallway.

Every click of her heels against the jeweled floor might as well have been cymbals crashing—and her pulse felt even louder.

And there was no end to their journey in sight.

In fact, there was *nothing* in sight, except for the twelve intimidating figures marching stolidly ahead of them under their silvery spotlights—which was probably why Sophie kept dragging her feet a little more with every step, even though her brain was simultaneously screaming that they needed to hurry up and get to work on the actual problems.

They'd had to leave the rest of their group behind, despite Sandor's vehement protests. The Councillors wouldn't even tell anyone where they'd be heading within the palace, or what exactly would be involved with swearing the oaths. All they'd shared was that it would be a different process than what any other Regent had experienced before. And as they'd led Sophie and her friends away, they'd added, "We'll return when the appointments are final."

Which made what Sophie and her friends were about to do feel very . . . *permanent*.

"Yeah, I'm probably never going to remember to call you Lady Sophie either," Biana whispered back. "Or wait—is it supposed to be something fancier because you're our leader? Captain Sophie? Master Sophie?"

Sophie cringed. "I hope not."

Dex leaned in. "Um, I'm pretty sure it's your call, since you're the one in charge—unless you want us to choose for you. How about Lady Sophie the Reluctant?"

"Very funny," Sophie told him as Biana covered her mouth to muffle her giggle.

"I kinda like Foster the Great," Dex went on, oblivious to her annoyance—or perhaps because of it. "But I still feel like we could do better. Hmmm. Wait! I've got it!" He paused for a beat, dragging out the suspense before he leaned in and whispered, "The Fos-Boss."

"Ohhhhh, I like it!" Biana breathed.

"I vote for that too," Wylie added as he leaned in.

"Then it's settled," Dex decided. "Unless you think Lady Fos-Boss is better."

"Yes!" Biana said, fighting to hold back another giggle. "That's the winner."

Sophie gave them each her deadliest glare. "If you call me either of those things, I swear I'll—"

"And she thought she was going to have a hard time bossing us around," Dex whispered to Biana and Wylie. "Looks like our fearless Lady Fos-Boss is a natural leader."

This time even Wylie had to muffle his laughter.

"You guys are worse than Keefe," Sophie grumbled, wondering if she could smother them with her frilly gown.

"I can't believe I'm going to officially be linked to you weirdos," Stina growled under her breath.

"You can still back out," Dex reminded her.

"Or you could try acting like you appreciate what the Council's doing for us today!" Stina whisper-hissed. "We're inside the Seat of Eminence, about to be sworn in as the youngest Regents ever. Could you maybe try behaving with a *little* dignity?"

Dex scratched his chin. "Nah. Annoying you is way more fun."

Stina gritted her teeth hard enough to make a cracking sound, and Sophie bit back a smile, wishing she could tangle the feeling around herself until it choked out the worries bubbling up her throat. Sure, the commitment she was about to make was huge and complicated and terrifying—especially given her past challenges with the Council. But . . . at least she was making it with friends.

Or *mostly* with friends—and they could handle Stina together.

"So . . . we have Lady Fos-Boss's title settled," Dex said, grinning when Sophie shook her head. "Any thoughts on a better team name?"

"No discussing team names until you're somewhere far beyond my range of hearing!" Councillor Emery shouted from up ahead.

"You're the one who came up with 'Team Prodigious,' aren't you?" Dex called back, clearly not the least bit ashamed to know that the Council had been eavesdropping on their ridiculous conversation. "That's why you're so sensitive about it, huh?"

A whole lot of muttering followed.

Then there was silence—until Wylie called out the question that Sophie had been wondering as well: "How much longer is this going to take?"

"Why?" Emery asked. "Do you have somewhere else to be?"

"No," Wylie admitted. "But . . . there's someone I need to talk to."

"Well, I'm sure they'll understand why this was your priority," Emery assured him. "Once we announce your appointments, that is."

"And when will that be?" Stina asked.

"Soon," Emery told her. "We want the public to be aware of your elevated status as much as you do."

Actually, Sophie would've been fine if her new title remained a classified secret. But she had a feeling she was the only one who wanted to avoid that particular attention.

"You'll wait until we have our *much*-cooler new team name, though, right?" Dex clarified. "So you won't have everyone making fun of Team Prodigious?"

Councillor Emery's sigh echoed down the hall. "Yes, I suppose that would make sense. You five need to figure that out as quickly as possible."

Which foolishly opened the door to a whole lot of team-name brainstorming between Dex and Biana. Sophie tuned them out somewhere between Team Hotness and Team Awesomesauce.

She shuffled closer to Wylie. "Is everything okay?" she whispered. "Nothing's going on with your dad—"

"No, he's fine," Wylie interrupted. "Well . . . as fine as he ever is."

Prentice was still recovering from all the years he'd spent trapped in the madness of his broken consciousness—and he'd probably never fully get back to his old self. His mind had been so shattered by the memory break that his memories had all but dissolved—including the information that Sophie had hoped to learn after she'd healed him, like what had made him call "swan song" before he was arrested.

"Did you mean you needed to talk to Linh, then?" she whispered. "To tell her about Tam?"

"No. She's probably going to feel a little left out because the Council didn't include her today. So dropping the Tam bomb on top of that seems pretty harsh. But I don't want her to think I kept it from her either, so . . ." He blew out a breath.

"That's super tricky," Sophie admitted. "If there's any way I can help, let me know."

"Actually . . . there is—but not with Linh." He chewed his lip for a couple of seconds before he leaned in, his voice barely louder than a breath as he told her, "I need a favor."

"Of course." Sophie would forever be trying to make amends for all the devastating things that Wylie had endured because of her. "What do you need?"

He glanced at the Council. Then at Stina. "I'll tell you later."

"Sure." She said nothing else out loud. But as he stepped away, she transmitted, *Or we can talk telepathically, if you give me permission to open my mind to your thoughts.*

Wylie was subtle with his nod, clearly not wanting the others to know they were still talking. And when Sophie stretched out her consciousness, his thoughts felt jittery—shuffling around her too fast, like a magician dealing cards for a trick. But she couldn't blame him for trying to make sure she only saw what he wanted her to see. She would've done the same thing if the roles were reversed.

What's going on? she asked.

More thoughts shifted—flickers of faces she didn't recognize, until Wylie settled on one that she did.

I . . . need you to promise me that you won't let Maruca join the Black Swan, he told her. *I've been trying to talk her out of it—but I need some backup in case I can't change her mind.*

Sophie studied the smiling face that was now filling Wylie's head. It was a younger version of Maruca than she remembered, with way less attitude in her expression. The blue streak was also missing from her hair, and she wore it natural texture—without a drop of makeup on her warm brown skin. Almost as if Wylie was trying to make Sophie see his second cousin as more of a little girl than she really was anymore.

Or maybe that was just how *he* saw her.

Why would Maruca want to swear fealty? Sophie had to ask. She didn't know her very well—just that Maruca used to be Biana's best friend, until they'd had a falling-out when Biana became friends with Sophie. But even after they'd patched things up, Maruca had never seemed the least bit interested in hanging out with them again—much less getting involved with all the dangerous stuff they did for the Black Swan.

Wylie explained as his mind tucked away the image of Maruca and replaced it with stomach-turning flashbacks from outside the troll hive at Everglen. *She got all fired up after watching what happened* to us during the Celestial Festival, and now she thinks we need all the help we can get—and I'm not saying we don't. Why do you think I'm becoming a Regent? But I don't want her caught up in any of this.

Sophie couldn't blame him for that—just reliving his memories was enough to make her want to lock up every single person she cared about to keep them safe.

I already tried reminding her about what happened to my mom and dad—and what happened to me, Wylie added quietly. *But she's convinced that she can handle it—and that the danger shouldn't matter anyway. And I'm sure she's going to get way more insistent once she finds out that Stina's part of this team—if she hasn't reached out to the Collective already. So I need you to make sure that if she HAS reached out, her offer gets rejected. And if she hasn't yet, then I need you to make sure that whenever she DOES try to join, the Collective tells her they're not interested.*

Okaaaaaay, Sophie transmitted slowly. *I'm not asking this because I don't want to help—I do. But . . . wouldn't it be better to go to Tiergan for this favor? I mean, he's actually PART of the Collective.*

He's only one vote out of five, Wylie corrected.

Yeah, but I'm ZERO votes, so . . .

But you're the moonlark. They listen to you when you argue with them—way more than they listen to Tiergan. Plus, I'm pretty sure Tiergan would end up backing down. The Collective has this whole thing about putting the needs of our world above everything else. Look at the things they've had you do—how many times have they almost gotten you killed?

Well . . . but like you just said: I'm the moonlark. All this stuff is what they made me for, no matter how dangerous.

Okay, but they've let your friends take the same risks, haven't they?

His eyes shifted to Biana, his gaze tracing over the scars that Vespera had given her. *If they see value in someone, that's all that matters. Especially if that person has an important special ability.*

He had a point—which was why it took her a second to catch what he was saying. *Wait—has Maruca manifested?*

Wylie's thoughts scattered like frightened birds.

I'm guessing that's a yes, Sophie noted. *And that it's something . . . pretty powerful.*

He didn't respond, which seemed to confirm her suspicion.

But what ability would it be?

Hydrokinetic?

Charger?

Phaser?

Shade?

Why would he be afraid to tell her any of those things? Unless . . .

Is she another Pyrokinetic? she asked. *Because if she is, she's going to need training—*

It's not pyrokinesis, Wylie promised. *And I still think it's a bad idea for Marella to be training with Fintan, by the way.*

So did Sophie.

Despite Fintan's claims that he simply wanted to save Marella from losing control of her flames—and all the precautions that had been taken with his icy prison—Sophie was sure he was planning another dramatic escape.

But none of that mattered at the moment.

You really won't tell me what Maruca's ability is? she pressed, still running through a list of options in her head.

What if Maruca was another Mesmer, like Grady?

Or a Beguiler, like Councillor Alina?

Or—

Not right now, Wylie admitted.

Why not?

He took a small step away from her, staring at his hands as he fidgeted with the Endal crest securing his cape. *Because I know what you're going to say—and I won't even blame you for it. But . . . we don't NEED her ability. Or if we do, we could find someone else. I know it's selfish, but . . . I don't want Maruca taking the kinds of risks she'd have to take. I've already lost enough family.*

Sophie's heart splintered at his words.

Okay, she transmitted. *I honestly have no idea if the Black Swan will listen to me about something like this—especially if Maruca's super insistent about volunteering. But I'll do everything I can to talk the Collective out of letting her join. And I can speak with Maruca, too, if you want. I don't think she likes me that much, so maybe I can use that to make her not want to work with me or—*

You can't let her know I talked to you, Wylie interrupted. *That'll just make her more determined to join. She thinks I'm treating her like a little kid, but that's not what it is. It's . . .*

I get it, Sophie said when his brain seemed to trip over the next words.

Wylie had watched his mom fade away right in front of him.

He'd spent more than a decade with his father locked away in Exile.

He'd been captured, interrogated, and tortured—and then got hurt again when he showed up with Dex to help Sophie and Fitz survive an ambush.

She couldn't fault him for wanting to protect Maruca from those kinds of dangers. She'd tried to do the same thing with her friends—*many* times.

I'll do my best, she promised again.

Wylie let out a breath. *Thank you. And . . . thanks for not pushing me to tell you what her ability is—and for not stealing that info out of my memories. I know you could find it in, like, two seconds if you wanted.*

I could, Sophie agreed. *But . . . you'll tell me when you're ready—or Maruca will. Either way, it's not worth damaging your trust.*

He turned back to look at her. *That's why you're going to make a great leader—and I don't just mean of this team. I had my doubts about Project Moonlark for a long time. I think you know that better than anyone. But . . . even with everything that happened to my dad, I can still tell . . . the Black Swan really got it right with you.*

Sophie glanced away, hoping he couldn't see the way tears were welling in her eyes, or how hard she had to blink to keep them from spilling down her cheeks.

Hearing those words from anyone was amazing—but from Wylie? After how much he'd hated her when she first got to the Lost Cities?

Thank you, she transmitted, wondering how her mental voice could sound choked when she wasn't actually using her throat. *That really means a lot.*

Yeah, well . . . that's why you're Lady Fos-Boss.

He winked as he said it, and Sophie clung to the tease, letting it rein her emotions back until they were much less sappy.

That's NOT what you guys are going to call me, she told him.

Wylie grinned. *Keep telling yourself that.*

"Uh, is there something you two wanna share with the rest of the team?" Stina asked, her voice jarringly loud after all the whispering and transmitting.

Sophie glanced down, surprised to see Stina's hand wrapped around her wrist.

She had no idea when that happened.

She also had no idea when they'd stopped walking.

Or how long everyone—including all twelve Councillors—had been watching her and Wylie.

But she hoped her red spotlight camouflaged her flushed cheeks.

"Just a trust exercise," Wylie said smoothly. "To make sure we can work together, since Sophie and I have a complicated history."

The Council looked mostly satisfied with the explanation.

Dex and Biana, not so much.

And Stina tightened her grip on Sophie's wrist.

"Is this where we're taking our oaths?" Sophie asked, yanking her arm free and turning to survey where they were standing, which was basically a dark dead end. She could see nothing but the faint outline of solid diamond walls and one small silver door that looked more gnome-height than elf-height.

"This is how we reach the place where we'll make our oaths," Councillor Emery corrected, because nothing with the elves could ever be quick or simple.

The door slid silently open as he approached, brightening the dark hall with a rectangle of light that spilled from wherever they were heading. The doorway itself stretched several feet deep, so it was impossible to see the room they were about to enter.

Emery's spotlight vanished when he reached the threshold, and he had to stoop and shuffle forward with strange, almost pigeonlike movements in order to pass through without conking his head—as did the rest of the Councillors when they followed one by one. They disappeared from sight after a few steps, but Sophie could hear their stumbling footfalls continue on, picking up a hollow tone once they'd entered the room beyond.

"I'm assuming there's a reason you guys didn't make the door taller?" Dex called after them, frowning at the abundance of untouched wall that could've easily been cut away to make the opening a normal size. "And a reason why the doorway's so deep?"

"Yes" was all Emery shouted back.

Sophie shared a look with her friends before Stina shrugged and followed the Councillors—and the amount of bending and slouching she had to do was both hilarious *and* impressive. Wylie didn't look nearly as graceful when it was his turn. Neither did Dex. But of course Biana found a way to saunter through the doorway like a celebrity on the red carpet. And Sophie was the clumsiest of them all—though, in her defense, her gown was also the poofiest, and the layers of tulle made the process a special kind of impossible.

The strange tunnel-like doorway turned out to have a second door on the other end, which slid shut as soon as Sophie passed through, leaving her no choice but to shove her way deeper into the crowded, tiny room. She bumped so many limbs along the way that she was sure she'd have a few bruises the next day. And her face ended up smashed into someone's armpit.

She didn't want to know whose.

Claustrophobia wasn't something she usually wrestled with, but she couldn't help staring at the low ceiling and curved diamond walls around her—which lacked any trace of windows or other doors—feeling like she'd just been locked inside a super-blinged-out, elf-size hamster ball, packed with *sixteen* other people.

The urge to shove everyone out of her way and pound on the only exit until someone let her out reared up hard—but she tamped it down, worming toward the edge of the group and pressing her back to the cool wall.

"This is the Paragon," Emery explained. "You five are the only non-Councillors to ever set foot inside of it."

"Lucky us," Sophie mumbled, sucking in a slow breath and trying not to wonder how the room got any fresh air. She didn't see any vents, or even any tiny gaps between the wall's honeycomb-shaped diamond bricks.

And it did *not* help when Councillor Emery pointed to the golden key securing his cape and told them, "You won't be able to return to the Paragon—or *leave*—without one of these."

"I know it's bit cramped," Councillor Oralie added, her lovely eyes flashing with sympathy as they met Sophie's. "But that's only temporary."

"How temporary?" Stina asked, sounding almost as miserable as Sophie felt.

"A matter of minutes," Emery promised. "Brace yourselves."

"For what?" Dex asked, but the Councillors were too busy bumping into each other as they struggled to reach their key-shaped cloak pins. Once their hands were in position, they each pressed their right index finger against the bit piece of the key, holding it there until a low rumble vibrated the floor.

"It's best if you keep your eyes open for this next part," Emery advised, drawing in a breath before he added, "Here we go."

The Councillors pressed their keys once more, and the floor rumbled again—harder this time. And then . . .

. . . nothing.

Seconds ticked by—so many that Sophie became convinced they'd be stuck in there for all eternity, or until they ran out of air, whichever came first. And she was about to start clawing at the walls when the Paragon rattled hard enough to leave everyone wobbling.

Sophie had barely regained her balance when the room seemed to roll forward and bounce up at the same time, triggering gasps and yelps and a whole lot of squealing and flailing—but only from Sophie and her friends. The Councillors barely seemed to notice as the Paragon blasted up and up and up some more—faster, faster, faster. Her eyes watered and her ears popped and her stomach dropped into her toes—which, she was stunned to realize, were no longer touching the floor.

"Why are we weightless?" she asked, trying to wrap her brain around the strange physics of their situation. By all counts, gravity should be pushing down against their upward momentum, shouldn't it?

"The Paragon is actually spinning *really* fast," Councillor Terik told her, swinging his prosthetic leg—which moved so much smoother when it wasn't having to support his weight. "So fast that your eyes can't see it. That's why it's best to keep them open—your brain believes the illusion and doesn't let your body feel the effects of the motion."

All Sophie could say was, "Oh."

And she had to force herself to stop thinking about it, because the more she tried to picture how fast they had to be spinning in order for any of that to be remotely possible, the closer she came to throwing up—and vomiting in a small, spinning room filled with sixteen other people could quickly reach nightmare levels of grossness.

"Shouldn't we be slowing down?" Biana asked, her voice calmer than the question probably should've merited. "We must be near the top of one of the towers by now."

"We are," Emery agreed. "Which is why we need *more* speed."

All twelve of the Councillors pressed the bits of their golden key-pins again, and a tiny whimper slipped through Sophie's lips as another rumble rocked the room and made her feet drift farther off the floor. She was pretty sure she now understood how Charlie would've felt in Mr. Wonka's Great Glass Elevator as he hurtled toward the ceiling of the chocolate factory. And she couldn't help imagining all of them getting cut to ribbons as they crashed through the roof of the diamond palace.

But there was no collision—no shower of jagged shards or fiery explosion.

Just a much louder rumble as the Paragon flooded with shimmering light, which Sophie assumed meant they'd somehow left the Seat of Eminence and were now flying over Eternalia. There was no way she was looking down to verify—not that she expected to be able to see through all the glittering facets of the spinning diamond stones. But on the off chance that she could . . . ignorance was better.

"Where exactly are we going?" Dex asked, shielding his eyes from the glare.

"To the Point of Purity for the Prime Sources," Emery told him, and Sophie was glad she wasn't the only one staring at him like he'd answered the question in a different language.

"Honestly," Bronte scoffed, "what is Foxfire teaching these days?"

Councillor Alina rested her hands on her hips. "Don't look at me—the Council set the curriculum, not the principal."

"And yet you haven't made any corrections—or even any suggestions—now that you've been appointed to our ranks," Bronte noted.

Alina rolled her eyes. "Yes, I've been a little busy cleaning up all the messes I inherited from the rest of you."

"The Prime Sources," Emery cut in, before any of the other Councillors could turn Alina's dig into an argument, "are sunlight, moonlight, and starlight."

"So . . . we're going into space right now," Sophie clarified, really hoping she was wrong about that. The elves had pulled off some amazing feats—but space travel in an oversize diamond hamster ball?

Without even giving them special suits to make sure they'd be able to breathe?

Or seat belts?

Or anything?

"Not quite," Oralie assured her. "The Point of Purity is a very specific spot in our atmosphere, where we can access the purest version of each type of light without any contamination or filtering. We should be there any second."

Except they weren't.

Five hundred and twenty-nine seconds later they were *still* climbing—and yes, Sophie counted. It was the only way to stop herself from thinking about how impossibly high they must be. And from wondering how they were ever going to get back down safely. *And* from noticing how stuffy it was getting inside the Paragon, thanks to all the bodies and the sunlight. The sweat trickling down her back felt like ants crawling on her skin.

Around the seven-hundred-second mark, the light shifted, fading from warm yellow to a soft blue, and Sophie was too relieved by the rush of cool air to wonder what that meant. She didn't even care when *cool* turned to *cold*. Or when *cold* turned to *shivering*. She just wrapped her cape tighter around herself and watched her breath puff out in tiny clouds, relieved to finally not feel like she was slowly melting away.

"Brace yourselves," Emery warned again—not that there was anything to grab ahold of. And it would've been nice if there had been, since the stop was about as smooth as a teenage driver slamming on the brakes.

Sophie was a few seconds from face-planting into the floor when strong hands hauled her back to her feet.

"Thanks," she mumbled, blinking at her savior.

She knew she was having a strange day when ending up in Bronte's arms wasn't even the weirdest thing that had happened.

"Give yourself a second to adjust to the altitude," Oralie told her, catching Sophie by her shoulders when she tried to stand on her own—and nearly collapsed again.

"How come you guys aren't affected?" Biana asked as both Councillor Darek and Councillor Liora helped steady her.

Councillor Alina and Councillor Zarina were keeping Stina upright, Councillor Clarette and Councillor Noland each had their arms hooked around Dex's elbows, and Councillor Ramira and Councillor Velia had lunged to catch Wylie when he'd toppled forward.

"We have these," Councillor Terik said, pointing to his key-pin—and looking far steadier than Sophie and her friends were, even with his cane. "A clever Technopath built altitude stabilizers into them, as well as some features that help with motion sickness and balance."

"I suppose we should've had something similar made for you," Emery murmured. "Hazard of being the first to share this experience. You're going to expose all the flaws in the system."

"Does that mean you're planning on appointing more Regents like us?" Stina asked, trying to tame her curls, which now looked like someone had rubbed her head with a balloon. "Or making more teams or whatever?"

"That depends on whether or not you succeed," Emery told her.

Dex snorted. "Great, no pressure."

"You should *absolutely* feel pressure," Emery said, and the diamonds in his crown seemed to glint with the warning. "You've had a lot of fun making jokes today, Mr. Dizznee, but I hope you truly understand the gravity of the responsibility you're taking on. Fail at your assignment and it's likely that people will perish."

"Yeah, what else is new?" Dex snapped back. "You realize how normal that is for us, right? We've been facing those kinds of odds for years—and by the way, some of those lives on the line? They're *ours* and all the people we care about. We don't get to hide away in the safety of our castles—"

"I'm sure you'll agree that what happened to Councillor Kenric proves we are anything but *safe*," Bronte cut in.

Silence followed, and Sophie had to steal a glance at Oralie, feeling her heart twist when she watched Oralie's eyes turn glassy. Clearly all the months since Kenric's death hadn't lessened Oralie's grief over losing the person everyone had suspected she'd secretly been in love with—and who'd obviously been in love with her, too.

"Fine," Dex conceded, "but you *have* to admit that you guys aren't exactly on the front lines—and I'm not saying you should be. All I'm saying is: Don't act like we don't get how huge the stakes are just because we still know how to have a little fun sometimes."

"Yeah, maybe we joke around because it makes all the tough stuff feel a little less terrifying," Biana added. "It doesn't mean we don't know what we're up against—we know that better than anybody." She held out her arms, letting the light catch the lines of her scars. "And we're still here—still fighting. So the only real difference is that now you guys are *supposedly* going to help us, instead of hindering us, like you have been."

"Exactly." Dex crossed his arms, eyeing each of the Councillors. "The way I see it, we're just going to keep right on doing what we've been doing. And whether this new arrangement fails, or succeeds, that's on *you*."

"It's always *on us*, Mr. Dizznee," Emery said through a sigh that sounded more weary than frustrated. "Being Councillors is a *tremendous* responsibility—one you need to start grasping more fully if we're going to work together. Which is why we brought you here today. We realize you're eager to get to work, and assure you that this will only take a few more minutes. But it's time for the five of you to understand the larger forces at play in our world, and how they shape the roles we've taken on."

All twelve Councillors reached for their pins again, this time pressing the filigree inlaid into the bow and triggering a squeaky rattle in the walls.

Sophie's ears rang as the honeycomb stones unfolded with extra panes of smooth, clear crystal that slowly rotated as the diamond stones eased apart, allowing the new pieces to snap together with the old and form a much wider globe. The floor stretched toward its new barriers, and within seconds the Paragon had doubled in size—maybe even tripled.

And the clear panes now served as windows, providing an impossible view of . . .

"I thought you said we *weren't* going into space," Sophie murmured, rubbing her eyes to make sure she was truly staring at the sphere of swirled blue, white, and green like she'd seen in hundreds and hundreds of pictures in human science classes.

She never thought she'd actually see the earth from up above—and it was so much more beautiful than she'd imagined.

And humbling.

And awe-inspiring.

And more than a little terrifying.

Everything she knew—everything she cared about—was so *very* far away. And she had no idea how they were supposed to get back, or how it was safe for them to be hovering so high up in this sparkly hamster ball contraption.

"Technically, we're not in space," Councillor Emery corrected. "We're at the very edge of our atmosphere, at the Point of Purity, where the force of the sunlight, starlight, and moonlight are all equal. As Councillors, we make this journey at least once a year, to remind ourselves where the true power in our world lies. It's not in us—or in anyone in our species—but in nature itself. We are fragile, flawed creatures. But by some strange fluke of chance, we're also conduits for these forces that surround us—and we're the *only* species on our planet capable of such a feat. Which makes it our responsibility to use that power for good—to maintain order and peace for *all* creatures, and to ensure that everyone continues to prosper. *That* is why we lead. Not for praise or privilege or honor or glory. But because it's our obligation. And all we hope for in exchange is a thriving, safe planet. Only when you truly believe that about us can you understand who we are, both as your Councillors and as people. The crowns and fanfare are simply a facade to look the part we've found ourselves having to play. They do not change the fact that what we *really* are is a group of twelve relatively normal individuals trying our best to be what people need. And *that* is why we must stay in power."

"Our rule will never be perfect," Bronte added quietly, "but at least we serve for the right reasons—and we will always strive to do what's best for our people. That's why we wanted the five of you to stand with us here today, in the center of all that drives us, so we can offer you the new oath that we've created."

Councillor Emery's gaze shifted to Sophie, and when he spoke again, his tone held a new level of authority. "Everything we do—right or wrong, good or bad, success or failure—is to serve the various species who need our help on this planet. We won't deny that we've made missteps, or that we've resisted change—but those days are now behind us. For too long we've clung to the old ways, relying on the tried and true because it had worked in the past. But it has failed us, again and again. So it's time to move forward. Time to embrace new views and new wisdom. And we stand here now, ready to swear to you that from this moment on, you can be assured of three things: *We will listen. We will learn. And we will adapt.* All we ask in return is that you be ready and willing to do the same. If you put your faith in us, we will put that same faith in you. For the good of everyone."

"For the good of everyone," the other eleven Councillors repeated, their diamond circlets glittering like stars. "We will listen. We will learn. And we will adapt."

"Your service to us will not be easy," Emery added, widening his gaze to include all of Sophie's teammates. "It will not be safe. And it will not always be what you wish it would be. But it will be vital. It will be game-changing. And together, we will bring our side to victory—assuming we're *on* the same side. Are you ready to accept this partnership?"

"A partnership in the loosest sense of the word," Bronte clarified quickly. "Your authority will technically be no different than the authority of any other Regent. And our authority will remain supreme. But . . . we will hear you out and keep an open mind. And the fact that I'm promising this after I've endured your ridiculous discussions of team names and titles for Miss Foster—and did so without inflicting on any of you, no less—should be more than enough proof of my commitment to this vow."

"We're *all* committed," Terik assured them. "The five of you are incredibly special children."

"Uh, who are you calling 'children'?" Wylie asked.

Terik smiled. "When you get to be my age—and certainly when

you get to be *Bronte's* age—you'll see why the term still applies. But you'll also see that it's not a bad thing. There's great power in youth. What you lack in experience, you make up for in innovation. And hopefully, by combining both perspectives, this new arrangement will be the solution we so desperately need."

"Which is why we must now ask for your commitment," Emery added. "We've sworn our oath to you. It's time for you to make yours to us—which will be a two-step process. First a vow, similar to what most Regents say, with slight modifications to reflect our unique situation. And the vow will be followed by a simple test to prove that you're each ready for the responsibilities and challenges ahead."

"Test?" Sophie and all of her friends repeated, sharing a nervous look.

"A *simple* test," Emery emphasized, "which will only take a few moments—and all of you should have no trouble completing it. But I assumed it would hold your focus from the moment I mentioned it, so I'm going to explain the details of the test first, even though it will technically be the second step in this process."

He led the five of them forward, and Sophie noticed that her legs weren't the only ones shaking as Emery had her, Dex, Biana, Wylie, and Stina line up in that order. He positioned them several feet apart and had them face the diamond-and-crystal dome with the rest of the Councillors behind them.

"We brought you here to experience the power of the Prime Sources," Emery said, stationing himself to their left. "Have any of you already detected their presence?"

"Yes," Wylie breathed, his hands trembling as he wrapped his arms around himself and closed his eyes. "They're . . . overwhelming."

"I'm sure they are for a Flasher," Emery agreed. "Just as I'm certain they're more intense for a Vanisher."

All eyes shifted to Biana, who'd started flickering in and out of sight like a strobe light. "Yeah, they're . . . wow," she whispered.

Emery nodded. "But even those without light talents can still feel each source if they concentrate properly. It's easiest if you stretch out your arms and hold your palms toward the windows."

Sophie had assumed he was only talking to her, Dex, and Stina— but when she glanced over her shoulder, all the Councillors had done the same.

"The sunlight is the easiest to identify," Emery said quietly. "You simply need to seek out the same warm tingle you're used to feeling on a bright summer day."

The instruction wasn't quite as simple as it sounded, given how freezing it was inside the Paragon. But Sophie knew from her skill lessons with Keefe that there was always more warmth around her than she realized. She just had to make her mind concentrate the right way. So she thought of that sweltering yellow glow she'd endured for most of their journey, focusing on the trickle of sweat she'd felt streaming down her back. And sure enough, she could still detect traces of that same heat prickling along her spine. She centered her mind on the feeling, and it was as if someone had turned on one of those human patio heaters, showering her with a dry, swirling warmth that erased her shivers, even though her breath was still clouding with every exhale.

"Sunlight is not a gentle heat," Emery continued. "It's an invisible fire that can burn all the way to your core if you let it—and that's still only the beginning of its power. The sun *always* has more to give—which means it can easily become too much if we draw upon it too heavily. So we must never let ourselves take more than we have a need for. Harnessing the sun is about respect and restraint."

"The moonlight is the opposite," Councillor Terik informed them, limping to stand beside Emery. "It's always cool and gentle and soothing. And it can sometimes be elusive. To find it, you must search for the soft calm you feel on a clear evening. It tends to linger in the quietest places."

He paused, giving them time to seek out the right sensation, and it took Sophie several breaths to home in on the feeling—a cold, silky caress down the back of her neck.

"The moonlight will always be there for us in our darkest hours," Terik continued. "But it's also ever-changing. Sometimes weak. Sometimes strong. It all depends on the day. So we must learn to embrace the force in all its varying phases—demanding as much as we can, but never pushing for more than it has to offer. Never expecting it to be more than it is. Harnessing the moon is about managing expectations."

"And starlight is the most varied of all the Sources," Councillor Oralie whispered as she joined Terik and Emery, placing one slender hand against a clear pane of crystal on the curved wall. "Each star will share only the faintest flicker—unless we ask it to give us more. Then it will pour out all we need in abundance. And even when we ignore its force, or wash it away with other light, it is *always* there waiting. You'll feel the starlight patiently thrumming in the background, like a steady, tingly heartbeat."

The last word helped Sophie center on the right sensation—a

pulsing shiver that felt like it was everywhere and nowhere all at the same time.

"Every star is different," Oralie added softly. "And calling on too many can muddle their energy. It's best to be deliberate when we reach for them, selecting the precise star we need and nothing more. Harnessing the stars is about choice, and utilizing them takes both knowledge and wisdom."

"We realize all of this likely feels a bit abstract," Emery said as Oralie stepped back from the window. "I'd wager some of you are even thinking, 'Why does this matter? Don't we mostly use light for leaping?' And you're not wrong. But light is the foundation of our world, and it affects *everything*. So the more we endeavor to understand and appreciate the unique attributes that each type of light comes with, the better we're also able to understand the needs of everything that relies on that light for existence. Which is why the test we've chosen is the same test we take ourselves every year: We want you to leap back to Eternalia using a beam made from all three Prime Sources. It will be no more challenging than any other leap you've made, but it will also feel unlike anything you've experienced. And it will help you to better comprehend the power at your disposal—and your position in relation to that power—in a way that nothing else truly can."

"You'll each make your leap with two of us at your side," Bronte added, "and those same Councillors will be your points of contact for as long as they serve and you maintain your title as Regent. You'll report primarily to Miss Foster, of course—given that she's your team leader—and she'll report to all of us, both for general updates and for any larger matters. But should you need further guidance on smaller issues, know that your assigned Councillors will always be available to you. And no—you don't get to pick who you'll be paired with."

Darek and Liora moved to stand beside Biana, while Clarette and Noland joined Dex, and Ramira and Velia stationed themselves by Wylie. Alina and Zarina went to Stina—who looked less than thrilled to be paired with her former principal—and Sophie realized they'd each been paired with the same Councillors who'd helped steady them when the Paragon had stopped moving.

So she wasn't surprised when Bronte and Oralie moved to stand next to her—but she *was* surprised that she didn't mind the idea of working so closely with Bronte.

Definitely a very strange day.

"Emery and I are at your disposal as well," Terik explained. "Think of us as the team's general overseers—those less closely involved in the nitty-gritty of it all, in order to maintain a wider perspective."

"Is everyone ready now?" Emery asked, and when Sophie, Wylie, Dex, Biana, and Stina had nodded, one Councillor from each pairing reached into their cloaks and removed a long silver chain that held a simple crystal pendant.

The crystals were swirled with three different colors—white, silver, and gold—and looked much cloudier than the stones the elves usually used to create leaping paths. But that did nothing to dull the vibrancy of the light that was refracted at everyone's feet when the Councillors held the pendants up to the windows. In fact, the paths were so bright that Sophie couldn't look directly at the beams.

"Now that everything's in place," Emery said, "it's time for you to make your oaths. And as I mentioned before, the vow has been slightly amended for this occasion. Regents generally say: 'I swear to use everything in my power to serve the Council and make our world a haven of peace, hope, and illumination.' But for you five, given that you're making this oath at a time when war threatens to cast its shadow over our world, we've made two small adjustments to the wording. The vow we're asking you to make is: 'I swear to *fight* with everything in my power to serve the Council and keep our world a haven of peace, hope, and illumination.' We'll have you make your oaths one at a time—and then you should let the Prime Sources carry you back to Eternalia, where your assigned Councillors will give you a few final instructions. Then your appointments will officially be complete and you can get started on your assignment. Is everyone clear? Good. Who would like to go first?"

"Shouldn't our fearless leader show us how it's done?" Stina suggested, smirking at Sophie.

"Actually, a true leader goes last," Emery corrected, "to ensure that everyone in their team successfully completes their task."

Stina's smile faded.

"I'll go," Wylie offered, and when his eyes shifted to Sophie, it took her a second to realize he was waiting for her approval.

That . . . was going to take some getting used to.

She nodded and he reached for Ramira's and Velia's hands, then cleared his throat and said, "I swear to fight with everything in my power to serve the Council and keep our world a haven of peace, hope, and illumination."

"May the Prime Sources carry you safely," Emery told him, and Wylie turned back to Sophie. Once he had her permission, he pulled

Ramira and Velia forward and the three of them stepped into the blinding light, vanishing in a shower of shimmer.

Biana went next, copying Wylie almost exactly. The only difference was the tiny wink she gave Sophie before the light whisked her, Darek, and Liora away.

Then Stina made a big fuss about it being her turn. It looked like she *wasn't* going to get Sophie's permission before doing anything. But at the last second Stina rolled her eyes and turned to face her new leader. "We good, Foster?"

Sophie considered the question, wanting to make sure she was being honest when she nodded.

Stina nodded back and huffed out an annoyed breath before she repeated the oath and disappeared with her Councillors in a particularly bright flash.

Then it was Dex's turn. And when his eyes met Sophie's, he looked more nervous than she'd been expecting. As if the reality of what he was agreeing to was finally hitting him.

"Ready to become Lord Dex?" she asked, trying to help him relax.

"You ready to become Lady Fos-Boss?" he countered.

The title didn't feel like a tease this time, and Sophie assumed that meant he was asking if they were making the right decision.

She honestly didn't know.

But they *never* knew if they were making the right decision. They just took their best guess and kept going.

So she told him, "I'll *never* be Lady Fos-Boss. But . . . everything else? Bring it on."

His dimples peeked out of the corners of his mouth. "Yeah, bring it on."

"And then there was one," Emery noted as Dex, Clarette, and Noland glittered away.

"The girl who changed our minds," Terik added, and Sophie couldn't tell if he meant that as a good thing or a bad thing.

She pressed her hands to her sides, refusing to tug on her eyelashes during such a crucial moment. Instead, she took her chance to ask the question she'd been wondering about since she first stepped into the Paragon.

"The day I first met you guys," she said, turning to Oralie and Bronte, "when you tested me to decide if I qualified for Foxfire, you were wearing the same cloak pins you are now. Does that mean you'd been up here before you went to Everglen—or came up here after you left?"

"Yes," Emery answered for them. "We all made the journey that morning, since we sensed that your arrival was sure to be a turning point in our world."

"We wanted to ensure that we had the proper perspective when we met with you," Oralie explained, "in order to make the best possible decision under such unexpected circumstances."

"We leaped straight from here to the gates of Everglen," Bronte added, "and I thought a lot about the Sources during our visit. In fact, the whole time I was there, I couldn't help wondering if someday you'd be standing up here beside us—and now, here you are."

He snorted when Sophie's jaw fell open.

"No need to look so stunned," he told her with a rueful smile. "I never said I was *pleased* with the idea. I could simply tell that this was where we were heading. Why do you think I pushed you the way that I did? I had to ensure that you were truly someone who could be trusted with the role you were surely meant to play. And I won't claim that my behavior toward you was always admirable—or fair. But . . . you bore it far better than I ever would've expected. And now, here we are, and I must say . . . you are certainly worthy."

Sophie's eyes burned worse than they had with Wylie's earlier compliment.

A couple of tears might've even spilled over.

She hoped no one noticed.

Oralie took Sophie's hand, gently twining their fingers together. "Are you ready to make your oath, Lady Sophie?"

Sophie nodded.

But instead of the vow, she found herself blurting out, "I have no idea what I'm doing."

Bronte took her other hand, guiding her closer to the beam of light. "I'll let you in on a secret, Sophie. One that you may or may not find reassuring. None of us know what we're doing."

Terik laughed. "No, we certainly don't."

"That does *not* make me feel better," Sophie told them.

But as the words left her mouth, she realized they weren't true.

Maybe this was what growing up meant—tackling the huge challenges, whether you were ready for them or not. And trusting that you'd figure out a way to get through it.

"You ready?" Bronte asked.

"She's ready," Oralie answered for her, offering a shy smile before adding, "The Empath would know."

Sophie tightened her grip on each of them—the two Councillors she'd first started her adventure in the Lost Cities with.

It seemed fitting to let them guide her into this next stage.

She only wished Kenric was still with them.

But she'd let his loss fuel her determination.

She owed him a victory. Hopefully this was how she'd get it for him.

"Okay," she said. "I swear to fight with everything in my power to serve the Council and keep our world a haven of peace, hope, and illumination."

Then, without a second's hesitation, she led Bronte and Oralie forward, and they each stepped into the light and let the Sources carry them away.

NINE

OPHIE HAD ENDURED LEAPS OF ALL
different speeds and sights and sensations during her
years in the Lost Cities—but she'd never experienced
anything that made her feel so . . . *small*.

She was a dust mote swirling in an endless sunbeam.

Plankton riding the crest of a tidal wave.

And yet, somehow, the journey still felt incredibly empowering—
and peaceful.

The Sources' threads of soft warmth and silky cold and subtle
tingles moved in perfect synchronization.

None of them tried to overshadow the others.

None fought to take control.

Each force did what it did best and relied on the others to handle
their own.

And the unity was so soothing—so steadying—that Sophie's
mind happily surrendered to the flow, trusting the light to keep her
safe and cared for during their travels.

She would've followed the Sources anywhere as they swirled and
spun and soared across the sky. But the powerful triad of light knew

exactly when it was time to let her go. And suddenly there was breath filling her lungs and solid ground under her feet, and her eyes were blinking through the too-bright glare as her body pieced itself back together and the light continued its adventures without her.

She wasn't sure if the test had been meant to remind her that she was both strong *and* insignificant, or to teach her the importance of balance and cooperation. Either way, she could definitely understand why the Council found it valuable to make that leap year after year after year.

The Sources had shown her a perfect example of how to lead without dominating—and made her feel powerful and humbled all at the same time.

Oralie and Bronte looked just as affected, despite how many times they'd experienced the phenomenon. Bronte's eyes were even a little bit misty.

"Where are we?" Sophie asked, squinting at the round room, which felt like a cross between a fairy princess's bedroom and a Middle Eastern palace. Arched windows broke up the shimmering walls, draped with wispy pink curtains and strands of beaded lace, and dozens of pink jeweled lanterns dangled from the domed ceiling. Pink silk cushions were piled across the ornate pink rugs. And the gilded dressing table and chair were inlaid with enormous pink tourmalines. Golden chests of all different shapes and sizes were stacked neatly around the table, along with two floor-length mirrors, which gave Sophie a rather pitiful glimpse of her now greatly disheveled appearance.

Her hair had morphed into a tangle-monster, and the smoky powder she'd brushed across her eyelids had gooped up in the corners.

"This is one of the readying rooms in the Seat of Eminence," Oralie told her, removing the pins from her bun and letting her long blond ringlets fall free. "To ensure that we're always able to present ourselves at our best. The rest of your friends are in four of the other rooms. There are twelve in all—one for each of us on the Council. I doubt it surprises you that this is mine."

"Are you sure?" Sophie teased. "This place really feels like Bronte to me."

Bronte snorted. "Mine has an empty mahogany table and a sturdy chair."

"It's one of the bleakest places I've ever been," Oralie noted, shaking her head. "Hence why we decided it would be better to leap you here."

"But I don't understand," Sophie admitted, remembering what Grady had told her earlier. "I thought the Seat of Eminence was designed to block light from coming into the building."

"It is," Bronte agreed. "But as Councillors, we have secret access points, in case we need to make a private visit or a hasty exit."

"And don't worry—you're perfectly safe here," Oralie assured her. "This room is protected by an abundance of security measures."

"We also won't be here long," Bronte added. "I can only handle so much pink."

"You'll tough it out as long as you have to," Oralie informed him. "Sophie needs to look her best when she returns as a Regent."

She pulled out the dressing table's chair and motioned for Sophie to sit.

"Uh . . . please tell me you're not giving me a makeover," Sophie mumbled.

The number of pots and vials and brushes and powder puffs on the dressing table was downright terrifying. And they'd already lost enough time.

"It'll be painless," Oralie promised.

"Somehow I doubt that will be the case—for both Sophie and myself," Bronte muttered.

Sophie had never felt such a strong bond with the pointy-eared Councillor in all her life.

Oralie clicked her tongue at both of them and patted the chair's cushion—which was, of course, pink—and Sophie realized there was no way she was getting out of there without a little primping.

So . . . time for a makeover.

From a *Councillor*.

Definitely the Weirdest. Day. Ever.

"Nothing too sparkly," she begged as she slumped into the chair, and Oralie spun her around and crouched in front of her.

"I'll stay true to who you are," Oralie promised, tilting Sophie's chin from side to side, studying each of her features for what felt like an eternity. Sophie had to start counting the passing seconds to stop herself from squirming.

She made it to seventy-three before a pucker formed between Oralie's perfect eyebrows. "Is something wrong?" Sophie asked, since forehead puckers were rarely good news.

Oralie shook her head. "Of course not! You just look so . . ."

"So . . . ?" Sophie prompted.

"It's hard to explain. You've changed since the first day I met you. You're . . . not a little girl anymore. Which is how it's supposed to be. I just wish . . ." Oralie bit her lip and looked away.

"Never mind. We should get started." She straightened up and grabbed a silky cloth from the table, spritzing it with something that smelled like jasmine. "I know you and your friends are eager to get to work."

"Are Dex, Biana, Stina, and Wylie getting makeovers too?" Sophie asked, hoping Dex would show up with his hair dyed black and styled all shaggy—because Emo Dex would be hilarious—and that Stina would end up with giant hair-sprayed bangs.

"I doubt it," Bronte told her, killing her dreams. "So you need to hurry, Oralie."

"I'll do my best. But this is important. Sophie's the leader. She needs to look the part. Especially for her big debut."

Sophie frowned. "I thought you guys hadn't decided when you'd be announcing our appointments."

"We haven't." Oralie wiped Sophie's eyes with the cloth she'd prepared, then set to work brushing out Sophie's tangles. "But that doesn't mean we can't start building buzz. We're going to have you and your friends and family leap home from outside the Seat of Eminence. That way people will see you in your finery and wonder what's going on. Should get the rumors and gossip spreading."

"Oh. Great."

Bronte barked a laugh. "I think you and I understand each other far better than we realized, Miss Foster. But try to remember that there's been a turning of the tide, so to speak. Gossip can now be a good thing for you. You're no longer a girl steeped in suspicion."

"Why is that?" Sophie asked, turning to look at him, even though she could tell Oralie wanted her to hold still. "I mean . . . what happened at Everglen was a disaster—and I barely did anything except run around trying not to get eaten. I don't really get how seeing that could've inspired people to trust me."

Oralie set down the brush and dabbed a cool pink gel on the apples of Sophie's cheeks. "You know what I think it was? Out of all the people there, you were the one who could flee from the danger the easiest. Everyone else needed to get their hands on a leaping crystal. But you could've teleported away—and your trollish bodyguard even tried to convince you to do exactly that. And still, you stayed. That kind of loyalty means something to people."

"As it should," Bronte agreed. "Why do you think you're here with us now? Though I wish we weren't *here*." He gestured around the room as Oralie smeared Sophie's lips with a balm that tasted like lushberries. "So while Oralie finishes whatever nonsense she's doing, I'll walk you through the Articles of your Regency. The more we multitask, the sooner we can escape this pink monstrosity."

Oralie flung one of the powder puffs at his head, showering his face with a cloud of glitter.

But Sophie was all for Bronte's plan—even if the term "Articles" had her bracing for a bunch of thick, boring books she'd be expected to read from cover to cover in order to learn all the various laws and procedures of the nobility.

Instead, Bronte grabbed one of the larger chests resting at her feet and flipped back the lid to reveal . . .

"I have to wear a *crown*?" She scowled at the gilded circlet resting on a black velvet cushion. The band was decorated with curls of gold that hooked together to form pointed spirals, and tiny diamonds were dotted throughout the design. The main focal point, though, was an oval ruby that glittered at the circlet's center.

The delicate headpiece was actually quite pretty, in that horrifying, everyone-will-definitely-be-staring-at-her-when-she-wears-this kind of way. But she would've preferred the jewel not be bloodred.

"It's only for official occasions," Oralie assured her. "Like elections or special announcements—or today, when we're trying to get people's attention."

"I guess." That was still a whole lot more crown time than Sophie wanted.

"And remember, we decided on the starlight circlet," Oralie told Bronte, spraying Sophie's face with something that smelled citrusy, "because the glow from the lumenite will draw more attention."

"Uh, how many circlets are you giving me?" Sophie asked as Bronte lifted the velvet cushion, revealing a nearly identical silver circlet hidden underneath. Then he lifted *that* cushion and there was a third nearly identical glowing white circlet, which had to be the one Oralie meant.

"There's one to represent each of the Sources," Bronte explained.

So . . . *three* crowns.

Ugh.

"Occasionally we may request that you wear a specific one—like today," Oralie explained, leaning back as she dusted Sophie's forehead with one of the powder puffs. "But you'll generally be able to choose your favorite. The important thing will be making sure that everyone on your team is wearing the circlet for the same Source as you are, so the five of you come across as unified—and the same thing goes for your cloak clasps."

Before Sophie could ask, Bronte lifted another smaller trunk and flipped back the lid to reveal three pins—one gold, one silver, one lumenite—each in the same swirled shape as the pattern woven throughout her circlet. It reminded Sophie of some of the Celtic symbols she'd seen, only the spiral was a little looser.

"It's the symbol we created for your team," Bronte explained, handing her the gold pin to examine. "Each of the three lines represents one of the Prime Sources, and the design shows them evenly uniting. Hopefully it will remind you of the need for proper balance in your collaboration."

"Do you not like it?" Oralie asked, pausing in the middle of lining Sophie's eyes with black, smudgy pencil.

"No, it's fine." Sophie ran her finger along the smooth metal curls. "It just . . . feels a little weird that I've never heard people talk about the Sources before. Seems like they're super important."

"The Sources should definitely be covered better in the Foxfire curriculum," Bronte admitted. "I'll have to make sure that Magnate Leto has that oversight corrected when sessions resume. But most people will likely still see them primarily as light and nothing more. Focusing on the power behind them is more of a Council way of thinking, which is why we thought they'd be a fitting symbol for your team, since you'll be collaborating with us rather uniquely."

"But something else bothers you about the pins," Oralie pressed, placing her hand on Sophie's shoulder, probably to remind her that she couldn't hide anything from an Empath.

Sophie sighed. "Well . . . I guess I'm just wondering if these pins mean I can't wear my Ruewen crest anymore."

"We'd prefer that you didn't," Bronte admitted. "At least until people no longer need regular reminders of your authority. That's the point of all this"—he motioned to the gilded chests at her feet—

"to ensure that people will see past your youth, and any of the previous scandals they may remember, and recognize that you must be obeyed and respected. Particularly those with authority themselves, like the leaders of the other species. That's going to be essential for you to succeed with your assignments."

"I guess that makes sense," Sophie mumbled, reaching to remove her Ruewen pin. But her fingers didn't want to unfasten the clasp.

"Grady and Edaline will always be your family, with or without their crest on your cloak," Oralie assured her.

"It's not that," Sophie argued—though it was a *little*.

Having a family crest meant a *lot* to a girl who'd been adopted.

"It's just . . . I don't know—this all feels so much bigger than I imagined when Edaline first told me about the Regent thing. I mean, it's not like Grady wears a special cloak clasp with a custom designed symbol, or a circlet—and he's an *Emissary*."

"But you're a new kind of Regent," Bronte reminded her. "In fact, we considered creating a wholly new title for you and your friends, to help highlight the difference to everyone. But we feared that would end up causing too much confusion—as well as a bunch of Regents seeking appointments to the new level. So we asked our gnomes to put together these Articles for all of you instead. The circlets, clasps, and cloaks should sufficiently communicate your exalted status, while also feeling specific to your team."

"Cloaks?" Sophie repeated, letting out a sigh when Bronte pointed to three more of the chests on the floor.

"One silver, one white, and one gold," he told her. "I'm sure you can guess the meaning for the colors at this point. And in case it's not clear, you should be mixing up which Source you choose for each item. So you'll be wearing the starlight circlet today—and you're holding the sunlight clasp. Which means you should wear the moonlight cloak." He flipped open the center trunk to reveal a neat bundle of folded silver with some sort of patch sewn to the fabric. "The patch is one final demonstration of your new status—and your Foxfire uniforms will need to be affixed with it as well, once sessions resume, since it's a noble school." He reached for another small chest and showed her the stack of round patches inside, handing her one so she could study the design.

The palm-size circle had a bright red border and the same symbol from her circlet and cloak clasps swirling in the background—though the three lines alternated colors this time, one gold, one silver, and one white. But the main focus was the detailed silhouette stitched on top of everything—a howling dire wolf.

"We've assigned each of you an individual mascot," Oralie explained, "to represent the role you'll play for your team."

"And I'm . . . a dire wolf?" Sophie asked. "Shouldn't mine be . . . you know . . . ?"

"A moonlark?" Bronte guessed.

"I mean, it seems logical, right?" She was surprised she even had to suggest it.

Bronte shook his head. "No offense to the Black Swan. The name they chose for you is not without its significance. But we think it's high time for people to see you as more than an experiment. More than a survivor. More than a girl left to fend for herself in a world where she didn't truly belong. You're a leader now, Miss Foster. Not a defenseless little bird. And you're part of a team, not struggling alone. So we wanted you to show our world—and your enemies—that you rule your pack, and have the claws and teeth to take anyone on."

Sophie studied the wolf silhouette again, hoping it hid the tears she could feel forming.

She'd never thought she needed the Council's support—but having it meant *everything*.

Even if the pressure of their expectations was also pretty nauseating.

"The change has already happened inside you," Oralie assured her, tucking Sophie's hair behind her ears. "I can feel it. And I can see it. Now we're just helping you dress the part."

"Exactly," Bronte said, passing Oralie the glowing lumenite circlet. "Trust us."

"I do," Sophie told them, trying to hold still as Oralie went to place it over her head. But at the last second, she couldn't stop herself from blurting out, "But you need to know I'm unmatchable."

Oralie froze.

Bronte sighed. "I'm assuming that has to do with the lack of information about your genetic parents."

Sophie nodded, wondering if Bronte was yet another person who'd been expecting this to happen.

Oralie didn't seem surprised either. More devastated.

"I'm trying to find out who they are," Sophie assured them, in case they were about to take her title away.

"You shouldn't do that!" Bronte warned.

"Why not?" Sophie asked, surprised by the snap in his tone.

"Because no good can come from it." Bronte kicked aside several pillows as he turned to pace the length of the room. "Remember, the Black Swan has kept their identities hidden by choice. I'm sure that means they have good reason for the secrecy—and I think this is an instance when we should trust their judgment. Uncovering the secret will surely cause a tremendous amount of turmoil for the donors—and it's possible that their turmoil could ripple through our entire world. Their identity could also renew the scandal surrounding your unconventional past, right when public opinion has finally shifted in your favor."

"And what about the scandal of being unmatchable?" Sophie countered. "How do you think people are going to feel when they see me parading around with your fancy Regent symbols on my special cloak—and my *crown*—knowing I'm even worse than a bad match?"

"You're not *worse*," Bronte insisted. "And if you remain single—"

"Don't!" Oralie slammed the circlet down on the dressing table hard enough to make Bronte pause midstride. "You can't expect Sophie to consider the kind of commitment you're about to suggest. Not at her age. I'd had time to review *all* of my match lists—and I was still far too young. I had no inkling of the sacrifice I was making."

Bronte cleared his throat. "I realize that you may have certain regrets," he told Oralie, "but can you honestly tell me that given the chance to do it all again, you'd do anything differently?"

Oralie tilted her head to stare at the lanterns twinkling above them. "No. But my decision was *my choice*. What you're suggesting for Sophie wouldn't necessarily be."

"Not everything can be as fair as we want," Bronte argued. "Nor as ideal. But I never said any decisions needed to be made today. I simply felt it was important to point out that all of this is technically an avoidable scandal."

"It's also avoidable if I can provide the matchmakers with my genetic history," Sophie noted.

"But *that* would be a very bad idea." Bronte resumed his pacing. "In my experience, when the Black Swan wants something to stay hidden, they have a way of making that happen—at any cost."

"I thought the Council trusted the Black Swan," Sophie reminded him.

"We do," Oralie said quietly.

"But trust doesn't cover everything," Bronte noted. "And in this case, what it means is that we believe the Black Swan to generally be working for the good of our world. That doesn't mean we don't still expect them to bend or break any rules they deem necessary in order to attain their goals. And they've already told you that they cannot and will not reveal your parentage, yes?"

Sophie reluctantly nodded.

"I'm also assuming they've asked you not to investigate, right?" When she agreed again, he told her, "Well, then it's safe to conclude that they'll do whatever it takes to ensure you can't defy their decision. And think of what they allowed to happen to Prentice in order to keep your location secret. Do you want to risk that your quest to find your genetic family could lead to another similar tragedy?"

Sophie's heart stalled. "The Black Swan wouldn't—"

"Wouldn't they?" he interrupted. "They know this secret affects their moonlark in many unfortunate ways. And *still* they've kept it hidden. Do you honestly not see that as proof that nothing will stop them from keeping this truth safe? And if you agree with my assessment—as you should—then are you truly willing to say,

'Hang the consequences,' and embark on such a quest solely for your own personal benefit?"

Sophie's mouth was so dry that her tongue felt superglued to the roof of her mouth. So the words came out slightly garbled as she said, "I have no idea. But if I don't, and people find out I'm unmatchable, how can I be a Regent—"

"Because we say so," Oralie interrupted, taking Sophie's hands. "This was a Council decision. All that matters to us is that your team needs you—and *we* need you."

Sophie closed her eyes, letting the wonderful words float around her brain before she forced herself to remind them, "But you didn't know about my match status—"

"Perhaps we didn't know this specific development," Bronte cut in quietly. "But all of us have long assumed that there are sure to be many surprises ahead with you, Miss Foster. Not all of them ideal. And still, none of us hesitated to make our oath to you, did we?"

"No," Sophie mumbled, wondering how this could possibly be the same Bronte who'd been so against her in the beginning.

"Your title is settled," Oralie reminded her. "Your match status changes nothing. And if anyone questions that decision, you'll have the full support of the Council."

"You will," Bronte agreed. "So I implore you, Miss Foster: Keep this team your focus. And the danger to the dwarves. And whatever else the Neverseen might be planning for Tam—as well as any further assignments we may ask you and your friends to take on. Anything beyond that will be a distraction at best and a danger at worst. Promise me you'll put it out of your mind."

She knew what he was trying to get her to commit to. And she couldn't deny he'd raised some valid concerns.

But the best she was willing to give him was, "I won't lose focus—and I won't do anything that would endanger anybody."

"I truly hope that's the case," he murmured.

"It is," she promised.

Painful silence followed, until Oralie cleared her throat and reached for the circlet. "We shouldn't keep the others waiting. They need their leader—assuming you're still willing."

Sophie stared at the glowing crown, wondering how long she'd actually get to keep it. She wasn't convinced she could truly count on the Council to stand at her side if the public turned against her.

But . . . she had to agree that the Black Swan might go to great lengths to stop her from finding the information she needed.

The choice felt overwhelming—until she remembered the leap she'd just taken.

How freeing it had felt to surrender to the Sources' power.

All she'd had to do was let go and rely on something bigger than herself to carry her through.

So she nodded, and Oralie set the circlet gently around her forehead.

The metal felt cool and heavy against her skin, but she could tell she'd get used to the weight of it. The pressure wasn't more than she could handle.

"I'm sorry," Oralie whispered before she stepped back.

"For what?" Sophie asked.

"Many things." She adjusted a strand of Sophie's hair. "But mostly for the fact that you've needed an ally so many times—and I haven't been there. I promise that's changing."

"It is," Bronte agreed. "You're a Regent now—see for yourself."

Oralie tilted the mirror, letting Sophie study her reflection. And she barely recognized the girl staring back at her.

The pink blush on her cheeks should've made her look softer. So should the wavy tendrils framing her face. But the bold lines highlighting her eyes made her look older instead.

Pretty—but *fierce*.

Different—and proud of it.

And that glowing crown . . .

"May I?" Oralie asked, pointing to Sophie's Ruewen crest. When Sophie agreed, Oralie unfastened the clasp, and Sophie's cape fell away from her shoulders, sliding to the floor as Oralie draped the much heavier silver cloak in its place, fastening it with her new golden Regent clasp and arranging the drape of the fabric so the howling wolf patch hung visibly over Sophie's heart. Then she stepped back, giving Sophie another moment to study herself.

And this.

This was the kind of girl who commanded attention.

The kind of girl who didn't care what anyone thought of her—because she knew exactly who she was.

The kind of girl who wouldn't let anything matter. Not scandals or gossip or frightening responsibility.

This girl could handle it all—and would.

Sophie wasn't sure if any of that could truly be said about her—yet.

But she wanted it to be.

Oralie nodded, her eyes shimmering as she made one final

adjustment to Sophie's cape. "Perfect," she whispered. "You're ready."

"Yeah," Sophie agreed. "I think I am."

Everyone had clearly been waiting on Sophie for a while when she returned with Bronte and Oralie to the dark, spotlighted room where she'd left Grady, Sandor, Della, Tiergan, and Vika earlier. But she also wasn't the only one of her teammates who'd had a Councillor makeover.

Stina's transformation was nearly as drastic as Sophie's. No giant hair-sprayed bangs—sadly—but her new look might've been even better. Something about her peach cheeks and glossy lips and tamed curls had turned Stina into someone who actually looked . . . friendly.

Her smile even seemed sincere when she spotted Sophie—though the mascot the Council had chosen for the silhouette in Stina's pink-bordered patch was a kraken. So clearly everyone still had realistic expectations.

Wylie's dark hair was too closely cropped for there to be much change to his overall style. But the regal finery definitely gave him a much more confident air.

Sophie had a feeling that out of all of them, Wylie would have the most people bowing and curtsying—though she also noticed that one of his hands kept fidgeting with his new golden cloak pin. He probably missed his Endal crest as much as she missed her Ruewen one, which was now pinned to the chain of her home crystal and tucked under her cape.

His patch had an opalescent border that changed colors as he moved, and his mascot was a huge winged lizard—which she assumed was a dragon until she noticed the ridge of spikes down its back and the fact that it only had two legs. She didn't know enough about wyverns to guess why the Council chose that particular creature to represent Wylie. But it sure made him look cool.

Dex's mascot, on the other hand, was . . . probably not what he would've chosen. If it weren't for the two tiny eyes stitched onto the round, fluffy silhouette in the center of his green-bordered patch, Sophie wouldn't have even known it was a tomple. But the dust-eating poofball actually did seem like a good fit for Dex once she thought a little more about it. Tomples weren't just adorable—they were *useful*. And even though they might look cuddly, they also had six spindly insect legs hidden under all their fur and could cause plenty of chaos.

And while Dex's makeover wasn't the hilarious Emo-tasticness that Sophie had been wishing for, his hair had been styled with a cute little swoop in the front that really suited his features, and his new silver cloak made his shoulders look extra broad. His glowing circlet also gave his periwinkle eyes a proud twinkle, and Sophie wished she could be there to see the joy on his parents' faces when he walked through the door to Rimeshire in his new finery and explained his appointment. She'd known Dex was special from the minute she'd met him—and his family had *always* believed in him. But now *everyone* was going to see him as Lord Dex—a handsome, important Regent, and a member of Team Still-Needs-a-Better-Name.

And then there was Biana—proof that some people were *born* for moments like these. Now that she had a circlet, Sophie already couldn't imagine Biana without it. And the look in Biana's eyes seemed to say, *I've just made my own Vacker legacy, and I can't wait to show you what I'm going to do with it.*

Her overall style was more muted than normal—neutral tones on her eyes, cheeks, and lips, with her hair pulled back into a simple knot at the base of her neck. And yet somehow that made her even more striking. The Council had chosen a kelpie for Biana's mascot, and while Sophie—once again—didn't know much about the creature, she *did* know that kelpies were beautiful and elusive and a tiny bit sparkly. So it seemed like an excellent decision.

And when she noticed that Biana's patch was bordered in purple, she realized that each of their patches' colors matched the colors of their spotlights—which made her wonder if the Council had somehow known that her spotlight would be Inflictor red before she'd gotten there, or if their gnomes had set to work as soon as she stepped foot in the Seat of Eminence. She also realized that the jewels in the centers of their circlets were color-coordinated to their spotlights—ruby for her, pink tourmaline for Stina, opal for Wylie, emerald for Dex, and amethyst for Biana.

The Council had truly thought of everything. And Sophie had been so busy studying her friends that she'd forgotten they weren't the only ones who'd been waiting for her—until Grady lifted her into a crushing hug, spinning her around a couple of times before he set her down and leaned back to study her.

His eyes took in every detail of all her new accessories, lingering the longest on her cape's patch.

"Apparently I'm not just a moonlark anymore," Sophie told him, too embarrassed to share the Council's reasons for choosing her mascot while the rest of her friends were close enough to hear.

"I guess not," Grady agreed, his voice thoroughly choked up. "You okay with that?"

The best answer she could give him was, "We'll see."

He pulled her back into a hug. "How are you *really* holding up?" he whispered in her ear. "I know this must be a lot."

"It is," she whispered back. "But . . . I think you were right. It's time to take this step. We're going to need all the allies we can get to stop the Neverseen."

He hugged her tighter. "I'm so proud of you, kiddo. Wait—can I even call you 'kiddo' anymore? You look so grown up."

"There's always Lady Kiddo," Dex suggested, striding up beside them and earning a chuckle from Grady. "Or you could join the cool kids and call her Lady Fos-Boss."

Grady's eyebrows shot up.

Sophie shook her head. "Don't ask—and that's not happening."

"It so is," Dex insisted. Then his dimpled grin faded, and he reached up to adjust his circlet. "*All* of this is really happening, huh?"

Sophie nodded.

And as she listened to Sandor lecturing the Councillors for taking his charge into *space* without his protection, and to Biana telling Della all about her light leap with the Sources, and to Tiergan quietly assuring Wylie that he was so incredibly proud of him—even to Vika promising Stina that she was sure to be the most famous of all the Hekses—she was hit with the rare sense that for that one moment, things were exactly the way they ought to be.

They had a ton of work and drama and problems ahead—and probably lots of bickering and almost dying. But they'd deal with all of it, because they all had one thing in common.

"I know what our team name needs to be," she realized, having to repeat the words louder for everyone to catch them.

"Oh yeah?" Dex asked. "Hit us with it, Lady Fos-Boss."

Sophie sighed. "Seriously, that's *not* my name."

"Keep telling yourself that," Dex, Wylie, Biana, and Stina all said in unison, because of *course* the first thing they'd all agree on would be the need to continue annoying her.

But she'd deal with her title issues later.

For now, she turned to the twelve Councillors and told them. "You wanted something respectable. And we wanted something that fits who we are—"

"And something that isn't an epic fail," Dex jumped in, earning himself glares from all of the Councillors. "I'm still particularly fond of 'Team Dex-Is-the-Greatest.'"

Sophie cleared her throat, giving Dex a *please-not-now* look. "So *I* think," she continued, "we should be Team Valiant. It sounds official. It means brave and heroic. And if we want, we can always shorten it to Team V."

Silence followed, long enough that Sophie started to worry she'd gotten it wrong.

Then Dex applauded.

A slow clap—but still genuine.

And when Biana, Wylie, and—reluctantly—Stina joined in, Team Valiant was officially born.

Biana even made sure to repeat the name a little louder than necessary as they stood on the steps outside the Seat of Eminence, making plans to head home for the night and meet up the next day to discuss all the huge problems they needed to start tackling.

They pretended not to notice the elves that had stopped to stare—exactly the way the Council had hoped that people would. But Sophie could already hear the whispers starting.

"Is that Sophie Foster?"

"And Dex Dizznee?"

"And Biana Vacker?"

"And Wylie Endal?"

"And Stina Heks?"

"It looks like they're part of the nobility!"

"They can't be!"

"But they're wearing circlets."

"And what's that symbol on their pins?"

"One of them said something about a team—what do you think it means?"

Sophie held her breath, waiting to hear the answer.

And it made her heart swell, even if it also made her stomach extra twisty and sour.

"Looks like the Council's finally doing something."

TEN

WHOA, EDALINE WASN'T KIDDING about the whole 'Lady Sophie' thing," Keefe murmured, making Sophie jump—and then reel on Sandor for not giving her a heads-up that she had people waiting for her in her bedroom.

Sandor shrugged. Clearly he was still annoyed with her for leaving the planet without him—as if the edge of the earth's atmosphere was somehow the perfect spot for a Neverseen ambush.

Then again, Bo hadn't warned her about her visitors either.

His white-knuckle grip on his sword—and the satisfied smirk on Ro's face—probably had something to do with that.

And Edaline must've gotten sidetracked by all the hugging and crying and asking fifty thousand questions and forgotten to mention that there were a smirking boy and an ogre princess waiting upstairs.

All Sophie knew was, she was going to yell at all of them later, because now she had to face a Keefe-and-Ro Inquisition while still wearing a crown.

Sandor and Bo were wise enough to wait in the hall.

Keefe whistled as he crossed her flowered carpet and made a

slow circle around her. And Sophie braced for a record-breaking amount of teasing. But his voice actually sounded serious when he asked, "Sorry, was I supposed to bow?"

"If you had, I would've flung a pillow at your head," she told him with a grin he didn't return. "And you can forget the Lady Sophie thing, too."

"Thank goodness," Ro said, dropping her feet from where she'd had them propped on Sophie's desk. "I never would've been able to pull that off with a straight face. And, uh, please tell me this isn't your permanent new wardrobe."

"Parts of it are," Sophie admitted, pointing to her new cloak clasp as an example. "But I'm done with the dress. And this."

She tried to yank the much-too-conspicuous circlet off of her head, hoping the humiliating way it got tangled in her hair at least proved that she was still the same clumsy mess she'd always been.

She knew she should probably tuck the obnoxious accessory safely into one of the gilded chests that Grady had brought home from the Seat of Eminence. Edaline had supposedly conjured them all into Sophie's bathroom.

But she didn't feel like being tidy.

She felt like getting into normal clothes as fast as she possibly could.

"What about that patch?" Ro asked, pointing to the wolf silhouette on her cloak. "What's that all about?"

"Long story," Sophie mumbled, dumping the circlet on her bed and stumbling into her closet to ditch her cloak, gown, and heels.

"I like stories," Ro called after her. "Unless it involves a lot of speeches about how you elves get to boss everyone around because you think you're so pretty and powerful and sparkly. Then we can skip that snorefest."

Sophie pulled on a pair of leggings and called back, "There was definitely some of that going on. And a lot of talk about the differences between sunlight, starlight, and moonlight."

Ro started making very loud snoring sounds.

"You would've enjoyed all the horrible team name suggestions that Dex and Biana kept bugging the Council with, though," Sophie shouted over the abundance of snorts and gurgles. If that was what Ro actually sounded like when she slept, poor Keefe probably had to sleep with a pillow over his head. "I thought Emery was going to exile them at one point."

"Okay, *now* I'm interested," Ro informed her. "And let's hope Team Fancypants was the winner. Because I can *almost* forgive you for wearing all of those sparkly accessories if that's what you're making your stuffy Councillors call you."

"Wait," Keefe said, before Sophie could respond. "Dex and Biana were there?"

Sophie nodded, then realized he couldn't see her. Which actually made it a little easier to tell him. "Yeah. And Wylie. And *Stina*. I guess the Council decided I'm way more successful when I have backup—and they're not *wrong*. But I'm still trying not to be insulted that they built this whole team because I'm useless alone. Oh—and you'll love this. They wanted to name us Team Prodigious."

"Wow," Ro said. "You guys shut that down, right?"

"First thing we did," Sophie agreed, pulling on a blissfully boring gray tunic and wishing all clothes could be so unassuming. "The Council was *not* happy about it."

She waited for Keefe to make his own team name suggestions, but he stayed noticeably silent. And when she made her way back to her bedroom, she found him turned away, fussing with the sleeves of his embroidered gray tunic as he stared out her wall of windows.

"Everything okay?" she asked.

"Pretty sure he's pouting," Ro told her.

"I'm not pouting," Keefe argued—in a tone that definitely sounded pouty. "I just love how it took you less than a day after your little chat with Bangs Boy to cut me out of everything."

"Hey, I had no say in this!" Sophie reminded him. "If I got to pick the team, do you really think Stina Heks would be on it?"

"Probably not—but that doesn't mean you would've included me," he countered.

Sophie sighed. "I won't lie, if the Council had wanted you involved in all of this . . . yeah, I would've made Ro keep you away. Because this is exactly the kind of thing that Tam was warning us about. And I think it's more important for you to be focusing on your memories, anyway. But, if it makes you feel any better, your name did come up. Dex actually pushed for you to be swapped in, instead of Stina—and even Grady agreed that you would've been the better choice for the 'team's Empath.'"

"He did?" Keefe asked, perking up a little as he glanced at her over his shoulder. But his smile faded just as fast. "The Council shot them down because of my mom, huh?"

There was no point denying it.

"Would you have honestly wanted to swear an oath to the Council?" she asked instead. "Doesn't seem like your kind of thing."

"It's not," Keefe agreed. "I just didn't realize it was your kind of thing either."

"Honestly? Neither did I." She made her way closer, watching the ocean shimmer with glints of pink and orange from the sunset. "But . . . it sounds like we're going to need the Council's help to deal with King Enki as we try to figure out what the Neverseen are planning in Loamnore. And if Mr. Forkle's right that the Neverseen are also trying to turn the public against the Councillors, then it's probably pretty important for us to be allies. So . . . I'm giving it a try. But it's also good that they left some of our group out. That way you, Fitz, and Linh will have a clearer perspective and can let us know if it seems like we're getting sucked into anything weird. And you can look into anything we don't want the Council knowing about. Well . . . Fitz and Linh can do that last part. *You* can focus on your memories—and staying safe."

"Great," Keefe muttered.

"Hang on!" Ro said, stomping over to join them by the windows. "Did you just say that Pretty Boy's not a part of this?" Her mouth fell open when Sophie nodded. "But . . . aren't you two, like, a package deal? Team Obnoxious-Telepaths?"

"We usually are," Sophie agreed, ignoring the "obnoxious" part of that nickname. "But the Council wants to separate us. They think I rely too much on my telepathy and am not taking full advantage of my other abilities. So they want me to work on stuff without Fitz and see if it helps me widen my focus."

Ro blinked. "Wow! Okay—I officially take back every bad thing

I've ever said about your Councillors! They're my heroes! All hail the sparkle-fied twelve for breaking up the Great Fitzphie!"

"They didn't break us up," Sophie argued, her face burning when she realized how that sounded. "They just thought it was worth seeing what happens if we don't work *as* closely *as* often—and they promised they'd let Fitz join the team if it turns out I need him."

"You won't," Ro assured her. "Right, Hunkyhair?"

She elbowed Keefe, who'd gone back to staring at the ocean.

"Come on, Captain Sulky," Ro said, elbowing him harder. "There's really nothing you want to say?"

"Nope." He scooted away before Ro could elbow him again, earning himself an epic ogre eye roll.

And he looked so miserable—so *un*-Keefe—that Sophie decided she was willing to sacrifice herself on the altar of humiliation if it got him out of his funk.

"You know what Dex has everyone calling me now?" she asked. "I'm sure you'd be proud of him."

"The Mysterious Lady F?" Ro guessed.

"Ugh, I wish. Nope, it's . . . Lady Fos-Boss."

The confession was almost worth it when Keefe couldn't help giving her a quick smirk.

"I knew I liked that boy," Ro announced. "In fact, I even tried out one of his little tricks—see?"

She pointed to Sophie's desk, and it took Sophie a second to figure out what she meant.

"You changed Iggy's color?" she asked, heading over to his cage, where, sure enough, the tiny imp had yet another new look. His neatly trimmed, gold, sparkly fur was now a much poofier ice blue with tiny crimps.

"Huh, I figured he'd be pink and purple," Sophie admitted, pointing to Ro's colorful pigtails.

Ro tossed her head, swishing her hair in the process. "Uh, no, I'm not sharing my fabulous style with anyone—much less a creature who spent the last hour eating his own toenails. But I thought it was only right to save your imp from being sparkle-fied—and I was *going* to be nice and turn him your favorite color. But apparently your favorite color is *teal*—and yeah, yeah, we all know why. But, um, do you realize how many of the nastiest little microbes are that color?" She shuddered. "I couldn't do that to you—or the little dude. So I went with a nice ice blue. The kind of color you can't help but love. Classic. Reliable—"

"We get it," Keefe interrupted. "Iggy's blue. Good job. Can we please talk about *anything* else?"

"Okay," Sophie said, slipping her fingers through the bars of Iggy's cage and scratching his fuzzy cheeks until the room was filled with the sound of his squeaky purr. "How about you tell us what's wrong?"

"Nothing's wrong," Keefe insisted.

"Then why are you being Lord Grumpypants?" She'd hoped the tease would snap him out of it, but he just went back to fidgeting with his sleeves. "Come on, Keefe. Something's clearly up. You haven't even made any Lady Fos-Boss jokes yet."

"Or Team Prodigious jokes," Ro added.

He shrugged. "They're not my jokes to make. I'm not part of the team."

"And that bothers you?" Sophie guessed. "No, don't shrug again—I'm serious." She stepped closer, forcing him to look at her. "You know it doesn't change anything, right?"

"Well, I mean, it kinda does," he corrected. "You're in the nobility now. You have a crown! And Councillors to report to! And I have . . . a bunch of mostly empty notebooks."

"They won't stay empty," Sophie assured him. "And the more you fill them, the more valuable they're going to be."

He didn't look convinced.

"So you never told us," Ro said, filling the tense silence. "What team name did you go with? Team Awesomesauce?"

"Dex campaigned pretty hard for that," Sophie admitted. "And Biana tried for Team Sparkles a couple of different times. But I sold them on Team Valiant—and I know it's not super clever or exciting. But the Council said they'd only approve something respectable."

"Respectable," Ro scoffed. "That's always the problem with you elves. You like to be so *dignified* and *diplomatic*. This is war! If you want to send a message to your enemies, you form Team Ruthless. Or Team Bloodbath—though I guess you also don't put a bunch of scrawny kids in Team Bloodbath."

"No, you don't," Sophie agreed.

She honestly would've rather been Team Prodigious.

"But then what's the story behind the wolf patch?" Ro asked. "I'm not gonna lie, I'm hoping it's because Team Valiant has a howl-y battle cry."

Sophie had to disappoint her again.

And as she explained the Council's reasons for choosing her new mascot, she couldn't remember why the dire wolf had felt so cool or empowering.

"Hey," Keefe said, fanning the air as her mood plummeted, "don't let us ruin this for you, Foster. It's a big deal. I'm sorry I've been grumpy. I was just surprised, is all. And I was up way too late, so I think I'm tired."

"Were you drawing more of your memories?" she asked, grateful for the subject change—and the apology.

"I did a few. Nothing important. But . . . I was mostly working on something else. That's why I stopped by—but . . . maybe it's not a good time. You've had a crazy day and—"

"It's about my biological parents, isn't it?" Sophie interrupted.

Her heart felt like someone tied it to a massive anchor as he reached into a pocket hidden in his tunic and pulled out the blue notebook they'd started their planning in the day before.

"Wow, that's even more dread than I felt yesterday," he mumbled, fanning her emotions away. "Are you *sure* you want to keep looking into this?"

"Honestly, I have no idea what to do," she admitted. "Bronte gave me this whole long lecture on why I shouldn't find out who my genetic parents are, and it kinda got in my head."

Keefe stood up straighter. "Does that mean you told the Council you're unmatchable?"

"Only Bronte and Oralie." She made her way over to her bed and sank onto the edge. "I wasn't planning on saying anything. But I kinda freaked out when they were crowning me—started imagining giant crowds of elves chasing me through the Lost Cities with torches and pitchforks, shouting, 'Burn the unmatchable girl!' And

I figured it'd be less humiliating to risk losing the title now, before anyone even knows it was an option."

"And Bronte freaked out?" Keefe assumed.

"Of course he did—but . . . not the way I'm sure you're thinking. He was actually strangely awesome about the unmatchable part."

Ro snorted.

"No, really. I mean, he didn't offer to order the matchmakers to make my lists even without having my genetic parents' info or anything—and of course he brought up the whole 'it's not a problem if you just stay single forever' argument. But . . . he also said the Council would stand by me if people made a fuss about it. And it kinda sounded like he meant it." She picked up the circlet she'd tossed aside earlier, tracing her fingers over the symbol for her new team. "It's a little hard to believe him, but . . . I don't know. I kinda do."

"I can feel that," Keefe said, sitting down beside her. "So why all the extra dread?"

"Because he also brought up something I hadn't thought of before, and now I'm not sure what to do about it." She stared at her reflection in her circlet's ruby, feeling just as fragmented as she repeated Bronte's warnings about what the Black Swan might do to protect their secrets.

And she'd expected Keefe to agree that they truly were valid concerns—or to at least need some time to think about it.

But he was already shaking his head before she'd even finished. "Nah, I don't buy it. For one thing, it's not like the Black Swan did the memory break on Prentice. That was all on the Council. They kept pushing and pushing and pushing, no matter the consequences—

and that's *totally* different than the kind of digging you're doing. I'm pretty sure you'd never shatter anyone's sanity to find out what you want to know."

"I wouldn't. But it doesn't have to be as drastic as a memory break for someone to get hurt. And that's what makes this so hard. Because if you really think about it, *I'm* the only one who'll get any benefit out of finding my biological parents. Everyone else gets a ton of drama. And there really *is* a chance that the Black Swan might try to stop me, so who knows what kinds of problems that might cause? And if I'm aware of all of those risks, and I still search out my genetic parents anyway, I'm . . . being selfish, aren't I?"

"Maybe," he admitted. "But . . . you're allowed to be a little selfish sometimes. And it's not like you aren't making huge sacrifices too."

"I know. But if something really bad happens because of this, that's gonna be pretty hard to live with." She set her circlet gently on her nightstand and tugged out an itchy eyelash. "I just wish I knew *why* the Black Swan won't tell me who my genetic parents are, you know? I'm not trying to gamble with people's lives, but I'd like to not have mine get totally messed up either—especially without even understanding what's really at stake."

"I get that," Keefe said quietly, "and . . . I actually have a theory about why the Black Swan won't tell you—and it might even explain why Bronte got so pushy with you today."

"Okay," Sophie said when he didn't continue. "Are you going to tell me?"

"I can. But . . . you're not going to like it."

"What else is new?" Sophie scooted back farther on her bed, deciding she might as well be surrounded by fluffy pillows if she had to get hit with bad news. She grabbed Ella, too, burying her face between her floppy ears. "Okay, what is it?"

Keefe stood up to pace, passing her enough times to seriously ramp up her anxiety.

"You're making me wonder if suspense can actually kill me," she warned.

"Sorry. I'm just trying to figure out how to do this without freaking you out like I did yesterday. Actually, wait."

He hurried back to her bed and nestled into the pillows beside her, setting the blue notebook in his lap and pointing to her hand. "Turn your enhancing restrictors off. That way I can calm you down if you need me to."

"It's really *that* bad?" Sophie asked, tapping her thumbs and forefingers the way Tinker had shown her.

"I guess we'll find out." Keefe placed one of his hands near hers—without touching—and drummed his fingers against the front of the blue notebook with the other. "So . . . yesterday, I said I didn't think your genetic parents would be people you know, because it would be too hard for them to pretend around you—and I might still be right about that. *But.* As I started trying to make lists of possible DNA donors, I realized the biggest clues we have are your abilities. I mean, yeah, it's not *always* that telepathic parents have telepathic kids or whatever. Sometimes genetics decide to get funky and do their own thing. But it also happens consistently enough that it's safe to assume your biological parents have at least some of your abilities. Do you see where I'm going with this?"

"Sorta," Sophie said. "I've always assumed one of my parents must be a Telepath."

"That's where I started out focusing too, since your telepathy is so strong, and it seemed fundamental to the Black Swan's plans for you. But then I remembered that one of the few things we know for sure is that Mr. Forkle wanted you to be able to heal broken minds, since he knew there was a chance that could happen to some of the order. And to be able to do that, you need *two* abilities, right? Telepathy and . . ."

"Inflicting," Sophie finished slowly.

He tapped the notebook harder. "Yeah . . . so I started thinking about how *rare* inflicting is."

Sophie's insides scrunched together.

He was right—she wasn't going to like this.

"There's only one other registered Inflictor," she mumbled.

"I know." Keefe scooted his hand even closer to hers—but still not quite touching. "And it's someone whose whole life would be turned upside down if people found out he had a child. In fact, the news would pretty much turn everything upside down—at least for a little while. And it happens to be the same person who just gave you a big speech trying to convince you not to look into your genetic parents—even promising that the Council would stand beside you being unmatchable if it came to that. He basically said anything he could to get you to leave it alone."

He stopped there, giving her a chance to leave the rest unspoken.

But there was no point hiding from it.

She reached for his hand, focusing on the soft blue breeze that rushed into her mind as she whispered, "You think Councillor Bronte is my biological father."

ELEVEN

E DON'T KNOW ANYTHING FOR certain," Keefe reminded Sophie as she tightened her grip on his hand.

And she tried to believe him—tried to focus on the soothing colorful breezes he kept sending into her mind.

But her head was spinning in fifteen different directions. And the only thought that seemed to stick through all the chaos was: *Seriously?*

Out of *all* the people the Black Swan could've picked to be her biological father, they chose *Councillor Bronte?*

"It's just a theory," Keefe insisted.

"But it makes sense!" She honestly couldn't believe she'd never suspected him before—and not just because of the Inflictor thing.

Maybe *this* was why Bronte had been so hard on her when she'd first met him.

Mr. Forkle had already admitted that the Black Swan had been forced to bring her to the Lost Cities earlier than they'd originally planned, because the Neverseen were getting too close to finding her. So what if Bronte had been trying to get her exiled because he wasn't ready to deal with the fallout if people figured out that she was his daughter?

And what if he'd stepped up the meanness even more after she'd manifested as an Inflictor, because he thought it would keep people from suspecting any connection between them?

And maybe the reason he'd been so cruel when her abilities were "malfunctioning" was because he'd taken such a huge risk in order to make her an Inflictor—and then it was looking like it had all been for nothing.

None of that excused the awful things he'd said and done to her, of course—but she wasn't trying to decide if Bronte was a good guy.

She was trying to decide if he was her *biological father.*

And . . . he had to be—didn't he?

It even explained why he'd started being nicer once her abilities had been healed. Then Project Moonlark was back on track, and enough time had passed that he could relax a little without people suspecting him of anything.

Who knew? Maybe he'd even felt a little bad for treating his biological daughter so coldly—though *that* sounded mostly like wishful thinking.

"I . . . don't know what to do with this information," Sophie admitted, rubbing her left temple as she pictured Bronte's face, trying to see herself in his sharp features.

She ended up with a mental image of herself with piercing blue eyes and huge, pointy ears—and a laugh bubbled up even as tears welled and her hands curled into fists, legs itching to run, *hide*—

"Easy there, Foster," Keefe said, sending her more calming mental breezes.

The soft rushes of color whisked across her consciousness, soothing any raw nerves.

But for every wave of panic that Keefe's winds were able to ease, there was another stronger surge ready in its wake.

"I get it—this is huge," he told her, pulling her out of her pillow nest and spinning her to face him better. "But try to remember that even if it *is* true—and we *don't* know if it is—it's also not *bad*."

"How can you say that?"

"Well . . ." He dragged his free hand down his face. "For one thing . . . Bronte's not a murderer. Or part of the Neverseen—and I'm not saying that to compare your life to mine—"

"I know," Sophie assured him, squeezing his hand as tightly as she clung to the reminder.

Some of Bronte's behavior over the last few years had strayed pretty close to "villain territory."

But he *wasn't* a villain.

In fact, if he really had been part of Project Moonlark, that technically made him even more solidly one of the good guys.

Plus, she'd already known that she was going to hate the people who'd donated their DNA to the Black Swan and then abandoned her—especially if they'd been lying to her ever since she'd gotten to the Lost Cities.

But . . . maybe *that* was why this revelation stung like lemon juice in an open wound.

She'd actually been starting to like Bronte as a person—starting to trust him as an ally. She'd even been glad that he was one of her points of contact on the Council.

And now?

"How am I supposed to work with him?" she whispered, trying to focus on the most important question—because this was so much bigger than her personal drama.

She'd become a Regent to be able to tackle the problems with Tam, the dwarves, and the Neverseen—and if this got in the way . . .

"Bronte can't know that I know," she realized.

"Why?" Keefe wondered. "Isn't that why we were doing this?"

She pulled her hand free and scooted back as far as she could, trying to save Keefe from the nausea clawing up her throat. "It was, but . . . I didn't really have a plan for what I'd do if we actually found either of my genetic parents—and I never thought we'd learn something like *this*. It's like you said: If anyone finds out Bronte's my biological father, it would turn our world upside down. He'd have to resign as a Councillor. And there'd have to be another election—right when the Neverseen are trying so hard to destroy the Council's authority. And all of that will take up time we should be using to figure out how to protect Loamnore or how to get Tam away from your mom. *That's* why Mr. Forkle wanted me to let this go—and why Bronte did too. If I don't, it's going to make an enormous mess of everything."

"Okaaaaaaay," Keefe said, dragging out the word. "But if you never tell anyone . . ."

He stopped before the part she was trying *so* hard not to think about. But they both knew what he wasn't saying.

If she never told anyone who her biological father was . . . she'd be unmatchable forever.

"I know," she whispered. "But . . . what can I do?"

Keefe had no answer.

And she hated the Black Swan so much in that moment—more than she'd ever hated them before. There was no way they didn't know what would happen if they used a *Councillor* for Project Moonlark. And clearly they didn't care. Giving her a chance at a normal, happy life didn't matter, as long as she was able to inflict pain on people—an ability that didn't even work very well.

The Neverseen had special headpieces to block her, and her lack of control always took out more good guys than bad guys.

A tiny, rational part of her knew that her inflicting was also the only reason Alden was awake and functioning—and Prentice, too. But her anger at the moment was so much stronger.

"Hey," Keefe said, reaching out like he was going to hug her—then stopping at the last second and patting her awkwardly on the shoulder. "It doesn't matter, okay? Like I said yesterday, no one's going to care about your matchmaking status—or no one who matters, anyway. And now you even have the Council promising to back you up if there's any drama."

"Yeah, because Bronte wants to keep his job," she grumbled. "And he's clearly hoping I'll make it easy on everyone and just stay single forever—like *him*. Ugh, that's probably why he thinks it's no big deal to expect that!"

Same with Mr. Forkle, actually.

She punched one of her pillows, but it wasn't nearly satisfying enough. She needed something more *destructive*, so she twisted and tugged and clawed at the silky fabric, hoping for a dramatic *rip* and a spray of feathers.

But pillows were a whole lot tougher than she realized they could be.

Keefe gave her another reassuring shoulder pat—but when she flung the pillow aside and buried her face in her hands, she heard him growl something that sounded like "screw it." Then his arms wrapped around her and she sank into the hug, not realizing she was crying until she felt her tears soak into his tunic.

"All right, Foster," he murmured into her hair. "I think we're getting *way* ahead of ourselves here. So let's back it up and try to focus on the facts for a second, okay?" He waited for her to nod against his shoulder before he said, "Okay, fact number one: We have absolutely no idea if Bronte is *actually* your biological father. I mean, yeah, it's a solid theory. But it *definitely* could be wrong—just like you were wrong about Forkle, Kenric, and Jolie. So try to let go of all those nightmare scenarios I'm sure you're imagining right now—at least until we have actual proof. Which brings me to fact number two: We need to prove whether or not this is true. And thankfully, it shouldn't be hard to do. We just need to get you, me, and Bronte in a room. Then I'll grab his hands while you ask if he's your father—and boom. My mad Empath skills will get you your answer."

"But . . . then he'll know I know," Sophie reminded him. "And if he *is* my father—"

"Then at least you guys will understand each other," he supplied for her. "And let's face it—it's not like you're going to be able to hide this. Every time you look at him, you'll be a puddle of panic and rage. It's better to get it out there, find out the truth, and then figure out where you go from there."

Sophie sighed. "I guess you're right."

"Of course I am—how many times do I have to tell you I'm a genius before you start believing me?" He laughed, and Sophie could feel the soft vibration where her cheek was pressed against his chest. "Anyway, back to my brilliant facts—and moving on to number three! Once you confront Bronte—"

"Hopefully in a super-dramatic way," Ro cut in, making Sophie and Keefe both jump so hard that Sophie's forehead crashed into Keefe's chin.

"Forgot you weren't alone?" Ro asked, raising her eyebrows as Keefe pulled away from the hug.

Sophie totally had.

And Ro wasn't the only eavesdropper she should've been thinking about.

"Whatever you've heard," she called to Sandor and Bo, and maybe Flori, if she was back from her patrols, "it's—"

"Not to be repeated," Sandor finished for her, leaning his head through the doorway. "Yes, I know. Have I ever given you any reason to doubt my respect for your privacy?"

"No. But this is *way* bigger than anything I've asked you to keep secret before," she felt the need to point out.

"I'm well aware of its significance—and its implications. And that's all the more reason to trust that the information is safe with me. You also have my word that it's safe with anyone under my command." The promise was made along with a grunt that sounded like maybe Sandor had kicked Bo to make sure he got the message. "And that's true regardless of whether your suspicions turn out to be correct. I also agree with Mr. Sencen—and you know how much it pains me to say that. This is still only a theory—the kind of theory that absolutely must be proven before you decide what to do with the information. And for the record, I *will* be there when you confront Councillor Bronte—and I *don't* recommend resorting to dramatics."

"Aw, come on, Gigantor!" Ro whined. "How many times does a girl get a chance to stomp into a room and demand to know if someone's her daddy? Bonus points if she can squeak out a few tears—and then follow it up with a face slap!" She let out a wistful sigh. "Should we also take bets on what the verdict's going to be?"

"No bets!" Sandor ordered, stalking closer to Sophie and waiting for her to make eye contact. "I think it's also important that you understand something very clearly, Miss Foster. If Bronte makes any threats during this confrontation—verbal or otherwise—I *will* subdue him. It won't matter that he's a Councillor and could cause *diplomatic issues* for me. My job is to protect *you*."

Sophie tried to swallow, but a lump had lodged in her throat. "Bronte wouldn't—"

"Wouldn't he?" Sandor interrupted. "We both know the things he's already put you through. And if this theory is true, it's a secret he's gone to great lengths to protect. There's no telling what he'll do if he fears exposure. In fact, I almost wish you'd go to Mr. Forkle for confirmation instead. He can't inflict pain or threaten you with Exile."

"Yeah, but he's a way better liar," Keefe argued. "And he won't be nearly as caught off guard, since I'm sure he already assumes Foster's looking into this. So his reaction would be much harder for me to gauge."

"Bronte knows I'm looking into this too," Sophie reminded Keefe.

"Yeah, but he won't expect you to make progress this quickly. Plus, you're supposed to check in with him all the time about your

Regent stuff anyway, right? So if you call a meeting with him, it won't seem nearly as suspicious as it would if you demanded another Forkle chat. The only trick will be coming up with a reason for why I'm there with you. Maybe we can say I want to make a case for joining Team Fancypants—"

"Team Valiant," Sophie corrected.

He smirked. "Yeah, I'm pretty sure I'm never gonna call it that. Just like I'm pretty sure you're gonna have to get used to me calling you the Lovely Lady F."

She tried to smile, glad he was back to his old, teasing self. But she knew her eyes didn't sell it.

"Stick to the facts, Foster," Keefe begged, taking her hand again and sending another soft breeze into her mind. "Remember, there's still a good chance we're wrong about all of this. Genetics are weird. Look at Dex. He's a Technopath, and his mom's a Froster, and his dad's Talentless—and no, I don't think that's because his parents were a bad match. Marella's parents were matchmaker-approved, and neither of them are Pyrokinetics like she is. So you and Bronte both being Inflictors might not mean what we think it means."

"Exactly," Ro said. "For the record, I'm totally on Team Not-the-Daddy."

"You are?" Keefe asked.

"Yup! I've seen the dude, remember? I mean, personally I think all of you elves are scrawny and weird-looking—but that doesn't mean I don't know how to tell which ones of you are technically 'prettier' by your elf-y standards. And Councillor Pointy Ears? Meh. No way his daughter could be our little blond hottie right here."

"Unless she gets that from her mom," Keefe reminded Ro, and

part of Sophie's brain wanted to wonder if that meant Keefe was agreeing with Ro's "blond hottie" assessment—but that was definitely not something she needed to be thinking about at the moment.

Or ever.

"I know you're trying to make me feel better," she said, pausing for a much-needed eyelash tug. "But we all know what's going to happen here. Bronte's going to confirm that he's my father. And then he's going to beg me not to tell anyone and—"

"And *then* you'll have to decide what you're going to do," Keefe jumped in. "That was the third fact I was getting to, before we were so rudely interrupted by my nosy bodyguard. You *do* have a choice here, Foster. I know you think outing Bronte will cause some epic, world-destroying scandal. And I'm not saying it won't cause some temporary chaos while he steps down and there's the election and stuff. But . . . Bronte's not exactly winning the prize for Most Beloved Councillor, you know? I'm pretty sure most people aren't going to be sad to see him go. And it's not like we've never had a Councillor step aside because they wanted to get married or have kids or whatever."

"Uh, that's a little different than someone stepping aside because they secretly donated their DNA to an illegal experiment and then lied to everyone about it for years and years," Sophie argued. "Think of how outspoken Bronte's always been about the Black Swan— how many times he's gone after them and tried to convince everyone that the Black Swan was the enemy. He even . . ."

"'He even' what?" Keefe asked when she fell *very* silent. "And what's with the fresh blast of panic?"

He tried to send her more mental breezes, but Sophie yanked

her hand back, needing a clear head to think through this new revelation.

This was the kind of thing she had to be really, *really* sure of.

"So. Remember what you said earlier about suspense killing you?" Keefe asked after a couple of minutes. "I think I might be getting there."

"Same," Sandor and Ro agreed.

"Sorry, it's just . . . do you realize what this means?" Sophie whispered, afraid to give the words too much volume.

"Not yet, but we might, if you try actually explaining it," Sandor suggested.

Sophie nodded, swallowing several times to pull together enough voice to tell them. "The Council was the one who ordered the memory break on Prentice when they were looking for me. And Bronte pretty much led that charge, didn't he?"

"I think so," Keefe agreed slowly. "I know he was definitely a big part of it."

Sophie wrapped her arms around herself, needing that extra bit of support. "Right. So . . . if he was *also* secretly part of Project Moonlark . . . he basically forced Prentice to sacrifice himself for no reason. Or maybe he did it for show, to cover up his own involvement? Either way, that's . . ."

There were no words for that level of ugliness.

And she might be biologically *related* to someone capable of it.

"Definitely not gonna argue with the disgust you're feeling there," Keefe told her, his face scrunched like he'd licked something sour. "If Bronte *is* your biological father, he has some *serious* explaining to do—but remember: That has nothing to do with you. I can give you the 'our families don't decide who we are' speech again if you need me to. Also . . . in a weird way, this might be good news. I mean, not for Prentice or Wylie—or Alden, given how much that memory break messed him up too. But . . . it'd mean you wouldn't have to feel bad about outing your connection to Bronte—because someone that heartless? They shouldn't be a Councillor. In fact, he probably shouldn't be anything except a prisoner in Exile. And I know you're worried that any scandal will help the Neverseen discredit the Council—but not if we're cleaning house. Not if we're saying, 'Ugh, this guy is creepy. Let's change him out for someone we can actually trust.'"

"I guess," Sophie said—though she was pretty sure it would never be that clear and easy. Especially since Bronte's "creepy" decision raised a lot of questions about the Black Swan as an organization— questions she'd definitely want answered herself.

And it would surely destroy whatever favor she'd recently gained.

But . . . if anyone was a pro at being unpopular, it was her.

And she'd still be able to focus on the dwarves and Tam and the Neverseen—even if they stripped away her Regent title. Biana, Dex, Wylie, and Stina could be in charge of anything that needed to be handled more officially, and she'd work with Linh and Marella and Fitz on everything else.

And speaking of Fitz . . .

She knew it was a gross, selfish thought to have after any of the things they'd been discussing. *But* . . .

If Bronte really was her biological father, she actually did have a good reason to expose him.

And *if* she exposed him, she'd be halfway to the solution to her matchmaking conundrum.

"*There's* the hope I've been waiting for," Keefe said, grinning as he fanned the air—though his smile looked . . . tired. "See? It's not all doom and gloom."

"It's a mess," Sophie insisted.

"It *might* be a mess," he corrected. "Don't forget fact one and fact two."

Sophie nodded, not sure if it made her a terrible person to suddenly be hoping that Bronte was her father. Life would be drama and chaos for a while, but . . . then it would be settled. One hurdle down.

"How soon do you think you can get me in a room with Bronte?" Keefe asked.

"I'll talk to him tomorrow and see what he says," she decided. "I'm sure he'll let me schedule something—it just might be a few days or weeks from now. And I don't think I'll be able to push him without it seeming weird."

"Well . . . name the date and time, and I'll be there."

"Thank you," Sophie told him, choking up a little.

He shrugged. "Eh, don't go giving me too much credit, Foster. Thanks to you and Ro—and Bangs Boy—it's not like I have a very busy or exciting schedule these days. It's either this, or sit at home while Dad of the Year complains about how I should be studying or honing my empathy instead of drawing—which does at least give me an excuse to doodle some very unflattering cartoons of him and hide them around the Shores of Solace for him to find."

He flashed a particularly smug smirk, but Sophie could see the sadness behind it.

And it had her pulling him back into a hug.

Keefe had so many huge family problems of his own, and yet

here he was, spending all this time helping her deal with hers—after staying up late figuring all of this out.

"Thank you," she repeated, wishing he didn't feel so tense in her arms. "I mean it, Keefe. I don't know if I'd be able to get through this without you."

"Yes you could," he argued, finally relaxing as he leaned into the hug to whisper, "You're Lady Foster. The Dire Wolf of Team Fancypants. And I gotta say, you look awfully cute in a crown."

Heat burned from the top of her head to the tips of her toes—and even though she knew he was teasing, she was sure her cheeks were blushing.

"And I know I keep saying this," he added quietly, "but I want to make sure you don't forget it. No matter what happens with Bronte, or whatever else we learn about your biological parents, or whether you stay unmatchable or not, it's all going to be okay. I *promise*."

And the funny thing was, in that moment, she actually believed him—or she did right up until someone cleared their throat *very* loudly.

She dropped her arms and scrambled back, bracing for a particularly humiliating conversation with Grady. But all the blood seemed to leave her body when she glanced toward her bedroom door.

Because it wasn't Grady.

And it wasn't Sandor or Bo—who she was definitely going to murder later for not warning her that she had another visitor.

And not just any visitor.

Fitz.

Her heart officially shut down on her.

And her brain was still struggling to process how he could look so handsome and so *furious* when his teal eyes met hers and his lips parted to ask something she couldn't hear over the roaring in her head.

It took one, two, three breaths before he repeated the question.

"You're unmatchable?"

TWELVE

HIYA, FITZY," KEEFE SAID, LOOKING and sounding infinitely calmer than Sophie was feeling as he gave Fitz a quick chin nod and stood up to greet him—though he also shot Ro a look that said, *Your punishment for not warning us will be LEGENDARY.* "Didn't know you'd be stopping by."

Fitz snorted. "Clearly."

Keefe smirked. "Wow, someone's grumpy. Did Biana kick your butt in bramble again? He haaaaaaaaaaaaaaaaates to lose," he stage-whispered to Sophie. "But I guess you probably already know that about your boyfriend."

Sophie had a feeling he'd used the last word *intentionally*—and she chose to *not* correct him for the same reason, even though the label felt especially tenuous at the moment.

"Or is it because Biana's making you call her 'Lady Biana' now?" Keefe asked. "Your girlfriend's totally been doing the same thing, in case you were wondering. Isn't that right, Lady Fos-Boss?"

Sophie scowled. But she knew what Keefe was doing—both with the girlfriend comment and the nickname. And even though both made her fidgety for completely different reasons, she had to give him credit for how casually he was changing the subject. He'd almost made *her* believe that nothing had happened.

Then again . . . nothing *had* happened.

It wasn't like she couldn't be friends with Keefe—or wasn't allowed to let him help her through a hard time.

She didn't understand why she felt so . . . "caught"—until Fitz went back to the question that her overwhelmed brain had managed to bury.

"Seriously, Sophie." His accent sounded sharper than usual. "What did Keefe mean about you being unmatchable?"

"I . . ."

She knew she needed to add a lot more words to that sentence. But the only other sounds she seemed to be capable of making were much closer to dying animal noises.

"It's one of those Things That Only Happen to Foster," Keefe jumped in as Sophie tried to calculate the odds of successfully flinging a piece of furniture through one of her bedroom windows, levitating to freedom, and teleporting to a new life—maybe with Silveny, Greyfell, and their twin babies in a nice, peaceful meadow somewhere. "You know how it is. She always has to be all *mysterious.*"

"Actually, I *don't* know," Fitz snapped back. "But apparently *you* do?"

Keefe sighed, shaking his head a few times before he looked Fitz right in the eyes. "Trust me, dude. You don't want to do this."

"Pretty sure I do," Fitz countered. "If you're trying to—"

"How about I stop you right there?" Keefe interrupted, holding up his hands. "Because I *know* you don't want to turn a situation that's already been super stressful for someone you care about into something even harder for them. And we both know I'm not talking about me here."

Fitz gritted his teeth and looked away, tearing a hand through his hair. "I just want to know what's going on with my girlfriend. I didn't realize that was a lot to ask."

His eyes darted to Sophie, and there was such betrayal in his stare that it took her a second to realize he'd just used the *g* word.

It was the first time he'd ever called her that, and it should've made her all floaty and fluttery. But the hurt in his tone filled her whole body with something sour and slimy.

Keefe looked pretty miserable too as he slowly backed toward her bedroom door, giving the two of them as much space as possible.

Or maybe getting ready to flee.

She wouldn't have blamed him.

This was why he'd made her swear she'd talk to Fitz before he agreed to start helping her. And even though she'd made that promise less than twenty-four hours earlier—and had lost most of that time to the Regent appointment process—that didn't change the fact that she hadn't held up her end of the bargain.

Plus, *she* was the one who'd chosen to hide everything from Fitz in the first place.

"I'm sorry," she told both of them, glad her mouth seemed to be regaining the ability to form recognizable words. She even managed to hold Fitz's gaze as she added, "I . . . should've told you sooner."

"Then why didn't you?" he asked.

She closed her eyes, scraping together the courage to give an honest answer. "Because . . . once I told you, then it'd be real. And I wasn't ready to find out what would happen next. I'm still not, but . . ."

She forced herself to tell him *everything*. From the color of the gown she'd worn that day in Atlantis—teal, of course—to the names of her matchmakers—Brisa and Juji—to how close she'd come to vomiting when she saw the ugly red letters that would define her future if she couldn't make them go away. And how she'd spent days hiding out, hoping Mr. Forkle would give her the information she needed to fix everything—but of course the Black Swan let her down. So now she was stuck going rogue with her own investigation, which Keefe was helping her with—but only because Ro had forced the information out of her. And even though her voice was pretty wobbly at that point, she ended with the theory that Keefe had come up with about Councillor Bronte, as well as their plan to find out if it was true, and the very mixed feelings she had about the whole thing.

"I'm sorry," she repeated when she'd finished, squeezing her eyes as tight as she could. She definitely wasn't ready to see the look on Fitz's face as he processed all of those bombshells.

And then, it got very quiet.

The only sound was a bit of whisper-hissing out in the hallway from Grizel—Fitz's bodyguard—who was also Sandor's girlfriend, and who seemed to be less than thrilled that her boyfriend had kept her totally in the dark about all of this as well. And Sandor, being Sandor, was unapologetically defending his need to protect his charge's secrets—which was great for Sophie. But was probably going to earn him another one of Grizel's humiliating punishments involving tight pants and dancing.

"Anything you want to say?" Ro finally asked, and Sophie couldn't tell which boy she was talking to. She still hadn't worked up the courage to open her eyes.

Keefe was the one to speak up, and his voice sounded even farther away. "You get that the reason Foster went to the matchmakers was for you, right?" he asked Fitz. "And you know what a big deal that was for her, don't you?"

Ro muttered something about foolish boys, which made it impossible to translate Fitz's tone when he told Keefe, "Yeah."

More silence followed, and Sophie went back to imagining which piece of furniture would be the best to fling through a window for her teleporting escape. And as the seconds stacked into minutes, she started to wonder if everyone had left.

Then she felt her mattress shift, and someone sat beside her on the bed.

"Okay." Fitz's voice was quiet, but she still flinched at his sudden closeness. "I don't want this to be a big fight. So will you please just promise me something?"

She forced herself to look at him, needing several seconds for the world to blur back into focus. And her heart stumbled a beat when she found his gorgeous face staring at her *without* all the anger and betrayal she'd last seen in his expression.

He was the kind of handsome that made her eyes tune out everything except him, and her brain shut down—which was probably why she nodded without bothering to ask what she was promising.

"I just want you to remember *this*," he told her, running a hand through his dark hair as he scooted even closer. He stopped when their legs touched, and that tiny contact between them felt like fireworks in Sophie's veins. "I want you to remember me sitting here with you, *not* freaking out or causing any of the drama you've been worrying about, okay? I know I haven't always been great about that—but I'm working on it. So I need *you* to work on trusting *me*—because having you avoid me like you've been doing *really* hurts. And finding out you've been hiding something this important totally sucks. And knowing you confided in other people before telling me makes it even worse."

She hung her head. "I know. I'm really, *really* sorry."

He tilted her chin back up, leaving his warm fingers resting there—which made it very hard to concentrate as he told her, "You don't have to apologize, Sophie. Just try not to do it again. Especially the avoiding me part. I've really missed you."

Her heart and stomach seemed to be competing over which could flutter the hardest. "I've missed you too."

"Yeah?" He flashed one of his breathtaking smiles, and she needed a moment to remind herself that this was actually happening.

This beautiful, perfect guy she'd had a crush on from the moment she'd first stared into his impossibly teal eyes was really saying these things, and looking at her like she meant something—even knowing what the matchmakers had said.

And his fingers were really tracing up her jaw, triggering a new explosion of tingly fireworks as his gaze shifted to her mouth and he leaned closer.

Closer.

"Uh, not to ruin the smoochy-smoochy time," Ro interrupted at the absolute last second—making Fitz snarl, "Are you kidding me?"

as Sophie tried to decide if she wanted to die of embarrassment or launch the heaviest thing she could find at Ro's head.

Ro shrugged, unrepentant. "Thought we'd left, didn't you? Nope! Someone had to keep an eye on you two. And what kind of chaperone would I be if I didn't remind you that Pretty Boy hasn't *actually* said what he thinks about the whole unmatchable thing? In case that matters to you."

"Stay out of it," Keefe warned, adding a whole new level to Sophie's humiliation.

She hid behind her hair, suddenly glad that Ro had interrupted.

The thought of kissing Fitz in front of Keefe was more than just awkward. It felt . . . wrong, somehow.

"I *am* staying out of it," Ro insisted. "It's not like I'm dragging them to separate corners—though we all know I *could*. I just figured I should make sure that our sweet, innocent little Blondie noticed that her teal-eyed wonder boy left out that crucial detail, since I know it's kinda hard to think when a cute boy is leaning in with his eyes all heavy-lidded and his lips all puckery. And I thought she might want a little further clarification before she got lost in all the 'YIPPEE! HE'S KISSING ME'—but what do I know?"

Fitz's glare could've withered forests. "And *I* thought the fact that I was about to kiss her made it pretty clear how I feel."

"Does it, though?" Ro asked, tapping her chin with a painted claw. "I mean, I guess it could. *Or* it could mean you're in the mood for some lip-on-lip action—and hey, no one's judging you. Smooching rocks! But, if you really care about your Lovely Lady Foster, I'm guessing you'd want to make it clear that all the panicking and obsessing she's done about her match status these last few days doesn't bother you—assuming it doesn't, of course."

"Of course it doesn't!" He turned back to Sophie, and repeated, "It *doesn't*."

"Really?" she whispered, feeling like she could finally breathe freely.

He reached up to tuck her hair behind her ears. *"Really."*

Sophie closed her eyes, letting the simple word chase away the doubts and worries she'd been carrying since she'd left the matchmakers' office.

Her heart felt lighter—faster. Her head, clearer than it had in days and days.

Right up until the moment when Fitz added, "I promise we'll find your genetic parents and make this whole mess disappear."

Ro sucked in air through her teeth. "Ooooooooooooooo, you were sooooooooo close."

"Seriously, stay out of it!" Keefe ordered.

But Fitz had already turned back toward Ro. "What's wrong with offering to help? Keefe clearly is. And I would've been helping already, if she'd told me what was happening." His gaze shifted to Sophie, and his forehead crinkled with concern. "I'm sure finding your genetic parents is going to be super complicated and exhausting—and you already have a ton of other stuff going on with the dwarves, from what Biana told me. So I just wanted you to know that I'm here for *anything* you need, okay? *Anytime.* No matter what. We're in this together."

He held out his hand, and Sophie tried to come up with something to say.

But her head felt so *messy*.

All of the questions and confessions had shaken up her brain—left her thoughts scattered and twirly. And her emotions were even more chaotic—all tangled up like a bunch of wriggling snakes.

So she tapped her fingers to reactivate her enhancing-blockers and took the hand he'd offered, mumbling the only thing she could think of: "Thank you."

Fitz tightened his hold. "You don't have to thank me. This is what boyfriends do."

Her breath caught.

There was that word again.

And it felt different this time—and not just because Fitz was the one using it.

It was more like . . . they were discussing something that had already been decided.

Maybe they were.

Fitz knew everything about her matchmaking status now—and he hadn't run screaming away.

Yet.

He reached for her other hand. "Speaking of helping—hear me out on this, okay? I know you and Keefe have a plan—and I'm not saying it's a bad one. But I really think *I* should be the one to go with you when you confront Bronte."

Ro sniffed. "Of course you do."

"Um, reading his thoughts will be way clearer than trying to translate his emotions," Fitz argued, "and this is the kind of thing we need to be absolutely certain about."

"It is," Sophie agreed. "But . . . I've been in Bronte's head. It's really not a great place for a Telepath."

"But you went in alone," Fitz reminded her. "Now we'd be taking him on together."

Ro clapped her hands, jumping up and down. "Oh! Oh! This is the part where he's going to remind you that you're Cognates!"

"Well, we are!" Fitz snapped back, looking like he'd had about all he could stand of Ro's interruptions.

Sophie was equally done with them.

She also knew that Fitz was right. Reading Bronte's thoughts *would* be more conclusive than reading his emotions.

She just . . . didn't want to do it.

She'd learned the hard way, many times, how painful unguarded thoughts could be—even from people who loved her. So to hear what *Bronte* thought about being her biological father—whether or not he actually was?

No thank you.

She'd much rather let Keefe do the reading, so she wouldn't have to hear anything more than "Yep, it's Bronte" or "No, it's not," and then figure out how to live with either answer.

She just didn't know how to explain that to Fitz.

The conversation still felt so . . . delicate.

"I think Bronte will get suspicious if he knows you're going to be there," she said carefully, "since we were going to tell him the meeting was about having Keefe join Team Valiant. The Council already made it pretty clear that they want you and me to work separately for a while—"

"Yeah, what's that about?" Fitz interrupted.

The bitterness in his voice was hard to miss.

"Don't feel bad, Fitzy—you're not the only one who didn't make the cut," Keefe told him. "In fact, I'm kinda thinking you, me, and Linh should start our own team—Team We're-Having-More-Fun-Than-You-Are! Instead of crowns, we can wear tunics that say 'You Wish You Were This Hot.' And all of our mascots will be gulons. You with me?"

Fitz didn't smile.

"Okaaaaaaaaaaaaaay," Keefe said, backing up a step. "Well, at least you'll have more time to focus on finding Alvar. You making any progress with that?"

"None," Fitz admitted, looking even sulkier. "I swear I've searched every single inch of Everglen. There should've at least been a trail showing which way he went. He was . . . pretty messed up."

Sophie tried not to shudder.

She tried even harder not to wonder what it had to feel like to believe you'd willingly killed your traitorous older brother—and then find out later that he managed to get away. It had to be such a strange mix of anger and guilt and frustration and pain.

And instead of being there for Fitz, she'd ignored him and avoided him.

Because of stupid matchmaking.

If she really *was* his girlfriend, that probably made her the Worst. Girlfriend. Ever.

"Whoa. The mood is getting *low* in here," Keefe said. And when his eyes met Sophie's, it looked like he wanted to ask her what was wrong. Instead, he turned to Fitz and added, "All the more reason we need to make Team We're-Having-More-Fun-Than-You-Are! a thing. Come on, Fitzy—I'm sure Linh would be okay with you as our fearless leader. Then you can order everyone around and I can call you Lord Bossypants. It's a win-win!"

"You know what I don't get?" Fitz asked, turning back to Sophie—

and even though he was ignoring Keefe, she noticed the corners of his mouth were twitching, like he might've been trying not to smile. "Everyone knows how rare Cognates are—and you and I are some of the most powerful Cognates *ever*. So why would the Council think splitting us up is going to be a good thing?"

Sophie shrugged. "They said they think it'll help me focus on my other abilities, since I don't use them very often and the Black Swan gave them to me for a reason. But honestly? I think they're just randomly changing things up, trying to push us all out of our comfort zones to see if it makes a difference."

"Yeah—it'll make it *worse*," Fitz muttered.

"Probably," she agreed. "That's why I already made them promise to add you to the team if I need you."

"*If* you need me?" he repeated.

Sophie couldn't tell if he was teasing or moping. Maybe a little of both.

And after all the ways she'd neglected him, she . . . owed Fitz a little reassurance. Even if Ro would forever torment her for it.

So she leaned a little closer, telling herself to be brave as she reached up and smoothed the crinkle between his eyebrows with the tip of her finger.

Pretty sure I'll always need you, she transmitted.

"Aaaaaaaaaaaaaaaaand they've gone into full Fitzphie eye-staring mode—so that's our cue!" Keefe announced, fumbling for his home crystal.

He hooked his arm around Ro's, but she locked her knees. "Nope, I have one more question for Pretty Boy, first."

Sophie and Keefe groaned.

Fitz crossed his arms and tilted his chin up. "Okay, hit me with it."

Ro flashed all of her pointed teeth. "If Sophie can't find out who her genetic parents are, does that change anything for you?"

He frowned. "Why wouldn't she be able to?"

"Doesn't matter," Ro told him. "Just answer the question."

"But . . . the question makes no sense!" Fitz argued. "It's not like the information doesn't exist. If we needed to, we could pull it right out of Forkle's brain." He glanced at Sophie. "Wait—should we just do that?"

"It's plan Z," Keefe told him.

"Huh. Any reason why it's not plan A?" he asked.

"Because . . . it's icky," Sophie mumbled, "and I don't want to be that kind of person unless I have no other choice. Especially for something like this."

"'Something like this,'" Fitz repeated slowly.

Sophie sighed, trying to figure out how to explain without making everything worse. "It's just . . . I already thought matchmaking was unfair to certain people. And now I've turned out to be one of those people. And that seems like proof that I was right and the system's seriously broken—not something I should use as an excuse to violate someone's privacy."

All Fitz had to say to that was, "Hmm."

Ro elbowed Keefe. "Nothing you want to say, Hunkyhair?"

"Yep! Time to go!" He held his crystal up to the fading twilight, and Sophie wondered when it had gotten so dark outside—and how she hadn't noticed.

Ro shook her head. "Fine. Be that way. But you still didn't answer my question," she reminded Fitz.

"Because it was a dumb question," he argued.

"I figured you were going to say that," Ro told him. "So I have a new question for you. And be careful. In fact, *don't* answer until you've put some serious thought into it. There's no wrong answer—but that doesn't mean there isn't one that's *right*."

Keefe sighed. "You have ten seconds until I tackle you."

"Try it," Ro told him, keeping her focus on Fitz. "Ready for your question?"

"I'm definitely not scared," he countered.

"We'll see." She batted her eyelashes—but her smile was anything but sweet as she asked, "If Sophie decided she *didn't* want to find out who her biological parents are—and didn't want anyone else to look into it either—what would you say?"

Fitz frowned. "Why would she do that?"

Ro clicked her tongue. "I told you not to answer."

"I didn't."

"If you say so." She glanced at Keefe. "And since *you're* still not going to say anything, I guess that's the best I can do. For now."

"What does *that* mean?" Fitz asked, but Ro had already dragged Keefe into the light. They were gone the next second, nothing but a shower of glitter—though Sophie could've sworn Keefe mouthed the word *Sorry* as he left.

Fitz blew out a breath, pinching the bridge of his nose. "Well . . . that was weird."

Sophie nodded, trying to figure out how to fill the silence now that they were alone—or as alone as they could be next to a hallway filled with eavesdropping bodyguards.

But her brain couldn't come up with anything useful.

She missed how much easier things used to be between them.

Comfortable.

Friendly.

This dating thing was so much more complicated than she'd realized—if they even *were* dating.

And it got a whole lot worse when Fitz asked, "So . . . would you?"

"Would I what?"

"You know . . . do what Ro was asking. Decide you don't want anyone to find out who your biological parents are."

"Oh."

She dropped her gaze to her hands, knowing this was another one of those questions where there was definitely a *right* answer.

But she couldn't make herself say those words.

So she gave Fitz the same answer he'd given Ro. "Why would I do that?"

And Fitz looked relieved. "Exactly."

THIRTEEN

I THINK I'M GOING TO CALL YOU THE DROOL-
monster from now on," Stina announced, and Sophie's head
snapped up so fast, she slammed the back of it against the
braided bark of Calla's Panakes tree.

She reached for her chin, sighing when she discovered that it *was*
a little slobbery.

And the smirks on Dex's, Wylie's, Biana's, and Stina's faces
made her wonder if she'd also been snoring.

She wiped the drool away with the side of her sleeve and scowled
at Bo, Sandor, and Flori, who were patrolling the nearby pastures
along with Lovise and Woltzer. Clearly her bodyguards had no inter-
est in protecting her from *humiliation*.

The last thing she remembered was petting Wynn and Luna in
the shade, waiting for the rest of her team to arrive for their first
planning session. But the alicorn twins seemed to have abandoned
her. And if the crick in her neck was any indication, she'd been
conked out for a *while*.

"Couldn't sleep last night?" Biana asked as Sophie rubbed the back
of her head, finding the tender spot where she'd bonked it on the tree.

"Not really," Sophie admitted.

No matter what images Silveny had tried sending—soaring through starry skies, galloping across pristine beaches, grazing in quiet meadows—Bronte always crept into the dream, lecturing her or scowling at her or threatening to exile her. And when he'd held out his arms and asked, "Who needs a hug?" she'd decided she was never sleeping again.

But then she'd gone outside to brainstorm for the first meeting of Team Valiant, and Wynn and Luna had been all snuggly, and the air had been filled with a soft, whispering breeze that felt like Calla was singing to her through the swaying leaves, and the day was warm and quiet, and the grass was soft and squishy, and . . . now she would probably forever be the Droolmonster.

But there were worse nicknames.

And thankfully, she didn't remember dreaming at all—score one for Panakes-napping!

Maybe she'd start camping out there at night. At least until she got an answer to the Bronte conundrum. Which . . . might take a while, if she kept being such a wimp.

She'd planned to hail Bronte that morning to schedule the meeting with her and Keefe. But the thought of hearing his voice and seeing his face on that tiny screen—and then asking him the dreaded, potentially life-changing question, and having to face whatever new reality came with his answer . . .

"You okay?" Biana asked, plopping down beside Sophie on the grass and reaching out to brush some of the fallen pinkish, purplish, bluish petals out of Sophie's hair. "Fitz wouldn't tell me what you guys talked about last night. But he said it got a little . . . intense."

"Uh, I think I speak for all of us when I say, *ew*," Dex complained as he sat down next to Biana.

Biana shoved him. "That's not what he meant. And gross—he's my brother! He knows not to tell me that kind of stuff."

"Um, there's nothing to tell!" Sophie emphasized.

"Okay, but why *not*?" Stina asked, joining them on the grass. "We're talking about kissing *Fitz Vacker*, aren't we? *Fitz! Vacker!*" She curled her arms around her knees and stared dreamily at the swaying branches. "How are you not—"

"All right, just so we're all clear," Biana interrupted, holding out her hands like stop signs. "I'm good with Sophie dating my brother. It's a little weird, but . . . whatever. But that doesn't mean I want to *hear* about it."

"YUP!" Dex agreed.

"And *I* really don't want to *talk* about it," Sophie added. "So how about we all just pretend it's not happening?"

"But it *is* happening, right?" Stina pressed, tossing a handful of flowers at Sophie like confetti. "You're done with all the pointless denial?"

Sophie honestly wasn't sure if she knew the right answer to that question.

And all of her friends were watching her now, waiting to hear what she had to say—though Wylie looked like he was mostly wondering how much of this kind of drama he was going to have to deal with as a member of Team Valiant, and when he sat, he positioned himself a couple of extra inches away from them.

Sophie knew she could change the subject—demand they focus on the reasons they'd met up in the first place. But . . . Dex and

Biana still didn't know about her unmatchable status. And Stina and Wylie should probably be in the loop too, thanks to the potential Bronte ramifications.

"Fine," she said, tugging out an itchy eyelash and making a mental note that the next time she had huge, life-changing news, she needed to gather everyone together and tell them all at the same time so she didn't have to keep reliving the same stressful conversation. "There's something I should probably tell you guys, and I really don't want it to be another big, drawn-out thing. So I'm going to say it really fast, and then you guys each get to ask *one* question, and then we're done talking about it. Deal?"

Stina's eyebrows shot up. "Wow. The Droolmonster's bossy today."

"That's because she's Lady Fos-Boss," Dex said, flashing a smug, dimpled grin.

"And we'll take the deal," Biana decided for all of them.

Which meant it was time for Sophie to explain the whole messy situation *again*—though she was pretty proud of herself for condensing it down to one long run-on sentence. She blurted it out as fast as she could, then leaned back against Calla's tree and focused on arranging some of the Panakes blossoms into a tidy circle.

She didn't want to see how much pity was now being directed her way.

"All right," she said, clearing the squeak out of her throat, "one question each. Who wants to go first?"

"I will." Dex leaned closer, and Sophie braced herself for something especially awkward. But all he asked was, "Are you okay?"

When she looked up, she found his eyes shining with the kind of deep, honest worry that could only be found in the stare of someone who'd "been there."

That's when she realized . . .

Even knowing firsthand how much scandal and scorn came with defying the matchmaking system, Dex still talked about how he might choose to not register, as a protest. So . . . rough as the drama would be—it also *had* to be manageable.

And he *must* also believe he'd find someone who wouldn't care whether or not his name was on their lists, or how the rest of their world would label their relationship.

She needed to remember all of that, in case the search for her biological parents spiraled into disaster.

"It hasn't been fun," she told him—but she actually felt like she meant it when she added, "but I'll get through it."

"If you ever need to talk, I'm here," he promised.

"Thanks."

He started to lean back, but Sophie reached out and pulled him in for a hug.

Dex lost his balance for a second. Then he wrapped his arms around her, squeezing as tight as he could. And when he let go a few seconds later, his cheeks weren't red, and he didn't look shy or nervous or fidgety.

He looked . . . like her best friend.

"Okay, *my* turn," Stina announced, reminding Sophie that she still had three more questions to go. "And *I* won't be getting all sappy."

"Shocking," Sophie deadpanned, leaning back against the Panakes again.

"You *really* think Bronte's your biological father?" Stina asked, crinkling her nose like she couldn't picture it—which might've been the best compliment she'd ever given Sophie.

Sophie added a few more blossoms to her flower circle. "I think there's a strong enough possibility that I need to look into it—and not just because of the matchmaking stuff." She glanced at Wylie, wondering how much more she should say. It seemed wrong to raise the horrible possibility when she could be on the complete wrong track.

But . . . if it *was* true, he could probably use some time to mentally prepare.

"The thing is," she said carefully, still holding Wylie's stare, "if Bronte *was* part of Project Moonlark, it makes what happened to your dad a whole lot creepier."

Wylie straightened—and his voice was about fifty degrees colder when he said, "I want to know the second you find out anything."

"You'll be the first person I hail," Sophie promised.

"*Before* you hail Mr. Forkle," Wylie clarified. "If this is true, I want to be there when you confront him—make him look me in the eyes while he explains what happened."

Sophie nodded. And when she saw how tightly his skin was stretched across his fisted knuckles, she added, "Remember: I've had wrong theories before."

Wylie frowned. "Like who?"

Sophie hesitated, so he added, "That's my one question."

"Welllllllll," Sophie said, shifting her weight as she tried to figure out how honest she should be. "I'm not sure if it's weird to tell you this, but my first theory was actually your dad—because everyone kept mentioning his name and getting strange looks and not telling me why. But that was before I knew how Project Moonlark was connected to what happened to him. And it was before I met you . . ."

"And saw how much we look alike?" Wylie finished for her, grinning as he pointed to his dark skin.

Sophie laughed and nodded. "So after I ruled him out, I thought it might be Mr. Forkle, since he's a Telepath and he was the one who rescued me from the kidnappers and healed my abilities and stayed in the human world to keep an eye on me. But . . . he says it's not him."

"He could be lying," Stina noted.

"Oh, I know. But . . . the longer I'm around him, the more it doesn't feel like he's the one—especially when you consider the whole 'secret twin' thing. The Forkle brothers were the *only* people who could do most of the stuff they did for me, which makes those good deeds seem way less significant and more like . . . they were just doing their *job*, you know?" Sophie shrugged. "I also wondered if it was Councillor Kenric, since he was always so nice to me and he was a Telepath and he gave me his cache. But Forkle said he's not—and with Kenric being dead . . . I don't really see why he'd bother lying."

And now that she'd fully realized what it would mean if one of the Councillors had been a part of Project Moonlark, she *really* hoped Kenric was *not* her biological father. The thought of him letting Prentice get hurt to keep his secret safe made her insides churn.

Plus, it would devastate Oralie.

Then again, she supposed all of *that* could be a reason for Mr. Forkle to lie to her about Kenric. Maybe she shouldn't rule him out as her biological father after all. . . .

"What about your biological mother?" Stina asked, and Sophie pulled her legs into her chest, needing to be in another Sophie-ball.

"You already had your turn," Biana reminded her.

"Yeah, but Wylie asked her about 'other *theories*'—that covers both parents," Stina argued. "Besides, I'm sure this little search is going to keep popping up in all kinds of messy ways, so we should be prepared."

Sophie went back to arranging fallen flowers, definitely not loving when Stina made good points. "I've only had one theory for my genetic mom," she said through a sigh, "and you can't repeat it to *anybody*. I don't want it getting back to Grady and Edaline."

Stina's eyebrows practically launched off her forehead. "You think it was Jolie?"

"I *thought* she was," Sophie corrected. "Past tense." She glanced at Biana and Dex, trying to remember if she'd ever told them that as she explained, "Everyone kept telling me I look like her—and she was part of the Black Swan, so . . . I had to wonder. But Forkle said no, and I don't think he'd lie about something that close to home."

"Yeah, I don't think he would," Dex agreed.

"Me neither," Biana added. "I also don't think he would've let you live with Grady and Edaline without them knowing—that would be too weird for them when they found out."

Sophie nodded. "Exactly. The Black Swan is difficult, but . . . they've never been *cruel*."

At least, she hoped they hadn't been.

Once again, her mind strayed to the awful implications of Bronte being her biological father—and the list seemed to be getting worse the more times she went through it.

"You don't have any other theories for your biological mom?" Stina asked.

Sophie rested her chin against her knees. "I guess it's possible that Keefe came up with some and hasn't told me yet, because we got sidetracked by the Bronte thing. But otherwise, nope. I can't think of anyone."

Everyone got really quiet, and Sophie decided to focus on adding another layer to her circle of Panakes blossoms—anything to stop her brain from wondering who they might be considering.

She'd moved on to a third flower level, and it was starting to look more like a leaning pile when Stina clamped her hands over her mouth and gasped, "I bet I know who it is!"

Just like that, every part of Sophie was sweaty.

"An *actual* theory?" Biana clarified. "Because this isn't something to joke about."

"I *know*. One look at Little Miss I'm-Gonna-Vomit-Any-Second over there—and her team of surly bodyguards—makes that pretty clear. So of *course* it's an actual theory—and a good one too." Stina squinted at Sophie, as if she was mentally comparing her against whoever she was imagining. "Wanna hear it?"

Sophie curled into an even tighter ball. And she *knew* she was going to hate herself for this, but . . . "Who?"

Stina grinned, dragging out her dramatic pause until even Wylie was groaning and saying, "Never mind."

Then she told them, "Lady Cadence Talle!"

If Sophie's life had been a movie, the soundtrack would've screeched to a stop right there—and the narrator would've chimed in with a comment like, *Definitely didn't see that one coming!*

"Lady Cadence," Sophie repeated, testing the words on her tongue.

They tasted sour and disappointing, like a low-calorie human dessert.

And there were plenty of shocked murmurings in the background from Sandor.

"I mean, I guess she's technically Master Cadence," Stina corrected. "But yeah—she's your linguistics Mentor, right? Think about it! You're both Polyglots. And she saved your butt when King Dimitar tried to haul you off to an ogre work camp for breaking into his brain. And she was off living in Ravagog until the Council dragged her back to mentor you, so no one would ever suspect her. It's perfect!"

"That . . . actually does kinda make sense," Dex admitted.

"She doesn't look like Sophie, though," Biana argued. "Her hair is, like, raven-feather black."

"So? Maybe Sophie looks like her dad," Stina countered. "Or maybe Sophie's hair color is another one of the things that comes from what the Black Swan did to her genes—like her eye color. And who knows? If we put Sophie next to Lady Cadence, we might spot all kinds of similarities we've never noticed, now that we know to look for them. We should do that!"

Wylie placed a hand on Sophie's shoulder. "You okay?"

At some point he'd scooted closer to her.

She hadn't noticed.

Just like she hadn't noticed that she'd started trembling a little.

Her brain was too busy replaying every moment she'd spent with Lady Cadence—and the memories were so . . .

Awful.

Miserable sessions, where Lady Cadence went out of her way to make it clear how unhappy she was about having to be Sophie's Mentor—and how unimpressed she was with Sophie's talent.

All the horrible, stinky detentions where Sophie had been singled out for additional punishments—though technically some of that was Keefe's fault.

All the endless lectures and sighs and scowls and criticisms.

"Seriously," Wylie said, squeezing Sophie gently until she looked at him. "Need us to change the subject? Or should you have your bodyguards take you inside for a break?"

"No, I'm fine," Sophie mumbled, shaking her head to clear it. "It's . . . a solid theory. Definitely worth looking into."

"It can be worth looking into without you being *fine*," Wylie pointed out.

"I know. But . . . changing the subject doesn't actually change anything," Sophie reminded him. "Neither does going inside and hiding from it."

"Yeah, I know," Wylie said as Sophie hugged herself as tightly as she could. "I learned that after my dad was exiled—and even more after I lost my mom. I think that's why Tiergan was so big on making me talk it out. It's like . . . giving your brain permission to think what it's thinking and feel what it's feeling, instead of shoving it all away. So . . . if you need someone to listen . . ."

He raised his eyebrows expectantly, and Sophie knew he had a point. But she needed a good, solid eyelash tug before she told him, "I was just thinking . . . couldn't at least *one* of my biological parents be someone who's been a *little* nice to me?"

"Or maybe that's *why* they've been so mean," Biana suggested, scooting closer and wrapping an arm around Sophie's shoulders. "Maybe they think it makes them seem less suspicious."

"Great, so they care way more about themselves than they ever will about me," Sophie muttered.

"That kinda makes sense though, doesn't it?" Dex asked, scooching closer too. "I mean, don't take this the wrong way, but . . . Project Moonlark was a pretty selfish thing for all of them to do. I'm not saying I'm not glad the Black Swan did it, since it's why you exist, and you're awesome. But they *were* also experimenting with your life in ways that were bound to cause problems for you—and that didn't stop them from doing it. So, I'm just saying . . . anyone who helped with the project *probably* has some issues—especially the people who didn't even want anyone knowing they were involved."

"Plus, your adoptive parents are *awesome*," Biana added. "And it sounded like your human parents were too. *That's* the family that matters. Who cares about your genetic parents? You got what you needed from them. You exist. The rest?" She shrugged, as if to say, *Who cares?*

Sophie wanted to share that attitude.

But . . . she *did* care.

And telling herself she didn't wasn't going to change that.

Biana cleared her throat. "I know you're probably getting sick of this conversation, but . . . I still haven't asked my question."

"You're right," Sophie said, sitting up to put a little space between her and Biana. She had a terrible feeling that she was about to get hit with a question about what the unmatchable thing meant for her and Fitz's relationship, and since she still didn't know for sure, having a small buffer seemed like a good idea.

But Biana placed her palm over Sophie's gloved hand and asked,

"Will you *please* let us help you with this? I know you're going to say that it all has to be up to you since it's such a personal thing—but our team will work best if you're able to focus on being our leader. So why don't you let us give you a hand?"

"Because there's nothing for you to do," Sophie insisted. "I'm sure we'll have to test Lady Cadence the same way we're going to test Bronte—and that needs to be done by me and an Empath."

"Oh hi! In case you've forgotten, *I'm* an Empath," Stina reminded her.

Sophie was still struggling to process the realization that Stina had technically just volunteered to help her with something she didn't *have* to help her with, when Biana added, "And who said it has to be you for the other part?"

"Um . . . we're searching for *my* biological parents."

"Right, but *anyone* can confront them," Biana argued. "In fact, I bet if it was one of us, we'd get a more telling reaction, since the person will be way more caught off guard. Just like I bet they'd be way less suspicious if one of us set up the meetings to ask the question. And then you could stay out of the whole thing and spend your time being the moonlark and Lady Fos-Boss—"

"And the Droolmonster," Stina chimed in.

"If the Droolmonster part means she actually gets some sleep, I vote for that," Dex added.

Wylie nodded, and Biana tightened her grip on Sophie's hand. "I know it goes against everything your brain is telling you right now. But *please* let us handle this. I promise we'll keep you updated on everything—*and* we'll be careful!" she shouted over her shoulder to her bodyguard.

Woltzer shouted back something about how Biana better not even *think* about ditching him as Sophie stared at her pile of Panakes blossoms, tempted to punch it until the flowers were flattened.

The idea of anyone learning anything about her genetic parents before she did sounded pretty unbearable.

Then again, so did the idea of being there for the confrontations.

Basically, there was no way to *not* have it be awful—so which option would be the least stressful?

"Keep in mind that if *I* were in charge of this," Biana added gently, "I'd already have a meeting set up with Bronte—and not because I think you're slacking or anything. It's just that reaching out to him isn't a *thing* for me like it is for you."

"How did you . . . ?" Sophie started to ask, but her question trailed off when Biana smiled.

"Because you didn't tell us what time you have a meeting scheduled for—and I know you would've if you had one arranged," Biana told her. "And you also didn't complain about Bronte being stubborn and not agreeing to meet yet. So I'm assuming that means you haven't contacted him—and no judgment here. If I were in your position, I'd *dread* having to talk to him and stall doing it as long as I could. *That's* why I want to help. I can save you from the hard parts—*and* get stuff taken care of faster. It's a total win-win."

Sophie snuck a glance at her teammates, and all four of them were nodding—as were all the bodyguards in the background—which made her eyes get that familiar burning feeling.

But she was *not* going to cry, so she cleared her throat and stood to pace. "Well, maybe we can give it a try—but only if turns out you guys have time. First we need to make sure we're really focusing on all the big stuff this team was created for—which is what we're *supposed* to be meeting about today, remember? I swear, this unmatchable thing is the worst distraction ever. Thank goodness everyone knows now, and I don't have to have this horrible conversation again."

"What about Linh?" Biana asked, killing the dream. "And Marella?"

Sophie paused midstep, not sure if it would be smarter to sink back to the grass and never get up again or to run far, far away.

"I can tell them," Wylie offered. "I'm supposed to see Linh today, and she's been training with Marella a *lot*, so I'm sure Marella will be there."

"You . . . wouldn't mind?" Sophie had to ask.

It was an awkward enough conversation when it was *her* news. She couldn't imagine doing it for someone else.

"It'll be easy," Wylie promised. "I'll just repeat what you told us, and let them know you're kinda over talking about it—but if they really have questions, they can hit you up. Sound like a plan?"

Sophie nodded, barely resisting the urge to tackle-hug him.

"Are you going to tell Linh about Tam?" Biana asked.

Wylie fidgeted with his wyvern patch. "I actually already did yesterday. She took it better than I'd expected, mostly because she was relieved that Tam hadn't given Sophie their signal. I guess if Tam were hurt, or if things were getting to be more than he could handle, he would've used some sort of code word and asked Sophie to pass it along to Linh without her knowing what it meant."

"What's the word?" Dex asked.

"Linh wouldn't tell me. She said it works best if she and Tam are the only ones who know it. They came up with the trick when they were banished, since they never knew what kind of problems they might find themselves facing."

"Okaaaaaaaaay," Sophie said, replaying her conversation with Tam again to make sure she hadn't accidentally missed any crucial code words that she should've passed along. "But Gethen would've learned the code word when he probed Tam's memories, wouldn't he?"

"I asked the same thing," Wylie admitted. "But Linh told me Tam's prepared for that, since he always figured the biggest threats were the Telepaths on the Council. I guess he has a way of shrouding a few of his most important memories using shadows. *No one* can see them. So Linh thinks the fact that he didn't use their code word yet is proof that Tam doesn't need any help right now and we should try to leave him alone. And she also said it's a good thing Keefe's taking Tam's warning seriously. She claimed her brother would *never* pass along a message like that unless he was convinced the threat was real."

"And Keefe is *really* going to cooperate?" Stina asked. "'Cause . . . that doesn't sound like Keefe Sencen. . . ."

"But you've met Ro, right?" Biana reminded her. "She'd totally drag Keefe off to Ravagog and lock him in a dungeon if she had to."

Stina shrugged. "Not saying she wouldn't *try*. But I bet you anything Keefe will find a loophole."

Sandor and Bo snorted their agreement.

And Sophie definitely shared all of their concern—but she forced herself to shove it aside. Right now, she needed to stay focused on the more immediate issues. "Did you tell Linh about Team Valiant, and was she upset that the Council didn't include her?"

Wylie scratched at his closely cropped hair. "I . . . don't know. I feel like it *might've* bothered her—but all she said was, 'I'm not surprised.' And she did sound like she meant it when she told me it's actually better, because right now, her focus needs to be on making sure the Neverseen can't keep using her as leverage against her brother. I guess that's why she and Marella have been training so hard. She wouldn't tell me what they're planning—just that it's an elemental thing. I think they're trying to combine their abilities somehow."

"Coooooooooooooooooooooool," Dex breathed. "Fire and water could be *awesome*."

"Um, don't they cancel each other out?" Stina wondered.

"They can," Wylie agreed. "When I was there, that seemed to be what they were practicing. Marella would spark a flame, and Linh would immediately drown it with water, and then Marella would evaporate the water to steam. But I know the elemental abilities are a little bit different than other abilities, so I wouldn't be surprised if they can find a way to merge the two."

"I guess," Stina said, turning to frown at Sophie. "Does anyone else think it's weird that the Black Swan didn't give their moonlark any elemental abilities?"

"They may have, and she just hasn't manifested yet," Dex countered. "Forkle's always been super vague about how many abilities they gave her."

"But hopefully I'm done," Sophie jumped in. "Five is *enough*. And Linh didn't have any theories about what the Neverseen might be planning for Tam?" she asked Wylie, beginning to understand why people often complained about the challenges of keeping her and her friends focused on a single topic.

Wylie shook his head. "No. But she said we should definitely talk to Lady Zillah. Apparently Tam did a *ton* of late-night training sessions that he wouldn't let Linh go with him on because he said they were too dangerous."

"That . . . doesn't sound good," Dex murmured.

No, it did not.

"Okay . . . so when would be a good time to meet with Lady Zillah?" Sophie asked. "Is everyone free tomorrow?"

"Why do we all have to be there?" Stina wondered. "Isn't the point of us being a team so that we can do five things at once and then loop back and fill each other in on what we've learned?"

Once again, Sophie had to admit that Stina had a valid point— and she surely had some serious Stina-bragging in her future for conceding. But time was of the essence, so she said, "All right. Who wants to be in charge of meeting with her?"

"I get the impression she's *not* a fan of Flashers," Wylie said, "so it might be better if it's not me."

"Actually, I think it *should* be you," Sophie realized.

Lady Zillah *did* have some very strong opinions about how overrated Flashers were—and light in general—particularly since Shades were generally looked down on in the Lost Cities.

But after leaping with the Sources and feeling the potency of that glowing power—and how cooperative it was—Sophie didn't want to lose track of the bigger picture.

If shadows and shadowflux were going to be the Neverseen's focus, perhaps the best countermeasure would involve light in some form.

"Maybe bring Stina with you," Sophie suggested, "as a buffer."

Miraculously, Stina didn't argue.

She even agreed to take notes and give Sophie a full update once they'd learned everything they could from the Shade Mentor.

Which left Team Valiant with the bigger challenge they needed to be focusing on—the threat that felt so huge, it made Sophie want to hand her wolf patch to an adult and say, "Shouldn't this be your job?"

"Okay. Moving on," she said, trying to sound as leaderlike as she could. "Since it sounds like King Enki might be difficult to work with, I think we want to prepare as much as we can before we visit Loamnore."

"Uh-oh, are you about to give us the 'we need to do lots of research' speech?" Dex asked. "Because it's not too late to change your mind!"

"We *do* need to do research," Sophie insisted. "But it doesn't have to be hours and hours in the library. I think, in this case, we'd be way better off going straight to the source."

She motioned for everyone to follow her, and there was shockingly little debate as Sandor, Bo, Flori, Lovise, and Woltzer took the lead and their whole group made their way down the flower-lined path through Havenfield's rolling pastures—though Biana and Stina *did* get sidetracked when Wynn and Luna came trotting over for some nuzzling.

"Are we teleporting somewhere?" Dex asked when they made it to the Cliffside gate.

"You'd better not be," Sandor warned as Sophie squatted to undo the lock.

She shook her head. "Not today." And she couldn't help grinning when she noticed how relieved Stina looked by the news—but her smile faded when Dex turned very pale.

"Are we going where I think we're going?" he whispered.

Sophie nodded, wishing she'd thought to check with him when she put this plan together. "Is that a problem? If it is—"

"No, it's fine," Dex interrupted.

But it didn't sound fine.

"You don't have to worry," Lovise told him. "You have me now."

"Um . . . where are we going?" Stina asked.

Sophie chewed her lip, wondering if she should course-correct—or if that would only embarrass Dex.

"There's a cave down there," Dex explained, making the decision for her. "It's . . . where Sophie and I used to practice alchemy."

"You mean the cave where the Neverseen grabbed you guys?" Biana asked quietly.

"Yeah," Sophie admitted. "But we don't have to—"

"Yes, we do." Dex stood up taller. "If you can go back there, so can I. Plus, we have *five* bodyguards with us."

"Six," Sophie corrected. "Which is why we're going there—you'll see what I mean in a minute."

"Then lead the way," he told her, gesturing to the now unlocked gate.

Sophie studied Dex a second longer and was about to reach for his hand—but Biana beat her to it, making Dex jump a little as their fingers twined together.

Sophie smiled, definitely not missing the pink flush across Dex's cheeks as she pulled open the gate. "Okay, let's do this."

Sandor, Bo, and Woltzer drew their swords and marched down the stairs ahead of them, with Flori and Lovise promising to bring up the rear.

"I know that's supposed to make us feel safe," Stina murmured, watching the muscled bodies disappear around a bend in the stairs. "And it *does*. But . . . it also makes it worse somehow, doesn't it?"

"I know what you mean," Sophie admitted.

Having bodyguards meant *needing* bodyguards.

But that was just another reason why they had to stay focused. None of them would ever be safe as long as the Neverseen were out there.

She had a feeling the rest of her friends were thinking the same thing, because the mood of their group shifted during that descent. And by the time they made it to the stretch of rocky beach leading up to the infamous cave—where their guards were already completing a thorough safety inspection—their jaws were set, shoulders squared, eyes determined.

"So . . . care to tell us what we're doing here, Lady Fos-Boss?" Biana whispered as they slowly crossed through the cave's dark entrance.

Sophie rubbed at her arms, trying to scrub away the goose bumps that had popped up from the damp sand and the brisk air and the bad memories. It wasn't her first time back in the cave since her abduction—but that didn't make the flashbacks of cloaked figures and drugged cloths any less vivid. "Mr. Forkle suggested I talk to my dwarven bodyguard—Nubiti—to see what she can tell me about Loamnore," she explained. "And I figured we should have that conversation somewhere that won't bother her eyes."

She headed as deep into the shadows as her courage allowed, then turned and stomped her feet in the pattern that Sandor and Grady had taught her, sending grains of sand flying.

Seventeen painfully silent seconds passed before the ground

rumbled and a small creature emerged from the earth, shaking sand out of her brown, shaggy fur.

Nubiti's nose was pointed, and her eyes were squinted slits, even in the darkness. And her voice was as raspy as tumbling pebbles when she dipped her head with a bow and asked, "How can I help you, Miss Foster?"

"Have you been listening to our conversations these last few days?" Sophie asked, proud of herself for sounding casual, even though her brain got a little weirded out talking to dwarves. It was like chatting with a child-size mole.

"I have," Nubiti confirmed, studying her hands, which had plenty of long, sharp claws for digging. "You wish to ask me about a threat to my city."

"Wow, so you guys really *can* eavesdrop that clearly?" Wylie asked, tilting his head to study Nubiti from a different angle.

"Your voices carry far deeper into the earth than you realize," Nubiti informed him. "Listening poses no challenge—though *understanding* can be more difficult. Your species worries about such unnecessary things."

"Does that mean you don't think Loamnore's in danger?" Sophie wondered.

"No." Nubiti's voice was much calmer than Sophie felt as the small dwarf crouched and ran her claws through the cold, clumpy sand. "The threat is as real as the worry you're carrying—and the solution as elusive as your dreams. Our king has done what he can, but he cannot recover what has been lost without first finding it, and there is no trail for us to follow, which is the true mystery."

"Anyone else confused?" Dex whispered.

"I am," Biana agreed, and Sophie noticed the two of them were still holding hands.

But she made herself concentrate on what Nubiti was saying. "I'm a little confused too," she admitted. "*What* was lost?"

Nubiti scooped up a fresh handful of sand and fished out a delicate piece of blue sea glass. "You already know that some in my species have abandoned their people and formed an alliance with these Neverseen from your world. I do not claim to understand their motivation, nor can I guess their plan. But before they left Loamnore, they . . . altered the magsidian."

The last word was whispered, and yet it still seemed to bounce around the cave, echoing out of the shadows.

Magsidian was a rare, onyxlike stone that only the dwarves were capable of mining, which was why the elves used it for security in Exile. The dwarven guards could sense the presence of the gem and know if a visitor had permission to be there, since they'd only given pieces of the stone to the Council.

The Black Swan had also acquired at least one piece as well, which they'd once given to Sophie to use to find them.

Magsidian changed properties depending on how it was shaped and faceted.

"We have stones placed very specifically throughout our city," Nubiti went on, tucking the shard of sea glass among the shaggy strands of her fur, "carved to serve many needs. And several of those stones were changed before the deserters left—which is not new information. Your Council is well aware, as is your father, Miss Foster. Many inspections have been made on the altered magsidian—as well as many repairs. But no stone can ever be the same after it is altered.

Each new facet causes a permanent change. So we have been left with a network that can achieve the same purpose, but it is *not* the same."

"Is that what you meant by 'lost'?" Sophie asked, trying to piece together what Nubiti was saying.

Nubiti shook her head. "I meant the lost shards of magsidian," she said as she bent to scoop up another handful of sand.

"Shards?" Sophie glanced at her friends, hoping some of them were following this better than she was.

Stina seemed to be, because she asked, "You mean the pieces the deserters chiseled away when they altered the magsidian in Loamnore?"

"Yes. They cut at least a dozen shards, some no larger than a splinter, some similar in size to this." Nubiti fished a second piece of sea glass from the sand—green this time, and about the size of a small Lego. "And there is no telling what those stones can do," Nubiti warned as she tucked the green glass among her fur. "They are new shapes, new sizes—and for some reason we cannot feel them, no matter how thoroughly we search."

"That doesn't sound good," Dex mumbled.

"It's not. Especially given what I now suspect is the source of the stone, after listening to your conversations." She moved to the wall of the cave, trailing her claws along the jagged edges in the rock. "Some stone comes from the earth. Other stone falls from the sky. Magsidian is a blend of both—something new, created by a dark collision."

"You mean a meteor?" Sophie asked.

"Yes and no. It was no ordinary rock that fell and fused with all it touched. None of my people have a name for it because none of us witnessed the impact. But the stone tells its own tale. One of shadows and energy. One that feels *elemental*."

She left the word hanging there, waiting for someone to grab ahold of it and make the connection that would forever raise the stakes of what they were dealing with.

And as the leader of Team Valiant, Sophie knew it was her job to step up to the task. So she whispered, "You think magsidian is made of shadowflux."

FOURTEEN

COULD MAGSIDIAN WEAKEN TAM'S ability if it were cut the right way?" Biana suggested, earning a round of murmured agreement from the rest of her teammates as Sophie added the question to the list they were building.

Nubiti had tunneled back into the sand not long after she'd led them to the shadowflux-magsidian revelation, and they'd decided that the meeting with Lady Zillah now needed to be their top priority. Stina had hailed the Shade Mentor as soon as they'd made it back to Calla's Panakes tree, and Lady Zillah had been her usual intense, uncooperative self. But she'd agreed to have a "brief conversation" with Stina and Wylie the next day if they met her at her office in Mysterium at noon—sharp. And she'd emphasized that it would be *brief.* Which meant that Wylie and Stina needed to be prepared in order to make the most of their limited time. So Sophie had rushed to her room for a notebook and they'd all gathered under the swaying branches as they brainstormed—with Wynn and Luna trotting around, causing plenty of distractions.

But figuring out what to ask was proving to be more challenging than Sophie had expected.

The problem was, everything they'd discovered seemed so *abstract*.

So . . . magsidian was made of shadowflux—at least partially. And the dwarves who'd joined the Neverseen had stolen some pieces of the rare stone before they left. And for some reason, the rest of the dwarves couldn't feel any trace of those shards the way they could with other magsidian, so they had no way of finding or recovering them.

But what did any of that *actually* mean?

And what did it have to do with Tam?

Nubiti hadn't seemed to know, and was very reluctant to say any more about it than she already had.

And since there was no guarantee that Lady Zillah would know much either, they were trying to come up with a mix of specific *and* broad questions, hoping that *something* might help them figure out what to do with this new information.

So far, including the question that Biana had just added, they had:

> *Did Lady Zillah know about the connection between*
> *shadowflux and magsidian?*
> *Are there any other physical manifestations of shadowflux*
> *that they should be aware of?*
> *What happens if magsidian comes into contact with*
> *shadowflux?*
> *Would any of the Shade skills that Tam had learned*
> *be more dangerous around magsidian?*
> *Could magsidian weaken Tam's ability if it were cut*
> *the right way?*

"Do you think we should ask either the Council or the dwarves to give Lady Zillah a piece of magsidian to experiment with?" Wylie asked after Sophie had finished reading their list out loud again.

"Probably," Sophie told him. "But I don't know if it'll do much good. She knows a lot *about* shadowflux, but she can't call for it or control it herself."

Still, that was why Sophie had already taken the time to talk to Grady, hail Councillor Oralie, and have Flori tell Mr. Forkle what they'd learned from Nubiti. And they'd all wondered the same thing Sophie had—the one question she'd managed to ask Nubiti before she disappeared underground again: Why had Nubiti waited so long to tell anyone about this?

Apparently, that had been King Enki's decision.

Nubiti had only made the connection between magsidian and shadowflux a couple of days earlier, when she'd overheard Mr. Forkle sharing his fears about Tam and the dwarven city with Sophie. And she'd gone straight to her king to see what he wanted her to do. But he'd disagreed that there was any cause for concern. He felt that the cuts they'd made to repair the damage in their existing magsidian network had not only fixed the sabotage, but had enhanced their overall security so well that it more than addressed any potential threats that might arise from the stone's origin. So the last thing he wanted was to have the elves demanding explanations for how the system worked. He preferred to keep that information classified.

He'd actually ordered Nubiti *not* to share her theories with anyone in the Lost Cities. And she'd been trying her best to follow that order—but she was also worried that King Enki had spent too long underground, away from the dangers thriving on the planet's surface, and was severely underestimating their enemies. So she'd decided that if any elves reached out to her, she'd lead them to the information. That way she wasn't disobeying, but she was still passing along a warning in case the connection between shadowflux and magsidian was significant. And while Nubiti hadn't asked Sophie to cover for her whenever she and her friends met with King Enki, she'd looked immeasurably relieved when Sophie had promised to make it seem like they'd made the discovery on their own—since, in a way, they had.

"Anyone have anything else to add?" Sophie asked, scanning their list again and wishing it were longer.

"I think that covers it pretty well," Dex assured her. "Especially since her answers will probably make them come up with additional questions while they're there."

"And you don't think we should *all* go?" Sophie had to ask.

When they'd decided to split up for the meeting, the conversation hadn't felt nearly as important.

"Ugh, don't go getting all 'I have to be a part of everything' *now*," Stina grumbled.

"This isn't about *me*," Sophie insisted. "I just think it might be good to have all of us there, since any of us could catch something the others don't."

"Eh, I think that'll freak Lady Zillah out," Stina argued. "You heard her—she already sounded super suspicious. And I can't really blame her for that. It's gotta be weird having your only prodigy working with the enemy—"

"Tam's not working *with* them," Biana interrupted. "He's basically their prisoner."

Stina shrugged. "Just because he's not doing it by choice doesn't mean he's not still *helping* them. And hey—I'm not judging. I'd probably make the same decision if the Neverseen were threatening my parents. But that doesn't change the fact that every time he cooperates, he's technically contributing to their plans. And I'm sure Lady Zillah's not happy that the stuff she taught Tam might be used to hurt someone—or lots of someones, depending on what the Neverseen are getting ready for. So I'm betting she's a little nervous to answer questions about Tam's lessons. And if five of us show up when she's only agreed to meet with two of us, I think she'll freak out and refuse to cooperate."

"Stina's right," Biana agreed, crinkling her nose like those words pained her a little. "I think we should let her and Wylie handle this. If we feel like they missed something, we can always ask for another meeting—and if Lady Zillah won't agree, we'll just show up at her office and not leave until she answers our questions."

"I guess." Sophie studied the questions one more time to make sure her photographic memory had completely captured them before she tore the page out of her notebook and offered it to Wylie. "You're meeting briefly with Lady Zillah at noon, right? Then I'm going to hail you guys at one for an update—and I want to know *everything* she said. Take notes if you don't think you'll be able to remember it all."

She wouldn't let go of the paper until he nodded—even when Stina mumbled something about bossy Droolmonsters.

"I'm assuming you'll update Dex and me after that?" Biana asked.

"Of course," Sophie promised.

"Good. And I'll hail Bronte as soon as I'm home to see if I can set up a meeting—but I doubt he'll agree to anything right away. And I should probably update my dad about some of this and see if he has any thoughts or advice—or, wait, am I allowed to do that? Is all of our team information classified?"

"From the general populace, yes. But Alden's an Emissary with the highest level of clearance, so it won't be a problem," Grady told her, making all of them jump—and making Sophie wonder how long he'd been eavesdropping.

Apparently long enough for Grady to also know to ask, "Why do you need to meet with Councillor Bronte?"

Biana's eyes darted to Sophie, and Sophie gave the tiniest possible head shake.

Grady and Edaline were being way cooler about the search for her biological parents than Sophie had ever expected them to be. But she had a feeling the Bronte theory might be a bit too . . . *head-explode-y*, given the implications. So it seemed better to wait until she had confirmation before she hit them with that kind of bombshell.

Plus . . . she *really* didn't want to have to live through any more Bronte-related conversations. She'd already had enough of those to last two lifetimes.

"I wanted to see if he knows when we'll be announcing our appointment as Regents," Biana told Grady—which sounded like a perfectly legitimate explanation to Sophie.

But Grady did *not* look convinced.

Sophie was bracing for him to call them out when Dex jumped in. "So does that mean I *can't* tell my parents about anything we're working on?" he asked. "Since they're not Emissaries?"

"If you were a normal Regent, the answer would be yes," Grady admitted. "But your age might change things. Your family may have a right to know at least a little about what you're investigating, in case it puts you in danger. So you should probably double-check with the Council."

"What about the Black Swan?" Wylie wondered. "The Council must assume I'm going to tell Tiergan."

"Probably. But it can't hurt to verify," Grady suggested. "They may want all communication with the Black Swan to funnel through Mr. Forkle."

"I guess I can ask," Wylie said, shoving some Panakes blossoms into his pocket as he stood and pulled out his home crystal. Stina and Biana did the same, right down to collecting some of the healing flowers to take with them—which was smart, considering how many lives the Panakes blossoms had saved.

But Dex stayed seated in the soft grass, and it was clear that he was lingering for a reason.

Sophie had no idea what he needed, but for the first time in a long time, she didn't feel any awkward worry about it. Even when Biana noticed—and frowned a little—Sophie just smiled and asked her to let Fitz know she'd hail him as soon as she caught up on a few other things.

And once Biana had leaped away—and Grady had wandered off to help the gnomes with the gorgodon feeding—Sophie almost wanted to hug Dex again, so they could marvel at how far their friendship had come.

But *that* probably would've been a little weird.

Plus, she didn't want to distract him from whatever he'd stayed there to tell her.

"So what's up?" she asked as Dex stood and offered a hand.

"I checked in with Keefe this morning," he said, helping her to her feet, "to find out when he wanted to go to the Forbidden Cities so I could set up the cameras to watch for that guy he remembered. But Ro started shouting in the background about chaining him to a porch swing. So he said I needed to talk to you, and then he launched into this long speech about how we both needed to bring him back a bunch of biscuits to apologize for ditching him—at least that's what I think he said. There was a lot of talk about Jammie Dodgers and Jaffa Cakes and Digestives—*no* idea what those are. But he said you'd know—or that you *should*, and if you didn't, I needed to tell you to be ashamed of yourself."

"Uh, except I grew up in America, not England," Sophie argued, even though she actually *had* heard of a few of those cookies— *biscuits*—whatever she was supposed to call them. But she doubted Dex cared about human regional snack variations. So she focused on the actual important subject. "When do you want to go?"

He shrugged. "Totally up to you. I know we have a ton going on."

"We do. But Keefe's missing memories are super important too. So whenever you're ready, we should get moving on that."

"I'm ready," Dex assured her. "I know exactly what I need to do. I just need to get there. We could seriously go now if you wanted."

"Now?" Sophie repeated. "You don't need any tools or—"

"Nope, got all the tools I need right here." He held out his hands, wiggling his fingers with a proud grin. "And it shouldn't take me long either. Five to ten minutes, tops."

"I'm going to interrupt right there," Sandor said, stalking over with his hand gripping his sword. "Because I know what you're thinking. And *no*."

"I wasn't—" Sophie tried to argue, but Sandor shook his head.

"Yes, you were. And I repeat: no."

"I agree," Lovise added. "No one is going to any Forbidden Cities right now. Don't even think about it."

Sophie hadn't been—at least not seriously.

But . . . now that they were making her *really* consider it, she had to ask, "Why not?"

The sun hadn't set yet, so they had time before she'd need to go to bed.

And she didn't have anything urgent to do—which might not be true the next day, or the day after that. Things changed quickly when it came to the Neverseen, and the Council, and all the projects they were juggling.

If they actually had a free moment, they should probably take advantage of it.

"You need more time to prepare," Sandor told her, grabbing her shoulders and pressing down like he was afraid she might try levitating any second.

"Do we, though?" she countered. "You heard Dex—all he needs is five to ten minutes. And our clothes aren't *that* elf-y."

She gestured to her outfit: a blue silk tunic with embroidered purple flowers along the waistline, paired with black gloves, black leggings, and knee-high black boots.

It might not be "fashionable" in the human world—or maybe it was. She'd been gone long enough that she had no idea—not that she'd ever really cared about that kind of thing. But either way, she knew no one would think she was wearing anything strange.

And Dex's gray jerkin kind of made him look like he was wearing a vest—which would probably blend in super well in London. Didn't their businessmen wear waistcoats?

She'd also definitely seen enough pictures of London to teleport them there—though she wasn't sure which part of the city to head for. They'd need to go somewhere with a lot of security cameras, so . . .

Maybe Big Ben?

Or the Tower Bridge?

Or that big Ferris wheel thing—what was it called? The London Eye?

"Stop thinking about it, Sophie," Sandor ordered. "It's not happening."

"What if I say you can come with us?" she countered.

Bringing a seven-foot-tall gray goblin to London definitely wouldn't be ideal. But if it got Sandor to cooperate . . .

"I'm sure Grady has an obscurer we can borrow," she told him. "And you can wear one of his hooded capes, just to be safe. It's London—it'll be foggy and raining and you'll blend right in. But *just* you," she added, glancing at Bo. Bringing an ogre to a human city would be a terrible idea. "It'll be such a quick trip, I'm only going to need one bodyguard."

"Exactly," Dex jumped in.

"You're not going *anywhere* without me," Lovise told him, grabbing his arm and pulling him to her side.

"Fine," Dex told her, "we'll get you a cloak too—though it's seriously ridiculous. The whole thing will be *super* fast. I bet if we'd left already, instead of standing here arguing about it, we'd be back by now."

"The length of the trip is not the issue!" Lovise snapped. "It takes seconds to deliver a killing blow or to steal away a hostage. What you need is proper preparation! We cannot embark on such an excursion without scouting the area, planning escape routes, gathering the necessary weapons—"

"Eh, you're forgetting about the power of spontaneity," Dex interrupted. "It's the easiest way to stay ahead of your enemies: Don't plan anything. Just do whatever you need to do the moment you need to do it and leave them struggling to keep up."

The glare Lovise shot him made it clear she was *not* a fan of being spontaneous.

"Dex has a point," Sophie insisted.

"I have a better one," Sandor said, crossing his arms and straightening to his full height. "I can end this right now by calling for your father and asking what *he* thinks of this plan. Is that what you want me to do?"

"No need," Grady said behind them, and everyone whipped around to find him standing with a bundle of swizzlespice—and Wynn and Luna bounding around him, begging for the treats.

His eyes met Sophie's, and between the deep creases across his forehead and the hard set of his jaw, Sophie assumed Sandor was about to be *very* smug.

But after Grady finished unleashing a shoulder-heaving sigh, he mumbled, "I can't believe I'm saying this—especially since I've only caught bits and pieces of *why* this needs to happen, but . . . assuming there's a good reason, they might as well go now. They're Regents, so the Council won't punish them for visiting a Forbidden City. And Dex has a point about spontaneity. The Neverseen would definitely expect us to calculate a visit like this for days—or at least hours. Going so suddenly—especially for such a brief amount of time—probably *is* the safest way to do it. And as far as the humans go"—he tossed the swizzlespice to the begging baby alicorns and reached into one of the many pockets lining his pants, fishing out a small black orb—"I've learned to keep an obscurer on hand, since I never know when you guys might need one in a hurry."

"You're *seriously* okay with this?" Sophie asked as he handed the gadget to Dex.

"'Okay' isn't the right word," he told her. "More like . . . I'm resigning myself to the fact that among a number of less-than-ideal options, this one might not be completely horrible. But I'd recommend going soon, before I change my mind."

Sophie had to blink a couple of times to make sure she was truly awake and living this rare moment of cooperation.

"I trust you," Grady told her, holding her gaze before he shifted focus to Dex and added, "and I trust *you*. And I trust *Sandor* to keep you both safe. And I trust that all three of you will be back in *ten* minutes. Not eleven. Not twelve. Definitely not thirteen. *Ten*— maximum. Which does mean that nine and under is perfectly fine."

He unfastened his navy blue cloak and held it out to Sandor, who looked far from thrilled as he pinned it across his shoulders. The fabric barely hung past his thighs, but when he stooped, he looked kind of like an old, hunched man—with a quick glance, at least.

"And Lovise is going to need this," Edaline said behind them, making everyone spin around again. She snapped her fingers to conjure up a bundle of thick black fabric and handed it to Dex's bodyguard before moving to stand beside Grady. "That's the longest cloak I own. You'll still have to hunch, but it'll only be for ten minutes—right?"

She directed the last question to Sophie, smiling when Sophie nodded. And Sophie was struck by such an overwhelming mix of shock, gratitude, and love for her adoptive parents that it nearly knocked her back a step.

Grady and Edaline had been through so much heartache, and yet they'd still welcomed her into their family, loving her despite all the stress and danger she'd brought into their lives. And somehow they'd gotten to a point where they trusted her enough to support a crazy plan like this?

It made her remember what Biana had said about Grady and Edaline being the family that mattered. And she found herself sprinting over and pulling them into a strangle-hug.

Grady laughed. "Don't get too grateful there, kiddo. Remember, I'm only giving you ten minutes. Then I'm turning on the trackers that Sandor sews into your clothes and sending Bo after you."

Bo flashed a rather ominous, pointed-toothed grin, and Sophie found herself needing to check with Dex. "You really can get it done that fast, right?"

He looked a *little* less certain than he had a few minutes earlier— but he squared his shoulders and told her, "I've got this."

"You do," she agreed.

"*We* do," he corrected, holding out his hand.

Sophie gave her parents one more squeeze before she pulled away and reached for Dex, leading him through the pastures, toward the Cliffside gate.

She figured they might as well jump this time. Make it a true leap of faith.

And even though Sandor and Lovise were clearly less than thrilled with this development, they made no further protests—even when their small group stepped to the cliff's edge.

Waves churned below, and a cold, salty breeze whipped through Sophie's hair as she rallied her concentration and pictured where they were heading.

"Okay," she said, grabbing Sandor's hand as Lovise clung to Dex. "Let's go to London!"

"What is this place?" Dex asked, squinting through the bars of the iron-and-gold gate, at the large stone structure beyond, which looked . . .

A little plain, if Sophie was being honest.

Sure, there were intricate columns. And rows of windows. And a *very* recognizable balcony. And Sophie was positive that if she went inside, she'd find an abundance of chandeliers and tapestries and antiques and paintings—not to mention the immaculate flower beds and pristine lawn behind them, along with a huge, fancy fountain.

But . . . after living in a world of jeweled cities and crystal castles, there just wasn't as much sparkle as there should be—especially considering where they were.

She'd been planning to take Dex to Westminster Abbey, but as they'd crashed their way through the void, she'd realized that if they were looking for a spot in London with a lot of security cameras, Buckingham Palace was probably the best place to go.

"This is the queen's residence in London," she told Dex as she tried to find a less crowded spot to stand in, even though no one seemed to be paying them any attention.

Dex squinted at the palace. "Their queen is a white-haired lady, right? I think I saw some pictures of her when I was researching about the cameras."

"Yeah, Queen Elizabeth," Sophie said. "I don't know much about her. Just that she likes little dogs and wears a lot of hats. And I think that flag means she's actually here right now." She pointed to the red, gold, and blue standard flying from a pole in the center of the palace, instead of the British Union Jack. "Same with the fact that there are four of those guys instead of two."

She nudged her chin toward the four members of the queen's guard, standing stolid and motionless in what appeared to be narrow blue houses. The soldier's faces looked blank, but Sophie had no doubt their eyes were seeing everything, and it made her hope the obscurer was keeping them hidden—especially when she noticed their guns.

"So wait—the dorky guys in the red coats with the big furry hats are *important*?" Dex asked, covering his mouth to block a giggle. "And you had the nerve to complain about our Foxfire uniforms!"

"Hey—*I* never had to wear anything like that. That's strictly a British soldier thing!"

"Soldier?" Dex repeated, frowning at the guards. "So . . . is that uniform supposed to be intimidating? Because I feel like if a dude marched up to an army of ogres wearing *that*, he'd mostly get laughed at."

"Goblins definitely wouldn't be able to suppress their snickers," Sandor noted, his lips twitching with a smile.

"I think it's supposed to be traditional," Sophie told them, shrugging. "I don't know. Like I said, I grew up in the U.S. Soldiers wear camouflage over there."

Dex shook his head. "It's so weird to me, the way humans divide up their own species. Don't they realize they'd be stronger as a larger, united group?"

"I don't think they care," Sophie admitted. "They don't know that they *need* to be stronger, you know? They have no idea that there are elves or goblins or ogres or trolls or dwarves or gnomes to think about."

And Sophie was struck, in that moment, by how truly *other* she felt standing there, watching the crowds of tourists posing for selfies outside the palace, with buses and cars driving past and a light drizzle peppering her skin—and it wasn't just because London was such a very different place from San Diego, where she grew up.

The air felt too heavy in her lungs—thick from all the pollution. And the smell of chemicals and car exhaust turned her stomach.

And the *noise*.

Even with her mind shielded from the bombardment of blaring human thoughts, everything was still so very loud. Shouted snatches of conversations. Sirens and car horns. The steady banging of some nearby construction project.

It made her *truly* appreciate how peaceful and calm the Lost Cities always felt, despite the problems her home was facing.

And yet, even with that thought rattling around her mind, she couldn't help taking another look at the humans around her. And all she could see were smiles and hugs and laughter.

Humans definitely posed a challenge.

But . . . they were worth protecting.

Sandor cleared his throat, snapping her out of her strange musings when he warned them, "You've now used up one minute and thirty seconds of the ten minutes your father gave you. So I suggest you get to work."

Dex nodded, leading their group along the perimeter of the palace, studying several of the black cameras before settling on one that jutted out from the wall on a hooked black arm.

"Can I get a boost?" he asked Lovise, who didn't look thrilled about the idea of lifting Dex onto her shoulders so he could reach the camera more easily—and Sophie wasn't in love with the position either, mostly because it would draw all kinds of attention to them if the obscurer stopped working.

Sandor kept one hand gripping his sword as he scanned the crowd for signs of a threat.

And Sophie stood there doing . . .

Nothing.

"Need any help?" she asked Dex, craning her neck to see what he was up to.

He'd pressed his fingertips against the camera, murmuring something under his breath that she couldn't hear. And whatever he was doing made the camera flash.

For one nerve-racking second, Sophie was sure they would be spotted. But then Dex let go and told Lovise to put him down.

"Okay, we're all set!" he announced, pointing to the panic-switch ring he always wore. "Now I'll get an alert anytime their camera network records anyone who looks like that guy Keefe drew. Hopefully it'll only take a few days for him to show up in the system. I'll hail you the second I hear anything. And look at that—we still have at least five minutes to spare! Man, I'm good! Come on, Sandor, you can say it. Who's the Lord of Awesome?"

Sandor gritted his teeth. "I'll save any compliments for when we're safely back at Havenfield five minutes early."

Which definitely would've been the smart thing for them to do.

But Sophie had spotted a cluttered shop and decided that cheering up Keefe was a better use of that extra time. So with Dex's help at a nearby ATM, she was able to make a very creative withdrawal through her elvin birth fund, and she used that cash to buy all the weird British biscuits that Keefe had requested—plus some called Hobnobs, and some called Custard Creams, and several bars of Cadbury chocolate, and a few boxes of proper English tea.

And as they leaped home—with thirty seconds to spare—she couldn't believe how easy it had been.

Maybe Dex was onto something with the whole "spontaneity" thing.

But she should've known that the universe would never let her day end with something so easy.

Mr. Forkle was waiting for her in the Havenfield pastures—along with Grady and Edaline—and the dented line in the grass made it clear that all three of them had been pacing.

"What's wrong?" Sophie asked, dropping her bag of biscuits.

"Nothing," Mr. Forkle told her, shuffling forward and retrieving her snacks with his ruckleberry-swollen hands.

"Then why are you here?" she countered, glancing over his shoulder at Grady and Edaline, who looked . . . tired.

Or maybe "wary" was a better word.

Mr. Forkle handed Dex her bag and turned to pace again, his bloated legs moving slower than usual.

Sophie assumed he was about to demand a lot of information about why they'd been in London. Instead, he told her, "I'm here because I never anticipated the Council's decision to appoint you as a Regent. And as far as I know, my brother didn't either. It makes me wish he were here, so we could talk through the implications together. But *that* . . . is not possible." He cleared his throat. "So it seems the best option is to allow you to make your own decision, even though it will be no simple choice."

"What decision?" Sophie asked, jumping when Dex hooked his arm around hers.

She hadn't noticed how unsteady her legs felt until she had someone to keep her better balanced.

"It's multifaceted," Mr. Forkle told her, "so I think it might be best to take you somewhere that will help the advantages *and* consequences feel far more real than they ever will standing here, surrounded by sunshine and grazing animals."

"*Sunset,*" Grady corrected.

"Grady's right," Edaline said. "If this is going to be a long, drawn-out process, don't you think it would be best to wait until the morning?"

"I wondered the same thing before I made my way over," Mr. Forkle admitted. "But . . . I fear I may have already waited too long."

He turned to Sophie, offering her his right hand as his left hand held a crystal up to the light.

A *blue* crystal.

The kind that only led to the Forbidden Cities.

"Come with me, Miss Foster, if you think you might be ready," he said quietly.

"Ready for what?" Sophie asked as Sandor jumped in front of her and Dex tightened his hold on her arm.

"*You* may come with us," Mr. Forkle told Sandor, shuffling around him with an unexpected amount of agility. "*You* may not, Mr. Dizznee. This is a moment best kept between Miss Foster and me."

Dex raised his eyebrows at Sophie, clearly not sure if she wanted him to let go.

Sophie felt just as uncertain, since that meant it probably had nothing to do with where they'd just been.

"Ready for *what*?" she repeated.

Mr. Forkle stepped closer, offering his hand again. His eyes had never looked more ancient—or more desperate for her to listen to him—as he said, "Ready to face the truth behind one of your powers."

FIFTEEN

SOPHIE RECOGNIZED THE ELEGANT TUDOR manor with cut-glass windows and its vibrant green lawn even before the world had fully glittered back into focus. And the realization of where she was made her smile *and* feel like she'd had her legs kicked out from underneath her at the same time.

"This is my human family's house," she whispered, needing to say it out loud to make her brain accept it.

As that reality sank in, so did the icy panic. "Are they in danger?"

"They're perfectly safe," Mr. Forkle assured her, tightening his grip on her hand to stop her from sprinting up the driveway and tearing open the front door.

Sandor drew his sword anyway, sniffing the air as he scanned every tree, shrub, and shadow.

"You can relax," Mr. Forkle told him. "I've taken numerous precautions to ensure that our visit today poses no risk to Miss Foster's family—or to ourselves. Including bringing one of these." He removed an obscurer from his pocket. "What would the neighbors think if they saw a goblin warrior waving around a sword?" His smile faded as his eyes shifted back to Sophie. "After what happened with Vespera at Nightfall, I've made it a habit to check on your family every single day. Most of the time I simply observe them through a Spyball. But occasionally I'll hail your sister to ask a few questions or—"

"You do?" Sophie had to interrupt.

She couldn't decide if she was touched, nervous, or really, *really* jealous when he nodded.

"It's the best way to assess their situation," Mr. Forkle explained. "Though sometimes I'll also leap here to walk the grounds and search for signs of trouble—which I've never found any trace of, by the way. And none of that has anything to do with why I've brought you here. I simply wanted you to know that your human family is being *thoroughly* monitored and protected." His forehead creased with a much deeper kind of wrinkle than the lines caused by the ruckleberries. "I'm the one who dragged them into all of this without their knowledge or permission, so you have my word that I'll do everything in my power to ensure that nothing bad will ever happen to them again."

"Then why are we here?" Sophie asked.

Mr. Forkle turned his face toward the sun, which Sophie realized was still several hours away from setting.

Her brain had started to calculate what that meant as far as the relative time zones between where she lived at Havenfield and where they were—until he told her, "I brought you here to give you your missing memory back."

Sophie froze as something dark and buried—but never gone—stirred deep inside of her, and a pair of terrified green eyes flashed through her mind, along with a piercing scream.

Sophie, please—stop!

She stumbled back, crashing into a wall that was both lumpy and solid and somehow moving, not realizing it was Sandor until he spun her around, taking her shoulders and shaking her gently.

"Do you need us to get you back to Flori?" he asked, his voice even squeakier from the worry. "You've gone pale, like you do whenever the echoes are stirring."

"No," Sophie said, refusing to give the darkness that kind of control again.

She closed her eyes, imagining her mental strength as a glowing sphere, letting it grow bigger and bigger and bigger until she could shape it into something more useful. She chose a giant cartoon-size mallet, then pictured it pounding at the threads of black that were curling into a much-too-familiar clawed shape—*Bang! Bang! Bang!*—until the darkness was nothing more than a smear of shadow.

She washed away the last of the black by replaying her happiest memories.

Silveny nuzzling her tiny babies after they'd safely emerged from the makeshift hive.

Fitz twirling her around in his arms.

Dex hugging her without any awkwardness.

Keefe clinging to her hand, like she was the only thing holding him together.

Grady and Edaline telling her they loved her.

"Okay," she whispered. "It's under control now."

"I still think we should take you home and have you rest," Sandor said, turning to Mr. Forkle. "Surely you agree."

Mr. Forkle dragged his hands down his face. "I . . . should've thought to bring Flori. It slipped my mind, like so many things, now that there's only half of me. Though, honestly, this entire process seems determined to be fraught with challenges. I'll never understand why one failure seems so ready to chain itself to another and another. But that has been the case from the minute this memory became a part of our story. And each new trouble seems to outdo the others—though I suppose nothing has been worse than the moment at the hospital."

"You mean when my allergy nearly killed me?" Sophie clarified, pulling free of Sandor to prove she could stand on her own.

"Definitely not a moment I want to live again," Mr. Forkle whispered. "And yet, it may be unavoidable. . . ."

"Um, what does *that* mean?" Sophie asked, backing a step away, as if Mr. Forkle was about to lunge for her with a giant syringe full of limbium.

He cleared his throat several times, then straightened and smoothed his hair. "All will be fine, Miss Foster. One problem at a time."

"Okay, now I want to know what *that* means too," Sophie noted.

"As do I," Sandor agreed, positioning himself between Sophie and Mr. Forkle.

Mr. Forkle's laugh was mostly a wheeze. "I suppose I can't blame you for those reactions. But I assure you, this visit is entirely about returning Miss Foster's memory."

Sophie's head rang with another ghostly scream.

"There, see?" Sandor said as Sophie imagined another giant glowing mallet smashing the newest shadows to smithereens. "You're not up for this. We need to take you—"

"No," Sophie interrupted, stumbling away from everyone to get some fresh air.

She'd spent years trying to beg, bribe, trick, or steal back her missing memory—and then weeks running from it after she'd recovered that terrible piece.

But . . . not knowing didn't change anything.

Whatever had happened, *happened*, whether she remembered it or not.

Sophie, please—stop!

"I'll be fine," she said, taking slow, steady breaths as she closed her eyes and replayed more happy memories.

"I don't think you will be," Sandor said quietly. "At least wait until we're somewhere that Flori can help—"

"You are," a muffled voice told them as the ground parted by the nearest tree and Flori emerged from among the tangled roots. She shook the dirt and pebbles out of her plaited hair and sang a few soft lyrics to make the tunnel close behind her, each blade of grass falling perfectly back into place as if the hole had never been there.

"How did you—" Sophie started.

Flori flashed a green-toothed smile. "Nubiti and I have recently discovered that the language of the earth is connected to the language of everything that grows within it. I can't understand every word she says, but I can catch the basics, and it makes her able to reach me immediately—and the same is true when I need to reach her."

Mr. Forkle frowned.

Sophie could tell his mind was flooding with just as many questions as hers was. But he simply stomped twice and called, "Thank you," toward the ground, before he repeated the sentiment to Flori.

Flori nodded, already humming her healing song as she made her way to Sophie's side and took her hands, swaying back and forth. Sophie closed her eyes, unable to deny how much it helped to feel the soft sounds sinking under her skin like one of Elwin's balms. And when Flori was finished, she had to hug the tiny gnome.

"You did not need me this time," Flori whispered, trailing her fingers across Sophie's shoulders. "You're growing stronger and stronger with each brighter day. But I'm still happy to make your struggle easier, so you can save your energy for the larger battles."

Sophie squeezed her tighter, breathing in Flori's earthy scent, which reminded her so much of Calla that it made her heart both lighter *and* heavier. And when she'd soaked up every possible drop of strength, she let go and stood to face Mr. Forkle. "Okay. If you want to give me back my memory, I'm ready. But . . . I don't understand why you brought me here to do it."

He turned to the stately manor, his gaze centering on one of the upstairs windows. "You're not the only one who needs to have a memory returned."

"What?" Sophie raced in front of him, shaking her head so hard, it made her neck hurt. "*No.* We're not doing that. Amy doesn't . . ."

Her voice trailed off as her sister's screams flooded her mind.

Sophie, please—stop!

"No," she repeated as Flori started humming again.

Mr. Forkle wrung the edge of his cape. "How much have you remembered?"

"Not much," Sophie admitted. "Just that . . . I hurt Amy somehow. She was *begging* me to stop." Her voice cracked, and she turned away, wiping her eyes. "What did I do to her?"

"That is a question better shown, not told," Mr. Forkle said as he slowly stepped around her.

Sophie scrambled in front of him again. "Maybe it is—but you're only showing it to *me*. She doesn't need to know that."

He slipped by her again, his steps more determined. "She disagrees."

The words took a couple of seconds to sink in. "Wait. Amy knows about this?"

"Of course. We talked at length this morning. Mind you, I didn't give her any more specifics than I've given you. But I made it clear that it was a difficult moment for both of you, and that I thought it would be best if you faced those complicated truths together. And she agreed. She's far stronger than you're giving her credit for. She's . . ." His steps faltered for a beat, and his voice had thickened when he added, "She's something I never expected. I knew I'd be aiding your parents in the birth of one child, and that it was possible they might have children on their own afterward. But I'll admit, when your mother told me she'd gotten pregnant again, I was mostly concerned about how that would complicate things for you. Your differences from humans would be more noticeable with another child providing a constant direct comparison—and your sister had no problem teasing you as she got older, which sometimes posed a challenge, like it did in your lost memory. But . . . there was something so *special* about the bond you two formed. And that connection shouldn't be ignored, especially when you're facing a decision like this."

"And what decision is that?" Sophie demanded.

"One thing at a time," he told her. "First, we must give you all the facts."

"But—"

Loud barking cut her off.

They'd gotten close enough to the house for her family's beagle—Watson—to realize they were there and switch into guard-dog mode.

"It's fine," Mr. Forkle promised when Sophie, Sandor, and Flori all froze. "As I said, Amy knows we're coming. And in case you're wondering, I asked her to clear your parents from the property. She said she'd invent an urgent errand to send them away on."

That was probably better—the idea of facing her parents now that she'd been erased so thoroughly from their memories would be a special kind of misery.

And yet, the part of Sophie's heart that would never forget how it felt to have them tuck her in at night and kiss her cheeks and call her "Soybean" felt like it had been jabbed with a sharp pin at the missed opportunity. So she had to ask, "Why couldn't they be here? I thought seeing me can't trigger anything anymore, now that I'm . . . you know . . . gone."

"That's correct," Mr. Forkle told her, placing a hand on her shoulder. "But it would be very hard to explain why a strange adult male is at their house asking for alone time with their daughter and another young girl, don't you think?"

Sophie grimaced. "Yeah . . . They'd definitely call the police."

"As well they should," Mr. Forkle agreed. "And that's why we should stop stalling. I doubt your sister was able to buy us more than a couple of hours—and while returning the memory itself won't take long, you two will need time to process and discuss. So once again, I have to ask: Are you ready?"

He offered her his hand again, and Sophie reluctantly took it, letting him guide her the rest of the way up the path, to a short flight of stone steps that led to the front door.

Watson's barking grew more desperate, his paws scratching at the other side of the door, but Sophie was too busy taking in all the tiny unfamiliar details to care. The house had a new welcome mat since the last time she'd been there, the kind that said WIPE YOUR PAWS in big, bold letters, surrounded by doggy paw prints. And three pairs of beat-up sneakers were lined against the wall, along with a few pots of prickly succulents. But what really caught Sophie's eye were the wind chimes.

Dangling from the highest eave, the chimes were gleaming silver interspersed with strands of dangling crystals, and they were so sparkly and fancy, they looked like they belonged in the Lost Cities.

In fact . . .

"Are those leaping crystals?" Sophie had to ask.

"No, but they look like it, don't they?" Amy's familiar voice said behind her, and Sophie's heart wedged so hard in her throat, it nearly choked her as she turned toward the now open door and faced her younger sister.

Amy's smile was shy, her green eyes watery and darting between her feet and Watson, who she held tightly by his collar—though the beagle had gone *very* still now that he was facing a goblin warrior. "That's why I had Mom and Dad buy them," Amy added, swallowing hard as she shifted her gaze up to the chimes. "It seemed like there should be something around here to represent . . . everything. You know?"

Sophie nodded, her voice not working as she studied her sister more closely.

Amy's hair was longer and straighter, with a few soft layers framing her face. And her skin had picked up a whole bunch of freckles. Somehow the combination made her look so much older than Sophie wanted her to be and much too young for what they were there for, all at the same time.

She still couldn't find any words, so she threw her arms around Amy and pulled her into the tightest hug she could manage.

"I take it that means you've missed me?" Amy grunted out as Watson broke free from her hold and started thwapping Sophie with his wagging tail.

Sophie cleared her throat, realizing she needed to get herself together.

She was supposed to be the strong one—and she knew she should say something fun and teasing—keep the mood light given the heaviness they both had coming. But she blurted out, "I have to tell myself not to hail you every single day."

A shiver rocked Amy's shoulders, and her voice sounded choked as she whispered, "Me too."

They'd been ordered not to communicate unless it was an absolute emergency—part of the deal they'd struck with the Council in order for Amy to keep her memories of the Lost Cities.

And speaking of memories . . .

"You're sure you want to do this?" Sophie asked, pulling back to meet her sister's eyes—the first time they'd *really* faced each other since she'd gotten there. "Whatever happened between us that day, it . . . seems like it was pretty bad."

Amy chewed her lip and went back to staring at the wind chimes. "Bad like . . . what happened to Mom and Dad?"

"No," Mr. Forkle assured her. "What happened was an accident. Nothing more."

Amy nodded, shifting her focus back to Sophie. "Then I want to know. I want to know *everything*. The good *and* the bad. You're my sister, and . . . that's how it works with family."

She emphasized the last word, and it nearly undid Sophie.

A few tears leaked from her eyes, but she blinked hard to fight back the rest.

"You're really doing okay?" she whispered, tucking Amy's hair behind her ears. "It's not too hard, hiding everything you're hiding?"

Amy shrugged. "I mean . . . sometimes I wish I had some mallow-melt, but . . ."

"I'll bring you some," Sophie promised, not caring how many rules she'd have to break to make that happen.

"What about you?" Amy asked, studying Sophie like she was checking her for injuries. And somehow, even though Sophie's right hand showed no new scars, Amy's focus lingered there.

"Oh, you know how it goes," Sophie told her, forcing a smile. "Lots of near-death experiences. But nothing I can't handle."

Amy didn't look convinced. But she changed the subject. "How about the cute boys? Still trying to decide which one makes your heart flutter the hardest? I haven't changed my vote, by the way, in case you were wondering."

Mr. Forkle cleared his throat. "I realize you two have lots to catch up on. But now really isn't the time. I'm assuming your parents will be home soon."

Amy sighed. "I mean, I convinced them to go to the boring farmers market they always spend hours and hours at, since apparently looking at stalls of avocados and tomatoes and fresh-churned butter is super exciting when you get old. But I don't really know when they'll be back."

"Then we should get started," Mr. Forkle said gently, turning to Flori and asking her and Nubiti to keep watch for the parents' return.

Amy and Sophie shared a long look—and Amy seemed every bit as nervous as Sophie felt. But her determination was clear.

"We're doing this?" she asked Sophie.

Sophie fought the urge to tug on her eyelashes. "Yeah, I guess we are."

Amy nodded, taking Sophie's hand.

And they clung to each other as Amy opened the front door wider and they stepped aside to let Mr. Forkle take the lead.

SIXTEEN

I SHOULD WARN YOU THAT THIS PROCESS WILL be painful," Mr. Forkle said, his wheezy voice slicing through the silence of Amy's dim bedroom.

Sophie jolted off the bed, where she'd been lying beside her sister, attempting to relax. "Why? It didn't hurt when you gave my other memory back."

"Yes, but *that* moment didn't involve this level of pain," Mr. Forkle reminded her. "And I can't separate the visuals from the sensations that go with them. It all comes back together—though you'll only experience a shadow of what you endured the first time, since our brains have a way of filtering trauma to help us move past it. And the pain will fade once the memory settles into the correct place in your mental timeline and no longer feels *present*. But you both need to prepare yourselves for some intense discomfort. Especially you, Amy."

"Oh good," Amy mumbled. "You know, you left that part out when you explained this to me."

"Same," Sophie said, narrowing her eyes at Mr. Forkle.

Sandor added a goblin death glare from the doorway.

Mr. Forkle raised his hands, giving them all the universal *What?* gesture. "Does it change anything?"

Sophie and Sandor said "yes" at the same time that Amy said "no."

"Seriously?" Sophie asked her.

Amy looked just as stunned by Sophie's answer. "You really don't want your memory back anymore?"

"I didn't mean it changed anything for *me*," Sophie clarified, earning a snort of protest from Sandor. "*I* still need to know what happened. But you don't—and if it's going to cause intense pain, why would you put yourself through that?"

Amy sat up to face her, probably trying to look strong and confident as she told Sophie, "We've been over this already."

But the way she'd bent her legs crisscross-applesauce style made her look very, *very* young.

"Please, Amy," Sophie whispered. "Don't be so stubborn. Just let me go and—"

"No!" Amy caught Sophie's wrist before Sophie could grab her home crystal, throw open the curtains they'd drawn to make the room feel more private, and leap far, far away. "I can handle a few minutes of pain, Sophie."

"How do you know?" Sophie countered.

Amy shrugged. "I got through it the first time, didn't I?"

"Not necessarily," Sandor argued. "The Black Swan took this memory away for a reason."

"The pain had nothing to do with that," Mr. Forkle insisted. "Sparing you both the trauma was a *bonus*—not the necessity."

"And what was the 'necessity'?" Sandor demanded.

"That will be obvious once I return the memory," Mr. Forkle

told him, earning himself another vicious goblin glare.

"See?" Amy said to Sophie, as if they'd somehow solved everything.

Sophie shook her head, trying—and failing—to pull her wrist free from Amy's death grip. "I don't understand why you want to remember me hurting you."

"Because that part doesn't matter. It was an *accident*," Amy reminded her.

"Not completely." Fresh tears stung Sophie's eyes as she scraped together the words for her confession. "I've had one flashback from that moment, and . . . it was of you *begging* me to stop whatever I was doing. I'm assuming that means I had some control over what was happening."

"Wrong," Mr. Forkle told her. "It was . . . an unanticipated chain reaction."

"Yeah, well, that *chain reaction* had me make a six-year-old scream in pain," Sophie snapped back, twisting her arm a different way and wondering if her sister had figured out how to channel strength when she lived with the elves because seriously—*how was she so strong?* "Everyone realizes that, right? Amy was just a kid."

"So were you," Mr. Forkle noted. "You were a terrified nine-year-old with no idea what was going on or how to stop it. In fact, you *couldn't* stop it. So there was no *fault* in the situation. Just unfortunate happenstance that I wish I'd anticipated. Truthfully, if anyone's to blame, it's me for not being prepared or noticing what was going on until it was too late. So please stop taking that responsibility upon yourself, Miss Foster. You know the dangers that come with guilt."

Sophie winced as her mind flashed to an image of Alden's pale, lifeless face after his mind had shattered from his regrets over Prentice.

"You have *nothing* to feel guilty for," Mr. Forkle assured her. "And I need you to start believing that, otherwise we can't proceed any further—and you're going to need the information in this memory for the decision you have ahead."

"What decision?" Amy asked.

"One I can't explain yet," Mr. Forkle told her. "Not until your sister's in a proper position to make it."

"It's a new power, though, right?" Sophie guessed, surprised at how calmly she could ask the question.

But it was the only explanation that made any sense.

In fact . . .

"I'm assuming I manifested another freakish ability that day and used the power to hurt Amy," she admitted as the pieces of a nauseating theory snapped together. "So you and Livvy decided to reset my brain with limbium, and then discovered I was allergic to it and had to rush me to the hospital so the human doctors could save me. And then you took the memory away so I wouldn't know what I was capable of and so Amy wouldn't figure out that I wasn't human. And now you're going to make me relive it all so you can ask me to let you almost kill me again to turn that creepy ability back on."

Stunned silence followed the outburst. And Sophie tried to use that shock to finally pull her wrist free from her sister's death grip—but Amy held strong as she turned to Mr. Forkle and asked, "Is that what happened?"

"It's . . . on the right track," he admitted, causing Sophie's queasiness to level up. "But it's still wrong in several significant ways. So I urge you to keep an open mind, Miss Foster. I can tell that you think you already know what your decision will be once the choice is presented—but I assure you, it's not as simple as you're imagining—"

"Uh, it is if you're going to do something that could kill her," Amy interrupted, shaking Sophie's arm until Sophie looked at her. "You're not going to agree to that, are you?"

"She better not," Sandor growled.

"And *this* is why I'm giving your memories back," Mr. Forkle told them, "to avoid these kinds of hasty conclusions. For the record, no one will be asking anyone to put their life in serious danger, so can we please focus on what we're here for?"

Sophie studied his face, searching for some clue to what was coming, but the ruckleberries made him impossible to read.

"Fine," she said quietly. "But I still don't agree with you dragging Amy into this. Haven't we put her through enough?"

"*You* haven't put me through anything," Amy argued. "I mean it, Sophie. I'm never going to blame you for what happened."

"Even if that's true," Sophie mumbled, torn between wanting to believe her and knowing how impossible it would be for Amy to keep that promise, "I'm sure this will end up being your most vivid memory of me—and I hate that, since it's not like you have a lot of good ones to make up for it."

"Uh, are you kidding?" Amy asked. "I have *tons* of good memories! Why do you think I fought so hard to keep them? And I don't just mean the stuff in the Lost Cities—though the whole flying-with-an-alicorn thing is pretty hard to top. But there's also this." She pulled back the quilt on her bed, uncovering something white and fluffy.

"Is that Bun-Bun?" Sophie asked, feeling a tug in her chest when Amy held up the well-loved stuffed bunny.

Bun-Bun had been Amy's version of Ella ever since Amy was four years old, and Sophie couldn't believe her sister had been allowed to keep him through all the moves and identity changes. His shaggy fur wasn't as white as it used to be, and he looked matted in a few places—but that made him more perfect, since it proved he was the real, original stuffed animal.

"Do you know why Bun-Bun's my favorite?" Amy asked quietly, making his ears flop from side to side.

Sophie shrugged. "I figured you liked how soft he was."

"Well, I *do*. But the real reason is because of you." She held Bun-Bun closer to Sophie's face and squeezed his neck to tilt his head a little, pitching her voice higher and squeakier as she said, "Hey there, Miss Sophie. Who wants to play?"

And just like that, Sophie was seven years old again, making Bun-Bun talk to Amy the exact same way.

Amy cleared her throat, pulling Bun-Bun back and staring into his shiny black eyes. "I didn't say it enough, but . . . you were a good sister. Still are, even if we don't get to see each other. I always know you're out there, taking risks I wish you wouldn't take. Being Miss Superhero Elf."

"Ha, I'm *so* not a superhero," Sophie corrected, focusing on the joke so she wouldn't get all teary again.

"Please—you even wear a cape!" Amy teased back. Her smile faded just as fast, though. "Promise me you'll be careful, okay? Especially with whatever choice he's going to have you make."

Sophie choked down a lump in her throat. "Only if you promise that if your missing memory turns out to be more traumatic than you were expecting, you'll ask Mr. Forkle to erase it again."

"I'm not going to need that," Amy argued.

"Promise me anyway," Sophie pressed.

Amy rolled her eyes. "Fiiiiiiiiiiine. I promise. Ugh. So bossy."

They shared a smile—but it felt both happy *and* sad. And Amy broke eye contact first, shifting back to studying Bun-Bun.

"Remember the song you made up for him?" she asked. "And the little hoppy dance?"

"Please demonstrate both," Sandor jumped in. "Along with anything else that would make good blackmail."

"Another day," Mr. Forkle said, peeking through the curtains of the nearest window, probably checking for signs of Sophie's human parents. "We can't afford to waste any more time. Are you two finally ready?"

"I am," Amy said immediately.

Sophie chewed her lip, taking another look around Amy's bedroom.

Nothing made the gap between their lives feel wider.

The room wasn't small—but it was nothing like Sophie's enormous suite at Havenfield. And it wasn't plain, but the painted blue walls and scuffed wood floors definitely weren't the same as a glass ceiling strung with dangling crystal stars, or flowers woven into the carpet, or windows with sweeping ocean views. The twin bed looked like a shoebox compared to Sophie's sprawling canopied bed, and the closet could probably only fit about one tenth of Sophie's clothes and shoes.

And yet, Amy's room had all the tiny personal touches that Sophie was still struggling to add to hers.

The saddest part was, Sophie didn't recognize any of those additions.

Aside from Bun-Bun, all the stuffed animals and knickknacks were new. And the smiling friends in the photographs were all strangers. Sophie had also never heard of the boy band that Amy had *lots* of pictures and posters of on her door—though their hairstyles reminded her a little of Tam's.

And something about that distance between them made her whisper, "Please don't hate me for whatever happened that day, okay?"

Amy pulled her closer, offering her Bun-Bun to hug. "You don't have to worry about that, Sophie. I loved you even when I didn't remember who you were. I'd get this weird ache sometimes, right here." She pressed her fist against her chest. "I didn't know how to explain it, but it felt like . . . something was missing. And then you showed up and my memories triggered and it was like, 'Ohhhhhh, *this* is what I was looking for.' *That's* why I don't want any more gaps in my past. I just want to know my life is complete again, if that makes sense."

"It does," Mr. Forkle assured her, his voice a bit thick. "And it's a very *mature* reason for doing this."

Sophie knew why he was emphasizing the word—and hated him for having a point.

Amy wasn't the bratty little nine-year-old that Sophie had left behind when she moved to the Lost Cities. Nor was she the terrified six-year-old begging Sophie to stop whatever she was doing.

She was a girl who'd watched her parents get abducted and

managed to stay clearheaded enough to keep herself hidden from the Neverseen.

A girl who'd learned that everything she'd been told about her life—and the world—wasn't real, and then had to spend months hiding with strangers in a secret underwater city while she worried every day about the people she loved.

And now she was a girl who'd chosen to lie to *everyone* in order to keep the secrets she'd learned about her past and the Lost Cities.

If memories meant that much to her, she probably *could* handle this.

So Sophie took Bun-Bun and slowly lay down next to Amy on the narrow twin bed.

Amy lay back beside her, and Sophie wedged Bun-Bun between them.

"Are you ready?" Mr. Forkle asked, striding closer.

The sisters reached for each other, tangling their fingers together as they nodded.

Mr. Forkle clapped his hands. "Excellent. Then let's begin. Keep in mind that the memory will take a moment to register in your consciousness after I return it. And once it does, it will feel detached—as if you're watching something happening to someone else. Try not to think too much during that initial confusion, as it will only slow your mind from making its own connections—and once those connections form, the sensations will take over. I'd recommend locking your jaw so you don't bite your tongues when the pain hits. That part should pass within a few minutes. If it doesn't, I have sedatives—"

"No sedatives," Sophie interrupted.

"Yes, Miss Foster, I figured you'd say that. But I still wanted both of you to know that the option is available. And Flori is right outside if you feel the echoes stirring."

"Echoes?" Amy asked.

"Loooooooooooong story," Sophie told her.

"And now is not the time," Mr. Forkle noted. "Right now, I need you each to focus on taking slow, deep breaths, dragging each one out longer than the last."

Their breathing quickly fell in sync, and there was something so soothing about the steady rhythm of matched inhales and exhales.

"It's also important to note that some of your memories will feel very abstract," Mr. Forkle added quietly, "given the mental state you were in when they happened. And you'll still have gaps that you'll need me to fill in, since quite a lot occurred after I rendered you both unconscious. And while I'll do my best to answer your questions, please bear in mind that there are certain things I won't be able to explain—not because I'm holding anything back, but because there are parts that even I don't fully understand. In fact, I'm hoping the two of you might be able to provide some additional insights. We'll see soon enough. For now, keep breathing. Slooooooooow and steeeeeeaaaaady."

They'd each taken ten more breaths when he urged them to close their eyes and hold the next one. And when Sophie did as he asked, she felt his shaky fingers press against her temple.

"Here we go," he whispered. "Three . . . two . . . one."

The last word came with a rush of cold, like someone had poured a glass of ice water into her brain, and Sophie clamped her jaw shut to keep her teeth from chattering.

The chills numbed her thoughts, leaving her head quieter than it had ever been before, and she soaked up the silence, loving every second—right up until the noise took over.

It felt like someone clicked on a movie projector at full speed and full volume. And the images were too jumpy to make any sense.

But each new breath brought more focus, until Sophie could recognize two little girls—one blond and one brunette—surrounded by murky green.

They started out talking. But talking shifted to teasing. And teasing turned to taunting as the voices grew louder and louder.

Angrier and angrier.

Sophie couldn't make out any of the individual words.

But she could feel them cutting deeper and deeper.

Sinking into sensitive places.

Raw places.

Dangerous places.

Poking and prodding and pulsing.

Exposing powerful new nerves that sent tingles rocketing through her.

Her hands burned—fingertips humming with a strange, itchy energy.

And her head . . .

There was So. Much. Pressure.

Too much.

It boiled and bubbled inside her skull, growing darker and darker and darker—and Sophie gasped as her consciousness dropped fully into the moment, the sensations completely taking over.

Her stomach twisted.

Limbs thrashed.

Brain churning churning churning with emotions so intense, it felt like they were tearing and scratching and shredding—and maybe they were, because something deep inside her mind seemed to unravel, leaving . . . an opening.

A new pathway.

And the darkness surged forward.

Turning hotter.

Wilder.

She felt herself cry out at the same moment she did in the memory as her fury shifted from black to red and poured out of her mind.

Aimed at a single target.

Sophie, please—stop!

Amy's screams clawed through Sophie's ears, and she couldn't tell if they were from memory or reality. The lines between both had blurred, and she was caught up in the frenzy.

Beyond her body.

Beyond the world.

Nothing but pure, unbridled force.

Powerful.

Unstoppable.

"*Sophie!*"

The new voice demanded attention—familiar in some ways, and unexpected in others. And with that thought, Sophie felt her mind divide.

Part of her clung to the girl she *is*.

The rest stayed trapped with the girl she used to be.

And each "Sophie" was frightened and fearless and furious.

But Present-Sophie felt clearer. She could recognize the desperation in Mr. Forkle's voice as he called her name over and over and over, and she knew she needed to listen.

Past-Sophie heard nothing but a ghost in the darkness.

His pleas were lost.

She was lost.

Buried under her newfound power that was consuming everything it touched.

She didn't recognize the warm pressure in her palms for what it was.

But Present-Sophie did, and she knew that Mr. Forkle was clinging to her. She heard him gasp as the tingly warmth bled between their skin, his grip tightening and his voice gaining a newfound strength.

Sophie, STOP!

His command was loud enough to reach even Past-Sophie—but she didn't know how to obey.

STOP! he repeated, filling her mind with happy thoughts.

The red rage quickly burned those away.

STOP!

STOP!

STOP!

I can't! she tried to tell him, but the words were there and gone much too fast.

Heat tingled in her palms again, and the next time Mr. Forkle spoke, his voice was laced with joy.

And hope.

And happiness.

And love.

Each emotion flooded her mind with warmth and light, melting away the black and the red until there was nothing but soft golden shimmer, like a perfect sunrise.

An awakening.

Past-Sophie was too tired to face it—and didn't resist the sticky sweetness that trickled across her tongue.

Present-Sophie gagged from the memory of the cloying sedative that Mr. Forkle must have given her.

And as Past-Sophie happily floated into the fuzziness, too weary to wonder what she'd done, Present-Sophie knew there *would* be consequences.

Sophie clung to the word, and the thought triggered a surprising ripple of information as the two parts of herself tangled back into one and the memory tucked itself away—buried under all of that unexpected truth.

Everything she'd seen and felt and learned was now solidly in her *past*.

But new questions stretched into her future as Sophie's mind translated the vague, blurry feelings and pieced together what had actually happened.

She'd inflicted on her sister that day—lost control during a fight and unleashed a tempest of pain.

But that wasn't the discovery that left her shivering and shaking.

No, she was trembling because Mr. Forkle hadn't been able to call her out of the frenzy until he'd touched her hands.

Then she'd *enhanced* him.

And he'd *inflicted* on her.

SEVENTEEN

OU."

It was the only word that Sophie could pull from the pounding chaos in her brain.

A question.

An accusation.

A revelation.

"Yes," Mr. Forkle told her, his voice raspy, as if he'd been shouting in the present—not just in the past.

There was another sound too, one that made Sophie want to slap herself when she recognized it, because where were her priorities?

"Amy?" she asked, swaying from a head rush as she pulled herself upright.

It took a few seconds for her eyes to focus—and then there was her sister, curled into a tight ball, rocking back and forth as whimpers rattled out of her.

Her face was pinched.

Forehead sweaty.

Skin a troubling greenish-gray.

"She'll be fine in another minute or two," Mr. Forkle promised, which sounded more impossible with each pained noise that Amy made. "Truly, Miss Foster. Her memory of what happened simply runs longer than yours, since I sedated you first that day, in order to ensure that you couldn't lose control again. And your sister also regained consciousness very briefly after Livvy arrived to help, so she has those extra moments to relive as well. But her mind should settle right . . . about . . . *now*. See?"

Amy's body stilled and her moans fell silent—but she still looked far too ill for Sophie to be impressed.

Sophie choked down the bile coating her throat, though the sourness remained when her sister didn't move. "Is she unconscious?"

"She's somewhere between awake and asleep, finding her path back to reality." Mr. Forkle pressed two fingers onto each of Amy's temples and closed his eyes, nodding at whatever he saw inside her head. "These kinds of things take longer for humans to process. But don't worry—she's past the pain. Her mind's simply struggling to understand that the sedative it thinks it's feeling was actually in her system years ago and wasn't something she took today—though I wonder if it'd be easier to give her some now and let her rest. She looks more exhausted than I'd hoped."

"That's what happens when you help someone relive being tortured," Sophie muttered. "But . . . I don't think we should sedate her unless she asks us to. I'm sure my—*her*—parents will freak if she doesn't wake up when they come home."

"I suppose that makes sense," Mr. Forkle agreed, moving one of his hands to Amy's wrist to feel her pulse. He counted under his breath and nodded. "Actually, her vitals are bouncing back nicely. She should be lucid in the next few minutes. And there's still no sign of her family returning?" he asked Sandor, who'd marched over to one of the windows to check through the curtains.

"Flori has signaled that we're clear—for the moment," Sandor informed him, stomping back to his post in the doorway. "But the sooner we leave, the better."

"Agreed," Mr. Forkle said.

"We're not going anywhere until Amy wakes up and we make sure she's okay and answer her questions," Sophie reminded them.

"That's the *plan*," Mr. Forkle corrected, "but we'll have to adjust if her parents return—which is why I tried to start this process as soon as we got here."

"Excuse me for trying to save my sister from *this*." She pointed to Amy, whose eyes were squeezed so tight, they looked like angry lines.

Sophie reached out, brushing back strands of Amy's sweat-soaked hair off of her forehead and tucking them behind her ears—stalling as she worked up the courage to ask, "How badly did I hurt her that day? My memory . . . wasn't exactly clear."

"No, it wasn't," Mr. Forkle said quietly. "All the more reason you can't blame yourself for what happened. You had no idea what was going on."

"I didn't," Sophie agreed, stopping herself from mentioning all the things she *did* know, now that she had the advantage of hindsight to translate what had happened between her and him.

She had *lots* of questions.

Maybe even a few accusations.

But she wasn't going to let him sidetrack her.

"You didn't answer my question. How badly did I hurt her that day?"

Mr. Forkle checked Amy's thoughts again before he answered.

"Inflicting is all in the mind, so she suffered zero physical trauma. Why do you think I didn't bother bringing Elwin or Livvy with us today?"

Sophie had a feeling that Elwin and Livvy would strongly disagree with that decision—and Sophie wasn't sold on it either, given the greenish pallor lingering on her sister's skin.

But once again, Mr. Forkle was changing the subject.

"We both know the pain is just as real as an actual injury," Sophie insisted. "Probably worse."

Mr. Forkle sighed. "It can be, yes. And I won't lie, what your sister experienced that day—and again now, to a smaller extent—was . . . let's just call it indescribable, and leave it at that, okay?"

Sophie brushed back another strand of her sister's sticky hair.

Didn't she owe it to her to learn every detail about what Amy had endured?

"Sometimes knowledge is simply knowledge," Mr. Forkle said, guessing what she'd been wondering. "My brother and I shared every single memory throughout our entire lives—except one. He held back the details of the pain he experienced from his final injury, and I'm sure he did that because he knew I would've relived it over and over, trying to make amends for the fact that I get to carry on and he doesn't. So he eliminated that as a possibility for me. And from what I know of your sister, I've no doubt that she'd want the same for you—just as you would for her if the situation were reversed."

"Maybe," Sophie admitted, blinking hard to keep any tears from forming. "It's just . . . I can still hear her screams."

"And I'm sure you always will," he said quietly. "But . . . I think we should also acknowledge the fact that you just mentioned them without needing Flori to sing your echoes to sleep. That's a *tre-mendous* victory, Miss Foster. One that's not worth jeopardizing—especially for knowledge that will do no actual good."

Sophie sighed. "I guess—unless Amy needs to talk about what happened. If she does, I'll let her share every awful detail."

She didn't care if it brought the shadow monster back in full force—she'd do whatever Amy needed to help her recover from this nightmare.

"Fair enough," Mr. Forkle told her. "Though, I think you're also overlooking a very important aspect of what happened. Your sister's screams came from more than just pain. She was also witnessing something her brain couldn't begin to comprehend—and she was terrified that the red light was killing you."

Sophie frowned. "Red light?"

He nodded. "Your inflicting operated very differently that day. It worked the way we designed it to—or mostly, anyway—and the emotions were channeled out of your mind in a single, targeted red beam that flashed and struck like a bolt of lightning."

Sophie tried to picture it, but the only thing she could come up with was some cross between an alien mind trick and an exorcism—and she *really* didn't want to imagine herself that way.

And once again, her head flooded with questions about what had actually happened between Mr. Forkle and her during those terrible moments.

But she had to stay focused on the most important information.

"That's the big *choice*, isn't it?" she asked. "You want to reset my brain so my inflicting will work differently."

"So it will work *properly*," Mr. Forkle corrected, which wasn't any less terrifying. "Your ability was designed to target whoever or whatever you were feeling threatened by, rather than taking out everyone in the vicinity the way you do now. That would make the power much more effective, don't you think?"

"I suppose," Sophie said slowly. "But what happened to the whole 'no one will be asking anyone to put their life in serious danger' promise you made earlier?"

"I was about to remind him of the same thing," Sandor growled.

"I said *serious* danger," Mr. Forkle argued. "This time the procedure will be much more minor. We don't have to reset Miss Foster's *entire* brain, like Livvy did to her that day—or like I did the day I healed her abilities. We only need to reset her inflicting, which will require a significantly smaller dose of limbium."

"Okay, *but* . . . I'm still deathly allergic to it, even in a small dose," Sophie pointed out, surprised she even had to say it. "The elixir Dex gave me only had a drop in it, and it still made Bullhorn lie down beside me, and Elwin was barely able to bring me back."

"I'm not saying there won't be risks," Mr. Forkle said carefully. "But the risks will still be less dangerous this time than your previous experiences, both because of the much more limited problem we're addressing and because of our increased knowledge and practice. Livvy and I have been researching allergies for months, wanting to be prepared in case this day was ever upon us. And I feel very strongly that we've now perfected our remedy."

"Does that mean you won't have to use any needles?" Sophie asked.

"I wish." He reached for her hand, peeling back the fabric of her glove until he'd exposed the star-shaped scar he'd accidentally given her when he'd healed her abilities. "This time I know to administer the injection into your leg, so I shouldn't leave another mark like this. But . . . it still needs to be an injection. That's the fastest delivery method, and with allergies, every second counts."

Sophie wished she could argue.

But she'd felt how close it came the other times when they'd triggered her allergy.

There was zero margin for error.

"I'll have Elwin and Livvy with me for any emergencies," Mr. Forkle promised, pulling her glove back into place and releasing her hand. "And I think it might be wise to have Mr. Sencen and Mr. Vacker there as well, since they both have ways of keeping your mind and emotions steady and focused. And if there's someone else you'd like to have there—like perhaps your parents?—that can be arranged. But know this: No matter what, I *will* keep you safe. That's my job."

"No, that's *my* job," Sandor corrected. "And if you think I'm going to let you—"

"It's *Miss Foster's* decision," Mr. Forkle interrupted.

Sophie snorted. "Right. Just like it was my decision the day you reset my abilities. I could either stay *malfunctioning*, or risk my life to fix everything—and bonus: It was the only way I'd be able to heal Prentice and Alden. That's not much of a choice, is it?"

"It *is*," Mr. Forkle insisted. "And this time it's even more so. You've managed just fine with the way your inflicting currently operates."

"Have I?" Sophie asked, thinking of all the times her vision had cleared to reveal her friends writhing in pain or unconscious around her.

The Neverseen had even started counting on it when they planned their ambushes, letting her take out her bodyguards for them—although that raised another question.

"Is the ability even worth it?" she asked, her voice almost a whisper. "The Neverseen always wear those caps to block me."

"Actually, that would be one of the biggest advantages to resetting your ability," Mr. Forkle corrected. "The red beam is designed to target the heart, not the head. The Neverseen would have no way to shield themselves from that kind of attack, and the blow would be infinitely stronger because the emotions are so much rawer and more vulnerable there."

Sophie sighed.

That *would* be a significant improvement from what she could currently do.

"I'm sorry," Mr. Forkle said, clearing his throat. "I realize this is probably the last thing you feel like enduring. I haven't forgotten how much you've already been through. It's also my fault. What Livvy and I did to reset your brain clearly went awry."

"Clearly," Sophie muttered, "considering I almost died."

"Yes, you did. I still have nightmares about it sometimes." He stared at his hands, wringing his fingers back and forth. "It was *me* with you that day, in case you were wondering. Not my twin brother. It's why I was chosen to be the one to reset your abilities the second time—everyone felt I had 'experience' with the situation—though truthfully, both times I've never felt so out of my depth or terrified in all of my life." He cleared his throat again. "That first time, when I heard the screaming and saw what was happening, I hailed Livvy for help immediately. Then I carried you and your sister into my house, hoping no one else in the neighborhood had noticed anything. By the time Livvy got there, I'd already erased both of your memories—but of course, I had to erase another from your sister when her sedative wore off not long after Livvy's arrival. I hadn't wanted to overdo how much I gave her, considering she was so small and had just been through such an exhausting trauma. But I clearly underestimated—the first of many mistakes I made that day."

"I'm assuming the second mistake was when you gave me limbium?" Sophie guessed.

"Actually, that was the third. The second was before Livvy came up with the idea of limbium. I grew impatient and gave you a half dozen other medicines I thought might help, and ended up making you vomit all over yourself."

Sophie cringed. "This just keeps getting better and better."

"That was my thought too. And then we gave you the limbium, and I got to discover exactly how dire things could truly get. You started making a horrible sound as your airway closed off, unlike anything I'd ever heard before, and then your whole body was convulsing and I just . . . froze. If Livvy hadn't been there, I don't know what would've happened. I might've lost you. She was the one who kept you breathing and suggested we rush you to the nearest human hospital. Her reasoning was flawed—though we didn't know it at the time. She suspected our treatments were negatively reacting with some human toxin or virus that you'd been exposed to, which sounded logical enough. And it got you to the place that saved your life, which was all that mattered. Then Livvy had to go, so no one could wonder who she was or how she knew you, and your human parents arrived, and I just sat there, watching you hooked up to those horrible machines, hoping nothing irreparable had happened. And when you woke up . . ."

His voice choked off, and he dragged a hand down his face, lingering on his eyes.

She couldn't tell if that meant he was crying.

Part of her was glad she couldn't tell—her world made so much more sense when Mr. Forkle was a strong, reliable presence, even if his stubbornness drove her crazy at times.

"When you woke up," Mr. Forkle continued, his voice steadier this time, "it felt like one of those 'miracles' that humans are always going on about. You were *you*. Your inflicting had been switched back off, and everything else seemed fine. And you and your sister both had no idea what had happened between you."

"Wait," Sophie had to interrupt. "Aren't you always saying that abilities can't be switched off once they've been triggered?"

"For ordinary elves, yes," Mr. Forkle agreed.

Sophie groaned, knowing this was going to lead to another "let me explain how very weird you are" speech.

And sure enough, he told her, "In your case, I made your genes slightly more flexible in certain ways. That way, if something we'd planned needed adjusting, we'd have the option of doing so— which has been both an advantage and a disadvantage. I often wonder if that flexibility is the reason we've had to reset things in your mind."

He tilted his head and sighed in a way that seemed to say, *It's so challenging experimenting on someone.* Which definitely helped Sophie choke back any fuzzy feelings she might've been fighting when she'd thought he was crying.

"Anyway," Mr. Forkle said, moving the conversation back to what they'd been discussing. "I swore I would be a thousand times more vigilant from that moment on to ensure that nothing like that ever happened to you again, and yet, somehow I still managed to misunderstand the role that the limbium had played in your allergy until it happened again. And I didn't anticipate any problems when I triggered your inflicting, either. So imagine my horror when I heard Mr. Dizznee's account of how your inflicting had operated in Paris and realized our enhancements to the ability had somehow been switched off. I'd hoped the problem was connected to all of the other glitches you were experiencing during that same time, and that once I reset your abilities, all would go back to the way we originally designed it. But it didn't recover as well as your other abilities. And now, here we are."

"Okaaaaaaay," she said, trying not to drown in that deluge of information. She had a feeling she'd be wading through it for weeks and weeks to come. But at the moment she had one very important question. "Why would resetting the ability again change anything? We already know it didn't help—"

"It's not an exact science," Mr. Forkle interrupted. "Nor does the limbium affect everything evenly. I was so focused on your telepathy that day—and the gaps in your mental blocking—that I didn't give your inflicting the care that it needed. I also failed to realize that your inflicting was working incorrectly even before you faded, and therefore needed a much more fundamental adjustment. This time the ability would be my entire focus, and I'd target it differently."

"But you still can't guarantee that it will work, right?" Sophie pressed.

"There are no guarantees with any of this," Mr. Forkle reminded her. "It's all theoretical until we implement the treatments and see what happens."

"Great. So . . . basically, you're asking me to trust you with my life—*again*—while also admitting that you don't *actually* know what you're doing," Sophie had to point out. "Awesome."

"I don't blame you for feeling that way, but—"

"Good, because it's true!" Sophie jumped in. "I'm pretty sure I'd be better off—"

Her snarky comment was interrupted by a soft moan from her sister, who uncurled her legs and rolled onto her back.

"Amy?" Sophie asked, cringing as her sister opened her eyes and Sophie saw how red and puffy they looked.

Amy's voice sounded like bits of crumbling gravel as she whispered, "Sophie? You're still here?"

"Of course I am. Where else would I be?" She offered Amy the bottle of Youth that Mr. Forkle had just handed her and helped Amy sit up for a drink.

"I don't know," Amy admitted after downing half the bottle. "I guess I thought . . ." She looked away, tears streaming down her cheeks. "Those things I said to you—"

"I don't even remember them," Sophie assured her. "Seriously. In the memory it was just a bunch of noise. I couldn't separate out the words—and I don't want to know," she added when Amy opened her mouth, like she was going to repeat everything. "Whatever you said doesn't matter—unless *you* need to talk about it," she added, remembering her earlier vow.

Amy pulled her knees into her chest, wrapping her shaky arms around them. "I'm just so sorry, Sophie. I can't believe what a brat I was."

"Um, you were six," Sophie reminded her. "I'm pretty sure everyone's a brat when they're six."

"Yeah, well that still doesn't excuse what I said," Amy mumbled.

"And what you said doesn't justify my reaction," Sophie argued. "*Nothing* justifies what I did to you."

"It's not *what you did*," Mr. Forkle corrected. "It's *what happened*. You need to start making that distinction. Inflicting is an incredibly volatile ability. And it manifested for you very young and very suddenly, in the midst of a situation where tempers were already running too high—*and* you had no knowledge of what was happening to you. *Anyone* would've lost control under those circumstances."

"I guess you would know," Sophie noted, finally calling out the huge revelation she didn't know what to do with.

Honestly, she didn't *want* to know what to do with it, because it was surely going to lead to other conversations she didn't have the energy for.

But she *had* to ask, "Why didn't you tell me you're an Inflictor?"

Amy and Sandor both drew in sharp breaths.

"I'm not," Mr. Forkle said quietly as he stood and paced to the other side of the room.

"I know what I felt," Sophie argued. "Inflicting's the only way you could've flooded my mind with emotions like that."

"It is," Mr. Forkle agreed, squinting at Amy's photographs.

"It wasn't regular inflicting either," Sophie pressed. "You sent me positive emotions. Even Bronte can't do that."

She winced at the name, deciding to save the questions that went with it for later.

"That doesn't make me an Inflictor," Mr. Forkle insisted.

"I'm fairly certain that it does," Sandor noted.

"Yeah, isn't that how talents work for you guys?" Amy asked. "If you can do the thing, that means you have the ability? If you can't, you don't?"

"Not in this case." Mr. Forkle turned to the room's largest window, parting the curtains and scanning the yard. "All I have is a handful of dormant Inflictor genes, which I wasn't ever supposed to be able to use. They were simply part of a test."

"A test," Sophie repeated, not sure why the word made her stomach feel so squirmy until she realized, "You're talking about Project Moonlark."

"I am." Mr. Forkle turned back to face her. "Despite our abundance of research, much of our genetic work was purely theoretical—and I wasn't about to implement those theories on an innocent child and risk that something could go seriously wrong—even with the flexibility we were designing. Every tweak planned for your genes had to be properly vetted before I allowed it to be added to your genetic code. And since I wasn't willing to risk anyone else's safety, it meant playing the role of test subject myself. My brother and I split it up—he tested your Polyglot genes and I tested your inflicting. That way we could examine the effects in isolation."

"What about her teleporting?" Amy asked. "And that other one—what's it called again?"

"Enhancing," Mr. Forkle said, beating Sophie to it. "Both of those abilities were 'unplanned side effects' of our other genetic modifications, so we weren't aware that we needed to test them. In fact, we didn't know about the teleporting until Miss Foster discovered it while trying to escape the Neverseen's attempt to capture Silveny. And the enhancing I discovered during this incident."

"Because it triggered the same time as my inflicting," Sophie guessed.

Mr. Forkle's smile was equal parts impressed and reserved. "I'd wondered if you would notice that part of the memory, with all the other chaos happening."

"I did," Sophie told him. "And I'm assuming it had something to do with your inflicting, since you were only able to do that after you touched my hands."

"That's my assumption as well—and it was definitely a surprise, in case you're wondering, as well as a true testament to the strength of your enhancing ability, considering the ridiculously insignificant amount of Inflictor DNA that's a part of me." He lifted the hem of his tunic to reveal a palm-size round blotch on his hip where the skin was so pale, it almost looked translucent. And when the light hit the patch, his skin shimmered with tiny flashes in every color of the spectrum.

Amy gasped. "Did that hurt?"

"Of course," Mr. Forkle told her, lowering his shirt back into place. "Definitely one of the top ten most painful things I've ever experienced. But that was a price I was willing to pay in order to guarantee that everything we were planning for your sister would be both safe and effective." His eyes shifted to Sophie. "I know you're frustrated by the guesswork that sometimes comes into play with your abilities, and I wish I knew a way to eliminate that completely. Someday we'll hopefully get there. In the meantime, I hope this at least proves how far we're willing to go to ensure your safety."

It did and it didn't.

Whatever he'd done to himself—whatever risks he'd taken—still hadn't spared her from staring down another 'this could kill you' decision.

"I don't understand," she said, sticking with a safer answer for the moment. "How can your DNA be different right there?"

"The same way that someone's DNA can be different in a place where they've been exposed to intense radiation," Mr. Forkle explained.

Amy sucked in a breath. "But radiation like that would kill you."

"It would," Mr. Forkle agreed. "Or, at the very least, it would certainly make me very, very sick. Which is why our team had to devise a much safer method for our tests. Calla was the one to realize that light was the answer, but we needed something stronger than any of the Sources on their own—or even any of the Sources combined. Something *elemental*."

"You used quintessence," Sophie realized, shivering as her palms remembered the burns she'd suffered after she'd accidentally bottled some of the fifth element during a school assignment. "Wait—does that mean the DNA in my hands—"

"No," Mr. Forkle cut in. "Those burns were from exposure to the extreme cold of Elementine—not exposure to the quintessence itself. I also had to prepare a sample of my altered DNA and apply it to my skin *before* we added the quintessence, in order for the exposure to have any lasting effect on my genetics. Plus,

Elementine is far too aggressive to be used for that kind of a delicate task. The fusion only succeeded when we used the quintessence from Phosforien."

"Uh, there are different kinds of quintessence?" Sophie asked, trying to linger on the part of his explanation that didn't sound like something straight out of a sci-fi/horror movie.

"Of course. Each of the unmapped stars generates a different variation. I thought you knew that." Mr. Forkle frowned when she shook her head. "Why else would the locations of those five stars be kept secret? The quintessence from Elementine is the least stable, but also the most powerful, which makes it extremely valuable for creating substances that need to be somewhat explosive or all-consuming—like frissyn. The quintessence from Marquiseire is incredibly abrasive, which makes it the best choice when something needs to be broken down on a cellular level—and yet its abundance of shimmer also makes it reflective, which allows it to be the most versatile of all the iterations of the fifth element. I guarantee we've only scratched the surface of Marquiseire's many uses. The quintessence from Lucilliant is the coldest and the darkest, but also the most balanced, which makes it particularly valuable when something needs to be preserved. The quintessence from Candesia is the weakest—almost smoky and sluggish in nature—but it's also the safest form to turn to, and best for subtle shifts and changes. And Phosforien is the most colorful and vibrant—full of life and energy—which is what made it optimal for our DNA tests."

He lifted his tunic again, and the flash of colors did remind Sophie of the neon glow she remembered Phosforien having.

"Didn't you notice how varied each of the leaps were when

we sent you and Mr. Sencen on that rather convoluted journey?" Mr. Forkle asked. "When we were trying to isolate how the Never-seen kept tracking you?"

"I did. But I thought those jars were just *light*," Sophie admitted. "Well, four of them, at least. I thought quintessence only came from Elementine."

His frown deepened. "Strange. I planted details about all of this into your mind years ago—the same time I gave you the location of the unmapped stars and the formula for frissyn. Odd that it didn't trigger with everything else—and it's even weirder that it's not triggering right now, given that we're actively discussing it."

"Great," Sophie mumbled, slumping down on the bed. "Another way I'm malfunctioning."

"Any error for this would be on my part, not yours," Mr. Forkle assured her. "There's no perfect method for implanting memories into someone else's mind—and I was very concerned about the information triggering too early, especially since I knew you'd be exposed to so many human teachings during your schooling and I wasn't familiar enough with their curriculum to know what words to avoid. I must've hidden certain things too well."

Amy scooted closer and gave Sophie's hand a gentle squeeze. "You okay?"

"Oh sure." Sophie couldn't tell if the tightness in her chest was from tears she was holding back—or laughter. "Just another typical day in my life as the moonlark. It's always an adventure—and apparently I'm not the only one here who knows what it's like to be an experiment."

"You're not," Mr. Forkle agreed, absently rubbing his hip.

And Sophie wanted to keep sulking—but there were still too many important things to discuss. So she forced herself to straighten up and ask, "Does that mean if I enhanced you right now, you'd be able to inflict again?"

"I highly doubt it. As you probably noticed in your memory, the ability only activated for me when I kept failing to get through to you. So I'm assuming adrenaline and desperation were factors. Plus . . ."

"Plus . . . ?" Sophie prompted when he didn't finish the sentence.

"Well," he said, turning back to the window. "This is my own personal theory, so take it with a grain of salt—as humans love to say. But I've long been curious about whether your enhancing was also affected by everything that happened to your abilities that day. It's hard to know, since we didn't make any of our own tweaks to the power—and it works perfectly well as it is. It's just that . . . it must've taken a *tremendous* amount of strength to temporarily trigger an ability hidden in such an insanely small percentage of my DNA. And I can't help wondering if that means you actually have more to give, and that this new reset—*if* you choose to do it—will boost your enhancing back up to that level."

"*New reset,*" Amy repeated, tugging on Sophie's arm to make Sophie look at her. "I think I missed that part when I was still recovering from the memory. Is that as dangerous as it sounds?"

"It's worse," Sandor told her, with a glare at Mr. Forkle to make it clear he was still bitter about the way his objections had been silenced earlier.

"Then you're not going to do it, are you?" Amy asked.

"I don't really have a choice," Sophie admitted. "If I don't let them reset me, I'm stuck with a broken ability—or *two* broken abilities, apparently."

"The enhancing is only a theory," Mr. Forkle reminded her. "And neither ability is *broken*."

"Right. They just don't do what they're supposed to do," Sophie argued as a dark laugh bubbled out of her chest. She turned back to her sister. "Remember Dad's blue car? The one that was in the shop so much, he called it his Lemonmobile? That's . . . me. Everyone loves to tease me about how often I end up in the Healing Center— and *some* of that is the Neverseen's doing. But I swear the rest comes from the fact that I'm basically defective."

"No, you're *not!*" Mr. Forkle snapped, stalking closer with such intensity that Sophie shrank back, leaning on her sister. "I understand your frustrations, Miss Foster. And I'm not going to tell you how to feel. But I hope you also remember at least *some* of the incredible things that you—and only you—are able to do, as well as the tremendous things you've accomplished because of those powers. I realize it's not easy being one of a kind. I also understand how natural it is to fixate on the negative, particularly in a moment like this, when you're facing another complication. And I won't deny that we've run into unexpected challenges. But none of that makes you *defective*. You . . . are my greatest success." He stepped closer, reaching for her hands. "Never lose sight of how special you are, Sophie. You're unique in a way that no one else ever can or will be—and only part of that comes from our experiments, by the way. The rest comes from *you*. From the bright, brave, brilliant girl you naturally are. And I hope you know that as far as all of us involved with your creation are concerned, you exceed our expectations every single day."

The words were some of the most wonderful things that anyone had ever said to Sophie.

But for some reason, they only threw kindling on her anger.

Maybe she was tired and frustrated and sick of being manipulated.

Or maybe she just needed answers.

Either way, she finally snapped back with the question she'd been avoiding. "Does that include Councillor Bronte?"

Mr. Forkle frowned. "What do you mean?"

"The people involved with my creation," Sophie clarified. "That includes Bronte, right?"

"Why would it?" Mr. Forkle asked.

Sophie rolled her eyes. "You're really going to make me say it?" When he stayed silent, she sat up straighter, holding his stare as she said, "Fine. I know Bronte has to be my biological father."

Amy sucked in a breath. "He's the pointy-eared guy we rode the alicorns with, right? The one who let me keep my memories?"

Sophie nodded, not taking her eyes off Mr. Forkle, whose expression was as inscrutable as ever.

"Well?" she prompted. "Anything you have to say to that?"

He cleared his throat. "I suppose I should've realized you'd jump to that conclusion, given the rarity of his ability. And I won't deny that I studied his DNA as I developed the tweaks I made to your inflicting. But that's the full extent of his involvement in Project Moonlark—and he has no idea he was even a source of inspiration. I gathered the sample of his DNA without his permission and conducted all of my research without his knowledge."

"And I'm just supposed to believe that?" Sophie argued.

"I would hope so, since it's the truth." He looked away, shaking his head. "You've also met Bronte—and seen how he treated you and our order. Can you honestly see him agreeing to be a part of Project Moonlark?"

"I don't know—that could've been his way of trying to cover up his involvement," Sophie countered.

Mr. Forkle sighed and reached up to rub his temples. "It wasn't. And I'm only going to say this one more time, Miss Foster: Councillor Bronte is *not* your biological father. So I need you to put that thought out of your mind—and call off any investigations you and your friends might be making into it—before you start rumors that could cause a nightmare of drama and headaches."

"If you don't want us investigating, you should tell me who my genetic parents are," Sophie told him. "That's the only way it stops."

"I've told you—I can't do that."

"Why not?" Amy asked when Sophie didn't bother.

"I can't tell you that, either," Mr. Forkle said, and Sophie mouthed his answer along with him, nailing the words *and* his inflection. "I *can't*," he added, when he noticed Sophie's mimicry.

"Maybe not," Sophie said quietly. "But I can't let it go, either. And . . . I can't trust someone who's hiding things from me."

"I'm hiding them for good reason," Mr. Forkle assured her.

"Even if that's true," Sophie told him, "you're also asking me to trust you with my life—*again*. Asking me to swallow something I'm deathly allergic to and trust that whatever remedy you give me—using another huge needle, by the way—will stop the reaction before I die. I'm supposed to do all of that, and you won't even trust me enough to tell me a simple truth about my life that I deserve to know."

Mr. Forkle turned away, pacing across the room.

"Is that what this is, then?" he asked, his voice ominously low. "'Tell me who my biological parents are or I won't let you reset my inflicting'?"

Sophie hadn't realized it was until he spelled it out that way.

"Yes," she said quietly.

"That is . . . unfortunate," he gritted out as he paced back the other way.

"It is," Sophie agreed, refusing to worry that she was being stubborn or selfish.

She'd taken every single risk the Black Swan had ever asked of her—plus dozens more.

And they repaid her by hiding the one secret she'd ever demanded in return.

Silence followed—nothing but Mr. Forkle's shuffling steps and Sophie's pounding heart for thirty-seven breathless beats.

Then he told her, "Well then, if that's your decision, I guess we're done here."

Sophie nodded, proud of her legs for not shaking as she pulled out her home crystal and stood to face him. As Sandor moved to her side, she transmitted a promise to Amy that she'd hail her later.

"I guess we *are* done," Sophie told Mr. Forkle, holding his gaze as she raised her crystal to the light.

And she didn't hesitate when she leaped away.

EIGHTEEN

SOOOOOOO . . . THESE ARE DISAPPOINT-ing." Keefe took a second bite from a round Digestive biscuit and crinkled his nose. "Are they supposed to suck up all the spit in your mouth and turn it into a paste? Is that, like, something humans find delicious?"

"Maybe you're supposed to dunk them in milk?" Sophie suggested, trying not to spray crumbs as she struggled to swallow the bite she'd taken. They really did win the prize for Driest. Cookies. Ever. "Actually, I think you're supposed to eat them with tea."

"You *think*?" Keefe asked, shaking his head and stuffing the rest of the Digestive into his mouth. "You're failing me with your human knowledge, Foster."

"For the thousandth time, I grew up in the U.S., not the U.K.!" she reminded him. "We had Chips Ahoy! and Oreos and E.L. Fudges!"

"Hm. Those *do* sound more fun than a Digestive," Keefe conceded.

"I'm sure you'd especially enjoy the E.L. Fudges," Sophie told him. "They're shaped like tiny elves."

Keefe dropped the package of Jaffa Cakes he'd been in the process of opening and scanned the beach in front of them. "Okay, where's the nearest cliff? You need to teleport me somewhere to get some of those immediately."

"She most certainly does *not*," Sandor corrected from his position in the doorway that connected the patio they were on to the rest of the Shores of Solace.

Sophie couldn't tell if he'd chosen that spot to keep an eye on both the house and the shoreline, or if he was there to keep Lord Cassius away from them. Either way, she was just glad Sandor hadn't fought her—*too* hard—about the visit.

"Aw, come on, Gigantor!" Keefe whined. "We're talking about elf-shaped cookies! I need this in my life!"

"So do I!" Ro added. "Do you have any idea how much fun I would have smashing them?"

Sophie laughed, and Keefe leaned back against the arm of the large cushioned swing they'd been sharing, watching the sun slowly sink toward the ocean.

"*There's* the smile I've been waiting for! It's about time, Foster! I wasn't sure how many more biscuits I'd be able to stomach. I mean, these weren't too bad"—he picked up the Jammie Dodgers from the stack of cookie packages piled between them—"but note to self: Next time Foster shows up out of the blue, clearly upset over something she's been worrying about all day and yet refuses to talk about, stick with mallowmelt for the cheer-up process."

Sophie's gaze dropped to the pack of Custard Creams they still hadn't opened. "I didn't need cheering up. And I'm not worrying about anything."

"Uh, do I *really* need to remind you that I'm an Empath?" he asked.

"Or can I just pelt you with the rest of these Digestives? It'd be way better than having to eat them."

He wasn't wrong about anything he'd just said—but Sophie still stuck with the safer topic.

"I'm not feeling a whole lot of gratitude from you here for all the effort I went through to bring you back your biscuit shopping list—plus bonus treats," she pointed out.

"You mean having Dizznee pull some money from your birth fund and then hitting up a shop for a couple of minutes?" Keefe asked. "Yeah, Dex told me all about how *not* exhausting that was last night, when *he* checked in to tell me how things went for you two in London, while *someone* was off doing *something* with Mr. Forkle that was clearly both frustrating and intense—as most things with Forkle tend to be."

"Hey, I still thought of you!" Sophie argued, ignoring the obvious nudge he was giving the conversation. "That counts for something."

"It does indeed, Foster," Keefe said quietly, fidgeting with another Digestive. "It does indeed."

A beat of silence followed before he cleared his throat and added, "But do you really think you're going to be able to leave here without telling me what happened with the Forklenator? If you do, you're going to be sorely, sorely disappointed—and covered in biscuit crumbs."

"Don't worry, she came here to talk to you about it," Ro jumped in. "The cookies were just her excuse. You gonna deny it?" she asked when Sophie turned to scowl at her.

Sophie definitely wanted to.

But . . . Ro was right.

Sophie had spent the day avoiding Grady and Edaline's questions about where Mr. Forkle had taken her—and ignoring whoever kept hailing her on her Imparter. And after a few hours of that, her bedroom had started to feel smaller and smaller and smaller. She'd been ready to beg Silveny to fly her somewhere far away when she'd noticed the bag of biscuits on her floor, and the next thing she knew, she was teleporting to the Shores of Solace again and claiming she'd wanted to bring Keefe his London cookies before they got stale.

"The thing is," she said, scooting back as far as she could on the swing, since space felt important in that moment, "I made a decision yesterday—and it probably wasn't the right decision, or the smart decision, but I made it anyway because . . . I just had to. And I'm sure I can take it back if I want, but . . . I *don't* want to. And I figured you might understand that better than a lot of other people would."

"Soooooooo, what you're saying is, you think I'm the king of bad decisions," Keefe said, laughing when Sophie fumbled for an apology. "Relax—I know what you meant. I'm just giving you a hard time. And you have a point. I'm not necessarily great at doing what I'm supposed to do and giving people what they want. *And* I'm not usually sorry about it either."

"Don't forget about all of the self-sabotage!" Ro added. "I can happily provide numerous examples." She ducked when Keefe flung the package of Digestives at her. "That all you got, Cookie Boy?"

Keefe rolled his eyes and turned back to Sophie. "*Anyway* . . . how can I help?"

Sophie dropped her gaze back to the packs of biscuits, tracing her gloved fingers along the logo for the Hobnobs. "I guess I just wanted to talk to someone who might not judge me for what I decided, since I'm pretty sure most people are going to say I made the wrong call—and they're probably right. I know what the smart thing to do is. I'm just so *sick* of always being the good little moonlark, you know?"

"Sorta?" Keefe said, waiting for her to look at him. "I mean, you came to the right place—this is definitely a judgment-free zone. But it miiiiiiiiiight help if you tell me what the decision actually was. Just, you know, for clarity."

Sophie gave in to the urge to tug on her itchy eyelashes as she explained what had happened in her missing memory, and how Mr. Forkle wanted to reset her inflicting and enhancing, and why she'd refused and leaped away.

"So . . . you chose to *not* let the Black Swan almost kill you—*again*," Keefe said when she'd finished. "And you think people are going to judge you for that?"

"They should," Sophie mumbled. "I have the chance to have an ability—or maybe two abilities—that might actually help us take down the Neverseen. And I know better than anyone how badly we're going to need that kind of power."

"Yeah, but you also know better than anybody what it feels like to almost die from a huge allergic reaction," Keefe countered.

"I do," Sophie agreed.

Her sister had said pretty much the same thing when Sophie had hailed her to check on her after she'd leaped back to Havenfield. Amy had been firmly on Team Don't-You-Dare-Let-Them-Convince-You-to-Risk-Your-Life-Again.

But . . . Amy was also human.

She didn't *really* understand the gigantic problems the entire planet was facing, or how they threatened the safety of *every single species.*

"The thing is," Sophie admitted quietly, "that's not why I said 'no' to what Mr. Forkle was asking. I'm used to pain. I don't *like* it—but it's not like it's a deal-breaker or anything. And I'm not *that* worried about surviving, since I'm pretty sure Mr. Forkle, Elwin, and Livvy would find a way to get me through. I even know how valuable the abilities might be. I just . . . I'm sick of everyone telling me to trust them when they clearly don't trust me. And I'm *really* tired of no one caring about what I want when it comes to . . . pretty much anything. I mean, would it be so hard for someone to say, 'Hey, Sophie, we get how rough this is for you and we want to do something to make your life a little easier'? Is that *such* an unreasonable dream? Especially since all I've been asking for is a tiny bit of personal information?"

"That one hundred percent makes sense," Keefe promised, and Sophie felt her shoulders relax a little—until he added, "which is why I have to ask why I feel so much guilt coming from you when you say it. And yeah, it's definitely guilt—don't try to deny it. The same stuff that can shatter your sanity if you let it get out of control, so . . . we kinda need to figure out how to stop you from feeling so much of that, okay?"

Sophie curled her knees into her chest, focusing on the subtle swaying of the swing in the cool ocean breeze. It made it easier for her to say, "I guess it's because I'm being selfish. And I'm supposed to be better than that."

"Because you're the moonlark?" Keefe asked.

She nodded. "The entire reason I exist is so I can use my abilities to stop the Neverseen. I didn't have parents who loved me and wanted to have a child to add to their family—"

"Neither did I," Keefe pointed out. "I'm here for my 'legacy.'"

"I know," Sophie said, hating that Keefe had to live with that. "But . . . at least for you, doing the right thing means ignoring all of their plans. It's the opposite for me. I was created to do a job. A pretty important one, from what I can tell. And here I am, refusing to do it simply because I'm trying to find a way to make my life a little more normal. And that's just . . . really selfish and silly of me. It's like an Imparter saying, 'Hey, I'm sick of you telling me who to hail all the time—I'm not going to do it anymore until you tell me why you made me a square!'"

"Uh, but you're *not* an Imparter, Foster—though I appreciate the little voice you just did there to really sell the character," Keefe teased. "But in all seriousness . . . I see what you're trying to say. The thing is, though, the Black Swan didn't make a gadget. They made a *person*. So they're going to have to deal with the fact that you have a mind of your own—and a pretty darn smart one too. It's okay to trust yourself sometimes. If something feels wrong to you, it probably *is* wrong. And if it feels like someone's taking advantage of you, they probably are."

"I guess." Sophie sighed, hugging her knees tighter. "But . . . I keep thinking about how I'm going to feel if someone gets hurt the next time we run into the Neverseen, and I'll have to wonder if I could've stopped it if I hadn't been so stubborn and agreed to fix my inflicting."

"But you *shouldn't* do that." Keefe reached toward her, and for a second she wondered if he was going to take her hand—but he grabbed the Jammie Dodgers instead. "I know you're not going to believe me when I say this, but I'm going to say it anyway because you clearly need to hear it—and I think it might even be why you came here to talk to me. *So* . . . listen closely: It's *not* your job to protect anyone, Sophie. No matter what you think—or how many abilities you have—or what plans the Black Swan had when they created Project Moonlark. The only *job* you have is to be Sophie Foster. And *you* get to decide who Sophie Foster is."

"Yeah, I guess you're right," Sophie said, turning back to the sunset. A sad smile curled her lips as she added, "I *don't* believe you. But . . . thanks."

"Anytime." Keefe crunched on another cookie, and Sophie closed her eyes, letting everything he'd said float around her head for a few more seconds.

It sure would've been nice if her life really could be that simple.

But the world was far, far too complicated.

"So . . . how goes the memory searching?" she asked, needing to fill the silence.

He shrugged. "Nothing new so far—and *nice* subject change. Don't think I didn't notice."

Sophie snatched the Jammie Dodgers away from him and pulled out another cookie, twisting the two halves slowly back and forth, determined to find a way to separate them. "What about our other project?"

Keefe's eyebrows shot up. "If you mean the Bio-Mommy-and-Daddy Quest, I . . . wasn't sure you'd be in the mood to talk about that after yesterday."

Sophie gave her cookie another careful twist, finally feeling the stubborn jam separate. She held the two halves up triumphantly, then licked the raspberry off of her fingers. "I don't know—I'm kinda feeling more determined than ever to find out what Mr. Forkle's hiding from me."

Keefe flashed his widest grin yet, leaning back and giving her several slow, proud claps. "You hear that, Ro? Our sweet little Foster's bringing the fight to the Forklenator."

"I like it!" Ro agreed. "Now if only she'd realize—"

"So what do you think?" Keefe jumped in, before Ro could finish that sentence. "Was Forkle telling the truth about Bronte? Or lying to throw you off track?"

"No idea," Sophie admitted. "I mean . . . he seemed pretty surprised when I said it. But I guess that doesn't really tell us anything."

"Does that mean you still want to go ahead with the awesome-Empath-gets-all-the-answers plan?" he asked.

"Is *that* what we're calling it?" Sophie wondered.

Keefe smirked. "I'm also good with calling it Keefe-to-the-Rescue!—but that applies to so *many* things, you know? Plus, then I'd need you to start calling me your *hero* and swooning occasionally in my presence."

Sophie flung half of her cookie at him, and the raspberry side splatted perfectly against his cheek, suctioning on.

"Oh, you wanna start the biscuit war, Foster?" Keefe asked, not even bothering to remove the Jammie Dodger from his face as he snatched the box of Jaffa Cakes and tore it open. "Because I can bring it."

Sophie was tempted.

A cookie fight sounded way more fun than discussing biological-parent theories.

But she'd already lost the majority of the day to a mix of fuming and sulking and avoiding everybody.

So she set down the other half of her jam-covered weapon as a cookie surrender and caught Keefe up on what she'd discussed with the rest of her teammates—how she'd agreed to let Biana and Stina help, as well as Stina's theory about Lady Cadence.

Keefe whistled at that last revelation. "Wow, that does kinda make sense. I don't know how I missed her when I made my list—and if she *is* your bio-mom, *please* tell me we can dump a bunch of curdle-roots on her head for lying to you."

"I'd be good with that," Sophie told him, needing an extra second to work up the courage to ask, "So . . . you have a list?"

"A short one, yeah." He hesitated for a beat before he offered, "Want me to go get it?"

Sophie chewed her lip. "Maybe just tell me one of the names as a start?"

"Sure—though you don't know any of them, so I'm not sure if it'll mean a whole lot. But one of the genetic-mom options is Lady Pemberley. She's blond and a Telepath, so it seems worth looking into. But she's also married and has a kid, and I kinda feel like we're looking for someone who lives alone, since they'd be putting their family in danger by getting involved in all of this."

"Makes sense." Sophie told herself to leave it there, but somehow she still found herself asking, "So . . . she has a kid?"

Keefe nodded. "A son. Actually, I think you've met him—his name's Dempsey. He was a Level Six when you were a Level Two, and I feel like I remember you showing him who's boss in a splotching match one time."

"That does sound familiar," Sophie agreed.

She didn't recall him being all that nice—though she *had* just defeated him in front of the whole school and splattered his face with bright orange goo.

"Want me to see if Biana and I can coordinate a confrontation for Lady Pemberley?" Keefe offered.

"I don't know," Sophie admitted. "I think we're going to need to be careful about how many people find out what we're searching for. The more times we're wrong, the more we risk that rumors will start flying and my biological parents will go into hiding—or at least be prepared to lie if we confront them."

Plus, it could cause a lot more speculation about her matchmaking status, but Sophie wasn't in the mood to remind him about that.

"I was wondering about that too," Keefe said, finally peeling the Jammie Dodger off his face. "We might need a new strategy."

"Like what?" Sophie asked.

He popped the cookie into his mouth, then licked his thumb and set to work removing the sticky jam residue left on his cheek. "Still working on it. Might have to get a bit creative."

"I like creative!" Ro agreed.

Sandor muttered something unintelligible—though Sophie was pretty sure she caught the word "ridiculous."

"In the meantime," Keefe said, swiping the last of the raspberry smear off of his face, "you still haven't answered the extra-super-duper-important question, Foster."

"And what's that?" Sophie asked.

He motioned for her to lean in closer, like he was afraid his father might be eavesdropping.

"The question is"—his eyes locked with hers—"when are you taking me to go get some of these magical E.L. Fudge thingies? Because they're officially a *need*, Foster. I neeeeeeeeeeeed tiny elf-shaped cookies in my life. I can't believe you've never brought me any before! In fact, I kinda feel like that's a betrayal of our friendship!"

The question was so unexpected that Sophie couldn't stop the loud snort-laugh from bursting out, which of course was followed by a fit of embarrassed giggles.

"You're not laughing your way out of this one either, Miss F!" Keefe warned her. "I expect another cookie delivery ASAP—and this time it needs to have all those kinds you mentioned, plus anything else shaped like an elf. And you'd better be able to answer all my questions about them and not give me any excuses about . . ."

"About?" Sophie asked when his voice trailed off—right before she realized his eyes were focused on something over her shoulder.

Or *someone*.

Sophie had never thought she'd hope to turn around and find Lord Cassius standing there watching her—but she definitely would've preferred him over the handsome, teal-eyed guy with the crossed arms and the surly brow.

"Hey, Fitzy's here!" Keefe said, shooting a quick glare at Sandor— though this wasn't totally Sandor's fault.

Fitz hadn't come through the door that Sandor had been guarding, instead using a side patio entrance that Sophie hadn't even noticed. Grizel stood several steps behind him, and Lord Cassius loomed several steps behind her, tucked in the shadows of the arched doorway, almost like he'd intentionally *snuck* Fitz onto the patio.

Then again, that didn't explain why Ro and Sandor hadn't warned them that they had visitors—unless the reason for that was because no one needed a warning.

Once again, Sophie had to remind herself that she and Keefe weren't doing anything wrong.

Keefe had asked for biscuits.

She'd brought him biscuits.

Then they'd talked for a bit—*because they were friends.*

And Fitz *knew* they were friends.

"You need to get in on this, Fitzy," Keefe said, holding up the box of Jaffa Cakes. "Foster and Dizznee proved that they'll do anything I ask them to"—he made a dramatic, evil laugh—"and brought me a bunch of human cookies. They're mostly disappointing, I'm not gonna lie. *But!* There are still a few we haven't tried, and who knows? They might be the life-changing ones. *And* you can help me convince Foster to go get us these elf-shaped cookies I'm just now learning about—though I also think she owes us all an apology for not telling us about the elf-shaped cookies sooner, don't you? *And* I think she needs to use her teleporting way more often. I'm thinking we should give her a weekly Forbidden Cities item to track down for us. Maybe then I'll finally be able to try Ding Dongs. I don't know what they are—but I read something about them in my research, and I mean, they're called 'Ding Dongs,' so I'm here for it. You with me?"

He held up his hand like he was hoping Fitz would stride over and give him a high five.

Fitz did not.

"Looks like you're having an interesting day," Grizel said, her voice extra husky as she sauntered over to Sandor.

"You have no idea," Sandor squeak-murmured. "And I'm pretty sure it's about to get worse."

Sophie had the same feeling, especially when she forced herself to meet Fitz's eyes and was *not* gifted with one of his perfect smiles.

"Have you tried hailing me today?" she asked, really, really, *really* hoping he hadn't.

"Three times," he told her.

Even Keefe winced at that.

Okay, so maybe *that* was why Sophie felt so bad.

"I'm sorry," she said, standing up from the swing to face him. "It's been kinda a rough day—but I guess that's not a very good excuse."

"It isn't," Fitz agreed.

Silence followed, and Sophie wished Keefe would break it with another ramble about E.L. Fudges.

But he was too busy glaring at his father, while Lord Cassius raised one eyebrow back at him.

She cleared her throat and took a few steps toward Fitz—stopping before actually reaching him. "How did you know I was here?"

"I didn't," he admitted, "though maybe I should've guessed?"

"Yeah, we were working on"—she glanced at Lord Cassius and corrected the rest of that sentence—"that project Keefe's helping me with—trying to come up with an alternate strategy in case we need to be a little subtler." And because she didn't want him to think she was hiding anything from him, she added, "We also talked through a couple of other things I still need to tell you about."

"How come you're here, Fitzy?" Keefe asked, jumping in before Fitz could ask any of the harder questions, like when Sophie had been planning to tell him about those things or why she hadn't come to him first. "Finally ready for that bramble rematch? If so, I say loser has to eat the rest of the Digestives." He pointed to the slightly smashed package he'd tossed at Ro earlier.

"Actually, Fitz is here to help me," Lord Cassius interceded, smoothing the sides of his hair.

Keefe's eyes narrowed at his dad. "With what?"

"With a new project of my own." Lord Cassius studied his cuticles as he added, "It's not lost on me, Keefe, that you've been drawing so tediously lately because you're attempting to sort through your memories, searching for fragments of things your mother might've erased. I don't understand why you're working by hand when it would be so much more efficient to have a Telepath assist you with a task like that—and clearly Miss Foster would be more than willing. But regardless of your foolish planning, your little mission got me wondering whether your mother dared to erase anything from my mind over the years."

"I bet she did," Keefe warned him. "It sounded like she had a Washer on standby in case we saw anything or heard anything she didn't want us to."

"Yes, that's the conclusion that I reached as well," Lord Cassius noted, his eyes and voice darkening as he said it. "I've worked with Telepaths before, searching for clues your mother might've let slip around me. But we weren't checking to see if anything had been stolen away. So young Mr. Vacker here has agreed to help me search my memories yet again. And this time, we'll see if I can find what your mother tried to hide from me."

NINETEEN

YOU'RE GOING TO SEARCH MY DAD'S memories?" Keefe asked, shaking his head when Fitz nodded. *"Why?"*

Fitz's shrug didn't look quite as casual as he probably wanted it to. "Someone has to."

"Okay, but why *you?*" When Fitz didn't answer, Keefe turned to his father. "Why not ask whoever you worked with last time? Or Quinlin Sonden? Or Alden? Or Tiergan? Or even Forkle?"

Lord Cassius smoothed his hair again. "Young Mr. Vacker has proven to be every bit as powerful as any of them. Perhaps even more so. And he has a much more flexible schedule."

"Yeah, but that's not why you picked him," Keefe argued.

"It isn't," Lord Cassius agreed, his eyes flashing with enough glee that Sophie could guess his ulterior motive.

He'd chosen his son's best friend *knowing* it would make Keefe uncomfortable—probably as punishment for all the times Keefe had rebelled.

"Mind you, the ideal candidate would've been young Miss Foster," Lord Cassius added. "But she's always so busy with *you.*"

Before Sophie could formulate a response—or even parse out what Lord Cassius was implying—Ro patted the side of her breastplate and told him, "Sounds like it's time to bust out my *extra* fun bacteria buddies. Get ready to lose a *lot* of body fluids, Lord Snootypants."

"Nah, save 'em for when it'll really be worth it," Keefe told her, stalking over to his father and tilting his head. "You wanna share all of our family secrets with the Fitzster—you do that. *I* have nothing to hide."

"Neither do I." Lord Cassius flashed a particularly oily smile before turning his attention back to Fitz. "I'm assuming you'd like to visit with your friends for a few minutes—be my guest. But don't keep me waiting too long. I'll be in my office."

Keefe whistled as Lord Cassius left the way he'd come. "Wow. Have fun with that, Fitzy."

He sounded so calm and casual that Sophie *almost* believed him. But she knew Keefe better than that. She'd seen the terrified, broken version of Keefe tucked behind his mask of snark and indifference. And she couldn't blame him for being bothered by this.

He didn't try to hide the abuse he'd suffered—but he definitely wasn't an open book about it either. And now Fitz was going to read the extended, annotated version, complete with sound and visuals.

"I'd like to go on the record and make it clear that I was against this idea from the start," Grizel informed all of them.

Fitz rolled his eyes, and Sophie stepped closer to him, keeping her voice low as she asked, "Why would you agree to this without telling us?"

"Uh, maybe I *tried* to tell you but someone ignored my hails— even though you promised you weren't going to do that anymore?" he snapped back.

There was nothing Sophie could say to that except, "Sorry."

"Yeah, me too." Fitz looked away. "And just so you know, I agreed to do this to *help* Keefe. If Lady Gisela tried to hide something from Lord Cassius, we need to find it. And I figured Keefe would rather have someone he trusts poking around his father's memories— someone he knows won't tell anyone about anything he finds."

"Except none of those other people that Keefe suggested were strangers," Sophie couldn't help reminding him. "And some of them he'd even worked with before."

"Okay, everyone, relax! It's fine!" Keefe flopped back down on the swing and scooped up the box of Custard Creams. "This is definitely not worth you two having your first Fitzphie fight over it. Seriously. Spend as much time with my dad as you want, Fitzy—and if you feel like telling people all about the fun things you learn, fine by me. If Daddy Dearest is cool with you knowing exactly how awesome he is to live with, by all means, spread the Sencen shame!" He tore open the box and fished out one of the biscuits. "Ooo, these ones are fancy! Check that out!"

He held up one of the rectangular sandwich biscuits and pointed to the swirling filigree pattern on the top. "Looks promising, doesn't it? But there's only one way to tell."

Pale yellow crumbs showered his tunic after he took a huge bite, and he closed his eyes as he chewed. "Hm. Still a *little* on the bland side—but the cream center really helps. Definitely the best so far. You guys should get in on this."

"Ugh, I think I'm on biscuit overload," Sophie admitted.

"Better stop, then," Keefe told her. "We don't want you tossing your cookies—if you know what I mean."

He looked *very* proud of his wordplay, so Sophie let him enjoy it.

"What about you, Fitzy?" Keefe asked, shaking the package of Custard Creams. "You've yet to experience the wonder of a British biscuit. And trust me, if you're going to spend hours poking around my dad's brain, you could use a good sugar rush."

Fitz ran a hand through his hair as he made his way over, reaching for a cookie and—

Keefe snatched Fitz's wrist. "I knew it!"

"Knew what?" Fitz shouted, trying to wrench his arm away.

Keefe tightened his grip. "Shhhhh, let the Empath work."

"Ugh, a little help here?" Fitz asked Grizel, who was talking to Sandor, barely paying him any attention.

"No, this one's your mess!" Grizel called over her shoulder. "You can get yourself out of it!"

"Relax, Fitzy, no need to take your frustrations out on the poor innocent biscuits!" Keefe told him when Fitz's next escape attempt nearly sent the rest of the Custard Creams plummeting toward the floor. "I'll let go in a second. First things first. It feels like . . . Yep! There's definitely another reason you signed on to be my dad's personal memory boy. Something you're embarrassed of *and* super angry about, so . . . I'm guessing it has to do with your brother?"

Fitz muttered about Empaths as he stopped struggling.

"I take it that's a yes?" Keefe confirmed.

Fitz nodded. "Your dad said he knows how to find Alvar and offered to track him down for me if I help with this."

Keefe released Fitz's wrist. "Sounds about right. And okay, three things." He held up his right hand to count them off. "One: Take a Custard Cream. Seriously." He waited until Fitz had grabbed one of the cookies before he continued. "Two: Uh, you know my dad will claim *anything* to get what he wants, right? I mean, I'm not saying you made a bad call—hopefully you'll also find some juicy secrets my mom tried to hide. But just . . . prepare yourself for disappointment, okay? Odds are, my dad only knows one tiny, useless thing about your brother—if that—and you're going to want to punch him."

"And if that's the case," Ro jumped in, "punch away!"

"Oh, don't worry, I will," Grizel assured her.

"So will I." Fitz took a tentative bite of the Custard Cream. "Wow, human cookies are *dry*, aren't they?"

"You think that's bad, try the Digestives," Keefe told him.

"Yeah, uh, pass." Fitz finished his Custard Cream anyway—and reached for another, Sophie noticed—as he told Keefe, "I know learning anything useful from your dad is a long shot. But I'm not making any progress on my own, so . . ."

"I get that," Keefe promised. "I do. But what I don't get is thing three." He counted it off on his fingers as he asked, "Why didn't you just tell me this had to do with Alvar from the start? Did you really think I wouldn't understand?"

"Honestly?" Fitz stuffed the rest of his second cookie into his mouth, spritzing crumbs when he said, "I don't know."

Keefe nodded slowly, grabbing another Custard Cream and prying the two halves of the sandwich apart. "Life's . . . getting complicated, huh?"

"It is," Fitz agreed, examining a Jammie Dodger like it held the secrets of the universe.

"I swear, watching boys try to communicate is like watching amoebas," Ro told Sophie during the long silence that followed.

"You just stare at their blobby little bodies and think, 'How do these things even function?'"

"Hey, who you calling blobby?" Keefe complained, pulling back his tunic sleeves and flexing his arm muscles, which were pretty impressive—not that Sophie would ever tell him that.

Ro snorted. "You elves are so adorably puny."

"Aren't they?" Grizel asked. "I swear, I have swords that weigh more than some of them."

"Um, excuse me, I complete your training regimen every day," Fitz reminded her, "even with my healing leg."

"You do," Grizel agreed, before turning toward Ro and stage-whispering, "Do you think I should tell him that it's the same work-out we have our toddlers start with in Gildingham?"

Fitz scowled.

Keefe smirked. "I think the moral of this conversation is, females are cruel."

"They can be," Fitz said quietly.

He didn't look at Sophie as he said it—but the not-looking almost made it worse.

And Sophie was fairly certain that another apology wasn't going to get her out of this new mess she'd created, but she still had to transmit a quick *I'm really sorry.*

I know, Fitz transmitted back. *We'll . . . talk later.*

Sure, she thought, regretting every biscuit she'd eaten.

All the sugar and carbs churned in the pit of her stomach as Fitz cleared his throat and told Keefe, "I guess I shouldn't keep your father waiting."

"You shouldn't—and don't go easy on him in there," Keefe warned.

"You'll never find anything my mom hid if you let him push you around."

"Oh, don't worry, I have big plans to make this as miserable as possible for him," Fitz assured him.

Keefe grinned. "That's what I like to hear! If you need pointers for maximum annoyance, you know where to find me."

"I do," Fitz agreed.

"Wow, did they just fist-bump?" Ro asked.

"You bet we did!" Keefe told her. "That's what besties do, right, Fitzy?"

Fitz's nod couldn't necessarily be described as "enthusiastic."

But he still made the gesture.

Even gave Keefe half a smile as Fitz turned to head down the hall.

"Ugh, the one time I'd been counting on you to annoy Fitz into storming off so I wouldn't have to stand guard duty around your father," Grizel grumbled to Keefe, "you have to go and be all mature."

"What can I say? I like to keep people on their toes. Biscuit to ease the pain?" Keefe held out the pack of Jammie Dodgers.

Grizel snatched the cookies and stomped off after Fitz.

"Oh, but Fitzy?" Keefe shouted as Fitz reached the bend in the hall. "I want to know all the memories you see, okay? Not because . . . whatever. It's just possible there's something in his head that'll knock something loose in mine, you know?"

Fitz gave him a thumbs-up.

"Boys," Ro told Sophie. "They really are high-functioning amoebas."

"It's a good thing we're cute, right?" Keefe countered.

When Ro didn't agree, Keefe launched into a long pondering on whether Ro considered Bo to be a "hunky ogre," and Sophie decided to flee before the bacteria started flying.

But she couldn't leave without making sure Keefe was okay.

He assured her he would be—and the third time he said it, he *almost* sounded convincing.

He also promised he'd try to come up with a subtler plan for investigating the names on his list of possible biological parents. But Sophie wasn't holding out much hope on that front.

"Subtle" wasn't really a word that fit with "Keefe Sencen."

"Thanks again for the biscuits," he said as she dug out her home crystal. "And don't think I'm going to forget about the E.L. Fudges you owe me."

Sophie had no doubt she'd be hearing about them endlessly.

"I'll find a way to get you some," she promised, ignoring Sandor's protests—though those weren't as spirited as they normally were.

She wondered if that meant Sandor had already resigned himself to the fact that elf-shaped cookies were going to have to happen.

And Sophie was about to leap away when she realized she had one more thing she wanted to tell him. "Thanks for listening, Keefe. It . . . really helped."

Keefe's smile was slower than usual—but it lit up his whole face. "Anytime, Foster. And I meant what I said. You're not doing *anything* wrong. But if you change your mind and go ahead with the reset? I'll be right there to make sure you get through safe."

Sophie nodded. And she'd just pulled Sandor into the light when Keefe called after her, "Oh, and don't worry about the Fitzster. I'll talk to him."

Lots of ogre curses filled the air as the rushing warmth swept Sophie away.

· · ·

Back at Havenfield, Sophie lasted about ten minutes in her bedroom before the walls closed in. And she had to give Grady and Edaline credit. When they saw her stumbling down the stairs with her comforter, pillows, and Ella, all they'd said was, "What else do you need?"

Even Sandor and Bo didn't argue with Sophie's plan. They just set to work rearranging the nightly patrols to better cover Calla's Panakes tree. And thanks to Edaline's conjuring, it only took a couple of minutes to get a hefty mound of pillows and blankets neatly arranged under the swaying branches.

Wynn and Luna seemed to think the campout was the greatest idea that Sophie had ever had, and were snuggled up in her makeshift bed even before Sophie had added the final pillows.

Iggy didn't mind it either. He was snoring like a garbage truck within about thirty seconds of Grady setting his cage next to Calla's trunk.

"So . . . is this going to be a regular thing?" Edaline asked as she and Grady helped Sophie crawl past the tangle of alicorn legs to get under her covers.

"I don't know," Sophie admitted. "I just . . . couldn't breathe inside tonight."

"I know the feeling," Edaline told her, kissing Sophie on her forehead.

"And I'm not trying to be nosy, kiddo," Grady added. "But . . . I have to ask if this has anything to do with your meeting with King Enki."

"I have a meeting with King Enki?" Sophie asked.

Grady nodded. "The Council's taking you, me, and your team to Loamnore in two days—and since you clearly didn't know that, I guess that answers my question."

"Yeah," Sophie said, feeling a whole new set of worries stack up inside her brain. "Wow. I'm . . . getting really bad at this."

"Bad at what?" Edaline asked, lowering herself to the grass and petting Luna's sparkly rump.

"Juggling," Sophie admitted. "I used to be so much better at keeping track of all the things I needed to focus on. But now . . ."

She'd barely thought about the dwarves.

Or Team Valiant.

Or Tam.

The last one hit the hardest.

Especially when she considered how much time she'd spent focusing on herself—fighting about healing her abilities. Stressing about boy stuff, and matchmaking stuff, and her biological parents.

"Why is it so hard to remember what really matters?" she asked quietly, staring up at the stars.

"Because it *all* matters," Edaline told her, reaching for Sophie's hand. "And for the record, I think you do a pretty amazing job of juggling everything."

"Thanks," Sophie mumbled.

But she still needed to do better.

And she would.

Her mind put together a long to-do list as Grady and Edaline finished tucking her in. And she buried all the silly, selfish stuff down at the bottom.

She put Team Valiant at the top, since she'd never checked in with Wylie and Stina about their meeting with Lady Zillah. And even though she was dreading it, she needed to check in with Bronte and Oralie—find out when the Council would be announcing their Regent appointments.

Priorities, she told herself. *It's all about priorities.*

She repeated that over and over—along with a vow to not let herself get sidetracked again—as she closed her eyes. And as she slept, it felt like Calla's tree was cheering her on.

Singing about the perfect balance of the forest.

How every tree has its place.

And Sophie woke with the sunrise, ready to start fresh in the new day.

TWENTY

FRIEND! FRIEND! FRIEND! FRIEND! FRIEND! *No—that's absolutely NOT your friend!* Sophie transmitted for what had to be the twentieth time.

And once again, Wynn immediately countered with another burst of *FRIEND! FRIEND! FRIEND! FRIEND! FRIEND!*

Sophie reached up to rub her temples.

Bits of torn grass showered her lap, and she didn't want to know how much more was tangled in her hair. Probably half a pasture's worth, thanks to all the rolling around she'd done while tackling two baby alicorns and dragging them away from the gorgodon's enclosure.

Sandor had offered to help, but she'd wanted to handle this on her own. After everything she'd been through with Silveny and Greyfell, Wynn and Luna kinda felt—in a weird way—like a new obnoxious baby brother and sister.

Sophie wanted to prove that she could take care of them.

She just wished they'd cooperate a *little.*

FOR THE LAST TIME, she said, trying not to think about how sore she was going to be the next day, or how muddy her clothes were, *THE GORGODON IS NOT YOUR FRIEND!*

Wynn looked at his twin sister—some secret thought passing between them—before they both filled Sophie's head with a fresh chorus of *FRIEND! FRIEND! FRIEND! FRIEND! FRIEND!*

Sophie groaned, wondering if her brain could actually explode from the sheer volume of their transmissions.

Or maybe from her own frustration.

She'd thought dealing with Silveny was exhausting, thanks to the mama alicorn's demanding side, and her tendency to transmit almost everything in blocks of three. But that was *nothing* compared to the intensity of simultaneous mental shouting from two baby alicorn troublemakers.

And they showed no sign of stopping, or any remorse for how badly they'd frightened her.

In fact, they seemed to be building steam, their chants growing faster—louder. More high-pitched.

ENOUGH! Sophie snapped after the thirty-first *FRIEND!* crashed into her head.

She jumped to her feet, looming over the sparkly winged horses and giving them each her sternest glare.

She'd tried reasoning.

Tried begging.

All she had left was threatening.

If you won't promise to stay away from the gorgodon, she warned, *then I'm going to tell your parents where I found you guys today and let them decide how to punish you!*

Sadly, the words didn't have as much impact as Sophie had hoped.

Or any at all.

The stream of *FRIEND!* transmissions held steady, and Sophie was tempted to let Sandor take a stab at putting fear into them after all. Or maybe she'd call Bo over from wherever he was patrolling and let them face down an angry ogre warrior.

Instead, she stalked off through the pastures, making it clear that she was prepared to make good on her threat.

And Wynn and Luna galloped happily after her, as if they were heading off for an afternoon of adventure together.

It didn't help that Sophie had no idea where to actually find Silveny and Greyfell, and kept guessing places that turned out to be busts. The alicorns weren't confined like the other animals, because it was safer for them to have the option to teleport—though she might need to tell Grady and Edaline to reconsider that arrangement if Wynn and Luna didn't get over their inexplicable obsession with the gorgodon.

Sophie truly didn't understand the creature's appeal to the stubborn baby alicorns. Sure, sometimes she felt a little sorry for the unruly beast, since it was the last of its kind and had lived through some particularly horrible things. But it was also ugly and angry and seemed determined to destroy anyone and everything simply because it could.

Definitely not an ideal playmate.

And yet, Wynn and Luna were *convinced* that the gorgodon was their *FRIEND!*

No barrier seemed capable of keeping them away, either.

Sophie still had no idea how the twins had slipped past all the wire that Grady and the gnomes had carefully wrapped around the enclosure after the last time Wynn had paid the gorgodon a visit.

She'd checked everywhere for a gap, or a spot where the wire was loose, or for some sort of tunnel near the base—anything she could use to get Wynn and Luna out of there.

But there was nothing.

Even the gnomes who'd rushed over when they'd realized what was going on couldn't figure it out, and Sandor had been forced to slash a new opening with his sword for them to use as an extraction point.

And all the while, the gorgodon had been striking at Wynn and Luna with its venomous, scorpion-like tail—coming so close to death blows that Sophie had to keep shutting her eyes, unable to watch the horror that seemed about to unfold.

But somehow, each time, Wynn and Luna managed to keep on flying.

And when the gnomes had finally coaxed them out of the enclosure with an absurd amount of swizzlespice, they didn't even have a scratch on them—which was why Sophie hadn't felt guilty about channeling all of her mental strength into a baby-alicorn tackle and hauling them far away by their gangly little legs.

She'd tried her best to make them understand how lucky they were that she'd been outside and realized what was going on with enough time to get them away from the deadly beast before something seriously tragic had happened. But none of that had gotten through to the stubborn twins.

So it was time to let their parents take over—and when Sophie finally found Silveny and Greyfell grazing near the pterodactyl enclosure, she braced for some epic freaking out.

But both the mama and papa alicorns kept right on munching as Sophie recounted the story.

And when Sophie finished, Silveny didn't even bother raising her head when she transmitted, *BABY OKAY! BABY OKAY!*

It wasn't a question.

It was a *reassurance*.

As if she wanted Sophie to know that she'd been worrying for nothing.

Sophie glanced at Greyfell, hoping he'd take over as Overprotective Daddy. But he just shook his mane and chomped down another mouthful of grass.

I don't think you understand, Sophie told them, wondering if the danger had been somehow lost in the translation between their languages. Or maybe they didn't realize how bad it had been because she hadn't let herself scream while it was all happening, trying not to escalate the situation.

So she shared her actual memories from the morning, letting Silveny and Greyfell see exactly how close they'd come to losing one or both of their children.

And still, Silveny simply nuzzled Sophie's shoulder and transmitted, *BABY STRONG! BABY STRONG!*

Then Greyfell told Wynn and Luna to run along and play.

"I don't get it," Sophie grumbled after she'd stomped inside and recounted the whole harrowing tale again. Edaline had definitely looked shaken, and Grady had raced outside to check in with the gnomes at the gorgodon's enclosure—the kinds of reactions she should have gotten from Silveny and Greyfell. "How can they not care? They were *so* overprotective when Silveny was pregnant— shouldn't they be even more so now?"

"I don't think this has anything to do with not caring," Edaline assured her. "You've seen how they both dote on Wynn and Luna. I think . . . they just trust their children to handle themselves. Like Silveny said, 'BABY STRONG!'"

"But Wynn and Luna almost died!" Sophie argued.

"I know. But . . . they didn't. And obviously I can't speak for Silveny's decision-making—or Greyfell's, for that matter. But we all know that they both went through some pretty difficult things before they came to live with us. And even with our protection, they've still endured several attempts on their lives. The world isn't safe for sparkly flying horses. So maybe they're trying to prepare their children for that reality, knowing that Wynn and Luna are going to need to be strong and fast and brave if they want any shot of surviving. It's the struggle every parent faces as their children grow up. Trust me, we all wish we could lock our kids in a bubble and never let anyone or anything go near them—"

"And I'd be *happy* to arrange that," Sandor jumped in.

"I'm sure you would," Edaline said with a teasing smile. "But we're not going to. Because that's not how life works. If parents did that, our children would be miserable—and they'll inevitably step into reality someday anyway, whether we want them to or not. So the best thing we can do is teach them the skills they need to survive, even when that means letting them take big risks."

"Right, but . . . Silveny and Greyfell weren't teaching them anything today," Sophie argued. "They weren't even there watching!"

"That doesn't mean they haven't been doing things to prepare Wynn and Luna at other moments," Edaline reminded her. "Or, for all you know, they could've had a telepathic connection open the entire time that Wynn and Luna were in with the gorgodon, guiding them through what to do."

Sophie sighed. "I guess. Wynn and Luna just seem so young and tiny to be taking that kind of chance."

"Well, things *are* different with animals," Edaline noted. "*But*, it's also funny you should say that, since I have that same thought every time I have to step back and let you and your friends dive headfirst into one of your plans. No matter how brave and grown-up you get, you'll always be too young and tiny for the frightening things the Black Swan asks you to do."

Sophie became very interested in scraping at the dried mud on her gloves.

Edaline placed her hand over Sophie's, waiting for their eyes to meet before she said, "I know Mr. Forkle asked you to do something dangerous, Sophie. He wouldn't tell us *what*, but given the Black Swan's track record, I'm assuming the stakes will be *very* high. So . . . I'm trying to take some pointers from Silveny and tell myself, *SOPHIE STRONG! SOPHIE STRONG!*"

Sophie looked away. "It . . . might not happen."

"Really?" Edaline's voice sounded awfully hopeful, and she cleared her throat before she asked, "Any particular reason why?"

"I'm still trying to decide if I want to do it," Sophie admitted.

Edaline tightened her grip on Sophie's hand. "Well then, I'm very proud of you. It takes a lot of courage to remember that you really do have a choice in all of this."

Sophie wondered if Edaline would be so proud if she knew *why* Sophie was rebelling.

"If you need to talk . . . ," Edaline added.

"I know," Sophie told her.

Silence followed, until Edaline cleared her throat again. "See what I mean about being a parent? Here I am, *not* pressuring you—or Sandor—for more information, even though we all know I want to. And I'm not saying that as a hint, or to guilt you into sharing. I just bet you anything that Silveny wasn't nearly as calm as she seemed when you talked to her. I'm sure her head was full of things she stopped herself from saying because she's letting Wynn and Luna have their freedom, knowing that's the best thing for them in the long run."

"I guess," Sophie said, "but . . . why go through all that stress for *this*? It's not like they're going to run into a lot of gorgodons in the wild."

"No," Edaline agreed. "But I'm sure there's a reason."

"So . . . you're okay with Wynn and Luna hanging out in the gorgodon's enclosure, then?" Sophie had to ask.

"Absolutely not!" Grady said behind them, and Sophie wondered how long he'd been back inside. "The gnomes are wrapping the cage with a second layer of wire as we speak, following a new pattern to cover different spaces and gaps. And when they're done with that, I asked them to add a third layer in a third pattern, all of which should close off whatever weak spot the twins used to slip through today. But just to be safe, I've also asked Bo and Flori to keep an eye on the area as much as they can, to make sure we're not missing something. Silveny and Greyfell can be as permissive as they want to be—but *I'm* not letting anything happen to those babies on my watch."

Sophie definitely agreed.

Which was why she dragged herself back outside and spent the rest of the first part of the afternoon trying to get Wynn and Luna to make a new "friend" with one of the other, safer creatures living in Havenfield's pastures.

They weren't interested in the verminions, which Sophie couldn't blame them for. The giant purple rodents were particularly curmudgeonly—and had very large fangs.

And the mammoths and mastodons could far too easily trample the tiny alicorns, so Sophie steered them away from those.

She also didn't introduce them to any of the creepy giant bug things, since they gave her the heebie-jeebies.

Which really only left her top choice: Verdi—Havenfield's permanent resident. Sure, the neon green, fluffy T. rex struggled occasionally with her vegetarian diet. But Verdi and Sophie had been through enough together that Sophie knew Verdi would obey her command not to harm the alicorns. And Wynn and Luna did seem to enjoy swooping around Verdi's head until she let out one of her mighty roars.

But as soon as Sophie left them alone to play, Wynn and Luna raced off, heading straight for the gorgodon's enclosure.

"I know that look," Marella's familiar voice said from somewhere off to Sophie's left. "That's your *I want to strangle someone* look."

"You're not wrong," Sophie admitted, turning to face her pale, pixielike friend, who stood smirking at her while playing with a couple of the braids scattered throughout her long blond hair.

And Marella wasn't alone.

Linh was with her, looking fiercer than usual in a fitted orange tunic, with her shiny black hair pulled back into a severe bun.

She'd wrapped the strands in a way that left her trademark silver-tipped ends fanned out around the base of her neck. And her silver-flecked eyes were rimmed in dark liner that winged up at the corners.

But it was the third girl who Sophie really hadn't been expecting.

The last time she'd seen Maruca, her dark hair had been straightened. But now it hung in long, gorgeous dreadlocks, half of which were pulled into a complicated twist on top of her head. She still had a streak of blue in the middle, which made her turquoise eyes pop—though she'd also lined them with a shimmering gold liner that glowed perfectly against her rich brown skin. And her full lips were painted the same deep fuchsia as her silk tunic.

But Maruca didn't smile when her gaze met Sophie's. Instead, her jaw set with enough determination that Sophie tried to come up with somewhere else—anywhere else—she needed to be Right. That. Second.

Sophie hadn't forgotten the promise she'd made to Wylie to keep his cousin out of the Black Swan.

She just also hadn't been smart enough to plan what she'd say whenever Maruca turned up to make her request.

"Do you have a minute to talk?" Maruca asked, in a tone that was somehow both friendly and firm.

"Of course she does," Marella answered before Sophie could respond, batting her huge ice blue eyes. "Sophie may not spend as much time with us as she spends with her *other* friends, but she'd never *ignore* us—especially when we've made the effort to stop by for a visit."

"I wouldn't," Sophie agreed, raising her eyebrows in a way that hopefully made it clear to Marella that she meant it. "So . . . what do you guys need?"

"Oh, Linh and I are just here so Maruca doesn't wimp out," Marella told her, rolling up the sleeves of her white, lacy tunic—which was much crisper than Sophie would've expected. Everything Marella wore tended to look like it had spent a significant amount of time on the floor.

"And we wanted to cuddle the baby alicorns!" Linh added, her cheeks turning their usual soft pink tone as her gaze shifted toward the direction that Wynn and Luna had run off.

"Don't be fooled by their cuteness," Sophie warned. "They're little, sparkly, flying monsters."

"Is that why you look like you've been getting your butt kicked in tackle bramble for the last few hours?" Marella asked, and Sophie's face burned as she realized she was still covered in grass and mud and who knew what else, thanks to her wrestle session with Wynn and Luna—which really wasn't fair, considering how perfect and put together Marella, Linh, and Maruca all looked.

"Let's just say that babysitting twin alicorns isn't as fun as it sounds," Sophie told them, making a few halfhearted swipes at the grime on her tunic. There really wasn't much of a point—showering and changing would be the only actual solution. Best she could do was comb her fingers through the worst of the tangles in her hair.

"Well then, you deserve a break!" Linh told her. "I'll take it from here!" She called Wynn's and Luna's names and ran off to find them.

"That girl sure loves animals," Marella said, shaking her head as she watched Linh disappear around a bend. "I caught her talking to her murcat the other day—and not, like, 'Are you hungry, Princess

Purryfins?' which I could sorta understand. It was like a full-on conversation."

"Um. Hang on. She named her murcat Princess Purryfins?" Sophie had to ask.

"Don't even get me started," Marella grumbled. "Though I'm pretty sure she did it so Tam would have to say the words 'Princess Purryfins' on a regular basis—and I'm definitely all for that."

Sophie tried to smile. But not only did the anecdote remind her that she should be focusing a lot harder on getting Tam back—it also made it painfully clear how much she'd been neglecting her friendship with Linh.

Marella sighed. "I know I'm good at giving you a hard time for not hanging out with everybody equally. But . . . I do get how much you're dealing with, and how hard it has to be to keep up with all of it *and* occasionally sleep and eat and see your boyfriend."

It was a miracle Sophie didn't cringe at the last word.

Despite Fitz saying they'd "talk later," she . . . hadn't heard from him.

And she'd been too big of a wimp to reach out.

She was pretty sure that made her the worst girlfriend in the world—if she even *was* his girlfriend anymore.

Every day that was feeling less and less clear.

"Linh's doing okay," Marella promised, probably assuming that the sigh that slipped out of Sophie's lips was for something less selfish. "We've been training together every day—and it's super handy to have someone who controls water around when I meet with Fintan."

Sophie stood taller. "Linh goes to your Fintan lessons?"

Marella nodded. "Mr. Forkle thought it would be safer, since she can drown any flames. She's only gone once, so far, but the lesson went way better with her there. I think Fintan's impressed with her."

Absolutely none of that sounded like good news.

Sandor must've agreed, because he muttered a string of goblin swear words under his breath.

"Well . . . wow," Sophie mumbled, feeling *miles* behind the curve. "Anything I need to know about your lessons—or about what you and Linh are working on?"

"Probably. But that's not what we came here to talk about." Marella shot a meaningful look at Maruca, who'd been standing so quietly, Sophie had almost forgotten that she was there. "And I should go make sure Linh hasn't renamed the alicorns Prince Shimmernose and Princess Sparklefeathers or something. I swear, if she and Keefe ever get together, I'd feel super sorry for their kid."

"Does she like Keefe?" Sophie blurted out—her face heating about a million degrees when she realized how nosy she was being. "Never mind. I shouldn't have asked that."

"Probably not," Marella agreed. "But maybe not for the reason you're thinking? And on *that* bombshell—I'm out! Have a good chat, you two! Miss me!"

Marella gave a teasing salute before she wandered off in the same direction that Linh had gone, leaving Sophie with a little whiplash as she tried to figure out what that last comment was supposed to imply.

"Gotta love how unapologetically honest she is, huh?" Maruca asked, breaking the silence. "I'm trying to get better about doing the same thing—tell it like it is a little more."

Sophie cleared her throat. "Yeah . . . and I think I know what you're here to tell me."

"I know you do," Maruca said, tossing back a couple of her dreads. "Just like I know Wylie talked to you."

"You do?"

"Of course. He means well and I love him. But he's also a paranoid pain who makes me want to punch him."

"He's not *paranoid*," Sophie corrected gently. "Really bad things can happen to anyone who gets involved in this. Look at where Tam is right now."

"I know." Maruca stepped closer, clearly not backing down. "But I'm good with taking those kinds of risks. I know Wylie doesn't want me to—and that's sweet of him. I appreciate it. But that doesn't mean he gets to dictate my life for me. And since I'm sure you've had your share of people trying to make decisions for you because they think they know better than you do, I'm hoping you'll at least hear me out."

Sophie sighed and motioned for Maruca to follow her over to the shade of Calla's Panakes tree.

"Full disclosure," Sophie said while she sank down onto the grass, "it took me years to finally get on good terms with your cousin, and I *really* don't want to do anything to make him mad at me again."

"I get that," Maruca agreed, noticeably not sitting. "Just like I'm sure the next thing you're going to tell me is that you aren't in charge of who gets to join the Black Swan and who doesn't."

"Well . . . I'm not," Sophie had to point out.

"Maybe not. But come on—pretty much all the new members have been *your* friends," Maruca argued. "Don't even try to say there's not a connection."

"Yeah, well, for one thing, Mr. Forkle and I aren't really on great terms right now, so I'm not sure if I'm the best ally," Sophie admitted. "But even if I am, you realize I don't exactly love how many people I've dragged into this, right? If I'd never made friends with Tam and Linh at Exillium, he wouldn't be trapped with the Neverseen right now."

"And if you hadn't, Atlantis would be destroyed, and you guys would've been captured in Ravagog, and who knows what other stories I haven't heard?" Maruca countered.

"I know," Sophie said quietly. "I'm not saying I necessarily *regret* it. But . . . if something happens to any of you, I can't help blaming myself. And it'd be extra hard with you, because Wylie made me *promise* to keep you out of this. So . . . lots of guilt—and you know how dangerous guilt is."

"I do." Maruca's shoulders drooped and she stared at her hands. "Why do you think I'm here? I don't *want* to risk my life, or worry my mama, or Wylie, or anyone else. But you guys *need* me. I can keep you safe."

"How?" Sophie and Sandor asked in unison.

Maruca's eyebrows rose. "I take it that means Wylie didn't tell you?"

"About your ability?" Sophie clarified. "He told me you manifested, and he made it sound like you can do something pretty powerful. But he wouldn't tell me what it was."

"That's because he knows it changes everything," Maruca said, tossing back more of her dreadlocks. "Trust me. Once you know what I can do, you'll want me with you everywhere you go."

Sophie had a feeling she was going to regret this, but now she definitely had to know. "Okay, show me," she said, leaning back against Calla's trunk and crossing her arms.

Maruca nodded, looking both proud and nervous as she raised one hand, her fingers poised to snap.

Sophie assumed that meant she was about to reveal herself as a Flasher.

But the light that flared around Maruca was a glaring white curve that bent into a dome.

A force field.

"You're a Psionipath," Sophie breathed, stumbling to her feet.

"I am." Maruca snapped her fingers again, forming another perfect force field, this time around Sophie—which Sandor looked less than thrilled about, given that it separated him from his charge. "I saw how crucial the Neverseen's Psionipath was during the fight at Everglen. He kept his people safe *and* controlled all of you. And I can do exactly the same thing."

She snapped her fingers a third time, making both force fields disappear—then snapped again to form a single glowing dome around Calla's entire Panakes tree, caging her, Sophie, and Sandor in a wall of energy that grew thicker and thicker, until it was almost humming.

"I'm a Psionipath," Maruca emphasized. "I'm the piece you've been missing. And if you let me fight on your side, I can turn this game in our favor."

TWENTY-ONE

THE THING IS . . ." SOPHIE KNEW SHE WAS about to sound like one of the boring, lecture-y adults she'd rolled her eyes at *lots* of times over the last few years. But she needed to be *very* clear, and not get too wowed by the shiny force field glowing around them, even if her brain was screaming, *MARUCA'S A PSIONIPATH—THIS CHANGES EVERYTHING!*

She'd made a promise to Wylie to keep his cousin safe and out of the Black Swan—she had to at least *try* to hold up her end of that bargain.

"This isn't a game," she warned Maruca. "I've called it that before too, because it's easier to think of it that way. But it's not. It's *war*. Not the global, multispeciesial battle that Mr. Forkle thinks we're building toward—yet. But still. *War*."

Maruca didn't flinch at the word.

But she did *blink*.

And so did her force field.

The white light fizzled away for a couple of seconds before flickering back into place, like an old fluorescent light bulb.

"See?" Sophie asked, making sure to keep any triumph out of her voice. This wasn't about being right—it was about making Maruca understand the stakes. "That's all it takes. One moment of distraction. One second when you lose focus or let your guard down. I've seen it over and over—and I've done it myself, so I'm definitely not judging you for it, I promise. It happens sometimes. But when it does, people get hurt. Or die."

Maruca swallowed hard. "I *know*. But I only manifested a few weeks ago. I'm still learning how to control my ability. I haven't even told Magnate Leto yet, or been assigned to a Mentor. Once I start taking lessons, I'll be able to do a *lot* more."

"I'm sure you will," Sophie agreed. "But . . . maybe you should wait to get involved with the Black Swan until you're stronger and have had some time to practice. Because once the Neverseen know what you can do, you'll be their biggest target. And you'll be going head-to-head with Ruy, who's had *years* of training as a Psionipath—not to mention tons of battle experience. He's fast, and he's strong, and he knows all kinds of crazy tricks. And right now, you won't stand a chance against him."

"Not necessarily," Linh called from somewhere over Maruca's shoulder.

It took Sophie a second to spot Linh striding toward them, along with Marella—and Wynn and Luna, who trotted ahead and sniffed curiously at the force field.

"I saw the light," Linh explained, "and knew Maruca was going to need us for this next part."

"Next part?" Sophie asked.

Maruca let the force field fade so Linh and Marella could get closer.

"We might've had *one* other reason for coming here today," Marella admitted as she joined Sophie and Maruca in the shade. "Linh . . . thinks Ruy's been changed."

"Changed," Sophie repeated, not sure what to do with that word. "Changed how?"

"Don't you remember?" Linh's eyes glazed, as if her mind was focused on her memories instead of the present. "The night of the festival, when we were facing off at Everglen, my brother bound Ruy's wrists with shadowflux, and the darkness seeped into Ruy's skin. His fingers turned black and . . ."

"Ruy couldn't make another force field," Sophie finished, shivering as she remembered the way the shadowflux had poured out of Tam's palms—which meant he'd stored some of that horrible stuff inside of himself.

And the shadowflux had seemed more than happy to do his bidding.

"That's why the Neverseen fled," Marella said, reminding Sophie to pay attention. "They weren't so brave once they couldn't hide behind Ruy's handy little shields anymore."

Sophie pressed her arms to her sides, fighting the urge to reach for her eyelashes. "So . . . you think whatever Tam did to Ruy changed him *permanently*?"

"You don't?" Linh asked.

Sophie shook her head. "I figured it was just an injury he'd heal from after the battle."

She didn't even know abilities *could* be permanently changed.

Though . . . maybe "damaged" was a better word for it.

And wasn't that what had happened to her—twice?

Wasn't that why Mr. Forkle needed to reset her inflicting—and why she'd had to have her other abilities reset once before?

Then again, she was the only one with "flexible" genes, apparently.

She'd also come *very* close to dying both times her abilities changed—and Ruy had barely looked fazed by what Tam did at Everglen.

"I spoke with Lady Zillah," Linh said, crouching so she could be at eye level with Luna as she stroked Luna's silvery mane, "and I described what I saw and asked if she knew what skill Tam had used on Ruy in that moment. But she said shadowflux doesn't work that way. I guess once Tam calls for it, he can tell it to do pretty much anything he wants, as long as he's strong enough to *make* it obey. So there's no way to know exactly what command he gave the shadowflux. But . . . he didn't want Ruy to be able to shield Gethen and Vespera anymore—I know that much. He said something about having the newborn trolls go after the Neverseen instead of us, remember? Plus, Lady Zillah's always saying that shadowflux changes everything it touches, so the question isn't *whether or not* it changed him. It's *how much*. And the Neverseen have been *awfully* quiet lately—"

"They always are after one of their big attacks," Sophie reminded her. "That's how they operate. They show up, cause some huge disaster, and then disappear while they regroup and set up for their next plan."

"Maybe. But . . . they also took my brother." Linh's voice cracked on the last word, and she rested her head against Luna's neck, soaking up a baby-alicorn snuggle. "They have to be assuming we'll try to get him back, regardless of all the warnings they gave us. So you'd *think* they'd be doing stuff to scare us away or keep us too busy to plan a rescue—like they did when they attacked you and Fitz to keep you from focusing on Alvar. They also know Mr. Forkle is Magnate Leto now—*and* still alive—and they haven't made any moves against him. Or Tiergan. Or Juline. And they know you're an Enhancer—and that the alicorn babies are out of the hive and running around free at Havenfield—and they haven't tried to do anything about any of that, either. Doesn't that seem strange to you?"

Sophie noted that Maruca didn't look surprised by any of those revelations—and neither did Marella—as she told Linh, "Not necessarily. It hasn't been *that* long since Tam was taken."

It really hadn't been—even if it also felt like *forever*.

"The Council also didn't seem worried that the Neverseen had all of that information and hadn't made a move yet," Sophie added, still trying to convince herself she was right not to worry—even though she could hear Sandor mumbling about needing to talk to Bo, Flori, and Nubiti about security improvements.

"The Council doesn't exactly have the best track record for knowing what to focus on," Marella pointed out.

Which was definitely a valid point.

But Sophie didn't want to admit that, because she had a feeling this conversation was spiraling somewhere *very* dangerous, and she had to keep control. "I just know the Neverseen are strategic. They make *big* moves, not small ones. And they spread them out and take their time. So the fact that they haven't struck again isn't as telling as you think."

"Maybe," Linh conceded, nuzzling her nose into Luna's shimmery fur. "But you *have* to admit that it *could* also mean that they don't have their handy Psionipath to hide behind right now. Particularly when you think about how much the shadowflux affected you and Fitz. You can still feel it sometimes, can't you?"

Sophie flexed the fingers on her right hand, wishing they weren't weaker than they should be. "Only a little. I'm mostly better now."

"*Mostly,*" Marella emphasized. "And that's after how long? You and Fitz were in the Healing Center for *weeks*—and it's been even longer since you got out. So even if it's not permanent, there's a solid chance that Ruy's down for the count at the moment and the Neverseen are lying low because they know they're too vulnerable without him—which means if we make a move now, we'll catch them at their weakest."

"We might even be able to get my brother away from them."

Linh said the words so softly that Sophie almost wondered if she'd imagined them—until she saw the hope shining in Linh's eyes.

"Okaaaaaaaay," Sophie stalled, trying to figure out the right thing to say. "It sounds like . . . this has been on your mind for a while, if you already talked to Lady Zillah about it. So why have you waited until now to suggest it?"

"Because I knew it was still too dangerous," Linh said, calling Wynn over to her other side, so she was sandwiched between both baby alicorns. "Even without Ruy, the Neverseen are vicious, and I refuse to put anyone in a situation where they could get hurt—or worse. But . . . then Maruca stopped by and showed us what she can do, and . . . a plan started to come together. I just needed to think it through a little longer."

"I told them a couple of days ago," Maruca explained, "after Wylie said that he'd talked to you and that you were on his side. I thought it might help if I had some backup in my corner too. And then Linh told me about all of this, and . . . it does seem like perfect timing. So I promised her she can count on me for whatever she needs."

"Nothing with the Neverseen will ever be *perfect*," Sophie warned.

"Maybe not," Marella allowed, "but Maruca's ability is a game changer—"

"Or a *war* changer," Maruca cut in and corrected, "if that's what you want us to call it."

Marella shrugged. "Sure. Whatever. My point is, you *know* how important her ability is, Sophie. Especially right now, when the Neverseen don't even know she's a Psionipath or that she's working with us—"

"She's *not* working with us," Sophie felt the need to point out. "And technically, neither are you. You help out sometimes, but you haven't sworn fealty."

"I haven't?" Marella asked, fishing a very familiar necklace out from underneath her tunic—a black metal swan curving around a smooth glass monocle.

Sophie and her friends had each been given the same pendant after they'd officially joined the Black Swan.

"When did that happen?" Sophie asked, feeling even more out of the loop.

Marella tucked the pendant away. "Forkle suggested it after I agreed to take regular lessons with Fintan. He claimed that since pyrokinesis can be so all-consuming, it would be helpful for me to feel like I'm officially part of something bigger than my ability—but I'm pretty sure he mostly just wanted to lock me in on your side in case Fintan tried to recruit me."

"And you were okay with that?" Sophie needed to ask, despite the fact that the answer was already hanging around Marella's neck. There'd been a brief time, early in their friendship, when Marella had been bothered that Sophie had left her out of all the Black Swan–related stuff—but then Marella saw how dangerous it all was and hadn't seemed the least bit interested in joining anymore.

Marella shrugged. "Felt sort of inevitable at this point. Plus, the Council could come after me any day and try to shut down my ability training, so I figured it might be good to have some powerful people on my side who have no problem breaking rules when they need to."

"And I'll be part of the order as soon as I speak to the Collective," Maruca added, tilting her chin up defiantly. "We all know that once I show them what I can do, they'll let me join—even if you tell them not to, Sophie. But I'm hoping you won't do that. In fact, I'm *hoping* you'll put in a good word and speed things along. I know you made a promise to my cousin—but Wylie will get over it. I'll make sure of it. He needs to understand that just because he wants to keep me safe, it doesn't mean he gets to control my life. I'm not a little kid. *I* get to choose how I use my ability. And *I* choose to fight. So if he wants to protect me, he can fight beside me—or get out of my way. And if he doesn't? I'll knock him into a pile of mastodon poop and put a force field around him so he can spend some quality time with all that stink."

Sophie couldn't decide if she was intimidated or impressed.

Probably both.

"See why she's our secret weapon?" Marella asked with a huge grin. "She can handle this. And so can we. But we have to strike *now*, while the Neverseen are weak and unprepared and won't expect anything."

"Riiiiiiiiiiight," Sophie said, stalling again as she tried to find a nice way to word her next argument. "I mean, not to be the downer, but . . . I think you're forgetting that we don't actually know where the Neverseen are right now."

Linh stood, sending Wynn and Luna scattering. "Not yet. But I can find them."

"How?" Sandor demanded, beating Sophie to the question.

"Through Tam," Linh told him. "If Sophie will help me reach out to him."

Sophie's palms turned sweaty under her gloves. "You know Gethen will hear everything you say to Tam."

"But he won't understand it," Linh insisted. "Tam and I have a code. It's nothing fancy, just two 'I'm in trouble' phrases—one for me and one for him—plus some words we assigned other meanings to, in case we needed to communicate something beyond danger. And I think I've come up with a way to use that code to find out where he is without anyone knowing."

Sophie ignored the less-than-reassuring "I think" in that statement and focused on the bigger issue. "Okay, but . . . Tam doesn't know where he is."

"I'm sure he doesn't," Linh agreed. "But he doesn't have to. I'm going to ask him to send a signal that will lead me to him."

"What signal?" Sandor demanded as Sophie started picturing disastrous ideas, like super-conspicuous puffs of smoke.

"It's really hard to explain," Linh said quietly, "and I'll need Sophie's help to make it work. But . . . I think I can find him through the water."

Sophie glanced at Marella and Maruca, surprised by how readily they were nodding, as if what Linh had just said made perfect sense. "What water?"

"Any water." Linh raised her hand and curled her fingers, forming a tennis ball–size sphere out of the moisture in the air.

"Yeah . . . the thing is . . . it sounded like Tam was in some sort of dry desert cave the last time I talked to him," Sophie hated to tell her.

"Even if he is, there's *always* water." Linh wiggled her fingers, letting the sphere she'd formed unravel with a soft splash. "I realize this won't make much sense to you, but . . . when you enhanced me in Atlantis, I became very *aware*. It felt like I was connecting with water on a whole other level—like I was part of it, and it was part of me, and my consciousness had no beginning or ending because the water was everywhere and in everything. And I think, if you enhance me again, I can use that awareness to find Tam. I just need him to let his shadow touch water while I'm listening— and in order to tell him to do that, I need you to reach out to him telepathically."

"I'm not saying I won't," Sophie said—ignoring Sandor's protests. "But . . . you know contacting him puts him in danger, right? No matter what you say to him or how much the Neverseen understand, they'll still know we reached out and punish him somehow?"

"Why do you think I haven't asked you before?" Linh waved her hand, pulling the tears from her eyes and letting them glisten like tiny diamonds in front of her before she flicked her fingers and they vanished into mist. "I wouldn't put my brother at risk—or any of you—if I didn't truly believe this would work. I can find him, and we can bring him home safely."

Sandor opened his mouth, but Sophie cut him off. "All she's asking for right now is a telepathic conversation."

"Yes, but if this convoluted plan works, I need you to understand that you're not going *anywhere*—none of you are," Sandor informed them. "End of discussion. I will allow you to attempt to gather the information, in case it proves helpful to those who can safely carry out the kind of ambush you're describing—though I also seem to remember your last conversation with Tam triggering your echoes," he reminded Sophie.

"Then Flori can sing to me again," she told him. "But I doubt I'll need her. I'm stronger now. Especially here, under Calla's tree." She closed her eyes, breathing in the sweet floral scent and soaking up the breezy melody before she turned back to Linh, studying the determination in her features. "You know what's best for your brother way better than I do. And you know your abilities. And you've clearly put a lot of thought into this. So if you want to try . . ."

Linh nodded, lowering herself to the grass and crossing her legs as Sophie sat across from her.

"Is there anything you need me to do right now?" Maruca asked.

"Or me?" Marella added.

"You can keep an eye on Wynn and Luna," Sophie told them. "Apparently they have super-poor taste in friends. So if they try to go near the gorgodon—stop them."

Marella shuddered. "Ugh, I forgot that creepy beast lived here. I mean, I know we're supposed to be all about protecting animals and stuff, but . . . that thing's not natural. I can't believe the Council hasn't ordered it to be destroyed."

"And I can't believe the Council isn't resetting the Timeline to Extinction again," Linh said absently, gathering dewdrops off the fallen Panakes petals and letting them hover around her like twinkling stars.

"Why would they?" Sophie wondered.

"Because the gorgodon's the last of its kind," Linh reminded her. "Once it's gone, the species is extinct."

"Yeah, but it's not a real species," Marella argued.

Linh let her watery stars evaporate. "Being created doesn't make it any less *real*. Look at Sophie."

Sophie definitely wasn't sure what to do with that comparison— or Linh's point about the gorgodon. But that wasn't what she needed to be focusing on anyway. "Am I supposed to enhance you now?" she asked.

Linh shook her head. "Not until Tam's ready to send the signal. Once I connect to the water, it's all-consuming, and I need to concentrate on sending the message first."

Sophie tugged off her gloves anyway, since she still had her fingernail gadgets to block the ability, and she doubted Linh wanted all the crusty mud near her face. But she hesitated before reaching for Linh's temples. "I might be able to open a mental channel between the three of us, so you guys can communicate directly. I've never tried doing that over such a long distance, so I don't know if it'll work. But we can find out, if you want."

Fresh tears brimmed in Linh's eyes. "I'll be able to hear his voice?"

"That's what I'm hoping—but . . . no guarantees, okay?"

Linh nodded. But she looked so heartbreakingly hopeful that

Sophie almost wished she hadn't mentioned it until she knew whether or not it was possible.

"I'll also need permission to open my mind to yours," she said, closing her eyes and gathering her mental strength.

"Of course," Linh whispered, and Sophie pressed her fingers against Linh's temples and stretched out her consciousness, imagining it wrapping around both her and Linh like a sheer curtain.

Linh's thoughts poured slowly into her mind, and the world turned quieter.

Softer.

Reality drifting gently away.

It took Sophie a second to realize that the sensation reminded her of being underwater.

Is this what your head feels like all the time? Sophie asked, trying to remember if she'd noticed it the other times she'd communicated telepathically with Linh.

A little. But it's stronger when I'm trying to concentrate. The words rippled like waves. *I think better when I let the pull of the water fill my mind, if that makes sense.*

Not really, Sophie admitted. *But I'm not a Hydrokinetic. And it IS easier to focus this way.*

With the rest of the world muffled, she could feel each of her thoughts individually, stretching them into threads, which she used to tether Linh's mind to hers.

We'll see if that holds, Sophie transmitted, letting her mental energy pool between the two of them, the warm hum growing stronger and stronger and stronger. *If it does, you and Tam should be able to hear each other—assuming I can make contact.*

Thank you for doing this, Linh told her.

You don't have to thank me. I'll do anything I can to help you and your brother—I hope you know that.

I do. And I want you to know that this is my choice—what you're doing right now, and what I'm asking you to do if this works. If any part of this backfires, I won't blame you.

Let's hope we won't have to think about that, Sophie transmitted, squeezing her eyes tighter as the humming inside her mind turned crackly, like static—or maybe a better analogy would've been like a wave crashing toward the shore. She could feel her consciousness get swept up in the inertia, surging forward, forward, forward . . .

Brace yourself! she warned. *This next part will be loud.*

Linh nodded under her fingertips, and they both sucked in a breath as Sophie shoved the energy out of her mind in a blaring transmission.

TAM! PLEASE DON'T IGNORE ME!

PLEASE!

PLEASE!

PLEASE!

She repeated the call again and again, each transmission like a mental river, carrying her plea along with the rush, churning farther, farther, farther. But no matter how far the words flowed, only silence followed.

Do you think it would help if I call for him? Linh offered.

He won't be able to hear you until he lets me connect with his mind. Unless . . .

Unless what? Linh asked when Sophie didn't finish the thought.

I have a weird idea—and I don't know if it'll work, but . . . can you think his name for a minute? Just his name—and give it your whole concentration, like it's the only solid thing in your head.

Linh did as Sophie asked, and Sophie gathered up the sound, wrapping her consciousness around it until it felt like she'd formed an airtight bundle, with Linh's voice echoing softly inside.

A thought bubble of sorts.

Here goes nothing, she told Linh, letting her strange mental creation drift out of her mind, like a message in a bottle, floating through the space between her and Tam, drifting across the vast nothingness.

CAN YOU HEAR WHO I'M WITH? she transmitted, shoving Linh's plea farther and farther. *LINH NEEDS TO TALK TO YOU. IT'S IMPORTANT.*

More silence surrounded them, and Linh's disappointment was almost tangible as Sophie tried to edge her consciousness away from the headache looming ahead—a mental waterfall that would drag them both down into the pain if she didn't sever their connection before she reached it.

PLEASE, TAM—TAKE THE RISK.

TAM!

TAM!

TAM!

TAM!

TA—

A shadow darkened Sophie's mind—the rush both icy and eerie.

Linh gripped Sophie's wrists. *Tam?*

DO YOU HAVE ANY IDEA HOW DANGEROUS THIS IS??? Tam shouted.

The words were cold black stones.

Sinking through Sophie's consciousness.

Crashing into the darkness lingering below.

But Sophie focused on Linh's laughter, refusing to let the echoes stir.

It's nice to hear from you, too, Linh told her brother. *Good to know you're still as stubborn and surly as ever.*

Tam's thoughts seemed to stumble over themselves—stunned by the sound of his sister's voice.

But he recovered quickly, his consciousness tangling into another dark storm that battered around their shared minds as he thought, *SERIOUSLY, LINH—WE CAN'T TALK LIKE THIS! YOU DON'T KNOW WHAT YOU'RE DOING.*

Actually, I do, she assured him. *I know it's a risk. But I had to talk to you—and I need you to listen carefully. I need you to tell me if it's safe to swim in the ocean.*

THE OCEAN? Tam repeated—though Sophie could feel his thoughts swarming around each of Linh's words, beyond just those few. And several seconds later he asked—very carefully—*HOW WOULD I KNOW?*

Linh sat up straighter. *Can't you dip your toe in for me?*

The words hung there, and Sophie held her breath—feeling Linh do the same.

And for a moment, the cold shadows turned warmer and lighter.

But the blackness came crashing back before Tam finally answered. And he simply told her, *NO.*

Tam, you—

NO! Tam's shout was louder than thunder, and it drowned out every syllable of Linh's argument. *STAY OUT OF THE WATER.*

I can't, she told him. *You know I can't.*

WELL, YOU'RE GOING TO HAVE TO.

Tam—

NO, LINH. YOU DON'T GET IT. I LIKE IT HERE. DO YOU HEAR ME? I. LIKE. IT. HERE.

A shudder rocked Linh's shoulders, as if she'd been physically struck. *You don't mean that.*

I DO, he assured her. *I REALLY, REALLY DO. I'M EVEN MAKING FRIENDS. SO FORGET YOUR PLANS AND YOUR CODES. I DON'T NEED THEM. I DON'T EVEN WANT THEM.*

But—

NO! SOMEDAY YOU'LL UNDERSTAND, he told her.

I really, really won't, Linh countered, and Sophie wondered if she was intentionally mirroring his phrasing.

WELL . . . THAT'S NOT MY PROBLEM! Tam insisted, and his words formed a wall, shutting out everything else Linh tried to tell him. Leaving his mind so bitingly, painfully cold that Sophie knew they couldn't stay any longer.

Come on, Linh, Sophie thought, letting her consciousness slowly ebb away.

NO! Linh shaped her next thought into a tidal wave and slammed it into the darkness. *What am I supposed to do without you?*

Sophie didn't expect Tam to answer.

But he told Linh, *GO BACK TO CHORALMERE.*

Tam—

GO BACK TO CHORALMERE AND STAY THERE, he thundered. *AND DON'T EVER CALL FOR ME AGAIN.*

Then the shadows faded and Sophie's mind brightened and warmth poured in, like rays of dawn melting away the night—snuffing out the stirring echoes and leaving her head still and steady and silent.

"He's gone," Sophie said out loud, severing the final threads of the connection in case Gethen had somehow found a way to eavesdrop on that pocket of mental conversation.

"I know." Linh's voice sounded both watery and wobbly, and when Sophie's eyes came into focus, she found Marella and Maruca pulling Linh into a hug.

"Are you okay?" Sophie asked, knowing it was a pointless question. "I'm sure Tam only said that stuff because he was trying to protect you. He did the same thing last time—"

"No, he meant it." Tears streamed down Linh's cheeks, and she let them fall as she added, "I didn't realize how hard it would be to hear him like that."

"Like what?" Marella asked.

"So . . . stubborn and hopeless."

"Hopeless?" Sophie repeated.

Linh stared at the sky. "I think he's giving up."

Maruca hugged her tighter. "Didn't he understand that you were ready to rescue him?"

"He did. But . . . he didn't want me to. He told me to 'stay out of the water,' which wasn't part of our code—but it's what he said a lot when I first manifested and he knew I was about to make a mess of everything."

She dried her tears with her sleeve, but more replaced them immediately.

"You didn't make a mess of everything," Sophie tried to tell her.

Linh just looked away. "We can't reach out to him again. He won't respond—and he'll never cooperate. He doesn't want me to find him."

Sophie kept her face angled down, trying to hide her relief.

Even with Maruca's force fields, she couldn't see how any rescue attempt would end in anything other than disaster, nor could she imagine any possible scenario where Sandor would let them try.

"Why would he want you to go to Choralmere?" Sophie wondered, recognizing the name of the Song family's estate.

Tam had almost as many mommy and daddy issues as Keefe did—and he'd always been *very* opposed to the idea of giving his parents a single second of their time, now that he and Linh were free of them.

Linh stumbled to her feet, swiping at her smudged eyeliner. "He doesn't. That was the code."

"The code for when he's in danger?" Marella asked.

Linh shook her head. "No. The code for when *I* am."

TWENTY-TWO

DO YOU THINK TAM WAS JUST TRYING to scare you?" Sophie asked as she watched Linh pace around Calla's Panakes tree, taking slow, meticulous steps—as if Linh were trying to match her previous footprints with each revolution. "That way you'd abandon your rescue plan for him? Or to make sure you wouldn't risk reaching out to him again?"

"Or maybe those things are *why* he thinks you're in danger?" Maruca suggested. "And he was trying to tell you to lay off, so you'll be safe again."

Linh ignored Wynn and Luna as they trotted up beside her— even when they made some seriously adorable squeaky whinnies. "If any of that were Tam's reasoning, he would've just reminded me of the Neverseen's threats. Using the code means he doesn't want the Neverseen to know he's warning me. So I'm pretty sure that means they really are planning to come after me, either to kill me or capture me—or maybe to injure me the way they did to you and Fitz."

She said it so matter-of-factly that Sophie couldn't decide if she should be impressed by Linh's bravery or worry that her friend was in shock.

Shock seemed to be the answer when Linh casually added, "I just hope they don't send Tam to do it."

Sophie jumped in front of her, blocking her path. "Tam would never do any of those things."

"I know." Linh tilted her head back to stare at the sky. "And that'd be so much worse—seeing how they punish him."

"It's never going to come to that," Sophie promised. "I won't let it."

"Neither will I," Marella added.

"Same," Maruca agreed.

Linh's eyes brimmed with tears and she turned her face away. "I guess we'll see how it goes," she said as she broke her pattern of footprints to step around Sophie.

"We *will* see!" Sophie called after her. "And right now, we need a plan to protect you."

"I don't need protecting!" Linh reached up and pulled a pin from her hair, letting the long, silver-tipped strands fly free with the afternoon breeze. "I need to go back to Choralmere."

Sophie glanced at Marella and Maruca, glad to see they were equally as confused by that statement.

"Why?" Maruca asked for them.

"Yeah, that seems like the last place you should go," Marella added. "Isn't that the one place the Neverseen know to look for you?"

Linh shrugged, bending the clasp of her hairpin back and forth. "It's not like I'm hiding right now—or when I go home to Tiergan."

"No, but you should be," Sophie argued, "now that Tam gave us this warning. I'm sure the Black Swan or the Council can find some-where—"

"I *have* to go to Choralmere," Linh interrupted. "Otherwise the Neverseen will suspect that Tam's words had another meaning, and that'll put him in even more danger." Her voice thickened when she met Sophie's eyes and added, "I should've listened to you. You warned me that reaching out to him was too dangerous."

"We had to try it," Sophie told her.

Linh wouldn't have been able to stop wondering whether they were missing their chance to save her brother.

"And hey, Tam's probably relieved that he finally got to pass along that warning," Sophie added. "Who knows how long he's been carrying it around, trying find a way to reach you? Now we just need to figure out a plan to keep you safe."

"I'll be fine at Choralmere," Linh assured her.

"Will you, though?" Marella jumped in. "I mean, even without it being a super-obvious place for the Neverseen to find you, it's . . . not like you have an awesome relationship with your parents."

Linh stopped pacing. "I can handle my mother and father."

Sophie, Marella, and Maruca shared another look.

"Okay, but—" Sophie started to say, but Linh cut her off.

"I'm *going* to Choralmere!" She added a foot stomp for empha-sis, then turned her face to the wind and closed her eyes. "And I'm going to stay there, just like Tam wanted."

"So . . . you're moving back home?" Sophie had to clarify.

Linh nodded. "It's the best thing I can do for Tam. Please don't try to talk me out of it."

"I won't," Sophie promised, not sure what else to say.

Marella and Maruca seemed pretty stumped too.

But Sandor stalked closer, towering over Linh as he told her, "If that's your decision, you'll need protection."

"I have dwarven bodyguards," Linh reminded him.

"I'm aware." Sandor glanced at the ground, looking slightly skeptical that the dwarves were actually there. "But I think a more visible deterrent might be better, given the threat you're presently facing. I'll need time to arrange something more permanent, but for the moment I'm sure Bo would be willing to accompany you, provided Miss Foster agrees to stay here, where she's less likely to need his protection."

"Or I could go with Bo and Linh," Sophie countered, "help her get settled in and—"

"I appreciate the offer," Linh interrupted. "But it'll be better if I go alone. I doubt my parents know that Tam has been taken—I certainly haven't told them. And that conversation will go smoother without the complication of an audience."

"Linh—"

"I'll be fine, Sophie," Linh insisted. "I know how to handle my parents."

Sandor cleared his throat when Sophie fell silent. "That may very well be. But it's all the more reason I'm going to insist that you take Bo with you."

"I'm okay with that," Linh agreed, "as long as Sophie doesn't need him."

"She won't," Sandor assured her, "because she's going to remain here with Flori, Nubiti, and me, right?"

Sophie nodded, and Sandor marched off to find Bo and explain the new arrangement.

"My father's going to *hate* having an ogre patrolling the property," Linh said quietly, "so that will be fun, at least."

"You're sure about—" Sophie tried to ask.

But once again, Linh cut her off. "I'm sure."

"Yeah, well . . . I don't like this plan," Marella said, shrugging when Linh turned toward her. "Someone had to say it."

"I agree," Maruca added. "Maybe I should go with you—that way I can shield you if anything goes down."

"I'll be fine," Linh repeated for what felt like the millionth time, and the weariness in Linh's voice made Sophie leave it alone.

After all, Linh had started her day thinking she'd found a way to rescue her brother. And instead, she was now stuck moving back in with the people who'd failed her over and over, because they'd been ashamed that she was a twin. Plus, she'd picked up an abundance of new worries for herself and for Tam.

"We're going to get him back," Sophie promised, pulling Linh into a hug—which Maruca and Marella quickly turned into a group squeeze.

Linh nodded against Sophie's shoulder.

But there were tears in Linh's eyes when she ended the embrace, and she wouldn't look at anyone as she fished out a small, round home crystal that Sophie never realized she carried.

No one broke the painful silence, until Bo marched over to Linh and barked a bunch of orders about letting him take the lead and sticking by his side. And Sophie tried to think of something encouraging to say as Linh held her crystal up to the sun.

But every promise sounded so empty. So she went with the same assurance that Linh had said when she first found out that Tam had left with the Neverseen.

"Tam can take care of himself."

"I hope so," Linh whispered as she let the light carry her and Bo away.

Marella and Maruca left soon after—though not before Maruca made it clear that she *would* be talking to the Collective about joining the order. And Sophie didn't try to stop her.

If Tam's warning had proven anything, it was that they needed all the protection they could get.

Though it wasn't nightmares about cloaked figures coming for Linh—or coming for any of Sophie's friends—that had Sophie building another makeshift bed under Calla's Panakes that night.

It was Tam's voice, replaying in her head.

Shouting over and over, *I LIKE IT HERE. I'M EVEN MAKING FRIENDS.*

"We need to have a serious discussion about your leadership skills, Miss Foster," Bronte's sharp voice barked the next morning, jolting Sophie out of the dazed, half-sleepy state she'd been lingering in since sunrise. "And perhaps also about your strange choices for sleeping location."

Some part of her brain had been telling her that she needed to get up and get ready for a big day of super-important stuff.

The other part had decided that all of that stuff could wait a *tiny* bit longer.

And then a tiny bit longer after that.

And a little more after that.

As if she'd found some sort of strange mental snooze button—

which she was happy to keep hitting as long as it let her stay surrounded by baby alicorns and Calla's soothing songs instead of having to face reality.

And now her entire brain was telling her that the best solution to her current situation was to pull her blankets over her head and wait for Bronte to go away.

The only problem was . . . Bronte was right.

Part of the *stuff* she had to do that day was the rather important task of going to Loamnore with Grady and the rest of Team Valiant to meet with King Enki and examine the dwarves' security. And she'd planned to check in with Dex, Biana, Wylie, and Stina the day before, to make sure they were ready.

But then there was the chaos with Wynn and Luna and the gorgodon—and Maruca, Marella, and Linh showed up with their risky plan, and there was all the drama with Tam and . . .

It totally slipped her mind.

She also *still* hadn't followed up with Wylie and Stina about their meeting with Lady Zillah—despite her vow not to get sidetracked from that again.

And she couldn't even argue that they should've reached out to her when they didn't hear from her, because she'd ignored a bunch of hails after her standoff with Mr. Forkle, and there was a good chance that some of those had been from her teammates.

She was also pretty sure that she hadn't actually given Dex an assignment to work on.

And Biana . . .

Sophie stopped breathing when she realized who Biana had been trying to arrange a meeting with—and why.

The same person who barked again. "Miss Foster, I know you're awake."

Sophie held extra still, wondering if there was any way to trick her mind into playing possum for her. Lapsing into a vegetative state for a few hours seemed like the only viable option at that point.

Until another voice said, "Maybe we should let her rest a little longer," and Sophie's eyes popped open—as if her brain had decided, *You can ignore the grumpy Councillor, but not the nice one.*

And Oralie did reward her with a warm, reassuring smile.

But then Sophie's gaze followed the movement in her periphery, and before she could stop herself, she was focused on Councillor Bronte.

And there was something extra unsettling about his stare.

A wariness in his expression that she'd never seen before. Mixed with . . .

Was it pity?

Maybe even a dash of curiosity?

All of which swirled together into a nauseating reality.

He knows.

Biana must've followed through with her plan to confront him about being Sophie's biological father—and if Sophie'd had any doubt, the fact that Bronte broke eye contact first definitely settled it.

But he cleared his throat, ever the steady taskmaster, and asked her, "Do you need us to explain why we're less than satisfied with your leadership skills?"

"*Satisfaction* has nothing to do with it," Oralie corrected. "We understand that it's going to take some time for you to fully adjust to your new responsibilities, and we simply want you to know that we're here to help you organize and prioritize. I think it might be wise for us to come up with a schedule of things for you to do every morning and every evening until they begin to feel like a habit. For instance . . ."

Sophie tried to listen as Oralie listed off what were surely lots of helpful leadership suggestions.

But her brain was too stuck on other, much more selfish questions like, *Was Bronte, or wasn't he?*

And, *Did she even want to know?*

Mr. Forkle had already claimed Bronte wasn't, but . . . that didn't necessarily make it true.

"Sophie?" Oralie asked, and Sophie blinked back to proper focus, realizing that hadn't been the first time Oralie had called her name.

"Are you okay?" Oralie asked, reaching for Sophie's forehead like she was checking for a fever. "Should we hail Elwin?"

Sophie shook her head and forced herself to sit up—which turned out to be a mistake. An overwhelming head rush blacked out the world, and she would've collapsed back onto her pillow if Oralie hadn't grabbed her shoulders.

"You're sure you don't want me to call for Elwin?" Oralie checked. "Or at least for your parents?"

Sophie cringed at the last word.

And Oralie frowned, tracing her fingers down Sophie's arms— which made Sophie realize two things.

One: She was still in her jammies, which had both ruffled shorts *and* hopping jackalopes on the tank top. . . .

And two: Oralie was reading her emotions.

"You feel very . . . strange," Oralie said softly, closing her eyes and tilting her head. "The worry, I understand—though you're not in any trouble, despite what Bronte may wish you to believe. But there's such reluctance, and dread, and—"

Sophie pulled her arms away before Oralie could add anything else to that list of feelings.

"I'm fine," she promised, relieved to have her voice working. "I'm just . . ."

She needed an end to that sentence.

But her brain had run out of useful words.

Bronte sighed and stalked to the edge of the Panakes, brushing aside the curtain of weeping willow–esque branches to gaze out at the pastures. "Should I assume this means you haven't followed up with young Miss Vacker since she spoke with me?"

Sophie managed a nod.

Bronte shook his head. "Wonderful, so I'm going to have to endure this conversation a second time."

"What conversation?" Oralie asked.

Don't say it, Sophie mentally begged.

She may have even transmitted the plea.

But if she did, Bronte ignored her—and it turned into one of those surreal moments where everything seemed to switch to slow motion as he turned back around to face her.

Her ears were ringing so loudly that she couldn't make out any of the first words that crawled out of his lips—but then her brain caught back up to speed, and she managed to hear the most important part.

"For the record, Miss Foster, I most certainly am *not.*"

"Not what?" Oralie wondered as Sophie's body turned numb and noodle-y.

She flopped back onto her pillow as Bronte made a sound that was half growl, half groan.

"If you must know," he told Oralie, "I'm not her biological father."

Even from her horizontal vantage point, Sophie could see Oralie's mouth drop open.

"Why would . . . ?" Oralie stumbled to her feet, wrapping her arms around her waist. "I don't understand."

"Neither do I," Bronte admitted, tearing his fingers through his closely cropped hair. "Apparently Miss Foster has chosen to ignore my vehement recommendation that she stay focused on her far more pressing assignments, and has instead recruited her teammates into assisting with her ill-conceived search for her biological parents. And thanks to the unfortunate coincidence that she and I both share a rare ability, they've fixated on me. So I got to endure a rather ridiculous meeting with Miss Vacker the other day, wherein she accused me of participating in Project Moonlark *and* had Miss Heks test the veracity of my answer." His eyes narrowed at Sophie. "Which is why I feel the need to say, once more for the official record—or as official as we're going to get in these circumstances: I am *not* your genetic father, Miss Foster. By *any* means. And if you need to verify that I'm telling the truth, ask Councillor Oralie."

Oralie stumbled away from both of them, shaking her head hard enough to tangle some of her ringlets. "I don't want to be involved in this."

"Neither do I," Bronte noted. "And yet, here I am."

Oralie's rosy cheeks turned very, very pale. "If anyone found out . . ."

"They won't," Bronte assured her, "because there's nothing *to* find out. Isn't that right, Miss Foster? This whole convoluted theory was simply the wild imaginings of a few foolish teenagers. And now that they've seen it for its absurdity, they're going to let it go. Aren't they?"

His lips quirked with the tiniest hint of a smile when Sophie nodded.

"Excellent."

"It *is*," Sophie agreed, feeling her temper click back on now that the shock was finally wearing off. She held Bronte's stare as she told him, "It's a huge relief."

In fact, her head felt lighter than it had in days.

Minus twenty pounds of worry.

"Good," Bronte told her, his familiar scowl returning. "Because this is the end of this conversation. Understood? I want your word that no mention of this will be made to anyone else, ever again. Not to me. Not to your friends or family. Certainly not to anyone new." He strode closer, looming over her. "And I also want you to promise me that you'll listen this time and stop this foolish quest before you cause irreparable damage—and I'm not referring to any challenges you'll cause for the elves who actually *are* your genetic parents, though you'll likely destroy them with the scandal. Think of how many crucial tasks you've already neglected because you've allowed yourself to be so distracted—and before you try to deny it, keep in mind that *I* gathered an update from Miss Heks about her meeting with Lady Zillah once we'd moved past the ridiculous accusation. And not only did she and Wylie acquire several pieces of information that could prove vital in our visit to Loamnore today, but she also mentioned that you'd never bothered to follow up with them.

Nor had you responded when they'd reached out to you. And that kind of sloppy leadership cannot continue, Miss Foster. Councillor Oralie and I are happy to help you set up some systems for checks and balances—but none of them will matter if you choose to be sidetracked. It's time for you to focus, before someone gets hurt."

He was absolutely right.

And Sophie hated him for it.

She also hated herself for hating him for it—and for failing so hard at everything lately.

All the time she'd spent stressing and obsessing about her genetic parents and matchmaking—and what did she have to show for it?

Another disproved theory about her biological father, and a boyfriend she'd neglected so badly that he might not even be her boyfriend anymore.

And yet, despite all that, she still wasn't willing to promise what Bronte wanted.

So she told him, "I promise I'm going to adjust my priorities and concentrate on the bigger problems."

"Don't think I don't notice what you're doing there, Miss Foster," Bronte countered.

"I'm sure you do," she agreed. "But wouldn't you rather I be honest with you?"

He blew out a breath. "I suppose. So long as you're also ready to take your position as Regent more seriously."

She stared at her lap, tugging at the stupid ruffles on her shorts, which probably made it harder for him to believe her when she said, "I am."

"Good," Bronte told her, frowning when he glanced at Oralie, who still stood several steps away, her gaze fixed on the horizon. "Then go inside and get ready. To play the part, you first need to look the part—isn't that right, Oralie?"

Oralie didn't respond.

Bronte cleared his throat and turned back to Sophie. "The rest of your teammates should be here within the hour, so I suggest you hurry. We have much to discuss before their arrival. And then together, we'll all need to go over the protocol for meeting with King Enki, as well as some fundamentals for what to expect in Loamnore. In many, many ways the city is unlike anywhere you've been before. In fact, it can be downright disorienting. So the more you prepare ahead of time, the better."

Sophie nodded, knowing it probably didn't help instill Bronte with a lot of confidence when she gathered up her blankets, pillows, and Ella and stumbled toward the house with the giant bundle, tripping over her feet several times.

But she didn't feel right leaving all of that outside.

And it wasn't like she needed to impress him.

He wasn't her father.

Never before had those words been such a happy thing, and she repeated them with every step, feeling her smile grow wider and wider.

But it faded when Bronte called after her, "Remember who you are now, Miss Foster. And when you return, make sure you're wearing your crown."

TWENTY-THREE

ANYONE ELSE *REALLY* HATE THIS?" Stina asked, scrunching up her face as she took a cautious step onto the soggy ground in front of her. The mud suctioned around her foot, and she screamed and jumped back, nearly falling when her boot stayed lodged in the sludge. "Seriously," Stina grumbled, using telekinesis to retrieve her goop-covered shoe. "It's disgusting."

Sophie definitely wasn't going to argue with Stina's assessment of the situation—particularly as she waded another step into the bog and the squishy ground slipped away under her feet, leaving her with the thick, stinky mud now up past her knees. She could feel its curdled texture through the thin fabric of her leggings and was *not* looking forward to having the same muck directly on her skin. Her gloves stopped at her wrists, and the blue tunic she'd worn was unfortunately sleeveless, leaving lots of exposed arm—and she didn't even want to think about the fact that she was going to have to dunk her face and head under. . . .

The desert was also glaringly bright and annoyingly windy, and the temperature had to be at least a million degrees—even in the small oasis they'd reached after several long minutes of hiking. The patch of green and blue had seemed so mysterious and inviting when Sophie had first spotted it among the endless sea of rippled dunes—the kind of place where she might find a magic carpet. Or a genie's lamp.

But *of course* Bronte and Grady had led them past the cool, shimmering lagoon without even pausing to dip a toe in. They'd also ignored the much-needed shade formed by the clumps of lacy palm trees, instead heading straight for an icky brown quagmire on the far side of the oasis, bordered by scraggly grass.

The area kind of looked like something that'd be used as a camel potty spot—and it very well might be.

Sophie was trying *really* hard not to wonder about that as her next step sank her even deeper into the mud.

But she couldn't help glancing longingly at Sandor, who'd managed to find a place that was both well shaded and a little breezy to stand as sentinel while they went on without him. Goblins weren't allowed to enter the dwarven city, so Sandor was restricted to guarding Loamnore's entrance—and Woltzer and Lovise had been forbidden from joining them at all.

Sandor had been complaining *vigorously* about the restrictions— right up until he saw the mire of steaming mud they all had to sink through.

Then he'd become *much* more cooperative.

"You're sure this is the only way to get to Loamnore?" Stina asked, earning several heaving sighs from Grady and Bronte.

Oralie had decided to stay behind when they'd left Havenfield, and at first Sophie had found that to be a little strange. But now that she was experiencing the mud-drenched method of entry into the dwarven city, Sophie was pretty sure she understood why the pretty Councillor had decided to skip the visit to King Enki.

"For the fifth and final time, Miss Heks, yes—*this is our path*," Bronte snapped as he strode into the muck in all of his jewel-encrusted finery. Within three steps, he'd sunk past his waist. "Do you honestly think I would use it if there were any alternative?"

"Well, there *should* be an alternative," Stina muttered, stomping her boot to clean off as much of the gunk as she could.

Clearly she was in denial about the muddy fun she still had ahead of her.

"You'll be fine," Sophie promised. "Alden and I had to sink through quicksand at the Gateway to Exile, and it really wasn't that big of a deal."

Though, she couldn't help a tiny shudder as her mind flashed back to that scratchy, suffocating fall.

"The dwarves seem to like messy entrances," Dex noted, moving to the lead of their muddy group. He was even grinning, like he was actually enjoying the journey through the sludge.

"It's not about what we *like*," Nubiti corrected as her furry face popped out of a nearby patch of sand, and Sophie was pretty sure her dwarven bodyguard was smirking at all of them for squealing like schoolchildren—but it was hard to tell with Nubiti's squinted eyes. "It's that your species is useless at tunneling, so we've had to get creative in order to give you access to our world."

"Or you could just dig a tunnel," Stina argued. "Carve in some of those things called 'stairs'—maybe you've heard of them?"

"A tunnel like that would greatly compromise Loamnore's security," Nubiti countered.

"Yeah, but it wouldn't be gross!" Stina snapped back. "And wait a minute—Tam and Linh lived in a house in Loamnore for a while, didn't they? So how did they get back from the Lost Cities after school and stuff? Don't even *try* telling me they were diving into pools of sludgy mud all the time. No way that's what happened."

"That's true," Sophie realized, "Mr. Forkle gave them special magsidian pendants he'd gotten from King Enki."

"Perfect—where do I get one of those?" Stina demanded.

"That's not how it works," Nubiti corrected. "Accessing a residence is different than accessing the city as a whole. Each residence has its own unique security—and some are far more flexible than others, like the place where your friends stayed. And before you ask, no, accessing a residence doesn't mean you can then access the main city, just like visiting one of your estates does not then lead to any of your cities."

"Right, but our houses are scattered all over the planet," Stina reminded her, "and so are our cities, so that's a whole different thing. I've seen maps of Loamnore—your residences are *right here*."

"That does not mean there's a way for an elf to pass from one to another," Nubiti insisted.

Stina rolled her eyes. "Well, there should be. Seriously, this is the most ridiculous arrangement I've ever heard of!"

"Hey, we make everyone slide down a giant whirlpool to get to Atlantis," Biana reminded her, sounding surprisingly chipper for a girl who usually obsessed about her hair and makeup and was currently thigh-deep in poop-colored muck. "Fitz still talks about how freaked out Sophie was the first time she had to try it. He said he was about three seconds away from having to push her over the edge because she was frozen in place."

The sound of Fitz's name made Sophie's heart both fluttery *and* heavier—but she shoved all of those feelings aside.

She was *not* letting any boy worries distract her that day.

But she could tell Biana was watching her, waiting for some sort of reaction. So she announced to everyone, "I would've taken Fitz with me if he'd tried."

The threat might've sounded more ominous if she hadn't lost her balance on her next step—and she would've face-planted into the mud if Wylie hadn't lunged to grab her shoulders. The poor guy ended up sunken all the way to his chest as a reward for his heroics.

"Thanks," Sophie mumbled, not quite meeting Wylie's eyes.

She hadn't found the right moment to ask if he'd spoken to Maruca yet, but she had a feeling that if he had, he would've let her eat some stinky mud—and she probably would've deserved it.

But she'd worry about the Wylie and Maruca problem later. If her lecture from Bronte and Oralie had taught her anything that morning, it was that she had to keep her mind focused on the most pressing worry in each moment. And given that they were currently making a rather disgusting journey to have a meeting she definitely didn't feel prepared for, she needed to concentrate on figuring out what she was going to say to King Enki.

"I gotta admit," she said as the sludgy brown goop reached her chest, covering the silver moonlight clasp pinning her golden sunlight cape. "I don't really get why you made us wear all of our fancy Regent accessories if you knew we'd be mud monsters by the time we got there."

"The mud completes the ensemble," Grady teased, winking at her from near the center of the swampy pool, where he stood shoulder-deep, waiting for everyone to catch up to him.

"Or maybe I'll lose the stupid circlet when I get sucked under," Sophie muttered under her breath.

That *might* make the slimy experience worth it.

She'd made her team wear the glowing starlight crowns again, since it seemed like the most fitting choice for a visit to an underground city. But she'd felt a whole lot more like a silly little girl playing dress-up once she'd slipped it on.

"Feel free to hurry it up, guys!" Dex called from where he now stood beside Grady, the mud up to his chin—and creeping higher.

"Ah, but we can't," Bronte told him. "Because your intrepid leader is allowing one of your teammates to fall behind."

Sophie glanced over her shoulder, scowling when she found Stina *still* where they'd left her—and she really wished she'd noticed before Bronte had to point it out.

"It's just mud, Stina!" Sophie said, rolling her eyes as she turned around to face her. "You can shower it off later."

"Yeah, well maybe I don't *want* to shower it off later," Stina argued, backing farther away from the sludge. "I think I'll just wait here with Sandor."

"Not an option," Sophie told her, trying to think like a leader.

The Council had put Stina in Team Valiant for a reason. She was also their only Empath. And she knew lots about magsidian and shadowflux thanks to meeting with Lady Zillah.

"You have two choices," Sophie decided, placing her hands on her hips—even though most of her torso was under the mud, so the effect was somewhat muted. "You can wade in now on your own. Or I can have Sandor pick you up and toss you in."

"Everyone votes for option B, right?" Dex asked.

The chorus of "yes" was definitely unanimous.

"I hate all of you," Stina informed them as Sandor stalked toward her with a smile that looked downright gleeful. "Fine. I'll do it on my own—back off!"

She moved to the edge of the mud again.

And then she just stood there.

"Ten seconds," Sophie warned. "Then it's Sandor dunk time! Ten . . . nine . . . eight . . ."

Biana, Dex, and Wylie joined in the countdown as Stina made a noise that was part growl, part moaning whale.

"Four . . . three . . ."

Stina muttered a string of words that would've made Ro proud.

Then she shuffled into the mud, trying to move slowly and carefully. But two steps in, she lost her footing and . . .

SPLASH!

"For the record," Dex said as Stina burst back to the surface looking like a sludge beast and screaming like a banshee, "this might be the greatest moment of my life."

"Oh yeah?" Stina asked, scraping her muddy curls off her face and running toward Dex with pretty impressive speed, despite the resistance caused by the muck.

"Better?" Sophie asked Bronte as Dex received a thorough Stina-dunking and Biana scrambled over and tackled her.

"Not *quite* what I'd imagined," Bronte noted, dodging several splats of flying mud. "But I suppose the method was still effective."

"It was," Sophie agreed.

"I have no doubt that you can be an excellent leader, Miss Foster,"

Bronte told her, his voice a bit quieter. "*You* just need to believe that and truly commit."

It wasn't much of a compliment—but coming from Bronte, it was pretty huge.

"I'm trying," she promised, not sure if he could hear her over all the squealing and slopping and squishing sounds.

Stina, Biana, and Dex had dunked each other so many times, it was now impossible to tell their muddy forms apart.

"Is there a certain place where we're supposed to let the force drag us under?" Sophie asked Bronte. She'd been assuming it would happen naturally once their heads were covered. But Dex, Biana, and Stina were now muddy from head to toe and were still at the surface.

"Once you reach the exact middle of the pool," Nubiti explained, popping out of the sand again, "you'll want to close your mouth and eyes and surrender to gravity. We will do the rest."

The "we" in that statement felt strangely ominous. . . .

"I'm assuming there's a trick for how we breathe once we have to stay under?" Wylie asked Nubiti.

"No secret," Bronte told him. "Just hold your breath. And trust the trap."

Sophie winced at the familiar words.

She'd been given the same instructions the day that she and Alden sank into Exile—and considering how horribly that trip went, she had to remind herself that this time would be different.

This time they weren't going to the planet's most secure prison to meet with a murderous Pyrokinetic.

And she wouldn't be performing any horrible memory breaks—

nor would there be any surprise mental breakdowns or shattering consciousnesses.

Her abilities were also working properly this time.

Well . . . mostly.

"Do you not want to do this?" Grady asked, probably misunderstanding why her lips had dipped into a frown. "You don't have to."

"Uh, yes she does!" the blobby brown creature who sounded like Stina insisted as it stalked toward Sophie—but the other two mud monsters dragged her back, even after Stina latched on to Wylie, taking him with her as the four of them became a tangle of thrashing limbs and flying mud in the center of the mud pool.

"See you on the other side!" Biana's voice shouted from among the chaos, and Dex added, "TEAM VALIANT FOR THE WIN!" Then there were sharp intakes of breath and some strange gurgling sounds as all four teammates sank under the muck.

"They're going to make *quite* the entrance into Loamnore," Grady said—his smile fading when Sophie barely laughed. "You sure you're okay?"

"Of course." She waved a muddy arm at all the grossness around her. "How could I not be?" But the joke clearly wasn't going to fly as an answer. So she admitted, "I'm just . . . nervous. I meant to do more research before we came here, but there's been so much going on that this visit snuck up on me."

She glanced at Bronte, wondering if he'd call her out for focusing too much on finding her biological parents. But he was studiously examining his muddy fingernails.

Grady waded closer to Sophie, draping a muddy arm around her shoulders. "I'll let you in on a secret, kiddo. You could've spent the last week rehearsing for this visit every single day and you'd still be nervous—and there's nothing wrong with that. *I'm* nervous, and I've been to Loamnore numerous times! These kinds of assignments are intimidating. So don't be too hard on yourself, okay? You're doing *great*." He kissed her cheek, leaving a muddy chin print on her neck as he whispered, "And remember, you have *lots* of backup. Your friends may be goofballs, but they're also talented and fearless. And you know *I'll* never let anything bad happen to you."

"Thanks," Sophie told him, spinning to pull him into a real hug. "Guess we should probably catch up with the others, huh?"

"I'm pretty sure if we don't, they'll find a way to destroy something," Grady agreed.

Sophie had assumed that Bronte would go next, but he held back, so Grady went, telling her, "Point your toes when it's your turn—it'll make it go faster. And keep your mouth *closed*—trust me on that."

"I will," she promised, pressing her lips together to prove it.

Then Grady was gone—sucked down the mudhole, leaving Sophie alone with Bronte, and she straightened up, bracing for another lecture.

"Remember what I told you about King Enki," he said as she followed him to the center of the muddy pool.

Bronte and Oralie had given Sophie a *lengthy* lesson that morning, once she'd showered and changed, going over all kinds of tedious protocols.

When to bow.

Where to look—and where to *not* look.

Proper responses to various phrases the king might say.

The importance of using titles—and having good posture.

But above all, they'd emphasized two things.

Authority and *confidence*.

She needed to display an abundance of both if she wanted the king to take her seriously.

And Sophie had been feeling pretty daunted by all of that back when she had freshly styled hair and a ton of glittering diamonds on her tunic.

She wasn't sure how to pull it off as Lady Mud Monster.

But . . . she'd find a way.

"Are you ready?" Bronte asked.

Sophie tried to mean it when she nodded. But she had to add, "I'll try not to mess anything up."

"A worthy goal," Bronte told her. "But I think you should aim higher. I meant what I said earlier. I have no doubt that you'll be an incredible leader if you stop second-guessing yourself and commit."

Sophie looked away, not sure what to do with the compliment besides mumble a quick "thanks."

He nodded and stepped into position. But before the mud dragged him under, he cleared his throat and added, "For the record, Miss Foster, now that it's just you and me—or I suppose I should say you, me, and your bodyguards—I . . . may not be your biological father, nor have I ever wanted to involve myself in that kind of experiment. But . . . if you were my daughter, I'd be very proud."

His head disappeared into the sludge as he finished the last word, leaving Sophie staring at the mucky air bubbles he'd left behind, wondering if she'd imagined what he'd said—and trying to figure out what to do with that information if she hadn't.

The shock stayed with her as she stumbled to the center and pointed her toes, her mind barely registering the slight tug on her ankles as the muck dragged her down, down, down, much farther than she'd been expecting.

And yet, she felt nothing.

Thought nothing.

Just held her breath and sank through the darkness, waiting for solid ground to steady her again.

And when she found it, along with fresh air and just enough soft, flickering light to see, she . . .

Didn't know how to describe what was happening.

There was too much shouting, and laughing.

But mostly too much splattering.

So.

Much.

Splattering.

Tiny particles of brown were flying everywhere—kind of like a dust storm, but wetter and stickier and everything was somehow falling up, not down.

And the longer Sophie stood there, the lighter and softer and steadier she felt, until the air cleared, and her eyes focused, and . . . she didn't know where to look, or what to think, or how, or why, or . . .

Clean.

It seemed like a good word to start with.

Because she *was.*

Her skin was smooth. Her hair was bouncy and shiny. And her clothes were completely spotless.

There was absolutely zero trace of any mud, grime, or grossness.

And Dex, Stina, Wylie, and Biana looked just as immaculate—as did Grady and Bronte.

Which brought Sophie's mind back to the *how*—and she must've said it out loud, because Nubiti popped out of the sandy floor, pointed to one of the prism-shaped black stones set into the room's cavelike ceiling, and told her, "Magsidian."

"Magsidian," Sophie repeated, feeling goose bumps prickle her arms.

Nubiti nodded. "These particular shards are cut to draw the earth to them. It's how we clean up our visitors—and how we reinforce the cavern after someone's arrival."

Sophie squinted harder at the curved ceiling, and sure enough, it did seem to have a fresh layer of packed earth coating it. "That's . . ."

She knew she probably should say "amazing"—but now that she knew what magsidian was made of, she found herself saying "weird."

And what she *really* wanted to say was . . . "kinda scary."

"So where are we?" she asked, studying the rest of the bubble-shaped room, which didn't have much to see, honestly. The floor was made of packed, shimmering sand, and the ceiling was made of smooth, dark mud, and the walls were carved from a gray, marbled stone that had been polished to a perfect gleam. Every few feet there were arched nooks carved into the rock—lower than Sophie was used to, thanks to the dwarves' shorter stature—where delicate glass jars flickered with tongues of pale orange fire, providing just enough light to reveal two hallways ahead.

One was narrow, but bright enough to tell that it curved to the left.

The other was a wide, black void of nothingness.

"We call this our Visitor Center," Nubiti explained. "Those with permission to enter the city go that way"—she pointed to the path that Sophie very much hoped they were taking—"and those here for King Enki go this way."

"I thought we were starting with a tour of the city," Grady cut in when Nubiti turned to lead them toward the darker path.

"King Enki told me this morning that I must bring you to see him first," Nubiti explained—and Sophie definitely didn't miss the look that passed between Bronte and Grady.

Dex must've caught it too, because he asked, "Is that a bad thing?"

"No," Bronte said in a tone that wasn't convincing. "But it's rare for the king to change plans."

"It is," Nubiti agreed, not bothering to expand on that statement as she gestured for them to follow her into the shadows.

Grady sighed and reached for Sophie's hand—which didn't feel that strange until Bronte grabbed her other hand.

"It's best to keep contact," Bronte explained. "The King's Path is . . . unsettling."

"More unsettling than sinking through a gross bog?" Stina asked, reaching for Biana, who was already clinging to Dex.

Wylie completed their chain as Grady told them, "Unfortunately, yes."

Dex sighed. "Why?"

A curl of white in the shadows caught Sophie's eye, and it took her a second to realize it was Nubiti's smile as the tiny dwarf told them, "We had to make sure the path to our king is a journey no intruder wants to make."

"What about guests?" Sophie asked.

Nubiti's smile faded. "To King Enki you are one and the same."

TWENTY-FOUR

OKAY, SO BACK TO THAT LOVELY 'unsettling' description you gave us," Biana said to Bronte as their group stared at the dark path ahead, none of them seeming eager to make the first step. "What exactly does that mean we're in for? Steep drops? Eerie noises? Creepy-crawly things?"

"Really hope it's not that last one," Wylie mumbled.

Sophie definitely agreed.

"If it helps," Nubiti called from somewhere in the shadows—and the whole disembodied-voice thing did *not* make her next words very reassuring—"everything you're about to experience will live entirely in your minds. None of it will be real."

"None of what?" Dex asked.

"It's different for everyone," Grady told him, tightening his grip on Sophie's hand. "I don't fully understand the phenomenon, but something about the sensory deprivation makes us see things, and hear things, and sometimes even feel things that aren't actually there."

"And I'm assuming it won't be, like, pretty flowers and flying alicorns and rainbow glitter showers?" Biana asked.

"It is for some," Bronte admitted. "And those kinds of halluci-nations pose their own challenges. But the majority of us will find that the total absence of any light leaves us facing our worst night-mares."

"Wonderful," Dex muttered.

"Wait—*total* absence of light?" Wylie clarified.

Sophie frowned when Bronte nodded.

"I thought there was always *some* light," she argued, "and that we just had to find a way to make our mind concentrate on it in order to see it."

That was what she'd been taught during her skill lessons, when she was trying to improve her darkness vision.

"Not on the King's Path," Grady corrected. "Once we move far enough away from this room, there won't be *any* light until we reach the Grand Hall."

"How is that possible?" Wylie wondered.

Sophie could've guessed Nubiti's answer.

"Magsidian. The stones set along the King's Path have been cut to absorb every particle of light that comes near them, which makes those in my species lose their bearings unless they've been given something specific to guide them. But you elves have a much stron-ger reaction. The effect won't set in immediately, and when it does, I'll be here to keep you moving. But you must all count on becom-ing *very* disoriented. And those of you who've journeyed down the King's Path before should know that our security has changed in recent months. The magsidian has been altered, and that, in turn, has altered the Path's effect. There's no consensus on whether the experience is better or worse, but all agree that it's wholly different, and many have struggled because they thought they knew what to expect. So try to go in with the mind-set that what you're about to endure will be unlike anything you've survived before."

Sophie wasn't a fan of the word "endure" in all of that.

Or "survived."

But she tried to be a good leader and focus on what was most important.

"Does that mean the King's Path is where the dwarves who joined the Neverseen sabotaged the magsidian before they left?" she asked.

"It's one of several locations," Nubiti agreed, sounding far more casual than Sophie would've expected, considering the fact that they were discussing a security breach on the path to her *king*.

"Where were the other places?" Stina wanted to know.

"I'll show you during the tour," Nubiti promised. "Right now, I need you to start moving. You'll still have a few minutes before the disorientation hits if you need to ask any final questions. But keeping King Enki waiting would be a very unwise way to begin this visit."

"It would," Bronte agreed. "Particularly given the change of plans."

Sophie had a feeling the quick squeeze he gave her hand had nothing to do with reassurance and everything to do with the fact that she was supposed to take the lead.

So she allowed herself one long breath to gather her courage.

Then she dragged everyone onto the dark, unsettling path.

They'd only taken three steps before Sophie's lumenite circlet winked out—along with Dex's, Wylie's, Stina's, and Biana's—and Sophie hadn't realized how much the white light had been helping until it was gone.

"Within the next minute, you will no longer be able to see," Nubiti warned, sounding suddenly closer, "and when that happens, I need you to know three things. First: The Path is flat and true, so there's no need to seek out walls for balance. You can trust your feet not to fail you—even those of you who sometimes consider yourselves to be clumsy. Second: My voice is your guide, and you will be able to follow the sound regardless of how deeply you lose yourself. And third: The longer you linger, the worse the effect gets. So if you can hold on to one truth, it's that you must keep going, no matter what."

"This is sounding better and better," Stina grumbled.

"If you don't like it," Nubiti told her, "I suggest you move faster."

Sophie picked up the pace for all of them.

"How much longer do we have before the hallucinations start?" Dex asked.

"It varies from person to person," Bronte told him. "I've seen some lose themselves almost instantly, and others make it through a significant portion of the journey."

"The average is about ten minutes from the moment you hit the darkness," Grady added, "which for us should be right . . . about . . . now."

Sophie didn't need the verbal cue—she knew the second the light abandoned them.

The shadows shifted, turning blacker—thicker.

Erasing *everything*.

Up. Down. Left. Right. These no longer held any meaning.

She couldn't even feel the breath in her chest or the ground beneath her feet.

Ten minutes until the madness, she thought, determined to last longer. She counted off the seconds, hoping the focused task would keep her head clear.

How many seconds were in fifteen minutes?

Or twenty?

Working the math made her lose count, and she started over, making it to eighty-one before the darkness changed again, slamming against her with an eerie sort of chill that sank past clothes and skin and bone.

Into the heart of every cell.

Freezing solid.

But her body didn't shiver.

It sweated.

And the trickle down her back felt like icy fingers—tugging at her hair, her skin, her clothes—

No! Stop! Focus!

No one was touching her.

No one else was even there with her, except Nubiti and Bronte and Dex and . . .

There were more.

Why couldn't she remember them?

And what if there was someone else—someone she didn't know?

Nubiti had never said they'd be alone as they journeyed down this path.

And dwarves could pop out of the ground anytime, anywhere, their clawed hands thrashing through the sand, teeth glinting—

"What was that?"

Sophie didn't recognize the voice who asked.

She also couldn't see what they meant.

It was too dark. Too cold. Too empty. Too—

"Wait, what *was* that?"

This time the voice was hers—though it sounded shriller.

Shakier.

Broken up by heavy breaths.

But that was because she'd caught something this time.

A flicker of movement.

A darker shade of black.

Someone *was* there.

What was that? What was that? What was that?

So many flashes all around her, burning her eyes, making them tear up. But she must've made it past the darkness, because she could see again.

The hallway stretched endlessly in front of her.

And it was empty.

No one.

No one.

No one.

Her hands felt strange now.

Hadn't she been holding on to something?

And wasn't she supposed to be with . . . ?

She couldn't remember their names.

Sophie.

No—that wasn't it.

She needed several beats to realize that was *her* name. And she tried to tell the voice it wasn't being helpful, but it just kept repeating her name over and over—the sound echoing down the dark, empty hallway in front of her.

Urging her on.

Slowly she followed.

Counting her steps. Her breaths. The stones beneath her feet.

Anything.

Everything.

Millions of things.

Billions.

How long had she been there if she'd counted that high?

How many lifetimes had passed?

No—that couldn't be right.

She shook her head, trying to clear it and . . .

Her ears felt strange.

Longer.

Sharper.

Ancient.

"No!" she screamed, reaching for her face, but she couldn't feel it, couldn't find it.

"Yes, Sophie," a voice said behind her. "We've come *that* far. And this was always where we were heading."

She spun around and . . .

There.

There in the center of the hall.

A tall figure in a hooded black cloak with white eyes glowing across the sleeves.

The sight of it made Sophie want to kick and punch and vomit all over the floor—but she couldn't feel her body enough to do any of those things.

"Isn't it time to stop fighting?" the figure asked, raising its arms—but not to strike.

To embrace.

"This was always the endgame," it told her, no longer in a single voice.

A voice with four layers.

Gethen.

Vespera.

Lady Gisela.

The fourth she couldn't—wouldn't—let herself recognize.

But that didn't mean it wasn't there.

And it was the only tone she could hear when the figure told her, "This is our legacy."

"NEVER!"

She screamed the word so loud that her throat tore, pain arcing through her as she turned to run and run and run—but there were cloaked figures everywhere.

Hundreds of them.

Thousands.

A lifetime of enemies.

Closing in.

Welcoming her home.

"Sophie. Sophie. Sophie."

NEVER! NEVER! NEVER!

"Never is a very long time—but not long enough," all the figures told her, and it was in that same voice again.

The one she hated but didn't hate.

"Go away go away go away," she begged, curling in on herself as the figures closed in—black fabric all around, flowing and fluttering and flapping.

"This is my legacy," they told her. "Our legacy. Your legacy."

No. No. No. No. No. No. No.

Panic and fury flooded her mind—thicker and blacker than the darkness.

Like poison.

Like a *weapon*.

"I can stop you," Sophie told them.

"We'd like to see you try!" they challenged.

And she would show them.

She'd show *everyone*.

"Sophie!"

The voice was new and not new.

Familiar but strange.

And much, *much* too far away.

But it called for her anyway, repeating her name over and over and over.

Growing more desperate.

"Don't listen!" her enemies shouted. "Listen to us! We're your endgame! And you will never be able to stop us!"

"YOU'RE WRONG!" Sophie screamed. "I'M THE MOONLARK!"

She dived into her consciousness, letting the poisonous darkness boil and bubble and burn around her.

But it wouldn't be enough.

She needed to be so much stronger.

So she reached deeper.

Sank farther.

Past the walls around her heart.

To the reserves within.

Emotions so pure, so potent that there was no longer good or bad. Only unending power.

Sophie. Sophie. Sophie.

No—she wasn't Sophie anymore.

She was hate.

And love.

And victory.

And defeat.

And she was finishing this—once and for all.

Red rimmed the edges of her consciousness, and the darkness rose higher and higher, pressing against her mind, clawing out like a monster and—

"SOPHIE, STOP IT!"

The voice felt like a slap.

Or maybe she really had been slapped.

Her cheek stung and her breath was heaving and . . .

"Wait—where am I?" Sophie asked, feeling like she'd been dropped into a strange new body, and only parts of it were working.

She couldn't see.

And her ears were ringing.

And her legs were so, so shaky.

And her head . . .

Her head was *much* too heavy.

She let it fall forward, and then every part of her followed—falling, falling, falling—until something squeezed her arms and dragged her back upright.

"We're still on the King's Path," the voice told her, "so I need you to get it together."

The sharpness of the tone gave Sophie the piece her brain had been missing.

Stina.

She was talking to Stina.

And this . . .

This was reality.

Everything else . . .

"What's happening?" Sophie asked, shoving the lingering wisps of her nightmare to the back of her mind and trying to spot something—anything—to give her brain some focus.

But there was only the thick, endless black, and the more she stared into it, the more it stared back.

Looming over her.

Ready to devour.

"None of that!" Stina snapped as something squeezed Sophie's arms again.

Hands, she realized.

Hands that were shaking her.

"Stop it!" she whined.

"Then stay awake!" Stina ordered. "I don't think I can stop you from inflicting again."

"Inflicting?" The word was a kick to the heart. "Did I—"

"Almost," Stina corrected. "The pain knocked me out of the weird dream I'd been having. Something about unicorns and kelpies . . . and . . . I don't really know. They were chasing me, and . . . it doesn't matter." There was a rustling sound like Stina was shaking her head. "Then I realized what was happening, and somehow I got my legs moving, following the feeling until I found you and tried

to snap you out of it. I pulled your gloves off, but you still had those gadget things on, and I didn't know how to work them. So I tried smacking you—"

"I knew it," Sophie murmured, reaching up to feel her cheek—marveling that her arm and hand were willing to do that. It still felt like she was inhabiting someone else's body—a puppet with ten million strings, and she didn't know how to use any of them. "But . . . you stopped me in time?"

"I think so. I can't see anything, but I don't feel anyone in pain or anything."

Sophie sank with a sigh, and Stina had to steady her again.

"Seriously, Sophie, I'm having a hard enough time—"

"You two shouldn't be conscious," another voice interrupted from somewhere beside them, and Sophie wondered if her heart was going to be permanently stuck in her throat from the shock of it.

But the jolt brought a new level of clarity to her brain.

"Nubiti?" she whispered.

"Who else?" the voice—*Nubiti*—asked.

And she was close enough now that Sophie could feel Nubiti's breath on her cheeks as if her dwarven bodyguard was leaning in, studying her through the nothingness.

"You should've heard me guiding you," she told Sophie quietly. "But you didn't. No matter what I tried."

Stina snorted. "Big surprise, something about Sophie doesn't go the way it's supposed to."

"I guess I should've expected her reaction might be atypical," Nubiti conceded. "But that doesn't explain why *you're* functioning so clearly." Nubiti's voice shifted, like she was moving to examine Stina. "How are you awake?"

"No idea," Stina admitted. "I'm guessing it's an Empath thing. I felt Sophie's emotions spiking out everywhere, and they dragged me back—and be glad they did, because you'd be writhing in pain on the floor right now if I hadn't. We all would. I'm sure your king would love that. And, wait a minute, why is it so much easier to think all of a sudden? I had to fight so hard at first."

"So did I," Sophie added, and the thought felt like stretching her mind, waking up muscles she hadn't been using.

"I'm wearing a piece of magsidian that keeps my head clear so I can guide you down the Path," Nubiti explained. "You must be benefitting from the proximity to it."

"So wait . . . is everyone else still hallucinating right now?" Sophie asked, whipping around when Nubiti told her, "Yes."

She had to find them—help them.

But it was too dark.

And her body was so tired.

And she didn't know how to pull all the strings and make everything work yet.

"They're *fine*," Nubiti assured her. "It's all in their minds."

"That doesn't make it any less traumatic," Sophie snapped back, squeezing her eyes, trying to block any flashbacks of her creepy visions.

She'd have to face them someday—analyze what the hallucinations said about her deepest fears.

But she'd had more than enough of them for the moment.

"This is a horrible thing to do to people!" she told Nubiti. "How can you just stand by, letting them suffer?"

"Because this is how we protect our king! My people are small. And few. Who would ever fear us if we didn't give them a reason to?"

"I'm pretty sure all you'd have to do is show them that trick you guys do with the stomping-and-opening-up-huge-cracks-in-the-ground thing," Sophie reminded her.

"That is no *trick*," Nubiti huffed, "and it takes far more energy than you think. This is better. And safer. No enemy poses any real danger if they cannot even *find* King Enki, and if they're too frightened and weary to resist capture. Besides—the only weapon we're using is *darkness*. How is that cruel?"

Sophie wished she had a good answer, because Nubiti's points were valid.

But the Path was still so incredibly awful.

Nubiti let out a sigh. "Every moment we stand here arguing is another moment the rest of your group must endure their delusions. So why don't you take my hands and let me lead us out of the maze?"

"So the King's Path is also a maze?" Stina asked.

"Of course. Between the darkness and the endless twisting corridors, no one can get through unless we want them to. *No one*," she emphasized. "That's the point. To keep our Grand Hall as a safe haven. I know you doubt our security—"

"Don't *you*?" Sophie interrupted. "Isn't that why you told us about the magsidian?"

"I worry about certain places," Nubiti admitted. "But not about the King's Path. That's why I planned your visit to start with the tour of the city, so you would feel the difference. The Path is our masterpiece. Even you, with all your moonlark gifts, couldn't begin to brave it."

"Stina kinda did," Sophie noted.

"Not really," Stina admitted. "I mean, I did *way* better than you. *You* were a disaster. But . . . if your inflicting hadn't snapped me out of it, I'd still be thinking I was being chased by kelpies and unicorns. There might've been a talking murcat, too, and maybe a flock of boobries? I don't know—it was super weird and *really* overwhelming."

"Exactly," Nubiti said. "And we need to keep moving. I'm sure King Enki is growing frustrated with our tardiness—and you must not tell him about your strange reactions to the darkness. He will consider it an insult."

"How is it an insult?" Stina wondered.

"Because he says it is," Nubiti said, as if that was all that mattered.

And Sophie was ready to argue, but . . . maybe that's how it worked for kings.

They weren't just above the law.

They *made* the law.

"Time to hurry," Nubiti said, hooking an arm around Sophie's and dragging her forward as Stina flailed to keep her grip on Sophie's other arm.

"What about the rest of our group?" Sophie asked, wishing she could spot some trace of them in the darkness.

But no.

Nubiti's pendant might've cleared her head, but it didn't lighten the endless, overwhelming black.

"They will follow my voice," Nubiti assured her, calling out, "THIS WAY!" and Sophie thought she might've heard the sound of feet shuffling after them.

The steps were listless.

Loping.

Like zombies hunting flesh.

She shook her head to fight the fresh wave of panic. "This is a bad place to have a vivid imagination."

"Yes" was all Nubiti told her, then shouted, "KEEP UP!" and increased their pace even more.

Sophie counted their steps, glad her mind could stay focused on the numbers.

One hundred.

Two hundred.

Three.

Four.

Five.

On the five hundred and twenty-third step, there was light.

Blissful, glorious light.

Only a glimmer—and yet it burned and burned and burned.

Searing across Sophie's corneas.

Scorching into her brain.

And she didn't care one bit, because her thoughts were *clear* and her body was *hers* and she could see the rest of her group around her, stretching and blinking out of their dazes.

She wanted to run around hugging all of them—but that probably would've been a bad idea. Because as she settled back into reality, she took a longer look at her surroundings and realized they'd stopped in front of a very large, very fancy, very intimidating door made from thousands of pieces of every possible kind of metal intricately welded together.

The kind of door that surely led to the Grand Hall of a dwarven king.

Still, she couldn't listen to Nubiti's final instructions, needing to use those brief moments to make eye contact with everyone to ensure that they were okay.

They definitely looked weary, and haunted. But they gave her small smiles—and she gave them the same so they'd know not to worry about her, either.

And then there was an earth-shaking clang and a cringeworthy scraping, and Nubiti was guiding them into another dim, round room—enormous this time. And far more elegant.

The packed white sand making up the floor shimmered like a moonlit shoreline, and the earthy ceiling was flecked with silvery minerals like stars. A chandelier formed from interlocking rings of dangling, flame-filled glass jars cast a flickering orangey glow over everything. And the marbled walls had gorgeous swirled carvings inlaid with gold and silver and copper and lumenite and other metals that shone green and black and purple. Gemstones were set into the marble around the swirls: emeralds and rubies and topazes and sapphires and onyxes—though Sophie had a feeling some of the black stones were magsidian.

And in the center of it all, seated on a glittering black throne, was a small bald creature wearing white furry pants and a crown carved from a single piece of curved opalescent shell.

King Enki.

He snorted at their arrival. And his gritty voice sounded particularly gruff when he told them, "I don't like to be kept waiting."

TWENTY-FIVE

I 'VE NEVER SEEN A DWARF WITHOUT FUR," Stina whispered—though the words still felt *way* too loud in the echoey room. "It's . . . odd."

It totally was.

But that didn't stop Sophie from elbowing Stina in the ribs—and wishing she could do the same to Dex for letting one muffled snicker slip.

Clearly she should've warned the rest of her teammates about King Enki's unusual appearance ahead of time, so they would've been prepared for the surprise.

She'd have to add that to the list of ways she wasn't exactly killing it as team leader.

King Enki might look a lot like a plucked chicken with mottled peach, brown, and black skin. But to the dwarves, the fur-waxing was a statement of their king's power and strength.

Sophie wasn't sure *why* a fur-free king communicated either of those things—but it didn't matter.

She and her friends didn't have to understand it.

They just needed to show their respect—especially since they'd already arrived late, *and* had forgotten to bow when they entered, which Sophie only realized after someone cleared their throat beside her.

Then she turned and saw that Grady had dropped to one knee and Bronte stood stooped at the waist—each position reflecting their titles of Emissary and Councillor.

As Regents, Sophie and her friends were supposed to drop to *both* knees—which they immediately scrambled to do.

Dex, Stina, Wylie, and Biana were also supposed to lower their heads.

But Sophie had to keep her head held high to show her authority. Which made it a lot harder to not flinch when the king's gaze focused on her.

"My guards tell me you experienced some challenges on the Path here, Miss Foster," he called out, making Sophie wince. And even though there was quite a bit of distance between them, Sophie could hear his claws tapping the armrests on his throne.

Tickety tap. Tickety tap. Tickety tap.

She wished she could turn to Nubiti for guidance, since she hadn't forgotten her bodyguard's warning about how King Enki would consider her struggles along the Path to be insulting. But she forced herself to remember what Bronte and Oralie had taught her.

"It's Lady Foster," she corrected, trying to channel Keefe's smooth confidence as she held the king's stare. "Leader of Team Valiant. And yes, your security definitely did pose a challenge. Clearly it's been brilliantly designed."

Authority *and* deference.

That's what Bronte and Oralie had emphasized.

She needed to speak with *conviction.*

Demand recognition.

But also defer to the king's authority—and give praise any chance she found.

From the corner of her eye, she could see both Bronte and Nubiti nod their approval.

But her relief was short-lived.

"If you find our security so impressive," King Enki said with a lot more *tickety-tapping*, "I wonder why you've demanded this meeting to inspect it."

"You know very well why we're here," Bronte cut in, straightening from his bow.

"Do I?"

Tickety tap. Tickety tap. Tickety tap.

"Yes," Bronte insisted.

King Enki inclined his head, making the light glint off of the smooth opalescent circle of his crown—which probably would've been an impressive accessory if Sophie weren't so familiar with the creepy giant sand crab creature the shell came from. She could remember too many spindly, flailing legs to ever find it pretty.

"I *thought* I understood the purpose of this meeting," King Enki said, and Sophie blinked back to attention, "right up until yesterday, when I found myself playing host to someone from the Black Swan."

"The Black Swan?" Grady repeated, as Sophie blurted out, "Yesterday?" and Biana and Dex both asked Bronte, "Did you know about that?"

"We . . . were unaware of that meeting," Bronte told King Enki after a beat of silence.

"Clearly." *Tickety tap. Tickety tap. Tickety tap.* "Which seems particularly strange to me, since I was told that many of you kneeling in front of me are members of the order."

"We are," Sophie agreed, hoping it was okay to shift back to standing. Her knees were starting to feel bruised—the sandy floor was *much* more solid than it looked.

She didn't know how the rest of her teammates were managing to stay so still.

"Well, then surely you can understand why I find it both obnoxious *and* suspicious that these meetings weren't combined," King Enki informed her.

Tickety tap. Tickety tap. Tickety tap.

"Either you're wasting my time," he added, "or the Council's been overstating their supposedly improved relationship with the Black Swan."

"If we were, do you think Miss Foster would be with us?" Bronte countered. "And as a Regent, no less? Leader of a vital new arrangement in our nobility?"

"That's what I'm trying to determine." King Enki reached out his palm and curled his fingers—a gesture that Sophie had been told meant that she was supposed to approach the throne.

She didn't dare glance at any of her friends, knowing the worry in their eyes would shred her already frazzled confidence. And the twenty-seven steps she took to cross the room felt like twenty-seven miles. She had to lock her arms at her sides to be sure she didn't fidget as King Enki leaned closer, sniffing the air between them.

"So much fear," he murmured.

"Can you blame me?" she asked, hoping the question would earn her points, both as honesty and a subtle compliment.

"No, I suppose I can't."

Tickety tap. Tickety tap. Tickety tap.

"So . . . the moonlark now has a crown," he said, leaning back against his throne again. "And she's distanced herself from her creators."

"I haven't—" Sophie stopped herself, realizing that arguing with King Enki would only make things worse.

Instead, she straightened up, smoothing her golden cape and straightening the jeweled hem of her tunic before she told him, "I'll always be their moonlark."

"And what exactly does that mean?" he asked.

"Honestly? I have no idea," Sophie admitted, holding her breath through the silence that followed the confession.

And she cringed at the sharp sound King Enki finally made— until she realized it was a single barked laugh.

"I think I could enjoy your company, Lady Foster," he told her, looking even more surprised by the sentiment than she was. "If only you weren't here to criticize my city."

Sweat streamed down Sophie's back, and she sucked in a steadying breath. "I—"

"No need to deny it," King Enki interrupted. "And it may be unfair to hold it against you. It's not your fault your Council has chosen to use you this way—sending you to face me, hoping I'll be less inclined to offense if the criticisms come from a pretty young child." His gaze shifted to someone over Sophie's shoulder as he called out, "At least the Black Swan had the courage to face me leader-to-leader when they gave their unnecessary warnings!"

"Sophie *is* a leader," Bronte called back.

"Yes, and what an *impressive* team you've made her a leader of," King Enki scoffed. "Three children, and one who could hardly be called an adult. All still too afraid—or ignorant—to realize they could be standing."

"We're not afraid!" Biana shouted back, and Sophie tried not to flinch—or panic that the outburst would land Biana in a dwarven prison. "And we're not ignorant, either," Biana added. "We're just . . . really bad at bowing, apparently."

King Enki's lips twitched with what was either a smile or a sneer. "Such boldness," he said, turning back to Sophie.

Tickety tap. Tickety tap. Tickety tap.

"We may be young," Sophie said quietly—but not timidly. "But we've lived through more than you would expect. And we're not here to criticize. We're trying to help. The Neverseen—"

"Yes, one of your creators already gave me the whole story yesterday," King Enki interrupted. "I've heard allllllllllllllllll about how my people will be the next targets of these villains that you keep failing to defeat. Just as I've heard allllllllllllllllll of your worries about Shades and shadowflux and magsidian."

His gaze shifted to Nubiti on the last word, and Sophie wondered if that meant he'd realized that Nubiti had found a loophole to defy him.

Tickety tap. Tickety tap. Tickety tap.

Sophie's eyes followed the sound, and she realized his entire throne was a single carved block of magsidian.

"Impressive, isn't it?" King Enki asked, trailing his fingers across the stone. "This is the largest piece we've ever found. The ultimate seat of power."

"It's beautiful," Sophie murmured.

And it was.

The style of the throne was rougher than other ornate chairs usually used by kings and leaders—but there was something so elegant about its raw simplicity. It looked as if the dwarves had tried to cut the minimum number of facets into the magsidian—as if they wanted people to know that it was all their king needed.

Which made Sophie wonder what those cuts and carvings caused the throne to draw.

Justice?

Truth?

She didn't ask.

Instead, she shared what Stina and Wylie had taught her right before they'd left for Loamnore, when she'd finally had them give her an update on their conversation with Lady Zillah.

"Did you know that some believe shadowflux was the *first* element, existing long before anything else?" she asked.

"I suppose that theory makes sense. Darkness *is* the natural state of things. We have to work to add light."

Tickety tap. Tickety tap. Tickety tap.

"You don't like hearing that, do you?" he asked. "Given your species' obsession with anything that glows."

Sophie shrugged, hoping the gesture wasn't too casual. "Personally, I've always been a fan of both. I think light and darkness each have their place, and the trick is to keep the right balance."

He tilted his head.

Tickety tap. Tickety tap. Tickety tap.

"Was there a point to that piece of trivia you just shared?" he asked.

"I'm getting there," Sophie promised, daring a glance behind her.

The lighting was too dim for her to read Stina's and Wylie's expressions. But they weren't waving their arms trying to get her to stop, either.

So she told King Enki, "Some people also believe that since shadowflux was first, its influence can be felt in *everything*. Which would make it the most powerful of all the elements—and a power that strong can never truly be contained, even when we think it has been."

She gestured toward his magsidian throne.

"What are you implying?" King Enki asked.

"I don't know," Sophie admitted. "Everything about shadowflux feels so abstract to me. All I know for certain is that it's brutal. And unlike anything I've experienced. And it changes everything it touches."

Tickety tap. Tickety tap. Tickety tap.

"The Black Swan essentially told me the same thing yesterday. But I'm still failing to see what the information has to do with my people. I do not fear a few rebel elves—or a few traitors from my own kind. Our security is stronger than it's ever been."

"I hope you're right," Sophie told him. "But isn't it safer to double-check?"

"The Black Swan *did* check. I allowed them to search for an entire hour."

"Okay . . . then triple-checking won't hurt either, will it?" Sophie pressed. "I wish Mr. Forkle—"

"It wasn't him," King Enki interrupted again, leaning closer to sniff the air between them. "You really *didn't* know about yesterday's meeting, did you?"

Sophie shook her head. "Who did you meet with?"

Tickety tap. Tickety tap. Tickety tap.

She thought he wasn't going to answer. But eventually he said, "The rocky one."

"Granite?" she clarified.

King Enki nodded. "He's often our point of contact. But go on. You were saying something you wished about the Black Swan."

She had been, but she'd lost her train of thought, trying to figure out why Tiergan would've gone to Loamnore without telling her—or Wylie.

"Right," she said, trying to focus. "I was just going to say that . . . I wish the Black Swan had let us know that they'd be meeting with you. They're good at keeping secrets—which you probably know after so many years of working with them."

King Enki had often sided with the Black Swan over the Council.

"And I'm sorry if you feel like we're wasting your time, or doubting your power or your security," Sophie added. "I hope Loamnore isn't a target—and if it is, I hope the Neverseen end up writhing and sobbing in the King's Path from their hallucinations. Feel free to leave them in there if that happens."

That earned her a twitchy partial smile from the king.

"But I've watched the Neverseen win over and over and over," she added quietly. "And they generally strike the places we feel the safest. You were there when Lumenaria fell—and you've helped us rebuild our other fallen cities. Would you have ever imagined that kind of destruction would happen?"

Tickety tap. Tickety tap. Tickety tap.

"Fine," he told her after what might've been an eternity. "Make your unnecessary searches. Nubiti will take you around, answer any questions you have. But I want a report before you leave. And if you find nothing, this is the last I want to hear of this," he added, shifting his focus to Bronte.

"Thank you," Sophie told him, wishing her legs weren't so shaky as she dipped a full curtsy.

And she could tell that Grady wanted to hug her when she stumbled back to her group—and she wanted to bury herself in his arms—but they both had to settle for a pat on the shoulder and a "good job."

"That sounded *fun*," Dex mumbled.

"Not now," Nubiti told him. "He can still change his mind, and I want to show you where the other security adjustments occurred."

"Wait!" Biana said as Nubiti stomped her foot and revealed a new tunnel for them to take. "Aren't we going to search in here?"

"In the Grand Hall?" Nubiti shook her head. "That would be unnecessary."

"But we're *here*," Biana argued. "And it was a pretty horrible journey. And we know the security has been altered—"

"It hasn't actually," Nubiti interrupted. "There's nothing to alter in this room. The Grand Hall is defended by the King's Path and the royal brigade—our strongest warriors, who remain ready to strike whenever necessary." She pointed to the ground, and Sophie tried not to imagine an army of dwarves bursting out of the sand—it was a bit too close to her hallucinations.

"I still think we should look around before we go," Biana insisted.

"I agree," Dex jumped in. "Just in case there's something we're missing—especially since I'm pretty sure none of us want to have to come back here ever again."

Everyone seemed to turn a shade of green.

"I don't see how a quick look could hurt," Grady told Nubiti. "Especially since King Enki said we could search anywhere."

Nubiti heaved out a sigh. "Do what you must. But be quick. And quiet. And do *not* go near the throne. I'll explain to King Enki what's happening so he does not call for his guards—and if he tells us to leave, we will leave, understood?"

"I'll go with you," Bronte offered. "I need to have a few words with the king anyway."

Nubiti didn't look thrilled with that information, but she motioned for Bronte to join her as she made her way over to the throne.

"Let's split up," Sophie told her friends. "Dex, you and Biana start over there"—she pointed to the farthest part of the room—"and, Stina, you stay with Grady and start here, in the doorway. Wylie and I will take the middle."

Shockingly no one argued—or made any jokes about Lady Fos-Boss—as they set to work searching the walls and floor.

If only Sophie had any idea what they should be looking for.

"Did you know Tiergan met with King Enki yesterday?" she whispered to Wylie.

"No—and you can bet I'll be calling him on it," Wylie assured her. He glanced over his shoulder to where Bronte and King Enki had moved to a spot of shadowy quiet for some sort of intense whispered conversation. "I thought we were about to get kicked out of here."

"So did I," Sophie admitted, tracing her hand along one of the swirly gold carvings, which curled around a glittering black stone. "Is this magsidian?"

"No," Nubiti said behind her, making her jump. "That is onyx, for decoration. The only magsidian in this room is the throne."

"You're sure?" Sophie craned her neck to better see the abundance of black stones inlaid into the walls.

"All onyx," Nubiti insisted. "Magsidian would hinder the pull of the throne."

"Still seems smart to make sure," Wylie decided. "I mean, we're here, right?"

He snapped his fingers and a tiny sphere of pale white light hovered over his palm.

"Your light tricks have no place in our world!" King Enki shouted over to him.

"This will only take a second," Wylie called back before turning to Nubiti. "Onyx will shimmer when the light hits it. Magsidian will do . . . who knows?"

Nubiti sighed. "You're wasting your time."

"Maybe," Wylie agreed. "I guess we'll find out."

And for all of her stubbornness, Nubiti looked mildly curious as Wylie flicked his wrist and sent the glowing white sphere to the base of the wall, guiding it in wide, slow circles around the room and climbing higher with each rotation.

Sophie was pretty sure everyone was watching the way he lingered at each black stone, waiting for the telltale onyx shimmer. And with each confirmation, Nubiti grew smugger and smugger.

"I told you, there's no magsi—"

Her word was drowned out by a crackling buzz as the white sphere disappeared with a shower of sparks into the stone that Wylie had been testing.

"Uh, what was—"

It was all Sophie managed to say before the light blasted back out like a bolt of white lightning, aimed at a stone directly across the room, which absorbed the light the same way—crackling and sparking before the light blasted toward a third stone that ricocheted it toward the ceiling, aimed right for—

"TAKE COVER!" Nubiti screamed, dragging Sophie and Wylie to the floor as the bolt hit the chandelier and made every jar of flame explode.

TWENTY-SIX

*H*OW DO WE STOP THIS?"
That was the first question everyone shouted
as the shower of flames and jagged glass turned
into full-fledged blazes—tearing across the Grand
Hall's floor, fueled by the spilled chandelier oil.

And there seemed to be no answer—except to evacuate immediately—until the fires drew close to King Enki's throne and . . .

The flames vanished.

Sophie had never seen anything like it.

One second there was choking smoke and searing heat and her brain was screaming, *NOT AGAIN! NOT AGAIN! NOT AGAIN!*

And then . . .

Nothing.

Not a spark.

Or a wisp of smoke.

Or even a scorch mark to prove the flames had ever been there to begin with.

King Enki seemed just as stunned as they were by the development. He even burned his hand on the magsidian while he inspected his throne—which also miraculously turned out to be the largest injury anybody suffered that day.

Everything else was just cuts and scrapes from the broken glass and tiny blisters from the splattered oil.

And other than the shattered chandelier, the Grand Hall showed little sign of actual damage—though Sophie wondered if they'd find more once the room had better lighting again.

King Enki was understandably reluctant to bring in any more jars of flickering orange flames until he had a better understanding of what had actually happened to the chandelier. So the only illumination came from Sophie's and her team's glowing circlets.

Nubiti even had to borrow Sophie's crown when she crawled up the wall to inspect the stones that Wylie had accidentally triggered. And she was able to confirm that the stones definitely *were* hidden pieces of magsidian—cut with a pattern of facets she'd never seen before.

But there was no way to tell how long the magsidian had been there.

The stones could've been part of some elaborate sabotage planned by the dwarves who'd defected to the Neverseen.

Or, as King Enki immediately reminded them, the stones could just as easily have been a long-forgotten defense from the days of an ancient king.

Or anything in between.

All they knew for certain at the moment was: The stones weren't going anywhere.

Nubiti tried to pry them out—first with her claws, and then with a special tool—and nothing would loosen them. So she'd had to settle for covering the stones with a cementlike paste to keep any light away.

Which brought Sophie's group to the much trickier part of the conversation: the part where King Enki took back his offer to let them search other places in Loamnore, convinced their strange elf-y tricks would trigger more unexpected disasters.

Nothing would change his mind.

They tried promising not to use their abilities—or their skills. Not that King Enki understood the difference.

Tried pointing out that if they didn't find the problem first—and the Neverseen *were* behind it—they'd now seen exactly how easily their enemies could cause serious damage to Loamnore.

But the best they managed was persuading King Enki to let Nubiti conduct her own investigation without them—which wasn't a horrible compromise. But it meant Nubiti would need to take at least a few days away from her duties as Sophie's bodyguard.

Probably longer.

"Take as long as you need," Sophie told her as Nubiti handed back her circlet. "This is so much more important." She debated a second before she added under her breath, "I don't think those stones are from the past."

Nubiti looked somehow smaller as she whispered, "I . . . don't either. I did not want to argue with my king. But . . . the facets carved into the magsidian were so sharp and precise that they had to be cut with modern tools."

Sophie's insides tangled up tighter than her old human earbuds. "Keep me posted?" she asked. "And let me know if there's any way we can help?"

Nubiti nodded, grabbing Sophie's arm before Sophie turned to rejoin her friends. "You know what I can't stop wondering?" Nubiti asked, stepping closer so only Sophie would hear. "We saw how those stones react to light—but how will they respond to shadows?"

"I've been wondering the same thing," Sophie admitted. And Nubiti's raw honesty made Sophie lean in to share her own equally bone-chilling question. "But you know what really scares me?" she whispered directly into Nubiti's ear. "If the security on the King's Path relies on darkness to keep King Enki safe from intruders, what happens if the intruders have a Shade?"

"Three bodyguards is *fine*," Sophie told Sandor as he paced back and forth across Havenfield's living room.

"Right now it's only two," he reminded her. "I'm still figuring out other arrangements for Linh."

"Then two is *fine*," Sophie insisted, glad to know that Linh still had Bo protecting her. "Honestly, sometimes *one* feels like too many."

She'd hoped Sandor would smile at the tease. But there was no lightening the goblin warrior's scowl—not after Sophie's group had used a special magsidian pendant to leap back to where he'd been standing guard in the oasis and told him about the horrifying hallucinations and the almost-inferno and how Nubiti had stayed behind to conduct the search that they were no longer allowed to do.

Then they'd leaped back to Havenfield, and Bronte and Grady had gotten on their Imparters while Sandor had stalked off to get Flori, and within about five minutes the downstairs main room had become *very* full.

Everyone who'd gone to Loamnore was still there.

Plus Edaline, Sandor, and Flori.

And the entire rest of the Council.

And Elwin—who was hard at work treating all their cuts and burns with various ointments and poultices.

The only person noticeably missing was Mr. Forkle.

Given the Black Swan's secret meeting with King Enki the day before, Bronte and Grady had decided *not* to include him—or any members of the Collective—in their current conversation, which had started out as a long, brutal accounting of everything that had happened in Loamnore, followed by lots of panicked speculation, and had now somehow dissolved into another round of "How do we protect Sophie?"

But for once Sophie wasn't bothered by their overprotection.

In a way, she was going to need it.

The whole journey back to Havenfield, her mind kept replaying the question they'd shouted as the fire had erupted around them.

How do we stop this?

Seemed like a fitting way to sum up their current Neverseen situation.

And sadly, she had no idea.

But Sophie *did* know that if it hadn't been for Stina's well-timed slap on the King's Path, Sophie would've sabotaged their mission in Loamnore, which would've meant they'd never have discovered those magsidian pieces—not to mention the fact that she would've caused everyone excruciating pain while they were already struggling with horrific hallucinations.

If she'd needed proof that her inflicting was a problem—that was it.

Especially since Bronte hadn't come close to raging out on everybody.

She wasn't just malfunctioning.

She was becoming a liability.

And given what they were up against, they needed all the power they could get.

A knock at the front door interrupted her thoughts, and Sophie gave herself a quick eyelash tug as Grady asked, "Who could that be?"

Sophie already knew.

She'd hailed the wheezy, wrinkled figure who shuffled into the room, looking particularly uncomfortable—but whether his discomfort was from the bloating caused by the ruckleberries, or from the glares everyone was giving him, was anybody's guess.

"I thought we'd agreed to keep the Black Swan out of this conversation," Bronte grumbled, scanning each face like he was searching for a culprit.

"We did," Sophie said, proud of how steadily she stood. "I invited him for a different reason."

Her eyes locked with Mr. Forkle's as she added, "I'm ready to let you reset my abilities."

TWENTY-SEVEN

SOPHIE HAD PLANNED AHEAD FOR ALL OF the *What?*, *Why?*, and *How?* questions she knew she'd be getting after she dropped the "ability resetting" bombshell on everybody—but she wasn't prepared for how quickly the conversation shifted to a simple, "Okay."

"Okay," she said, echoing everyone as she studied the abundance of faces staring back at her. *Twenty-two*, to be exact, between friends, family, bodyguards, and Councillors—which made their speedy, unanimous agreement all the more unprecedented. "Does that mean you're *not* going to try to talk me out of this?"

"We can if it'll work," Grady offered, earning himself an elbow to the ribs from Edaline.

"What your consistently overprotective father meant to say," Edaline corrected, "is that you've obviously put a lot of thought into this decision—and it's also something you've experienced before, and that means you understand better than any of us exactly how dangerous and painful it's going to be. And if you've decided that it's worth the risk, you must have good reasons. So . . . we trust your judgment."

"Even if we're not happy about it," Grady added under his breath—

and Sandor, Dex, Biana, and Wylie snorted their agreement.

"Well . . . ," Sophie said, still struggling to process this unexpected cooperation. "Thanks."

And amazingly enough, that seemed to settle it.

No arguing.

No drama.

It was almost *too* easy—which made Sophie worry that there was some sort of trick or loophole she was missing.

"Are you doing this now?" Edaline asked Mr. Forkle, sounding much calmer than Sophie would've expected—though Edaline did also seem to be wringing her hands pretty tightly.

"Yes, if Miss Foster is truly ready," he agreed. And there was a challenge in the way he raised his eyebrows at Sophie—as if he was reminding her that her stubborn demand for information had been the reason they hadn't reset her abilities already, and that technically nothing on *that* front had changed.

"I need to fix myself," she told him, holding his stare. "That's my number one priority. So yeah—I'm ready. We'll figure the rest out later."

She added an eyebrow raise of her own with the final words— her way of challenging him back. Letting him know, *We're not done here—but this is more important.*

Then she made her way over to his side, hoping no one noticed the way her knees shook with every step. "Do we need to head to the Healing Center, or . . . ?"

"Your room here should work fine," Mr. Forkle told her. "It's probably best for you to be somewhere you're relaxed and comfortable. I'll hail Livvy and have her bring over the supplies."

"That better not mean you're thinking of doing this without me," Elwin warned, stepping in front of Mr. Forkle—which would've been a lot more intimidating if Elwin's tunic wasn't covered in pink fluffy dinosaurs.

"Quite the contrary," Mr. Forkle assured him, taking out his Imparter and tapping the silver screen. "I'd been planning on having you around as backup—"

"*Backup,*" Elwin scoffed, raking his fingers through his messy hair.

"I assure you, that's *not* an insult," Mr. Forkle promised. "Livvy's been researching and perfecting the treatment we're about to use for the last several months, so naturally she'll take the lead. But she'll need you at her side the whole way through. That's why I'm glad you're already here and on board with the ability reset. Saves me both an errand and a lengthy discussion. And if . . ." His voice trailed off as he turned back to the larger group. "Actually, that reminds me. Did I hear correctly that all of you *chose* to exclude me from whatever meeting I'm interrupting?"

Councillor Emery crossed his arms. "We chose to keep *any* members of the Black Swan out of the discussion."

Mr. Forkle's frown deepened. "I thought we were past these kinds of squabbles."

"Squabbles?" Bronte repeated. "Is that your way of trying to trivialize our concerns? As if we couldn't possibly have a valid complaint against your order?"

"No, it's my way of reminding you that you can come to me, or anyone else in the Collective, and raise your complaints anytime, and we'll do our best to address them—the way responsible adults do when they want to resolve an issue," Mr. Forkle corrected. "Holding secret meetings is childish."

"Funny you should say that," Bronte noted, "considering we're gathered here to discuss the problems caused by Granite's *secret meeting* with King Enki yesterday."

Mr. Forkle straightened.

"Ah, so you thought we weren't aware of your subterfuge?" Councillor Emery asked.

"There was no *subterfuge*," Mr. Forkle insisted. "We've made it abundantly clear that our current focus is on the dwarves, and that we'd be arranging a meeting with King Enki as soon as possible."

"And yet you didn't bother to tell us that you had a meeting *actually* scheduled," Bronte argued, "which nearly derailed *our* visit. King Enki accused us of wasting his time *and* of misrepresenting our working relationship with the Black Swan, since you clearly weren't keeping us informed. He seemed ready to cast us out of Loamnore, and the only reason he didn't was because Miss Foster managed to calm him down."

For what it was worth, Mr. Forkle did look sufficiently chagrined. "Well. I suppose it might've been wise if we'd better coordinated our investigations."

"Yes, it would," Councillor Emery agreed. "And it should be noted that *we've* made every effort to be forthright—"

"*Every* effort," Mr. Forkle interrupted. "Strange. I don't remember you informing us ahead of time that you'd be appointing several of our members as Regents—including Miss Foster."

"You didn't know about that?" Sophie asked, not sure what to feel when he shook his head.

She'd assumed the Black Swan was fully aware that the Council was offering her the title, since the Council appointed her right after she'd met with Mr. Forkle in his office—and her first assignment overlapped with things that the two of them had discussed. Plus, Tiergan was with them in the Seat of Eminence when they'd agreed to become Team Valiant.

But . . . now that she thought about it, no one had actually *said* the Black Swan knew she was becoming a Regent. And Tiergan had been confused about why he and Wylie had received a vague summons to be there.

All of which begged a different question—one Sophie probably should've thought to ask when Mr. Forkle admitted a few days earlier that the Black Swan had never anticipated her appointment to the nobility.

"Do you not want us to be Regents?" she asked.

Mr. Forkle dragged a hand down his face. "I have no problem with any of you having the title, nor with you allying yourself with the Council. But . . . it does complicate things. Particularly since delegating assignments to you and your friends has never been easy for those of us in the Collective—and I realize that may be hard to believe given the way we've been dragging you into our plans from your earliest days in the Lost Cities. But . . . the fact that you were always frustrated by how few and far between our notes were should prove how methodical we try to be—how thoroughly we explore all of the options before we choose to involve you. And the Council isn't nearly so meticulous—which isn't meant to be a criticism," he added when several Councillors made derisive noises. "It's simply a different method of operating. The twelve of you—as well as your many predecessors—have been handing off assignments to Regents and Emissaries for millennia. It's second nature to you. And I understand why—it's the only way a world as complex as ours can properly function. But the Black Swan has had to operate in the shadows for most of our existence, and our goal has always been to involve as few as possible to avoid detection—plus, we're well aware of the danger involved with our assignments and prefer to keep the risks to ourselves. So when I told you about meeting with King Enki, Miss Foster, it was with the assumption that the meeting would be arranged the way we always arrange anything we're involving you in—with someone in our order handling all the preliminary investigations and addressing as many potential pitfalls as possible before we ever brought you and your friends to Loamnore. And while I knew the Council worked at a different pace, it didn't occur to me that they might arrange a meeting with King Enki this fast, since your appointment—and the existence of your team—has yet to be announced."

"The public's lack of knowledge of Team Valiant is no reason for us to hold off utilizing the arrangement," Councillor Emery informed him. "Particularly with a sensitive meeting like this, which would've been kept classified anyway. But . . . I can see how you might've thought otherwise. Especially since I'm now realizing that we didn't mention the date or time of our meeting with King Enki to you. I suppose we assumed Miss Foster would pass that information along."

Which . . . Sophie probably would have, if she hadn't been fighting with Mr. Forkle about her biological parents. . . .

Yet another way her selfish focus was coming back to haunt her.

"In the interests of improving our communication," Councillor Emery added, "you should know that we're planning to announce the Regent appointments next week. We're still figuring out the exact date, time, and place. If you'd like an update once we've decided—"

"I would," Mr. Forkle told him. "And . . . for what it's worth, I *do* apologize for not informing you about Granite's meeting with King Enki—and I'm glad to hear that Miss Foster was able to salvage the situation." He turned to Sophie, and she was a little surprised by the level of pride radiating from his expression—like a dad whose kid had just hit a game-winning home run. "Does this mean you'll be willing to share what you learned while you were in Loamnore?"

"If you'll be willing to share what Granite learned with us," Bronte countered.

"But not right now," Sophie cut in when everyone nodded.

Mr. Forkle sighed. "Yes, I suppose I've sidetracked us from the reason you called me here, haven't I? All right then—why don't you go get settled into bed while I hail Livvy and let her know what's going on. I'd also still like to have Mr. Vacker and Mr. Sencen here—so long as that won't make you uncomfortable."

Sophie's mouth turned drier than the desert they'd hiked through earlier.

But she croaked out, "Of course it won't!"—even though she was pretty sure that seeing Fitz *wasn't* going to go well.

Then again . . . he couldn't stay mad at her when she was about to come super close to dying again, could he?

Maybe she'd finally found a perk to her allergy!

"I can hail my brother if you want," Biana offered.

"And I can hail Keefe," Dex added.

"Excellent," Mr. Forkle told them, clapping his hands as he turned to the Council. "I'm assuming you're planning to stay for this?"

"You are?" Sophie blurted out when Councillor Emery agreed.

She hadn't realized she'd be almost dying in front of such a huge audience.

"We want to make sure you're okay," Oralie told her, sounding so genuine that it melted a bit of Sophie's panic.

Or it did until Bronte added, "And let's be honest, we're all curious to see how this works—myself in particular, given that the ability being focused on is one that Miss Foster and I share."

"If you'd rather have privacy, Sophie," Edaline jumped in, sending an angry-mama-bear glare at Bronte, "I'm *sure* the Councillors will understand."

"No, it's fine," Sophie decided.

Given the lengthy discussion that Mr. Forkle and the Council had just had about working together, it didn't seem like a good idea to shut the Councillors out.

And who knew? Maybe they'd appreciate her a little more after they saw for themselves the kinds of things she put herself through in order to be useful.

"Just keep in mind," Dex warned the Council, "that if this goes anything like the time I accidentally gave her limbium, there's going to be a *lot* of Sophie-vomit. So if that's going to trigger a hurlfest for you guys, this could get really messy really fast."

"Actually, I think I have an elixir that will help with that," Elwin told him. "I'll grab some when I go back for Bullhorn."

"You're bringing your banshee here?" Grady asked.

Elwin nodded. "The last time I worked on Sophie's allergy, he was the only way I knew if something was or wasn't helping."

Right.

Because banshees could tell when someone was either close to dying—or *really, really, really* close to dying.

"Gotta say, it's not sounding like a whole lot of fun to be the moonlark right now," Stina mumbled. "And it's not feeling very awesome, either."

She fanned the air in front of her face the way Keefe always did.

"Wait. You can feel my emotions right now?" Sophie asked. "Without physical contact?"

"Some of them, yeah." Stina wrapped her arms around her stomach. "And it's a pretty miserable experience, so I think it might be proof that hanging out with you is ruining my life."

She said the last part in a friendly, teasing tone that Sophie never would've expected to hear coming from *Stina*.

And Sophie had zero words for a response.

"Most likely you're benefitting from the residual boost that comes from being around an Enhancer," Mr. Forkle explained. "It's a subtle effect—nothing like grabbing hold of Sophie's hands. But it can still cause small improvements to the abilities of everyone around her."

"Huh," Stina said—which summed up Sophie's thought on the subject as well.

She remembered Mr. Forkle mentioning something about that when he first triggered her enhancing, but then she'd been so busy getting used to the gloves that she'd kind of forgotten about it— especially since none of her friends had noticed a difference.

She wondered why Stina had. . . .

"Come on," Edaline said, crossing the room and draping an arm around Sophie's shoulders. "Let's get you settled into bed."

Sophie nodded, letting Edaline lead her up the stairs. But halfway to her room she changed her mind.

"I think we should do this under Calla's Panakes tree," Sophie decided. "I feel much calmer out there. And it's probably not a bad idea to be so close to all of those healing flowers."

Plus, Calla had been a part of Project Moonlark—and even though Sophie *knew* Calla's consciousness was technically gone, the thought of being surrounded by the Panakes' whispery songs while the limbium burned through her system made the whole process sound a little less awful.

"I think that's a great idea," Edaline said, snapping her fingers a few times. "I just sent blankets and pillows out there—I'll get you set up. Why don't you go change into fresh clothes while I do? Pick something extra soft and cozy for when you're . . ."

She looked away, and Sophie pulled her into a hug.

"I'm going to be okay," Sophie promised.

"I know." Edaline squeezed Sophie tighter. "But I'm still going to worry. It's my job as a mom—and I'm *very* good at it."

"You're good at *all* of the mom things," Sophie assured her, and Edaline found a way to hug her even harder.

They stood like that for a while, neither wanting to let go.

"All right, I've smothered you enough," Edaline eventually said, swiping at her eyes as she stepped back. "You go get changed. I'll set you up the most comfortable pillow-bed ever."

Sophie grabbed Edaline's hand as she turned to walk away. "I really am going to be okay, Mom."

"You are," Edaline agreed. And it actually *did* sound like she believed it. "You're my brave, brilliant, beautiful fighter."

Now Sophie had to look away and wipe at her eyes. "I love you."

Edaline leaned in and kissed her cheek. "I love you, too. So go get dressed. The sooner we do this, the sooner you'll be able to get some rest. You've had a long day."

She had.

And Sophie didn't say it, but she had a sour, sinking feeling that she still had a very long night ahead of her.

Sophie took Edaline's advice and wore her softest pair of leggings. But for a shirt, she went with the pink *Happy Shadow Thoughts* tunic that Linh had made for her when Sophie was recovering from the Neverseen's attack in the Healing Center.

Sophie hadn't touched the shirt since Tam was taken, because it brought up too many conflicting feelings.

But . . . it felt like a good time to remind herself why she was doing this.

If her inflicting could work the way it was supposed to, maybe the Neverseen wouldn't be able to hurt her again.

And maybe she'd be strong enough to get Tam safely away from their enemy.

Assuming he even wanted her to—

No.

Sophie shut down the unfair worry.

She wasn't going to doubt Tam like that.

She was going to focus on happy shadow thoughts.

And on fixing herself.

The Councillors and Mr. Forkle were grilling Wylie about what happened with the orb of light he'd made in Loamnore when Sophie made her way back downstairs—and part of her wanted to stay and listen. But she knew she didn't have the mental energy for that kind of conversation. She'd have to trust them to update her on anything they'd pieced together once she'd recovered from the ability resetting. For the moment, she needed to clear her head.

Edaline wasn't waiting for her at Calla's Panakes tree when Sophie made her way over. But Stina was.

"That's an interesting outfit you have on there, Foster," she called over her shoulder, adding another blanket to the pillow-mountain she was constructing.

"No, it's an *awesome* outfit," Biana corrected, appearing out of thin air beside Sophie and nearly making Sophie pee her pants.

Vanishers.

Biana tossed another pillow onto the pile. "I really need to get one of those tunics, for when . . ."

She didn't finish the sentence—and Sophie wondered if that meant Biana shared some of her worries about Tam.

"Where's Edaline?" Sophie asked instead, scanning the nearby pastures and hoping Wynn and Luna weren't anywhere near the gorgodon's enclosure.

"She's working with Dex to figure out how to keep Bullhorn confined to this area," Biana told her as she scooped up another pillow.

"Wow, this is turning into a huge fiasco, huh?" Sophie mumbled—then blocked Biana from adding the pillow to the pile.

If they made her bed-mountain any taller, she was going to need crampons and rope to climb in.

"Well . . . I mean . . . it's kind of a big deal," Biana reminded her. "You sure you're up for it after the day you've been having? First the King's Path. Then the exploding chandelier. Now this."

"Don't forget the mud," Stina added. "And the sandblasted hike."

Sophie shrugged. "There's never a good time to almost die."

"Okay, someone needs to get that embroidered on a tunic for our Mysterious Lady F immediately!" Keefe called out behind her, and when Sophie spun around, she found him striding up the path along with Ro.

His eyes darted to the sparkly silver letters shimmering across her tunic, and she could tell he *wanted* to make some sort of snarky comment.

But he held off, as if he didn't feel right making any Tam-Slams at the moment.

Instead, he turned to Biana and said, "Did I hear something about an exploding chandelier—because *that's* a story I need to hear."

"Uh, *yeah!*" Ro added.

Biana gave a brief retelling, and Keefe smirked at Sophie. "That sounds like our Lovely Lady F—can't take her *anywhere* without her trying to blow something up."

"Uh, excuse me, the explosion was Wylie's doing, not mine," Sophie argued. "And Biana was the one who suggested we search the Grand Hall."

"And it's a good thing I did!" Biana noted.

"It was," Sophie agreed. "We'll have to check in with Nubiti tomorrow and see if she found anything else."

"No, *we'll* have to check in with Nubiti tomorrow," Biana corrected, gesturing to herself and Stina. "*You* will be getting lots of rest."

Sophie rolled her eyes. "I'll be fine. I've done this before, remember?"

"Uh, yeah, and as someone who was there the last time you did this and saw you rocking the whole sweaty, slightly green look, I'm pretty sure you're gonna need to chill for a bit, there, Ms. Go-Getter," Keefe cut in. "Especially since they're probably not going to let you take any painkillers for the first twenty-four hours."

"I forgot about that," Sophie admitted, becoming very interested in kicking a couple of fallen Panakes blossoms. "Why does almost dying have to be the worst?"

"Pretty sure the answer's in the name," Biana said gently.

"So let's rename it!" Keefe suggested, making his way over to Sophie and draping his arm across her shoulders. "From now on, any time there's a disaster, we'll say, 'Wow, we almost Fostered it!'"

Sophie rolled her eyes.

"I'm serious," Keefe insisted. "We'll make it your big claim to fame!"

"So, when you challenged King Dimitar to a sparring match and he sliced a huge gash under your ribs . . . ," Sophie challenged.

"I totally Fostered it!" Keefe finished without missing a beat. "And when *you* projectile vomit all over the Councillors today, you'll be Fostering it hardcore—"

"And some of us are *super* looking forward to that, by the way!" Ro cut in. "I'm just wishing I'd thought to bring snacks."

"I can't believe you're joking about this," a familiar accented voice snapped behind them, and Keefe dropped his arm and backed away as Sophie slowly turned around, and . . .

There was Fitz.

Or rather, there were Fitz's shoes—right next to Grizel's big goblin feet—because that was all that Sophie had the courage to actually look at for the moment.

A painful stretch of silence followed.

Then Fitz's feet moved closer, and Sophie noticed that Grizel's feet stayed where they were and all the other feet around her quietly shuffled away, leaving her feet and Fitz's feet alone.

She held her breath, trying to brace for whatever Fitz was going to say.

But he didn't say anything.

He just wrapped his arms around her—gently at first.

Then hugging her so much harder.

Like he was afraid to let her go—and maybe he was. Because his voice filled Sophie's head, his consciousness slipping past all of her barriers so he could tell her, *I know you're trying to stop yourself from worrying too much—but I can't laugh about this, Sophie. This is serious.*

I know, she told him, digging her head deeper into the nook between his shoulder and neck and realizing how much she'd missed him—and how lucky she was that he still wanted to hold her like this after all the time she'd spent neglecting him. *But it'll be fine. Mr. Forkle said that he and Livvy have been researching the treatment for a while. And they're going to give me way less limbium than they gave me the last time.*

I still wish you didn't have to do this, he told her.

Me too. But . . . I can't keep pretending everything's fine when one of my abilities is broken.

It's not BROKEN, he argued. *Mr. Forkle told me he's just trying to make it fancier, the way they designed it to be or whatever.*

That's part of it—but . . . I almost took out everybody in Loamnore today because the dwarves' defenses made me get all rage-y. And think of how many other times I've messed everything up with my inflicting. Like that day at Grizel's training camp—if I hadn't—

DON'T, Fitz interrupted. *Don't you dare blame yourself for that—you know how strong Umber was. She would've taken out Sandor and Grizel if you hadn't, and probably hurt them a whole lot worse in the process.*

Maybe, Sophie conceded. *But . . . I still have to do this. The Neverseen won't ever expect the ability to change like this—and we can't pass up a chance to catch them off guard.*

His chest heaved with a sigh. *I know. That's why I'm here. Whatever you need—whatever it takes, I'm getting you through this, okay?*

She nodded against him, and he shifted slightly so he could pull her even closer, one hand tangling in her hair, the other reaching up to stroke her cheek.

"Okay, has everyone reached their Fitzphie overload point?" Ro asked. "Because I sure have. Besides, the doctor-lady's here, so aren't we supposed to get to the vomiting part now?"

"Livvy's here?" Sophie asked, pulling back from Fitz to check.

And sure enough, there was the Black Swan's physician, no longer bothering to wear her mask or use her code name.

"Hmm," Livvy said, tossing her braided hair and grinning at Sophie and Fitz. "Looks like a few things have changed since the last time I saw you two, and I gotta say, you sure make a good-looking couple."

"We do," Fitz agreed, and Sophie was so relieved that he still thought of them as a couple that it took her brain a second to register that he'd also called her pretty—and she probably would've melted into a puddle of mush right then if Fitz hadn't put his arms around her again.

The gesture felt protective this time, and his voice was all sharp edges as he told Livvy, "If you let *anything* happen to her—"

"Got it," Livvy interrupted, tossing her braids again, and Sophie noticed that they glinted with tiny yellow jewels, which matched the sunny glitter Livvy had brushed across her dark skin. "And you can ease up on the worry there, Pretty Boy. I'm not going to let anything bad happen to your sweet girl."

"Uh, you're still going to give her something she's deathly allergic to, right?" Fitz asked.

Livvy's smile faded. "Okay, I guess what I should say is that I'm only going to let some *temporary* bad stuff happen to your sweet girl—and then I'm going to fix it all and make her a thousand times better. So you don't have to worry, even though I get that you're all going to. And while we're being honest here, I'll tell you what I just told the worrying-adult brigade inside: Moments of this *definitely* aren't going to be pretty. So if you don't want to see that, you might want to skedaddle."

"I'm staying," Fitz and Keefe said, pretty much simultaneously, followed by Biana a half second later.

"What about you?" Livvy asked Stina. "You're new."

"I am," Stina agreed. And there wasn't a drop of snottiness in her voice when she said, "And I'm staying right here."

Things seemed to speed up after that as the rest of Sophie's audience made their way over and Livvy moved everyone into position. Sophie climbed onto her pillow-and-blanket mountain and tried to focus on the whispering melodies coming from Calla's tree as Livvy put Fitz on Sophie's left and Keefe on her right, so each boy would be able to hold one of her hands during the reset—Keefe to monitor her emotions, and Fitz to keep track of her consciousness. Then Grady, Edaline, and Mr. Forkle were lined up right behind them, along with Sandor and Flori, and Flori added her own soft humming to the Panakes' melodies as everyone else formed a half-moon curve around the tree—except for Elwin.

Elwin set Bullhorn on the pillow next to Sophie and moved to Livvy's side—and Sophie tried to concentrate on all of the serious medical stuff they then went over with her. But she didn't want to see the needle.

She knew it was there.

She'd caught a quick glance of the glass syringe filled with a thick blue liquid when Livvy handed it to Elwin.

And she knew it was the treatment that would save her life in the end.

But that didn't stop her mind from thinking, *Needle needle needle.*

She tried to distract herself by staring into Bullhorn's beady purple eyes, silently begging him not to freak everyone out as much as he had the last time.

"I'm going to be fine," she whispered to him.

Bullhorn snorted.

And her brain thought, *Needle. Needle. Needle.*

"You *will* be fine," Livvy assured her. "Regardless of what you choose, okay?"

Sophie nodded—and then her brain caught up to what Livvy had just said. "What do you mean 'regardless of what I choose'?"

"I mean you still have one more decision to make before we get started." She sat next to Sophie on the pillow-mountain and held out her hands, which were both curled into fists. "The thing is, as I was putting together this fix, I realized there were two ways to do it. We can go small"—she opened her left fist, revealing a tiny milky-white pill—"or we can go big"—she opened her right fist, revealing a larger pill that was shimmering emerald green. "Either one will trigger a reaction that will reset your inflicting."

"So what's the difference?" Sophie asked as Sandor and Grady already started calling for her to pick the white pill.

"The difference is, the white pill has a quarter of an ounce of limbium in it," Livvy explained, "plus some other stuff to target the inflicting parts of your brain. And the green pill has *half* an ounce of limbium, the same stuff to target the inflicting parts of your brain, *plus* some stuff that'll target one other place."

"Where?" Grady demanded before Sophie could ask.

Livvy chewed her lip. "Her heart."

Sophie reached for her chest, pressing her fingers against her ribs. "My *heart*."

Livvy nodded. "The power for most abilities comes from our brain—but everything I've read on inflicting says it works a little differently. Your brain switches the ability on, but the *real* power comes from here"—she pounded the fist holding the green pill against her chest—"because inflicting's all about channeling your emotions out into the world. And the emotions here"—she pounded her chest again—"are so much purer. So if we *really* want to see how strong your power can be, we should reset both places—head *and* heart. But we also absolutely don't have to. I want to be super clear about that. Everything we're trying to fix *will* be covered by this." She held up the white pill. "This will make it so your brain reins in your emotions the way we designed it to, and let you channel them in a much more targeted way. This is absolutely a solution."

"But the green pill's better," Sophie pressed.

"'Better' might not be the right word," Livvy told her, "because it *does* up the risks as well—and probably your recovery time too, since it's going to stop your heart for a few seconds, and that'll take a toll."

Now there were a lot more people calling for her to take the white pill.

Including Fitz.

And it did look so much simpler.

Small. Bland. Boring.

The green was so much more vibrant.

The color of life.

But also the color the elves wore to their funerals.

"You think I should take the green pill, don't you?" Sophie asked Livvy.

"I think it's your decision," Livvy corrected.

"But you *made* the green pill," Sophie reminded her. "You could've stopped at the white, but you knew you could probably do better so you kept going, right?"

Livvy sighed. "I'm a scientist, Sophie. I like pushing limits and solving puzzles. And your genetics are basically a playground for me. The last reset we did on you was completely mental, so part of me wants to know what'll happen if we stray into uncharted territory and tweak a few other things with your heart. *That's* why I made the green pill. And I've done everything in my power to make sure it's still safe for you. But 'safe' in this kind of situation leaves room for a lot of pain—and the potential for side effects. So the white pill really might be your better option. It's up to you and how hard you want to fight through."

Livvy held out both pills again as Elwin handed Sophie a bottle of Youth.

And it sounded like pretty much everybody wanted her to take the white pill.

She didn't hear a single call for green.

But there were definitely a few voices missing from the shouting.

Friends who were letting her decide.

But would probably take the bigger risk.

And the songs whispering through the air turned to melodies of boldness and bravery. Of tiny roots finding the strength to crack through solid stone.

"Just take the white pill, Sophie," Fitz pleaded. "You've risked enough."

She had.

Over and over and over.

And she was tired of it.

But the fight wasn't finished yet.

And what was the point of fighting if she wasn't going to put her whole heart into it?

"That's our girl," Keefe said quietly as Sophie snatched the green pill and gulped it down before she could change her mind. "Knew she was going to Foster it."

TWENTY-EIGHT

IRST THE WORLD TURNED ITCHY. Every nerve raw and tingling as a million buzzing things sprang to life under Sophie's skin, and she wanted to thrash and claw and scrape until they could scurry free and skulk away.

But she was pinned.

Trapped.

And then came the pain.

Time stopped as lightning flashed through her veins, and her blood caught fire, and a million needles and nails and spikes drilled into her brain.

And her heart . . .

Something was squeezing.

Crushing.

Closing off everything.

She couldn't breathe.

Couldn't think.

Couldn't function.

Everything was stopping, stopping, stopping as her insides twisted and writhed.

Resisting.

Rejecting.

Her body wanted to heave—wanted to purge—but something cold coursed through her, numbing and soothing and sweetening the sour enough to quell the urge.

She wished it could ease the other pain, which was swelling with every strangled breath, hammering with every stalled heartbeat, tearing with every prickle and squeeze.

But the agony raged on—harder and harder and harder until something tore open inside her.

A new wound she knew would never heal.

And the darkness she'd been carrying—hiding—crawled inside.

Nestled deep.

Made itself at home.

It wasn't a monster anymore.

It was part of her.

And with that thought a scream ripped out of her—guttural and primal.

Drowning out the other noises—other voices.

Distant sounds on the edge of everything that were too far away to actually be something.

People calling her name.

Offering promises and pleas.

None of them mattered.

Nothing could reach her.

Even the lulling melodies that slipped under her skin.

Her brain was too busy telling her, *Retreat, retreat, retreat.*

And her heart . . .

That still wasn't working.

And then, something soft and feathery slipped through.

A cool green breeze.

Floating and fluttering through her mind.

Swirling around her heart.

Keeping everything steady, steady, steady.

Despite the pain.

And the panic.

And the punishment her body was enduring.

Even the darkness turned sleepy.

Tucking itself away.

Hiding for later.

And Sophie kept drifting, drifting, drifting—letting the verdant wisps of energy hold her solidly in place, even though everything was fading, fading, fading.

Slipping so very far away.

Too far, maybe?

She—

Brutal, stabbing agony knocked her back to reality, and she felt herself cry out again as the world grew louder and louder.

Colder and crueler.

But there was also warmth.

And strength.

And air.

Blissful, beautiful air.

And with each glorious breath, time ticked slowly back to life.

Steady as a pulse.

Following a powerful new rhythm.

The voices were closer now—some shouts, some whispers. All saying the same thing.

Sleep now, Sophie.

Don't fight.

Give in. Give in. Give in.

Sweetness coated her tongue as another green breeze drifted in, and she let her consciousness follow it to a sweet, soft, soothing oblivion.

Awareness returned in stages.

Pain first.

Then nightmares.

And finally, a hazy fragmented reality where Sophie couldn't fully tell how much her blurry eyes were seeing and how much was still in her head.

"Where am I?" she asked, the words sticky and garbled and so much more exhausting than they should've been.

"In your room."

A smudgy form leaned over her, and it took Sophie's brain a second to morph the colors into the shape that matched the voice. "Mom?"

"Yes," Edaline whispered, leaning in to kiss Sophie's cheek.

Sophie blinked hard, willing her vision back into focus as Edaline pulled away, so she could study Edaline's expression.

"Wow, was it *that* bad?" Sophie asked, hating how swollen and shadowed and red Edaline's eyes looked.

"I'm sure it was far worse for you than it's been for us." Edaline swiped at the sweaty hair on Sophie's forehead, but it seemed to be plastered there. "How much do you remember?"

"I don't know," Sophie admitted. "It's sort of surreal as it's happening, so it's hard for me to connect it to anything physical, if that makes sense. Plus, my head's still really foggy."

Edaline nodded. "That's probably from the sedative."

"Sedative?" Sophie wanted to jolt out of bed in protest, but it felt like she had a woolly mammoth standing on her chest—and like maybe that mammoth had trampled her before it settled down, because she ached in every bone and muscle and nerve. "Last time I couldn't take sedativ—"

"Last time was different," Edaline interrupted. And there was a noticeable crack in her voice as she added, "Or so I hear, since I wasn't there. But last time they didn't have to do chest compressions until your heart started beating again."

"Chest compressions?" Sophie knew she needed to stop repeating things, but . . . chest compressions didn't sync with her scattered memories.

They *did* match the pain in her ribs, though.

"I don't remember that," Sophie admitted.

"Well . . . I guess that's good."

Something in Edaline's tone made Sophie wonder if Edaline wished she could've forgotten that particular moment too.

But Sophie had other questions—better questions. Most important: "Did it work?"

Edaline sighed. "They think so. But we won't know for sure until you inflict—and you need to get your strength back before we can try that. Which might be a slow process. *Not* as slow as it was with the echoes, I promise. It's just that Elwin and Livvy don't think we should give you any elixirs right now. That's why you're not on any pain medicine."

"Then why did they give me a sedative?" Sophie wondered.

"They only gave you a fraction of a dose to keep your pulse steady while the last of the limbium worked its way out of your system," Edaline explained. "They were afraid your pulse might stop again, otherwise. But if they needed proof that your body can't handle anything extra right now, the fact that you ended up knocked out for three days seems pretty telling."

"Three days?" Sophie wanted to throw off her covers and leap out of bed—but the woolly mammoth weighing her down was having none of it. "How could I lose that much time?"

"It's called almost dying," Edaline said gently.

"Actually, it's called 'Fostering' now," Keefe corrected—and it took Sophie a second to find him smirking at her from her desk, where his notebooks and art supplies were scattered all around Iggy's cage.

Keefe's hair looked as rumpled as his clothes, and Sophie wondered how many hours he'd been there.

Or how many *days.*

"I swear I haven't been, like, creepily watching you sleep or anything," he promised, probably misunderstanding her mood shift. "Elwin and Livvy had to rework some of the treatments they're planning for you, and they didn't want to leave you alone—but they also didn't want to set up an alchemy lab in here. So everyone started fighting over who would keep an eye on you—because everyone *wanted* to, not because they didn't," he clarified. "And Fitz definitely did, in case you were wondering, or worrying, or . . . he's been here a *lot*, okay? The only reason he's gone right now is because he'd promised my dad that they'd work through more memories, and you know how my dad is—he gets his way no matter what. And Dex, Biana, Stina, and Wylie have been around a bunch too, but they had some *Go Team Awesome!* stuff that the Council needed them to do with Grady today. And Flori and Sandor are reorganizing the security now that Nubiti's gone. And Edaline's here now, but she also has all the animals to care for. Meanwhile, I basically have nothing to do, thanks to Tammy Boy's warning—not that I wouldn't be here even if I did have stuff . . . I just . . . we figured you wouldn't want someone sitting here when they could be off investigating things—and I can draw anywhere so . . . it seemed like the most logical solution, you know?"

"Smooooooooooooooth, Hunkyhair," Ro told him. "Really, *really* smooooooooooth."

It sounded like Ro was inside of Sophie's closet, but Sophie wasn't propped up enough to be able to tell for certain—and if she was right, Sophie could only imagine what kinds of chaos the ogre princess might cause in there.

She sorta hoped it included shredding some of her ridiculously frilly gowns.

"So you've been here for *three days*?" Sophie asked, glancing from Keefe to Edaline, both of whom nodded—though Keefe looked way more fidgety about it.

"We left once," Ro admitted, "but only because I *made* Hunkyhair shower and change—and you're welcome, by the way. I swear the stench radiating off of him was making the flowers in your carpet wither."

"It was *not!*" Keefe argued. And Sophie had never seen him turn quite so red. "It also wasn't my fault," he mumbled. "Elwin and Livvy made it super hot in here because it was supposed to be good for your healing or whatever. So of course I got all gross and sweaty."

"We all did," Edaline added, trying and failing to wipe away the hair shellacked to Sophie's forehead again—which made Sophie realize she probably didn't want to know what she looked like in that moment.

Or what she smelled like . . .

"That doesn't change the fact that no one could go near Hunky-hair without coughing!" Ro called from the closet.

Keefe gritted his teeth, and Sophie had to laugh—and then whimper as the pain punished her for daring to use her chest muscles.

"I'm fine," she promised, but Edaline was already on her feet heading for the door.

"I need to let Elwin and Livvy know you're awake so they can check on you," Edaline called over her shoulder. "Try not to move too much in the meantime, okay?"

Sophie nodded.

But she still had to try to sit up—and then regretted it when prickles shot up her arms and down her legs.

Keefe snorted as he rushed over to help. "You listen almost as well as I do, you know that, Foster? Here."

He lifted her gently by the shoulders and eased her into a sitting position, propping her back and arms with extra pillows. "Better?"

She nodded, needing a second to catch her breath. "Definitely wouldn't mind if Elwin and Livvy let me take some pain medicine."

"Yeah. Me neither." He shook his arms as he backed away, and she realized his empathy was making him suffer through everything she was feeling—and she'd just made it worse for him by being stubborn.

She cleared her throat, planning to say, *Sorry.* But at the last second she changed to "Thank you."

"For what?" Keefe asked.

"For helping me sit up. And for staying here for so many days. And . . . for whatever you did to get me through the reset." Her memories were a scrambled mess, but she definitely remembered one thing. "You sent me a green breeze, didn't you?"

Keefe's gaze shifted to his hands, which were fidgeting with the loosened laces of his jerkin. "I mean, I can't always see the color of the emotions—and honestly, sometimes I'm not even sure what emotions I send. My ability gets a little abstract when you're enhancing me, so I don't always know what I'm doing. But I *do* know I wanted you to feel like whatever was happening was a fresh start, so it wouldn't be as scary for you, since your fear was spiking even worse than your pain."

"A fresh start," Sophie repeated, feeling her lips curl into a smile. "I guess that's a better way of looking at it than fixing my broken ability so I won't be useless or ruin anything else."

Keefe whistled. "It's kind of ridiculous how hard you are on yourself."

Sophie shrugged—then wished she hadn't when they both winced from the tearing sensation that zinged through her shoulder muscles. "I have to be hard on myself," she told him. "I have *lots* of people counting on me."

"You do. And I get it. But just . . . don't forget what I said before. The only thing you *have* to be is Sophie Foster. That's more than enough."

"Awwwwwww—good one, Hunkyhair!" Ro called, ruining the moment—not that it was a *moment* or anything like that. "Way to recover!"

Sophie cleared her throat, trying to move past the cloud of awkwardness now hanging over them. "So . . . Dex, Biana, Stina, and Wylie are working on Team Valiant stuff with Grady? Did they say what they were doing?"

"Not really. I'm not on the team, so . . . I don't get to know the secrets."

Aaaaaaaaaaaaaand, the awkwardness got a whole lot worse.

"Pretty sure it had to do with the dwarves, though," Keefe added quietly. "And Dex told me to tell you they'll stop by tomorrow morning to see if you're awake, so I'm sure they'll update you on everything then. After all, you're their Fearless Lady Fos-Boss."

Sophie sighed. "More like the Failing Lady Fos-Boss. No, really," she added when he opened his mouth to argue. "I totally forgot to check in with Wylie and Stina after they did . . . something I might not be allowed to talk about. And I forgot to give Dex and Biana anything important to do while Stina and Wylie were working on that. And I almost inflicted on all of them in Loamnore—and then had to have my abilities reset and ended up unconscious for three days. And who knows how much longer I'll be stuck in bed."

"See, but I seem to remember Bronte—*Bronte!* The-Dude-Who's-Tried-to-Have-You-Exiled-Almost-as-Many-Times-as-Dame-Alina-Has-Tried-to-Have-Me-Expelled, so you know he's *not* just being nice—saying that *you* were the reason King Enki didn't throw you guys out of Loamnore. And by the way, King Enki was mad because the Council *and* the Black Swan totally botched things with the scheduling. Your mistakes were nothing on that—and you're new at this. *Plus* . . . I mean . . . being a leader actually seems pretty hard."

"It is," Sophie admitted, staring at her hands—and realizing she wasn't wearing gloves. She also noticed a new bruise, the same size as the star-shaped scar it was next to, which she'd gotten the last time her abilities were reset. "Is that where they injected the allergy remedy?"

Keefe shook his head. "The main shot went into your leg. But then when Elwin had to start doing chest compressions, Livvy dug out a much smaller syringe with green liquid in it and stabbed that into your hand. Does it hurt?"

"Everything hurts." Sophie slid her hand under her blankets so she wouldn't keep staring at the spot that was surely going to be a new scar.

They needed a subject change—fast.

"So Fitz is at the Shores of Solace right now?" she asked.

"He is—and he's *not* happy about it. He didn't want to leave you. I heard him yelling at my dad before he left, saying the whole thing is a waste of time. But my dad still got his way—he always does. Someday I need to figure out how he pulls that off."

"I take it that means they haven't found anything useful?" Sophie asked.

"That's what I'm assuming. And I'm not surprised. I'm sure my dad's being super stubborn, and controlling, and hiding a ton of stuff, and basically sabotaging the process." Keefe plopped back onto the desk chair and propped his feet on her desk. "Plus . . . don't get me wrong. You know Fitzy's my Best Dude—"

"Best Dude?" Sophie interrupted. "Is that seriously what you're calling him now?"

Keefe nodded. "Until I convince him that we should call ourselves the Keefitzinator. Anyway, I'm not saying our Fitzy's not a super-powerful Telepath. He's just . . . better with the basic stuff when he's working alone, you know? And finding shattered memories seems like it might be a bit too fancy for him. Especially since my dad's *good* at dodging Telepaths."

Sophie chewed her lip. "If you want me—"

"Nah," Keefe cut her off, before she'd had a chance to make her offer.

"Why not?" she asked.

"Uh, for one thing, have you seen you?" he asked. "Hate to break it to you, Miss F, but you need some major bed rest."

"I meant after I'm better," Sophie mumbled, tugging at the parts of her hair that weren't plastered to her forehead and trying to hide behind the greasy strands.

"Oh, I know—but once you're better, you'll have *way* more important stuff to do than digging through my dad's creepy memories," Keefe insisted. "Besides, it's not like we even know for sure that we're going to find anything."

"Right, but—"

"Seriously, Foster. It's not worth it."

He wouldn't look at her as he said it. And Sophie had a feeling there was a bigger reason he was letting her off the hook.

And in case she was right, she decided not to keep pushing.

But they were running out of subject changes.

All she had left was, "Any luck with *your* memories?"

"I wish." He snatched the gold notebook off of her desk and tucked it into his cape pocket before picking up the silver one and slowly flipping through. "I've logged a bunch more stuff. But nothing useful. And Dex told me yesterday that he still hasn't gotten any hits from the London cameras, so . . . I don't know. Maybe the drawing I gave him wasn't good enough for the facial recognition."

"Or the guy might've moved," Sophie hated to tell him. "Humans do that way more than elves do."

"I know. I thought of that. But . . . London's the only lead I have, so . . ." He slumped lower in his chair.

"Well . . . it hasn't been *that* long since Dex set up the cameras," Sophie said, trying to be positive. "And the guy could've been on vacation. Or battling the flu and not leaving the house or something. Just because we haven't found him yet doesn't mean we won't."

Keefe looked about as convinced by those suggestions as she was.

She wished she could think of some brilliant solution, but . . . the man Keefe remembered could literally be anywhere on the planet, and they only had cameras searching *one* city.

If only they could tap into, like . . . a human spy satellite or something. Then they could at least cover a lot more ground. But she doubted Dex's Technopath skills stretched all the way to outer space—and even if they did, there would still be lots of places the satellite didn't cover because human tech wasn't *that* powerful. And the elves didn't . . .

"Wait," Sophie said, wincing as she straightened up. "Is Mr. Forkle still here?"

"He might be," Keefe said. "Why?"

"Go check," Sophie told him, wishing she'd thought of this sooner. "If he is, tell him I need to talk to him right now."

"About what?" Mr. Forkle asked from the doorway, and Sophie jumped—then winced.

"Whatever it is, it can wait," Livvy cut in, shoving Mr. Forkle aside to make her way over to Sophie, with Elwin right at her heels.

Edaline was with them too, and she held Sophie's hand the whole time that Elwin and Livvy did their exam—which was mostly Livvy asking, "Does *this* hurt?" before poking Sophie somewhere, while Elwin flashed various orbs of colored light around Sophie's body and studied her through his funny spectacles.

The answer, unfortunately, was always, "Ow, yes."

And the final verdict seemed to be that everything was on the right track—but Sophie still had a long way to go. They also didn't think she'd be up for taking any elixirs for at least another day.

Including pain medicine.

"Why is it so much worse this time?" Sophie asked, sucking air through her teeth as Livvy made her lie back flat again and her muscles punished her for the movement. "I mean, I know you messed with my heart a little, but last time you gave me *double* the amount of limbium so . . ."

"The heart is much more sensitive than people realize," Livvy said gently. "And so much more vulnerable. It can't defend itself the way the mind can—and I don't mean physically," she added when she noticed Sophie's frown. "From a physical standpoint, they're both vital organs, and any sort of serious strike or blow would be Game Over. But from an *emotional* standpoint, the brain can think through feelings and talk us into or out of them."

"Tell me about it," Ro muttered from Sophie's closet.

"See?" Livvy said. "The ogre princess knows what I'm talking about. It's a defense mechanism that the heart simply doesn't have. The heart feels what it feels, whether we want it to or not. So messing with it the way I did takes a much bigger toll, even on a physical level. This isn't a perfect metaphor, but . . . try to think of it as I poked a hornet's nest. And you got stung. And I'm really sorry."

"Me too," Elwin said.

Edaline squeezed Sophie's hand.

"The good news," Mr. Forkle told her, "is you made the right decision with the pill you selected. I can already feel your heart and mind communicating in ways they never have before."

Sophie's eyes widened. "Are you reading my thoughts right now?"

"Not in the way you're assuming," Mr. Forkle assured her. "I realize you haven't given me permission. So you're going to have to tell me what it is you needed to discuss—unless you want me to find the answer myself."

"No, it's fine," Sophie said, glancing at Livvy and Elwin and deciding it wouldn't matter if they heard. "I need you to do me a favor."

Mr. Forkle sighed. "If this has to do with—"

"It doesn't," Sophie interrupted. "I'm not focusing on that right now—though the fact that I trusted you with my life *again* when you *still* won't trust me with that information—"

"What information?" Livvy interrupted.

"It doesn't matter," Mr. Forkle insisted.

Sophie decided it *did*. So she told Livvy and Elwin, "He won't tell me who my biological parents are. Even though I deserve to know."

"You definitely deserve to know that," Elwin agreed, narrowing his eyes at Mr. Forkle.

"Some secrets must be kept, even from those deserving," Mr. Forkle countered.

Livvy groaned.

"I'm not saying that to pressure anyone into telling me right *now*," Sophie emphasized, turning back to Mr. Forkle. "But I need something else—and since I just took a huge risk for you, and you still won't give me the other information I really need, I don't think you should be allowed to say no to this. Especially since it's a very reasonable request."

Mr. Forkle pursed his lips, looking both wary and amused by her assertiveness. "That's quite the sales pitch, Miss Foster. But you realize you're going to have to actually tell me what you want before I can decide if I'll be able to help you, right?"

Sophie glanced at Keefe and said, "Show him the drawing."

Keefe's eyebrows shot up, but he didn't argue or question her. And as he flipped to the right page in the silver notebook, Sophie explained about Keefe's shattered memory and their plan to find the guy using the CCTV cameras.

"So this is why you and Mr. Dizznee went to London?" Mr. Forkle asked, taking the notebook from Keefe to study the man's face more closely. When she nodded, he asked, "Why do you need my help?"

"Well . . . so far, none of the London cameras have found the guy. And I'm starting to worry that it might be because he doesn't live in London anymore. It's been a few years and humans move around."

"They do indeed," Mr. Forkle agreed, turning to study the drawing from a different angle.

She waited to speak again until he met her eyes, hoping her stare made it clear that what she was about to demand wasn't optional. "That's why I want you to take Dex to Watchward Heath."

"What's Watchward Heath?" Keefe asked.

"Forkle's secret office," Sophie told him. "Or one of them, at least. He brought me there a few days ago and showed me how it gives him access to thousands and *thousands* of camera feeds—and that's exactly what we need. So now Mr. Forkle's going to take Dex there, and let Dex do his Technopath thing. And if our guy is anywhere on this planet—we'll find him."

TWENTY-NINE

"IF I AGREE TO WHAT YOU'RE ASKING," MR. Forkle said, glancing slowly between Sophie and Keefe, "and let's be clear that what I mean by that is, if I allow Mr. Dizznee to do his 'Technopath thing,' as you put it, to the cameras feeding into my private office, I expect to be fully kept in the loop on this project's progress from this point forward—and I don't mean simply with this particular memory. I mean with *all* of the memories you decide to investigate in the future."

He held Keefe's stare as he slowly flipped to the next page of the silver notebook, as if he was testing to see if Keefe would try to stop him.

"Flip all you want—I have nothing to hide," Keefe said, leaning back in his chair. "But I should warn you, that also means there's nothing else interesting in there. Mommy Dearest did a good job of making sure I wouldn't recover these memories. Why do you think Foster's pushing you so hard for this one?"

"What about the memories in those?" Mr. Forkle asked, pointing to the green and brown notebooks still sitting on Sophie's desk.

Keefe scooped them up and held them out. "I mean . . . if you're looking for a particularly inspired visual re-creation of the Great Gulon Incident, then you're about to be super excited. Otherwise, not so much. Oh, and if you flip the pages at just the right speed, you can watch the moment the gas erupts."

Mr. Forkle's lips twitched with a smile as he took the notebooks. "And here I thought you had nothing to do with that event."

Keefe smirked. "Not saying I did."

Sophie didn't bother asking. She'd been trying to get someone to tell her what happened during the Great Gulon Incident for *years* and had never gotten a straight answer.

And now definitely wasn't the time to sidetrack the conversation.

Especially when Mr. Forkle pointed to Keefe's chest and asked, "What about the notebook tucked away in your cape pocket? Are you going to show me the memories in there, or do you have something to hide after all?"

Keefe straightened up, placing his hand over the pocket, like he was afraid Mr. Forkle was going to try to snatch the gold notebook away. "How did you know?"

"I have very sharp eyes. Far sharper than you and your friends realize." He handed Keefe back the silver, brown, and green notebooks without paging through them. "Truthfully, Mr. Sencen, I neither want nor need to see your full recorded life history. I just need to trust that you'll come to me when and if you recover something pertinent. Given what happened with the Council and the meeting with King Enki, I'm realizing it's time for all of us to aim for a higher level of transparency."

"Said the guy who still won't tell me who my biological parents are," Sophie felt the need to point out.

"Ohhhhhh, she has you there!" Livvy added.

"She does indeed," Mr. Forkle said through a very long sigh. "But it sadly doesn't change where we stand on that particular issue. Sometimes a mystery must remain unsolved." His eyes locked with Sophie's. "And someday you'll understand why I had to protect this secret. In the meantime, I'm willing to grant your request. I'll bring Mr. Dizznee to Watchward Heath at his earliest convenience and let him program the cameras to search for the man in Mr. Sencen's drawing."

"And you promise you'll let us know the second you find him?" Sophie countered. "No holding back information while you conduct your own investigations?"

"Well, I suspect that Mr. Dizznee will program the feeds to notify him of any matches long before anything alerts me, so this is likely a moot point. But you have my word that *if* the cameras locate this mystery man and I'm the first to acquire that information, I'll pass it along to you and Mr. Sencen immediately—but note my use of the word 'if,' Miss Foster. I fear you're feeling a bit too confident in this plan's success and forgetting that there's no guarantee that we'll be able to find this man. Watchward Heath is an unprecedented monitoring system—but it's not without its gaps. The man may also have altered his appearance in some significant way since Mr. Sencen saw him in this memory—a change of hairstyle. Adding a beard or mustache. Gaining or losing weight. Even the simple inevitabilities of human aging, like wrinkles and hair loss, could be significant enough to make the cameras disregard him as a viable match."

The words might as well have been a giant pair of scissors, snipping the threads of excitement that had been stitching Sophie's newfound hope together.

She'd been living with the elves for long enough that she'd forgotten how much more humans change than the elves. Everyone in the Lost Cities stayed mostly static once they reached adulthood. An elf looked the same at thirty as they did at one hundred thirty and three hundred thirty and one thousand thirty and on and on and on. The only notable difference would be the points of their ears or how they chose to cut or style their hair.

Maybe that was even why the London cameras hadn't found the guy.

"Don't look so disheartened," Mr. Forkle told her. "I should be able to help Mr. Dizznee create some basic algorithms that will allow the cameras to predict the most likely appearance alterations and search for those as well. There will still be a margin for error, of course, but—"

"You would do that?" Sophie interrupted.

"Of course! That shouldn't come as a surprise to you, Miss Foster," he chided. "I fear you've lost sight of who I am. Allowed the fact that I'm unable to share information about your genetic parents to feel like an enormous chasm between us. When the reality is so much simpler. We're still on the same side. We still share the same goals. Still crave the same answers. So how about we endeavor to focus on those similarities from this point forward?"

He extended his hand for a handshake, and, after a quick glance at Keefe, Sophie reached out and took it.

"Excellent," Mr. Forkle said. "I'll explain all of this to Mr. Dizznee as soon as he returns from Loamnore this evening, so he can make any necessary preparations before I bring him to my office."

"Why is he in Loamnore?" Sophie asked.

Mr. Forkle released her hand. "That's classified information."

"Right. And I'm the leader of Team Valiant," Sophie reminded him.

"You are. But no one else in this room has the necessary clearance. And it's best if you don't use your telepathy right now."

"It's best if you don't do *anything* right now," Elwin added, before Sophie could suggest asking everyone to clear the room, "except drink a bottle of Youth, have some broth, and try to sleep. Give us at least the rest of today to get you a little stronger before you start diving into all the stressful conversations. Save the updates and worrying for tomorrow."

"Elwin's right," Livvy agreed, handing Sophie a bottle of Youth as Edaline conjured up a bowl of pale, purple-toned broth for her to eat. "I know you're itching to get back to work—and I get it. Believe me. But right now, your focus needs to be on your recovery or you're going to slow the process down. And the good news is, your friends are brilliant and talented and every bit as determined as you are, so it's not like you have to worry that nothing's getting done. They're out there right now kicking butt and taking names. And you have to be here. So make it worth it. Get as much rest as you can."

Sophie sighed and forced herself to take a bite of broth, which was somehow both a little sweet and a little salty. "What is this?"

"Panakes blossoms steeped with a few herbs Flori recommended," Edaline explained. "She thinks it'll speed your healing."

Sophie finished the whole bowl, and it eased some of the aching in her limbs, which made her want out of that bed even more.

"Try to sleep," Elwin told her, pulling her blankets back into place when she tossed them aside.

"But I've been sleeping for three days!" she reminded him.

"That wasn't restful sleep," Elwin insisted.

"It must've been, because I'm not tired," Sophie argued.

"I can fix that," Flori offered from the doorway. She padded over to the bed, singing a lullaby about windswept branches dancing in perfect harmony to the rhythm of the breeze, and the flowers on Sophie's canopy filled the air with their sweet, soothing perfume.

"That's not fair," Sophie grumbled through a yawn.

"Yeah, wow," Keefe said, rubbing his eyes as he stumbled to his feet. "If I don't go now, I'm going to be drooling on your desk—unless you need me to stay."

Sophie couldn't tell if he was asking her or her physicians. Either way, she told him, "Go home, Keefe. You've been stuck here long enough."

He shook his head, studying her with sleepy eyes. "I'm never *stuck* with you, Foster. Someday I'm going to make you see that."

"Sounds like I'd better get Hunkyhair home," Ro said, striding out of Sophie's closet in a silky pink gown that somehow looked both right and wrong with her armor strapped on top of it. "I was bored," Ro added when she noticed the way everyone was staring, like that explained her new fashion choices. "I'll bring the dress back tomorrow."

"Keep it," Sophie told her. "You . . . look really good."

Ro glanced down, sliding her hands across the shimmering skirt, then rolled her eyes and muttered something about sparkles going to her head.

"You look better," Biana told Sophie the next morning, glancing at Stina. "Doesn't she look better?"

"Does she?" Stina asked, with her trademark brutal honesty. "I mean, she's not so greasy anymore, but she's still awfully pale."

"It's fine," Sophie told Biana, before she could argue. Edaline had brought a mirror over when Sophie insisted on doing the sponge bath herself, so she was very familiar with her pasty skin and shadowed eyes and overall grayish pallor.

She definitely still had some major recovering to do.

The good news was, Elwin and Livvy had finally decided Sophie could have some pain medicine, so she could actually move without constantly wanting to say "ow."

Keefe had also been sweet enough to stay at the Shores of Solace that morning so she'd be able to have all the "classified" conversations with her team.

And Mr. Forkle had kept his promise and taken Dex to Watchward Heath. They were supposed to be there all day, since it was a *lot* of camera feeds for Dex to tweak. But it was progress, and Sophie could at least feel like she'd played some small part in making it happen.

The news from Loamnore was less encouraging.

Nubiti had found ten more magsidian stones hidden in the same corridors where the deserters had sabotaged other things before fleeing the city. And while none of the stones had exactly the same facets, they were all a similar size and shape, and their cuts followed a similar pattern—close enough to be clear that the same person or group had made all ten of the new stones, as well as the three they'd found in the Grand Hall.

And the stones were all hidden in places where magsidian wasn't supposed to be.

And all were impossible to remove.

And no one seemed convinced that the putty Nubiti had covered them with would solve the problem.

Wylie was still in the dwarven city, working with Nubiti to see if there was a way to determine how the stones responded to light without starting another fire.

"That's not the information we need, though," Sophie realized after Biana finished her update. "The Neverseen aren't going to attack with light. They're going to attack with shadows."

"You say that like it's a fact," Stina noted. "But we don't actually know if that's true. The way those stones in the Grand Hall reacted to light couldn't have been an accident. Someone planned that—lined them up so the beams would ricochet perfectly. So light has to be important too."

"I know," Sophie told her. "But no one's ever said that magsidian can't be cut to serve multiple purposes. I think we need to get a Shade down there and see what they can figure out."

Stina sighed. "I was afraid you were going to say that—so I'm calling 'not it' for being the one to convince Lady Zillah to go down there. She's . . . intense."

"I'm pretty sure it needs to be the Council who talks to her," Sophie realized, "since they'll need to work out the visit with King Enki. But someone needs to tell the Council—and make them understand that even if King Enki doesn't want to cooperate, we *need* to know what a Shade can do in Loamnore, both with these stones and on the King's Path."

"I'll talk to my Councillor contacts," Biana promised.

"And I'll hail Oralie and Bronte a little later," Sophie decided. "Is there anything else I need to know?"

Stina and Biana shared a look.

"More bad news?" Sophie guessed, sitting up a little taller to prepare for it. "Nothing with Linh, right?"

"No," Biana promised, glancing at Stina again. "It's just . . . Stina and I finally had a chance to meet with Lady Cadence."

Sophie stopped breathing. "You asked her?"

Biana nodded, eyes shifting to her feet.

Stina stood taller. "She definitely *isn't* your biological mother."

"She isn't," Sophie repeated with the last of the air in her lungs—still not quite ready to breathe again.

She isn't.

She isn't.

She isn't.

"That's good news, right?" Stina asked. "You didn't want her to be your biological mom, did you?"

"No," Sophie said, forcing herself to suck in some air—and triggering a whole lot of coughing—which unfortunately made her very aware of all the places she was still very sore from almost dying, even with the pain medicine. So there were several seconds filled with a lot of *cough*—"ow!"—*cough*—"ow!" before Sophie managed to grit out, "I'm definitely glad I'm not genetically related to her. But . . . do I want to know what she said after you asked her? Probably not, huh?"

"It wasn't that bad," Biana promised—and the "that" told Sophie everything she needed to know.

She held up her hands before Biana could continue. "Never mind. Whenever Foxfire's back in session, I'm going to have to train with her every week, and I'm pretty sure the only way I'm going to be able to do that without dumping curdleroots on her head is if I don't let you finish that sentence."

"It wasn't that bad," Biana assured her again. "But . . . yeah, you're probably right."

"She did say one interesting thing, though," Stina noted. "She said the Black Swan is too smart to have your biological parents' abilities match yours. It'd be too much of a giveaway—especially since your abilities are so rare. That kinda makes sense, don't you think? Like how Bronte *isn't* your biological father even though he's the only Inflictor? So I guess when we figure out more names, we should try to pick people who *don't* have your abilities."

"Great, so basically it could be anybody," Sophie grumbled.

"Not true," Biana argued. "You have a *lot* of abilities. And it rules out all of those."

"Yeah, but there are still way more abilities I *don't* have than abilities I *do*," Sophie countered, reaching up to rub her temples. "But it's fine," she said, trying to convince herself as much as them. "It doesn't matter right now. We're pausing the biological parent search."

"We are?" Stina asked.

Sophie nodded, feeling ten pounds lighter for having decided it. "It's just not the right time. There are too many huge things going on, and I can't keep letting it be a distraction. We can always pick the search back up once things calm down."

"I guess that's true," Biana murmured. "But . . . what about the whole unmatchable thing?"

Sophie sighed. "I'm just . . . going to have to deal with it. Fortunately, most people don't know about that yet, and it won't really be noticeable until our grade level starts picking up their match lists, which is still a little ways off. Hopefully I'll have it figured out before then. But . . . even if not, that doesn't change the fact that right now, we have to focus on the dwarves, and Keefe's missing memory, and whatever else the Neverseen are planning. And I need to get out of this stupid bed."

She tried to kick off her covers and regretted it when her legs proved to be extra achy.

"Want us to get Elwin or Livvy or Edaline?" Biana offered.

"No, it's fine," Sophie said, hating the next words she had to say. "I think . . . I just need to rest for a bit."

"I think that's a good idea," Stina agreed. "Seriously, Sophie. There's nothing wrong with taking the time you need to get better."

"Stina's right," Biana added, looking less uncomfortable with those words than she used to. "That's why you have us. Is there anything else you need us to be working on?"

"I can't think of anything," Sophie admitted, even if it felt like there should be dozens and dozens of things.

Did they really have so few projects and leads?

She tried to tell herself it didn't matter—that they were definitely on the right track with the magsidian stones they'd discovered, and that was going to give them a real advantage. But she still wished she could come up with something better to say than, "Just make sure you talk to the Council about getting Lady Zillah to Loamnore. And maybe check on Linh at Choralmere?"

"On it," both girls promised, and Sophie had to marvel for a second at how well they were all working together—even if bossing them around still felt really strange.

Stina leaped away after that to hail one of her assigned Councillors. But Biana lingered, and Sophie suspected Biana had a bigger reason than just helping her adjust her pillow and blankets.

"You're sure you don't want me to keep working on the Biological Parent thing?" Biana eventually asked, tipping her hand. "I swear I can do it without it being a distraction! I mean, I've managed to test Bronte and Lady Cadence and keep up with all my other responsibilities."

She had—which proved Biana was definitely better at multitasking than Sophie was.

But that didn't change Sophie's mind.

"I'm sure," she told Biana. "Things are getting way too real right now. It's starting to feel like it always feels right before something really big and horrible happens. And if I'm right, I don't want to have to wonder if we would've been better prepared if I hadn't wasted time on selfish, unimportant stuff."

"This isn't *unimportant*," Biana argued.

"No. But it's not *urgent*, either," Sophie had to remind her. "It can wait."

"I guess," Biana said, and the way she was chewing her lip made Sophie pretty sure that Biana was asking herself the same question she was.

Would Fitz wait?

THIRTY

HEY—YOU'RE UP!" FITZ CALLED ACROSS the pastures as he made his way over, and Sophie mentally thanked the universe that she'd decided to brush her hair and change out of her pajamas before she'd headed outside for a little fresh air and some baby alicorn snuggles.

It wasn't her first time out of bed since having her abilities reset—she'd managed that the day before. But she'd only been downstairs for a minute when her head got a little too spinny and her legs got a little too wobbly and Sandor had insisted on carrying her back up to her room.

So making it all the way outside to a nice shady spot under Calla's Panakes tree felt like a huge victory.

If only it hadn't taken her six days to get to that point.

And if only she hadn't been sitting on the grass with her forehead pressed against her knees, trying to fight off a dizzy spell when Fitz found her.

The worry crease between his eyebrows looked especially deep.

"I'm up!" she emphasized, offering him her best *seriously-I'm-fine* smile and wishing the flutter in her heart felt a little more like excitement and a little less like nerves.

After all, her boyfriend was here to visit her.

And he was very, *very* cute.

Fitz's fitted gray tunic made his shoulders look especially broad, and his dark hair was just the right mix of styled and tousled. And when his gorgeous teal eyes met hers and he flashed his movie-star-worthy grin, her brain definitely turned to melty mush.

Which was probably why she couldn't think of something better to say than, "I . . . didn't realize you were coming over."

"I know, I wanted it to be a surprise." He sat across from her in the grass, studying her for several endless seconds before his smile faded. "You still look really out of it."

Sophie let her hair fall forward, giving her a curtain of blond to hide behind. "Yeah, that's what Vertina told me too."

"Vertina?"

"She's this kinda annoying 'girl' programmed into Jolie's old spectral mirror. And she usually tries to get me to do more with my hair, or put on makeup, or wear fancier clothes or whatever. But today she was like, 'Wow, you look awful—why aren't you in bed?'"

"Well, I'm kinda with her on the 'why aren't you in bed' thing," Fitz admitted. *"But."* He reached up to tuck her hair behind her ear. "I *also* think you look really beautiful."

And with that, he scored all the boyfriend points *ever.*

But Sophie still didn't know what to do with the compliment—except maybe get choked up. And she *really* didn't want to do that again.

So she leaned back against the tree trunk, giving herself a little breathing room as she responded to the first part of what he'd said. "I couldn't lie around anymore. I *had* to move."

"Yeah, I remember having that same feeling when we were on bed rest in the Healing Center." He scooted closer to her side, and Sophie couldn't help noticing that his recovering leg still moved more stiffly than the other. "I just don't want you overdoing it and setting yourself back, either," he added quietly.

"I'm trying not to," she promised. "Honestly, the sunshine is helping a lot. And it's nice to have some distractions."

She tilted her chin toward the pasture to their left, where Luna was galloping by with a stalk of swizzlespice sticking out of her mouth and Wynn was racing to catch up with her, probably trying to steal it.

"They *are* pretty cute," Fitz noted. "Though, if you're looking for cute distractions, I'm more than happy to offer my snuggle services."

He flashed a teasing smile as he stretched out his arm and patted her shoulder, inviting her to lean against him.

They both pretended not to notice how long it took her to accept the invitation.

It wasn't because she didn't want to.

The boyfriend thing was still just so . . . *new*.

And she couldn't help running through a Humiliation-Risk mental checklist, trying to figure out if he'd be able to tell that she'd only had sponge baths for the last few days, or feel the nervous sweat pooling in the small of her back.

"Relax, Sophie," Fitz whispered. "I just thought it might help you to lean your head down a bit."

It *did* help.

And it definitely *was* distracting to feel his arm around her and hear the *thump thump thump* of his heartbeat against her ear.

But she couldn't relax.

"Have Livvy or Elwin said how much longer they think it's going to take before you're back to one hundred percent?" he asked as his fingers played casually with a strand of her hair.

"Not really," Sophie admitted. "But I'm guessing at least another week, since they're still trying to limit how much medicine I take. They also think it's going to set me back when I first test my inflicting."

His arm tightened around her. "When will you be doing that?"

"I don't know. Once Elwin and Livvy say I'm ready, I guess—though if they keep babying me, I might lose my temper and then there's nothing anyone can do to stop me."

She tried adding an evil laugh to the end of that statement, but the joke felt super forced. And she found herself once again missing the days when spending time with Fitz didn't feel so painfully awkward.

Sure, he'd always made her nervous—but most of those worries had been connected to the fact that she was super afraid he'd figure out that she liked him and not feel the same way.

She didn't have to worry about that anymore.

After all, he'd come by to see her.

They were *snuggling*.

And yet.

And yet . . .

She couldn't quiet the voice in the back of her mind that kept reminding her how important matchmaking was to Fitz.

And how soon he'd be able to start picking up his lists.

And how right now, there was no way her name would be on them.

She also didn't know how long it would take her to fix the situation or how Fitz *really* felt in the meantime.

Which probably meant they needed to have a long conversation—put all those fears and doubts "out there" and see where they stood.

That would be the mature, responsible way to handle the situation.

But . . . Sophie couldn't seem to make her mouth form those words.

Or *any* words.

So she just sat there, and the silence stretched between them, making Fitz feel farther and farther away even though they'd technically never been so close.

Fitz finally ended her misery by clearing his throat and murmuring, "So . . . I brought you a present. Well, *two* presents, actually."

"You did?"

Sophie turned her head enough to be able to see his face, and there was his perfect smile again, along with a teasing glint in his eye.

"Don't sound so surprised," he told her. "I used to bring you presents all the time!"

He had.

It'd been one of her favorite things.

Not for the gifts themselves, which were usually just silly trinkets. But for the fact that it proved he'd been thinking about her.

It was always so easy for Sophie to convince herself that a guy like Fitz Vacker would *never* be interested in someone as weird as she was. But every time he brought her some sweet, thoughtful gift that proved how well he knew her, she'd think . . . *maybe he could.*

"Anyway," he said, and she realized she was probably supposed to respond to his other statement. "Sorry I've dropped the ball on the gift giving lately."

"You don't have to apologize—"

"I do, though," he insisted, gently helping her sit up so they could face each other. "I totally meant to bring you something yesterday, after the Council's Regent Announcement. But my mom planned this whole dinner for Biana, and Keefe's dad nagged me to come over and work through more memories, and then I was worried it'd be too late and you'd be sleeping, and—"

"It's fine," Sophie assured him. "It wasn't a big deal."

Or, that's what she'd been telling herself, since she'd had to miss the big announcement.

She'd tried to go—that was why she'd dragged herself down-stairs. But much as she hated to admit it, Sandor had been right to haul her back to bed. There was definitely no way she could've stood in a fancy gown with a crown on her head and listened to the Coun-cil answer everyone's questions about the arrangement.

She would've passed out for sure.

So instead, she'd been the mysteriously absent team leader.

The one everyone was probably wondering about. Whisper-ing about—

"Here," Fitz said, distracting her with a tiny silver box tied with silky teal ribbon. "That's what I meant to bring by yesterday."

Sophie hoped he didn't notice the way her hands shook when she untied the bow and pulled open the lid to find . . .

"You have a charm bracelet, don't you?" Fitz asked as Sophie picked up the intricate silver charm—a howling dire wolf, just like her Regent patch.

"I do." She didn't wear it very often because Grady and Edaline had bought it after she was kidnapped, when they thought they'd be extending their annual commemorative charm tradition to another lost daughter.

But that didn't make it any less thoughtful and amazing of a gift. It was perfect.

Just like Fitz . . .

"I love it," she told him, tucking the tiny wolf safely back into its box and wishing she could think of something more meaningful to add than, "Thank you so much."

But *she* wasn't perfect—especially when it came to romantic gestures.

Fortunately, Fitz didn't seem to notice.

"Don't thank me yet! You still have one more gift—and this one's *special*. So special it comes with a speech." He held her gently by her shoulders, waiting for her to meet his eyes. "I know this boyfriend-girlfriend thing is hard for you. Don't shake your head—we both know it is. And that's okay. I get it. And I'm sure you remember me telling you that we'd go at your pace. I asked you to trust me. And then . . . I don't know, somehow things got a whole lot more complicated, and I felt like I didn't know what to do anymore. And I know that's probably made it even harder for you to trust me, so I want you to know that nothing's changed for me, okay? *Nothing.* Still no pressure. Still no time limit. Still your pace. And I've been trying to figure out how to prove that, and . . . this is the best I could come up with. . . ."

He let go of her shoulders and reached into his cape pocket, retrieving something as wide as a book but much thinner, covered in shiny teal paper.

And when Sophie unwrapped it . . .

"Oh wow," she breathed, needing a few seconds to even process what she was seeing.

It was a picture of her and Fitz, sitting under Calla's Panakes tree, just like they were right then. Only the scene was darker. And he was sitting even closer, with his hand cradling her cheek and . . .

"This is a memory," she realized.

His memory.

Of the night he'd just been talking about—when he'd promised he'd wait for her to be ready for all the relationship stuff.

He'd even captured the tears that had slipped down her cheeks while they'd been talking—and Sophie could feel new ones burning her eyes.

"How did you . . . ?" she asked, still trying to understand what she was seeing.

The gift looked more like a painting—but Fitz didn't paint, did he? And the style looked familiar. . . .

"Keefe helped me," Fitz admitted, before Sophie's brain could get there. "I started out projecting the memory—but . . . it didn't look quite right, because I don't have a photographic memory like *some* people. So there were details missing, and parts that were a little blurry. So I paid Keefe to paint over it and add in all the stuff my mind didn't get right."

"Wait—you *paid* Keefe?" Sophie asked, not sure why *that* was the part her mind had fixated on.

Fitz nodded. "Otherwise it's *his* gift—and it's not. This is from *me*. Just like I'm the one who wrote the words on the back."

Sophie hadn't thought to flip it over. But she did, and there, in Fitz's neat handwriting, was his simple plea:

Trust me.

"I do," she promised, feeling her tears spill over onto her cheeks. "I just—"

"I know," he interrupted, taking her hand and tangling her gloved fingers with his. "I get it. The unmatchable thing—it threw us both off. And I *really* wish I'd handled it better. I should've done everything I could to make it clear that it doesn't change *anything* for me. I'm still here, still waiting on you to set the pace. And I know it's all going to work out, Sophie. *We're* going to work out. Just trust me, okay? Talk to me. Lean on me. Don't hide or run away, or give up or . . . whoa."

"Whoa?" Sophie repeated, not sure what to make of the way Fitz was staring at their hands.

"You have gloves on," he said.

"I do . . . ," Sophie agreed. "Is that a problem?"

"What about your fingernail gadgets?" he asked, ignoring the question. "Are those on?"

Sophie nodded. "I always keep them turned on. It just makes more sense that way. Why?"

Fitz finally looked up at her, and his eyes were wide—and a little glazed—as he murmured, "It looks like your inflicting wasn't the only ability affected by the reset. Right now, even with all of that to block it, I can feel you enhancing me."

THIRTY-ONE

FITZ WAS RIGHT.

Sophie's enhancing was definitely stronger.

In fact, it took four layers of gloves *and* her fingernail gadgets to block the ability's effect on him.

And when she tried holding his hand without any barriers between them, it felt like lightning striking each of their palms. Fitz had to let go after a few seconds, so they weren't able to see exactly what the added boost allowed him to do with his telepathy. But Fitz did say it gave his mind a level of clarity he'd never experienced before.

The strangest part, though, was what they discovered throughout the course of the day, after testing the ability on anyone else they could gather: Everyone had a different threshold—and there didn't seem to be any logic to it.

Edaline, Elwin, Livvy, Biana, Dex, and Wylie all felt her enhancing fade as soon as Sophie added a second pair of gloves.

But Stina needed a third pair—and could feel a noticeable boost even without any physical contact.

Keefe needed six layers of gloves—and even then, he could still feel a tiny hum across his senses. But Sophie couldn't squeeze a seventh glove on over the others to see if it would help.

She expected Keefe to be very smug about how strong that meant his empathy was—or at least make an abundance of jokes about the thrill of holding his hand. But Keefe actually seemed . . . a little shaken.

Not as shaken as Grady—though that wasn't totally a surprise to Sophie.

The one and only time that she'd ever enhanced Grady, he'd told her afterward, "Never let me do that again."

But Sophie hated the distance it suddenly put between them.

Grady didn't want to risk exposure to the power, so he held back from hugging Sophie or reaching for her hand—or even standing too close. And the thought of that being her "new normal" made Sophie ill enough to reach out to Mr. Forkle and demand that he come to Havenfield immediately.

"I don't understand," she said, after they'd discovered that Mr. Forkle needed her to wear four layers of gloves to fully block her enhancing, and experienced the same jolt that Fitz had when he made direct contact with her fingertips. "Why wasn't it like this yesterday?"

"Because your abilities, like your body, are still recovering from the reset," Mr. Forkle explained. "As you grow stronger, so will they."

Sophie stared at her fingers, which looked like big marshmallows under all the layers of fabric. "So . . . this is how it's going to be now? I'm stuck with puffy fingers and people afraid to touch me?"

"No," he assured her. "You've simply entered another period of adjustment. Try not to panic, Miss Foster. There's always a solution.

And while it may be hard to see it at the moment, this is good news. You've now become far, *far* more powerful than your enemies."

"No, anyone who touches me is more powerful," Sophie corrected, "so really, *I'm* actually way more vulnerable."

Her imagination happily painted her a new nightmare.

A moonlark in a cage.

Forced to empower anyone who shoved their hand through the bars.

And the truly terrifying part was how easily her captors shifted in her mind, from the Neverseen to the Council—even to the Black Swan.

After all: Who wouldn't want to exploit a resource like that?

"We wouldn't," Mr. Forkle assured her, and she wasn't sure if he'd read her mind or if he'd simply noticed the way her eyes had narrowed with suspicion. "We would never use you against your will, Miss Foster. You *always* have a choice."

"How?" She held up her marshmallow hands. "This ability is automatic."

"I actually wonder if that's true anymore," he murmured, scratching his chin. "With a power this strong—and a brilliant mind like yours—I wouldn't be surprised if there's some sort of internal trigger you've yet to discover, one that allows you to rein in the ability through concentration or sheer willpower."

Sophie blinked. "If that did exist . . . how would I find it?"

"That would be up to you to determine," he told her. "Journeys of self-discovery must be embarked upon alone."

"Great," Sophie grumbled, making no effort to hide her eye roll. "You realize that's not actually an answer, right?"

"It is—it's just not the answer you seek," Mr. Forkle countered. "You want a ready solution, and I cannot give that to you. But I can assure you that if you become more mindful as you use this ability— more aware of the tiny shifts and connections occurring within you as it works—you'll likely discover whole new worlds of strength and control. Remember, this ability wasn't one we chose for you—it was one your genetics naturally dictated. Which likely means your genetics have given you the means to manage it on your own."

Sophie sighed. "That's still not helpful."

"It will be," he insisted. "You just need to give yourself a chance to process."

"Yeah, well, in the meantime, I'm stuck with eight zillion pairs of gloves and trying not to let my enemies get anywhere near me. Might as well lock me in my room."

"I'm on board with that plan," Sandor jumped in. "I'll happily stand guard at the door."

Mr. Forkle smiled. "That won't be necessary. Miss Foster simply needs to remember to rely on her friends."

He called Dex over and had Dex hold one of Sophie's fingernail gadgets in one hand while letting her fully enhance him.

"Oh wow," Dex breathed, his knees buckling the second her fingertips touched his skin—and miraculously, no one made any jokes about Sophie knocking a boy off his feet as Stina and Biana lunged to hold Dex steady. No one mentioned how many additional times Dex whispered, "Wow," before he pulled his hand free and sank to the grass, staring at the sky.

"Think you can make some adjustments to Tinker's design?" Mr. Forkle asked him after several seconds. "Create a more powerful shield for Miss Foster's ability until she learns how to manage it with her mind?"

"I think so, yeah," Dex mumbled, followed by a bunch of techy words that sounded like gibberish.

"I'll take him inside," Biana volunteered, hooking Dex's arm around her shoulders and hauling him to his shaky feet. "He's going to need a notebook to write this all down and make some sketches."

"See?" Mr. Forkle said, turning back to Sophie. "Your teammates are already working on a technical solution. And while they do that, I want you to get some rest—and spend the whole day in bed tomorrow if you can. Try to clear your mind of all other worries and start that mental journey."

"How?" Sophie asked.

Mr. Forkle smiled. "That's up to you. But the first step is sleep."

As it turned out, mental journeys were every bit as pointless and annoying as Sophie expected—and also, surprisingly exhausting.

Her mind didn't want to "clear."

Focusing on her breathing just ended up making her spend hours counting.

And when she tried to listen to her body, all it told her was that she was restless. And hungry. And really hated wearing so many pairs of gloves.

So Sophie literally tackled Dex with a hug the next day, when he showed up with Lovise and Mr. Forkle to deliver her newly designed fingernail gadgets.

The gadgets were clear this time and had to be worn on every finger—and the sequence of taps to activate and deactivate them was much more complicated. But once the gadgets were in place and active, they seemed to do their job perfectly, blocking her enhancing both for Dex and Mr. Forkle.

"You should probably test them on Keefe," Dex suggested, "since he was even more sensitive to your ability than we were. And I'd still recommend wearing double gloves—and keeping a couple of extra pairs in your pockets."

Mr. Forkle clicked his tongue. "Have you so little faith in your talent, Mr. Dizznee?"

"No. I just also know technology isn't perfect. It breaks. Or other stuff interacts with it. So it's good to have a backup plan."

Sophie nodded, pulling Dex into another hug, relieved that it still didn't feel a tiny bit weird between them.

"Thank you," she told him. "You saved me from being Lady Marshmallow Hands."

Dex grinned, flashing his dimples. "See, now I kinda want to take back the gadgets."

"Don't even think about it," Sophie warned.

"Oh, I'm thinking about it, Lady Marshmallow Hands," Dex countered.

Mr. Forkle cleared his throat. "In all seriousness, Miss Foster, I still hope you'll keep searching within yourself, because I feel quite strongly that you have more to discover. In fact, I'm regretting that I never made self-reflection and meditation into a habit for you when you were younger. I should've considered that the uniqueness of your abilities would require a measure of deep introspection, since only you can truly understand the workings of your mind."

Sophie wanted to roll her eyes and tell him how pointless everything she'd tried the day before had been. But it was easier to just say, "I'll do my best," and change the subject.

"What are you working on today?" she asked Dex.

"I asked Forkle to take me back to Watchward Heath, because I had a few thoughts about the cameras while you were enhancing me. The tweaks I made to the feed already are solid—but they're *slow* because there are so many different cameras. And I think I came up with a way to make it all work much faster. See? It's a good thing you had your abilities reset. I know you've been lying here regretting it."

She had, actually—though she hadn't even admitted that to herself.

She'd just lost so many days.

And now her enhancing was so much more complicated.

And she still couldn't even use her inflicting—still didn't even know if it worked any better than it had before.

"It was the right call, Sophie," Dex assured her. "Just give yourself time to adjust."

"Mr. Dizznee is very wise," Mr. Forkle told her. "And I've been meaning to add one more thing. I think it's quite telling that both Mr. Sencen and Mr. Vacker were so much more sensitive to your enhancing."

"Fitz needed the same number of gloves as you," Sophie reminded him.

"Yes, but my telepathy is far more honed than his, so for him to be at my same level is fascinating. And I realize you've always had strong connections with both boys in different ways. But I wonder if having them assist during the reset amplified those bonds. I think it might be worth exploring. I'd recommend working with both of them in tandem to see what you discover. Perhaps complete a few trust exercises."

Dex snorted. "You want Sophie, Fitz, and Keefe to do trust exercises together."

"I think it would be very enlightening," Mr. Forkle agreed.

"Oh, it'll definitely be that," Dex said with a particularly huge grin. "Can I, uh, be there when you do?" he asked Sophie.

"No, it'll work best if it's just the three of them," Mr. Forkle informed him. "Try it today, if you're up for it," he advised Sophie. "And if you're not, then I hope you'll work on more self-reflection."

Sophie couldn't decide which sounded more miserable.

But.

She already knew self-reflection was a total fail.

So even though she could definitely recognize the potential for disaster with Mr. Forkle's suggestion, she hailed Keefe and Fitz after Mr. Forkle and Dex left and invited them over to work together. And both boys reluctantly agreed to meet her in the Havenfield pastures in a few hours.

They started small—the three of them sitting in the shade of Calla's Panakes tree, testing Sophie's new enhancing-blocking gadgets to make sure Dex's design worked on both of them. And it did—though Keefe said he could still feel that same tiny bit of extra clarity he'd started picking up just by being around Sophie. But they decided that must be an Empath thing, since Stina had been feeling a similar boost for a while.

And then . . . it was time to pick a trust exercise.

"We could play something like Two Truths and a Lie?" Sophie suggested—and then immediately *un*-suggested it once she saw how excited Ro was by that idea.

But every other trust exercise she'd done with Fitz would be so much worse with Keefe as part of it.

So.

Much.

Worse.

In fact, Sophie was starting to think the best idea would be to feign exhaustion, flee to her bedroom, and hide under her covers until the boys and their bodyguards left.

But then Keefe stood, pacing past Sophie a few times before he asked, "This is about inflicting, right?"

"What do you mean?" Sophie asked.

"I mean, that's why you went through all of this, isn't it? And that ability comes from both the head and the heart, doesn't it?"

Sophie nodded.

"All right, then forget trust exercises!" Keefe decided. "Fitzy can cover the head stuff, I'll cover the heart stuff, you'll do your Ragemonster thing and you'll start getting a feel for your shiny, improved ability."

"I don't know what any of that means," Fitz said, glancing at Sophie, and Sophie was right there with him.

Keefe dragged a hand down his face. "I'm saying we focus on letting Foster practice inflicting. You and I will be here to make sure she doesn't lose control of anything. But that's what's most important, right?"

"But Elwin and Livvy think it's going to set back her recovery," Fitz reminded him.

"Right . . . but . . . if it's going to do that anyway, then why not test it out, let it set her back, and then she can focus on recovering?" Keefe countered.

"I don't think it works that way," Fitz insisted.

"And I don't know how to just . . . *inflict*," Sophie added. "I have to be angry and afraid—"

"So we'll make you angry and afraid," Keefe interrupted. "I mean, I feel like if there's one thing Fitzy and I both excel at, it's making you angry."

"I can help with afraid!" Ro volunteered.

"No, you can't!" Sandor warned.

"Actually, this might be a good idea," Grizel told him, stopping Sandor from drawing his sword.

"You can't be serious," Sandor snapped back.

"Why not?" Grizel asked. "We'll all be here to keep her safe."

"How can it be safe if there are no physicians to monitor her?" Sandor countered. "And why don't we see what her parents have to say?"

Round and round they went, and Sophie honestly didn't know which side she was on—but then it didn't matter because someone was clearing their throat behind them and they turned to find Mr. Forkle standing on the path, watching them. And he seemed . . .

Nervous.

It almost looked like he wanted to raise a crystal and leap away before any of them could ask why he was there.

And maybe that was because he knew Keefe would ask, "You found him, didn't you? The guy in my drawing?"

"We did," Mr. Forkle agreed. "Mr. Dizznee's latest adjustments gave us the speed we needed to also search the archive, starting with the year we estimated you first saw the man, since we knew his appearance would match most completely at that point."

"You have an archive?" Sophie had to ask.

"A very thorough one," Mr. Forkle agreed. "And . . . that's where we found him. The video didn't give us his location, but it did give us a name that Mr. Dizznee and I were able to search for in several human databases."

"You have access to human databases?" Sophie blurted out, even though she probably shouldn't have been so surprised—and she definitely should stop interrupting Mr. Forkle because Keefe looked ready to combust with impatience.

"We do," Mr. Forkle agreed, "and . . . I gave you my word that I'd let you know anything we found immediately. So . . . even though this goes against my better judgment . . . your mystery man's name was Ethan Benedict Wright II."

"Ethan Benedict Wright II," Fitz and Keefe both repeated.

But Sophie was stuck on a different word—one she almost didn't want to point out, since Keefe clearly hadn't noticed that Mr. Forkle had used it, and she hated to snuff out the triumph and enthusiasm she could see in Keefe's eyes.

Still, she forced herself to ask, "Was?"

And her heart thudded into her stomach when Mr. Forkle winced.

"What do you mean 'was'?" Keefe asked her.

"That's what I'm asking *him*," Sophie said gently. "Mr. Forkle said his name '*was*.' Not *is*. Did he legally change it?" she asked Mr. Forkle, trying to give Keefe what little hope she could.

Mr. Forkle sighed. "No. I said *was* because I found this." He reached into his cape and pulled out what looked like a crinkled printout of a newspaper clipping.

And at the top, in big black letters, was the word "Obituaries."

THIRTY-TWO

H E'S DEAD."

Sophie couldn't tell who said it.

There was too much roaring in her ears, between the cold ocean wind, her frantic pulse, and the ragged breaths she forced herself to take in.

But she knew exactly what Keefe was going to say next.

He looked like he couldn't decide if he was going to run off and pick a fight with the gorgodon or hurl all over his shoes as he told them, "My mom had something to do with this."

Not a question.

A fact.

"You don't know that," Sophie argued, snatching the obituary away from Mr. Forkle before Keefe could get his hands on it.

It took her overloaded brain three tries before any of the tiny black-and-white words sank in.

"Okay," she said, wishing the three short paragraphs gave a little more information. "It says here that Ethan Benedict Wright II, and"—her stomach turned—"his ten-year-old daughter, Eleanor Olivia Wright, were struck by a bus outside of the British Library and killed instantly." She told herself not to picture it. But she'd seen enough photos of London's famous red double-decker buses to paint a pretty gruesome mental picture. "That's . . . horrible," she whispered, clearing the thickness from her throat. "But it was an *accident*, Keefe. Either the bus driver got distracted, or Ethan and Eleanor forgot to look both ways before they crossed the street, or maybe—"

"Or maybe my mom had something to do with it!" Keefe finished for her, turning away and tearing his hands through his hair. "Come on, Foster. You don't think my mom could make it look like an accident? It wouldn't be hard. One quick mental shove with telekinesis or a blast of wind from a Guster and . . ."

Sophie squeezed her eyes tight, trying to block the fresh round of nightmare images.

"Accidents happen all the time in the Forbidden Cities," she insisted. "Humans rely on tons of super-dangerous things, and they just kind of go through life assuming nothing bad will happen to them—until it does."

"It's true," Fitz agreed. "I was stunned by that the first few times I visited. I couldn't believe they weren't all in a constant state of panic."

Keefe sighed. "So you guys really think it's a *coincidence* that the same human guy who got a letter from my mom—a letter she had me *illegally* bring to the Forbidden Cities and then went to pretty drastic lengths to erase all my memories of—just happened to die that same year? I bet you *anything*, if I had a way of knowing exactly what day my mom gave me that letter, we'd see that this 'accident' happened right around the same time."

Sophie sighed. "Okay, but why would your mom *kill* him and his daughter? Fintan made it sound like she was trying to recruit the guy—er, Mr. Wright," she corrected, realizing she should probably start using his name and trying to be a little more respectful of the dead.

"And Fintan also said the recruiting didn't work out," Keefe noted. "And the guy—Mr. Wright—would've known stuff about what my mom was planning, so she would've had to get rid of him to protect her secrets. And the daughter either got in the way, or my mom figured it was just easier to take out the whole family. Who knows?"

"But why risk her sanity on two murders when she could have had their minds wiped instead?" Sophie countered. "We already know she basically had a Washer on standby."

"Yeah, but—"

"If I might intercede," Mr. Forkle said, before Keefe could make his next argument. "I figured this is how the conversation would go, once I gave you that obituary. And it's the kind of debate that never actually leads anywhere because there is far too much speculation and far too little fact. It's also exactly the kind of all-consuming distraction that none of us needs when there are so many urgent matters that require our attention. So with that in mind, I did a bit of research before I came here, to see if I could fill in some of the unknowns and ease some of the worries."

"I thought you said you came here immediately," Fitz reminded him.

"I *did* come here immediately from Watchward Heath," Mr. Forkle insisted, "but I also completed some research before I left. And you should be thankful that I did—and even more thankful that I'm willing to share what I discovered, because I don't have to. This was never part of our arrangement. And my instincts are even cautioning me against sharing, claiming that none of you are ready for this sort of revelation. So I need your word that you'll stay calm and rational and avoid any reckless behavior, no matter how shocked and appalled you are."

"*Shocked and appalled?*" Ro repeated, making her way over to Keefe's side. "Wow, way to hype it, Forkle."

"I need everyone to be properly prepared," Mr. Forkle explained. "And that includes you bodyguards. You should be ready to prevent your charges from making hasty decisions."

"We always are," Sandor assured him.

"Just tell us!" Keefe demanded.

Mr. Forkle shook his head. "Not without your word—and you have to mean it. I need to know that level heads will prevail."

"Level heads," Keefe muttered under his breath. "Fine. Whatever."

"There is no 'whatever,'" Mr. Forkle informed him. "And there's no way around this. I'll say no more unless I have your word."

Keefe rolled his eyes. "Fine. You have my word. Ugh, it's not like this is the first time I've found out creepy news about Mommy Dearest."

"It isn't," Mr. Forkle agreed. "And that's why I need to hear you specifically say that you won't be reckless."

For a second, Sophie wondered if Keefe was going to tackle Mr. Forkle.

But he must've realized Mr. Forkle was serious because he gritted his teeth and said, "Fine—I won't be reckless."

Sophie and Fitz offered the same oath with a whole lot less venom—but that didn't stop Sandor and Grizel from moving to their sides. Sandor even hooked an arm around Sophie's shoulder to prevent her from leaping or teleporting without him.

"Very well, then," Mr. Forkle said, looking more wary than satisfied. "I suppose you're sufficiently prepared."

He turned to pace, and with each plodding step Sophie could almost feel Keefe's patience evaporating.

But somehow Keefe kept his jaw locked and waited.

And waited a little longer.

Until Mr. Forkle finally said, "I knew you were going to fear that your mother—or any member of the Neverseen—was involved in these deaths. So I had Mr. Dizznee set up a very specific set of search criteria for the archive. We checked all the footage from the week before the accident as well as the footage from the week after the accident, searching for black-cloaked figures as well as Fintan's, Brant's, Gethen's, Lady Gisela's, and Alvar's faces."

Fitz sucked in a very sharp breath at the last name. "Did my brother—"

"No," Mr. Forkle promised. "Though I suppose it's possible he used his ability as a Vanisher to hide from my cameras. But I have no record of him being in London during that time period."

"What about me?" Keefe asked. "Did you check to see if I was there?"

"I did," Mr. Forkle admitted, taking several agonizingly slow steps before he added, "and I found no trace of you in any of the footage."

Keefe blew out a huge breath, bending over and resting his hands on his knees.

But his relief only lasted a second before he demanded, "So who *was* there? Obviously you found someone."

"I did." Mr. Forkle glanced at the sky, and Sophie wondered if this was one of those moments where he was wishing he had his brother there to help him figure out the right decision.

But it was just him.

And he reached into his cape and withdrew a rolled piece of paper.

Keefe held out his hand expectantly, but Mr. Forkle gave the paper to Sophie, and she angled herself away from Keefe as she smoothed out the page.

"I feel that panic, Foster," Keefe told her as she studied the image that Mr. Forkle had given her.

A still from a video camera—a little too dark in certain places and too bright in others.

But there was no mistaking the fact that she was staring at Big Ben—London's most notable landmark.

And standing in front of it—in a black cloak with the hood flipped back, like the wind had just knocked it out of place—was Lady Gisela.

Keefe's mother.

THIRTY-THREE

DON'T MAKE ME RIP THAT PAPER OUT of your hands, Foster," Keefe told her, and Sophie blinked, wondering how long she'd been staring at the horrifying photograph. "I'll do it," Keefe warned. "I won't like it, but I'll do it."

"You'll try," Sandor corrected. "And *you* won't like what happens—but *I'll* enjoy it immensely."

"Hmm, that's a tricky dilemma," Ro noted. "It *would* be fun to watch my boy get goblin-clobbered. But I'm supposed to *protect* him—and if I do, then *I* get to clobber a goblin, so . . . decisions, decisions." She held her hands out on each side of her, dipping them up and down like a shifting scale.

"No one's clobbering anyone," Sophie told them, taking a cautious step toward Keefe, trying to figure out the best way to guide him through this latest nightmare.

He'd had his world ripped out from under him so many times already. . . .

But maybe that would make this easier.

"You know what I'm going to show you," she said carefully. "You guessed it from the beginning."

Keefe swallowed hard. "My mom?"

Sophie nodded.

His knees wobbled hard, and Sophie rushed to steady him—until she realized . . .

"It's fine," Fitz said when she glanced over her shoulder, hoping he couldn't tell that she'd momentarily forgotten he was there.

Keefe's going to need you right now, he transmitted.

He's going to need both of us, Sophie corrected.

Maybe, he conceded. *But you're better at this part.*

Sophie wasn't so sure about that—but she closed the distance between her and Keefe, keeping the photo pressed against her chest as she wrapped an arm around Keefe's shoulders.

"Show me," he told her—the words more of a plea than a command.

Sophie pulled him as close as she could and held up the photo.

Keefe sank to the grass, no longer able to stay standing, and Sophie sank down next to him, keeping the photo where he could see it.

And he stared.

And stared.

And stared.

Ro peeked over Keefe's shoulder. "Wow. Leave it to Mommy Dearest to make Lord Jerkypants seem like the good parent."

"She really did kill the guy," Keefe whispered. "And his *daughter*—what was she, ten?"

"Yeah," Sophie murmured, glad the obituary hadn't included a photo.

"I mean . . . I knew it," Keefe said, mostly to himself. "But that's different than *knowing* it, you know?"

Sophie bit her lip, trying to decide if what she wanted to say would make things better or worse.

Focusing on truth and facts seemed like it had to be the best way to go, though, so she reminded him, "Technically we still don't know that she killed them. I know coincidences are hard to believe, but they *do* happen. It *is* possible that she went and visited the guy, and then a few hours later he got hit by a bus—or that he got hit by the bus before their meeting and she was trying to figure out what happened."

"That photo is from after the accident," Mr. Forkle chimed in. "It has a time stamp."

Sophie's eyes took a second to find the string of tiny white numbers hidden in the corner, and if she was reading the time stamp correctly, then Lady Gisela had been standing in front of Big Ben at 8:14 p.m.

The obituary said the accident happened at 7:09 p.m.

"Does anyone know how close Big Ben is to the British Library?" Sophie asked, realizing how silly the question was as soon as she'd said it.

She was talking to elves, goblins, and an ogre.

And yet, Mr. Forkle told her, "I looked it up on the map before I left my office. It takes an average of fifty minutes to walk from one to the other—and significantly less time if one takes something they call 'the Tube.'"

"That's their underground train system," Sophie said, because that was so much easier to think about than the fact that Lady Gisela definitely would've had enough time to kill Ethan Benedict Wright II and Eleanor Olivia Wright, and then walk—or ride the Tube—over to Big Ben for a little sightseeing before she left.

"See?" Keefe asked, obviously picking up on her mood shift. "She killed them."

It was looking more and more that way.

But . . .

"We still haven't *technically* proven anything," she had to point out. "If this was a human murder trial and the only evidence the prosecution had was this photograph, there'd be plenty of reasonable doubt. It shows your mom nowhere near the scene of the accident—and I'm guessing she's not in the accident footage, either, otherwise Mr. Forkle would've brought that."

She glanced at Mr. Forkle to verify.

"Actually, there *is* no footage of the accident," he informed them.

"None?" Fitz asked.

Mr. Forkle shook his head. "As I said, the system at Watchward Heath is unprecedented. But it's not without its gaps."

"Well . . . that's . . . convenient," Fitz said slowly. "So the accident just *happened* to take place in one of the rare gaps in the Black Swan's surveillance? Nobody else thinks that's odd?"

"Oh, I think it's *very* odd," Mr. Forkle told him.

"And I think it proves my mom did it," Keefe added with a hollow sort of authority. "Come on, Foster, even you have to admit that's one too many coincidences."

Sophie sighed. "I just . . . I wish I understood why she would do something like that."

"Because she's a creepy psychopath!" Keefe crumpled the photo and flung it as far as he could—which wasn't all that far thanks to the wind.

"Keefe," Sophie called as he stood and stalked to the fence of the nearest pasture. But he ignored her, leaning against the rails with his back to everyone.

"Give him a minute," Mr. Forkle told Fitz when he moved to follow.

Sophie sighed again and used her telekinesis to retrieve the crumpled photo, laying it flat on the grass to try to smooth out the wrinkles.

"What do you think she's looking at?" Fitz asked as he squatted beside her.

"I don't know—does it matter?" Sophie wondered. "She's on a busy city street. She's probably trying to avoid a car or a pedestrian or something."

"But she's not moving," Fitz said. "See? Her feet are planted. And her head is turned to her right, her eyes focused on something taller than she is."

He traced Lady Gisela's invisible eyeline across the photo, following it up and off the paper, to some point beyond the frame.

"Well . . . maybe there's another building over there?" Sophie guessed. "Or a billboard?"

"What do *you* think she's looking at?" Mr. Forkle asked when Fitz frowned.

"I don't know," he admitted, squinting at the photo and tilting his head. "I guess it's not important."

"I wouldn't say that," Mr. Forkle corrected. "Do you know that for the entire five minutes and forty-three seconds of footage that I have of Lady Gisela standing there, she doesn't look away from that spot once? Even when the wind blew back her hood—which is the moment I captured for this still shot—her eyes remain trained on that single point."

"Do *you* know what she's looking at?" Sophie asked him.

"I have my theories" was all Mr. Forkle said. "But they're *just* theories. I checked the feed from every nearby camera and couldn't get a view of that portion of the street to confirm."

"Well that's . . . *also* convenient," Fitz said, reaching up to run a hand through his hair. "It's like she knows where your cameras are."

"That does appear to be the case," Mr. Forkle said, staring up at the sky. "And it's not altogether surprising, considering how rarely I've ever captured footage of any members of the Neverseen. I'd just been hoping that was because they stayed mostly underground or in their hideouts. But it seems they might know exactly how to evade detection. Which is particularly unsettling when you consider how *many* cameras I've hidden."

"They're *always* ahead of us," Sophie muttered, giving in to an eyelash tug.

"I wouldn't say *always*," Mr. Forkle said. "They—"

"What happened after five minutes and forty-three seconds?" Keefe interrupted, calling the words over his shoulder without turning around.

"I'm sorry?" Mr. Forkle called back.

"You said you only had five minutes and forty-three seconds of footage of her," Keefe clarified, still without looking at anyone. "I'm guessing it starts when she shows up. But what happens at the end?"

"She's simply gone," Mr. Forkle told him.

"So she light leaped?" Fitz asked.

"That's what I'm assuming," Mr. Forkle said. "But I have no record of her raising a crystal, so if she *did* leap away, she must've used one of the Neverseen's hidden paths—which, incidentally, is also what I believe she's looking at, tucked into that small portion of the street that's shielded from all of my cameras."

"You mean like the crystal that Dex and I found on one of the lanterns in Paris?" Sophie asked. When he nodded, she had to admit, "I've never really understood why that was there. Why go to so much trouble to hide a crystal in a Forbidden City when you could just use a home crystal or a pathfinder to leap away?"

"Because those can be lost or damaged," Mr. Forkle reminded her, "and the Lost Cities can only be reached through designated paths. That's one of the many ways we keep ourselves hidden from humans—and why our registry pendants all have a crystal in the pendant. It's a fail-safe, in case something unexpected were to separate us from all other paths. But for the Neverseen—and, admittedly, for the Black Swan as well—we have moments when our pendants must be removed in order to avoid the Council's tracking. And we take that risk most often when visiting the Forbidden Cities. So both of our groups have made the effort to hide a few emergency paths, to ensure we never find ourselves without a means to get home."

"So . . . you're saying you think one of the Neverseen's secret leaping crystals is hidden in London near that giant clock thing?" Keefe asked. "On a part of the street where they know the Black Swan can't see them?"

"That would be my guess," Mr. Forkle agreed. "And I know what you're going to say—"

"I say we go find it," Keefe interrupted.

Mr. Forkle sighed. "Yes, that's what I knew you were going to say. And I think you're misunderstanding what the crystal is—the hidden paths are not meant to go somewhere secret or significant, because they're left unguarded. All of the crystals the Collective has hidden leap to the most innocuous locations we could think of—places where we could blend in should we arrive unexpectedly, but that also have zero connection to our order in case our enemies find them."

"Okay, but just because *you guys* are smart enough to think of that doesn't mean the Neverseen are," Keefe argued. "And even if you're right, isn't it worth it to double-check?"

"Of course," Mr. Forkle agreed. "I plan to head there in the wee hours of the morning, once the streets are empty. And no—you're not invited to come with me. For *lots* of reasons, but the biggest one being that where you go, so do an ogre and multiple goblins and many of your friends, all of whom create far too much spectacle for such a simple task—even at that early of an hour."

"Uh, the ogre and goblins don't *have* to come with us," Keefe reminded him.

"Yes, we do!" Sandor stalked over to Sophie and grabbed her arm again to keep her at his side.

"You think Foster can't take you down right now if she wants to?" Keefe asked with a sharp, bitter laugh.

A very un-Keefe laugh.

Mr. Forkle must've noticed too, because he told him, "This is why I made you promise to stay calm and rational and avoid any reckless behavior."

"Yeah, well, then you proved my mom's a murderer, so excuse me for freaking out a little," Keefe snapped, tearing a hand though his hair.

Mr. Forkle narrowed his eyes. "Would it help if I promise to report back on everything I find?"

"No, because I don't want to know what *you* find. I want to know what *I* find. I've been to London. I've walked some of those streets—and who knows? Maybe I've even used that path my mom used to leave. I can't remember it because *SHE ERASED MY MEMORIES SO I WOULDN'T REALIZE SHE WAS KILLING PEOPLE*!"

He paused to catch his breath.

Mr. Forkle shook his head. "If Big Ben held any significance to you, the photo alone would've triggered the memory."

"That's not true and you know it! Memories aren't only triggered by sights. Sound plays a role too. Smell. Taste. Touch. Even emotions. So we all know my best shot at recovering the memories is to walk those streets again. And I *need* to get them back." His voice broke, and he looked away, tearing at his hair some more. "The guy's dead, Forkle. And his daughter. She killed them. And I might know why. I might've . . ."

He didn't finish the sentence, but Sophie could see the worry in his eyes.

The voiceless fear that he was partly to blame, because he'd delivered that letter.

Or maybe that he'd played an even larger role and had yet to fit those pieces together.

"I don't care about safe or smart right now," Keefe added quietly. "I care about finding the truth. Just let me walk those streets. That's all I'm asking."

Mr. Forkle dragged a hand down his face. "Fine. Give me a few days to properly prepare and I'll get you to London, and—"

"I see *zero* advantage to waiting," Keefe interrupted.

"And what about spontaneity?" Sophie added, realizing how close Keefe was to unraveling. "It worked great when Dex and I went, and—"

"That was a very different situation," Mr. Forkle cut in. "You were going somewhere totally random and leaving in a matter of minutes—not heading to a location with a proven connection to the Neverseen and planning to spend untold minutes wandering around. Also, I feel the need to point out that just because a somewhat reckless decision worked out once doesn't mean you can use that as a standard of measure for all similar situations."

Keefe's hands curled into fists. But it was the worry and panic dulling his ice blue eyes—mixed with something so much darker—that had Sophie transmitting, *I can sneak us to London tonight—but you need to stop fighting, otherwise Ro will be watching you too closely.*

She opened her mind to his thoughts so he could ask, *You're serious?*

Amazingly, she was.

She believed in the power of spontaneity.

Mostly, though, she'd seen Keefe like this before—dangling by such a very, very thin thread. There was too high of a risk that it would snap and he'd run off without her.

Can you slip away from Ro? she asked.

Can YOU slip away from Sandor? he countered.

I think so. Meet at the swings at your house at midnight?

That's too late, Keefe argued. *We don't know what Forkle means by "wee hours of the morning," and we need to be out of there before he shows up.*

Okay, how about eleven o'clock?

He chewed his lip and glanced at Fitz, who could clearly tell they were communicating telepathically.

Which meant Mr. Forkle could surely tell as well.

And the bodyguards.

"Thank you," Sophie said out loud, trying to cover. She sent Keefe a quick *Go with me on this*, before she turned to Mr. Forkle and said, "He said he'll wait two days and then he's going there on his own. Seems like a pretty fair compromise to me."

Mr. Forkle's forehead puckered, and Sophie couldn't tell if it was with suspicion or displeasure at being bossed around. All he said was, "I'll make the arrangements."

Sophie nodded, careful not to look at Keefe as she transmitted, *So we're on for eleven?*

You're sure you're up for teleporting after the ability-resetting thing? he thought back.

I'm fine. Just play it cool until eleven o'clock—but not so cool that Ro gets suspicious.

His mental voice sounded slightly wobbly as he told her, *Thank you.*

Yeah, well, remember that feeling of gratitude when you have to deal with however Ro punishes you. I'm pretty sure flesh-eating bacteria will be involved.

Probably, he agreed. *But it's worth it.*

He thanked her again. And right as she was about to sever the connection between them, he added, *Oh, and Foster? Make sure you bring Fitz.*

THIRTY-FOUR

YOU GOT AWAY FROM RO?" SOPHIE whispered, the words barely louder than the soft sigh of the waves lapping against the moonlit shore.

"Kinda," Keefe whispered back from somewhere in the darkness. She couldn't see him, but she could hear his footsteps on the patio, padding closer—which actually felt kind of ominous given the strange, shifting shadows cast by the swings. "I . . . might've laced her dinner with some of the amoebas she's been breeding to punish my dad when he's being particularly *fun*, and she hasn't been able to leave my bathroom ever since. I also barricaded my room juuuuuuuuust in case."

Sophie's jaw fell open, and it took her a minute to get her mouth working again. "Um, you realize she's going to kill you tomorrow, right? Like . . . you legitimately need to fear for your life."

"Oh, I know. I mean, I have a plan to make it up to her. But I also have an escape route ready to go." A hint of shine nearby caught her attention, and she realized he'd flashed a smile—something she hadn't expected to see after watching him spin so close to a breakdown earlier.

It felt like proof that she was doing the right thing—even if there was also a very good chance that it was a phenomenally bad idea to sneak away without their bodyguards like this.

We're being spontaneous, she told herself.

It worked before with Dex.

Spontaneous. Spontaneous. Spontaneous.

"What about you? How'd you get away from Sandor?" Keefe asked.

"Honestly? I have no idea," she admitted. "I set up my bed outside again—"

"You've been sleeping outside?" Keefe interrupted. "That wasn't just something you did for the reset?"

Sophie shook her head—then realized he probably couldn't see that. "I know it's ridiculous because my room is *huge*, but . . . it keeps feeling like the walls are closing in. And I figured tonight it'd also be way easier to sneak away if I was already outside. So I left the Cliffside gate unlocked, put a robe on over my clothes, and waited for Sandor to go check in with Flori. And then I threw off my robe, slipped on my boots, and ran for it—but I swear, Sandor must've guessed what I was planning because he caught up to me *so fast.* I totally thought it was over. But I channeled everything I could into sprinting and . . . I don't know. One second the cliffs seemed really far away and Sandor was *right* behind me, and the next I was at the cliff's edge and Sandor was too far back to do anything except shout a bunch of threats as I jumped."

"Maybe the ability reset amped up some of your skills, too?" Keefe suggested. "And your channeling is stronger now?"

"Maybe," Sophie agreed, not sure if she liked that idea.

Obviously, the stronger she was the better, but . . .

She was starting to feel like she was losing control of her own body, between the new enhancing gadgets and the extra layers of gloves—and pockets full of even more backup gloves—and the fact that she still had no idea how her inflicting worked.

"Don't worry about Sandor," Keefe told her, probably misunderstanding her mood shift. "Unlike *my* bodyguard, he's not one for revenge. You just have a lot of lectures in your future."

"Probably," Sophie said, trying not to think about the last thing Sandor had shouted before she'd cracked the sky and slipped into the void.

If something happens to you or your friends, you're going to have to live with it!

"Anyway," she said, choking down the bile on her tongue, "we should head out."

They'd be fine.

This was just a quick trip.

They were being spontaneous.

Spontaneous. Spontaneous. Spontaneous.

"I'm sure Sandor's guessed where I'm going and woken Grady and Edaline by now," she added, squinting at the dark silhouette of the Shores of Solace, half expecting lights to flare and shouting to erupt any second.

"What about Fitz?" Keefe asked, and Sophie could've smacked herself.

Had she seriously forgotten about her boyfriend *again*?

"I'm here," Fitz's accented voice whispered from somewhere over by the sand, and Sophie was glad the darkness hid her embarrassment from him. "Sorry to be a little late."

"Problems getting past Grizel?" Keefe asked.

"Nah, she was easy. I made it sound like I was sneaking off to talk to Sophie about something, and she agreed that we could use a little snuggle time."

No one seemed to know what to say to that.

Fitz cleared his throat. "Biana's the one who slowed me down. She cornered me with a billion questions, and I honestly wouldn't be surprised if she's about to appear with a 'TA-DA! I followed you!'"

She didn't.

"Well, that's good," Fitz said. "Does that mean we're ready?"

"I think so." Sophie took a deep breath to steady her nerves. "Will you do the levitating, Fitz?"

She wasn't sure how long her energy was going to hold, so she needed to conserve it. Plus, after the weirdness with her channeling, there was a chance she'd blast them all the way up to the Point of Purity or something.

"Of course," he told her. "Happy to be needed."

There was no chiding subtext to his tone—but Sophie still felt her cheeks burn when she thought about how little she'd relied on Fitz lately.

"Thank you," she whispered as she took his hand, holding her breath for the first few seconds, wondering if Dex's gadgets—and the three pairs of gloves she was wearing—would do their job.

They did for Fitz.

Not so much for Keefe—though he assured her the effect wasn't a problem.

"Do you think Mr. Forkle's right?" she asked as Fitz floated the three of them off the ground, fast enough to make her stomach lurch.

"Did that green breeze you sent me during the reset change our connection, and that's why you're so sensitive to my enhancing now?"

"I guess it's possible," Keefe admitted.

"What green breeze?" Fitz asked.

"Just an Empath trick," Keefe told him. "Nothing special."

Sophie was pretty sure it *had* been special—but she stopped herself from saying that. Because Fitz had helped her that day too. And even though she couldn't remember anything specific about it, she knew he'd done everything he could to guide her through.

"I *do* think Forkle's right about you being able to control the ability, though," Keefe added quietly. "I mean, I'm sure all of his 'journeys of self-discovery' stuff made you want to throw things at his head—"

"Yep," Sophie agreed.

"*But*, I don't think you have to be all deep and fancy-pants about it. I bet if you just treat it like solving one more Foster Mystery, you'll figure it out."

"Okay, but *how*?" Sophie countered.

"I think it's mostly about finding the source," Fitz told her. "Following the power in your fingertips to the reserves it's coming from and building some sort of . . . inner barrier that you can raise and lower whenever you want. Setting boundaries for yourself, if that makes sense."

"It does and it doesn't," Sophie hedged.

Several long seconds passed before Keefe told her, "See, I think it's simpler than that. I think the boundaries are already there and you just need to start bossing your abilities around. Think of it like . . . leading Team Awesome!"

"Team Valiant," Sophie corrected.

"Nope, I'm now officially naming your abilities Team Awesome," Keefe decided. "And it's time for you to show them you're their Lady Fos-Boss."

Sophie rolled her eyes. "You can't boss an ability around."

"Oh, I think you can, I think *you* can."

"I have no idea what that means," Sophie told him.

"Neither do I," Fitz agreed. "But more important, I'm pretty sure we're high enough now, and it's not exactly easy keeping us steady with all of this wind, so . . . think we can get to the teleporting part of this journey?"

Sophie stared at the glints of moonlight reflecting off the ocean far below, realizing this was one of those turning-point moments— the kind that could all too easily end up being something they'd look back on and think, *That's where it all went wrong.*

"Before we do this," she said, clearing the catch out of her throat, "I need you to promise me, Keefe, that you'll remember why we're there. I'm bringing you to London to see if it triggers your memories—*not* to go Neverseen hunting. So if we find a crystal to a hidden path, we're *not* using it."

"But—"

"We're *not* using it," Sophie repeated. "We're being spontaneous— not insane. Promise me you understand that."

It got really, really quiet.

"In case it matters," Fitz murmured, "I understand. And I promise."

More silence.

"I mean it, Keefe," Sophie told him. "Tonight is about investigat- ing only—*not* taking dangerous risks. If you won't promise that— and *mean it*—then I'm having Fitz set us back down."

Keefe sighed. "Fine, I promise."

"And *mean* it," Sophie emphasized. "Convince me that I can trust you."

"You can trust me, Foster," Keefe assured her, tightening his grip on her hand. "I know I've made huge mistakes in the past, but I'm trying to learn from them—and the *last* thing I ever want to do is let you down. Okay?"

Nothing about what they were doing felt okay anymore.

But . . . she believed him.

And they'd come this far.

Please don't let this be a mistake, Sophie thought, sending the plea to every star twinkling around them before she told Fitz, "Drop us!" and they plummeted into the void.

The time on Big Ben said 11:11 p.m., which probably meant that London was somehow on the same time zone as the Lost Cities—something Sophie would have to put more thought into later.

At the moment, her focus was on staying out of sight.

London was busier than she'd been expecting at such a late hour—a steady stream of cars and buses on the roads, pedestrians wandering every shadowed sidewalk—and while Sophie had managed to swipe Grady's obscurer before she left, their little group still felt very exposed.

It didn't help that their clothes stood out a lot more than Sophie had wanted. She'd tried her best—her magenta jacket and white ruffled tunic didn't look *that* different from the coats and shirts that some of the humans were wearing, and she'd layered different socks over her leggings to try to make the layered gloves on her hands seem like a fashion statement. But she'd decided to wear her cape, thinking its warmth might come in handy given London's reputation for cold, foggy weather. And Fitz and Keefe looked like boy princes in their capes and embroidered jerkins.

"We have to stay together," Sophie reminded Keefe, pulling him back to her side when he tried to head toward what might've been Westminster Abbey—she wasn't sure. She was still getting her bearings, trying to match the famous landmarks in front of her—each lit with a warm, golden light against the night sky—with the pictures she'd seen in human books *and* the photo they'd seen of Keefe's mom.

"Then come with me," Keefe told her. "The point is for me to wander around, right?"

"It is—but I didn't know it was going to be so crowded, so we need to figure out a strategy," Sophie warned. "It's not going to be easy moving as a group of three without bumping into anybody—and *don't* step into the street unless I tell you it's safe," she added, jerking him to a stop as he moved toward the crosswalk. "There are all sorts of rules about when it is and isn't your turn, and if you don't follow them . . ."

She didn't say any more, certain he remembered Ethan and Eleanor's obituary.

"Fine, but can we please get moving?" Keefe asked, and the frantic edge to his voice made him sound a lot more like he had earlier. He trailed his hand along the iron fence and narrowed his eyes, like he was trying to concentrate on the feel of the metal. Or maybe he was taking in all of the nearby sounds. "Nothing's familiar here. I need to find something familiar."

"You're going the wrong way," Fitz told him, pulling something crumpled out of his pocket.

It took Sophie a second to realize he'd brought the photograph of Lady Gisela—and it was hard not to hug him for thinking of that.

He pointed to the parliament building. "This is what your mom was standing in front of. It's just hard to tell which part of the building specifically, since it all kind of looks the same—and the clock is so huge that you can see it from lots of angles. Hmm."

He held up the photo and waved it around, like he was trying to piece it into a puzzle.

"Okay, but none of this is triggering any memories. Even the smell isn't familiar." Keefe sucked in a deep breath through his nose, coughing in the process.

"Yeah, the air here's *really* thick," Fitz said, crinkling his nose, "between the fog and the pollution and that weird damp smell. Are we near a river?"

"The Thames," Sophie agreed, pointing to the lights on the bridge ahead, which happened to be the same direction that Keefe's mom had been looking in the picture. "That might be a good way to go," she told Keefe, "since you can see a lot from the river, like the London Eye and the Tower Bridge and the Tower of London and—"

"A river doesn't sound familiar," Keefe interrupted. "What about the library? Which way do we go to find that?"

"I . . . don't know," Sophie admitted. "I've never been there before—or seen pictures."

And she hadn't bothered to look it up before they'd left, because she hadn't planned on walking that far.

Fifty minutes.

At night.

Just the three of them.

That would be a little *too much* spontaneity.

And they couldn't take the Tube. Not dressed the way they were—and not without knowing what stop they'd need to take. Plus, they didn't have any money to buy tickets, or a handy Technopath to help them make a birth fund withdrawal.

More important, though . . .

What happened if she brought Keefe to the scene of the accident and something about it felt familiar?

That was a kind of truth that there would be no going back from.

She hadn't considered that when she'd offered to bring Keefe to London—hadn't realized this little visit could make everything So. Much. Worse for him.

"Think we can ask someone for directions?" Keefe wondered.

Sophie shook her head a little too vigorously. "We can't let anyone see us."

"Why not?" Keefe argued. "You bought gelato in Florence! And you bought those super-dry biscuits with Dex!"

"I know, but . . ." She tried to think of a good excuse, and the best she could come up with was "We're already taking enough risks. No bodyguards. Elvin clothes. Zero preparation. Dark streets with too many shadows—and we know the Neverseen come here. I don't think we should add anything else to the mix."

"Fine," Keefe said, running a hand down his face. "We'll just . . . start walking and hope we see a sign or something."

"I think we should start by figuring out what your mom was looking at," Fitz told him, locking his knees so Keefe couldn't drag their group forward. "Once we start wandering, we might never find our way back here."

"I agree," Sophie said, jumping on any excuse to keep Keefe away from the library. "We need to know if there's a hidden path."

"Why?" Keefe demanded. "You already said we're not going to follow it. And Forkle's going to look for it later. And let's not forget that there's a chance Sandor's let him know we snuck off—and if he has, I'm sure Forkle will guess we came here. So we want to get as far from this place as possible, so he can't haul us back home before we're ready."

"But what if it's *not* a hidden path?" Fitz countered, dragging Keefe and Sophie down the sidewalk. "Knowing might be important. Come on—it'll only take a few minutes to find it."

But it took them ten minutes just to find the exact spot where Lady Gisela had been standing.

Then the real work began.

And with each passing minute, Keefe got antsier and antsier.

"It's hard to tell," Fitz said, squinting in the same direction that Lady Gisela was looking in the photograph. "I think it *might* have something to do with that sign for the Underground, but . . . I don't know."

"Maybe," Sophie agreed. "They could probably hide something pretty easily in all of that wrought iron. Though . . . would the beam of light really be able to reach her all the way over here? Seems like the crystal would have to be closer, wouldn't it?"

"Probably true," Fitz admitted, "unless the crystal's up high and angled to hit a pretty strong beam of sunlight."

"I guess," Sophie said. "But this is London. It doesn't get that many bright sunny days, so it seems like they'd have a lot of times when their path wasn't usable."

Keefe paced around the limited space covered by their obscurer. "Why are we still here? None of this is familiar."

"That's good, though, isn't it?" Sophie asked, keeping her voice extra chipper. "If you've never been here, then—"

"Then I still have no idea where I actually went," Keefe cut in, "or what I did. I thought that's why we came here—you said this was about triggering my memories."

"I know. Just . . . give us a few more minutes," Sophie pleaded. It was now 11:39. If she could stall the wandering a little bit longer— like, maybe until 11:45—they'd definitely have no time to get any- where *near* the library, because she was planning to use midnight as the "we need to get home and face the consequences of our actions" handy cutoff, but Keefe would still get fifteen solid minutes of exploring time. "I promise, we'll—"

"Wait," Fitz interrupted, placing a hand on Sophie's shoulder. "Did something just sparkle in that metal piece under the light bulb of the streetlamp?"

Sophie followed the angle of his stare, which *did* look similar to the angle that Lady Gisela's head had been tilted in the photo- graph.

And there *did* seem to be something glittering where he was pointing—but it was hard to tell with it being so dark.

"I guess it'd make sense to build the path into a streetlamp," she realized. "That way it's still usable on a rainy day. Maybe that's why they chose the lantern in Paris, too."

"Oh, that's true," Fitz said. "I didn't think of that. I'm going to levitate up there and check."

Sophie tightened her grip on his hand. "You can't. We only have one obscurer—and people would definitely notice a cute guy in a cape flying up to the top of the streetlamp."

"So what you're saying is . . . you think I'm cute," Fitz noted with a grin.

Keefe groaned. "If you guys go Fitzphie on me right now, I swear, I'll drag us all into the river."

"Or how about I levitate us up to the top of the streetlamp and we check for a hidden crystal?" Fitz countered.

"There's no need," a familiar voice informed them—a voice that made Sophie want to scream or hide or find something really sharp to fling.

But she did none of those things.

Neither did Keefe or Fitz.

They simply stared in fascinated horror at the black-cloaked figure striding through the middle of the street, making all the cars honk and swerve around them.

"Congratulations!" Lady Gisela shouted, tossing back her hood. A net of beaded silver covered her immaculate blond updo—probably some gadget meant to block abilities—and her ice blue eyes studied her son with the strangest mix of delight and disdain as she added, "You found what you were looking for!"

THIRTY-FIVE

A THOUSAND THOUGHTS SCREAMED through Sophie's head.

Strategies.

Problems.

Solutions.

But one word clawed its way to the front of the chaos.

Inflict.

This was why she'd reset her abilities.

The thing Lady Gisela wasn't prepared for.

Their chance for escape—for victory!

Inflict. Inflict. Inflict.

But when Sophie dived into her rage and terror, the darkness didn't boil over.

It stayed deep in her mind, stewing and brewing—waiting for . . . something.

A spark to the kindling.

A burst of energy.

A command Sophie didn't know—and couldn't figure out.

She wanted to wail and thrash and squeeze her brain until it surrendered—but she didn't have time for any of those things.

"Looks like the moonlark's learned some restraint," Lady Gisela said as she strode up onto the sidewalk, only steps away from them.

Her face looked extra pale in the glow of the streetlight, turning downright ghostly when her cheeks pulled into a warped smile. After Fintan's betrayal, Lady Gisela had been covered in curved scars—but those were gone now, replaced by skin stretched too tightly across her bones.

"How can you see us?" Sophie wondered as she backed up, positioning herself between Fitz and Keefe.

The pedestrians around them still didn't seem to be able to tell they were there—and no one seemed to see Keefe's mom anymore either. Several people were shouting to each other, wondering where the "freaky lady" had gone. Others were scurrying into the night, trusting their instincts over their eyes.

Sophie wished she could tell them all to run faster.

But they wouldn't hear her.

"Obscurers can easily be detected—and controlled," Lady Gisela explained to her. "And put the weapon away, Keefe," she ordered.

Sophie's heart stopped when she turned and spotted the goblin throwing star clutched in Keefe's right hand—and the hateful determination in his eyes.

His mom wagged a finger at him, like he was a naughty toddler. "None of that. We're going to have a quick chat—and we're going to keep it free of flying weapons, since those could hit any of these nice, innocent people trying to be brave and stick to their paths. You wouldn't want to harm anyone else, would you?"

"What do you mean 'else'?" Keefe spat through gritted teeth, rising so easily to her bait.

His mom smiled wider. "You know very well who I mean. Why would we be *here* otherwise?"

The blow was aimed perfectly, and Keefe stumbled back, his body shaking, shaking, shaking.

Sophie tried to reach for him, but he pulled too far away.

"You can drop the knife, Fitz," Lady Gisela added, and Sophie spun around, gaping at the finger-length dagger she hadn't noticed in Fitz's hand.

Apparently, she'd been the only one too naive to bring any weapons.

If something happens to you or your friends, Sandor had warned her, *you're going to have to live with it!*

But her abilities were supposed to protect her.

And this was supposed to be a quick visit.

A *spontaneous* visit.

"How did you know we were here?" she whispered, even though she could probably guess Lady Gisela's answer.

"Unlike the Black Swan, we monitor our paths closely," Lady Gisela told her. "This one in particular, since I knew my son's journey would soon lead you here. It actually took you longer than I expected for you to put everything together. It's been somewhat disappointing—though I suppose you've been busy playing mascot to the Council. Look at you, wearing their shiny Regent pin on your cape, even as you rebel. Such mixed signals. Such bravado. And I mean it, Fitz—*dagger down.*"

"Or what?" Fitz countered, raising the blade and squinting one eye—lining up his aim. "You keep giving orders, but all I see is a

Polyglot in an ugly cloak who knows how to manipulate her son's emotions. Without one of Ruy's force fields to shield you, I don't see why I can't end you right here, right now."

Lady Gisela inclined her head. "You know, I believe you really would do it. Such a dark side you've turned out to have. Particularly ironic given how much you condemn your brother—and yet I see more violence in your eyes than I've ever seen in his."

Fitz gripped his dagger harder. "I have no problem ending the *enemy*. My conscience will be clear."

"Will it?" Lady Gisela asked, raising one eyebrow when Fitz nodded. "You know, I almost want to let you do it. It's always fascinating to witness the folly of arrogance. But I'm not done with our Shade yet. So allow me to show you why you won't be hurling any weapons at me—and neither will my son. *This* is why you're going to cooperate for the rest of this conversation."

She backed up a step, giving her widest smile yet as she commanded, "Show yourself."

And the shadows in front of her thinned and faded—as if someone was peeling back a series of dark veils one by one, revealing a second black-cloaked figure with outstretched arms, standing as a living shield in front of Lady Gisela.

And Sophie knew—*knew*—who the figure had to be.

She clutched her stomach, trying to hold herself together as Lady Gisela pulled back the figure's hood, revealing a familiar face half hidden by dark, silver-tipped bangs.

And there was genuine fear in his silver-flecked eyes as Sophie whispered, "Tam?"

THIRTY-SIX

AUGHTER DRAGGED SOPHIE OUT OF her shocked daze.

Joyless, hysterical laughter that went on and on—until Keefe was clutching his sides and wiping tears from his cheeks.

"Enough with the theatrics," Lady Gisela told him.

Keefe snorted. "You're complaining about *my* theatrics? Isn't this the epic showdown you've been planning where you order Tammy Boy to kill me? Thanks for the warning about that, by the way," he told Tam. "As you can see, it worked super well."

Lady Gisela's eyes narrowed, studying Tam like she was seeing him for the first time—and making it glaringly clear that she'd had no idea he'd passed along any messages.

Which made the threat against Keefe all the more horrifying.

Sophie stepped in front of him.

"Oh, relax," Lady Gisela told her. "Like I said, I'm only here for a quick chat."

"Aw, but the setting is so perfect!" Keefe argued. "The misty air. The shadowy street. The strange human sounds—are those sirens?

Seems like an awesome moment to murder your only son, don't you think?"

Lady Gisela sighed. "Must everything be a joke to you?"

Keefe considered that for a second before he said, "I wanna say yes—but you know what I don't find funny? I'm *really* not a fan of you thinking you can scare me."

"I do scare you, Keefe. I *terrify* you. And only part of that is because of what you think you know about me." She took a step closer. "We both know that what really frightens you is how very alike we are."

"We're *nothing* alike," Keefe snarled, holding up the throwing star again.

"Go ahead," Lady Gisela told him. "I guarantee the only person you'll hit is Tam."

"Wow, look at you—cowering behind your little Shade," Keefe snapped back.

"If you realized how powerful Tam is, you'd be cowering too," Lady Gisela insisted. "But that's not what I came here to tell you. It's time to focus, Keefe. Time to listen. Time to stop fighting who you are and what you're meant to do. I've tried to be patient. Tried to push you and test you and prepare you any way I could. But you're still not ready, and we're drawing *very* close to the day when you *have* to step up and accept your legacy."

Keefe cracked up again. "Yeah, I'll get right on that."

"I hope you do," Lady Gisela told him. "Because you don't actually get a choice in the matter. Either you embrace the change or it *will* destroy you."

"What does that mean?" Sophie demanded.

Lady Gisela smiled. "You'll see."

Sophie glanced at Tam—and the horror in his eyes told her how seriously she needed to take these threats.

Ominous music filled the air, as if Sophie's life had turned into the climax of a scary movie—and it wasn't until the first *BONG!* that Sophie realized the sounds were coming from Big Ben.

Chiming midnight.

Telling them it was time to go.

BONG!

BONG!

BONG!

"Why don't you run?" Fitz shouted to Tam over the next *BONG!* "She's just a Polyglot—you're way stronger than she is. And we can keep Linh safe."

"There you go with your arrogance again!" Lady Gisela shouted back.

BONG!

"I swear, Tam's the only smart one in your entire group," she added. "The only one who knows exactly what will happen to everyone he cares about if he defies me." *BONG!* "The only one who doesn't lie to himself about his vulnerabilities." *BONG!* "But just in case he has a moment of foolishness—show them, Tam."

Another *BONG!* crashed through the air as Tam raised his hands—and Sophie braced for an attack, wishing they had Maruca there to shield them.

But no shadows shifted, and no darkness poured out of his skin.

Instead, the sleeves of his cloak slipped down to his elbows, revealing an almost blinding glow.

BONG!

Sophie's eyes burned as they tried to focus on Tam's wrists, but all she could tell was that the light had a strange sort of solid quality, wrapping around like bracelets.

Or bonds.

BONG!

And there was such shame in his stare.

But also such strength.

And such pride.

And Sophie knew that regardless of what the light was, or how the Neverseen were trying to control him, Tam was still resisting them any way he could.

So when his shadow darted toward hers during the final *BONG!* and filled her mind with a single word, she knew he meant it— knew it was the last warning she'd get before things turned really, really ugly.

GO! he told her.

And Sophie would have enough time to grab Fitz's and Keefe's hands and levitate them high enough to teleport away.

But she was done running.

And with that surge of absolute confidence, something clicked into place inside her.

All the dark rage and terror that had been boiling away in her mind turned red-hot and ready to burst.

And she wanted to unleash it all.

Wanted to let everything boil and burn.

But something green lingered in the corners of her mind, cooling her thoughts enough to remind her that the real secret to her power was staying in control.

So in one smooth motion she tugged her gloves free and tapped her fingers, reaching for the two people in her life who always kept her anchored. And she clung to them with all the strength she had, feeling heat and lightning shock through their palms as her feet lifted off the ground and her rage found a new kind of clarity.

A new level of focus.

A single target.

She had to make it count, so she reached into her heart, gathering all the emotions pooled there too, a swell of purple and blue that mixed with the red—hot and cold, fire and ice, rage and love, and fear and courage blasting out of her mind exactly where she wanted it.

She couldn't stop the frenzy once it started.

Had to let every drop of it pour out of her.

And when the fever faded and her feet drifted back to solid ground, she pulled her hands free and studied what she'd done.

Lady Gisela lay in a heap, limbs twitching, eyes rolled back into her head—in agony, but still alive.

And Keefe's eyes were on Sophie—not his mom. Pure worry was etched between his eyebrows as he asked, "Are you okay?"

"I am," she promised, amazed at how steady she was on her feet.

How clear her head felt.

How much energy thrummed through her body, despite how much she'd just blasted away.

Fitz cleared his throat. "So . . . that was new. Is that how you inflict now?"

"I think it might be." But they needed to focus on more important things. "Someone grab her," she ordered. "I'm not sure how long the frenzy will last, and we need to get her somewhere we can properly restrain her."

Tam was the closest, and his eyes looked dazed as he squatted down and heaved Keefe's mom over his shoulder.

"I told you to run," he mumbled.

"I know, but isn't this better?" Sophie asked. "Now we can rip that gadget off her head and probe her mind for all her secrets." She turned to Keefe. "Anything we want to know. Your missing memories. Your legacy. We can find it all."

Keefe blinked. "It's . . . almost over."

"It's not, though," Tam warned as he stumbled to his feet, his knees nearly buckling under Lady Gisela's deadweight. "There's so much more you don't know. Keefe's legacy is only one *tiny* piece."

"We'll figure out the rest," Sophie promised.

Tam looked so heartbroken when he shook his head. "You won't. That's why I have to do this."

His meaning clicked a second too late.

Just enough time for Sophie to shout, "DON'T!" and Tam to meet Keefe's eyes and tell him, "Stay away from me!"

Then darkness poured out of his hands despite the glowing bonds around his wrists, and the thick, inky black puddled on the ground.

"Stay away from me," Tam repeated as he stepped into the darkness, disappearing with Lady Gisela into the shadows.

THIRTY-SEVEN

THEY'RE GONE."

Sophie, Fitz, and Keefe all said the words at the same time—but their tones were completely different.

Sophie sounded shocked.

Fitz sounded furious.

And Keefe sounded . . .

. . . *broken*.

He started shaking right after, and Sophie and Fitz shared a look that seemed to say, *It's going to take both of us to get him through this*, without either of them needing to actually transmit the words.

So they pooled their consciousnesses together and wrapped the warmth around their shivering, crumbling friend before they leaped the three of them back to the safety of the Lost Cities.

A large crowd was waiting for them in the Havenfield pastures, despite the late hour, since Sandor had indeed woken Grady and Edaline with news of Sophie's reckless behavior—and word must have spread rather quickly from there, because they now found themselves facing Flori. And Alden. And Della. And Grizel. And Biana.

And Woltzer. And Lord Cassius. And Mr. Forkle. And Tiergan. And all twelve Councillors. And the rest of Team Valiant. And Lovise. And Elwin. And Livvy.

Even Marella and Maruca had turned up, since Marella had a way of finding out about *everything*.

The only people missing were Ro—who was still surviving the war between her stomach and the amoebas—and Bo and Linh, which was a *huge* relief, since Sophie had no idea how to tell Linh about Tam's betrayal, or whether they should even be calling it that.

Keefe, unsurprisingly, wasn't nearly as conflicted.

Once his shock wore off, there was a *lot* of yelling.

And kicking the ground.

And finding stuff to fling as hard as he could.

There was even one brief moment where Sophie was pretty sure he'd been crying.

That was when she led him over to Calla's Panakes tree and made him sit on her pile of pillows, wrapping him in one of the blankets to try to calm his shivers.

Soft melodies whispered through the leaves, and Sophie hummed along to help him find the rhythm.

"I know you can't understand the lyrics," she said quietly, "but it's a really peaceful song about shifting seasons and the forest growing stronger each day. Will you close your eyes and *try* to listen?"

He sighed. "It was almost over, Foster. We *had* her."

"I know." She hugged him as hard as she could—not caring who was watching. Surely no one would fault her for being a good friend after what Keefe had just gone through.

"We *had* her," Keefe said again. "And Tam would've been free if he'd just come with us."

Maybe not.

Sophie stopped herself from voicing the words.

Just like she stopped herself from reminding Keefe that when he'd been with the Neverseen, there'd been a moment when he'd chosen to help Alvar escape instead of fleeing with her and her friends.

They'd have that conversation later. Once Keefe had calmed down. And once *she'd* had more time to process what had happened—because even if Tam *did* have a good reason for what he'd done, it could still end up being the kind of mistake they'd all pay the price for.

"Just try to rest for right now," she told Keefe, calling Wynn and Luna over to snuggle with him. "I have to go answer more questions."

Keefe nodded blankly. "We had her, Foster."

"We did," she agreed. "And we'll get her again—for good this time."

She repeated the vow in her mind as she stood to head back to the group.

And maybe Keefe thought she couldn't still hear him as she walked away.

Or maybe it was too big of a worry to keep to himself.

But as he reached for a blanket, she heard him mumble, "We'd better do it fast. Otherwise I'm going to have to face my legacy."

Poor Fitz looked pretty shaken by whatever bombardment of questions he'd endured while Sophie was getting Keefe settled.

And Sophie didn't blame anyone for being upset—or for demanding answers.

She also felt seriously horrible for how much they'd worried everybody.

But when it came time to discuss proper punishment, she had a few things to say first.

"I know what I did was dangerous—"

"What *we* did," Fitz corrected, reaching for her hand—which was buried under several layers of gloves again.

"It was my idea," Sophie argued.

"Doesn't matter," Fitz insisted. "I chose to go with you—and I'd do it again."

"So would I," Sophie admitted, tangling their fingers together as she turned back to face the others. "That's what I was going to say. I know this was dangerous. And I know you're all stressed out and mad at me because of it—especially you, Sandor. And I get why. Just like I also realize how lucky I am that all three of us made it back unharmed. But . . . I don't regret going. And if I had to do it all over again, I'd still sneak away."

"Even though you didn't accomplish anything you set out to do by going?" Mr. Forkle asked.

"We accomplished some of it," Sophie argued.

"Yeah, we found their hidden path," Fitz added.

And if Lady Gisela was to be believed, they'd also gotten an answer to whether or not Keefe was involved in what happened with the accident—though Sophie was still holding out hope that his mom had been playing one of her mind games in that moment.

"We also learned that Lady Gisela's planning something for Keefe soon," Sophie added. "And that Tam's warning about what she wants him to do is probably true. And we saw those weird glowing bracelet things they're using to keep Tam in line—"

"Yeah, about those," Elwin interrupted, "when you get a minute, I'd love to see a projection of what they looked like."

"So would I," Wylie agreed. "I don't understand how light would control a Shade."

"I have a few theories," Elwin said, mostly to himself.

"Do any of those theories involve quintessence?" Mr. Forkle asked him, and Sophie's insides tangled tighter at the word.

"All of them, actually," Elwin admitted, which did not help Sophie's knotted-up feeling.

"Then it sounds like you and I need to have a longer conversation," Mr. Forkle said, rubbing one of his temples. "I'll project some images of the bonds for you—I've already seen Miss Foster's and Mr. Vacker's memories of them."

"You have?" Sophie and Fitz asked in unison.

"Yes. When you run off in the middle of the night, sending everyone you care about into a panic—and then turn up with stories of accidental showdowns against our enemies—you lose the right to insist I follow the rules of telepathy. Though, for the record, I *only* searched your London memories."

Sophie's eyes narrowed. "Pretty sure you wouldn't be okay with that logic if we tried to use it on you," she snapped back—but now wasn't the time for a huge fight. "Next time try asking. And . . . at least we learned something useful, right?"

"The showdown wasn't an accident, either," Fitz corrected. "Lady Gisela said the Neverseen have been watching that path, waiting for us to show up. She just didn't count on Sophie's inflicting being so strong."

"Which is the most important thing that happened tonight," Sophie jumped in. "We proved that I *can* handle problems by myself."

"Sounds like you handle them best when you're with Mr. Sencen and Mr. Vacker," Bronte noted.

"They did help," Sophie agreed. "So they should probably be a part of Team Valiant—but we can argue about that later. Right now, my point is"—she turned to Mr. Forkle—"you guys did your job. Now that my abilities are working right, I can tell, I'm . . . pretty powerful. *And* I have a bunch of crazy-powerful friends—and I can enhance them to make them even more awesome if I need to. So now . . . I think you guys need to realize that *sometimes* you're going to have to trust that we'll be okay without you—and yes, I *am* including you in this, Sandor. I'm honored that you're willing to risk your life to protect me—and most of the time I'm happy to have you at my side—"

"*Happy?*" Dex repeated. "I dunno—I've heard an awful lot of bodyguard grumbling."

"So have I," Biana agreed.

"As have *I*," Sandor emphasized.

"You're right," Sophie admitted, meeting Sandor's eyes. "And I shouldn't have done that. I wouldn't be alive right now if it wasn't for you—and I'm not saying I don't want your help anymore. I'm just saying . . . *sometimes* I'm going to need you to trust me to do things on my own—and while I know that's not going to be easy for you, at least tonight proves that I *can* protect myself."

Sandor gripped his sword, and Sophie braced for his usual determined declaration of "I go where you go."

Instead, Mr. Forkle jumped in. "We know, Miss Foster."

"You do?" Fitz asked, pointing to the rest of the bodyguards in their group, who were all grinding their teeth. "Do *they* know? 'Cause it doesn't really look like it."

"They're not happy," Mr. Forkle admitted, "which proves how fortunate we are to have their protection. Not only do they defend their charges faithfully, but they've even allowed themselves to *care*—which is truly remarkable when you think about it. But there's a reason I didn't leap to London and drag you all home by your ears—and I assure you, it's *not* because I didn't consider it, or because your families and bodyguards didn't want me to. In fact, there were times tonight when I suspected Sandor was considering taking my head off."

"I was," Sandor told him, his squeaky voice deeper than usual.

Deadly serious.

Mr. Forkle grinned. "Again, such astounding loyalty. And yet, despite that *pressure*, I chose to leave the three of you alone to fend for yourselves—and it was also *not* because I enjoy allowing you to risk your lives more than anyone else standing before you. Nor did I expect an uneventful evening. And still, I left you alone because I fear that as these challenges continue to escalate, our enemies are going to target each of you individually. And the better prepared you are for those moments, the more likely you'll be to survive them."

Dex cleared his throat. "Well, I feel all warm and fuzzy now."

"You're not meant to," Mr. Forkle informed him. "You're meant to take this very, *very* seriously. The stakes have never been higher— and I fear we're still far from the pinnacle. So if you want us to trust you, you must prove yourselves capable and ready. Which means, Miss Foster, that the next time you decide on a bodyguard-free mission, you'll discuss that plan *before* you put it into effect."

"I can do that," Sophie agreed, "as long as it doesn't turn into hours and hours of debating."

"It won't," Mr. Forkle assured her. "If you can articulate valid reasons that the task will have a better chance for success with a smaller group—and outline a brief plan of action—your parents and bodyguards have assured me that they'll agree. You'll also run into no problems from anyone in the Black Swan—or the Council."

"Really?" Sophie asked, studying the twelve intimidating faces she'd been doing her best to ignore up until that point.

"Trust is a powerful thing, is it not?" Councillor Emery asked.

"But it must not be abused," Tiergan added.

"It won't be," Sophie promised everyone.

"I hope not," Mr. Forkle told them, "because I've also convinced your parents and bodyguards not to punish you for running off the way you did tonight."

"I tried to tell Mom and Dad not to listen, but they're being *boring*," Biana told Fitz, "so *hopefully* they'll remember this the next time *I* cause a bunch of drama."

"Or you could choose to not cause any drama," Alden suggested, looking a little more tired than Sophie was used to.

But it *was* the middle of the night.

"It should be noted," Lord Cassius said, "that my son's bodyguard was not here to concede to this agreement—and considering the state I last saw her in, and her general temperament, it might be best for Keefe to not come home tonight. Not until I've had a chance to discuss all of this with the ogre princess."

Sophie couldn't imagine a single scenario where that conversation would end well. But when she glanced over to where she'd left Keefe, he was nestled into the pillows, sound asleep. So it didn't seem weird at all to say "he can stay here"—until Stina, Dex, Biana, and Grady all stared at her like she'd offered to cuddle with the gorgodon.

"I meant he can stay *there*," she explained—then quickly added, "and I'll obviously stay in my room tonight. I just—"

"That makes sense," Fitz jumped in. "If he actually fell asleep, we shouldn't wake him up."

And he sounded like he meant it—which made Sophie want to throw her arms around him and tell him he was the best, most understanding boyfriend ever.

But *that* also would've earned her weird stares.

So she kept her mouth shut, grateful when Edaline broke the silence by yawning and suggesting they all call it a night.

No one argued. Even when Sophie told her teammates she'd check in with them the next day—and told Mr. Forkle and Elwin she wanted to know what they had discussed about Tam's glowing bonds.

"Thank you," she told Fitz when he pulled her in for a goodbye hug before he leaped away.

"For what?" he asked.

"For trusting me," she whispered. And when he gave her one of his perfect smiles, she really, really, *really* wanted to kiss him.

But it had been a *very* long day.

And the timing still felt wrong—especially after everything that happened in London.

So she just hugged him again and told him, "Good night."

"I get why you've been sleeping out here," Keefe called without turning to look at Sophie as she made her way over to check on him the next day. "I seriously can't remember the last time I slept for so long."

It was already a little past noon.

But no one had wanted to wake him up earlier.

Even Grady had begrudgingly admitted that after the emotional turmoil of the day before, Keefe probably needed all the rest he could get.

"I think it must be Calla's songs," Sophie told him, trying not to grin when she noticed Keefe's hair, which looked like it had been chewed on by baby alicorns. "But Wynn and Luna help too."

"They do." He patted one of the pillows piled next to him, and Sophie took him up on the invitation, fidgeting a little when he turned to study her. "So."

"So," she repeated, not sure what else to say to that.

"I'm guessing you didn't sleep much, since you let me steal your spot, huh?" he asked.

"Actually, I did. *Really*," she added when he raised one eyebrow. "Silveny helped me fall asleep, which was nice, since she hasn't done that in a while."

"Aww. Is Mama Glitter Butt overwhelmed by the twins? I can see why. I woke up about an hour ago, and I've been watching them wreak havoc all over the pastures. That teleporting thing they do is *crazy*."

Sophie frowned. "Teleporting thing?"

"I think that's what it is. That thing where they slip in and out of sight?"

Sophie shook her head. "I have no idea what you're talking about."

"Really?" He craned his neck, trying to find Wynn and Luna—but they didn't seem to be anywhere nearby. "They only do it when they're running really fast. At first I thought they were vanishing or something, but then Luna ended up ducking in and out of the pterodactyl's enclosure, and you guys keep that locked, right? So I don't see how she could do that unless she's slipping in and out of the void."

Sophie's frown deepened.

Keefe's theory *would* solve the mystery of how Wynn and Luna kept sneaking into the gorgodon enclosure.

"But . . . you have to free-fall to teleport," she said, not sure if she was arguing with him or herself.

"That's what I thought too," Keefe admitted. "But you know what it kind of reminded me of? Remember that time at Everglen, not long after you and Dex were rescued? We were playing base quest and you did that Amazing Flying Foster routine, and we all wondered when you'd learned how to blink? Wasn't that before you figured out that you could teleport?"

"It was," Sophie said as her mind slowly dredged up the memory. She hadn't thought about that moment in months and months and months. "I actually realized later that some of the things I'd felt when that happened were things that reminded me of teleporting."

"See?" Keefe said. "Maybe it's something all baby alicorns do when they're learning how to master their power."

"Uh, except I wasn't a baby alicorn—and I'd be *very* careful with the next joke you make, Smirking Boy," Sophie warned, "because if it has the words 'horse girl' in it, I'm not giving you your present."

"You got me a present?" Keefe asked, his eyebrows rising when she patted the satchel slung across her shoulders.

"I did. Had to make a *very* special trip to go get it for you too—and enlist a little help to make it happen. So what were you going to say?"

"I . . . I don't know." He reached up to run a hand through his hair and seemed to realize for the first time that his current hairstyle could serve well as a nest for small animals—and his cheeks turned very, very red. He cleared his throat. "Does that mean I get my present?"

"I suppose," Sophie said, tempted to tease him more first, since he was so clearly thrown off his game. But she flipped open the satchel and pulled out the crinkly yellow-and-brown package, setting it proudly in his lap.

"You . . . got me E.L. Fudges?" Keefe asked, doing an adorable double take between her and the cookies.

Sophie nodded proudly. "Well, technically my sister stole them from my parents' pantry so I wouldn't have to deal with converting lusters to dollars and finding a grocery store and whatnot. It was hard enough convincing Grady and Edaline to let me teleport to see Amy without all of that. So a couple of cookies are missing, but Amy said they opened the package last night and they're still fresh. Besides, we all know what you really care about is—"

"The fact that they're shaped like tiny elves!" Keefe said, clapping his hands before he pointed to the label. "Hang on—*they call them 'elfwiches'*?"

"They do, Keefe. They do. And that's not even the best part."

"AHHHHHH LOOK AT THEIR LITTLE FACES!" Keefe shouted as he peeled back the plastic cover. "THIS IS THE GREATEST THING I HAVE EVER SEEN—EVER!"

"Greater than when you discovered Fitz slept with Mr. Snuggles?" Sophie had to ask.

"Um. *Yeah.* They have names, Foster. NAMES!" He held up one of the cookies and pointed to the name tag the little elf was holding. "This one's Ernie! AHHH AND THIS ONE IS FAST EDDIE!" he said, snatching a different cookie. "And this one is Buckets! And Elwood! I don't know who named these guys, but whoever they are, they're a genius, I tell you—a *GENIUS*. Also, I think Elwood kind of looks like me, doesn't he?"

He held the cookie up to his face and raised his other hand in a wave, just like Elwood's pose, and Sophie couldn't hold back her giggle.

"He has your smirk," she agreed.

"Yup, he's a good-looking elf-y cookie. And wait—there's writing on the back." He flipped the cookie over. "What does 'from the Hollow Tree' mean?"

"That's where the Keebler elves make their cookies."

Keefe snorted. "Of course they do—why didn't I think of that? Humans are my favorite. Though, this one says 'uncommonly good,' and this one says 'uncommonly made'—so it sorta seems like the dude deciding this stuff was running out of words, doesn't it? But whatever, he gave us Fast Eddie, so I'll forgive him. And wait, why does this one say 'dunk head first'?"

"The cookies taste best dunked in milk, so they're saying to dunk the head first before you eat it."

He blinked, turning the cookie back over to stare at the little elf. "Woooooooow, that got DARK. Poor Buckets. I didn't really think about how weird it was going to be, eating food with a little face on it staring at me—especially a little elf-y face. Look at his little ears! And his little hat! Humans are cruel. But here we go. . . . Sorry, Buckets, dude—know your sacrifice was for a noble cause." He raised the cookie to his mouth and flipped it at the last second, biting off the feet instead of the head. "I don't know why that seemed less brutal, since he totally has no legs now. But it made sense in the moment—and more important . . . eh."

"Eh?" Sophie asked.

"I mean—don't get me wrong. It's way better than those biscuit things you brought me last time. But it's still kinda dry and boring."

Sophie had to agree. And yet she still helped herself to a cookie, each bite tasting like childhood.

"Thank you, by the way," he said, tucking the extra cookies he'd pulled out carefully back into the container. "This was *really* amazing, Foster. No, I mean it—don't try to shrug it off. This . . . is the nicest thing anyone's ever done for me—by a *lot*."

"Well . . . I think that's mostly because your parents have set the bar *really* low."

"They have," Keefe agreed, and as his smile faded, Sophie wished she could take the words back.

But she'd gotten the E.L. Fudges for him because she knew he was going to need them.

"I'm done freaking out," he told her, clearly picking up on her worries. "I mean . . . the next time I see Bangs Boy, I'm going to kick him somewhere extra sensitive. But until then . . . there's nothing I can do, right? My mom's still out there, still planning my great 'legacy'—which apparently includes murdering a guy and his ten-year-old daughter—"

"You don't know that," Sophie interrupted. "That *easily* could've been another one of your mom's lies. And I thought of something we can do that might help us get a little closer to the truth—or find some other clues about what she's planning."

"Hmm. That *sounds* like good news—until your emotions hit me and it's a whole lot of DOOM and WORRY, so I'm guessing I'm not going to like this new tactic?"

"I'm sure it won't be your favorite, but . . . I also think it'll be worth it." She finished the last of her cookie, trying to get rid of the sour taste on her tongue. But nothing could block the fresh surge of bile that came with having to tell Keefe, "Fitz hasn't gotten anywhere with his search of your dad's memories. And I'm starting to think you're right. That kind of search might be a little more than his telepathy can handle. So . . ."

"You want to make it a job for Fitzphie?" Keefe guessed—which she probably should've expected, since the whole Cognate thing usually made them stronger together.

But . . .

"Actually, I think your dad has gotten too good at pushing Fitz around," she told him. "And the best way to find what we need is for me to take him on, one-on-one."

Keefe closed his eyes, looking about as green as the tree on the E.L. Fudge package.

"I can handle him," she promised.

"I know," he mumbled. "And I'm sure you're probably right. I just . . . ugh, I have a feeling this is exactly what he wanted."

"I thought of that," Sophie agreed.

She hadn't forgotten Lord Cassius saying, "The ideal candidate would've been young Miss Foster," the day he'd first told them he was having Fitz help with the project.

But it made her lips curl with a smile.

And Keefe's lips cracked with the tiniest hint of a smirk when she told him, "So maybe it's time your dad learns that he should watch what he wishes for."

THIRTY-EIGHT

LORD CASSIUS'S OFFICE WAS EVERY BIT as immaculate and elegant as Sophie had come to expect from the rooms in the Shores of Solace, with its wide ocean-view windows and beach-toned decor. The massive silver desk didn't have a single fingerprint dulling its shine. And the mother-of-pearl bookshelves were filled with books of the exact same height and width, with the same seafoam blue spines, as if he'd had them all rebound to match—or bought hundreds of the same volume purely for the aesthetic. The stiff white armchairs filling the center of the room looked as if they'd never once been sat in, and the marble floor was so heavily polished, it felt slippery under Sophie's shoes.

But one corner was different. Nestled near a small, flickering fireplace was a dark blue recliner that was so worn and well loved, it almost looked lumpy. And *that* was where Lord Cassius sat waiting, next to a small table strewn with scrolls and notebooks and a window with a perfect view of a hidden cove filled with dark rocks and beach grass and a stretch of smooth white sand.

"You seem surprised," he noted as Sophie and Keefe made their way over.

Sandor had chosen to stand guard outside of the office, mostly because they were fully expecting Ro to exact some sort of epic revenge and he wanted to ensure that Sophie wasn't caught in the cross fire.

Sophie shrugged. "I guess I assumed your office would be more of a personal shrine."

She'd heard plenty of stories about the life-size statue he had of himself, along with entire rooms displaying his accomplishments.

"At Candleshade, it is," Lord Cassius told her, his gaze turning somewhat distant as he added, "but not this office. This place is not meant to be seen by anyone other than me."

"Well then, lucky us," Keefe said, dragging one of the never-used armchairs closer to his father with a cringeworthy *SCREEEEEEE-AAAAAAAAAAAAAACH*. "Have a seat, Foster—you'll probably be here awhile."

Lord Cassius sighed. "Fitz has had no problem remaining standing."

"Yeah, well, Fitzy's been coming here hoping you'll feed him some tiny crumb of information about his brother—which I'm assuming you haven't done yet, because it keeps him from doing all the things you don't want him doing, like getting himself a stupid chair." He made a point of moving a second armchair over with an even louder *SCREEEEEEEEEEEEEEEEEEEAAAAAAAAAAAAAAAAACH* and plopped down onto it, propping his feet on his dad's cluttered table. "But *we* don't need anything, soooooooooo . . . we'll do what we want."

"If that's true," Lord Cassius said quietly, "I wonder why you're bothering with this at all."

Keefe shrugged. "Just trying to settle a bet. Lotsa people wagering on how fast Foster'll put poor Fitzy's skills to shame."

"We both know that isn't true." Lord Cassius's eyes focused on his hands, and he studied his fingernails as he asked, "What did your mother say to you yesterday—specifically? I heard the summary, but not her actual words."

"Why do you care?" Keefe countered.

"Because your mother is a master of saying one thing and meaning another, and you were always too afraid of her to properly learn how to speak her language."

Keefe snorted. "I wasn't afraid of her. I mean, I probably should've been, since she was sneaking around murdering people, but—"

"You were terrified," Lord Cassius insisted. "Because she gave you just enough love to show you how wonderful it could be if she truly cared for you—and then casually withheld the rest, leaving you wondering where you went wrong, and trying to figure out how to fix it, and being constantly afraid that you'd lose what little you had."

A beat of painful silence passed as Keefe shifted uncomfortably in his chair. "You sound like you know that feeling well."

It was Lord Cassius's turn to shrug. "Like father, like son."

Sophie could picture it all so clearly—the miserable dynamic that Keefe grew up with in his parents' cold, ostentatious tower. And all she wanted to do was squeeze into his chair so she could wrap her arms around him and prove that someone cared.

But she'd made Keefe two promises before he brought her there.

One: She'd do her best to avoid the memories she knew he probably wouldn't want her to see.

And two: No matter what she saw, she would never pity him.

What she was feeling in that moment definitely *wasn't* pity—but Keefe probably wouldn't see it that way.

"Okay," she said, taking a seat in the chair that Keefe had dragged over for her—and loving the way Lord Cassius's jaw tightened when she curled her knees up and rested her feet on the clean white fabric. "I'm pretty sure the one thing we all agree on is that none of us want this to take any longer than it needs to. And you already know how this works, since you've been doing it with Fitz, so you don't need me to explain anything to you, right?"

"Does that mean there won't be any fancy moonlark tricks to wow me with the wonders of your telepathy?" Lord Cassius asked.

Sophie matched his smug smile. "I don't need tricks to wow you. That'll happen naturally, when I crash through every wall you put up and find all the things you think you can hide from me."

Keefe whistled. "Okay, I'm not sure where all of this Foster confidence is coming from, but I'm here for it!"

Sophie's cheeks warmed a little—but not that much.

Because she *was* feeling confident.

Maybe her head was still thrumming from the unbridled force of her inflicting.

Or maybe it was because she'd been a Telepath since she was five years old.

Either way, she knew beyond any doubt that her mind was *powerful*.

And Lord Cassius, for all of his bravado, was very, very weak.

She double-checked her fingernail gadgets—and her four layers of gloves—before reaching for Lord Cassius's temples, since he was an Empath and his sensitivity to her enhancing would probably be stronger.

"The memories I want you to ignore are tinted purple," he told her.

Sophie shook her head. "That's not how this works. *You* don't get to decide what stays secret."

With that, she pressed her gloved fingers against his skin—relieved when no warmth from her enhancing sparked between them—and shoved her consciousness into his mind, without bothering to ask for permission.

His mental barriers shredded like paper, and she crashed into the center of his thoughts, where everything was . . .

Quiet.

And tidy.

And still.

Usually minds were a rush of color and motion and sound and energy—like being surrounded by thousands of flickering holograms, each broadcasting its own vibrant soundtrack.

But Lord Cassius's head was like stepping into a vast, pristine library—run by the kind of overzealous librarian who yelled at people for moving the books and took great pleasure in shushing anyone who made the slightest noise.

A lifetime's worth of memories loomed around Sophie in ten precariously arranged stacks. Houses of cards tinted red, blue, green, orange, gold, silver, pink, white, black, and purple—as if Lord Cassius had been categorizing each of his thoughts and experiences before meticulously tucking them away.

Sophie wasn't sure what the other colors meant—but she knew he wanted her to stay away from purple, so . . .

You're so much like my son, Lord Cassius thought as Sophie focused on the shaky tower of violet-stained memories, wondering what would happen if she slammed her consciousness against it.

Would it all come toppling down?

As soon as you know something's forbidden, he told her, *it's all you want. I often wonder if that's part of the appeal for—*

Sophie didn't bother listening to the end of that sentence, too lost in the purple-tinted memory she'd focused on. The scene was slightly faded and blurred, since Lord Cassius didn't have a photographic memory, but Sophie could still easily tell that she was watching a much younger version of him retrieve books from his locker in the Level One atrium at Foxfire.

He looked so uncannily like his son at that age that Sophie would've thought she was watching Keefe—if she hadn't known that Keefe had skipped that particular grade level.

Then again, Lord Cassius also lacked Keefe's easy swagger.

In fact, when she looked closer, she realized that his movements were rushed and tense, and the expression on his face was . . . nervous?

"Scared" actually might've been a better word for it.

She learned why a few breaths later, when a group of much taller, much more confident Level Threes sidled over to him, knocking his books out of his hands and messing up his hair.

Lord Cassius said nothing.

Did nothing.

But internally he swore that things would change.

Someday he would be better than everyone else—and then he would show them all.

The memory ended there—but something about the abruptness of it felt intentional. As if Lord Cassius had snipped off the rest, either to sort it somewhere else or to keep that part hidden.

So . . . I'm assuming you said the thing about the purple memories to distract me from the real stuff you don't want me to see? Sophie guessed.

Or I don't like anyone witnessing my moments of weakness, Lord Cassius countered—which might've been a believable explanation, if he hadn't had the answer ready to go.

Your mind games aren't going to work on me, she told him. *And I don't really get why you're bothering to play them. Searching your memories was YOUR idea—YOU wanted to find out if there was something that Lady Gisela hid from you.*

Yes, I'm aware. But that doesn't mean I'm willing to allow anyone to invade my privacy—and surely you've realized that something my wife stole wouldn't be tinted purple, or red or blue or green or any other color, since that means I'm aware of it.

Actually, that was a valid point.

This part of his mind was so organized—so *controlled*—that anything missing or out of place would've been glaringly obvious.

She needed to find the rest.

The parts he couldn't shape into the precarious narrative he wanted to display to the world.

The parts he'd tried to bury.

That won't help either, he warned, but Sophie was already poking and prodding at the corners and shadows—the cramped little nooks and the cold, empty stretches and . . .

There.

A tiny crack.

A flaw in his well-honed mental armor.

All she had to do was slip through and . . .

. . . down, down, down she went—careening through a dark, lonely void.

Hurtling toward a sea of nightmares.

But then her fall seemed to slow, and the air thickened around her, nudging her back up, until she could see a fuzzy gray path.

Everything about it called to her.

Welcoming her.

Guiding her.

As if Lord Cassius was providing her with an escape, to spare her from the shadows.

But it was another trick.

Another defense.

And Sophie wasn't afraid of the dark.

So she pushed back against the barrier and plunged straight into the mire. Sinking past glimmers of doubt and fear. Fighting her way through flurries of despair and hopelessness. Until she burst through to the other side, landing in an explosion of light and color and sound.

The *real* Lord Cassius.

Not the rigid construct he liked to present.

This won't help you, he insisted as she focused on the vibrant memories piled haphazardly all around her, like someone had tossed them away. *I may not like this part of myself. But I'm still aware of its presence.*

Why don't you like this part of yourself? Sophie asked, trying to process what she was seeing.

Most of the memories were brief flashes—snippets and scraps trimmed away from longer moments.

And many of them featured Keefe.

His smiles and laughter.

His pranks and jokes and art.

The same things Lord Cassius was always trying to force Keefe to change about himself.

And for a second Sophie was *furious.*

How dare he mentally edit his son?

Who was he to deny reality?

But then . . . she noticed the warmth.

It wasn't strong.

And it wasn't comforting.

But it was *there*—wrapped around each edited moment.

And she knew: *You love your son.*

Of course I do.

The words were a weary sigh, and Sophie's anger surged back.

WHY WOULD YOU BURY THAT?

Far, far away she felt Keefe give her shoulder a gentle, reassuring squeeze—which only added to her rage.

He deserved so much better.

You have no idea what he deserves, Lord Cassius argued, and Sophie wasn't sure if she'd transmitted the thought or if he'd read the emotions coursing through her. *Everything I withhold is for his own good. Love . . . convolutes things. If your creators had made you an Empath, perhaps you would understand that—though it's strange. Your*

mind focuses on feelings far more than any Telepath I've ever encoun-
tered. The way you homed in on that emotion just now—it was almost
a fusion of our abilities. I can't tell if that was taught to you or if it's
somehow inherent or . . .

His thoughts cycled through possibilities, and for a second Sophie
was right there with him, wondering if Mr. Forkle had trained her
mind to work differently than others', or if it was because she manifested so young—and grew up around humans—or if it was the
result of some small tweak to her genetics.

And then she realized . . .

You're not going to distract me, she told him. *What do you mean by*
"love convolutes things"?

A dark rumble shook everything around her. *I mean exactly that.*
And if you don't believe me—ask the question everyone's been whispering
since Gisela was outed.

It took Sophie several seconds to puzzle out what question he
meant.

You mean, "How did you not know she was part of the Neverseen?"

Exactly. How could an Empath—two Empaths, counting my son—
not realize they had a traitor among them? We should've sensed every
lie—every trick. But we missed them all. And while I want to believe
you'll find some stockpile of damaged memories that I can point to and
blame for the way she misled me, I fear the reality is simply that while it
may be nearly impossible for someone to lie to an Empath, it's far, far too
easy for us to lie to ourselves. Our emotions are stronger. Purer. So much
more overwhelming. And we cannot feel our own tells.

Your tells? Sophie repeated.

Another dark rumble. *I'm surprised my son's never mentioned it.*

Actually, no, I'm not surprised at all. I'm sure this is the last piece of knowledge he wants you to have.

What does that mean?

It means my son has plenty to hide. And all Empaths have a tell when we try to lie. It's instinctive. Unavoidable. Part of who we are. In fact, I strongly suspect it's why your creators didn't choose empathy as one of your abilities. What's the point of giving their moonlark an impenetrable mind if her heart will give her away every time?

I still have no idea what you're talking about, Sophie told him.

Yes, I'm sure you don't. And for a second he hesitated—debating whether he should share.

You realize I could pluck the secret from your mind with a single thought, right? Sophie reminded him.

I suppose that's a valid point. And it's not like this is a secret. It's just not particularly well known, either. Empaths have a physical reaction when we lie. You have to be reading our pulse to feel it, but it's always there. Our hearts skip three beats. One from guilt. One from fear. And one like a held breath, waiting to see if someone will catch us. It's completely involuntary—we can't even feel it in ourselves. Which makes it so very easy for our hearts to lead us astray. How else do you think I ended up married to a murderer?

The last word was a jolt, dragging Sophie's focus away from all of that strange new information.

And she found herself asking, *You REALLY loved her?*

She honestly couldn't imagine Lord Cassius loving anyone except himself.

You know almost nothing about me, he told her. *Or what I'm capable of feeling.*

True, Sophie conceded. *But you know what I'm realizing? I've been in your head for all of this time, and I haven't seen a single memory with her in it. Even down here, in the stuff you're trying to hide.*

Surely you've heard of coping mechanisms. Surely you can understand why I've spent the last several months painstakingly carving her out of my consciousness. I had to sort through my memories anyway, trying to find any gaps or inconsistencies on my own. And after I finished examining a moment, I'd sever any pieces with her and cast them away—the closest I can come to erasing her from my life.

Okay, but where are those pieces now?

It doesn't matter. I've already checked them.

That doesn't mean they won't trigger what you're looking for.

Once again, he hesitated.

And she had to remind him again that she *would* find everything on her own—and who knew what else she'd discover along the way?

It's a waste of time, he insisted.

But his mind still shifted and rattled, as if he were pulling open some sort of inner mental barrier, revealing a new light up ahead—a dim, icy glow that definitely wasn't inviting.

Sophie followed it anyway, into a chilly nook tucked into the darkest part of his consciousness where thousands of memories flickered in the shadows.

Thousands of glimpses of Lady Gisela.

Smiles.

Scowls.

Glares.

Laughter.

Though something about her always looked a little . . . calculating. Especially when she gazed at her son.

You see that too, Lord Cassius noted, and Sophie realized she'd transmitted that observation.

It just seemed so . . . obvious.

Hindsight brings a strange sort of clarity, doesn't it? Lord Cassius asked her. *It's so easy to hate yourself for missing something so glaring. But every moment has shades of meaning, and how we interpret it comes down to the knowledge we have in that instance. Like now, for example— you sit there stewing in your disgust for me, convinced I'm cruel and callous because that is the information you have. Just as I saw a wife and mother who was as determined as I was to help her son find success and reach his maximum potential—which, I suppose, IS still who she was. She just had a very different vision for his future, apparently.*

Sour dread mixed with Sophie's other emotions, and she couldn't tell if it came from her or Lord Cassius.

And I'm assuming you have no idea what she means when she talks about Keefe's legacy? she asked.

I don't—and I wish I did.

She could tell he meant it. Which was why she decided to answer when he asked again for the specific words Lady Gisela said to Keefe in London—and she didn't just tell him. She filled his mind with her memory of the conversation, letting him watch the scene play out for himself.

And when they got to the part where Lady Gisela told Keefe to "embrace the change or it *will* destroy you," something shifted in his mind again.

A soft quiver that grew stronger and stronger.

A mental earthquake that drove a deep rift through his consciousness.

And three new memories emerged, each one crackly and scratched, like watching a projection of a ruined piece of film—the same way Keefe's recovered memory had looked. The sound faded in and out, and the scenes sometimes played too fast or slow or dropped away altogether. But Sophie soaked up every detail she could pull from the damage.

In the first memory Lord Cassius found his wife nearly convulsing on their bed—with five empty vials strewn across the floor. Her mouth had a strange glow as she murmured to herself, "Embrace the change," over and over, and Lord Cassius scooped her into his arms and sprinted for Candleshade's vortinator to get her to a physician. The scene faded out after that, and faded back in when he was standing under the Leapmaster, with Lady Gisela begging him to take her back—to let her rest—swearing it was nothing he needed to concern himself with. She told him it was a treatment that took a few minutes for her body to accept. And he'd felt how strongly she meant the words—how desperate she was to be alone—so he'd brought her back to bed.

The second scene was much harder to watch.

There were five vials again, this time flickering and glowing on the bedside table. And Lord Cassius sat next to his wife on the edge of their bed as she tried to convince him to drink them.

The memory distorted most of their conversation, but Lord Cassius didn't seem to find anything familiar about what she was suggesting, so his other memory must've already been taken. And the soundtrack sharpened again as Lady Gisela promised, "This treatment will make you powerful in ways you can't even imagine. You just have to embrace the change."

She'd whispered something else Sophie couldn't hear, but whatever it was, it convinced Lord Cassius to gulp down each of the vials.

And then there was pain.

Burning and freezing and stabbing and tearing and crushing and twisting and writhing.

Unending.

Unsurvivable.

Except somehow, he did.

Somehow, when he stopped fighting it, he *became* the pain.

And then everything faded into a black, dreamless oblivion.

The third memory was the shortest.

Lady Gisela leaned in and licked a silver panel on a glittering crystal wall, and a small compartment popped open, with two tiny bottles inside. The glass was blacker than anything Sophie had ever seen—as if the bottles had been carved out of the void—and Lady Gisela seemed to be giving Lord Cassius a long list of vital instructions.

The memory only preserved three scattered pieces of what she said.

"When the timing is right."

"Embrace the change."

And "the beginning of our legacy."

THIRTY-NINE

SOOOOOOOOO . . . I'M ASSUMING THE crazy emotional spike I just felt means you guys had a breakthrough," Keefe said as Sophie's mind snapped back to the present. "And I'm *also* assuming it wasn't good news, seeing as how Foster's now as white as the armchairs, and Daddio reminds me of the way Ro looked after she ate those amoebas. In fact, we might wanna give him some room, so we're not in a splash zone if he goes projectile, like she did."

"If you think we're ready to joke about that," Ro called from the doorway, "you are sorely, *sorely* mistaken, Hunkyhair. But *you* can relax, Blondie," she added as Sophie jumped to her feet. "I don't hold *you* responsible for the Keefster's extremely poor life choices. Why do you think your bodyguard let me in?"

Sandor tilted his head in and nodded as Ro sauntered closer, tossing her pigtails—which were now a bright fire-engine red—as she leaned over Keefe's armchair and pinched Keefe's chin with her red-clawed fingers, smushing his lips into a fish face. "You can relax too, my foolish, *foolish* boy—for *now*. Because when I pay you back? You'll *never* see it coming. Count on that."

"I will," Keefe assured her, his voice distorted by the fish face.

"Good." Ro held him like that a second longer, squeezing his face even tighter before she dropped her hand and turned to Sophie. "So, what's this I hear about a breakthrough?"

"And don't try to sugarcoat it, Foster," Keefe added, rubbing his jaw, which now showed tiny dents from Ro's claws. "I agreed to this because I trusted you to tell me *everything*."

Sophie reached for her eyelashes. "I know, but—"

"We both know my imagination is probably fifty times worse than the reality," Keefe cut in.

Which was probably true. But she still had to warn him, "This is a lot to handle."

"Yeah, well . . . what else is new?" He forced a rather sad smile. "I'm serious, Foster. I don't care if it's a lot. I just want the truth."

Sophie studied him for a long second before nodding. "It'll be easier if I show you what we saw."

"Are you going to show him our *entire* conversation?" Lord Cassius jumped in.

The warning in his eyes tempted Sophie to say yes. But . . . Keefe didn't need his father's warped views on love distracting him from these new revelations.

Lord Cassius deserved to sweat a little, though, so she kept her answer vague. "I'm going to show Keefe everything that *I* think is important."

"Works for me," Keefe told her, leaning back in his armchair. "Hit me with all the creepy family stuff you want—it's *not* like it'll be a surprise."

Sophie hated how true that was as she reached for his forehead, making sure she had permission to open her thoughts to his before she pressed her gloved fingers against his temples.

I can handle this, Foster, he promised when his mental voice flooded her mind.

You have to, she told him. *The trust here works both ways. You're trusting me not to coddle you, and I'm trusting you to lean on your friends and let us help you through this.*

His mind got a whole lot quieter when he asked, *So it's that bad, huh?*

Sophie was about to say yes—but then she took a look at the thoughts flashing all around her. And Keefe was right: His imagination *was* worse than the reality. His head was a horror show of theories that felt very Dr. Jekyll and Mr. Hyde, with Keefe turning into some sort of evil, murderous monster at Lady Gisela's beck and call.

Your mom told us she didn't mess with your DNA, Sophie reminded him.

Uh, yeah, and my mom lies, Keefe countered.

I know, but . . . you're past manifesting age, right? And you still only have one ability.

Right, but I'm also supposed to "embrace the change"—remember?

Sophie felt herself flinch at the words and sucked in a deep breath, needing that extra second to work up the courage to tell him, *Those were the words that triggered the broken pieces we found of your dad's erased memories. You're SURE you want to see them?*

A tiny voice in the back of his mind said, *No.* But the rest of him told her, *Bring it on, Foster.*

When she still hesitated, he added, *It's not like I can hide from this.*

He couldn't.

No matter how much she wished she could protect him.

Okay, here goes, she warned, filling his head with the memories one by one, sharing them in the same order she'd seen them with Lord Cassius.

She offered no commentary, letting Keefe process everything himself. And he replayed each of the memories three times before his brain could form any coherent words—most of which were things he'd probably get in trouble for saying.

Please tell me it wasn't a mistake to show you that, Sophie begged when his brain started its fourth memory replay.

It wasn't, he assured her. *I'm fine.*

No, you're not. Sophie dropped one of her hands from his temples and reached for him, tangling their fingers together.

He didn't argue. Just clung to her as tightly as he could as they watched a fifth replay together.

Three things, Sophie told him as Keefe's Dr. Jekyll theories reared back with a vengeance. *First: Your mom talks about this being THEIR legacy—not yours. So it might not have anything to do with you—and I know you're going to argue with me on that, but you have to admit it's at least possible. Second: Whatever this was . . . your parents are fine. I mean, they're pretty awful people—but they were that way before any of this. So it's not like this changed them in any way that's noticeable. And third—and most important: This isn't triggering any new memories for you, right?*

She checked his nearby thoughts for any flashes of pain or glimpses of glowing vials.

No, he admitted, *but that might just mean my mom did a better job of burying it.*

I don't know, Sophie argued. *I don't think you can bury something THIS traumatic—especially when you're being given such a clear, direct trigger. You should've felt how fast it worked on your dad—and all it took for him was me sharing the memory from London of your mom telling you to "embrace the change." As soon as he heard those words, it set off this, like, mental earthquake, and his consciousness actually cracked as these memories came crashing through. So . . . if there was something in your past like this, I feel like you'd have gotten back at least the damaged pieces of it by now. And you haven't.*

The more she thought about it, the easier it was to breathe.

But Keefe didn't seem nearly as convinced.

His palm felt shaky in hers, and his thoughts were darting in so many directions, she couldn't keep up with them—except one.

One part of his mind stayed fixated on those eerie black bottles in the final memory.

There were only two of them, she pointed out, adding that to her list of reassurances.

Yeah, but—

"Are you ever going to bring me back into this conversation?" Lord Cassius interrupted. "Given that these are *my* memories, it seems like I should be a part of the discussion."

"I dunno—do you have anything useful to add?" Keefe asked as Sophie severed their mental connection and blinked her eyes back into focus on the present. "I mean, if you have any idea what that 'treatment' was—or what was in any of those vials—feel free to share," Keefe told his dad. "Otherwise, not sure what we need you for."

"Uh . . . that doesn't sound good," Ro noted. "Can someone maybe clue the bodyguards in?"

"Oh sure," Keefe told her. "Basically, it looks like Mommy Dearest definitely did experiment on me."

"No—she experimented on *me*!" Lord Cassius shouted, jumping to his feet and stalking toward his son. "You don't get to make this all about you."

"Yeah, well, you don't get to make this all about *you*, either!" Keefe snapped back. "Because I have a pretty strong hunch this all happened around the time Mom got pregnant with me, right?"

Lord Cassius reluctantly nodded.

"You're sure?" Sophie had to ask. Both of Keefe's parents looked exactly the same in the memories as they did now—and it wasn't like there'd been a calendar in the background.

"I'm sure," Lord Cassius agreed quietly. "The room in the first two memories is a room we only shared for a brief time. Once Gisela discovered she was pregnant, we separated ourselves."

The set of his jaw made it clear there'd be no further discussion on *that* topic—and Sophie was definitely good with that.

Keefe ran a hand down his face. "I'm guessing you don't know where the room in the third memory was?"

Lord Cassius shook his head. "Only that it was somewhere in Candleshade."

"Great," Keefe muttered.

"If you need me to go back there and smash more things, I'm happy to," Ro generously offered.

"Smashing would be bad," Keefe said. "We don't want to break those vials."

"You think they're still there?" Sophie asked.

"I don't know. It's possible. My mom said, 'When the timing is right'—and I haven't fulfilled my legacy or whatever yet."

"But it wasn't about *your* legacy," Lord Cassius reminded him. "She said 'our'—hers and mine."

Ro groaned. "Now *you* have a separate legacy? Is anyone else getting really sick of that word? Because I swear, every time I hear it, I wanna stab something."

"Right there with you," Sandor agreed quietly.

"Oh, I'm there too," Keefe agreed as well, tearing his hands through his hair. "The good news is—I'm pretty sure all the *legacies* are the same. Think about it—she talked about *their* legacy right around the time they made me, so . . ."

"Wait," Sophie said, leaning forward in her armchair. "You're saying you think those treatments were, like . . ." She wasn't even sure how to word it—and she really hoped she was wrong when she finished with, "An elvin fertility thing?"

"No, I think they were a mess-with-our-future-baby kind of thing," Keefe corrected.

But Lord Cassius shook his head. "Actually, I think Sophie might be onto something. Your mother was very concerned about getting pregnant. She went to a number of physicians beforehand, and I never understood why, because it seemed to happen quite quickly and easily—but maybe this is why. Maybe it seemed fast to me because she erased these memories."

"FYI, I *really* don't want to hear about Lord Hunkyhair's creation," Ro whined.

"That makes two of us," Sandor added.

And Sophie waited for Keefe to agree.

But he just leaned his head back against his armchair, staring at the ceiling.

"Sounds like I need to talk to some physicians," Lord Cassius decided. "See if any of them have heard of this kind of *treatment*."

"You should start with Elwin," Sophie told him. "Those vials almost seemed like they were filled with light—which doesn't really make sense since you can't *drink* light, but . . ."

Her voice trailed off as a sickening new thought occurred to her.

"I guess they could've been quintessence," she whispered, deciding to throw the theory out there.

The conversation couldn't necessarily get any weirder.

"I mean . . . the vials looked a little different than the vials of quintessence I've seen before," she added quietly. "But . . . there were five of them. And there are five unmapped stars. And each vial was different. And the pain they caused . . ."

Lord Cassius wrapped his arms around himself. "I'll hail Elwin and find out where he is."

"And you'll tell us what he says," Keefe said as he stood, making it clear it wasn't a request. "Feels like this is a good time for us to stop keeping secrets from each other, doesn't it?"

Sophie frowned when Lord Cassius agreed.

"You don't want to be there when he talks to Elwin?" she whispered.

Keefe shook his head. "I'm going to Candleshade to see if I can find that compartment."

"Oh." Sophie stood up to join him, trying to be supportive—and telling herself to be glad that his plan was something safe. But she still had to remind him, "It's just . . . Candleshade is *huge*—and there was nothing recognizable about that wall in the memory, was there?"

"Not the wall," Keefe told her. "But there was . . . a *feeling*. You probably didn't notice it, since you're not an Empath. But every time

I replay that memory, I get this, like, prickly sense right here"—he brushed his hands down his arms—"and I think it's triggered by whatever is in those vials. So if I search for that feeling at Candleshade, I should be able to follow it to that compartment."

"Assuming the vials are still there," Lord Cassius noted.

Keefe shrugged. "It's worth checking, right?"

"Um, just so I'm clear," Ro jumped in as Keefe dug an old home crystal out from one of his cape pockets, "your plan is to go room by room in a two-hundred-story tower, searching for some random elf-y feeling that might not even be there anymore because the thing causing it might be long gone?"

"It's either that or go with my dad and listen to him and Elwin chat about fertility stuff," Keefe reminded her.

Ro groaned again. "Fine. But I'm adding this to the list of things I'll be paying you back for."

"You do that," Keefe told her—and that seemed to settle it.

Sandor sighed as Sophie reached for Keefe's hand, and grumbled something about needing patience as he joined the light leaping chain.

And she honestly wasn't any happier about the project ahead of them.

But Keefe shouldn't be alone after everything they'd discovered. There was too big of a risk that he'd change his mind and run off somewhere much more dangerous.

And he'd endured an awful lot of boring, tedious things for her.

"Remind me to hail Dex, Biana, Stina, and Wylie a little later," she told Sandor, realizing she'd promised her teammates she'd be checking in on them that day.

"If you have other things to do—" Keefe tried to tell her.

But Sophie shook her head, channeling Sandor when she told him, "I go where you go."

Candleshade was somehow even bigger than Sophie remembered.

The glittering crystal skyscraper basically blotted out the sun.

And boy, was it depressing.

Keefe's house had always felt cold and unwelcoming—but now the once shimmering rooms were coated in dust and grime and were in total chaos from all the hasty previous searches. There was also quite a lot of smashed stuff that seemed to say, *Ro was here.*

If Keefe was bothered by the mess, he did a good job hiding it. But it probably helped that his search required his full concentration.

Room by room he'd close his eyes, feeling for whatever he'd picked up on in that memory, before he shook his head and moved on.

And Sophie tried not to sigh, or shuffle her feet—or do the math on how *endless* the search was going to be.

Ro was doing plenty of that for everyone.

But by the time they reached the fifth floor, Sophie had to at least voice a new theory she couldn't get out of her head. "So . . . if I'm right," she said quietly, wishing her voice didn't sound quite so echoey, "and those vials your parents took had some form of quintessence in them, that probably means the dark vials are—"

"Shadowflux?" Keefe finished for her. "Way ahead of you there, Foster. Why do you think I'm bothering with this? If it's shadowflux, we're finally on our way to figuring out how she's planning to have Bangs Boy off me."

"We are?" Sophie asked, not really seeing the connection.

If Lady Gisela already had bottles of shadowflux, what did she need Tam for?

And if she'd already drunk the bottles and needed more, couldn't Umber have provided that a long time ago?

"Yeah, okay," Keefe said, "I'm picking up on your skepticism loud and clear, Foster. And I *do* realize that even if we find the black bottles, they're going to raise a whole lot more questions than they answer. But at least it'd be progress, you know? An actual clue that ties right into Tammy Boy's Shade stuff?"

"True," Sophie agreed, trying to stay positive.

But after five more floors, positivity was feeling impossible.

They'd been there for at least an hour—and they still had one hundred and ninety floors to go.

"If we don't speed this process up, I'm going to start stabbing things," Ro warned when they made it to floor thirteen, and Sophie had to bite her tongue to stop herself from agreeing.

Sandor had no such qualms—and had apparently been working on the math in his head—and spelled out exactly how many hours they had ahead of them if they continued at their current pace.

"No way!" Ro informed them. "I seriously will murder some-one long before that. You mean to tell me our pretty little Blondie doesn't have some sort of elf-y ability to make this go faster?"

Sophie stopped walking. "I can't believe I didn't think of that. We should use my enhancing!"

"You sure you're up for that?" Keefe asked as Sophie peeled off her gloves. "You've kinda done a lot with your abilities the last few days, and you're still recovering from the reset."

"Enhancing doesn't do anything to me," she promised, tapping her fingers to turn off Dex's gadgets. "It's automatic, remember? Besides, it can't be more exhausting than spending ten million hours searching this place room by room. I bet you'll be able to search two or three floors at a time if I enhance you."

"*Please* let that be true!" Ro begged when Sophie held out her hand. "Please please please please please."

Sophie mentally made the same pleas as Keefe reached for her.

And as soon as her fingertips brushed his skin, the jolt nearly knocked them both over.

Ro and Sandor managed to steady them—but Keefe couldn't stop shaking.

"You okay?" Sophie asked when he closed his eyes.

"Yeah, I'm just . . . wow," he breathed. "I don't even know how to describe this. I swear I can sense the entire tower."

"I've never loved anyone as much as I love you right now, Blondie," Ro told Sophie, leaning down and giving Sophie a big ogre smack on the cheek. "It *almost* makes up for the fact that you didn't think of this the moment we got here. *Almost*."

Keefe shushed Ro, tightening his grip on Sophie's hand. "I think . . . there's something on the hundred-and-thirty-seventh floor."

"*The hundred-and-thirty-seventh floor?*" Ro repeated. "Um, your girlie here just saved your life. I'm betting by about floor twenty-five, I would've flung you out the window."

Keefe ignored her, clinging to Sophie as they stumbled over to the vortinator.

Sophie braced for an epic wave of nausea from blasting up so many floors at once. But either she was getting used to the spinning or Keefe was sharing some of his steadiness. Whatever the reason, she made it to the hundred-and-thirty-seventh floor with a clear head and a steady stomach.

Keefe stumbled toward the nearest room, which seemed to be one of Candleshade's many guest rooms—one that must've been spared during the previous searches because it was still clean and organized and nothing was smashed.

"Which way is the compartment?" Sophie asked, studying the nearest wall, searching for some sort of seam in the crystal.

"That way," Keefe said, pointing to the left. "There's something over there."

"You're sure?" Sophie asked, frowning when he nodded.

He was pointing to a window, and the compartment had very clearly been in a *wall*! But maybe—

"STOP!" Sandor shouted, jumping in front of Sophie and drawing his sword as he sniffed the air.

"What the—" Keefe started to ask, but Ro drew two daggers and shouted, "SHOW YOURSELF OR I WILL USE THESE!"

"I don't understand," Sophie mumbled. "Who are you—"

"YOU HAVE THREE SECONDS!" Sandor bellowed over her. "ONE . . ."

"TWO . . ." Ro joined in, aiming one of her daggers toward the glass. "I MAY NOT BE ABLE TO SEE YOU—BUT TRUST ME, I KNOW EXACTLY WHERE TO THROW THIS."

"THR—"

"ALL RIGHT!" a new voice shouted—and Sophie recognized it even before a pale, cowering figure blinked into sight next to the window.

Together, she and Keefe both whispered, "Alvar?"

FORTY

LVAR WAS HARD TO LOOK AT.

Not because he kept flickering in and out of sight—though he did, as if he were still hoping to vanish his way out of his current predicament.

And it wasn't because of the deep scars marring his formerly handsome face—though they were definitely cringeworthy. And there were more peeking out under his loose, rumpled clothes.

But no—what made it difficult for Sophie to meet Alvar's gaze was his expression: his wide, terrified eyes, paired with shadowed, hollow cheekbones and a trembling chin.

He looked exactly like the frightened, remorseful guy he'd been the whole time he'd had amnesia.

"You can drop the act," Sophie told Alvar as he pulled his bony knees tighter against his chest. "I'm not falling for it again."

"There's no *act*," Alvar said quietly, earning snorts from everyone. "I mean it. I made my choices, and I stand by them—I'm not going to pretend otherwise. But don't treat me like I'm still with the Neverseen. I'm not."

"I'm assuming that was *their* decision?" Keefe asked. "Let me guess—they weren't impressed with all of the time you spent setting up the world's dumbest scheme to open a gate?"

Alvar's jaw locked, and for a second his old arrogance had him sitting up taller.

But a coughing fit forced him to curl back in on himself.

"No," he rasped when the hacking had mostly eased. "Actually, they blamed me for how close I came to *not* opening the gate. And for how long I hesitated. And for what happened to Umber and Ruy."

"Ruy?" Sophie repeated. "So . . . Linh was right? Tam ruined his ability?"

"I don't know about *ruined*," Alvar corrected, his body flickering harder as he tried to stretch his legs. "But he was on bed rest when I saw him. And Gethen seemed worried."

"How long ago was that?" Sandor demanded, slashing his sword to make Alvar tuck his feet in again.

Alvar turned toward the window and ran a shaky hand through his dark, greasy hair. And when the light caught his face, Sophie realized how sunken his eyes were and how sweaty his pale skin had gotten.

"I don't know," he mumbled. "It's hard to keep track of time here. I only leave the tower when I have to find food, so the days all blur together. But . . . it's been a while. I chased them down as soon as I made it out of Everglen—and Vespera turned me away the second she saw me. Like I said, the Neverseen are blaming *me* for what happened, since I was the one who pushed them to expose my family's legacy."

"Oh good—there's that word again," Ro grumbled with a huge eye roll.

Sophie ignored her, forcing herself to meet Alvar's weary stare when he turned back to face her. "Was that really all there was to it?" she asked. "Luzia's hive and the experiments going on there—*that's* what you meant when you talked about the Vacker legacy?"

Alvar shrugged and then winced from the motion, which triggered another raspy cough. "That's as far as I got with my investigation. But do you really think that's the only thing my family's hiding? With *all* of their power, and *all* of their noble positions, and *all* of that history?"

"Why do you care?" Keefe wondered. "It's not like what they did has anything to do with *your* life. And you got to reap the benefits of being a Vacker."

"No, I got to grow up drowning in unrealistic expectations only to have all of that vanish when my parents had another son—as if that was some confirmation that I couldn't and wouldn't ever measure up," Alvar snapped back.

"Woooooooooooooooow, so this was all just about your brother being cooler and prettier than you?" Ro asked. "The whole 'They don't appreciate me, so I'll take them all down!' story?" She whistled. "Now *that's* pathetic."

"It was more than that," Alvar spat before lapsing into another round of coughing, and Sophie couldn't decide if he was actually sick or if he was faking it so they'd underestimate him.

"I don't care about the rest of the Vackers," Keefe told him, "or what creepy things you think they did or didn't do—you had parents who loved you! I'm pretty sure they *still* love you, even after all of the horrible things you've done. And you threw that away to join a group that can't even make up their mind about who's in charge, or what they want, or why they're trying to destroy the world—a group that left you behind when they fled Everglen, and left Umber for dead, and—"

"You want to talk about being left for dead?" Alvar lunged forward, but Sandor and Ro shifted their blades to block him. "I was left floating in a pod of orange goo while my brother and sister stood by watching! The same brother who'd threatened to carve me up with a knife earlier that night! The brother who stopped pressing buttons to try to save me as the pod filled up—did he tell you that? He *let* the tank fill, waiting for me to drown. He didn't know I was holding my breath and keeping my body temperature in check—and if he had, I guarantee he would've found a way to finish me. But *he* gets to carry on as the golden child, and I get *this*." He gestured to himself—how sickly and scrawny and awful he looked. "*He* gets to hide behind the Black Swan and their moonlark and pretend that makes us any different—"

"You ARE different!" Sophie shouted. "Fitz only did those things to stop you from hurting anyone else!"

"Keep telling yourself that," Alvar said, coughing so hard he had to lean against the window. "But I'll tell you this: If anyone's going to add to the infamous Vacker legacy, it'll be Fitz. Just wait and see."

"Well, fun as this is," Ro said, breaking the seething silence that followed, "we should get this charming prisoner to the Black Swan or the Council or whoever we want to hand him over to."

Alvar barked a wheezy laugh. "You're not handing me over to anyone."

Ro showed him all of her pointed teeth. "Wanna bet, Whiny Boy? That's what I'm calling you from now on, by the way, because that's all I've heard you do. Wah wah wah, nobody appreciates me—"

"They don't!" Alvar interrupted. "And it's always a mistake. You're making it right now. You should be cutting a deal with me." His eyes locked with Keefe as he added, "I know things."

Keefe applauded slowly. "Wow, that was the most desperate bluff I've ever seen."

"Was it?" Alvar asked. "Then how come I know why you're here? I also know what was in those little black bottles you're never going to find because they've been gone for years."

"How did—" Sophie started to ask.

"I heard you," Alvar told her.

"From the hundred-and-thirty-seventh floor," Keefe noted, raising one eyebrow. "*That's* the story you're sticking with? Need I remind you that I lived here—that I know how soundproof this place is? And don't try to pretend you were following us—I felt you up here. And if you'd somehow headed to this floor before us, we would've heard you use the vortinator."

Alvar coughed again. "The fact that you can't figure out how I did it only proves my value."

"See, and I'm pretty sure what it really proves is that when it comes to disappointing family members, I'll *always* win," Keefe muttered, stalking closer—and for a second Sophie wondered if he was going to punch Alvar. Instead, he leaned as close as he dared and asked, "What deal did you make with my dad?"

"What?" Sophie asked, but Keefe kept his focus on Alvar.

"My dad hailed you to warn you that we were coming here, didn't he?" Keefe asked. "He knows this is where you've been hiding— that's why he offered to give Fitzy information about where to find you."

Sophie sucked in a breath, feeling equal parts stunned at how fast Keefe had put all of that together and ashamed of herself for missing it completely.

"So again," Keefe said quietly—ominously. "What deal did you make with my father?"

Alvar, to his credit, held Keefe's stare. "Like I said. I know things. And you're not the only one with questions about your past. I offered to answer one for your father when he found me hiding out here, and he agreed to let me stay. And now here you are—desperately searching for two long-gone black bottles. And here I am, the only one who can tell you about them. I even know a little about your legacy. And I'm willing to share. But it'll cost you my freedom—and if you think you can pluck the information from my head, Sophie, remember, I grew up with a Telepath for a father. I know how to keep a secret. That's why I have nine fake stories tangled up with the truth, and you'll waste *months* trying to figure out which one's real. Or you can pretend you never saw me, and I'll tell you what I know as I leap away. Your choice."

"No deal," Keefe decided immediately. "If we let you go, the next person you hurt is on us—"

"Look at me!" Alvar interrupted before lapsing into another coughing fit. "Do I look capable of hurting anyone? I can barely stand up!" He pulled back his wrinkled sleeves, showing them how his arms were nothing more than skin stretched over bone. Same with his legs when he hitched his pants up to his calves. "I may have escaped that pod—but whatever was in that orange solution still killed me. It's just a slow, painful death—I'm sure my brother would approve."

"That doesn't mean you won't try to take someone with you when you go," Keefe argued. "Like, hey, maybe Fitz, since it sounds like you have a few *issues* with your brother."

Alvar laughed darkly. "Believe me, I've thought about it. And if there'd been any way . . ." He shook his head. "The truth is, if I went after Fitz, he'd kill me. And the one thing I have left is getting to choose how and where I die. And . . . I just want to be somewhere quiet."

"Prisons are quiet," Sandor noted.

Alvar laughed again, the sound morphing into yet another coughing fit. "I'm not going back to that miserable prison. And I'm not going through more Tribunals, or letting the Council parade me around like their little trophy."

"You deserve worse than that," Sophie told him.

"THIS IS WORSE!" Alvar shouted. "Don't you get that? You've already beaten me! All I'm asking for now is a chance to die on my own terms, and I'm willing to tell you what you want in order to get it—how can you pass that up?"

"Easily," Keefe told him. "Knowing you, you'll just feed us a lie—"

"And here I thought Empaths had a handy way of making sure that didn't happen," Alvar interrupted, sweeping his hair out of his eyes. "I'll let you hold my hand as I share what I know, so you can feel whether or not I'm lying. And when you see that I'm telling you the truth, you let me go, and I step into a beam of light and find somewhere else to hide for however long I have left."

"Are you even strong enough to light leap?" Sophie had to ask.

Alvar coughed. "That's my problem, not yours—and a risk I'm willing to take."

"How do you know I won't hold on to you even if you are telling the truth?" Keefe countered. "Pretty sure you're not strong enough to pull your hand free."

"Also a risk I'm willing to take," Alvar said quietly. "Because your mom planned everything *so* carefully—but I knew the moment I met you, you'll never be who she wants you to be. Remember that, okay? Consider it my parting gift, since I always liked you more than I liked my actual little brother."

Keefe turned away, and Sophie wished she had her gloves on so she could reach for his hand, knowing how hard those words must've hit him.

There'd been a time when Keefe had thought of Alvar like a brother too.

Looked up to him—wanted to *be* him.

And now . . .

"No matter what happens next, you can still be you," Alvar promised Keefe. "But you're probably going to have to fight a lot harder."

"What does that mean?" Sophie demanded.

Alvar shook his head. "That's all you get for free. If you want the rest, you have to let me go."

He crossed his arms, pressing his chapped lips together. And Keefe opened his mouth, clearly ready to tell Alvar where he could shove his bargain—but Sophie stepped in front of Keefe so he could see the look in her eyes as she told him, "I think you should take the deal."

Keefe blinked.

"I know," she mumbled, hardly believing the words herself. But that didn't stop her from repeating, "You should take the deal. Think about it—what do we gain by turning him over?"

"Uh, we make sure he can't cause any more trouble?" Keefe reminded her.

"I know, but . . . look at him," she argued. "Does he *really* look like a threat? And this might be our last chance to learn something about what your mom is planning before she makes her next move."

"But—"

"I let Brant go," Sophie reminded him. "He had information about the ambush on Mount Everest, and I let him go to get it—and I don't regret it, even with all the horrible things he did afterward. Sometimes, when there's no great option, you make the deal that gets you what you need to know right then—and if we decide to hunt Alvar down after that, I'm sure we can find him again."

Keefe chewed his lower lip so hard, his teeth left little dents. "Okay . . . but . . . if Fitz finds out—"

"I know," Sophie interrupted.

There was a decent chance Fitz would hate her for this forever—and if he did, she would have to deal with that.

But knowing that didn't change anything. "It's still the right decision," she promised. "Even with the fallout."

"I agree with Blondie," Ro chimed in.

Sandor let out a squeaky sigh. "I can't believe I'm saying this, but . . . so do I. Alvar won't get far in his condition. And I can't see him doing a whole lot of damage."

"He hasn't done anything this whole time he's been hiding here, right?" Sophie reminded Keefe.

Alvar flashed a tired smile. "Sounds like the majority has spoken. So are we ready to do this?"

Keefe stole another glance at Sophie.

"I'm sure," she told him, before he could ask.

"Okay," Keefe said, dragging a hand through his hair. "I . . . guess we are."

"One more thing," Ro told Alvar as he slowly struggled to his feet. "If you do anything—and I mean *anything*—that makes my boy or our pretty Blondie feel guilty for agreeing to this, I will find you and take *great* delight in making your final days as agonizing as possible."

"I believe you," Alvar told her, coughing as he pulled a crystal from his crumpled tunic—a crystal that looked like it'd been torn randomly out of a Leapmaster.

Keefe grabbed Alvar's arm before he could hold the crystal up to the light. "Secrets first—*then* you can make your little escape path."

"You *really* think I can run away?" Alvar coughed again, nearly toppling over in the process.

"Just tell us what you know," Keefe demanded, tightening his grip on Alvar's wrist.

Alvar cleared his throat, needing several gasping breaths before he said, "Your mom was very specific about the child she wanted. She wanted a son—and she wanted him to have a very unique ability. But she abhorred the idea of experimenting on her own kid, like the Black Swan was doing in Project Moonlark. So she did something to herself—and your dad—before she got pregnant. She never said what—but I know it involved the elements somehow."

"How do you know that?" Sophie demanded.

Alvar shrugged. "I'm a Vanisher. I know how to sneak around and eavesdrop—and I figured it might be good for me to have a little dirt on Lady Gisela if I needed it. Clearly I was right."

"And that's it?" Keefe asked, laughing when Alvar nodded. "That's the big mystery behind my legacy? That Mommy Dearest put herself through this super-painful thing and it failed completely?"

"How do you know it failed?" Alvar asked him.

"Uh, because I'm an Empath," Keefe reminded him. "Nothing unique about that!"

"And you're sure that's your only ability?" Alvar countered. "Your mother's a Polyglot, so her genetics are primed for manifesting twice."

"Except she didn't," Keefe argued. "My mom only has one ability."

"Does she? Or is that just what she wants everyone to *think*?" Alvar let that settle in before he added, "And how do you know she isn't waiting for you to manifest again?"

"If she is, she can keep right on waiting," Keefe told him. "I'm past manifesting age."

"Unless she's going to try to *trigger it*," Sophie murmured.

Embrace the change.

"My thought exactly," Alvar agreed. "For the record, I have no idea what the ability is supposed to be. But I know she called it 'game-changing.' And another time, I heard her say it was the foundation of her entire plan. Sounds like quite a *legacy*, doesn't it?"

"Watch it, Whiny Boy," Ro warned, pointing her dagger at his smug grin. "I can make it so you have to crawl into your little light beam."

Alvar's smile faded. "That's all I know," he told Keefe. "And you haven't accused me of lying, so clearly you believe me. Which means this is the part where you let me go."

"I . . . don't know what to do with that information," Keefe mumbled as he released his hold on Alvar's wrist.

"I'm sure you'll figure it out soon enough," Alvar told him as he hobbled into the light, adding, "Remember what I said," as he disappeared in a shower of sparkle.

"It's ridiculous, right?" Keefe asked Sophie in the silence that followed. "I'm not . . ."

There were a million ways to end that sentence.

But Sophie was pretty sure he'd planned to say, *I'm not you.*

And he wasn't—he wasn't part of some huge genetic project.

But maybe he didn't have to be.

"I'm not manifesting another ability," Keefe said—almost like it was a decision he had control over. "I don't care what she tries—it's not going to work."

Sophie had to stop herself from reminding him that shadowflux changed everything it touched—because she'd had a much more terrifying thought that she wasn't quite ready to share:

Lady Gisela . . . was messing with things she didn't understand.

And Tam *did* understand them.

And Tam knew what she wanted him to do to Keefe.

And he was certain it would kill him.

FORTY-ONE

O KAY," KEEFE SAID, CLAPPING HIS hands. "So . . . *that* happened."

"Keefe—"

"I'm fine, Foster," he interrupted in a squeaky voice that sounded anything but *fine*. "Seriously! Why wouldn't I be? I mean . . . sure, we just let a traitor go free in order to learn about how my mom did some freaky fertility thing to herself and my dad, so they'd have a kid with some weird mystery ability. But . . . you know what that means?"

"That you and our pretty blond moonlark probably understand each other better than anybody?" Ro suggested, batting her eyes when he turned to scowl at her. "What? I'm just saying! That's an awfully unique thing to have in common!"

"It is," Sophie had to agree.

Keefe shook his head. "Nah—it's two totally different things. Foster was, like . . . *planned* and *researched* and *tested* and *hidden away* and *monitored* and *guided* and *protected*. I mean, say what you want about the elves who signed up to be your secret genetic parents," he told Sophie, "but as far as the Black Swan goes, they tried really hard to do right by you. Meanwhile, my mom was apparently like, 'Eh, let's drink this stuff that'll almost kill us and see what happens to our baby!' And then it didn't work, so she was like . . . 'I know! Let's make a Shade do some stupid trick when my son's already way past manifesting age and see if that fixes it!' And then her Shade died, so she was like, 'No worries, I'll kidnap this surly guy with ugly bangs and make him take over!' So . . . *clearly* her planning skills need a little help—but I guess we already knew that because of how many times the Neverseen's plans have just been, like, *bizarre*."

"Keefe," Sophie tried again.

But he kept right on going, turning to pace the empty bedroom as he told her, "The more you think about it, the more it all makes *zero* sense, doesn't it? Like . . . I know we've joked about me being your nemesis before, but—"

"You're not my nemesis," Sophie assured him.

"I'm not," he agreed. "I'm older than you, for one thing. But . . . either way . . . it's looking like . . . I don't know . . . but you know what I do know? As I was *trying* to say before I was so rudely interrupted by my bodyguard—this means I now have a totally epic new way to disappoint Mommy Dearest! And—"

"Keefe!" Sophie jumped in front of him and grabbed his shoulders—both of them jolting from her enhancing. "Sorry," she said, dropping her arms. "I forgot I don't have my gloves on. And will you please take a deep breath and hear me out for a second?" She waited for him to nod before she told him, "Okay, first: I definitely agree that your mom's plan *sounds* pretty ridiculous—but that might be because we don't have all of the information. Or it might be because the pieces we've gotten came from damaged memories and Alvar. Or it might really be that crazy. Either way—you can't let that make you take this any less seriously—"

"Oh, I'm taking it seriously," Keefe assured her. "And I guarantee, Foster—there's no way I'm letting my mom trigger that ability."

"Good—because that's my second thing," Sophie told him. "Remember how you're *supposed* to be staying far away from the Neverseen—and anything that might possibly be connected to them? I've been letting that slide these last few days so we could make some progress on your missing memories—and we've ended up having a big showdown with your mom and a run-in with Alvar, so we're pretty lucky that something horrible didn't happen. And now we have a much clearer sense of the dangerous weirdness your mom is planning, so . . ."

Keefe backed up a step, shaking his head. "Uh-uh, Foster. You're not making me sit all of this out."

"No, that's *my* job," Ro corrected. "Remember that bet you lost?"

"Yeah, but—"

"There's no 'but'!" Ro interrupted. "And if you even *think* about rebelling, keep in mind that I still owe you some *major* payback for that amoeba stunt, so do you really want to find out what'll happen if we add 'violated the sacred terms of our bet' to the punishment I'm planning? You *know* how creative I can be, Hunkyhair. You *know* I'll make sure you're never quite the same."

Keefe sighed and sank onto the bed, propping his elbows on his knees and resting his head in his hands. "So . . . what? I'm just supposed to go back to drawing in my little notebooks while you guys deal with all of this?"

"Deal with it how?" Sophie asked, plopping down on the bed beside him. "You're making it sound like we have an actual plan—and you know that's not how this works! We're going to be stuck trying to puzzle out all of these random pieces of information for who knows how long. You won't be missing out on anything, except watching me fail epically at being Team Valiant's leader and Fitz's girlfriend."

"You're not *failing* at either of those things," Keefe assured her quietly.

"Oh, I definitely am," Sophie mumbled, kicking her heels against the bed. "I still haven't checked in with my teammates today, even though I told them I would. *And* I just let Alvar escape—and you know how much Fitz is going to love hearing *that*."

She stared at the verdigris bands on her thumbs, tracing her finger over the engraved initials—*SEF* and *FAV*. They'd been a gift from Fitz—a symbol of their Cognate connection. And she rarely got to see them now that she was always wearing gloves—which felt like a metaphor somehow. She just couldn't quite figure out the significance.

Keefe sighed. "Well . . . at least those are two easy problems to fix. We're done here, and it's still early enough for you to hail your teammates as soon as you get home, right?"

Sophie glanced out the window, noting that the sun was still a few hours from setting.

But she was sure it'd be dark by the time she was done talking to Fitz.

"Let me handle Fitzy," Keefe told her, obviously feeling her mood shift.

And Sophie started to shake her head, but he reached up, gently grabbing her chin.

"I know what you're going to say," he told her, ignoring the loud sighing sounds that Ro was making. "And letting Alvar go *wasn't* all your idea. Plus, *I'm* the one who benefitted from it."

"But—"

"Let me handle Fitzy," Keefe repeated. "He's my best friend, *and* I'm an Empath. I know how to get through to him better than anyone."

Keefe *did* seem to have a way of helping Fitz keep control of his temper. But . . .

"I'll only agree to this if you promise me one thing," Sophie said as he dropped his hand from her chin. "You have to tell Fitz that I was a part of what happened with his brother. No taking all the blame on yourself. I'm serious," she added when Keefe started to argue. "Promise me that, or I'm going with you when you talk to him."

Keefe nodded slowly. "All right, Foster, I promise I won't cover for you."

"Do you also promise you'll go back to focusing on your memories?" she pressed, and Keefe flopped back on the bed. "And that you'll do everything you can to stay far away from the Neverseen?"

He clearly wasn't happy about it. But he told her, "Yeah. I'll keep hiding from my legacy."

And they both tried to believe that his mom would let it be that easy.

Sophie wasn't sure how much Keefe wanted her to share about their recent discoveries when she group-hailed Stina, Dex, Wylie, and Biana. But she decided her teammates needed to know at least *some* of the details so they would understand what they were up against.

She left out all the stuff about weird fertility treatments and focused on the fact that Keefe's mom would probably be having Tam try to use shadowflux to trigger some sort of extra ability in Keefe.

And she reminded them that Tam thought the process would be fatal.

"Should we have Maruca stay with Keefe?" Stina asked. "That way she can put a force field around him if his mom shows up at his house or something?"

"Tam can break through force fields," Sophie reminded her, wishing that Shades weren't quite so powerful. Because Keefe probably *was* going to need extra protection. And Sophie had no idea what would actually be able to stop Tam.

"Have you told any of this to Linh?" Wylie asked, and Sophie fought back a tinge of guilt as she shook her head.

"I'll tell her," he offered.

"And I'll reach back out to Lady Zillah," Stina added, "and see if she has any ideas on how shadowflux would trigger an ability—or how to stop it, or . . . I don't know. Seems worth checking."

"It is," Sophie agreed, wishing she'd thought of the idea herself.

The best she'd come up with was to mention to Dex, "I don't suppose you can build a gadget—"

"That'll block shadowflux?" Dex finished for her. "I doubt it, since I don't really understand how that stuff works. But I'll still do some brainstorming."

"If you need me to enhance you again, let me know," she offered—and almost ended the conversation there.

But . . .

Biana deserved to know about Alvar.

The news did *not* go over well—especially the part about how Alvar was very likely dying.

And when Sophie asked, "Are you mad at me for letting him go?" there was an endless stretch of silence.

But Biana did sound like she meant it when she eventually told Sophie, "No."

That was all.

Just that one word.

But it was enough to give Sophie a trickle of hope that maybe Keefe's conversation with Fitz wasn't going as badly as she feared.

Part of her wanted to sit there, staring at her Imparter long after her teammates had clicked away, waiting to see if Keefe or Fitz would hail her. But she was getting better about remembering to focus on the bigger, less personal problems.

Sandor was updating Flori on everything, so Flori could pass a message on to Mr. Forkle. But the Council should probably know as well—and not just the bullet points, like Sophie had given her teammates.

The Council should have the whole story.

And since the idea of discussing fertility treatments with Bronte sounded about as fun as having her head chewed on by a T. rex, Sophie told her Imparter to show her Councillor Oralie.

The pretty blond Councillor's expression was impossible to read as Sophie filled her in on everything. The only noticeable reaction was a slight flinch when Sophie described how painful Lady Gisela's "treatment" had been.

"Thank you for telling me," Oralie said when Sophie finished. "I'll admit, I'm not entirely sure what to do with that information."

"Neither am I," Sophie said. "But I still thought you should know."

"We should," Oralie agreed. "And actually . . . it's helped me make up my mind about something I've been debating. Mr. Forkle told me that the strength of your enhancing has increased significantly since your abilities were reset, and that he's now hoping you'll be able to find the means within yourself to switch the power on and off in order to prevent anyone from taking advantage. I'm assuming you've not had much luck with that endeavor?"

"I haven't," Sophie agreed. "It turns out I'm not good at journeys of self-discovery."

"Few of us are," Oralie assured her. "And honestly, I think a 'journey' is the wrong way of looking at it. I think it's more about being aware of yourself and being mindful of your power and focusing on becoming fully aware of how everything within you is working in each moment."

"Okay," Sophie said, biting her tongue to stop herself from pointing out how that sounded even more vague and confusing than Mr. Forkle's suggestions.

Oralie laughed. "I realize that probably seems very abstract. Which is why I'd love to walk you through an exercise that might be helpful. It's something used in empathy training, but since my ability is also connected to touch, I think it could easily apply to enhancing."

"I'm game," Sophie told her, happy for any help she could get. "Did you want to try it now, or . . . ?"

"I suppose it would be wise to avoid delay," Oralie agreed, "especially since the challenges we're facing do seem to be gathering momentum. Can you come to my office?"

"Oh, you want to do it in person?" Sophie asked.

"The exercise works best if we can be in physical contact," Oralie explained. "But I'm just now realizing that it's late and you've had a trying day, so if you're tired, we can choose another time."

It *was* late.

And Sophie *was* tired.

And part of her still wanted to sit around waiting to see if she'd hear from Fitz or Keefe.

But her mind reminded her of the ominous words Oralie had just used.

Gathering momentum. Gathering momentum. Gathering momentum.

"Just let me tell my parents where I'm going," Sophie decided.

Oralie nodded. "I'll be waiting."

FORTY-TWO

SO . . . HOW DO WE DO THIS?" SOPHIE asked, ordering herself to relax as she surveyed the diamond-shaped sitting room that Oralie had led her to. But her heart still insisted on beating much faster and louder than it should—which was ridiculous.

Oralie was a nice Councillor.

A trustworthy Councillor.

A Councillor who'd always been on Sophie's side and had helped her numerous times.

She was Sophie's assigned point of contact for Team Valiant.

She'd even given Sophie a makeover!

And Sophie had been in that same sitting room once before, and nothing scary had happened—and surely nothing scary *could* happen in a room that was so sparkly and pretty and . . . *pink*.

Pink armchairs.

Pink jeweled ottomans.

Pink chandeliers.

Pink stones set into the glittering walls in intricate floral patterns.

It was basically Biana's dream space.

And Ro's worst nightmare.

But the Council had a strict "no bodyguards in the Councillors' offices" policy, so the ogre princess would never have to endure the sparkly pink overload.

Even Sandor had been forced to take up a post outside of the massive crystal castle—which meant that it was just Sophie and Oralie standing alone among all of that rose-colored shimmer. And it felt . . .

. . . awkward.

And overwhelming.

And intimidating.

It didn't help that Sophie had forgotten to curtsy when Oralie first opened the door. Or that Sophie hadn't thought to change before heading over, so she was still wearing a simple white tunic and gray leggings. Meanwhile, Oralie's perfect blond ringlets were crowned with her pink-tourmaline circlet, and her pink gown was made from different lengths of tulle, as if the skirt had been sewn together from oversize, pearl-lined rose petals.

"It's probably best if we sit," Oralie suggested, and Sophie obediently sank onto one of the throne-size armchairs.

As soon as she was settled, another chair floated off of the floor and drifted much closer before lowering gently back down.

"Does my telekinesis surprise you?" Oralie asked as she took the seat that was now right across from Sophie, sitting with the kind of regal posture that made Sophie feel like a gorgodon.

Sophie sat up straighter, folding her gloved hands and resting them neatly in her lap. "I know it shouldn't. I just don't see people use it very often."

She often forgot about it herself—which was silly, since it would make a ton of stuff so much easier.

Oralie smoothed the sleeves of her gown. "I'll confess, I find myself wondering more and more what price we pay for emphasizing ability over skill. How much stronger would our world be if we embraced the powers that unite us instead of narrowing our focus to that which sets us apart?"

"I . . . don't know," Sophie mumbled when she realized that Oralie was waiting for an answer.

"Sorry," Oralie told her, "I've gotten off topic, haven't I? I brought you here to walk you through a countdown exercise."

"Countdown?" Sophie repeated as her brain started picturing a whole lot of things that went *boom!*

"It's painless, I promise," Oralie assured her. "Think of it as a way of guiding your mind to a different sort of awareness—one without pressure or judgment. A method of acknowledging what you're experiencing and allowing yourself to *feel* it. These types of exercises are essential in empathy training, since Empaths must learn to separate our own emotions from those we're reading—and not judge, condemn, or interfere with either feeling. But as I said earlier, I think, with a few tweaks, this kind of exercise could also be very useful for helping you isolate how each of your abilities functions and learn to better control them—especially your enhancing, since that's another touch-based power. Did you know Empaths have to train ourselves not to automatically read the emotions of everyone our hands come in contact with?"

Sophie shook her head, "I always thought it was like my telepathy, and you had to concentrate in order to take a reading—at least around elves."

Human thoughts broadcast straight into her brain like radio transmissions unless she shielded her mind, and Keefe had made it sound like human emotions were equally bombarding.

"We have to concentrate if we want to *translate* what we're feeling," Oralie corrected, "but the basic act of sensing emotions is somewhat second nature, and it takes practice and training to teach ourselves to leave the feelings where they are and not pick them up."

"Pick them up?" Sophie echoed.

"That's part of the visualization technique we use. It's like"—she reached for her forehead, running her fingers across several of the pink tourmalines—"I'm touching this circlet right now—but that doesn't mean I have to do this." She lifted the circlet off of her head and set it on a jewel-inlaid table beside her.

"And picking up an emotion is different than translating it?" Sophie asked.

"It is. We can *feel* without *understanding*. But it's far better to leave the feelings where they are—particularly if they're intense or negative. Empaths need to set limits to save ourselves from the emotional overload we'd suffer if we had to feel all things from all people at all times—but I've sidetracked us again, haven't I?" she asked, her cheeks flushing even pinker than her gown. "Sorry, I just want you to see that there *is* a method to all of this—and proven success—since as we work through this there may be moments when you'll wonder what the point of it all is."

"It's fine," Sophie assured her. "I trust you."

Oralie's lips pulled into a smile, and her blush shifted to more of a rosy glow as she murmured, "I'm glad to hear it."

"And wait—does that mean Keefe might be able to stop himself from picking up my emotions through the air?" Sophie wondered.

"*That* I don't know," Oralie admitted. "Especially given what we now know about the rather unique origins of Keefe's abilities. My gut tells me there *is* a way for him to take control—but that may be because I prefer to believe that nothing is beyond our grasp. Which is why I'm excited to try this exercise on you. It's honestly always bothered me that enhancing is viewed as such an unruly, automatic thing. I'd love to disprove that notion."

"So would I," Sophie admitted, holding up her hands and wiggling her fingers, which looked especially marshmallowy thanks to all the layers of gloves.

"You should take those off before we begin," Oralie told her. "And remove the gadgets that Dex designed for you as well. You can set them here so they're not in contact with you at all—just in case they have any latent effect."

She flicked her wrist, making the jewel-inlaid table float to a spot right beside Sophie, and as Sophie piled her gloves and fingernail gadgets there, she noticed that Oralie hadn't bothered to put her circlet back on.

"I want you to feel comfortable as we work through this," Oralie explained before Sophie could ask about it, "and I thought it might help if I didn't look so much like a Councillor."

"But you *are* a Councillor," Sophie felt the need to remind her.

"I am," Oralie conceded. "But for this moment, just think of me as a Mentor. And try to see this as nothing more than another one of your many Foxfire ability sessions."

"I guess I can do that," Sophie agreed, deciding not to point out how often her ability sessions were stressful disasters—particularly the one that was *also* mentored by a Councillor.

"Try to relax," Oralie said, holding out her hands.

Sophie leaned forward to take them—then pulled her arms back before their fingers connected. "My enhancing's *extra* strong with Empaths," she warned, "so I don't know if that'll be too distracting."

Oralie frowned. "Only with Empaths?"

"Also with Telepaths," Sophie corrected. "Any idea why?"

"Not necessarily . . ." Which wasn't really an answer, but Sophie decided not to point that out either. "I'm sure I can handle your enhancing—but maybe it's better if we hold each other's wrists. That way our palms and fingertips don't directly connect, since that's where both of our abilities are the most sensitive."

Oralie stretched her arms out a little farther, and Sophie held her breath as she grabbed onto Oralie's wrists at the same time that Oralie grabbed onto hers—and both of them jolted from the shock of sparks that zinged up their arms.

"Sorry," Sophie mumbled, trying to pull her hands free.

Oralie tightened her grip. "It's fine, Sophie. Actually . . . I think this might be helpful. It's a whole other world of clarity." She tilted her head, studying Sophie like she was seeing her for the first time. "You are so brave. So determined. I can feel that now more than ever. But I feel your nerves—and while I understand them, I want you to acknowledge your nervousness, and then let it go. As I said, this is simply an exercise. Try not to overthink it."

"I'll try." Sophie took a slow, deep breath. Then another. And another. "I should warn you: I'm not very good at clearing my head."

Oralie smiled. "I know the feeling. But the good news is, the point of this exercise is to become *more* aware—not less. And I'll be guiding you to the proper kind of focus. Are you ready to begin?"

"I guess," Sophie hedged, taking another deep breath before closing her eyes. "What do I do?"

Oralie cleared her throat. "I'm going to walk you through a count-down of sorts, that focuses on each of your abilities—starting with your telepathy, then your inflicting, then your teleporting, then your talent as a Polyglot, and finally your enhancing. So to begin, I want you to think about how it feels to be a Telepath—and I don't mean to use the ability now. That would make it too difficult for you to focus. Fortunately, you have a photographic memory, so you should be able to recall the experience vividly. So remember the last time you opened your mind to someone else and searched their thoughts. And as you visualize that, I want you to give me five words—five sensations—that define the way your telepathy works. What is it like to open your mind to someone else's consciousness? And not what you hear or see or learn. How does that *feel*?"

"Um . . ."

Sophie had a hunch she was going to be *very* bad at this, but she squeezed her eyes tighter and tried to do as Oralie instructed.

Technically, the last mind she'd searched was Lord Cassius's—and she did *not* feel like reliving that wonderful experience. So she pictured the mental conversation she'd had with Keefe afterward, which still hadn't been pleasant, since she'd had to show Keefe those horrible memories. But . . . there was always something so natural about using her telepathy with Keefe. She barely had to try to let her consciousness reach for him and . . .

"I guess there's usually a stretching sensation," Sophie said quietly, "as I reach for the other person's thoughts. Is that the kind of feeling you're looking for?"

"It's a wonderful start," Oralie assured her. "But I think for the purposes of this exercise, it might be better to focus on a more emotional sensation, rather than such a physical one."

"Okay, but . . . I don't know what that would be," Sophie mumbled.

"All right. Well. I'm not a Telepath, but would you say that you're forming connections when you use the ability?"

Sophie nodded.

"Perfect. So let's make the first word 'unifying.' Does that help you see what kind of sensations we're looking for?"

"Maybe?" Sophie said.

Oralie smiled. "You'll get it, I promise. Just try to really visualize the *experience*."

Sophie sighed. "Well . . . telepathy usually makes me a little tired by the end."

"Okay—and *why* does it make you tired?" Oralie asked.

"Uh . . . I guess it's that the whole process is kind of draining? Like, I can feel my mental power pouring out of me the longer I stay connected."

"Good," Oralie told her. "So 'unifying,' 'draining'—what else? We need three more."

Ugh, she might as well have asked for a million.

And they still had to do this with four more abilities?

"Really think," Oralie told her. "Embrace your memories of the experience without trying to edit them into the answers you think I want to hear."

Sophie blew out a breath. "Um, okay, well . . . this is going to sound like I'm contradicting myself, but . . . using my telepathy also feels a little *energizing*."

"Good! Not a contradiction at all. An experience is never one thing. Exercise is both invigorating *and* exhausting, isn't it?"

"True," Sophie admitted.

"Okay, 'unifying,' 'draining,' 'energizing'—what else captures the *feel* of being a Telepath?"

"Well, it's kind of . . . *inspiring*," Sophie said, feeling her cheeks burn with the confession. "People have so much more going on in their heads than we realize."

"I'm certain they do. Same thing can be said for emotions, by the way—but that's beside the point. Excellent! 'Unifying,' 'draining,' 'energizing,' 'inspiring'—you just need one more."

An answer floated through Sophie's mind, but it didn't feel like the right word.

"Just say it," Oralie told her, gently squeezing Sophie's wrists. "I can tell you've thought of something."

"I did, but 'frightening' sounds so negative."

"There's no negative or positive here. Only the truth of your experience. And *isn't* it frightening to wander through someone's mind?" Oralie pressed.

"It . . . can be."

Something about admitting that out loud and recognizing the sensations made Sophie's heart feel a tiny bit lighter, and her head hummed with a rush of new energy that made her mind feel stronger and sharper.

"See?" Oralie asked. "There's power that comes with acknowledging the *truth* of what we experience, without measuring it as good or bad, positive or negative. It simply is what it is. And for you, telepathy is *unifying, draining, energizing, inspiring,* and *frightening.*"

"Yeah, I guess it is." Sophie sat up taller, feeling much less intimidated when she said, "Okay, what's next?"

But then she remembered it was her inflicting.

"I know this isn't your favorite ability," Oralie told her. "And I debated about whether I should make it fourth in the countdown, or third. But given your newfound control, and the untold depths of this power, I think it's best to give it that added bit of discovery. So relax, take a deep breath, and give me four words that sum up the feeling of inflicting—and again, don't try to censor them or shape them. Be honest about the experience."

Sophie chewed her lip, replaying that overwhelming moment next to Big Ben.

And she realized she'd already found her first word. "'Overwhelming.'"

She added "empowering" right after, which felt a little strange to admit, given that it was such a dark ability, but . . . it *was* empowering to know that she could face her enemies and not have to hide or cower anymore.

"What else?" Oralie asked, and it took Sophie a lot more emotional digging to realize her inflicting was both *unsettling* and *refreshing*—but it was. Owning the dark feelings inside herself would never be a comfortable process—but purging them all felt like a reset.

And when she repeated all four terms out loud—"overwhelming, empowering, unsettling, refreshing"—she felt her heart lighten again, along with another hum of energy that flooded both her mind and her chest.

Another burst of strength, right at the core of the ability.

The same thing happened after she decided that teleporting was *liberating, surprising,* and *alarming.*

And again when she realized being a Polyglot felt both *humbling* and *uplifting.*

"Down to enhancing," Oralie said softly, "and while I'm sure there are many words to describe the experience, I want you to choose the one that feels the most defining to you—and remember, it should be about *your* experience with the ability, *not* how it affects anyone else."

A word popped immediately into Sophie's mind, but—

"No," Oralie said before Sophie could even finish the thought, and she gave Sophie's wrists another gentle squeeze. "Don't edit yourself. What word did you just think of?"

Sophie shook her head. "It wasn't the right word."

"How do you know?" Oralie countered. "Tell me and we'll see what happens."

Sophie sighed. "I thought of 'frustrating,' because I can't control it—but that's why we're doing this, so . . ."

"We are. But you're on the right track. How does the ability make you feel? How do you feel about the gloves and the fingernail gadgets and the fact that someone could use the ability against you?"

"I . . . hate it," Sophie whispered. "It's so *restricting.*"

As soon as the word left her lips, she felt her heart shift—and not just lighten. It was more like . . .

Like it settled into a slightly new position.

The *right* position.

Uncovering a small, delicate thread underneath.

A raw nerve.

Another rush of energy hummed around it, and Sophie let it soak in, feeling the nerve twist and tighten until it felt like . . .

A string on a violin—and when she let her will slide across it, she felt the tiniest *tug* in her chest, zinging down her arms, all the way to her fingertips, where . . .

. . . her enhancing flickered off.

"Whoa," Sophie breathed, blinking her eyes to focus on Oralie, who was flashing the brightest, loveliest smile Sophie had ever seen. "I can't believe that worked. *How* did that work?"

"Honestly, it's a little abstract even for me," Oralie admitted. "But I think it comes down to the raw honesty of the exercise. You separated yourself from all of the preconceived notions of what you *wanted* your abilities to be, or what you thought they *should* be, and found the pure, simple truth—that for every advantage they bring, they also carry a complication. And you can own the challenge of that without being daunted by it because the responsibility of each ability is something you were *made* to carry, *made* to control, *made* to overpower."

"I guess that sorta makes sense," Sophie murmured, dropping one of Oralie's wrists so she could rub her chest. "Unless I just turned off my enhancing for good."

Oralie shook her head. "Try turning it back on—without fear or doubt. Turn it back on because you *want* it to be on."

Sophie wasn't sure what that meant, but she closed her eyes and felt for that same fragile nerve, thinking of all the good things her enhancing brought, and when her heart stepped up a beat, she let that rhythm slide down that new nerve ending and . . .

Another soft tug had her fingertips buzzing with enough energy to make Oralie's wrist flinch in her grasp.

"Sorry, should I let go?" she asked, but Oralie tightened her hold.

"No," she murmured, "it's fascinating to feel the emotional shifts you're experiencing. Such confidence and wonder and confusion and pride. I strongly suspect that the more you focus on whatever you're doing to affect the power, the more you'll notice subtleties that will allow you to even decide how *much* you want to enhance someone, so that it's no longer an all-or-nothing ability."

"Really?" Sophie asked, rubbing her chest again.

"Is that where the control pulls from?" Oralie asked, pointing to Sophie's hand, where her fingers massaged a spot close to the center of her ribs, just to the right of her heart.

"I think so." Sophie switched her enhancing off again to test it. "Yeah, that's where I feel the tug."

Oralie smiled. "I knew enhancing had to rely on the same inner strength as empathy! It explains so much!"

"It does?" Sophie asked.

"Well . . . it at least explains why your enhancing is so much stronger on Empaths."

"True," Sophie agreed. "Though my enhancing's also stronger on Telepaths—but that might be because of what Lord Cassius said. He said the way I use my telepathy reminds him of an Empath," she explained when she saw Oralie's confusion. "I pick up on emotions with my thoughts, I guess, without having to be in the emotional center. Have you ever heard of anyone doing that?"

"No," Oralie admitted, turning her head to study Sophie. "But given your unique history, I can't say I'm surprised."

"Yeah, neither am I," Sophie admitted. "Though it makes me wonder . . ."

"Wonder what?" Oralie pressed when Sophie didn't finish.

Sophie shook her head. "I'm not supposed to be thinking about that right now."

"Well, I don't know what you mean—but it's clearly upsetting you." She ran her thumb across Sophie's wrist to remind her she could feel everything Sophie was feeling right now. "It might help to at least talk about it."

Sophie sighed, reaching up to tug out an itchy eyelash. "I was just thinking about something that Lady Cadence told Biana and Stina. She said she thinks the Black Swan wouldn't have given me the same abilities as my biological parents because that would make it too easy for people to figure out who they were. And if she's right . . . their genetics would probably still affect me in certain ways, you know? And so many things about me are similar to Empaths, so . . . maybe that's what one of my parents is."

Oralie went silent.

"Don't worry—I'm not going to get all distracted by this like I was before," Sophie promised. "I told Stina and Biana and Keefe to stop coming up with theories and questioning people about whether or not they're my biological parents until everything settles down with the dwarves."

Oralie frowned. "Wait . . . does that mean . . . you thought Lady Cadence was your mother?"

Sophie's cheeks burned as she nodded. "It's not like I *wanted* to be related to her or anything. But . . . she's a Polyglot, so it seemed worth looking into—but Biana and Stina were pretty convinced that she was telling the truth when she said she's not. And if she's *also* right about her theory, then the abilities don't really tell me anything anyway— unless *I'm* right that the abilities would still affect me in certain ways. It kinda makes sense, doesn't it? Especially if it's an Empath?"

"No," Oralie told her—so firmly and immediately that Sophie should've been disappointed.

But.

But.

She'd . . . also felt a tiny shift in Oralie's pulse.

Three skipped beats.

And Sophie's own heart tripped over itself when she remembered what that meant.

"So . . . ," Sophie said slowly, wanting to make sure she hadn't imagined the tell, "you *don't* think one of my biological parents could be an Empath?"

"I honestly haven't given it a lot of thought," Oralie told her, pulling her wrist free.

But before she did, Sophie felt it again.

Three skipped beats.

And Oralie could've been lying for any number of reasons.

But . . . Sophie couldn't stop her brain from reminding her that *Oralie* was an Empath.

A *blond* Empath.

Who'd always supported the Black Swan.

And the fact that she was a Councillor would definitely explain why her identity had to be kept secret.

And the more those thoughts swirled around in Sophie's head, the more solid they started to feel.

The more settled.

Final.

Real.

So before she could think it through or change her mind, Sophie lunged forward, grabbing Oralie's wrist as she blurted out, "You're my mother . . . aren't you?"

And when Oralie said, "No!" there were three more skipped heartbeats.

FORTY-THREE

OU *ARE*," SOPHIE BREATHED, STILL
not letting go of Oralie's wrist. "You're . . . my
biological mother."

Oralie met her gaze, and Sophie searched
Oralie's face—her features—for some similarity.

Some final confirmation.

But it turned out that Sophie didn't need it.

Because this time Oralie told her, "Yes."

And there were no missed heartbeats.

Just a pulse that was hammering as loud and fast and erratically
as Sophie's.

And for a long breath, they just stared at each other.

And stared.

And stared.

Until Oralie said, "Sophie, I . . ."

And Sophie waited for her to finish that sentence.

And waited.

And waited.

And *waited*.

But all she got at the end was Oralie telling her, "I . . . can't do this."

"I don't care!" Sophie shouted, tightening her grip on Oralie's arm.

Oralie could drag her across the floor if she wanted to—but she didn't get to run away from this conversation.

Not after . . .

Sophie's mind played through every smile that Oralie had given her over the years.

Every kind word she'd ever said.

They used to mean so much.

But now they would never be enough.

There were too many lies.

Mountains of them—piling up in Sophie's head.

Smothering her.

Crushing her.

"I know you're angry," Oralie murmured—and Sophie had to laugh.

"Did you figure that out on your own?" she asked. "Or because you're an Empath?"

Empath. Empath. Empath.

Her biological mom was an Empath.

Her biological mom was Oralie.

COUNCILLOR Oralie.

And with that word came another avalanche of realizations.

Accusations.

"You let the Council threaten to exile me!" Sophie snapped. "And you let them force Dex's ability restrictor onto my head! And you let them banish me! And—"

"I'm one vote, Sophie," Oralie interrupted. "*One. Vote.* Out of twelve. I did as much as I could—but I could only do so much."

"Right," Sophie said quietly. "You had to make sure no one would ever find out the truth—because if they did . . ."

Her voice abandoned her as the full reality of her situation clicked in.

No one could ever know.

It was the same realization she'd had when she'd thought her father was Councillor Bronte—only so much worse.

Because Oralie was beloved by the people.

Vital to the Black Swan.

Essential to the Council.

She was the only one who could keep everyone honest.

Even though she'd lied and lied and lied.

And if Sophie told anyone the truth . . . If Oralie was kicked off of the Council . . .

The loss.

The chaos.

It couldn't happen.

Even if it meant . . .

Oralie sighed.

And the soft sound felt worse than a slap.

"This must be so tiring for you," Sophie told her. "Having to actually face your daughter and admit how much you've ruined her life."

"Ruined?" Oralie repeated.

Her tone was flat.

Emotionless.

And it wasn't fair.

She didn't get to be calm about this.

"I'm unmatchable!" Sophie shouted, needing something to throw or kick or . . .

The jeweled table.

Her free arm flipped it over, sending everything on it clattering across the floor.

Her gloves.

Dex's gadgets.

Oralie's circlet.

It landed at Sophie's feet, and she wanted to step on it with her full weight, jump up and down until the metal was a bent tangle and the jewels were a smattering of glitter.

But then Oralie told her, "Go ahead."

And the rage shifted.

"You don't get to tell me what to do!" Sophie said, kicking the circlet across the room so she wouldn't be tempted anymore. "You don't get to pretend like you care—"

"I *do* care!" Oralie insisted.

Sophie laughed. "You let me be part of an experiment! Left me with humans for twelve years! Ignored me as much as you could once Fitz brought me here—"

"I've *never* ignored you!" Oralie argued.

"Really?" Sophie countered. "Then where were you when Grady and Edaline freaked out and canceled my adoption?"

Oralie flinched. "Alden and Della—"

"Alden and Della stepped in and offered to raise *your* daughter," Sophie jumped in. "And you were just going to let them."

"Sophie, I couldn't—"

"No, I get it," Sophie told her. "You couldn't let anyone know. Just like you can't let anyone know now, even though I'll be stuck being unmatchable—"

"Sophie—"

"Just like you couldn't stand up for Prentice!" Sophie added—and somehow Oralie managed to turn even paler.

A ghost of her pretty pink self.

"I didn't know Prentice was hiding *you*," she whispered. "When I found out . . . I've never been so ill."

"But you knew he was part of the Black Swan," Sophie argued. "And I'm assuming you knew they were the good guys, since you volunteered your future child for Project Moonlark."

"You don't think the Black Swan could ever have a traitor?" Oralie asked her. "Back then, everything was murky. There was no clear line between the Black Swan and the Neverseen as far as anyone could tell. Some people didn't even believe there were two groups. And I'd been given zero information—"

"You must've been told something if you were willing to give them your DNA!" Sophie pressed.

"Yes, I was told that I could help them create something—"

"Some*thing*," Sophie interrupted.

"A wake-up call," Oralie clarified. "A force for change and good, who would make our world pay attention in a way that no one else ever could. Make people see things for what they *are*, not what we thought they were."

"And you thought, 'Sounds like a perfect job for my child.'"

"No," Oralie said, turning toward one of the windows and staring out at the stars. "I thought it sounded like the only way I'd ever be able to *have* a child."

She left the words there, waiting to see what Sophie would do with them.

But Sophie couldn't bring herself to care. "So I get to be unmatchable now—and Prentice had to spend years in Exile with a broken mind—because you wanted to have it all."

Oralie shook her head. "Prentice spent years in Exile because of a dozen different misunderstandings. And you . . ."

Once again, Sophie waited for Oralie to finish that sentence.

And waited.

And waited.

And waited.

Until she finally had to ask, "That's it?"

"I . . . don't know what else you want me to say," Oralie admitted.

Sophie wanted to tell her, *How about "I'm sorry"? Or how about "I'll fix this"? Or how about "I love—"*

But she shut down those thoughts.

If Oralie couldn't think to say them on her own, then they weren't worth hearing from her anyway.

So all that was really left for Sophie to say was, "It's late. Grady and Edaline are probably starting to worry."

Oralie nodded, still staring at the stars. "They're good parents, Sophie. Far better than I ever could've been."

"They *are*," Sophie agreed. "But you don't get to take credit for them."

"Don't I?" Oralie hesitated a beat before she reminded Sophie, "Alden and Della tried to adopt you after Fitz brought you here. And

I convinced Bronte to push the rest of the Council to deny their request and assign you to Grady and Edaline. I didn't know they'd momentarily lose their way, but . . . I knew you needed each other."

"We do," Sophie told her. "But that still has nothing to do with you."

"No, I suppose not," Oralie murmured.

Seconds ticked by, until Sophie finally let go of Oralie's wrist.

Her fingers had long since gone numb. And there was nothing else she needed to ask—no more lies or excuses she wanted to hear.

She stood and stumbled toward the door to find Sandor.

Oralie stayed where she was.

But she did call one question out to Sophie before she left.

Oralie could've said anything to her daughter in that moment. And all she wanted to know was, "Are you going to tell anybody?"

"Maybe," Sophie told her, because she wanted to leave Oralie worrying and hurt.

But Oralie was an Empath.

Surely she heard the lie in the word.

FORTY-FOUR

SANDOR TOOK ONE LOOK AT SOPHIE'S expression as she emerged from Oralie's crystal castle and asked, "Is there anything I need to know?"

And he was wise enough to let it go when Sophie told him, "It's just been . . . a *very* long day," as she dug out her home crystal.

It *had* been a long day.

In fact, Sophie couldn't believe that only that morning, she'd leaped to her sister's house to pick up Keefe's E.L. Fudges before heading with him to the Shores of Solace to search Lord Cassius's memories.

She wanted to flop into bed and sleep for a week.

Maybe a month.

Possibly a year.

But the pastures weren't empty when Sophie and Sandor leaped back to Havenfield, and Sophie had to swallow back a sigh—which probably made her a horrible person, given that the tall, handsome figure pacing back and forth along the moonlit path was her boyfriend.

But there was only one reason Fitz would be there waiting for her that late.

And she really wasn't sure she had the energy for that conversation.

She also didn't seem to have much of a choice.

"I can insist that you need your rest," Sandor leaned in and whispered, and Sophie couldn't decide if the unsolicited offer proved that her bodyguard was far more astute than she'd realized, or if her lack of enthusiasm was *that* obvious.

In case it was the latter, she straightened up and forced her lips into what she hoped was a convincing smile as she told him, "Thanks, but I've got this. Maybe you and Grizel can give us a little space, though?"

"Only a *little*," Sandor emphasized before making his way over to where Fitz's bodyguard had just stepped out of the shadows.

He offered Grizel his arm, and Grizel took one quick glance at her charge before she hooked her elbow around his with a wide smile. And as the two goblins wandered arm in arm toward one of the nearby pastures, Sophie couldn't help envying their ease.

They made the idea of a "happy couple" seem so much simpler than it was turning out to be.

Sophie hoped she'd have the same thing someday.

But for the moment, the best she could do was keep her smile in place as she made her way over to where Fitz stood waiting for her.

"Sorry—have you been here long?" she asked. "I was . . ."

She tried to think of something to say that might save her from having to use the name she definitely wasn't ready to use yet.

Before she could, Fitz told her, "Grady told me you went to meet with Councillor Oralie. What did she say?"

"Say?" Sophie repeated, realizing how many different ways there were to answer that question.

"About Alvar," he clarified, and both words dripped with so much venom, Sophie was surprised the grass didn't wither around them.

"Oh . . ." She stalled, trying to remember Oralie's exact words. "She said . . . she wasn't sure what to do with that information."

Fitz huffed out a bitter laugh, turning away and tearing a hand through his hair. "Am I seriously the only one who realizes how dangerous he is?"

"*Was,*" Sophie corrected gently. "You should've seen him, Fitz—"

"Yeah, I *should've,*" Fitz jumped in, without a drop of sadness or sympathy over his brother's sickly condition. "But you and Keefe apparently decided not to include me after you took over the project that *I* was working on."

Sophie closed her eyes, taking a second to remind herself that Fitz had every right to be upset.

But for some reason that felt hard to believe at the moment.

"You know what?" she said, wrapping her arms around herself. "Can we not do this right now? It's late. It's been a superlong day. You're clearly upset—"

"OF COURSE I'M UPSET—YOU LET ALVAR GO!" Fitz shouted over her, and somewhere from the shadows Sandor cleared his throat.

Sophie shook her head in that general direction, trying to tell Sandor, *I'm fine—please don't interfere.* And thankfully, no bodyguards came charging over.

"Okaaaaay," Sophie said, giving up on the whole wait-for-tomorrow plan. She motioned for Fitz to follow her over to Calla's Panakes tree, hoping the soft melodies would clear both of their heads. "I'm assuming Keefe told you *why* we chose to make a deal with your brother."

"He did. And it might've made sense if you weren't a Telepath—and yeah, I know, Alvar claimed he's *so* great at hiding stuff. But come on, Sophie. That's a load of garbage—and I would've told you that if I'd been there! And hey, we could've taken him on as Cognates! You really think we couldn't have found that secret *and* dragged Alvar back to prison?"

"I don't know," Sophie admitted, reaching up to rub her temples. "The thing is, Fitz, it's not like I planned any of this. It all just sort of happened. I didn't know we'd end up at Candleshade, and I definitely didn't know your brother would be hiding out there, and . . . I just tried to make the best decision I could in the moment—and if you'd seen how awful Alvar looked . . ."

"I still would've dragged him to prison!" Fitz insisted, tearing his hands through his hair again as he stalked a few steps away from her. "And the thing is, Sophie—okay, fine, maybe you didn't know how it was all going to go today. But you knew you were going there to search Lord Cassius's memories. And you knew I'd been working on that already, and—"

"Exactly," Sophie cut in. "He'd already figured out how to hide things from you."

Fitz huffed out another bitter laugh. "Wow. So that's what you think, huh? I'm such a pathetically weak Telepath, even Keefe's jerk of a dad can shut me down?"

"Of course not!" Sophie promised, moving closer. "I *never* said that, Fitz. I just . . . I know that Keefe's dad is good at getting around Telepaths. And you hadn't found anything yet, so—"

"So you thought the moonlark needed to swoop in and take over? The leader of Team Valiant? *Lady* Sophie Foster?"

"Wow," Sophie said, kind of wanting to smack him for that bratty sarcasm.

But she took a deep breath and reminded herself where it was coming from.

"I'm sorry," she said, reaching for his hand. "If I could go back and do it all over again . . ."

She was supposed to finish that sentence with, "I'd bring you with me."

But . . . she wasn't sure if that was actually true.

And she didn't want to lie.

So she just left the blank there for Fitz to fill in, holding her breath, hoping hoping hoping it would be enough.

His fingers twined with hers, and she felt her shoulders relax.

"I just . . . want us to be on the same page again," he said quietly.

"Me too," Sophie told him, meaning it. "I don't know why this is so hard, but—"

"Wait, where are your gloves?" Fitz asked, lifting her hand up to study it.

"Oh. I guess I left them in Eternalia," she realized, still avoiding the name she didn't want to think about.

Her gloves were scattered across that shimmering floor, along with her fingernail gadgets. So it was apparently a good thing she'd left her enhancing switched off.

"Am I crazy, or are Dex's gadgets gone too?" he asked, squinting at her nails.

"They . . . are," Sophie said. "I . . . can control my enhancing now."

"Seriously?" He tightened his hold on her like he needed to test it. "That's amazing! How are you doing it?"

"It's . . . hard to explain. There was this . . . exercise, and . . ." Against her will, her mind flashed to the look on Oralie's face the moment they'd both realized it had been a success. She'd looked so genuinely happy and proud and—

"Hey, are you okay?" Fitz asked, stepping closer and pivoting with Sophie as she tried to turn away.

"I'm fine!" she said with a notable squeak to her voice, blinking hard—but not hard enough to catch all of her tears.

"No, you're not fine," Fitz said, wrapping his arms around her and pulling her against him. "What's wrong?"

"Nothing. It's just been a really long day."

"It has," he agreed, trailing a hand gently down her back. "But I wish you'd tell me what happened. It feels like it's more than just the stuff Keefe told me."

"I'm fine," Sophie insisted, paired with a very "not fine" sniffle.

"Did something happen with Councillor Oralie?" Fitz guessed—and Sophie couldn't help flinching. "I take it that's a yes?"

"No, it's . . ." Once again, Sophie didn't know how to finish that sentence.

And this time, Fitz didn't fill in the blanks for her.

"What?" he asked, leaning back to study her face. "I know there's something, Sophie. Why won't you tell me? You can tell me anything."

She shook her head. "Not this."

"Why not?"

Fitz blew out a breath when she stayed silent, and Sophie realized she was going to have to give him something.

"The thing is . . . ," she said, backing up a step to clear her head. It was too hard to think with his arms around her.

"The thing is," she repeated, "I really can't tell you this. I can't tell anyone. You'd understand why if you knew, but . . ."

Fitz snorted. "You know who you sound like, right? Isn't that the kind of junk Forkle keeps telling you when you ask about your biological parents?"

Sophie flinched again.

And it gave her away.

"Wait," Fitz said, his eyes widening as he studied her. "Is *that* what this is about?"

Sophie shook her head hard, trying to stop him from following that train of thought any farther.

But Fitz had already decided. "You found out who your parents are—*that's* why you're so upset! And I get it, Sophie." He took her hands again, gently tugging her closer. "That must be so impossible to process. I get why you're not ready to talk about it yet—so don't worry, I'm not going to pressure you. And I won't ask who they are."

"Good," Sophie told him, surprised by the snap in her tone.

But Fitz . . .

Fitz was smiling.

Not a huge dopey grin or anything, but . . .

He looked so *relieved*.

And as much as she hated it, she needed him to understand. . . .

"I can't tell you who they are, Fitz," she said, pulling her hands away. "Not now—not ever. Though, for the record, I only figured out one. They each don't know who the other is, remember?"

Fitz's eyebrows scrunched together. "Does that mean you talked to one?"

Before she could find a way to dodge that question, he jumped to the conclusion she'd *really* been hoping he wouldn't.

"Wait. Is it Councillor Oralie?"

Sophie shook her head once again, hating the lie—but she had to stop this.

"I told you I can't tell you anything—and I thought you just said you weren't going to ask."

The snap was back in her voice—even sharper this time—and Fitz definitely noticed.

His jaw even locked for a second, and his face was all harsh shadows and angles.

But he took a steadying breath of his own before he said, "You're right. Sorry. You'll tell me when you're ready."

Sophie had to laugh at that.

Ugly, snorty giggles.

Because he Just. *Wasn't*. Listening.

"No, I won't, Fitz. I told you—I can't tell anyone. Why do you think I'm so upset? I can't tell anyone—and I'm going to have to live with what that means."

Fitz blinked as he processed that, not seeming to notice the tears gathering in her eyes.

It felt like he was staring right through her as he decided, "It's definitely Councillor Oralie."

And Sophie didn't know if she wanted to scream or sob or shake him really, really, *really* hard until he finally heard what she was trying to tell him.

But she was too tired for any of that.

Fresh tears streaked down her face as she begged, "Please stop guessing, Fitz. Please. This is going to be awful enough. Just please. Please let it go. Please."

"Okay," he promised, closing the distance between them and pulling her into a hug. "I'll leave it alone."

"Thank you," Sophie whispered, sinking into the hug.

And for that one quiet second, everything was good.

Or as good as it could be.

And then Fitz asked, "But . . . what about the match?"

And Sophie leaned back, meeting his eyes, trying to find the will to say the words he surely already knew were coming.

But after the day she'd had, she didn't have anything left.

Fitz nodded slowly, his face shifting back into lines and shadows. "So . . . that's the plan, then? You're just going to keep this all a big secret and live with the consequences—and you didn't think you should at least discuss that with me first?"

"Discuss it with you?" Sophie repeated.

"Um, yeah—you're not the only one this affects!"

And there it was.

The truth they'd been dancing around, finally forcing them to face it.

"You . . . don't want me to be unmatchable," Sophie mumbled.

"Of course I don't! No one wants that, Sophie—no matter what they're telling you. And *you* don't want it either—you know you don't."

"I don't," Sophie agreed. "But I don't have a choice."

"Really? Because it seems pretty simple to me. You're fifty percent of the way there to fixing everything."

The sound she made was somewhere between a sigh and a weary laugh. "No, I'm not, Fitz. How many times do I have to say this? I. Can't. Tell. Anyone."

"So . . . what you're *really* saying is . . . protecting that secret is more important than your future?"

"Sort of?" Sophie said, wanting to feel angry but instead feeling very, very sad.

She wished she didn't have to explain the next part, but she forced out the words. "I can still have a future, Fitz. It'll be a little more complicated, but . . . what else is new?"

She knew she was mostly trying to convince herself in that moment.

But she really, really, really needed Fitz to agree with her.

Instead, he said, "I . . . don't think you've thought this through. But of course you haven't. It's late. You've had a long day with lots of huge stuff. So . . . can we just agree to not make any decisions right now?"

"We?" Sophie repeated.

"Uh, yeah. Like I said—this affects both of us, doesn't it? Shouldn't we decide it together?"

He actually said the words quite sweetly.

Gently.

Maybe even a little tenderly.

But they were still all wrong.

"No, Fitz—it's my life. *I'm* the one who makes this decision."

Fitz straightened up. "Just like that."

She nodded.

"And you're not going to put any more thought into it," he pressed.

"You've just made up your mind, and that's it—everything's settled?"

Sophie nodded again. "If you understood why—"

"WELL, I DON'T!" Fitz interrupted. "Because you won't tell me! And apparently I'm not even supposed to be guessing—*and* I'm just supposed to be super okay with this too! Like it isn't going to also ruin everything for me."

And that was it.

Right there.

That was the cold, hard reality they'd both been trying to pretend away.

There was something eerily calming about having it "out there."

Like some giant toxic cloud had been lifted off of them, clearing Sophie's head enough for her to say, "So . . . I guess that leaves us nowhere, doesn't it?"

And for one second, she held her breath, hoping she was wrong.

But Fitz sighed and said, "I think it does."

And his eyes were heartbreakingly sad as he held his home crystal up to the moonlight and slowly glittered away.

FORTY-FIVE

SOPHIE?" EDALINE ASKED, SLOWLY sitting down beside her on the cold, damp grass. "What's wrong?"

Sophie wanted so badly to assure her that everything was fine.

But she didn't know how to be brave at the moment.

She'd sunk to her knees after Fitz had left and had been there ever since, watching the fluttering Panakes blossoms fall all around her, wondering how long she'd have to sit there until she was completely buried by flowers.

As far as life goals went, complete petal submersion seemed like her best option—and it was definitely better than admitting to herself that some small part of her had stayed, hoping that Fitz would come back.

She wouldn't have needed some big, dramatic apology—though she wouldn't have *minded* a little begging.

But she would've been good with a simple *We've both had tough days—can we start over tomorrow?*

Instead . . . they really were broken up—which felt so strange, since they'd barely been together.

She'd still been getting used to thinking of him as her boyfriend. They hadn't even kissed!

And now . . .

Now there would be so many ugly, painful, awkward, messy moments and conversations ahead.

She might even lose a few friends.

And she just couldn't deal with any of it.

"You don't have to tell me what happened," Edaline promised as she wrapped an arm around Sophie's shoulders. "But I *would* love it if you'd be willing to answer one question for me, okay? Just so I have some idea of which direction to focus my worrying."

Sophie's stomach twisted at the last word, and she realized how knotted up her insides were. It felt like everything was one big tangle and she'd never unravel it all.

She didn't want Edaline feeling the same.

So she forced herself to nod, and Edaline pulled her a little bit closer and whispered, "Did something happen with Fitz? Or Councillor Oralie?"

The correct answer was *both*.

And Sophie's lips started to form the word, but . . .

She couldn't give Edaline the truth.

And she wondered if maybe *that* was the real reason that Mr. Forkle hadn't wanted her to look into her biological parents.

He'd known the burden that would come with it.

The role she'd have to play.

The lies she'd have to tell, over and over.

And she hated that in a strange way, her breakup was a good thing.

It meant she could tell Edaline, "Fitz," and have a perfect excuse for the tears that streamed down her cheeks.

One ugly truth to cover everything she was hiding.

"Oh, sweetheart, I'm so sorry," Edaline said, shifting to pull Sophie into a full hug.

And as Sophie sobbed against Edaline's shoulder, some tiny piece of her crumpled heart smoothed itself out again.

Because as much as she hated The Liar Who Didn't Deserve to Be Mentioned, she also knew—with absolute certainty—that she didn't need her.

That mother had given her life.

This mother gave her love.

So did her father.

And her human parents had once done the same.

And *that* was all that mattered.

She was officially done with her biological parents.

In fact, she hoped she never found out who her father was.

"Do you want to sleep out here again?" Edaline asked, snapping her fingers to conjure up a giant pile of pillows and blankets when Sophie nodded. In record time, Edaline had set up a huge bed for Sophie to crawl into, and even conjured up Ella while Sophie settled under the covers.

"Will you stay with me?" Sophie whispered as Edaline kissed her good night. And she didn't care if the request sounded silly or childish.

She wanted her mom.

And Edaline didn't hesitate to lie down beside her, pulling an extra blanket over them both.

Wynn and Luna snuggled in around their feet, and Calla's songs filled the air with melodies about seeds taking root and growing stronger every day, and Silveny flooded Sophie's mind with images of the two of them soaring higher and higher and higher—leaving everything behind.

And even though tears still stung Sophie's eyes and she was pretty sure the knots inside her would never fully unravel, when Edaline whispered, "Everything's going to be okay," Sophie believed her.

And Sophie whispered, "I love you, Mom."

"I love you, too, Sophie—more than anything."

"We need to talk," Mr. Forkle's wheezy voice said behind Sophie, and she was proud of herself for not jumping.

She'd had a feeling he'd be stopping by. That was why she'd stayed outside in the pastures, choosing to sit near the gorgodon, where she knew they wouldn't have any eavesdroppers. Plus, it gave her a chance to see that Keefe had been right: Wynn and Luna *were* using their strange teleporting style to sneak into the vicious beast's cage—which made it a little less terrifying to watch the three creatures "play."

But only a *little*.

"Do you think Wynn and Luna are drawn to the gorgodon because it's the last of its kind and they sorta know what that feels like?" she asked without turning to look at Mr. Forkle.

"I suppose that's possible," he said, and she could hear his footsteps bringing him closer and closer. "But you might also be giving two stubborn baby alicorns more credit than they deserve. Children don't like when things are forbidden. It tends to make them want it all the more."

The comment felt like a dig, and Sophie refused to acknowledge it. Instead, she decided to take control of the conversation.

"I know what you're here to talk about," she told him. "And I'm really not in the mood. So here's what you need to know: I'm done searching for my biological parents. And I'm not going to tell anyone what I know, even though it's already messing up my life. So you can skip the lecture or the pep talk or whatever you were planning. You're already getting what you want. I'll be the good little moonlark."

Mr. Forkle sighed and sat down on the grass beside her—which looked like a pretty uncomfortable process given how swollen the ruckleberries had made him. "Fair enough," he said quietly. "And for what it's worth . . . thank you."

Sophie sat up straighter.

She wasn't sure if that was the first time he'd used those words with her—but either way, it felt . . . different.

A real acknowledgment that she was making her own decision— even if it still didn't feel like she had a lot of choice in the matter.

"I did actually come to give you an update as well," Mr. Forkle added after a few seconds. "Nubiti sent a report from Loamnore— and it's good news. She's figured out how to remove those pieces of magsidian. So while it would be unwise to let our guard down, it's looking quite promising that we may have managed to thwart the Neverseen's plan before they could fully put it into effect."

Sophie couldn't return his smile. "It . . . can't be that simple."

"It's not. Apparently removing the stones is quite a dangerous process, so it's going to take at least a week to get through all of them. And given yesterday's revelations, there's a strong chance that what was being planned in Loamnore has nothing to do with Lady Gisela's plans for Mr. Sencen's *legacy*. So there is still plenty of work to be done. But it's positive progress all the same. I've already updated the Council—I trust you'll see to updating your teammates?"

Sophie nodded, wondering why the idea of that felt so nauseating.

Until she realized . . .

Checking in with her team meant checking in with Biana. And there was a very good chance that Biana knew about the breakup—and might've already told the rest of the team as well.

Suddenly it seemed absolutely essential for Sophie to help Grady and Edaline feed all of the animals. After all, she needed to show them that she was doing fine—keeping busy—not sitting around moping over boy problems.

Cleaning her room felt equally important.

And she definitely needed to sort through all of her gloves, since she'd decided she would still wear a pair every day, until switching her enhancing on and off felt like second nature.

She also decided to polish up all of the Articles of her Regency—though *that* was a mistake and made her think of the day she'd gotten them, and how Councillor Not-Her-Mom had brushed her hair and gently applied makeup and pretended to be so outraged when Bronte discussed the realities of being unmatchable. She'd even sat there so calmly while Bronte told Sophie not to try to find her genetic parents—and she'd surely been able to feel everything Sophie was feeling.

But she'd said nothing.

Done nothing.

Just lied and lied and lied.

And Sophie couldn't help wondering what would happen if she requested a new point of contact on the Council.

Surely she and Councillor Not-Her-Mom weren't going to be able to work together.

She spent the next several hours trying to come up with an unsuspicious excuse for reassignment when she realized . . .

It was sunset.

And she'd wasted a whole day because of personal drama.

And there were too many important things going on for her to let that happen.

So she grabbed her Imparter, giving herself three seconds to panic about the awkward conversation ahead. Then she hailed her teammates to share Nubiti's discovery.

And the strange thing was . . .

Nothing felt different.

Biana was friendly.

The conversation stayed focused on the dwarves, and removing the magsidian stones, and whether or not they should try to get permission from King Enki to search Loamnore one more time to make sure they hadn't missed something. They also tried to come up with theories about what Lady Gisela might be planning for Keefe—but didn't really get anywhere. And Dex admitted he wasn't making much progress on creating a gadget to keep Keefe protected.

So there was still *lots* to keep them busy.

And Sophie tried to stay focused.

But a tiny part of her brain kept thinking: *Fitz hasn't told anybody.*

And she tried to tell herself that he surely would soon—tried to order her brain not to read anything into it.

But . . .

She still felt the tiniest glint of hope.

It wasn't even a full spark—and she did her best to smother it.

But it was still there.

A glimmer of possibility.

A faint whisper that maybe . . . *maybe* once pride had faded and tempers had cooled . . .

Nope, she couldn't let herself go there.

Before she went to bed, she even forced herself to pack away all of the tiny gifts he'd given her—and she also made herself sleep in her room.

She needed to find her new normal—cling to it with all the strength she had.

But Fitz's face still crept into her dreams.

And when she made her way down to the pastures the next morning and noticed teal ribbons tied around Wynn's and Luna's necks, Sophie's heart did about fifty backflips—and then did fifty more when she saw the tiny folded notes dangling from each of the bows.

Her hands shook as she untied them, and she needed a deep breath before she read them—and then the world was spinning and her vision was dimming and she had to drop to her knees to keep herself from passing out.

Because the notes weren't in Fitz's familiar writing.

One had particularly loopy, pretty letters—so at odds with the harsh, threatening words:

You think you're safe.
And you think you've thwarted our plans.
But you're wrong.

We can destroy everything you care about.
We can finish your friend.
And that will only be the beginning.

Or you can meet us in Loamnore tomorrow.
10 p.m. in the main marketplace.
Don't be late.

The second note was somehow even worse.

It was stamped with the same symbol that Sophie had seen on the letter that Keefe had delivered in London: two crescents forming a loose circle around a glowing star.

And across that, in Lady Gisela's familiar handwriting, it said:

Bring Keefe.
~XOXO

FORTY-SIX

HOW DID THIS HAPPEN?"

That was the question that everyone kept asking after Sophie handed the Neverseen's notes over to Sandor and unleashed a hurricane of panic and confusion.

How did this happen?

How did the Neverseen get past Sandor's abundant security?

But what Sophie wanted to know was: *What are we going to do about it?*

No one had an answer.

And they needed to find one—fast.

So she hailed all of her teammates and told them to come to Havenfield. Same with Linh, Marella, and Maruca. And Keefe, since it sadly didn't seem like they'd be able to keep him completely out of this.

The only person she *didn't* hail was Fitz—but she didn't need to because she told Biana to take care of that.

That was how she was going to survive this breakup.

Delegating!

Avoiding eye contact!

Hiding!

All of which were particularly easy to do later that day, given the size of the crowd that had crammed into Havenfield's living room once everyone made their way there to argue about their next move: Grady and Edaline, Mr. Forkle and Tiergan, Lord Cassius, numerous bodyguards, all of Sophie's friends—and, of course, all twelve Councillors.

And thankfully, The Councillor Who Didn't Deserve Sophie's Time seemed to be using her own avoidance strategies: keeping her head down, hiding her face behind her ringlets, and standing in the center of all the other Councillors.

Sophie pretended not to notice her.

She also pretended not to notice that Fitz had chosen to stand on the opposite side of the room from where she was hiding in the shadows of the staircase.

"Everything okay?" Keefe asked, and Sophie jumped, wondering how long he'd been there.

Surely long enough to read her mood, so she told him, "Um, the Neverseen just gave us an ultimatum—and they tied it around Wynn's and Luna's necks."

"Yeah, and their notes didn't even rhyme!" he added, clicking his tongue. "I mean, seriously, how hard is it to shape a threat into a clever couplet or two?"

He elbowed her when she didn't laugh, and sighed when she glared at him.

"In all seriousness," he told her, "you *don't* have to worry. I'm *not* going to let my mom hurt anyone."

"See, and I'm more worried about her hurting *you*," Sophie countered.

"Nah. She needs me. Remember: I have a *legacy*. In fact, I should probably give myself a title at this point—but the Legacyanator doesn't have quite the right ring, does it? What about *Lord Legacy*? I could see that embroidered on a tunic."

Sophie shook her head. "You're not going to make me laugh about this."

"Challenge accepted!"

Keefe said something else, but it was drowned out by the arguing, which seemed to have reached a whole new decibel. Sophie hadn't been paying attention, since it was basically the same conversation they'd had before the Celestial Festival—in that exact same room, no less—with everyone fighting over who should and shouldn't go and trying to anticipate what the Neverseen were planning.

They'd had an equally long debate before their venture into Nightfall—*and* before the ogre Peace Summit in Lumenaria. *And* before they'd headed into Ravagog. *And* before they'd tried to ambush the Neverseen on Mount Everest.

Even the night Sophie had gone to have her abilities healed had taken all kinds of discussion.

That's what they did.

Overanalyze.

Overprepare.

And it never worked.

We can't keep doing this.

The words started out like static in the back of Sophie's mind, but the more they repeated, the louder and louder they grew until she heard them ringing through the room and realized she'd actually *said* them.

All heads turned her way, and Sophie tilted her chin up, trying to look confident as she repeated, "We can't keep doing this."

"Doing what?" Mr. Forkle asked.

"This." She waved her arms at everyone. "All of this exhausting scheming. It never works. The Neverseen *always* have some twist planned, and then everything falls apart."

"That's how these things go," Mr. Forkle reminded her gently. "For every move, there's a countermove."

"But this isn't a game!" Sophie snapped. "It's a battle in a longer war."

"The same principle applies," Mr. Forkle noted.

"Yeah . . . well . . . I'm tired of guessing and reacting," Sophie informed him. "There has to be a better way."

"Like what?" Councillor Emery wondered.

Which was a very good question—and Sophie was about to admit that she had no idea, when she realized . . . she might.

"I think it's time to take a stand," she told everyone. "Time to show the Neverseen they're not in charge, like they clearly think they are—and go to Loamnore on *our* terms."

"And what would those terms be?" Mr. Forkle wanted to know.

"Well." Sophie pictured the Neverseen's notes in her head. "First . . . we position ourselves in the Grand Hall instead of the main marketplace, and make the Neverseen come to us. That way, they don't get to rely on whatever trap they've laid—since we all *know* there has to be one—and instead we make them come to the safest, hardest-to-reach place in the entire city."

"Um . . . but doesn't that mean *we'd* all have to go through the King's Path again?" Biana asked, turning a little pale.

"I'm sure once we tell Nubiti what's going on, she can get us enough magsidian to make it so we pass through unaffected," Sophie told her. "Especially since being in the Grand Hall puts us in the best position to protect King Enki."

"Really?" Marella asked. "Kinda sounds like we'd be leading the Neverseen straight to him."

"Assuming they even come after us," Stina added. "Which they might not."

"They will," Sophie assured everyone. "I don't know why, but they clearly need us in Loamnore—otherwise they wouldn't have gone to so much trouble to get our attention. And I'm sure they've been planning this all along, so we have to assume they have a way past all of the city's security—even the King's Path—and that they picked the main marketplace for a reason. So we get there early and set up in the Grand Hall instead and make it clear that that's where we are. If King Enki wants to be somewhere safer, that's his call. But we stand our ground and say, 'You want us? Come and get us.'"

"And then what?" Wylie asked.

"Then . . . I don't know," Sophie admitted. "Probably a fight of some sort."

"Oh, is that all?" Grady grumbled, falling silent when Edaline put a hand on his shoulder.

"I know that sounds scary. But I can control my inflicting now," Sophie reminded him. "And they might not have Ruy—and Maruca can keep all of *us* shielded and—"

Wylie cut her off with a grunting sound.

Maruca rolled her eyes at him. "Whatever you're about to say, stop it," she said, tossing her dreads. "This is happening. I'm help-ing. And you need me, bad."

"We do," Sophie agreed.

"You also need your bodyguards," Sandor informed her.

"Probably," Sophie said, "but goblins aren't allowed in Loamnore."

"Oh, I think I can convince King Enki to make a few exceptions," Councillor Alina chimed in.

"Better include an ogre, too, then," Ro added.

"I'll do my best," Alina said with the kind of mysterious smile that made Sophie wonder if she was planning to use her beguiling on the dwarven king.

"Does that mean you're in favor of this plan?" Councillor Bronte asked Alina.

Alina shrugged, smoothing her hair. "I have to admit, it sounds more promising than everything else we've been discussing. Sophie's right—we're never going to be able to anticipate every-thing the Neverseen are planning. So maybe it's better to just say, 'Forget this—here's what *we're* doing.' I'm sure King Enki would certainly appreciate the authority it demonstrates, rather than let-ting him see us capitulating to the Neverseen's demands."

Councillor Emery exchanged a look with the other Councillors. "I suppose."

"I still don't see why the Neverseen would come to us if they've set up a big thing in the marketplace," Stina pressed.

"Well . . . we'd have Keefe," Biana reminded her.

Keefe clapped his hands. "Oh goody, I get to be the bait! Should we make it extra dramatic and have you guys, like, tie me up or some-thing?"

Sophie shook her head. "Nope. Because *you're* not going to be there."

"Uh . . . you saw the note," Keefe pointed out slowly. "I'm the only one invited by name."

"Which seems pretty desperate, doesn't it?" Sophie countered. "And if we're taking a stand, we're taking a *stand*." She turned toward the group, meeting most of their eyes before she added, "Tam warned us what would happen if we let Keefe get near the Neverseen. And I saw the way Lady Gisela reacted when she realized he'd done that. We *have* to take that warning seriously. So Keefe's not going anywhere near the dwarven city. And if the Neverseen don't like it—tough. *That's* the point of this. Showing them that they're not calling the shots anymore, and proving we're stronger and smarter than they are."

"You *seriously* think it's a good idea to show up in the wrong place at the wrong time—without the person the Neverseen told us to bring—and hope they don't immediately make good on all the threats they made in their note?" Fitz asked, and the heavy skepticism in his tone hurt more than anything he'd said to Sophie the night before.

Apparently, she wasn't just losing her boyfriend.

She'd lost her friend—and even Fitz's faith and trust in her.

Which made her eyes sting and her nose burn, and she told herself, *Breathe, breathe, breathe,* because she was *right* about this, and if she started crying, she'd lose all of her credibility.

But the tears were still welling up, turning everything blurry, and—

"Okay," Keefe said quietly, and Sophie spun toward him.

"Okay?" she asked.

He nodded, wrapping his hand around hers, twining her gloved fingers with his.

And Sophie almost started to smile—until Keefe's back straightened and he said, "Wow, I can't feel your enhancing at all right now."

The change probably did surprise him—but there was something off with his tone.

That was when Sophie noticed the glare that Fitz had aimed at her and Keefe's hands—and she couldn't believe he'd look at them like . . . like . . .

She didn't know.

But he was wrong.

And she didn't want Keefe to feel awkward. So she pulled her arm back and told him, "Yeah . . . I learned how to control it."

Which of course reminded her of the other person in the room she was trying so hard to avoid.

"Well," Keefe said, frowning a little as her mood plummeted, "I *knew* you could do it."

Her cheeks heated. "Thanks."

"What do you mean by 'okay'?" Fitz demanded, not letting them change the subject. "'Okay' what, Keefe?"

Keefe huffed out a breath. "I was saying *okay*, I think Foster's right. If I'm there, then my mom's pulled off at least half of her plan already, and I'm not really a fan of making it that easy for her. If she wants to force me to face my legacy, she should at least have to come and get me, right? Plus . . . I promised Foster I'd stay away from the Neverseen. And I don't think this note gets to change that."

"*Seriously?*" Fitz's eyes narrowed when Keefe nodded. "Wow, you really hate Tam *that* much? Because he's the one who'll pay the price if you're not there—you get that, *right?*"

"He's also the one who told Keefe to stay away," Sophie argued. *"Twice."*

"Yeah, well . . . just because he's willing to sacrifice himself, it doesn't mean we should let him," Fitz countered. "Plus, who knows? Maybe the way they'll punish Tam is to hurt Linh. Did anyone think about that?"

All eyes turned to the silent Hydrokinetic, and Linh let go of Maruca's and Marella's hands and drew the moisture in the air toward herself, bending it into a small floating sphere. "Water's felt different the last few days," she murmured, closing her eyes. "Darker, somehow. And . . . I think that's my brother. I think he wants me to see how powerful he is, so that I'll be willing to trust him. And if that's what he wants . . ."

No one seemed to know what to say to that.

Or maybe Sophie did. "He might also be warning you to stay away—and even if he's not . . . that might be a really smart idea."

"She's right," Marella told Linh. "If you're there, the Neverseen can use you to control Tam."

Linh stared at the swirling orb of water. "But if there's a fight, you're going to need me. *You're* going to need me," she emphasized to Marella.

"Actually, I don't think an underground city is the best place to unleash a Pyrokinetic," Bronte admitted. "Particularly after the fire we already started the last time."

"Welcome to Team Too-Cool-for-Loamnore!" Keefe told Marella and Linh. "Are we all agreed that they need to bring us back souvenirs?"

"I'd rather they get back my brother," Linh said, her voice barely louder than a whisper—which definitely brought home the full reality of what they were about to be facing.

"If there's *any* way," Sophie promised.

Linh nodded.

Mr. Forkle cleared his throat. "So this is our plan, then? Mr. Sencen, Miss Redek, and Miss Linh will remain behind while the rest of us head to the Grand Hall?"

"For the record," Councillor Emery said before anyone could answer, "*we*"—he gestured to the other Councillors—"feel it's unwise to completely ignore the dwarves' main marketplace. And given that there are so many of us, surely it would be wiser to divide up and send some to each location?"

No one could think of a reason to argue with that.

"Additionally," Councillor Emery added, "we'd like to make two things very clear. First: We want King Enki to see that the Council stands with his people. So six of us will be going with you—three to each location—while the other six will remain in Eternalia. And second: We'd prefer that any members of the Collective sit this one out, to add greater import to the presence of the Councillors."

Tiergan raised his eyebrows. "If one of you gets hurt or killed—"

"Then we're not as powerful as we should be," Bronte cut in.

Grady started to insist on coming, but Sophie begged him and Edaline to stay at Havenfield to protect Silveny, Greyfell, Wynn, and Luna. She didn't care that the alicorns could teleport. She wanted someone keeping an eye on them—and if it kept her parents safe, all the better.

Which left them with the question of who would go where—and

Sophie told everyone, "I'll be in the Grand Hall—and let's not waste too much time arguing about this."

Fitz immediately volunteered to be in the main marketplace.

He tried to cover it—tried to claim it would give the two teams a way to communicate telepathically through him and Sophie. And everyone seemed to buy that.

Except Edaline.

And Keefe.

"Anything I should know, Foster?" Keefe whispered as he leaned in, his eyebrows scrunching together.

Sophie nodded. "You should know that I'm *very* grateful you agreed to stay out of this so I didn't need Ro to tie you up somewhere."

"Though I'm game for that, if you change your mind!" Ro jumped in.

A tiny smirk curled Keefe's lips. "Fine. Avoid my question. But know I'm onto you, Foster. And also know that my cooperation comes with one requirement."

"Does it now?" Sophie asked. "And what's that?"

He waited for her to meet his eyes. "You have to take Ro with you—you guys are going to need her way more than I do. And don't look at me like this is all part of my evil plan to sneak into Loamnore. I'm the one who volunteered to stay back, right?"

"I'll keep an eye on my son," Lord Cassius offered, making both Sophie and Keefe cringe. "And I'll ensure he stays where he should."

"How convenient that it means you won't have to risk your life either," Keefe noted.

Lord Cassius shrugged. "Physical confrontation with your mother is something I'd prefer to avoid."

Sophie couldn't necessarily blame him for that.

And miraculously, it didn't take *that* much longer to settle the groups.

Dex, Stina, Fitz, and Biana would go with Councillor Bronte, Councillor Darek, and Councillor Zarina to the dwarves' main marketplace, along with Woltzer, Lovise, and Grizel.

And Sophie, Maruca, and Wylie would go with Councillor Noland, Councillor Liora, and Councillor Oralie to the Grand Hall, along with Ro, Sandor, and Flori. They'd have one less person—but they'd also have a Psionipath, which Sophie felt a little guilty about, since the other team was likely heading straight into a trap.

Then again, she also wasn't sure how having Councillors who were a Vociferator, a Conjurer, and an Empath was going to do her group a whole lot of good—and she *really* wished she could think of an unsuspicious way to trade Councillor Lyingcurls to the other group.

"All right," Mr. Forkle said, and then seemed to realize that he wasn't technically a part of the mission—and definitely wasn't in charge—before he turned to Councillor Bronte.

"Everyone should go change, gather any weapons, and say your goodbyes," Bronte told them, being his usual uplifting self. "We'll notify Elwin to make sure he's on standby at the Healing Center, and meet back here in an hour and head to Loamnore. That should allow us to be in position about an hour before the Neverseen's deadline."

"And we'll notify King Enki about what's happening," Emery added.

With that, everyone scattered to do as Bronte had suggested.

And it all felt very real as Sophie changed into one of the out-fits that Flori had designed for her before their last showdown with their enemies, with all the extra pockets to hold goblin throwing stars and tiny daggers.

She also donned her Regent Articles—even the crown.

It was time to show the Neverseen that she was a *leader*.

And the glow from the lumenite would come in handy in the dark.

Keefe was still waiting for Sophie when she came back down-stairs, his eyes widening as he studied her outfit. But instead of com-menting on it, he asked, "So, what's going on with you and Fitzy?"

"Seriously?" she asked, wishing she didn't feel so much heat burning her face. "This could—potentially—be the last time you ever see me, and *that's* what you want your final words to be?"

"I can think of plenty of things he'd rather say," Ro offered from where she sat perched on the bottom stair. "One thing in particular."

Keefe rolled his eyes at both of them and told Sophie, "This will *not* be the last time I see you, Foster. Don't even say that!"

"I agree," Grady said from the doorway, where he stood with Edaline before striding closer and dragging Sophie into a strangle-hug. "You *will* come home safely."

"I'll do my best," she told him, wanting to stick with promises she could actually keep.

Edaline joined the embrace, whispering how proud she was, and how she knew Sophie could handle anything.

Then they were gone, and it was just Sophie and Keefe again. Alone—well, if they ignored Sandor and Ro.

And Keefe chose to ask, "Seriously, what's up with you and Fitzy?"

And maybe it was because this really could be the last time they ever talked to each other—but Sophie didn't want to lie, or dodge the question.

She just couldn't seem to make herself say the words either.

So she grabbed his hand and pressed it to her collarbone—as close as she could get to her heart without it getting awkward—and said, "You're the Empath. You tell me."

Keefe closed his eyes, and his forehead got all crinkly.

And he whispered, "I'm sorry."

She shrugged, unable to talk—but proud of herself for not crying.

Their eyes met, and she could see the worried questions he wasn't asking.

But all he said was, "Head in the game, Foster. Don't you dare let this distract you."

"I won't," she promised, dropping his hand and backing up a step.

"And when you see Mommy Dearest," he added, his eyes darkening, "tell her next time I'm calling the shots."

Sophie nodded.

But if things went the way she was hoping, there wouldn't *be* a next time.

"Looks like everyone's gathering outside," Ro announced. "So we should probably join them—and whoa, the Councillors all have their hair pulled back, and they're wearing these silver suit things that make them all look the same. It's kind of freaking me out."

"They do that sometimes," Sophie told her. "Are their cloak pins shaped like glowing golden keys?"

"Yep—gotta love how you elves *always* have to be glowy or sparkly—even going into battle."

The word was an icy splash of reality.

But Sophie also found it somewhat comforting knowing that the Council must have visited the Point of Purity on their way there, to remind themselves that there were bigger, brighter forces with so much more power than any earthly creature.

If only they weren't going somewhere so very dark and far away from those Sources.

Sandor and Ro headed for the door, and Sophie fought the urge to turn and hug Keefe goodbye.

Instead she told him, "Stay safe."

"I will if you will," he bargained. "Oh, and Foster? Fight hard. Don't hold anything back. And I'll see you soon."

FORTY-SEVEN

OKAY, WHOEVER CAME UP WITH THE whole 'let's make the elves sink through a stinky bog in order to get to Loamnore' idea needs a good, hard smack," Maruca grumbled, shaking her dreadlocks to make sure the mud was truly gone—or that's what Sophie assumed Maruca was doing.

It was hard to tell, since all Sophie could see through the dim, flickering light were the faint silhouettes of her group after they'd scattered to various positions around the bubble-shaped room. The Grand Hall felt so much darker and colder than it had during Sophie's last visit, and she kept trying to let her darkness vision take over—but she had way too many worries shattering her focus. So the only other distinct shape she could make out was King Enki's magsidian throne—a shimmering shadow in the center. Empty at the moment, since the king insisted on pacing the perimeter with two of his guards.

King Enki had evidently decided that it would be unwise to replace the ruined chandelier until all of the strange magsidian stones in the walls had been removed. And Nubiti hadn't had a chance to extract them yet—which Sophie was hoping wouldn't come back to haunt them.

The dwarves who'd defected to the enemy had likely planted those stones—and now Sophie was inviting the Neverseen to come to the room for a showdown. But by the time she'd realized the oversight, it was far too late to change their plans.

At least they were aware of the vulnerability.

And they were definitely used to improvising.

But King Enki had also forbidden Wylie from using his ability in case the light triggered another reaction. And Sophie doubted he'd be thrilled if Maruca formed any glowing force fields either. So they would have to save those tricks for absolute emergencies.

The only light that King Enki allowed in the Grand Hall came from two tiny, flickering sconces on either side of the massive door—though he'd permitted the Councillors to keep their glowing cape pins and let Sophie and Wylie wear their lumenite circlets. His own crown glowed as well, and was by far the brightest point in the room—flaring with a silvery gleam that made Sophie's eyes water every time he passed by the position she'd chosen, which was an equal distance between the throne and the door.

"I didn't realize tredgeon shell glowed like that," Sophie admitted, surprised the dwarven king would want something so bright near his sensitive eyes.

"It doesn't. This is my battle crown," King Enki told her. And as he reached up to run his fingers across the smooth, simple band, Sophie realized the light reminded her of the cuffs she'd seen on Tam's wrists in London—though Tam's had glowed far brighter.

"Is the crown made of lumenite?" Sophie wondered.

King Enki snorted. "*I* would never wear a crown made of something so common."

Sophie ignored the insult—but might've allowed herself half a smile when Ro coughed something that sounded like "awfully smug for a tiny hairless dude" from wherever the ogre princess had tucked herself away in the shadows.

"What *is* the crown made of, then?" Sophie asked King Enki.

He didn't answer—but Nubiti crawled out of the sandy ground near the center of the doorway and told her, "Ethertine. It's almost as rare as magsidian—but far less useful and therefore much less valuable."

Which sounded like a strange choice as a material for the king's battle adornment—but . . . his other crown was made from a giant sand crab's exoskeleton, so clearly the dwarves had very different taste from elves.

"I've never heard of ethertine," Councillor Noland said, his voice booming even from his post on the opposite side of the room.

"I have," The Councillor That Sophie Wished Wasn't There informed them—from a spot much closer to Sophie than Sophie wanted. "I believe it's formed when lightning somehow connects with starlight, isn't it?"

"Something like that," King Enki hedged.

"Ethertine," Sophie repeated, letting the word roll around in her head. "What does it do?"

"I wonder what makes you all think you have the right to ask me so many questions?" King Enki snapped. "Am I not a *king*? I may not be on my throne at the moment, but that does not lessen my authority! And is it not enough that I've given so many of your kind free rein in my city—and provided my guards to protect you? I've even allowed you to fill my halls with the stench of ogre sweat and goblin breath and gnomish feet!"

"Okay, *whoa*," Ro said, stepping into the flickering light near the doorway, brandishing two of her daggers.

The metallic hiss of an unsheathing sword rang through the air on the other side of the room, and Sophie followed the sound to a massive shape that had to be Sandor.

"Save your weapons for the enemy," Nubiti commanded. "In here you will only find allies."

"Will they now?" King Enki countered, stalking toward Nubiti as two more dwarven guards popped out of the ground to flank him. "I don't remember giving you permission to speak for me."

Even in the dim light, Sophie could see Nubiti grit her teeth. But she dropped obediently into a deep bow and told King Enki, "I'm sorry, my king. I did not mean to offend."

"I should hope not," he told her, angling his head to sneer at her prostrated posture before turning back to pace.

Nubiti continued bowing until King Enki had completed five full circuits around the room. And she kept her chin tucked when she told him, "We may be grateful for their presence before this day is done."

"I find that highly unlikely," King Enki huffed, pausing to survey the silhouettes around him—which he could likely see clearly. "But if this is what it takes to protect my city . . . so be it."

"It will be over soon enough," Nubiti told him, slowly rising to her furry feet.

King Enki resumed pacing. "Let's hope that's the case."

Sophie couldn't have agreed more.

She'd lost track of how long they'd been waiting in that shivery, shadowy room, but her legs were growing wobbly and her arms were feeling twitchy and she was ready for *something* to happen.

"Is your king always this cuddly?" Ro asked Nubiti—louder than she should have.

King Enki laughed. "Oh, I assure you, I am *far* from cuddly."

He stomped his foot, and a low rumble reverberated through the room, followed by the sound of crumbling earth.

It was too dark to see the crack heading for Ro until the ground beneath her feet had already fallen away—but somehow the ogre princess managed to leap to safety, tumbling into the shadows and stopping with a painful grunt, followed by a lot of spitting and coughing.

"Anyone else have anything they want to say?" King Enki challenged.

Councillor Liora stepped toward him, and her glowing clasp illuminated enough of her face to show the tension in her expression as she dipped her head in a bow and told the dwarven king, "Only if you'll allow me to fully express our gratitude for your hospitality."

King Enki inclined his head for a long second, and Sophie found herself holding her breath until he said, "You may."

Liora dipped her chin again and launched into a list of such exaggeratingly magnanimous praise that Sophie wondered how Liora managed to say it all with a straight face.

"I'm sorry," Nubiti whispered, suddenly at Sophie's side. The tiny dwarf's voice was barely audible when she added, "My king is in a very strange mood today. I suspect his crown is affecting his temper."

"Ethertine can do that?" Sophie asked, careful to keep her voice hushed.

Nubiti nodded. "It's been known to heighten emotion and dull inhibition—at least for those in my species. Something about the way the light affects our eyes . . . It's why some choose to adorn themselves with it in battle—though I've never seen my king with that headpiece before. He must be very worried for our people."

None of that was good news.

But Sophie tried to set aside the fear and focus on the useful information. "So ethertine affects every species differently?"

"We're all unique creatures, aren't we?" Nubiti countered.

They were.

And that *could* mean that Sophie was right about the theory slowly pulling together in her brain—but it also sounded so absurd that she needed a deep breath before she whispered, "Do you think, on an elf, ethertine might work like . . . mind control?"

Nubiti dragged her foot slowly through the sand. "Your species is very sensitive to light—more sensitive than any other. And your minds are known for their power. So . . . anything is possible."

It was. . . .

"And ethertine is really made of starlight and lightning?" Sophie asked.

"That's one of the common stories," Nubiti told her. "But if that were true, every thunderstorm with a break in the clouds would create more, and ethertine is incredibly rare. So I think it must require a specific *kind* of starlight."

"You mean quintessence," Sophie guessed.

"That has always been my presumption—more so now that I better understand the origin of magsidian."

"So . . . ethertine from quintessence, and magsidian from shadow-flux," Sophie said, mostly to herself.

And if Lady Gisela wanted to control a Shade . . .

"I'm going to check on the other group," Nubiti said as Sophie's mind raced through the possibilities. "I'll be moving back and forth between you as needed. Hopefully you're never both in dire straits at the same time. . . ."

"Hopefully they're never in dire straits—period," Flori corrected from somewhere in the nearby shadows.

"Of course." But Nubiti's grim tone made it clear how little hope she held for *that*. "Stomp in your regular pattern if you're in trouble while I'm gone," she told Sophie. "I'll check back as soon as I can."

She dived back into the ground, disappearing without a word.

And then there was silence.

Restless, endless silence.

Stretching so long that Sophie realized they surely had to be past the Neverseen's deadline.

And still, there was nothing—and Sophie wondered if she should reach out to Fitz telepathically, to see if his group had seen or learned or discovered *anything*.

But the thought of hearing his voice in her head made her chest feel much too heavy.

"Think the Neverseen are playing with us?" Maruca called from the darkness after several more painfully long minutes.

"Oh, I'm *sure* they are," Wylie muttered, the glow from his circlet swaying slightly, as if he were shaking his head. "I wonder if we should—"

Blaring sirens cut him off—and the high-pitched wails stabbed Sophie's ears like tiny needles.

"What *is* that?" Councillor Noland shouted as three of the king's guards locked arms in the dim glow near the door to form a furry barricade.

Sandor and Ro appeared behind them, their blades glinting in the flickering light.

"*That* is a warning alarm that Nubiti installed at the main entrance of the marketplace," King Enki explained. And he seemed so calm— so steady—as he stood before his throne with the glow from his crown making the magsidian shimmer all the more.

He didn't even flinch as a second siren joined the other, adding shrill, screechy sounds to the headache-triggering din.

"And that's the alarm Nubiti installed at the market's back gate," King Enki informed them.

"Does that mean we're in the wrong place?" Maruca yelled to Sophie.

"Or it means they're coming for us next," Wylie reminded her.

"Take cover!" Sandor ordered—but there was no way that Sophie was hiding.

She pulled two throwing stars from her pockets, aiming them toward the door.

Waiting. Waiting. Waiting.

But the door stayed safely barricaded.

Not even a thump on the other side.

And a third siren blared to life with a series of painful squawks.

"Additional alarm in the heart of the marketplace," King Enki told them.

And still nothing happening at the Grand Hall.

"Shouldn't we go help them?" Maruca asked, voicing the question that Sophie was pretty sure they'd all been thinking.

And Sophie had no idea—she'd been so *certain* that the Neverseen would come find them that she'd never considered a backup plan.

"I think we should go!" Maruca decided, and her silhouette sprinted toward the door.

"Wait!" Sandor commanded, waving his sword to block her as he sniffed the air. "Something's . . . shifted."

"You're feeling that too?" Ro asked, ducking into a crouch and pointing her daggers toward the darkness.

"It's the shadows," Flori added—and Sophie followed her voice to a spot behind King Enki's throne. Flori's huge gray eyes shone in the darkness—looking so heartbreakingly sad as she said, "I should've seen this."

Then the alarms went silent.

And all the shadows shifted—the entire room lightening.

Brightening.

Revealing three black-cloaked figures in front of the throne.

"Finally," Lady Gisela said, tossing back her hood and offering a cold smile as her eyes met Sophie's. "I wondered how much longer it would take you to notice us. Now, where's my son?"

FORTY-EIGHT

Y OU GUYS CAN STAY RIGHT THERE!"
Maruca shouted at the Neverseen, and Sophie
squeezed her eyes shut as a searing white flash
shredded the darkness.

She held her breath, counting the next few seconds—waiting,
waiting, waiting to see if the light would trigger a reaction from the
magsidian.

And when she made it to ten with no fiery explosions, she opened
her eyes, and . . .

Safe.

It was a strange word to think, given their current situation—
but it mostly summed up what Sophie felt when she saw that Lady
Gisela *and* both of the other cloaked figures were now trapped under
Maruca's force field.

She just wished Lady Gisela would've looked a *little* more upset
about it.

Instead, Lady Gisela clapped her hands and said, "Well! This
is a surprise! And once again—bravo for your brilliant recruiting,
Sophie. You found yourself a Psionipath—those are very hard to

come by! I would know—I've been looking. Maybe someday I'll take this one. . . ."

Maruca's smile glinted in the light of her force field as she told Lady Gisela, "Try it."

But Sophie's eyes locked with Wylie's, and she knew he was feeling the same sickening dread that she felt.

Especially when Lady Gisela told Maruca, "Maybe I will," before she turned back to the two cloaked figures trapped under the glowing dome with her. "Then again, you might be a little too inexperienced for me."

"Uh, I caught you, didn't I?" Maruca argued.

"Did you? *Am* I trapped?" Lady Gisela wondered. "Or am I just enjoying some rather convenient protection from Sophie's inflicting?"

"I don't like this," Ro whispered in Sophie's ear—and Sophie barely managed not to squeal, wondering when the ogre princess had snuck up beside her. "She's way too happy to be under that little shield," Ro added. "So I say you tell your girl to drop her force field and let me and Sandor take them down. We should have them on the ground in seconds—and if things get weird, you do your rage-girl thing. Either way, we save all the talky talk for once Lady Creeptastic is locked in a cage."

It was actually a smart plan.

But before Sophie could give Maruca the suggestion, Lady Gisela called out, "Whatever you and the princess are plotting over there, Sophie, I wouldn't recommend it. Clearly you haven't noticed how off your Psionipath's aim was."

"Psh, my aim was perfect!" Maruca snapped back.

"It was," Lady Gisela agreed. "For *me*. You trapped us in here with some very handy hostages. Show them, Tam."

Sophie was too stuck on the word "hostages" to feel the full impact of the name—until the shadows within the force field shifted, revealing the reality of their situation. Then her stomach lurched and her heart stopped and her head was pounding, pounding, pounding—and Sophie didn't want to know which one of the black-cloaked figures was her friend.

Because the figure on Lady Gisela's left had a dagger pressed against King Enki's throat.

And the figure on Lady Gisela's right held a dagger to Flori.

"I think we all understand the situation a little better now, don't we?" Lady Gisela asked as Sophie tried to remind herself, *Tam's being controlled.*

It wasn't him doing this horrible thing.

It had to be the ethertine.

He didn't have a choice—even if another part of her brain was screaming, *THERE'S ALWAYS A CHOICE!*

"Ah ah ah," Lady Gisela said as Maruca raised her arms. "No unraveling my precious force field—not unless you want the dwarves to be without their king, or Sophie to live without her favorite little gnome. That's how hostages work—in case you didn't realize. Now you have to do what I tell you or . . ." She nodded at the cloaked figures, and they pressed their blades even farther into King Enki's and Flori's skin.

Maruca's hands curled into fists, and her eyes were so wild with panic and fury and regret that Sophie stole a second to transmit to her, *This isn't your fault. Accidents happen. You were trying to help, and no one blames you. Just try to stay calm now, okay?*

She didn't have time to see if Maruca nodded, because Lady Gisela was telling Wylie, "No Flasher tricks either. And don't look so devastated, Sophie—this is honestly a good thing for everybody. I'd imagined we'd be stuck fighting a big annoying battle until all of you were sufficiently subdued. This was such a time-saver! And if you feel that rage of yours brewing, perhaps you should remind yourself that right now, no one's gotten hurt—and you can keep it that way if you cooperate."

"Cooperate how?" Sophie spat back, meeting Flori's eyes and mentally promising to get her out of this.

Lady Gisela clicked her tongue. "That doesn't sound like the tone of someone ready to play nice. So let's do a quick show-and-tell to make sure you fully understand the stakes—especially you three in the silver over there!" She waved at the three Councillors before stomping her foot in a very specific pattern.

Five dwarves burst out of the floor near the Grand Hall's entrance. And when *they* stomped their feet, cracks snaked every direction until the room was a maze of deadly pits and ledges.

"Is that clear enough for you?" Lady Gisela asked, pointing to the deep gouge in front of Sophie, which had stopped mere inches from her toes. "Are we ready to have a nice, calm conversation about the fact that I gave you one very clear, very simple instruction and you thought it would be fun to disobey me?"

"See, but there isn't much to say," Sophie told her, feeling her confidence return—because *this* was why she hadn't let Keefe come with them.

This was what *always* happened when they faced the Neverseen.

They'd make a mistake, or a small miscalculation, and the Neverseen would seize the advantage.

But there was nothing to seize.

Lady Gisela could make all the threats she wanted—cause all the theatrics. And Vespera was welcome to show up too. Or Gethen. They could have a great big Neverseen reunion.

And nothing would change the fact that Keefe wasn't there.

Sophie mentally repeated the reminder as she tapped her foot, trying to be subtle with the motion.

She had no idea what was happening in the marketplace, or how much danger the group over there was in. But surely if Nubiti was busy, there were other dwarves she could send as backup.

Lady Gisela sighed. "I don't understand why you insist on being so afraid of my son's legacy, Sophie. I'm trying to give him the best life—the best world—I can possibly give him. That's what parents do. We reach for the stars for our children."

Sophie snorted. "This isn't about Keefe—this is about you! You're so desperate to be right about whatever creepy thing you're planning that you'll do anything to keep it going. No matter how much it hurts your son—or how clear he makes it that he wants nothing to do with you."

"He doesn't know what he's resisting!" Lady Gisela argued.

"That's because you keep refusing to tell him!" Sophie snapped back. "It's almost like you know he'll still reject it—and reject you."

"What a strange conclusion for the moonlark to come to," Lady Gisela murmured. "You've never rejected your creators, have you? And they made you their *experiment*."

Sophie had to laugh at that. "You love to get all high and mighty about how you're not like the Black Swan. But at least the Black Swan lets me have a choice in what happens to me! Oh, and by the way—that treatment you did to yourself and Lord Cassius? That *totally* counts as an 'experiment.' And I'm sure whatever you're planning to do next is even worse. So you can stop deluding yourself. You've been experimenting on your son his entire life."

Lady Gisela shook her head. "Trust me, there's no delusion. Project Moonlark twisted and tweaked your genetics until you became something *other*. And the Black Swan may be okay with that—but I would never do that to *my* child. All stellarlune does is use the natural forces in our world to bring out someone's full potential!"

"Stellarlune?" Sophie repeated, trying to stay focused—trying not to glance at the blond, ringleted Councillor across the room to see how she was reacting to all of this.

Lady Gisela smiled. "I see what you're doing, Sophie. Stalling. Keeping me talking. Hoping I'll say too much, all while waiting for the others in the marketplace to come save you. But I assure you, Vespera is keeping them *very* busy. Her plans are always so much more convoluted than mine."

"Right, because this *isn't* convoluted," Wylie muttered, waving his arms around the room. "And I love how you're totally ignoring the fact that your boy's not here."

"He's *not*." Lady Gisela turned to glare at Sophie. "And clearly you're very proud of the stand you've taken."

"I am," Sophie agreed.

"And yet, for all your bluster, you failed to consider that *I* might be stalling as well. *And* you forgot the most important truth." Lady Gisela stalked to the edge of the force field before she added, "I know my son *way* better than you do. That's why I left him his own message."

Ro groaned and muttered a string of words that seemed to cover every ogre insult ever created. "I'll kill him."

"I'm sure you'll try," Lady Gisela told her, stomping her foot again, making two more dwarves crawl out of the floor.

And with them was a sand-crusted, disheveled blond guy who was very clearly not tied up or restrained in any way.

Keefe coughed a few times and shook the dirt out of his hair before he stole a quick glance at Sophie. And his smile looked more sad than sheepish as he shrugged and told her, "Couldn't let you have all the fun without me."

FORTY-NINE

YOU PROMISED!" SOPHIE SHOUTED AS Ro screamed, "WE HAD A DEAL!"

"I know." Keefe shuffled his feet, tapping his toe against the floor as the dwarves who'd dragged him there disappeared into the sand. "I'm sorry."

"That's it?" Sophie glanced at Ro, wondering which one of them looked more eager to launch a dagger at Keefe's head.

"That's all you have to say?" Ro added.

And Lady Gisela must've seen the murder in their eyes because she clapped her hands and called out, "All right, everyone—take a deep breath! Let's not forget that there are hostages to consider! So keep those weapons tucked away. And I don't like the way that some of you are trying to move right now either—especially you three." She pointed to the Councillors, who'd been silently skirting the perimeter of the Grand Hall, moving toward the door. "Wishing you could go back to cowering in your crystal castles?"

"As opposed to cowering behind a force field?" Councillor Noland shouted back.

"Wait—what *hostages*?" Keefe asked.

And then his eyes seemed to notice, for the first time, the daggers being held at Flori's and King Enki's throats—and he stumbled back, shaking his head.

Sophie assumed he was fighting the same mix of frustration and horror and disgust that she was.

But Keefe had focused on the piece she'd missed. "You're holding the DWARVEN KING hostage?" he shouted at his mother. "In the middle of HIS CITY? Right by HIS THRONE?"

Lady Gisela shrugged. "It'll be fine, so long as you cooperate."

Keefe whistled. "Yeah, keep telling yourself that. You're in a *way* bigger mess than we are."

Sophie had to agree—but she couldn't share Keefe's smugness.

The Neverseen rarely made mistakes—and when they did, they were *disasters*.

Vicious, bloodthirsty newborn troll–level disasters.

And now they had a dwarven king being held at knifepoint.

And while King Enki was being shockingly quiet and submissive for the moment—surely it was only a matter of time before his guards came charging in.

What if they blamed her and her friends, since one of them had made the force field that first trapped him?

Would the Councillors be able to smooth over a situation *that* fraught?

"Oh, stop with the wide-eyed-glancing-over-your-shoulders-with-panic thing," Lady Gisela told her. "You look as pathetic as your little friends cowering behind your goblin—who's supposed to be protecting you, isn't he?"

"Don't worry about me," Sophie told her, glad to see that Sandor had positioned himself between Wylie and Maruca, since she had Ro near her. "You're the one who's going to be facing down an army of angry dwarves. Is all of this really worth it?" She waved her arms around the damaged throne room, imagining the depths of King Enki's fury. "Whatever crazy thing you're planning—"

"There's nothing *crazy* about this!" Lady Gisela corrected. "Though those who lead the charge *are* often seen as such. And I'll endure the scorn, and the risk, and the sacrifice, and the work, because I'm building something lasting. I'm building a—"

"If you say 'legacy' right now," Ro interrupted, "I'm seriously going to hurl—and it *won't* smell good, so others will follow, and it'll be a great big barf-fest. And usually I'm all for that! But . . . you've got a knife pressed to my sweet little gnome-y friend's neck, so I'd rather we all stay focused, okay? At least till the army of angry dwarves gets here."

"Shouldn't be too much longer!" Keefe added.

Lady Gisela smiled. "Oh, but it will be—because that army is currently very, very busy in the main marketplace, thanks to Vespera's intricate little plan. Her style's a bit much. Though she has a true flair for the *dramatic*—but you know that already, don't you, Sophie? I'll admit, I'm a little surprised that you haven't so much as asked about your other friends. You really should be *much* more worried."

"They can handle themselves," Sophie assured her, choking down a tiny stab of guilt.

Lady Gisela smirked. "You mean like your group? You lasted, what? Thirty seconds? Long enough to form one very foolish force field and end things before they even began?" Her smile widened when Maruca hung her head. "And now here we are, me in complete control and—"

"I wouldn't exactly call this complete control," Keefe corrected, "since, you know, the second you tell Tammy Boy to lower that force field, you're going to have to face the wrath of Foster's inflicting—which, bad news for you, is even more powerful when I'm here. Why do you think I decided to stop by?"

"*That's* why?" Sophie asked, reeling toward him. "Seriously?"

"Much as I'd love to watch my son try to dig his way out of *that*," Lady Gisela jumped in, "that's *not* why he's here—nor is it because of any threat you think I made in the note I left him. Or whatever mind games you think I've played. The simple truth is, my son is here because deep down he *wants* to fulfill his legacy. He *wants* to become everything he was made for."

"Wow, you know me so well," Keefe deadpanned. "Please, tell me more about my hopes and dreams."

"Go ahead, hide behind your sarcasm and your attitude," Lady Gisela told him. "I see the truth in you, Keefe. I always have. You're an artist. A *visionary*. And you know the future I've created for you is your chance to be on the right side of history."

Keefe blinked for a second, his mouth forming several different words before he choked out a laugh. "A *visionary*. Sure—that's *exactly* why I'm here."

"Then why *are* you?" Sophie asked again. "Why couldn't you just keep your promise?"

Keefe sighed and shuffled his feet. "I . . . kept thinking about what you said—about wanting to come to Loamnore on *our* terms. And I realized that in all your talk about taking a stand, you never said anything about an exit strategy. So I thought I'd bring you one just in case—and . . . it looks like we're going to need it. Good thing Linh has dwarven bodyguards."

The words were still swimming through Sophie's head when he tapped his toe again, and she finally realized what he was doing.

Dwarven bodyguards.

A signal.

And sure enough, the floor rumbled, and two dwarves burst into the room—directly under Maruca's force field—and before Lady Gisela could finish shouting, "Stop them!" the new dwarves grabbed their king and Flori and dived back into the sand.

Safe.

"There go your hostages!" Keefe taunted while Lady Gisela turned to the cloaked figure on her left and told him, *"NOW."*

Then everything went dark.

The force field.

Sophie's and Wylie's circlets.

The Councillors' cloak pins.

The sconces by the door.

It was disorienting.

Overwhelming.

And Sophie wanted to run—wanted to hide—but this was her chance.

Focus, she told herself, opening her mind, searching for Lady Gisela's thoughts.

If she could find her, she could inflict, and this would all be over.

But the darkness was so thick, it seeped into her consciousness.

Making her eyes heavy.

Her mind foggy.

"Is that all you've got?" a new voice asked—one that felt familiar, but Sophie's cloudy brain couldn't place it, until a blazing ball of orange flared to life, stinging Sophie's eyes and filling the room with heat and light from a flickering fireball hovering over the hands of a girl who wasn't supposed to be there.

"Did I not mention?" Keefe called from somewhere in the shadows. "I brought friends."

"And fire beats darkness—every time," Marella added, her smile glinting in the light of her flames.

"Does it?" Lady Gisela called—and Sophie tried to track the sound of the voice, now that her head was clearing.

But the fire was snuffed out, and the sleepiness settled in and—

Another new voice shouted, "Stop it, Tam!"

Sophie was pretty sure every person was thinking the same question.

But the only voice that whispered it out loud was dark and haunted.

A ghost in the shadows.

"Linh?"

The darkness thinned, and a black-cloaked figure melted out of the shadows, tossing back his hood as he strode forward, and another fireball flashed to life—blue this time, and casting a wide enough glow to reveal Linh standing next to Marella, still shaking sand out of her hair.

"How are you here?" he whispered, his silvery eyes turning glassy.

"Our bodyguards," she told him, reaching out to gather his tears, letting them shine through the air around them. "And Keefe."

The room dimmed again.

Marella swelled her fireball brighter, and Linh grabbed her brother's arm, not letting him disappear.

"You shouldn't be here," he murmured. "I told you not to be here."

"I know," Linh said, adding his fresh tears to the others. Surrounding them in their own kind of starlight. "But I *am* here. Because we're stronger together."

"For the record, Hunkyhair," Ro called from somewhere behind Sophie, "*that* was the answer you should've given."

"And much as I hate to break up this *touching* brother-sister bonding moment," Lady Gisela added, her voice echoing around the room—everywhere and nowhere—"NEUTRALIZE THE HYDRO-KINETIC!"

Tam straightened, his body turning soldier-rigid, and his eyes clouded as he raised his hands, opening his mouth, but . . .

He shook his head and stumbled back—crying out in pain and curling his arms around himself and shaking, shaking, shaking.

Linh scrambled toward him, but Tam raised his hands again, this time like stop signs. "Stay back! It's not safe! *I'm* not safe!"

He pulled down his sleeves, revealing the glowing bonds on his wrists—which definitely were brighter than King Enki's crown.

Sophie could barely look at them.

And every time she tried, it felt *wrong*.

"Think there's any way a Flasher can break those things?" Sophie asked Wylie, who was already making his way closer—with Maruca and Sandor right behind him.

"I'll try my best," Wylie promised.

"And it will never work," an unfamiliar female voice told him. "Only the person who sealed the bonds can unseal them."

"And I'm guessing that was you?" Keefe called into the darkness.

"It was," agreed the voice, which had to belong to the other member of the Neverseen—who was clearly the person they needed.

More fire, Sophie transmitted to Marella, and Marella made her blue fireball double in size.

Heat licked Sophie's cheeks as she searched the brighter space, relieved to finally see all of her friends.

But there were still too many shadows and cracks and crevices.

Keep her talking, Sophie transmitted to Keefe as she opened up her mind.

She was finding this girl—*now.*

And she was *making* her set Tam free.

"That didn't bother you? Treating someone like that?" Keefe called to the girl, obeying Sophie's request. "Didn't make you wonder what they'd do to you if they were willing to do that to him?"

"You're wasting your time," Lady Gisela told him. "Glimmer's more loyal to our cause than anyone I've ever met."

"*Glimmer,*" Keefe repeated. "Wooooow. Okay, then. How'd you pick *that* name?"

"Am I the only one wondering what we're still doing here?" someone whispered in Sophie's ear—arguably the last voice that Sophie wanted to hear. "This is a standoff now," her biological mother informed her, "and our side seems to be out of moves—and King Enki's surely rallying the troops. We need to get out of here."

"How?" Sophie whispered back. "Tam can't leave with those things on his wrists, and Linh's not going to leave her brother, and I'm not leaving anyone behind. And even if we had a fix for all of that, *how* are we supposed to get out of the city?"

Keefe was right—they *didn't* have an exit strategy.

And *his* hadn't worked.

Which was strange.

He'd dragged even more of their friends into danger—he wouldn't have done that unless they were essential to his plan.

And all Marella had done was make a couple of flames.

And all Linh had done was say hi to Tam.

Was that really all that was supposed to happen?

That was when she noticed the way Keefe kept shuffling his feet as he tried to draw out the conversation.

The very deliberate, repetitive pattern—as if he were calling for more dwarves and nothing was happening.

Which made her wonder how bad it was in the main marketplace.

What was Vespera doing?

It had to be something *huge* for King Enki to wait this long to come after the elves who'd pressed a knife to his throat.

Bile soured Sophie's tongue, and she wondered if it was a mistake that she hadn't reached out to Fitz—but were they supposed to do that if things went bad?

She closed her eyes, deciding it had to be better to *know.*

But as she stretched out her concentration . . . she heard it.

A low, audible rumble in the ground.

"I guess that means it's time," Lady Gisela said, her voice echoing everywhere as the ground shook beneath their feet.

"Time to find out what happens when you take a *king* hostage," Councillor Liora told her. "Don't expect us to speak in your defense."

"Oh, I won't," Lady Gisela assured her as a dozen dwarves burst out of the floor—and a dozen more after that.

And Sophie shouted to her friends, "Raise your hands!"

Like humans did when they faced the police, to make it clear they posed no threat.

It's going to be fine, she told herself. *Keefe's the one who helped rescue him.*

Surely this is only between him and the Neverseen.

But when she glanced toward the dwarven king—who now stood blocking the door—his eyes were fixed on her.

And they were *not* friendly.

He held her stare as he raised his leg and slammed his foot down hard enough to crack the floor and . . .

Then there was chaos.

And Sophie understood why humans loved to say "it was all a blur," because her brain had no way to process what had happened.

Screams and gasps and grunts and pain—but only for a few heartbeats—and then Sophie realized she was now on the floor, limbs bound, something heavy on her back.

And she wasn't the only one.

She couldn't turn her head much, but she could see Keefe and Maruca and Wylie and Sandor and Ro.

Only Keefe was conscious.

And Sophie's mind fixated on the "how"—*how* the dwarves could strike so fast, so true, and take out their group in seconds.

But when she found her voice, she shoved down those questions, focusing on the fact that she needed King Enki to know. "We weren't a part of this."

She expected him to argue.

But he told her, "I know."

"Then why?" Sophie wondered, still trying to figure out the misunderstanding as King Enki crouched in front of her.

"Your Council and your Black Swan have come to my city many times—telling me to trust them and no others. Begging for my help. My faith. My fealty. Offering their help in exchange, as if I haven't noticed how many times they've failed. As if my people haven't had to help them rebuild, over and over and over, after their defeats. As if I didn't wonder if they ever had a victory. And then they came to me again, telling me they were now allies. Stronger. Smarter. And they told me the next attack would be in my city. Promised to stop it. Told me to trust. But they had no plan. And they sent me *children*. So I knew how it would end. And I made my own alliance. With the ones who *win*."

Sophie's mouth went dry.

And her heart pounded harder, harder, harder as she strained her neck, searching the prone figures around her for any sign of a black cloak.

"Don't struggle," King Enki told her as she tried to twist free, reaching for the strength in her core. "And don't dare use any of your abilities. Your friends are unconscious now—but I can finish them easily, starting with your goblin, ogre, and gnome."

Keefe barked a vicious laugh. "You're seriously allying with the people who had a knife to your throat a few minutes ago instead of the people who helped you escape?"

King Enki marched over to where Keefe lay struggling against the dwarf holding him. "If you think I couldn't have knocked the Shade to the ground and stabbed him with his own weapon—or simply tunneled away—you're a bigger fool than I imagined."

"Then why . . . ?" Sophie started to ask.

But it wasn't hard to figure out.

Not with hindsight, at least.

"You needed to wait for Keefe to arrive," Sophie said, certain Lady Gisela was nearby listening. "So you let King Enki play hostage."

"It wasn't my *most* clever improvisation—but it got the job done," she agreed. "Though King Enki still owes me one more thing."

King Enki sighed. "If you go back on your word—"

"I *won't*," Lady Gisela assured him.

"Then so be it," King Enki said, and Sophie twisted and fought, but it didn't matter. She could only watch as he dragged Keefe over to his throne and dropped him onto the seat—then placed his crown over Keefe's head.

Keefe looked like he was trying to thrash and kick, but his body wouldn't—couldn't—move.

"It's the magsidian," King Enki told him. "I carved new facets in the throne this morning to make it draw body heat. There's no way you can resist the pull. So I'd save your energy. It sounds like you're going to need it."

With that he stood tall and turned to Lady Gisela and said, "My debt is fulfilled—do your ceremony."

"It's not a ceremony," Lady Gisela corrected. "It's a transformation. The beginning of a brilliant new legacy. And it starts now."

FIFTY

O . . . MY LEGACY IS . . . *KING OF THE dwarves*?" Keefe asked, trying for a smirk—but it looked too much like a grimace. "Gotta admit, I did *not* see that coming!"

And somewhere out of Sophie's line of sight, there was a very loud sigh.

"You really will make a joke out of *anything*, won't you?" Lady Gisela asked from the same direction.

"Um, you just had King Enki shove me onto his throne and *crown me*—what else am I supposed to think?" Keefe argued. "Where is he, by the way? I feel like he owes me a bow—and an 'As you wish, King Keefe!'"

He tried to crane his neck to search the shadowy Grand Hall, but the pull of the altered magsidian throne must've been too strong to allow him the motion.

Sophie wasn't having much better luck with her own ability to move.

The dwarf pinning her to the scratchy, sandy floor was hyper-vigilant—*never* lightening the pressure on her back and shoulders, even when it made Sophie cough. And the ropes binding her hands and feet were so tight, even the slightest twitch made them slice into her skin.

Part of her wanted to thrash anyway.

She could handle the pain.

But . . . she was the *only* one from their group—besides Keefe—who was still conscious. And while she was sure that wasn't an accident, she didn't want to give Keefe's mom any reason to change her mind.

So she held still.

Swallowing her questions.

Thinking, thinking, thinking.

Trying to come up with a way out of this.

"The king left," Lady Gisela told Keefe. "Said something about not wanting to witness the further desecration of a royal relic and dived into the floor—and I suppose I can't blame him. It is a lovely throne. But I need the magsidian. And the ethertine in your crown. I had that made specially for you, by the way. Just for this. And it wasn't easy. It was even harder convincing King Enki to wear it as his own to keep anyone from getting too suspicious. But it was worth it—everything came together, despite the few hiccups we had along the way."

"Am I supposed to say thank you?" Keefe wondered.

"Yes, Keefe, you should. And someday, you *will*. For now, you're welcome to keep hating me."

"Didn't realize I needed your permission for that, but okay. Great!"

Yet another sigh. "I resigned myself to the role of the 'bad guy' long ago, Keefe. It's unfair. And inaccurate. But if that's how you need to see me to process what's about to happen—so be it."

"Uh, it's not about what I *need*. Like . . . are you seeing this situation? You attacked all my friends. Left them all unconscious over there—"

"Not *all* of them," Lady Gisela corrected. "Sophie's still awake—for *now*. In case we need her."

Sophie's heart stalled at the sound of her name.

And there was no need to stay silent anymore, so she asked, "Need me for what?"

"To ensure my son cooperates."

There was a dark edge to the words that made it clear she wouldn't be looking to Sophie for pep talks.

"Now that we understand each other," Lady Gisela said firmly, "we should get started. The deal I made with King Enki only buys me so much of his patience."

"What'd you have to give him?" Keefe asked.

"Nothing you need to concern yourself with."

"Aw, come on—I'm curious! Like, what's the going price for ultimate betrayal these days? And was the 'ruining your son's life' part of the fee—or was that just a fun bonus?"

He nailed the joke *almost* perfectly—but Sophie still caught the hurt laced through it.

And she wondered how his mother could reject it so easily.

But Lady Gisela stalked closer—finally stepping into Sophie's line of sight—and Sophie's hands clenched into fists at the way she loomed over her son. "For the *last* time, I'm not destroying anything. I'm allowing you to become something vital. And I need you to accept that, because the harder you fight what's about to happen, the more you'll suffer."

"That's riiiiiiiiight," Keefe said, and the smugness in his tone made Sophie wonder if he'd be propping up his feet and slouching across the throne if he were capable of moving in that moment. "I'm supposed to—how did you put it? 'Embrace the change'? Yeeeeeeeeaaaaaaaaah. Hate to break it to you, but . . . I'm not feeling very embrace-y. Thanks for playing, though!"

Lady Gisela shook her head, grabbing his chin and pinching it as she angled his face toward her. "This isn't a joke, Keefe. And it's time for you to stop thinking that you have any control over what's about to happen. You don't. There's no getting out of this. You can't stop it. And neither can *you*."

She glanced over her shoulder at someone Sophie couldn't see—but Sophie recognized the deep, weary voice all too well as Tam told Lady Gisela, "I've resisted the bonds before."

"Not for this firm of a command—but let's also not forget that I have your sister right there." She pointed roughly in Sophie's direction. "She's unconscious right now. But I can wake her up if you need motivation. Or maybe it would be better to make sure she never wakes up again—and you can drop those hands *right now*," she added, shaking her head. Her eyes shifted to Sophie as she called out, "Are all boys this stubborn and angsty?"

"Pretty sure they are when you're holding them prisoner and threatening to torture their friends and family," Sophie snapped back.

Lady Gisela shook her head again. "Don't you get it? That's a *gift*. Freedom isn't always as wonderful as we want to believe. Choice comes with responsibility. With consequences. With *guilt*. I'm sparing all of you from that—yes, even you, Sophie. Why do you think I went to such ridiculous lengths to leave you completely powerless? Do you realize how challenging that is? You have *five* abilities! Honestly, if you didn't insist on working with friends, I'd probably never be able to thwart you. But all those moving pieces and variables give me room to play. It still takes time—this moment right now has been *months* in the making. And you're lying there hating me. Surely still trying to figure out some way to resist me—which doesn't exist, by the way—completely missing the fact that thanks to my hard work, you'll be able to go home tonight, comfortable in the knowledge that you truly tried your hardest and that it was simply an impossible situation. You're welcome."

Keefe barked a bitter laugh. "That's right, ladies and gentlemen. Mommy Dearest wants us to thank her for being so evil!"

Lady Gisela rolled her eyes. "Never mind. Time to focus."

She waved Tam closer, and when he stepped into Sophie's line of sight, it was impossible not to stare at his glowing bonds.

Sophie knew how it felt to be powerless—but she couldn't imagine how much worse it would be for someone else to have *control*.

And not just anyone.

Lady Gisela.

Sophie's insides squirmed just thinking about it. And she wondered how much it had cost Tam to give her that warning about Keefe.

How desperate he'd been to avoid the exact situation they were now in.

I'm sorry, Tam, she transmitted. *This isn't your fault. I hope you know that. No one's going to blame you.*

He angled his face away, but Sophie could still see how hard he was blinking.

And she wanted to say more, but Lady Gisela clapped her hands, demanding attention.

"What's about to happen couldn't be simpler. On my command, Tam, you'll launch a bolt of shadowflux at the stone in the wall that I showed you earlier. You *shouldn't* have to do anything else, but since this is all untested—and I'm assuming you'd prefer my son to survive this—"

"Eh, I don't know if that's a safe assumption," Keefe interrupted. "Bangs Boy and I aren't exactly besties. Also, it's super awesome hearing how 'untested' this is."

Sophie had gotten stuck on that same word.

"Still trying to convince yourself this isn't an experiment?" she spat.

"Assuming you'd prefer my son to survive this," Lady Gisela repeated to Tam, ignoring Sophie and Keefe, "you'll monitor the reaction and step in as needed. The command I'll be giving you is to rely on your instincts—"

"And then you'll let me go?" Tam cut in. "That's what you told me. I train with you. I hear you out about all your *reasons*. I do the thing. And then I'm done and my sister is safe and my friends are safe and these are gone"—he patted the bonds on his wrists—"and it's up to me if I want to come back."

He stole a glance at Sophie after he said it, as if he were worried she might hate him for bargaining about this.

What other choice do you have? she transmitted to reassure him.

And she held her breath, whooshing it out as a sigh of relief when Lady Gisela told him, "Yes, Tam. That's the deal."

"And did you just say 'do the thing'?" Keefe jumped in.

"What else am I supposed to call this?" Tam countered.

Keefe considered that for a second. "Fair enough."

"Yes, well, while Tam is 'doing the thing,'" Lady Gisela said with an eye roll, "Glimmer will send a bolt of light at the crown to activate the ethertine to balance the reaction."

"That's what the crown's for?" Sophie asked.

She hadn't meant to blurt out the question—and Lady Gisela must've guessed why she was asking because she told her, "Ethertine only affects Shades the way you're thinking."

And Sophie's heart lightened ever so slightly.

Everything was still terrible.

This was still happening.

But at least she wouldn't have to wonder if that crown would somehow affect Keefe's mind.

"Back to what I was saying," Lady Gisela added. "After Glimmer adds light to the reaction, it's a waiting game—don't ask how long, because I don't know. And Keefe: You already know your job. You have to *embrace the change*. Don't fight it. Don't fear it. Even when there's pain. Think of it as being forged by fire."

"Who's jealous of my life right now?" Keefe wondered.

The panic hidden behind the joke nearly broke Sophie's heart—but it also made her realize . . .

Even if she couldn't save Keefe from this—

Maybe she could get them *through*.

So as Lady Gisela showed Tam where to stand, Sophie stretched out her consciousness, making sure she had Keefe's permission to slip into his mind.

I'll be with you the whole time, she promised. *I won't let anything bad happen to you.*

Pretty sure you can't control that but—

Uh, yes I can. I mean . . . I can't stop any pain—I wish I could—but . . . I've been in broken minds and lost minds and ogre minds and gnomish minds and so many other types of minds—and I've done healings and probes and all kinds of fancy Telepath things that will sound super boring, so I'll stop there. And the one thing I've seen over and over is that we all have . . . an inner sense of self. I'm probably not explaining this very well, but just . . . when I've had to heal people, THAT'S how I've done it. I just find that true piece of themselves and bring it back, and that makes them THEM again. So when this goes down, I'll be right here with you. And I'm not going to let you lose YOU. Trust the Telepath. My other abilities may let me down sometimes, but this one always comes through.

They locked eyes across the room, and Sophie's heart ached when he let his walls come down, showing her all the fear and fury and doubt and worry and hate he was feeling in that moment because of what was about to happen.

Trust the Telepath, she repeated.

I do. And she could feel how strongly he meant those words. *I'm . . . really glad I met you, Sophie.*

Me too, she told him, hoping he could feel how much she meant it too.

"Are we ready?" Lady Gisela asked, clapping her hands again and snapping Sophie back to the cold, shadowy reality of that dim, miserable room.

But she could also still feel the warm hum of the mental connection between Keefe and her. Like their minds were holding hands—

which might've been the goofiest, sappiest thought she'd ever had. But it helped her feel a little less devastated, seeing Keefe alone on that cruel throne that had been rigged to trap him there like flypaper, crowned with a responsibility he should never have to carry.

She was pinned and tied up and too far away to reach him.

But they could both still hold on.

Hold on, she told Keefe, in case he needed the reminder too. *I'm here,* she added as Tam stepped into position. *We'll get through this. Like I said: Trust the Telepath.*

I do, Keefe promised again.

And because he was Keefe, his lips pulled into a smirk as he focused on the wary Shade standing across from him, and he said, "So here we are, Tammy Boy. It's just you and me in this epic showdown we always knew was coming. Bangs Boy versus the Keefster."

Tam didn't smile.

And his voice was raw—almost ragged—as he told Keefe, "I *tried* to warn you."

"I know," Keefe told him. "And I *tried* to listen."

"I know," Tam said quietly. "And . . . here we are."

"I'm pretty sure it was inevitable," Keefe agreed. "So I want you to know three things, okay? The truest things you'll ever hear." He waited for Tam to nod before he told him, "Number one: I still don't like you." Tam's lips twitched at that, but he stayed silent as Keefe added, "Number two: I will always make fun of your bangs." That earned Keefe an actual smile. "And number three: I don't blame you, okay? I get it. You have to do this. And I have to face my legacy. So let's stop being angsty and get it over with."

Tam looked away, his eyes finding Sophie's, and his expression was both an apology and a confession. But he didn't need to give either.

"Just . . . do the thing, Tam," she told him.

Sometimes the only way out was through—and she *would* get them through this.

She had to.

Had to. Had to. Had to.

Tam nodded and raised his arms—then turned back to Lady Gisela and reminded her, "We have a deal."

"We do," she agreed. "But you still have to hold up your end."

He nodded again.

Then he took a very long breath, tugged on his bangs—hard—and told Keefe, "I'm so, so sorry," as threads of shadowflux poured out of his hands.

Tam twisted them into an arrow, checking his aim twice before launching it at the magsidian stone high on the wall, triggering a flash of eerie black lightning.

The ricochets happened even faster than they had with Wylie's ball of light—the dark energy turning the air shimmery as it blurred from stone to stone, showering Keefe with black sparks that fortunately didn't seem to hurt him.

Neither did the final swirling beam that blasted into the throne, shaking the room—the world—as it sank in.

For one second nothing happened, and Sophie knew Keefe was about to ask if that was it.

And then the throne . . .

"Melted" wasn't really the right word—but Sophie couldn't think of anything better. She'd never seen anything like the sludgy black syrup that somehow dripped up instead of down.

Keefe unleashed some creative words as it slicked around him, coating his legs.

His torso.

His chest.

His body should've collapsed to the floor by then, but the liquid darkness kept him suspended—spinning him around in slow rotations as it coated every inch of him.

Pooling thicker and thicker, like a goopy cocoon.

"Embrace the change," Lady Gisela said as the inky oil oozed toward his face.

I'm here, Sophie transmitted. And she could tell Keefe wanted to scream, but he didn't want the shiny sludge to pour into his mouth. So he clamped his lips tight and squeezed his eyes shut as his handsome features disappeared into the goo.

"Now, Glimmer!" Lady Gisela ordered, and the other black-cloaked figure stepped forward, blasting Keefe's crown with a swirling beam of rainbow light.

The metal melted into a blinding silvery syrup that trailed down Keefe's face in thin streams, coating the darkness in thin threads.

This looks as weird as I'm assuming it does, right? Keefe thought— and Sophie wanted to laugh and cry at the proof that he was still him.

It definitely does, she admitted. *I'll show you my memories later. It doesn't hurt?*

Not yet. It's just really cold and strangely sticky, and I'm going to shower for a year after this, but—

The thought cut off as the darkness sank in, disappearing under his skin, making his limbs thrash and flail, and in his head Sophie could see the agony take over.

His consciousness tried to flee from the pain—and she understood why.

But she stayed with him.

Hide if you need to, she told him. *But I'm here.*

I'm here. I'm here. I'm here.

And she was.

Every time he retreated, her thoughts followed, sending him warmth and strength and reminders that this would soon be over.

Soon. Soon. Soon.

I'm here. I'm here. I'm here.

And she was there the moment the darkness reached the deepest part of his consciousness. The raw, ragged space he'd tried to wall off.

Embrace the change, Keefe, she told him. *I won't let you lose yourself.*

And she didn't.

She clung to the threads of him as the shadows poured in—filling every crack and cranny.

Making everything smooth.

New.

And a blinding flash of light sealed it shut.

Don't go, Sophie pleaded as Keefe's consciousness faded—terrified she might be losing him after all of that.

Tired, he told her.

And she was sure he was.

But she didn't want to let go.

Tired, he repeated. *Tired. Tired. Tired.*

And his head turned fuzzy and warm.

Okay, she told him. *Sleep now. I'll still be here.*

Sleep, he repeated.

And his mind went silent.

FIFTY-ONE

H OW IS HE?" LADY GISELA ASKED AS Sophie blinked back to the shadowy present and found Keefe's mom leaning over her—definitely *not* who she wanted to see. "Don't try to deny it, Sophie—I knew you'd use your telepathy to stay connected to him during the transformation. Why do you think I left you conscious?"

"I thought that was so you could torture me if he wouldn't cooperate," Sophie snapped back.

"Well . . . I didn't say it was the *only* reason, did I?" Lady Gisela countered, with the kind of smile that made Sophie's skin feel crawly. "My point was: You're predictable. I knew you'd monitor Keefe's thoughts today. Just like I *knew* you'd stage a standoff in this room—exactly where I needed it. All I have to do is *not* suggest something to you, and I can count on you to plan it for me, since you and I think so much alike. So, I'll ask you again: *How is my son?*"

For a second, Sophie's brain got stuck on the whole "a creepy murderer says we think alike" thing and couldn't decide if it was absurdly hilarious or utterly terrifying.

But then she realized the much more important detail: *She finally had a bargaining chip.*

"Untie me and I'll tell you," Sophie offered.

Lady Gisela pursed her lips. "Nice try. I've experienced the wonder of your inflicting already—not interested in a repeat."

Sophie considered that. "What if I promise I won't inflict? I mean it," she added when Lady Gisela raised an eyebrow. "Think about it: What good is inflicting really going to do for me? Even if I take you out, I'd still have Glimmer to deal with, wouldn't I? And how many dwarves are here—besides the one I'm *really* getting sick of, who's pinning me right now? I'm guessing at least a couple—and more can pop out of the ground anytime. Not to mention I'm stuck in the middle of a city run by a king who's already betrayed me, so . . ."

Her stomach twisted as she realized how horrifyingly true all of that was.

That *had* to win for The Worst Mess She'd Ever Been In, didn't it?

But she'd worry about that later.

This was definitely a moment for *one problem at a time.*

And right then, she wanted that stupid dwarf off of her back—and she wanted to move her arms and legs and get up from that scratchy ground to check on Keefe up close.

And Lady Gisela looked like she still wasn't ready to agree to that, so Sophie added, "Need I remind you that all of my friends are currently tied up and unconscious, and there's no way I'm leaving them behind? And Keefe can't even survive a light leap right now, and—"

"He can't?" Lady Gisela interrupted.

Sophie shook her head. "You just filled his body with an insane amount of freaky darkness and weird light—do you really think his body can break down and not fade away?"

"Probably not . . . ," Lady Gisela murmured. And as the blood drained from her face, Sophie realized she'd just found her first real advantage.

Lady Gisela had a flaw in her exit strategy.

A pretty massive one.

It also confirmed that Lady Gisela *had* been planning on taking Keefe with her when she left—and there was no *way* Sophie was letting that happen.

All the more reason she needed to get back on her feet.

"So, see?" she said. "You don't have to worry about my inflicting. And if you untie me and get this dwarf off of my back, I'll tell you what I saw in Keefe's head during your creepy experiment."

"It wasn't an experiment!" Lady Gisela corrected. "It was a *transformation.*"

"Yeah, well, I almost lost him during that *transformation*— several times. And when the shadowflux sank in . . ."

"Yes?" Lady Gisela prompted when Sophie didn't finish.

Sophie shook her head again. "Untie me and I'll tell you. Otherwise forget it."

Lady Gisela huffed out a breath.

She glanced toward where the throne used to be, and Sophie followed her gaze, feeling her heart sink when she saw Keefe's crumpled position on the floor.

His mom had left him there—limbs bent and twisted. Skin pale and sweaty.

And his eyes . . .

"What's wrong?" Lady Gisela asked.

But Sophie couldn't answer. Her brain was too busy replaying the last things Keefe had said to her before his mind went quiet.

Tired.

Sleep.

But he definitely *wasn't* asleep.

His eyes were wide open, staring unblinkingly at nothing.

And even in the dim light, Sophie could see that he was breathing much too fast for someone sleeping.

"*What's wrong?*" Lady Gisela demanded.

"I don't know," Sophie admitted, because this wasn't just a bargaining chip anymore. "You have to get him to a physician—and you're going to need my help, since I'm the only one who can teleport."

Lady Gisela barked a sharp laugh. "Do I really look that foolish?"

"Do you actually want me to answer that?" Sophie snapped back. "Do you think I like this idea either? Do you think I *want* to leave my friends tied up and unconscious?"

Lady Gisela set her jaw. "I can't let you teleport away with my son—"

"*Look* at your son!" Sophie interrupted. "Does he look okay to you?"

"He doesn't," a new voice agreed when Lady Gisela stayed silent.

It took Sophie a second to realize it had to be Glimmer. And Sophie had no idea how to feel about that. Especially when Glimmer added, "I think you should listen to her."

"So do I," Tam agreed, and Sophie wanted to smack herself for forgetting about him.

She wasn't completely alone in this nightmare after all.

Tam proved how true that was when he told her, "Don't worry, I can keep everyone here safe until they wake up. You just focus on getting Keefe to Elwin."

"I'll need to get to the surface to teleport," Sophie realized. And without Nubiti, she had no idea how to get through the King's Path.

"You should use the path we took," Glimmer told her, sounding surprisingly genuine. "King Enki showed it to us—it's a straight shot once you go down one level. I'm sure the dwarf holding you will take you down."

"No, he won't," Lady Gisela informed them. And there was a strange tone in her voice.

Bitterness maybe?

Frustration?

"Why not?" Glimmer asked, beating Sophie to the question.

Lady Gisela dragged a hand down her face. "Because it's not part of our bargain."

"Your *bargain*," Sophie repeated, realizing there was only one person Lady Gisela would be talking about. "You agreed to let King Enki keep the prisoners if he helped you trap Keefe on his throne."

"That was part of the deal, yes," Lady Gisela admitted. "And he was particularly clear about wanting to make sure you were among them. So there's no way that dwarf is letting me undo your bonds."

"There definitely isn't," the cruel little creature agreed, shoving Sophie's shoulders harder into the sand.

"But if you explained to King Enki that I'm the only one who can take Keefe . . ." Sophie stopped herself there, not sure she could bring herself to argue that Lady Gisela should bargain for *Sophie's* freedom and leave the rest of her friends captive.

And it wasn't *just* her friends.

There were three unconscious *Councillors* tied up on the floor near her—and there might be three more on the floor of the main marketplace.

And *more* of her friends. Who she *still* hadn't checked on—hadn't really even thought of.

And now she was thinking of abandoning them?

But what else was she supposed to do—unless *they* could help?

She could reach out to Fitz telepathically, explain what was happening, and . . .

What?

Expect them to come charging in to save the day?

It was a lovely, lovely thought.

But not particularly realistic.

If her friends were in a position to help, they would've already been there.

Plus, if she and her group had been overpowered so easily, the odds were . . .

"That wasn't our deal!" Tam snapped, saving Sophie from finishing that devastating thought.

"Oh, relax," Lady Gisela told him. "I made an exception for your sister. You and she will be free to go with me and—"

"That wasn't our deal!" Tam insisted again. "You said my friends would be *safe*."

"Yes, well, technically they are. As far as I know, King Enki has no intention of killing them—well, maybe the Councillors, but . . ." She shrugged. "You can't save everyone, Tam."

"Maybe not," he admitted as the room slowly darkened. "But that doesn't mean you stop trying."

The dwarf pinning Sophie shifted his weight, bracing for the new threat—and Sophie wondered if that meant Tam was already free of his bonds.

But she should've known that Lady Gisela would never give up control until she absolutely had to.

"This is not a moment to mess with me," Lady Gisela warned, stalking closer to where Tam must've been standing. "I'm trying to figure out a way to help my son—I don't have time for another one of your temper tantrums. So let me be *very* clear. If you make one more move against me—*One. More. Move*—I'll cancel our deal and keep you as my handy little Shade pet as long as I want."

Silence followed—the kind that grew heavier and heavier, until it felt like the whole room was being smothered.

Then someone asked, "Shade pet?"

But it wasn't Tam.

Glimmer.

She was also the one to ask, "You'd seriously go back on your word?"

"Of course she would," Tam cut in. "That's what I keep telling you."

"I know. But . . . I want to hear it from her," Glimmer said—and the dwarf pinning Sophie shifted his weight again.

Sophie took her chance to slide forward and twist—only gaining a couple of inches. But it was enough to give her a clear view of where Tam stood with his hands fisted at his sides. The light of his bonds flickered from his shaking, as if Tam was using every drop of his restraint to stop himself from lashing out at Lady Gisela—who stood a few feet away with her hands on her hips.

Glimmer stood between them, still hiding behind her cloak and hood as she folded her arms and said to Lady Gisela, "You haven't answered my question. Would you seriously go back on your word?"

Sophie tried to guess how Lady Gisela would answer—but it wasn't an easy question.

A "no" canceled her threat.

But a "yes" would make Tam even angrier.

"The thing about being the leader of a movement," Lady Gisela eventually told Glimmer, "is that you have to be willing to do *anything* to further the cause. Alliances. Bargains. These things only work as long as they're useful. Once they're not . . . you make the necessary adjustments."

Another weighty silence followed.

And this time Tam was the one to break it.

"See what I mean now?" he asked Glimmer.

Glimmer nodded. "Yeah, I think I do. . . ."

Lady Gisela blew out a breath, shaking her head. "I'll deal with you two later."

And that seemed to be the end of it as Lady Gisela turned away to pace.

Until Glimmer called after her, "The thing is . . . I don't think you will."

Lady Gisela spun back, but Glimmer had already grabbed both of Tam's wrists, and her palms flared with a golden light so bright, Sophie had to squeeze her eyes as tight as she could.

It took several blinks for her vision to focus—and then . . .

There was Tam.

Teeth clenched.

Arms raised.

Wrists *bare.*

His bonds lay broken at his feet—and the dwarf pinning Sophie lunged for him.

Glimmer whipped an orb of glaring blue light toward the dwarf, and the beast burrowed into the ground to shield his eyes.

And Lady Gisela was fumbling in her pockets, likely searching for a weapon—but a bolt of shadows crashed into her chest, sending her tumbling head over feet, again and again, until she slammed face-first against the wall.

"That one was for you, Keefe," Tam said, turning to where Keefe still lay crumpled on the floor. "And this one's for *me.*"

Everything went black.

And then there was only sound.

Crunching and cracking.

Snarls and skittering and rustling.

Grunts and huffs and footsteps.

And Sophie could only lie there, thrashing against her bonds and worrying every nearby noise was a dwarf, come to drag her away.

"Here," Glimmer said, making Sophie shriek as she flashed a silver orb and appeared beside her, holding a dagger.

She reached for Sophie's bonds, and Sophie had to remind herself, *This is the girl who set Tam free,* so she wouldn't panic.

But . . . it was *also* the girl who'd turned Tam into Lady Gisela's little Shade pet in the first place.

And the dagger Glimmer was using was probably the same one she'd used to threaten Flori. . . .

So Sophie felt a *lot* better once the bonds were gone and the knife was safely tucked away.

"Thank you," she murmured, wishing she could throw back Glimmer's hood and see who she was dealing with. For all she knew, this could be another trick—another trap. Someone pretending to be loyal and helpful and setting them up for a future betrayal. But her options were limited. The only choice right now was to take the risk and hope it wouldn't blow up in their faces, because what mattered most was, "I need to get Keefe out of here."

Glimmer nodded. "Tam's making sure no dwarves carry him away. And I can help you get closer. But without a dwarf's help, I'm not sure how to get you to the path we used."

"Well . . . I guess I'll have to take him through the King's Path," Sophie decided. "And run really, really fast."

And find her way through the maze without anyone to guide her . . .

And fight through the nightmares and hallucinations without losing herself . . .

"I guess that's the only option," Glimmer agreed, sounding even less optimistic than Sophie was trying to be.

Glimmer snapped her fingers, and her silver orb drifted to Sophie, hovering over her shoulder like her own personal moon.

"Follow my light, and it will guide you through the safest path."

"You're not coming with me?" Sophie asked her.

Glimmer shook her head. "I'll stay here and guard your friends until they're conscious."

Sophie flinched, wishing she hadn't forgotten how many other people needed her.

And she didn't *love* the idea of leaving everyone's safety in the hands of a stranger wearing a Neverseen cloak.

But Sophie was in *one problem at a time* mode, and Keefe was her current project.

So she followed Glimmer's light across the cracked floor, barely missing several dwarves who tried to tackle her along the way. And when she made it to Tam, he'd already hefted Keefe over his shoulder.

"We'll do the teary friend-reunion thing later," he told her as he transferred Keefe to her arms—and it took Sophie a few tries to find the best position to hold him and channel extra strength to her muscles.

"Going to try for the King's Path?" Tam asked.

"Unless you have a better idea," Sophie said, holding out one last hope.

But Tam shook his head. "I wish I did. Especially since I'm pretty sure King Enki's waiting on the other side of the door. I keep hearing thumping—don't you?"

She hadn't noticed it before, with all the other chaos, but now that he'd mentioned it . . .

There was a noticeable *THUMP!*

"Great," Sophie mumbled. "Well . . . I'll try levitating over them."

"That could work," Tam agreed, neither of them wanting to admit how impossible the plan was. "And if he catches you, we can try trading you for Lady Gisela. Maybe he'd go along, since it sounded like she'd made him other promises."

"So Keefe's mom is still . . . ?" she started to ask, not sure how to word it.

"She's alive," Tam told her. "For now."

And there was really nothing else to say to that.

THUMP!

"Okay," Sophie said, "time to take on an army of angry dwarves! This day just keeps getting better and better."

"Glimmer's going to blast them with light when you open the door. It should blind them for a few seconds. And yes, you can trust her," he added before she could ask.

Sophie nodded, glad he was willing to acknowledge how shaky their alliance felt. "I'm guessing you know more about her? Like . . . why she was with the Neverseen?"

And why Lady Gisela had said that Glimmer was more loyal to their cause than anyone she'd ever met . . .

"I do," Tam agreed. "I'll tell you more later. For now, I'll try to keep all the dwarves away from you as you head to the door."

"Thank you." Sophie glanced at the pale, unconscious guy in her arms, reminding herself why they were sticking with this disastrous plan.

Keefe's eyes were still open, staring at nothing.

His chest was still rising and falling too fast.

THUMP!

"Okay, here goes!" she said, and took off for the door, trying to pace herself, knowing she had a long journey ahead.

And the first challenge turned out to be the door itself.

It was *huge*. And *heavy*. And she didn't see a handle anywhere. And . . .

She was so focused on the door that she didn't see the dwarf crawling toward her until they had already lunged—and with Keefe's extra weight, dodging was impossible.

The impact sent them tumbling, tumbling, tumbling—a tangle of legs and arms and fur—and Sophie tried to fight back, but she couldn't let go of Keefe, and then she was pinned and—

"It's okay, Sophie!" the dwarf shouted. "It's me. Nubiti!"

"Nubiti," Sophie repeated, needing another second for the panic and adrenaline screaming though her head to quiet.

Nubiti. Nubiti. Nubiti.

Except . . .

"I'm on your side!" Nubiti promised when she felt Sophie tense. "I know what King Enki did to you—if he even deserves the title of king—and I've been trying to—TAKE COVER!"

She grabbed Sophie's shoulders, barely managing to roll their tangled group away before something black whisked over their heads and exploded in a shower of shadowy smoke.

"SHE'S ON OUR SIDE!" Sophie called out to Tam. "IT'S OKAY. HOLD FIRE!"

"Wait—he's on *your* side?" Nubiti asked when she realized who Sophie was shouting to.

"He is. And so is the Flasher in the Neverseen cloak. Or, she says she is, and . . . I'm trying to trust her. She's the one who broke Tam's bonds so he could take on Lady Gisela."

Nubiti sighed as she stood. "It appears we've both been misreading the situation."

THUMP!

Sophie tensed again—and Tam and Glimmer went back to their positions.

Nubiti shook her head. "That's not what you think it is. This is the problem with battle—you lose proper communication and . . ."

Her gaze focused on Keefe, and her voice trailed off.

"I need to get him to Elwin," Sophie said, not bothering to get into the whole messy story because she'd realized something *way* more important. "You can take me to the better path! Glimmer said they used one that goes straight from here to the surface, but that I'd need a dwarf to take me down a level to use it. And since all the dwarves here were trying to kill us, I didn't think it was an option, but now you're here! Please tell me you know what I'm talking about."

"I do," Nubiti said, leaning closer to Keefe and waving a hand in front of his open eyes.

He didn't blink.

"I can take you to that path," Nubiti said slowly. "And I can distract the guards who patrol it as much as I can. But you will need to run *very* fast—and you'll be carrying—"

"I can do it," Sophie promised, refusing to share Nubiti's worries.

She'd just been given a *much* better chance of getting Keefe to Elwin, and she wasn't going to waste it because of doubt.

"I'll run faster than I've ever run before," she added, saying the words out loud to make them real. "I'm getting Keefe to the Healing Center."

THUMP!

"Ah yes," Nubiti said, "I should let them in before you go—let them know this area's been secured."

"Them?" Sophie asked, struggling to heft Keefe back into her arms and shift his weight to maximize running speed.

And she assumed Nubiti was going to tell her about a loyal band of dwarves she'd been fighting with.

But when Nubiti cranked open the door, it was one of those movie moments, where all of the heroes find their way back to each other and they can't decide if they want to laugh or cry or make the biggest group hug ever.

Because there, standing in the doorway, looking like they'd definitely been fighting some epic battles—but *winning* them—were Councillor Bronte, and Councillor Darek, and Councillor Zarina, and Woltzer, and Lovise, and Grizel.

And Dex.

And Biana.

And Stina.

And Fitz.

Fitz.

His eyes only held hers for a second—but it was enough for Sophie to see that he was alive, so she'd happily take it.

And she tried to figure out the right thing to say to all of her friends—some sort of celebration *and* apology for forgetting to check in on them.

But then she realized . . .

None of them were smiling.

None of them were really even looking at her—their focus instead on the pale, unconscious, blank-stared boy in her arms.

And the devastation in their expressions was both a gut punch and a jolt of energy. Because it reminded Sophie of where she needed to be focusing.

She'd save the hugs and stories for later.

Right now . . .

"Sorry, I have to go," she mumbled. "Things . . . haven't gone very well—though there has been one really good thing. But I'll let Tam tell you about it."

"Tam?" Biana asked, her eyes scanning the room—and getting caught on all the unconscious forms spread across the floor.

"Tam will explain that, too," Sophie promised. "And tell you who Glimmer is. I have to go. I'm sorry."

She avoided all of their stares as Nubiti crouched to dig a hole in the sandy floor.

But right before Nubiti dragged her in, Fitz's accented voice filled Sophie's head.

You don't have to be sorry, he transmitted. *You're doing the right thing. Take care of him, and we'll take care of whatever else we have to deal with here.*

Thank you, Sophie transmitted back as the sand swallowed her whole, scraping and scratching and scuffing her skin raw while her lungs burned and burned, desperate for a fresh breath.

But she barely noticed the discomfort, because Fitz sent her one more transmission.

I'm glad you're okay. And . . . I've really missed you. All of this is so much harder without you.

I feel the same way, Sophie agreed.

She wanted to say more, but the sand spat her back out, and she gulped down the fresh air, coughing bits of sand out of her lungs.

"Honestly, I think I'd rather sink though mud," she told Nubiti, shaking her feet, trying to get the sand off her boots—and then she lowered her voice to a whisper as she studied the long, empty hall stretching in either direction. "Is this the path?"

Nubiti nodded, pointing to the left. "That will take you to the surface. I'll go the other way and see if I can draw the guards to me."

"Okay, then," Sophie said, not wanting to waste any time or strength on lingering or worrying.

It was time to just . . . *begin*.

She took one second to stare into Keefe's unblinking eyes and transmitted, *Stay with me. I'm getting you to Elwin.*

"Run fast, Sophie," Nubiti whispered as Sophie hefted Keefe over her shoulder and took off down the hall, starting with a jog, giving her legs a moment to find their stride before she pushed them to go faster.

Faster.

Faster.

Faster.

She didn't think about what might be behind her, or how much farther she had ahead. She just centered her mind on one foot in front of the other.

Go.

Go.

Go.

Her muscles throbbed, and her chest heaved, and the hall echoed with scurries and hisses and screams—but she tuned it all out.

Stay with me, Keefe.

Stay with me.

Stay with me.

Almost there.

And they were.

The path curved enough to show her the exit—still forever away. But she could make it.

Go.

Faster.

Stay with me, Keefe.

We've got this.

But some of King Enki's guards had clearly been waiting for her—jumping out of the shadows.

Stomping their furry feet.

And the ground rumbled hard, nearly knocking Sophie over as cracks shredded the path ahead, trying to force her to turn around.

But she'd come too far.

Too far.

Faster.

Faster.

Faster.

She'd jump the cracks if she had to.

Or levitate.

Or . . .

She didn't finish the thought, because her instincts took over.

Focusing on the friction of her feet.

The rush of her sprint.

The thrill of the speed.

It felt like flying.

No.

It felt like *falling.*

And with that thought, warm, tingly energy burst out of her mind, unraveling a tiny thread in the space in front of her, a gap just wide enough for her to charge through, and . . .

She didn't know how to describe it.

Somehow she just sort of . . . skipped.

One second the cracks were there.

The next, they were already behind her.

And when she pushed more energy out of her mind . . .

She skipped again.

And again.

Farther leaps each time.

The energy replenishing itself by the power of her sprint.

And she realized she was no longer in Loamnore.

She'd made it to the desert, kicking up clouds of sand as she ran.

Which meant it was time to levitate, but . . .

Maybe she didn't need to.

A fresh rush of warm energy flooded her brain. Fueled by the triumph of freedom and escape. And she shoved it out of her mind, telling Keefe, *Stay with me, stay with me, stay with me,* as a crack split the space in front of her and she charged into the void.

FIFTY-TWO

THE GOOD NEWS IS, HE'S ALIVE," ELWIN said, snapping his fingers to form an orb of purple light around Keefe's torso. "And his vitals are strong."

That *was* good news.

And Sophie was grateful for every heartbeat and every rise and fall of Keefe's chest—even if both were definitely a little too fast at the moment.

She was also extremely happy that Bullhorn was paying them *zero* attention. He'd barely lifted his little banshee head when Sophie had stumbled into the Healing Center and handed Keefe over to Elwin.

But.

"What's the bad news?" she asked, wrapping her arms around her knees and curling into a Sophie-ball.

Elwin had made her lie down on the cot next to Keefe's when he saw how wobbly she was from her crazy run. And of course he'd also insisted on checking her for injuries.

But *she* was fine.

Nothing to worry about.

Except the fact that Keefe was *still* staring blankly at nothing. And when she'd tried listening to his thoughts, his mind was gray and silent.

"The bad news," Elwin said, running a hand down his face before adjusting his iridescent spectacles, "is that I have no idea what's going on. I've never heard of the treatments you described. I mean . . . obviously Lady Gisela's been playing with the elements, trying to affect abilities. And I'm *assuming* the reason she used magsidian and ethertine instead of pure shadowflux and quintessence is because the elements would've been more . . . I guess 'organic' is the word I'm looking for, since they'd fused with the earth when the stones were formed. And I think that was probably a smart call, by the way. I think that's why I'm not seeing any echoes."

"None?" Sophie asked, sitting up.

Recovering from her own echoes had been one of the hardest things she'd ever done. So if Keefe wouldn't have to endure that . . .

"See?" Elwin said. "More good news."

"It is." And she tried to smile.

But she still noticed the way Elwin's frown deepened every time he flashed another orb of light and squinted through his spectacles.

First blue.

Then red.

Orange.

Yellow.

Green.

And Keefe just kept right on staring at nothing.

"Is he in a coma?" she had to ask.

Elwin shook his head. "I think it's more that his consciousness is tucked away right now, because the rest of him is in so much flux."

"Flux?" Sophie repeated, hating that word.

"Well . . . judging by all the shifts I'm seeing in his cells, I'm pretty sure he's going through a kind of . . . transformation."

"Great," Sophie mumbled, hating *that* word so much more.

And she couldn't stop her brain from flashing to the nightmares she'd seen in Keefe's head—the scenes that had reminded her too much of Dr. Jekyll and Mr. Hyde.

"Easy now, Miss Dramatic. For the record—I see these same kinds of shifts whenever anyone manifests. So my guess is, Keefe's getting a brand-new ability."

That . . . sounded less scary—and matched the things Alvar had told them.

But . . .

"*What* ability?" she wondered.

"I guess we'll find out when he wakes up."

Sophie sighed, telling herself not to cry—but her tear ducts wouldn't obey. "I *hate* that his mom gets to change him like this."

Elwin sat beside her on the cot, offering her a soft handkerchief. "Okay, I'm usually not the one who has to say all the smart, pep-talky things. So bear with me on this, okay? The thing you have to remember is . . . *everything* changes us. Every day we live. Every person we meet. Every experience, good or bad. That's what makes us who we are. What shapes our thoughts—our decisions. And the changes always work on two levels: *what happened* and *how we respond.* So, yes, this . . . is going to change Keefe—just like it's going to change you and me and everyone else who cares about our favorite Lord Hunkyhair. But . . . that's just *what happened*. We all still get to decide how we'll respond. And if I know Keefe, he'll find a way to become even more awesome. Trust me, Sophie. Nothing will ever stop Keefe Sencen from being Keefe Sencen. Think of how many things have already tried."

And *that* . . . was probably the best point he'd made.

Keefe had survived *huge* betrayals and years of mind games and abuse.

And he'd still sounded like *him* before his mind went quiet.

Just tired.

Which made her wonder. "Do you think we should give him a sedative?"

Elwin clutched his chest, then spun her toward him and flashed an orb of orange light around her head. "Okay, who are you, and what did you do with the sedative-hating Sophie Foster?"

"I wasn't saying for *me*," Sophie reminded him. "I just know Keefe really wanted to sleep when it was all over. And that doesn't look like sleep."

"It is and it isn't. It's a kind of restful wakefulness—and yes, I realize those seem like opposite things. But that's the only way I can think to describe it. And since I know so little about what's happening to him, I'm a little reluctant to mess with it. I think it's better to keep a very close eye on him and let this run its course."

"Wait—you're not giving him *any* medicine?" Sophie asked. "Not even a painkiller?"

"I'm not sensing any pain. And like I said, I don't want to interfere."

Sophie slumped out of his grasp, curling into a ball again. "So . . . I brought him here for nothing."

Elwin snorted. "Gee, thanks."

"Sorry. It's just . . . I left everybody in Loamnore because I thought I was helping Keefe—"

"You *did* help Keefe."

"Yeah, but . . . not enough to make up for leaving my friends to face an army of angry dwarves without me—not that I was much help, honestly. Or *any* help." She shook her head, resisting the urge to punch her pillow—that was never as satisfying as she wanted it to be. "I don't get it. Sometimes I'm *so* powerful—like in London, when I inflicted. Or when I was running here, and I figured out this new way to teleport—"

"You did?" Elwin interrupted.

She shrugged. "I think that's what happened. I'll have to test it later—but, so . . . How come I can do *that*—and then other times be basically useless? My plans fail—or are 'predictable,' apparently. Or I get overpowered by dwarves. Or I get sidetracked by the wrong things, or—"

"Okay, I'm sensing that you could keep this Sophie-bashing going for quite a while, so I think it's best to stop you right there. And first: I have to say, I love that in the same conversation, you can tell me you figured out *a new way to teleport without really even trying* and then beat yourself up for not being powerful enough. Sounds like someone's expectations for themselves might be a *little* too high."

"But . . . I'm the moonlark!"

"You know what, Sophie? I'm going to tell you something I don't think people tell you enough, even if it means I'm going to have to be smart and pep-talky again. You *are* the moonlark. But you're also *Sophie Foster*. A *real* person with *real* flaws and *real* limitations—and that's not a bad thing! Honestly, if you got everything right all the time, you'd probably be kind of annoying." He grinned when her eyebrows shot up. "You know it's true. No one likes a show-off. And you know what else you'd be if you did everything perfectly all the time? Boring. And you know that's true too. Just look at the friends you've chosen. Are any of them perfect?"

She wanted to say that Fitz seemed pretty close sometimes.

But she wasn't sure if they were still friends.

That moment when she was leaving . . . the things he'd said . . .

She wasn't sure that was really enough to fix them.

And she couldn't decide how she felt about that.

She also didn't understand why things between them always had to be so fragile.

And she definitely couldn't believe she was obsessing about this when Fitz was probably still down in Loamnore fighting traitor dwarves.

She really didn't have the energy for an endless conversation with all of the gruesome play-by-play. But she had to know one thing.

Are you safe?

She transmitted the words over and over, wondering if they'd even reach him. She didn't want to distract him if he was still in the midst of everything.

But Fitz heard her.

And he must've been just as worn out as she was because he transmitted back, *Everyone safe. Please don't worry. We'll talk soon.*

"Well," Elwin said, standing and stretching, "I should hail your parents and let them know you're here—and safe. Should I tell them you'll be staying here tonight?"

"Is that okay?" Sophie asked.

She knew she was definitely avoiding reality, and all the "what happened" conversations, followed by everyone asking her, "What now?"

But she'd also promised Keefe she'd be there for him through this. And she wasn't done yet.

So once she'd assured her parents that she was fine and safe and sorry for not coming home and would tell them everything later—and of course that she loved them—she opened a tiny channel between her mind and Keefe's.

I'm here, she told him.

He didn't respond.

But she didn't need him to.

She just wanted him to know she was there.

So she told him about her new teleporting.

And her conversation with Elwin.

And how she was so scared for him—but also so proud of him—and that it didn't matter if some things about him changed.

He'd always be her friend.

Always be Keefe Sencen.

And when she couldn't stay awake anymore, she let her eyes flutter closed. And in that last flicker of her vision, she saw Keefe's eyes close too.

Keefe slept through the next day—and Sophie chose to stay in the Healing Center with him.

And everyone else in the Lost Cities woke up to a forever-changed world.

It definitely wasn't every day that a dwarven king faced a multi-speciesial Tribunal in Eternalia, where all twelve Councillors—as well as the leaders of the four intelligent species that had been affected by his crimes—unanimously voted that he be exiled for high treason and sentenced to the somnatorium.

And since Nubiti had been the one to capture and overthrow King Enki, by dwarven law, she had inherited the dwarven crown.

Queen Nubiti.

The title had a nice ring to it—though Sophie wasn't sure she wanted to picture her former bodyguard shaved bald.

And Queen Nubiti's first task would be to hunt down any dwarves who'd supported King Enki's rebellion and see that they were properly punished for their treachery. Odds were, any remaining traitors had already fled to the Neverseen. But when Edaline came to check on Sophie after the Tribunal, she said that Nubiti had given an inspiring speech, vowing to prove that Loamnore was a haven for justice and an eager ally of all the other worlds.

And Sophie was sure that Nubiti *would* do everything in her power to keep that promise.

But it would be a *long* time before Sophie would ever want to go back to Loamnore.

And yet, the Black Swan and the Council apparently followed the Tribunal with a rousing speech of their own, standing united before the crowd and claiming the events in Loamnore as a victory—which *might* have made Sophie throw her bottle of Youth across the Healing Center when Grady first told her.

Victory?

Didn't they care about what had happened to Keefe?

Or the fact that all of the Neverseen had gotten away *again*—except Glimmer, who didn't count because she'd chosen to defect?

And how about the fact that—in Sophie's group, at least—the Councillors had done basically nothing, and the Collective hadn't even been there?

But then Edaline had gently reminded Sophie that her group had gotten Tam back, and that everyone who'd gone on the mission had also come home alive.

And Sophie had begrudgingly admitted that those things did count for *something*.

Plus, when Dex, Stina, and Biana stopped by to share their account of what had happened in the main marketplace, it did sound like a pretty clear win for their group—though it helped that Gethen and Vespera had left almost immediately.

Stina and Dex were convinced their success was because of their "mad fighting skills and super-awesome gadgets."

But Biana had a different, much more interesting theory.

Biana thought Vespera *wanted* her plan to fail—at least a little.

After all, Lady Gisela had *forced* Vespera into their alliance, and Vespera had made it clear that they had opposite visions. So maybe Vespera had decided that the perfect moment to take control was when Lady Gisela was distracted by all of her grand schemes for her son's legacy. It would explain why Vespera and Gethen had shown up, triggered every single alarm, said a bunch of half-truths to get everyone riled up, and then fled, leaving the dwarves to fight for them—which definitely didn't have the spectacle and flair of

Vespera's usual schemes. And it would give Biana's group time to finish up their fight and head over as backup against Lady Gisela.

And if Biana was right—Vespera had *almost* gotten what she wanted.

Tam had knocked Lady Gisela out—and bound her with shadow-flux bonds.

But somehow, Lady Gisela had still gotten away.

Tam felt responsible, because he'd only bound her hands, thinking he was making her feel what she'd done to him, and he hadn't considered that leaving her feet unbound would give her a chance to walk away if she regained consciousness.

But Sophie couldn't help wondering if Glimmer had something to do with it—and Sophie wasn't the only one who thought that.

In fact, after talking to all of her friends, it sounded like they wanted to know *a lot* more about the mysterious Flasher before they'd be willing to trust her—and Glimmer was being awfully secretive.

"She won't even take off her cloak!" Linh vented to Sophie the next morning, when she'd stopped by the Healing Center to check in. "She left the Neverseen *two days* ago, and she won't even *lower the hood*. I'm ready to blast it off of her with a tidal wave."

Sophie smiled, watching Linh stomp back and forth. "Remind me never to get on your bad side."

But she definitely understood why Linh was being so protective.

She'd just gotten her brother back.

And Glimmer wouldn't even give them her real name.

Plus . . . Sophie had realized something else—something she decided not to point out until she'd had time to ask Glimmer a few more questions.

But . . . Glimmer didn't have bonds on her wrists forcing her to do anything.

And yet, she hadn't hesitated at all before blasting the ethertine crown on Keefe's head.

"I don't trust her," Linh mumbled, gathering the water in the air and shaping it into a bird, making it fly around the room. "And Tam thinks we should invite her to live with us."

Sophie sat up straighter. "You're not going to let her, right?"

Linh's waterbird swooped to Linh's shoulder.

"I told him if he tries it, I'll have a rain cloud follow her everywhere. Which isn't that scary of a threat, but . . . I didn't know how angry to make Tam. He's . . . hard to read right now." She sent the waterbird flying again.

"He's been through a lot," Sophie told her, which Linh already knew—but Sophie couldn't think of anything else to say. "How's he doing?" she added quietly. *"Honestly?"*

Linh sighed. "He's . . . different."

The word made both of them turn toward Keefe, who still hadn't woken up—or stirred even slightly.

"How's *he* doing?" Linh asked softly.

Sophie sighed. "Elwin says all his vital signs are normal and we just have to be patient. And when I checked his dreams, it was something about an army of elf-shaped cookies—don't ask," she added when Linh's eyebrows rose.

"Well . . . that sounds like a very *Keefe* dream," Linh decided.

"It does," Sophie agreed. "But . . . I wish he'd wake up."

He hadn't woken up the next day either—the *third* day—even after Sophie decided to transmit the plea over and over.

Wake up! Wake up! Wake up!

Keefe! Keefe! Keefe!

When that didn't work, she tried bribes.

Then threats.

Ro had even stopped by and screamed right in his face.

"He's just trying to get out of his punishment," the ogre princess decided, "because he knows I owe him for the amoebas *and* breaking our bet."

She started listing off possibilities—*loudly.*

Trying to scare Keefe awake.

"For the record, I vote for anything that includes a shaved head," Fitz said from the doorway.

And Sophie made a sound that was somewhere between a gasp and a squeak.

But she couldn't help it.

This was the first time she'd seen him since Loamnore.

He'd checked in telepathically a few times—but only quick questions and single-sentence answers.

And now, there he was.

Looking gorgeous and perfect and . . . nervous.

And *she* looked like someone who'd run straight from Loamnore to the Healing Center and hadn't left for three days, relying on hasty sponge baths and borrowing Elwin's colorful pajamas.

Of course the jammies she had on at the moment were covered in tiny aardwolves.

"Is this a bad time?" Fitz asked when Sophie didn't say anything, and his eyes darted to Ro.

"Let me guess," Ro grumbled. "You two want to be alone?"

"We won't be alone," Sophie reminded her, pointing to Keefe.

Plus, Sandor was with Elwin in the other room.

"YOU HEAR THAT, HUNKYHAIR?" Ro shouted. "YOU'RE GOING TO BE FITZPHIE'S ONLY CHAPERONE. DON'T YOU THINK YOU SHOULD WAKE UP FOR THAT?"

Sadly, still no reaction from Keefe.

But Sophie and Fitz were definitely cringing.

Ro tilted her head to study them, and her lips stretched into a smile. "All right, guess I'll leave you two alone to talk. Have fun!"

Then she was gone, and all that was missing was a background soundtrack of crickets chirping.

"Sorry I haven't come by before," Fitz eventually said, tearing a hand through his hair. "I've been trying to find Alvar."

Sophie slumped back against her pillow. "If you came here to—"

"I didn't!" Fitz interrupted, holding out his hands. "Sorry, didn't mean to make it sound like that. I just meant . . . I thought Alvar might know a bit more about this transformation or whatever— something that might help us know if Keefe should be awake by now or not."

"It feels like he should be, doesn't it?" Sophie asked quietly.

Fitz nodded. "But . . . I'm pretty sure I was unconscious for longer than that after I was exposed to shadowflux."

"You were," Sophie agreed. "But . . . Elwin was also sedating you."

"Yeah. True." He tore his hand through his hair again.

And the silence swelled again. Until Sophie said, "I'm guessing you couldn't find Alvar."

He shook his head, and she waited for him to point out that if she hadn't let Alvar go, they wouldn't have to find him.

But he just said, "Not yet. But I'll keep looking. I promise. I mean . . . I *know* Keefe's going to be okay. I *know* he's going to wake up and have some really cool new ability and drive us all crazy with it. But . . . the waiting's hard."

"It is," Sophie agreed, tugging on her eyelashes.

She'd started wishing on them every time one slipped free.

Please wake up, Keefe.

Please, please, please.

"It helps to keep busy, though," Fitz added quietly. "That's why I'm here. I know you haven't wanted to leave Keefe alone. But . . . I'm guessing you're dying to go home and take a shower, change your clothes—"

"You trying to tell me I smell bad?" Sophie interrupted, smiling when Fitz's eyes widened. "I'm kidding. I know that's not what you meant."

"I know," Fitz said, staring at his feet. "I just . . . wasn't sure if you'd ever tease me again."

Sophie sucked in a breath.

Fitz paced to the other side of the room, dragging a hand down his face so hard, it made his features get all stretched.

"The thing is, Sophie—I know this isn't the right time or place to do this—and I know I'm the one who messed everything up. But . . . I just . . . I need you to know that I miss you, okay? I miss my girl-friend. So if there's anything I can do to fix it . . . let me know. Even if all you want to be is friends, I'd take that. I just . . . I miss you. And I wanted you to know that. And now I can't stop rambling, and it's making this really awkward."

It was.

But it also made it sweet.

And when their eyes met, Sophie felt the familiar flutter in her chest.

But.

"I miss you, too, Fitz. You have no idea. And I will do anything for us to be friends again. But . . . *just* friends. For now, at least. There's just . . . too much going on. And it was so much harder than I thought it would be, and I don't know if that means I'm not ready or . . . I just know I can't handle a boyfriend right now. But I'd really love my friend back. Can we do that?"

Fitz closed the distance between them, grabbing her hand and giving it a soft squeeze.

A friendly squeeze.

"Yeah, we can do that."

Sophie squeezed his hand back. "Thank you."

They stood like that for a few seconds, and the really amazing thing?

It wasn't awkward.

Not even a little bit.

Even when Fitz met her eyes and said, "Well then, as your friend—and Keefe's best friend, by the way—how about you take me up on my offer? Even if you only go for a few hours to shower and change—"

"Back to the shower hints again," Sophie interrupted. "You really must think I smell bad."

"No. I think you just need a break," Fitz corrected. "That's all."

A break.

Maybe he was right.

"Okay," she decided, stretching her legs as she slowly crawled out of her bed. "I'll be back in a few hours."

Fitz plopped down on one of the empty cots. "And I'll be here. Probably throwing Prattles at his head, but hey . . . might wake him up."

Sophie laughed, loving how easily they were already starting to joke with each other again.

"Thank you," Sophie told him.

Fitz flashed one of his perfect smiles. "Anytime, Sophie. *Anytime.*"

FIFTY-THREE

E DALINE TOLD ME I'D FIND YOU OUT here," a familiar voice said behind Sophie, and Sophie curled her knees into her chest, too tired to sprint for the cliffs and teleport away.

She was also too tired to realize for several more seconds that she didn't actually need the cliffs to teleport anymore.

And she was definitely too tired to tell Silveny about how she could teleport like Wynn and Luna now, and find out if there was anything she needed to know about that.

That had been her plan when she'd headed outside and settled under the swaying branches of Calla's Panakes—she was going to have a nice long chat with the exuberant mama alicorn and take her mind off of everything.

But the thought of hearing Silveny chant, *Keefe! Keefe! Keefe!* had made Sophie's stomach fill with bubbling lava.

So she'd just sat there, watching the petals fall and trying to pick out the words to some of the drifting melodies—but there was too much noise in her brain.

Too many unanswered questions.

Too many worries.

Too many truths she wished she could unlearn.

And the noise only got louder when the person behind her said, "We really need to talk, Sophie."

Clearly, ignoring the person wasn't going to make her go away.

Refusing to use her name hadn't been working very well either.

So Sophie took a long, steadying breath and gave her eyelashes a soothing tug before she forced herself to face her biological mother.

Of course Oralie looked as pretty and perfect as ever, from her fluttering pink gown to the shiny pink gloss painted across her lips. She must be so disappointed every time she saw her daughter's boring tunics and lack of makeup—which actually made Sophie feel a little better about the whole mess.

Until she let herself wonder if Keefe had felt the same way every time he'd defied his parents—and if that same thrill had played a role in why he'd gone to Loamnore after he'd promised to stay away.

The line between *defiant* and *destructive* was a razor's edge.

"What do you want?" Sophie asked, needing to get this conversation over with.

Oralie lowered herself to the grass and fanned out her gown like a Disney Princess. "I can see why you like spending time out here. It really is remarkable."

"What do you *want*?" Sophie repeated.

Oralie sighed, her gaze turning distant as she reached out her hand, catching one of the falling blossoms. "I want so many things, Sophie. That's always been my problem."

Sophie rolled her eyes. "Yeah, I'm really not up for the whole 'here's my sad backstory' conversation—"

"I know," Oralie told her, blinking back to the present. "That's not what this is. I'm here because I need you to help me."

Sophie shook her head. "That's a super-bad idea. I'm sure someone on Team Valiant—"

"It's about Keefe's legacy," Oralie interrupted.

Sophie froze—wondering if she'd ever be able to hear that word without wanting to vomit.

She doubted it.

But her jaw also tightened. "If this is some ploy—"

"It's not," Oralie assured her. "I . . . think I know how to find out more about what Lady Gisela's planning for him—and what she did to him."

"You *think*," Sophie emphasized. "Yeah . . . forget it—I'm done with theories and guessing."

Oralie grabbed Sophie's arm to stop her when she tried to stand. "So am I. Don't forget—I was in Loamnore too."

"Yeah, doing nothing," Sophie muttered.

Oralie flinched. "You're right. I didn't do enough. None of us on the Council did—and not just that day. All the days before. King Enki's treason didn't happen overnight. And if we don't change the way we do things, it could happen again. We have to start facing our world's darker truths instead of washing them away. *That's* why I'm here." She stared at the sky for a second before focusing on Sophie. "In Loamnore, Lady Gisela said 'stellarlune,' and I can't get the sound of it out of my brain. It feels familiar but unfamiliar, like it *should* connect to something—but that something isn't there anymore."

Sophie groaned, dropping back to the grass hard enough to send

Panakes petals scattering. "*Please* tell me you don't think Lady Gisela messed with your memories."

Oralie shook her head, making her circlet shimmer in the sunlight. "She didn't. *I* did. Or . . . *they* did—whoever *they* are."

"I have *no* idea what that means," Sophie told her.

"Don't you?" Oralie stretched out her arm and snapped her fingers, making a tiny glass sphere the size of a marble appear in the center of her palm.

A *cache.*

Sophie's heart changed rhythm. "You're saying stellarlune is a Forgotten Secret."

"It's part of one, at least. *This one.*" She raised the cache to Sophie's eye level—and when the light hit the glass, it caught the tiny blue crystal set into the middle.

The *only* inner crystal.

"You only have *one* Forgotten Secret?" Sophie had to ask.

Kenric's cache had glittered with *seven.*

"Empaths shatter more easily, so the Council has to be very selective with how often they involve me in their more fraught situations. And the only challenge that they've ever decided was desperate enough to need my help was this one." She tilted her hand, letting the cache roll slowly around her palm. "And . . . it had something to do with stellarlune. So I'm willing to help you access the memory—but only if you promise we'll face this truth together."

Sophie plucked the cache from Oralie's palm, watching the light shift in the tiny inner crystal, which was more of a pale blue than a deep blue. "If this is your idea of mother-daughter bonding . . ."

"No—this is about trust. If I show you what's in this cache, I'll be violating some of the most fundamental vows I've made as a Councillor. And you're the only person I'm willing to take that risk for."

Sophie snorted. "Right, because my very existence violates a ton more vows you made."

Oralie sighed, but admitted, "That too."

There was no warmth in her voice—no regret in her eyes.

But . . . maybe Sophie didn't need there to be.

She didn't need another mother.

She needed answers.

That's what Oralie was offering her.

One, at least.

One truth that had been erased.

And Sophie wanted it.

Needed it.

And Keefe might never wake up without it.

But her conscience still forced her to say, "I thought the Forgotten Secrets were things that could damage your sanity if you remembered them."

"They are. That's another risk I'm willing to take. The question is, are you?" She let the question dangle for a second before she added, "It's going to get ugly, Sophie. And I can't guarantee your safety—or mine. All I can offer is truth—and I'm ready to get started. *If* you're ready to trust me."

She held out her hand, asking for her cache.

And Sophie hesitated only a second before placing it gently in Oralie's palm, pressing her hand over it to seal their bargain.

She didn't need to weigh her options or think through consequences or doubt herself or stress or panic.

She could do all of that later, as she fought her way through.

Right now, only one thing mattered.

"I'm ready," Sophie told Oralie, doing her best to channel Keefe's confidence as she added, "Bring it on."

ACKNOWLEDGMENTS

So . . . raise your hand if you're mad at me for that cliff-hanger!

pauses while the entire Keeper fandom raises their hands

I know . . . I know. I'm probably going to need to go into hiding until book nine comes out.

Must. Write. Faster.

In all seriousness, though, despite how cruelly I treat you guys with my endings, I hope you know how much I love each and every one of you. We're on an epic journey together with this series—a glorious sleep-deprived adventure! (for me, at least)—and I truly wouldn't be here without you. Thank you for reading. Thank you for trusting me to guide you through this story. And thank you, thank you, thank you for not throwing your books at my head (these things are heavy!). ☺

I worked some of the longest hours I've ever worked in my life to get this book done in time. But the truly amazing thing is how many people at Simon & Schuster suffered through the same schedule with me—and how many more work tirelessly every day behind the scenes to make sure this series finds its way to stores, schools, libraries, and readers. It's such an honor and a joy to work with so many inspiring people, including Liesa Abrams Mignogna—my endlessly patient editor—and Jon Anderson, Mara Anastas, Chriscynethia Floyd, Katherine Devendorf, Rebecca Vitkus, Chelsea Morgan, Elizabeth Mims, Karin Paprocki, Mike Rosamilia, Adam Smith, Stacey Sakal, Cassie Malmo, Lauren Hoffman, Caitlin Sweeny, Alissa Nigro, Anna Jarzab, Nicole Russo, Jessica Smith, Sara Berko, Michelle Leo, Jenn Rothkin, Ian Reilly, Christina Pecorale, Victor Iannone, and the entire sales team. And Jason Chan never ceases to wow me with his gorgeous cover illustrations.

I'm also incredibly lucky to work with my brilliant and supportive agent, Laura Rennert, who truly is my lifeline in this chaotic business (same goes for everyone else at Andrea Brown Literary and Taryn Fagerness Agency).

And I'm in awe of how hard Cécile Pournin and Mathilde Tamae-Bouhon—and everyone at Lumen Editions—work to get my books translated for French readers every year, despite my down-to-the-wire deadlines.

To all the booksellers, the teachers, the librarians, the bloggers, and the #bookstagrammers who go out of your way to support this series: Please know that I see you. I adore you. And I would not be where I am without you. You truly are my heroes.

This year has been an interesting year for me, filled with some of the greatest joys and biggest challenges I've ever faced. And all of that madness might've unraveled my creativity if it weren't for a host of supportive, inspiring people.

Debra Driza: I know I already dedicated the book to you—but I have to thank you here, too, because I *truly* wouldn't have survived this deadline without you. Thank you for the snacks, for the *abundance* of iced tea, and for talking me through Every. Single. Plot hole. Here's hoping for many more Shannon-and-Deb writing days in the future!

Thank you, Faith Hochhalter and Brandi Stewart, for being an endless source of wisdom on all things book/event related, and for all of the texts, calls, and hilarious GIFs. I'm so glad this business brought us together. *jazz hands*

Thank you, Kelly Ramirez, for proving that some friendships truly do last a lifetime, and for providing excellent pep talks, perfect distractions, and an abundance of Instagram wisdom.

Thank you, Kari Olson, for always making yourself available for a desperate brainstorming session—and for all the cute animal picture motivation. (The aardwolf mention in *Legacy* is for you!)

Thank you, Alexander Morelli, for teaching me about mindfulness exercises (best deadline coping mechanism ever!) and then not judging me for twisting one of them around to serve my plotting purposes. You saved the hardest scene in the book!

Thank you, C. J. Redwine, for being my writing check-in buddy on the longest deadline days, Sarah Wylie for the wonderful e-mails (and for not judging my long gaps between replies), Amy Tintera for putting up with my really long text messages, and Roshani Chokshi for always being fabulous (and inspiring me to try to be the same).

Thank you, Kasie West, Renee Collins, Bree Despain, Jenn Johansson, and Candice Kennington, for letting me crash your writing retreat—it was just the boost I needed to get back into the rhythms of writing.

Thank you, Allison Bennett, for being there for that first very long, very hard phone call, and for all the advice after. And thank you, Nadia and Roland, for continuing to be the best niece and nephew ever. (And I have to give Jeff Bennett a shout-out here too!)

And of course—of *course*—thank you, Mom and Dad, for helping me get my house reorganized into perfect writing spaces, for bringing me meals and groceries and anything else I needed. I know I say this every year, but maybe this time it'll actually happen: Here's hoping the next book will cooperate and I'll actually get to sleep!

Hi there, Keeper fans! Consider this your friendly reminder: If you snuck back here to spend a little time with our favorite silver-banged Shade before reading *Legacy*—**STOP! TURN BACK! SPOILERS AHEAD!** Even the next paragraph is iffy, so I'd recommend fleeing now.

*pauses for one more **SPOILER ALERT***

Okay! The scenes you're about to read take place simultaneously with what's going on throughout the course of *Legacy*, to give you some glimpses into Tam's side of the story. There are several references to moments you've already seen through Sophie's eyes, but now you'll get to see Tam's reactions and hopefully get some deeper insights into what our sweet, angsty boy is going through.

Happy reading!

First Day

Don't talk to anybody.
Don't listen to anybody.
Don't make friends.
Don't let them break you.

They were the words that Tam had repeated to himself every morning before he headed off with Linh to Exillium.

The rules he forced himself to follow.

The only way to survive.

And they were going to get him through this.

Hopefully he'd learn something useful too.

Tam studied his tiny, stuffy room, smirking at the ridiculous touches someone had added—as if they thought he'd look at the embroidered pillows and the jeweled moon jars and think, *Oh, I guess I'm not a prisoner, because they gave me a mirrored tray with . . .*

Is that a sparkly cat statue?

He rolled his eyes and tried to decide if it would be better to gather up all of that junk and shove it under the bed to show them exactly what he thought of it, or to leave it where it was.

What he *really* wanted to do was shred the pillows, fling the moon jars against the walls, and smash that stupid, shiny cat.

But this was a long game.

Best to start slow. Test the water.

"How did you sleep?" Lady Gisela asked behind him, and Tam kicked himself for flinching—but he hadn't heard the door open.

"Awesome," he told her. "Nothing says 'sweet dreams' like a concussion. You should try it sometime. I'd be happy to knock you out."

Lady Gisela sighed. "This will go much easier for you if you cooperate."

"Pretty sure it will go easier for *you*," Tam countered, spinning around to face her.

Her hair was pulled back into this supertight bun that looked like it had to be giving her a headache, and the skin on her face had this weird, stretched look to it. It almost looked like it hurt when she moved her mouth.

Tam really hoped it did.

"I know how to deal with stubborn, snarky boys," Lady Gisela told him.

"I can tell. Thanks for the cat statue!"

Her eyes narrowed, and Tam realized he should probably ease off a bit. It was only day one. He needed to figure out the boundaries before he started slamming against them.

"I'm not the enemy, Tam," she told him, and it was really, *really* hard not to laugh—until she added, "But I can be if you insist on being difficult. You're here for a reason, and I *will* make sure you fulfill it."

"Great. Looking forward to it."

"You should be. Now come on. Gethen's waiting."

Tam's stomach dropped. "Gethen?"

"Our Telepath." Lady Gisela's smile stretched wider. "He's very much looking forward to spending the day with you."

"I'm sure he is," Tam mumbled as he followed her down a dim, narrow hallway, trying to keep his back straight, head held high.

But a whole day with a Telepath . . .

Tam wouldn't be able to hide much.

And this prisoner-of-the-Neverseen thing just got a whole lot more complicated.

After the Warning

"So settle a bet for me," one of *Them* said, dropping into the chair across from Tam in the hideout's small study.

Tam gripped his book so hard, the spine crackled.

Her face was hidden by the cowl of her cloak. But he recognized her voice.

It was the one who'd put the bonds on his wrists.

The one who'd told him, *It'll be easier this way, I promise*, as she'd turned him into Lady Gisela's little Shade pet.

The Flasher who called herself "Glimmer."

Apparently she thought he didn't care about what she'd done to him, because she pointed to his forehead and asked, "So, the fact that you never wear your hood—is that a protest? Or because you want everyone to see your awesome bangs?"

Tam went back to reading.

"You don't talk much, do you?" When he still didn't respond, she sighed—then leaned closer and whispered, "Gethen's mad at you."

Tam gripped the book again.

Of course Gethen was mad at him.

He couldn't hide his whole conversation with Sophie—he'd known that the second he'd let her into his mind.

But hopefully he'd hidden the part that mattered.

And hopefully Sophie believed him.

"Be careful, Tam," Glimmer told him as she stood. "I don't think you realize what you're doing."

No. He knew exactly what he was doing.

Don't let them break you.

After Linh

"I seriously don't know how you can make any sense out of that journal," Glimmer said, taking the seat across from Tam and plopping a book about light theory down on the study's table. "Shades are weird."

She sat at his table a lot, either ignoring him or trying to trick him into talking to her.

So Tam tried to tell himself it was nothing unusual.

Nothing to worry about.

No one knew anything.

He'd shrouded his conversation with Linh in hundreds of layers of shadows. There was no way Gethen could've found the memory.

And yet, Glimmer leaned close and said, "I know something's wrong."

Tam kept his eyes on Umber's precise writing.

"I heard you crying last night," Glimmer added, her voice softening in a way that reminded him of his sister.

And it made him break his rule and talk.

"What do you want?" he asked, keeping his voice low—sharp.

"I just . . . don't understand why you have to be so stubborn," she said to him. "You don't have to be all alone here. You could have friends."

Don't make friends.

Not that he needed the reminder. He snorted and held his arms up, showing her the bonds she'd put there. "You think *we* can be friends."

Her head angled down, making her cloak fall even farther forward. "I think there's a lot you don't understand," she murmured.

"And I think there's a lot *you* don't understand," Tam countered. His voice low. Ominous. "Whatever reasons you have for being here are *wrong*. And whatever you think you know about these people is wrong too. They only care about themselves, and when the time comes, they *will* betray you." He pointed to his bonds again and told her, "Just like they made you trap me."

Silence stretched between them.

Then Glimmer grabbed her book and stalked away.

After London

"What happened?" Glimmer demanded, shoving her way into Tam's room and closing the door behind her, pressing her back against it like she was trying to keep everyone out. "Where did you go? Why is Lady Gisela *unconscious*?"

Tam curled up tighter on his bed.

He couldn't talk.

Couldn't think.

Couldn't stop shaking, shaking, shaking.

Glimmer crouched beside him, and her hood shifted in the process, giving Tam a glimpse of her long black hair.

Not that it mattered.

Nothing mattered.

Not after what he'd just done.

"What *happened?*" Glimmer asked again. "You can tell me."

Don't talk to anybody.

"You can trust me," she added.

Don't listen to anybody.

"I'm your friend," she promised.

Don't make friends.

And it hit Tam then, the absolute absurdity of his situation.

Friend.

She was the reason he'd just had to help Lady Gisela escape!

Laughter burst out of him at the reminder—cold, erratic sputters.

And when the frenzy passed, he told her, "You're *not* my friend."

The room dimmed with the words.

"I could be," Glimmer said quietly. "I keep trying."

"WHY?" Tam demanded.

Glimmer shrugged, picking up the tiny cat statue from his bedside table and trailing her finger along its curved tail. "It gets lonely here."

"THEN GET OUT OF HERE!" he shouted. "Seriously, Glimmer. See these people for who they really are."

"I *do!*" she insisted, reaching up to adjust her hood. Covering the few strands of her hair that had broken free.

Tam shook his head. "Then at least . . . just get out of my room."

Glimmer took the cat statue with her.

Last Night

"So . . . this is it," Glimmer said, leaning against the side of Tam's doorway. "One more thing and . . . then you're out of here."

Tam let out a dark laugh. "One more *thing*."

"What else am I supposed to call it?" Glimmer countered.

Which was true.

There were no words for the horror Lady Gisela was going to force him to do.

Or *try* to force him.

Please don't let Keefe be there.

Please, just ONCE, let Keefe do what someone tells him to do.

Another dark, bitter laugh slipped through his lips as he considered the chances of that.

And please don't let Linh be there.

Don't let her see me like this.

"Wow, you really are always gloomy, aren't you?" Glimmer asked, crossing her arms. "I thought you'd at least be relieved that it's almost over."

Tam shook his head, trying to decide if Glimmer could really be that naive, or if she was following some script Lady Gisela gave her to keep him hopeful and compliant.

"You *really* think she's going to let me go after I 'do the thing' or whatever you want to call it."

Glimmer nodded without the slightest hesitation. "You guys have a deal. Once you hold up your end, she'll hold up hers."

"Wow, you *really* believe that, don't you?" Tam wondered.

"Of course. It's only fair."

"Fair," Tam repeated, wondering why he was still talking. It didn't matter.

Don't make friends.

But he had to know. "Okay, tell me this, then," he said slowly, stalking closer. "If I'm right—if Lady Gisela goes back on her word—would you do anything about it?"

"What do you mean?"

"I mean"—he held up his wrists, showing her his bonds—"*you're* the one with the power to set me free. And *you* think our deal is fair. So if I hold up my end—and Lady Gisela doesn't hold up hers—would you step in and let me go?"

Glimmer backed up a step. "I . . . I don't know."

Tam snorted. "That's what I thought."

"Hey—you're asking me if I'd betray—"

"Someone who would've just betrayed me," Tam finished for her. "I'm asking if you'd betray a traitor to do the right thing."

"I . . . I don't know," Glimmer repeated.

"Well," Tam said slowly, pulling his sleeves back down to cover his bonds. "Maybe you should figure that out."

He flipped his hood up over his head, covering his face.

Time to go.

Don't let them break you.